SARMATIA

GOTHS

BLACK SEA

ARMENIA

BYZANTIUM

ANCYRA

CAPPADOCIA

CAESAREA

Tigris

ASIA

PERGAMUM

Euphrates

CTESIPHON

EPHESUS

SYRIA

PALMYRA

RHODES

DAMASCUS

CRETE

TYRE

SEA

JERUSALEM

ARABIAN

DESERT

ALEXANDRIA

HELIOPOLIS

MEMPHIS

Nile

EGYPT

RED
SEA

Persian
Warrior

The
Unconquered Sun

The Unconquered Sun

by R. Dulin

The Macmillan Company, New York

The
Unconquered Sun

1 The slave girl coughed; then

again said gently, "Lady, your father wishes to see you."

Her brown, pretty face, simple yet not without a trace

of the slyness natural in domestic slaves, showed such

eagerness that Severina thought: She knows . . . every-

body knows. How strange that she is glad. I suppose all

women grow excited at a time like this.

Conscious of the trembling of her limbs, she said in a voice she
tried to keep even but only succeeded in making cold, "Thank you,
I heard, Lalage."

The girl clasped her hands; obviously she expected even her reserved mistress to show some emotion at this particular summons.
But Severina, her expression distant, waited a few moments till the
faint shivering spell had passed and then said with an effort, "Tell
my father I will come to him soon." She was surprised how matter-
of-fact her words sounded.

In the mirror Severina watched the girl silently withdraw and guessed at the disappointment, even resentment, behind her deferential manner. The whole household must have buzzed for days! How absurd of her parents to maintain such a show of secrecy, falling silent with significant looks at each other when she approached and then resuming conversation about some triviality or other.

Now that she was alone, Severina could think with less agitation. The few minutes she delayed in this room before she left to confront her father were the last of her youth, her freedom, the last in which she would think of herself simply as somebody's daughter. A few minutes more and a breach would open in the closed circuit of her life—and everything would change, for ever.

She stared in the mirror as if for a farewell view of a self that soon would be dissolving. A thin girl, with something of the awkwardness of adolescence still in her carriage, tensely regarded her. Fine aquiline features, with troubled brown eyes below delicately penciled brows, a smooth forehead, tall rather than broad, unadorned black hair drawn straight back and clubbed simply in country style. A patrician face, almost overrefined, with intelligence and its own severe and sensitive beauty, but lacking robustness and a vital glow.

Patrician! Severina smiled faintly. A few generations back her father's family were dour, hardfisted Spanish peasants who had prospered by loans at exorbitant rates to less provident neighbors during crop failures. After reaching a certain magnitude, their wealth seemed to grow of its own accord, bringing its owners a corresponding growth of consequence. Her great-grandfather became an Equestrian, bought himself a mansion in Rome and, so that he could ocupy it with the proper assurance, a family tree. Researchers have a tariff of charges for ancestors; he paid top price and got the best. His son, her grandfather, who was enrolled in the Senate, used to boast of his kinship with the revered Spanish soldier Emperor, Trajan.

True enough, in the present time there were not many families, even in the capital, whose patrician claims had greater substance. Dwindling fertility, most marked among the wealthy and self-indulgent nobles, had extinguished many ancient houses. A more rapid destruction had been wrought by the Emperors who had fol-

2

lowed the philosopher Marcus Aurelius some eighty years ago. They had waged continual war on the senatorial order, which—rightly— regarded most of them as usurpers whose only authority was the sword. The Emperor's anger, their suspicion, their insatiable greed had been visited upon the senators, hundreds of whom had been butchered or driven to suicide, while their possessions, down to the last slave and the last acre, had been forfeited to the Imperial Treasury.

No doubt that was how the leathery, intense faces of her tough Spanish forebears had been transmuted into the refined and pallid aristocratic faces of the present age. Constant strain had made the nerves more tender; the eyes less blunt but more penetrating; the ear, alert for the whisper of peril, more sensitive. The women of her family, ruling over sumptuous households, had often trembled lest the clatter of hooves on the road signaled the approach of messengers of ruin or the tyrant's executioners. They had been lapped in luxury and sapped by fear. The combination was like some powerful chemical that burned out grossness, making the body more delicate, the mind more subtle, but which lowered the vitality of the organism, so that it had a less tenacious hold on life.

She glanced round the familiar, virginal room: its narrow wooden bed, plain clothes chest, oval bronze-framed mirror, and single stool beside a low table suddenly had a forlorn look, as if they knew they belonged to a past that was being discarded. Crossing to the door, she stood there a few moments, irresolute. A footfall sounded distantly along the corridor and, coming to herself with a start, she set out through the women's quarters for her father's favorite room.

The house, extended rather haphazardly at different periods, was huge and sprawling. At this time of day, many of the numerous domestic slaves were scattered over the place, dusting, polishing, scouring in the perfunctory way they worked unless one of the understewards was there to see that they applied themselves. A murmur of talk rose from them, which instantly stilled as Severina drew in sight; all inclined their heads. Her cheeks burned, for she felt their conversation had been about herself and that, once she had passed, their curious or even mocking eyes clung to her back and they whispered eagerly together. Still, she managed to keep her ex-

3

pression composed and her step unhurried. She was grateful to find that the peristylium, the colonnade-enclosed interior garden of the house, was deserted and she sank down on a stone bench beside one of the graveled paths. Not daring to linger, she rose abruptly after a minute and moved on.

Outside her father's room, her heart seemed to contract. She leaned forward a little, left arm pressed against her side, shaken by the tumult of her emotions.

After a little while, she pushed her right hand deliberately forward, as if it were someone else's unwilling hand. The door opened.

Her father looked up to see her motionless, in the doorway. He smiled. "Come in, my dear," he said in his most benevolent tone.

Facing her father, but at a little distance on a separate couch, her stepmother sat relaxed; at Severina's appearance she had turned her head to smile welcome. The room was spacious and rather coldly elegant, with a few couches and miniature tables of delicate craftsmanship and little else to distract the eye from its connoisseur pieces —two bronze heads of hollow-cheeked philosophers, each solitary and impressive on a plain pedestal in its corner, and against the wide window a superb vase, also in severe dark bronze, spoil from the far-off sack of Corinth. At the center of the tesselated floor a shaggy Neptune reared his trident in a sober-hued design over a train of sea divinities. Altogether, her father seemed in a perfect setting; her stepmother looked cheerfully out of place.

Marcus Ulpius Severinus was a neatly made man, rather below middle height. He had a lean and nervously handsome aquiline face, clean-shaven, with the same finely proportioned bone structure as Severina's and his eyes, though hard and calculating, were the same deep brown as her own. The crescent of close-cut hair round his bald crown was iron-gray and his skin, furrowed from either nostril to the tips of his thin mouth, had also a grayish tinge. In his expression was a certain unmistakable complacency. It was as though he strangely blended with the austerity of a scholar the self-approval of a successful man of affairs.

Her hands resting on her broad lap, Severina's stepmother gazed at her with placid affection. Drusilla was a comfortable-looking woman, with regular, rather heavy features and a complexion much

4

fairer than her husband's or her stepdaughter's. The intricate tower of curls into which her thick auburn hair had been tugged and twined and coiled at her morning toilet by her ornatrix was absurdly in the latest fashion. Yet even its elaborate artifice did not take from her effect of matronly warmth and simplicity. There was about her an air of common sense and natural calm, as if to have a pedantic and rather condescending husband and an intellectual daughter one could never properly understand were part of a woman's normal experience, to be accepted good-humoredly.

Of her true mother Severina retained only one vivid recollection—a woman, obviously young but with face ravaged, as though with fever, staring at her from sunken eyes whose darkness was accentuated by the black patches beneath; gesturing feebly in her direction with a gaunt hand; and muttering something unintelligible. Severina had forgotten the circumstances, but she guessed that the negligence of some slave had permitted her to wander into the room where her mother was dying. It was for years a horrifying picture that returned to mingle with her nightmares; even now it was a disturbing memory, to be forced back into some far recess of her mind. Still she had never really missed her mother; there was soon another kindly adult woman to watch over her meals and games, choose her clothes, banish with a hug and good-night kiss the unease she felt in the quiet and loneliness of her twilit bedroom, nurse her during her frequent illnesses. For her father had married again within a few months of his bereavement. Probably Drusilla's pleasant matter-of-factness had been a healthy influence on a highly strung only child, so Severina now appreciated. She felt a close natural affinity with the rational outlook of her father, who had personally planned and supervised her education, an uncommonly literary one for a girl, but between her and Drusilla there was, despite the gulf in tastes and interests, a genuine if temperate affection.

"Come in! Come in!" repeated her father genially, as Severina hesitated in the doorway. Suddenly she realized he was wearing the formal tunic of his rank with the broad purple stripe. That meant he had just returned from some official visit—connected with herself, she was certain. The Senate, of which he was a leading spokesman, much admired for his mastery of the frigidly classical style of oratory

5

then in vogue, would hardly be concerned with her. No . . . her father was a respected adviser of the Emperor Valerian. He must just be back from the Palace!

Prompted by some defensive impulse, Severina ignored the empty couch on her father's left hand and sat down on the same couch as Drusilla, though at the opposite edge, holding herself rigidly upright. In the crisis that was engulfing her she felt her stepmother's nearness some protection.

"Yes, Father," she said quietly.

Severinus looked at Drusilla. He had always felt a certain contempt for his second wife—she came of a middle-class family. Nor had she any pretensions to culture: she never read a book. Still, she had brought him a rich dowry at a time when an unlucky lawsuit seriously diminished his resources; and on the death of her uncle, an immensely wealthy army contractor, she had inherited a second fortune. Besides, there was no denying it, she could be shrewd enough in her judgments and she managed their complicated household without fuss. These considerations gave her a status in his eyes, despite her plebeian origins and the fact that she regarded his passion for the arts as a kind of amiable oddity.

Drusilla smiled encouragingly at him and nodded. "Severina, my dear," he began, "I have something to say to you."

A moment's silence. Then, "Yes, Father," repeated Severina with the same forced calm. Reading the strain in the girl's flushed face, Drusilla motioned more emphatically to her husband.

"We have been thinking—your mother and I—about your future," he went on carefully. "You're over seventeen, you know. We feel . . . well, it's getting to be time you were married."

She had anticipated his remark, even the way he phrased it. But the words fell like a blow upon her heart and she stared at him, stricken.

Severinus saw her unconsciously shake her head slowly, an act of instinctive rejection, and he frowned. Though he would never have demeaned himself by showing her warmth, he was fond of his only child after his fashion and was sensitive, as her stepmother rarely was, to her mood. It was because he divined so accurately what she felt that he began to grow irritated. She was so much like

6

himself that it seemed unreasonable of her not to accept his viewpoint.

He plunged on: "All your friends—most of them, at any rate—are already married. Why, that little Clodia, she's only sixteen and she already has a child!"

"It's Claudia, Balbus's daughter," commented Drusilla placidly. "And she's over seventeen—the same age as our Severina."

"Sixteen—seventeen, what odds?" he said peevishly. "The fact is the Emperor has been talking to me about you, Severina."

She had guessed as much, but it did not lessen her anguish.

"Valerian is surrounding himself with these Illyrians—a parvenu tends to favor new men, I suppose," continued Severinus drily. "They're all the rage today. He wishes, he tells me, to wed the vigorous young Rome they represent to the cultured and majestic older Rome represented by the Senatorial nobles. Wed quite literally . . . for, in short, my dear, he has impressed on me what pleasure it would give him to see you married to a distinguished Illyrian. When the Emperor talks like that, we have no option but to obey."

Severina recalled how her father liked to describe himself—though only among intimate friends—as the last philosopher in an age of slavish timeserving and darkening superstition.

"Obey?" she echoed, in a bitter whisper. "Why?"

Her father's delicate nostrils twitched; he breathed audibly. Though he could not fully appreciate the tremendous impact on a sensitive young girl of sudden news that she was being married off to a complete stranger, his conscience was pricking him. No doubt he was not behaving quite like a man of principle. But there it was. The Emperor's wish was a command—the matter was closed. He knew his daughter's recoil was a momentary thing, an irresistible cry of protest before surrender. But because he disliked having to exact from her something she was painfully unwilling to yield, he lost his temper.

"Be a sensible girl, Severina," he snapped. "Do you want to ruin me? Your duty is to marry as the Emperor wishes. If he says an Illyrian, then an Illyrian it must be!"

"Which . . . Illyrian?" asked Severina, through clenched teeth.

Drusilla sat upright; her husband looked wary.

7

"Well," he went on in a more affable tone, "you really should feel flattered. The man the Emperor has in mind is"—here he paused from oratorical habit, though he had no wish to prolong Severina's suspense—"Lucius Domitius Aurelianus. You must have heard of him—Aurelian, the famous general!"

Severina's brows knitted. She knew vaguely that the Illyrians, from the Western Balkans and the Danube provinces, were the Empire's finest soldiers, the core of the Legions. But Lucius Domitius Aurelianus . . . Aurelian? The name meant nothing. She could easily enough have recalled the names of most of the Greek leaders at the siege of Troy, but Rome's living commanders were unknown to her.

Seeing her unhappy bafflement. Drusilla moved over and placed an arm around her shoulder. "It's a good match, darling. Really it is. Aurelian's a great hero, a brilliant soldier!"

Severina drew away, her glittering eyes fixed on her father. "How old is he?" she demanded.

Her father gestured, embarrassed. "I don't exactly know . . . not within a year or two. . . ."

Severina's heart turned to ice. She cared little whether Aurelian were handsome or ugly, rich or poor, famous or obscure. Only that he should not be old, that she should not have a loathsome old man forced on her body!

She looked despairingly round at Drusilla. "How old is he?" she repeated.

Her stepmother's smile was warm with reassurance. "Aurelian's a little over forty . . . forty-three perhaps. He's in the prime of life. After all, he's an active service officer!"

Severina sighed. He was certainly elderly. But at least her husband would not be some bowed and withered graybeard drooling over a young girl's flesh. Aurelian began to take misty shape in her mind. Suddenly, from nowhere, a man she had never known existed was advancing to take possession of her!

"Why?" she murmured. "Why this Aurelian?"

Her father looked relieved. The question was a sensible one. Severina's rational habit of mind was reasserting itself.

"It's natural enough, my dear, when you come to think of it. Aurelian is an army commander, one of the Empire's foremost sol-

8

diers; we are one of Rome's most illustrious houses. Of course, there has been a matchmaker of sorts—my kinsman, Ulpius Crinitus."

He smiled rather sourly, for Crinitus was wounding to his pride twice over. First, by being the son of a freedwoman, a German barbarian at that (actually she was a slave concubine at the time the uncle of Severinus, his father's scapegrace younger brother, had begotten Crinitus). And again, less excusably, by having distinguished himself so greatly in the Army that his reputation outshone that of any other member of his family.

Severina could recall seeing this brilliant though rather dubious second cousin of hers once only—some six years ago when, visiting Rome on duty, he had coolly billeted himself on them. He was a burly, loud-voiced, chuckling man, with a broad but firm-fleshed face, a kind of crust worked by wind and weather on his tanned cheeks and small, lively gray eyes each flanked by rays of humorous wrinkles. There was a swagger, a dash of the devil-may-care about him that startled Severina and obviously jarred on her father.

Crinitus had seemed to keep their rather staid household in an uproar for the whole week of his stay. His booming voice could be heard everywhere, often raised in rather indelicate jokes, at which he himself was the first to laugh. He drank a lot, though fortunately the wine seemed only to add to his great good humor. His manner with the maids smacked rather of the streets of a garrison town than of the most cultured environment of Rome.

He was popular at once with the servants and with Drusilla he got on famously. Severina at the time was fascinated but baffled by him. On his arrival, he had eyed her undeveloped body narrowly and chuckled, "Time you were a woman—eh?" Leaving her with hot cheeks, he had gone off to fish among his baggage and returned with a rough wooden box, from which he produced a huge brooch magnificently wrought in gold, showing an antler-proud stag in flight with hind legs curiously elongated and forelegs coiled, while his flanks seemed to heave with his panting; the blend of artifice with nature in it was quite unfamiliar to Severina. He pushed it into her hands, pressed her fingers over it and said: "I took it from the wife of a Scythian chief I slew (here he made the comically exaggerated imitation of a fierce sword thrust and burst out laughing). I had the chieftainess—you have her brooch!" Scandalized, her

9

father had glared at Drusilla, who had hurried her off on some pretext. After that, she had been kept away as much as possible from Crinitus, but the brooch remained her most valuable—and cherished—personal ornament.

When Crinitus left, he had planted a hearty kiss on her forehead and embraced her with clumsy warmth. At long intervals, other handsome presents, purchases as well as spoils, would arrive from him, accompanied by some banteringly affectionate message.

"Aurelian took over from him on the Rhine some time ago," her father was saying. "Crinitus seems to have taken a great fancy to him. He spoke to our respected Emperor about him—and you. Now Valerian, as you'd expect, has come to think the whole proposal his own—he is most enthusiastic."

Severina, less agitated now, studied the floor; she felt completely helpless. The Emperor, two great commanders and her own father, a pillar of the Senate, had been conspiring about her. The whole massive machinery of the Roman State appeared to be crushing her into subjection. It seemed treasonable, almost impious, to resist.

Drusilla gave her husband a look; he nodded and rose. "I must be going," he said, as casually as he could, addressing them both. "The President . . . he's expecting me . . . about tomorrow's debate." He came over and stood a few moments looking down on Severina's bent head. He had been in no hurry to lose his daughter to some stranger, although Drusilla had been urging for a year now that they find her a husband. Nor could he feel overjoyed about the Emperor's choice of bridegroom. Aurelian was a man of no family or fortune, a common soldier who had fought his way up from the ranks. He might be difficult to handle, too—people said he was a harsh disciplinarian. Still, the match had certain advantages, there was no doubt of it. To have a formidable soldier as son-in-law would strengthen his position enormously. As for Severina . . . he shrugged his shoulders rather unhappily. "A pity she wasn't a boy!" he thought and placed his hand for an instant, almost diffidently, on her lustrous black hair.

She looked up and said, smiling wanly, "It's all right, Father!" —interpreting the rare caress as an appeal, though in reality it had been prompted by something like compassion.

10

Once her husband had gone, Drusilla took the girl's head on her own strong shoulder. "Aurelian's coming to Rome next month. You'll be very happy, trust me!" Severina's lip trembled. As a high-born Roman maiden she had little conception of romantic love and she had always known that something like today's happenings was inevitable. Yet in spite of her masculine education (or perhaps because it had made the Olympians familiar figures in her thoughts) she had had her vague dreams of a radiant, godlike youth, whose arms would be a haven from the harsh, incomprehensible world. Instead . . . instead, they were handing her over to an aging man . . . set in his habits . . . infirm, probably . . . some rugged Illyrian swordsman . . . shaggy . . . uncouth of speech . . . a loose-tongued roisterer, like Crinitus. The inconsistency of these pictures suddenly struck her and she almost smiled at herself. At the same time, deep within her, something had awoken, trembling and expectant, that took no regard of Aurelian's age and manners, only of the fact that he was a man. As Drusilla stroked her head, very gently, she struggled to find relief in words from these bewildering emotions and the confusion of her thoughts, but all she managed to say at last was, "Oh, Mother!"

2

A SINGLE lamp, hanging from a wooden stand, was burning in the middle of the lofty Praetorian tent, the acrid smoke, which at intervals obscured its yellow flame, adding a tang to the smell of damp earth. Nearby three men sat in attitudes of ease round a small table of undressed pine, on which stood a wine jar, a pitcher, and some drinking-pots, all of coarse earthenware; the men's shadows stretched across the trampled grass and wavered on the streaked and shabby leather walls.

Neither the raw night chill nor the fumes seemed to trouble them, so absorbed were they in their conversation. Two of the men were listening intently to the third, a Military Tribune by his insignia. He was slim and good-looking in a youthful way, with curly chestnut hair tumbling over a broad brow, and his voice was eager and melodious. As he spoke his sparkling dark eyes were fixed across the table on a tall, strongly built man—perhaps ten years older than himself—whose muscular neck emerged from a leather jerkin. The last of the trio was a brawny First Centurion with a hard-bitten face. His thick lower lip protruded a little, truculently; his knotted forehead showed the effort he was making to follow.

"Luckily your wine is stronger than your logic," said the Tribune, smiling. He tipped the jar over the rim of a pot, judging the flow of wine carefully. Then he took up the pitcher, shook it to hear the contents swish and poured a slow trickle of water into the pot, diluting the wine to his taste. "What about you, Aurelian?"

The long-limbed man in the jerkin raised his head—there was a suggestion of force even in the casual movement—and pushed a mug forward.

"Just a little—half and half." His voice, though conversational in pitch, was firm and resonant, as if capable, when necessary, of compelling attention across a wide parade ground.

"Mucapor?" asked the Tribune, turning.

"No water for me, philosopher!" the Centurion answered with a hoarse chuckle. He grasped the jar's neck in one sinewy hand, a pot in the other, and tilted them expertly together. "Not a drop spilled, see!" he exclaimed, holding up the pot with the wine gleaming a little short of the rim. He took a deep draught and smacked his lips.

"To resume," said the Tribune. "It is obvious that as the peoples of the Empire must unite in its defense, so must their gods. Such is our peril now that Rome needs all her gods, even those that once fought against her, even those she once tried to suppress."

"But Demaratus," said Aurelian carefully. "Are not the gods already united? You said yourself that all are manifestations of one Supreme God."

The Centurion grinned. "Ay, you did that—you can't get away from it!"

Demaratus looked more boyish than ever as he laughed. "I'd

12

thought you would say that," he observed, addressing Aurelian. "There is, as I pointed out, one Divine Essence, one unknowable Godhead from which all the gods emerge whom men worship. But since we cannot, either by sacrifice or prayer, reach this ultimate Divine Unity, so pure and remote it is, we must for practical purposes concern ourselves with the various outward forms in which alone we can apprehend it. You follow?"

Aurelian nodded. The Centurion scratched his ear with a look of worried concentration.

"Some of these gods are more powerful than others." Demaratus was speaking more slowly, so as not to outrun the understanding of his audience. "Perhaps it is because men pray to them more often and more fervently and prayer, particularly from the heart of chaste and upright worshipers, is a source of power to a god, just as levies and tributes strengthen a monarch on earth."

"One moment!" Aurelian was frowning. "What of the barbarians? When we meet them in battle their gods fight our gods. Does that mean one part of the Divine Essence fights another?"

"Exactly!" Demaratus sipped his wine, enjoying the moment. "Just as the race of men, though one, is divided against itself, so the Godhead. Why, there is evidence on every hand of conflict in the Heavens—good wars with evil, even one good with another good. Obviously there are combinations and concentrations among the gods at certain times in certain causes—you could call them alliances. Now we three here honor Mithras above all: we are initiates of His mysteries, and because of our common faith we can talk like brothers, regardless of rank. But we would be foolish to disdain the help of other gods. Terrible dangers threaten Rome: we should muster the greatest number of gods we can on her behalf!"

"Where's your Greek subtlety leading us?" growled Aurelian. "You'll have us begging the god of the Christians for help!"

Mucapor gave a scornful grunt.

"Better have Him with us than against," retorted Demaratus. "You yourself must fear Him, Aurelian, for you don't enforce the edicts, though there is a regular persecution in many towns. And you are quite right. Look what happened to Nero. He turned the Christians into living torches—and he died miserably himself. Come to our own times—take Decius. He incurred the enmity of this Christ by persecuting His followers and there's no need to remind you, Aurelian, how he met his end!"

At this reference to the Emperor who with an entire Roman army had been slain by the Goths nine years before, Aurelian with a wry expression rubbed his left shoulder.

"Still feel it, General?" asked the Centurion, remembering that Aurelian had been wounded in the great disaster.

"When it rains," answered Aurelian curtly. He got up, walked to the entrance of the tent and drew the hanging back. "Did you hear something?" he muttered.

By the thin starlight between the scudding clouds his trained eye could make out faintly the silent lanes of tents. A light glimmered from the guard tent, at the camp boundary.

He turned his head toward Demaratus. "You may be right," he said thoughtfully. "We shouldn't antagonize any god, not even this Christ." Then he looked out again into the night that overhung Pannonia.

Of course, Demaratus was a clever Greek word-spinner, but even clever words can be ill-omened. That reference to Decius was an untimely one. The name was an evocation of defeat—of defeat by the Goths.

He stood there troubled, conscious of his scarred shoulder, his thoughts ranging far into the immense gloom.

Some Gothic raiding parties had been reported on this side of the Danube. There was no certainty about their numbers and the direction in which they were moving. They might loot a village or two and run for it; they might be lunging deep into the province. He had made all the necessary dispositions, but if this proved an incursion in force, the situation could quickly become very serious. With a scowl he looked over the sleeping camp—he did not relish the thought of a battle against the Goths, not with this scruffy mob! On the Rhine where he had relieved Crinitus and, more recently, during a tour of duty as Inspector of Camps, he had found discipline everywhere breaking down in the Army. But here in Pannonia, to which he had come almost a month ago with a handpicked staff, including Demaratus and Mucapor, the demoralization was worst of all. The

14

catastrophe in which Decius had perished weighed on the soldiers' imaginations. The Balkan Legions had forgotten the habit of victory; the Goths had established a moral ascendancy over them.

With narrowed eyes Aurelian tried to penetrate the darkness around the guard tent where the light went off and on as though men were passing and repassing it. Some unusual activity was taking place there, for it was not yet time for the normal sentry reliefs. A sense of foreboding grew on him. The night seemed full of menace. Shadowy pictures invaded his mind of barbarian bands, swift and silent, padding over the shrouded Pannonian plain.

Yes, Demaratus was right: if it came to a battle they would need the help of every god they could persuade. If only he had a year to build up his formations and lick the men into shape! The Legions were down to half, a quarter even, of their paper strength; cohorts dwindled to two or three hundred; centuries shrunk to a mere handful. And the soldiers, though they were of tough Illyrian peasant stock, most of them, had gone to pieces. On his arrival he had found half of them wandering over the countryside, terrorizing the villagers. They had been involved in the rebellion of one of those accursed pretenders the Empire seemed to breed on every side. It soon had come to grief and what with one thing and another, they had drawn no pay for months. Nothing made a soldier more sullen than a grievance over pay. Sullen—and dangerous. It was all very well for Valerian, far away from the province, to decree fitting punishment for mutineers. But an unpaid soldier was a trained killer with a seething heart and a sword in his hand.

He had begun by paying the men part of their arrears. That step, taken on his own responsibility, was one of the things he would have to account for when he visited Rome next month for the staff talks—and, of course, to get married.

Even in his mood of disquiet thoughts flickered through his mind about the bride the Emperor was bestowing on him. He had little sentiment about the matter; it was not uncommon for a senior officer to have his wife thus chosen; and, in his own case, he knew it was a mark of Imperial favor and a means of advancing his career. Still he wondered briefly and half-absently, what this Ulpia Severina really was like. Valerian's letter had described her as "young, of great beauty, exceptionally talented, and of noblest family." To Aurelian it sounded like the routine extravagances of court rhetoric. At any rate, there was no doubt she was young, surprisingly young, and of a distinguished family—she was a Senator's daughter and cousin of sorts to Crinitus.

He quickly dismissed the subject. More pressing concerns engaged his thoughts. He needed time. His action in paying the men had certainly put them in better heart. Nearly all had returned to their standards and he had been able to assemble the bulk of the two weak Legions under his command in this training camp and to start the laborious task of turning them into disciplined soldiers. If only he had a year, one quiet year. . . .

But since the death of Decius none could confidently reckon on a whole year of peace along this stretch of frontier. The most alarming feature of the situation was that there were no reinforcements he could call up speedily if a grave emergency broke. Now that winter was over, Valerian would be returning shortly to Asia to resume personal command of Rome's main army in her bitter war with Persia. Already he had summoned to his aid the two best Legions from the Lower Danube, leaving the defenses of the Balkans dangerously undermanned.

With a sigh Aurelian turned back into the tent where the murmur of Demaratus' voice had hardly stilled for a moment. Mucapor caught his eye and grimaced as Demaratus said: "Once skepticism was the fashion. Who's a skeptic now? What have unbelievers in common but their unbelief?"

Aurelian stiffened. "Wait!" he said, his tone peremptory. "What was that?"

Instantly there was quiet. The informal atmosphere in the tent was transformed. Aurelian's authority had asserted itself in four brief words, a harsh, dominating presence.

Some faint disturbance was gnawing the edge of the silence. Suddenly a tiny but insistent and increasing sound occupied the ear. After a while they identified it: two men, in armor, were approaching the tent at the double.

Aurelian sat down calmly at the table. "Take these away!" he said to Mucapor, indicating the drinking vessels.

A few moments later, the Guard Commander bulked in the entrance to the tent; his brow glistened. "General," he panted, "a messenger from Fort Quintilian." He turned and beckoned. A tall, sandy-haired soldier, whose face was drawn and dejected, stumbled in after him.

Making an effort, the soldier saluted smartly. "Our commander, Lucius Prudens, sent me, sir," he announced, half-stammering. "The men have run away."

There was a suppressed gasp from Demaratus. Mucapor shuffled. Aurelian looked steadily at the soldier.

"Stand at ease. Tell me what happened—quickly," he said, not raising his voice.

The man glanced haggardly at the Guard Commander, as if for support in telling his shameful story. "A patrol went out—they found the Goths advancing . . . thousands of them . . ."

"Exactly how many thousands?"

There was a brief pause. "Two or three," amended the soldier in a low voice. "They got back—our patrol, I mean. There was panic when the news spread. Some men started running. Then everyone seemed to bolt."

"Your Commander, Lucius Prudens . . . ?"

"He grabbed some of them, swearing and punching right and left. But they swarmed past him—he got knocked over. A lot of them made for this camp. He yelled to me—I was orderly—to get the horse and report to you. There was someone already on it. I had a fight before I could drag him off. I should have got here hours ago, but the horse went lame."

Aurelian stared at him, calculating. A mob of Roman soldiers, getting on for two hundred of them, in terror-stricken flight at the mere report of approaching Goths. No doubt the Gothic vanguard were already in the empty fort, which dominated a strategic road junction; they must have rushed word back to their chiefs that the way to Sirmium lay open.

"Guard Commander," snapped Aurelian. "All Centurions here inside ten minutes! Never mind about dressing properly. Warn the duty detachment to be ready to parade any moment—full marching order. We'll be leaving soon for Sirmium—yes, I'll be with them.

Get all the cooks up—a day's hard rations for every man. Off you go— Oh," he added, as the Guard Commander saluted. "Get someone to collect a meal for this man."

He turned to Demaratus and Mucapor. "Fort Quintilian's twenty miles from Sirmium—the Goths will be at the gates by nightfall. We'll be there first. I'm leaving within the half-hour. Get two more cohorts off as soon as they're ready, the Second and Fifth. The rest follow at dawn. Send an alert to the Cavalry camp: tell Herennianus we're concentrating at Sirmium. You, Mucapor, will bring up the rear guard. Strike the tents; stack them. Seize a few wagons somewhere to load essential stores. Put a guard on what you leave behind: it would take a year to get replacements."

Twenty minutes later, the camp was blazing with lights, when Aurelian strode onto the parade ground where the two hundred men of the duty cohort were cursing and rubbing the sleep from their eyes. A subdued growl traveled round: "Old Hand-on-Hilt!" The muttering stilled. A Centurion barked and the men stamped to attention. More orders clanged on the night air. A long column emerged from the parade ground and threaded through the camp toward the main gate, propelled by the curses and the husky, insistent "left, right!—left, right!" of the Centurions.

The rhythmic trampling diminished down the dirt road that ran toward the Sirmium Highway.

Just before dawn they were still marching strongly when they came up with the first of the fugitives from Fort Quintilian. One of the scouts dropped back and sought out the Centurion, who gave the brusque command, "Javelins ready, men!" and reported to Aurelian. There was a swift, laconic murmur between them. As the files pressed forward they soon saw the runaways in a disorderly line at the roadside, blinking stupidly at the apparition of Roman soldiers marching confidently toward the terror from which they themselves had fled. In the bleak twilight, they looked haggard and shamefaced. Most of them still had swords in their scabbards: none of them bore a shield.

The Centurion bawled. The rear half of the column halted with a crash, while the rest carried on for another twenty paces or so and then, at another sharp command, also stamped to a standstill, leaving an interval in the center of the formation.

"You there!" rasped the Centurion at the fugitives, with an abrupt, sideways scooping motion of his hand toward the gap. "Pile your arms and get fell in, d'you hear!"

First two or three obeyed, and then, with a sluggish, fearful motion, the rest followed. Swords clinked onto a swiftly growing heap. The disarmed men formed up with scared eyes where the Centurion's gesture had scornfully indicated.

"Anyone see what became of your Officer?" called the Centurion, hoarse and menacing.

The men froze. After a moment heads began to shake, repudiating any connection with the fate of Lucius Prudens, while there were one or two mutters of "No! No!"

The Centurion's shrug was ominous. He conferred briefly in a low voice with Aurelian; then his word of command jarred again on the ear and, in the first gray light, the march was resumed, the rear ranks of the column collecting, as they passed, the surrendered weapons of the runaways.

As the darkness ebbed, the imprint of former raids became plainly visible over the countryside. Blackened walls of roofless huts . . . fruit trees with branches wrenched off to feed barbarian camp fires . . . an occasional villa in ruins amid gardens fast reverting to wilderness.

Already the first laden farm wagons were trundling on to the road, for through the night the alarm had sped from village to village. Dejected peasants in plaids or rough woolen coats and trousers prodded the slow yoke oxen with goads; while, seated precariously aloft amid blankets and pots and pans and baskets and squawking hens, their women, some of them with babies at the breast, gazed sullenly at the soldiers who once again had failed to protect their homes. Even the solemn, sleepy-eyed children stared down in hostile silence at the rows of helmets flowing past.

By the time they came within sight of Sirmium, the column, urged on by the tireless blasphemies of the Centurions, was pushing its way past long, crawling processions of carts and through crowds of even more pitiable evacuees, who trudged along, many humping outsize bundles.

It still lacked several hours to noon when the feet of Aurelian's men rang on the cobbled street behind the main gate of Sirmium. In the center of their formation, picked up at intervals along the dozen miles of highway they had tramped, marched some fifty disarmed and dispirited men, surrendered runaways from Fort Quintilian.

Though a provincial center and military headquarters, Sirmium had suffered from the general decay and depopulation. Not only the hovels in the narrow lanes of the poorest quarters, but many of the more substantial houses lining the main road, were dilapidated and some were semiruinous.

In the prosperous neighborhood near the Forum, not a few mansions were empty, with only caretakers and their fierce watchdogs behind the blank outer walls and barred gates; for wealthy people were tending to emigrate from the disturbed frontier region to the more tranquil South.

Already in the town's open spaces and vacant building lots, refugees were installing themselves with the routine born of experience; some making up beds for the youngest children, worn out with their hurried and comfortless flight; others seeking water and kindling to cook a meal.

Knots of onlookers stood here and there at the roadside as Aurelian's troops swung by. But there were no cheers; only an anxious murmur, as if the column's size caused disappointment. The men, eager to rest, stepped out briskly; soon they were wheeling through the gateway of the barracks. This was a commodious complex of one-storey buildings capable of housing a thousand troops and a mass of warlike stores. The runaways from Fort Quintilian were herded into a dingy shed and a strong guard posted outside with orders to strike to kill if a breakout were attempted.

Aurelian was making a quick inspection of the armories when one of the headquarters clerks came hurrying up. "Someone from the Town Council to see you, sir."

The Councillor was fretfully pacing about in the orderly room, a thin, sour-faced man, who looked as if he had suffered so long from a disordered stomach that he had forgotten the taste of a satisfying meal.

"I'm Aulus Saturninus," he announced in a precise and peevish voice. "Acting Chief Magistrate. My senior colleague's ill. What a shocking business this is, General! We haven't begun to recover from the last attack and here the Goths are again."

"Yes, they're here again," said Aurelian, "yet there still isn't a proper organization to deal with all these refugees."

The Magistrate looked resentful. "The peasants? What can we do? We would have to find staff, accommodation, stores of every kind. Who's going to pay for it? Taxation is crippling, as it is!"

"Pretty helpless, aren't you?" said Aurelian.

The Magistrate drew himself up. "It's no privilege to be responsible for administering a town like Sirmium these days. I'm prepared to hand it over to anyone you nominate. We could avoid all this trouble if only the government kept a proper garrison here."

Aurelian shrugged. He had no wish to involve himself in a wrangle with this carping civilian.

"Let's get to business," he said sharply. "Sit down." The Magistrate took the stool he indicated, but his face was still rigid with righteous indignation.

"First," said Aurelian. "How many German and Sarmatian slaves have you in Sirmium?"

"Why do you want to know?"

"How many?" repeated Aurelian, a clang in his voice.

"I should say—at a guess—two to three hundred."

"They're to be rounded up. Today. Every one of them. I'll lend you a squad of soldiers. Lock them up in small batches—and, till I give you the word, put them on the smallest rations that will keep them alive."

"I must protest, General!" snapped the Magistrate, who had bobbed up and down while Aurelian was speaking. "These men are valuable property. Many are public slaves. Who's going to sweep the streets and stoke the furnaces at the baths?"

"I could suggest some who'd benefit from the exercise," Aurelian said tartly. "Anyway, it's an order, justified by the emergency. Don't you see, man, what could happen if the Goths attack? These barbarian slaves are itching to win their freedom. All they need do is rush one of the gates—the Goths would be in your streets in a matter of minutes."

The Magistrate looked shaken.

"Next point," Aurelian resumed. "I want all wineshops closed. Never mind the loss to business," he added, as the Magistrate's mouth automatically opened. "I shall have four thousand soldiers in Sirmium tonight. Their tongues will be hanging out, after their forced march. I can't have the only Roman army for hundreds of miles rolling in the gutters."

Outside, there was the noise of a detachment arriving and a series of sharp commands: equipment dropped with a clatter on the pavement.

The Magistrate pursed his lips. "Very well," he said, without enthusiasm.

"The same applies to the brothels—close them," said Aurelian. "It will stop men going absent. No need to get excited—it's only for one night. We're leaving tomorrow."

"What!" exclaimed the Magistrate, jumping up. "You're going away?"

"Don't worry!" answered Aurelian drily. "We're not deserting you. We're marching against the Goths."

The Magistrate stared at Aurelian, his expression slowly growing a little more amiable. Then he said with a strained-looking smile, "Well, General, you can rely on the Council to do everything we can to support the Army. I trust you will do my wife and myself the honor of dining with us today."

"Too busy, thanks," said Aurelian. "I can't snatch an hour to see my mother. She's here in Sirmium . . ."

He broke off as heavy and hurried footfalls approached along the corridor. A soldier of the guard clumped in. "Message from the walls, sir. Patrol of Goths in sight."

"You must excuse me," said Aurelian. A few moments later the startled Magistrate was alone in the room.

22

Followed by a dozen soldiers Aurelian walked along the ramparts. From his lofty viewpoint the patrol, still distant, looked like a slow trickle of dots over the plain; twenty to thirty of them, mounted no doubt on captured ponies. As usual, he felt a hot gust of hatred, not entirely free from apprehension, at the sight of Goths. Never before on her northern frontier had Rome to contend with such an enemy, so numerous, so united, so determined and skillful in aggression; a restless, mobile, fiercely warlike people, from whose tremendous series of impacts the Empire was reeling. He could picture them, a multitude of uncouth, shaggy men and ruddy-cheeked, sturdy women, plodding silently south from the desolate Baltic shore, on and on through the immense dank forests, trampling down or swallowing up the tribes in their path, until they issued into the light and air of the endless Sarmatian plains. There, in one prolific generation, they had spread their settlements from the foothills of the Caucasus to the Dacian frontier, which had simply dissolved at their presence. They allied their characteristic German battle fury with a most un-German cohesion. They fought stubbornly and with cunning and were fertile in stratagem; they were as formidable in defense as in attack. Already they had broken the self-confidence of the legions and—first of all the barbarians to do so—had slain a Roman Emperor in the field.

At intervals on the walls of Sirmium stood batteries of catapults, ungainly but powerful engines, whose stone missiles could smash any assault by ill-equipped barbarians. Their condition, however, was poor. For a long time nobody had bothered to protect them against the weather with tarpaulins or dismantle them and store the sections under cover, a wanton neglect that was part of the general loosening of grip in the Empire. Aurelian stopped at a trio of catapults that seemed in rather better state than the others, perhaps because they stood in the lee of a tower. He heard the men exclaim; they were pointing over the battlements. The Goths, still squat figures rammed down on squat horses, were drawing near and making gestures which he could swear were derisory. His brow darkened. "Check over those catapults—quick as you can!" he called to the men. A couple of minutes passed, while the Goths jogged onward,

23

growing slowly bigger and bigger. "Cable's perished on one—two look all right, sir," a soldier shouted. "Bit mucky, though!"

"Load!" commanded Aurelian, not taking his eyes from the Goths, who now were nonchalantly riding into extreme range. The men ran to the tower and returned with stone roundshot from the heap at its base. They tugged at the catapults: back in a stiff motion swung the arms and the two missiles were hoisted into place. The Goths were watching now, unimpressed.

"Let 'em have it!" rapped Aurelian. Creaking, the lever of one catapult jerked free and slapped over viciously. The shot whined in a swift perceptible arc toward the Goths, struck the ground near them and bounced past, spattering them with earth and tiny stone splinters. Their formation halted abruptly and began to recoil. Before they could retreat more than a yard or two, the second stone tore right across their fringe, bowling half a dozen over. The others fled, leaving men and horses writhing on the ground. The soldiers cheered and Aurelian smiled grimly; it was good to see Goths run in panic.

About an hour before dusk, one thousand men had formed up in a hollow square in the parade ground of the Sirmium barracks; they were fully armed, except that none bore javelins. Most had marched fast and far that day. They were weary and a bit jumpy with the expectation of action—early and bloody action, since old Hand-on-Hilt was their commander—and there was muttering in the ranks. A reverberating bellow from the senior Centurion froze all tongues; there was a swift twofold crash as the men stamped and stiffened to attention. Aurelian, followed at a few paces by Demaratus, Mucapor, and three other officers of his staff, appeared and took up position facing the square.

The next moment the feet of many men were heard marching with desperate smartness to viciously compulsive timing from a Centurion whose voice seemed to lash like a whip round their calves. Into the center of the hollow square filed almost one hundred and fifty bareheaded men, without armor or weapons, the day's haul of the fugitives from Fort Quintilian. They formed up in two ranks, facing Aurelian.

"Soldiers!" Aurelian did not appear to shout, but his voice grated in every ear. "Look at these men! They shamefully betrayed their standard. They ran from the enemy. They abandoned a Roman fortress and placed Sirmium and the whole province in danger."

The hush that followed was charged with foreboding. Most of the runaways had hung their heads as the words flailed them, but a few looked about them piteously or with a show of defiance.

"The penalty for cowardice in action is death," the implacable voice resumed. To those screened from Aurelian by the double row of runaways it seemed disembodied, assailing them from every side. "By virtue of the authority vested in me as your General, I impose this penalty on one man in ten. Sentence will be carried out at once!"

The shuffle of one overstrained young soldier sounded monstrous in the appalled silence.

A decimation! The dreaded punishment which maintained the iron military discipline of the Empire's great days had fallen into disuse, partly because ignominious routs had become so common that it would have been grossly wasteful of trained soldiers; partly because the unruly temper of the Legions, who felt themselves masters of the State, made it dangerous to practice mass executions among them.

There was a faint murmur, wordless, menacing. The oldest soldier present could hardly remember anyone who claimed to have been eyewitness of a decimation—and here was the General decreeing death, instant, shameful death, for ten—twelve—fifteen perhaps of their own comrades!

Before the mingled wrath and horror could voice itself in a universal growl, Mucapor strode forward, harsh-faced, a brutally overbearing figure who inhibited any noise but his own. At a deliberate pace, he walked along the front of the runaways, counting aloud, in a monotone. At ten, he grabbed the shoulder of a shrinking, white-cheeked wretch and pulled him forward. "You!" he bawled. "Fall in over there—you, too," he added, seizing the corresponding man in the rear rank.

With an automatic movement the men who had escaped selection closed up, rejecting the condemned.

25

Tensely, staring, the parade watched Mucapor repeat the cold-blooded process again . . . again . . . again. . . . Soon fourteen men huddled together with stupefied expressions at a point midway between the diminished ranks from which they had been taken and Aurelian.

Mucapor turned toward the nearest barracks building and blared, "Forward!"

At once three burly men appeared; the foremost carrying a long, broadbladed sword naked on his shoulder; the others straining behind with a massive wooden block. Immediately in their rear marched a squad of stalwart legionaries, from the First Cohort, Mucapor's own. Each grasped two javelins.

Hypnotized, the condemned men saw the executioner's assistants set the block carefully down; adjust its position; then come over and with the same methodical calm seize one of their number, strip him swiftly to the waist and draw him, unresisting, away.

So intense was the stillness that the blade's swish could be plainly heard and the soft thump of the falling head caused a visible tremor.

"Next!" rasped Mucapor; a second man was hurried to the block.

The parade watched spellbound; now that the ritual of killing had begun, every man felt rooted to his place. Only the ministers of death and their victims made any movement. So rapidly and efficiently were the condemned being dispatched that five men died almost soundlessly except for a yelp, cut short by the headsman's blade, from the last of them.

Then the spell snapped. The sixth victim, a huge, tousled man, eyes bulging, throat working, wrenched himself free from the executioner's assistants and flung himself toward Aurelian. Before anyone could intervene, he was on his knees, clutching at Aurelian's legs, babbling for mercy.

His incoherent cries unnerved the onlookers; a low moan went up; the alignment of the ranks suddenly grew less precise; trembling hands fumbled toward sword hilts.

Aurelian gave the supplicant one bleak look and motioned: the executioner's assistants seized him under the armpits and dragged him away.

Again the hiss of the great sword; again that soft, dreadful thump.

26

Aurelian raised his arm. "Enough! Let the rest return to the ranks."

Mucapor bent on Aurelian an almost imploring look of balked bloodlust; then turned with a scowl on the survivors. "Off with you, scum," he snarled, swinging the nearest one round and propelling him in the direction of his unit.

It was a few seconds before the stunned men grasped that they had been reprieved. Two or three tottered and all walked as though dazed. There was much shuffling and stumbling while they raggedly fell in. As the lines dressed, one pitched forward in a faint; the others ignored him.

"Men!" The cold authority in Aurelian's voice beat down mutinous thoughts. "Remember: a Roman soldier never runs from the enemy!"

There was a pause: then he resumed in a tone that was almost comradely: "And now we can go out and look for those Goths!"

He made a sign to Mucapor who stepped back smartly and wheeled to face the parade.

"All units will draw forty-eight hours' rations tonight. The disarmed unit will report to the stores, to be issued weapons. Reveille at dawn. Everyone on parade one hour later!"

The other Centurions took up his commands, adapting them to their own formations. Their shouts mingled in a masterful uproar. The soldiers were caught up in the intricate maneuvers for disentangling a complex of units tightly arrayed in a confined space. They had no time to mutter, hardly to think.

Before the last formation had tramped off, the corpses had been hauled away, and the only reminder of the evening's gruesome ceremonial was the sight of the executioner's assistants scouring the spot where the block had stood.

3

FOR three days Aurelian with almost four thousand men moved cautiously but steadily against the Goths, who retreated slowly, keeping just beyond reach of his advance guard. He had left behind all heavy baggage, including the cumbrous entrenching tools. Wideranging patrols beat all woods, scrambled to the skyline of the neighboring ridges, probed the dense undergrowth of the ravines. A little way inside this mobile screen, columns alert for instant action double-guarded the flanks of the main formation. No fortified camp with palisaded mound and ditch protected the army at night; instead the men bivouacked in naturally strong positions, round which pickets in depth made it certain that the alarm would be given in ample time at any hostile approach.

Still the Goths fell back and back, with a disdainful calm. Aurelian's cavalry consisted of one hundred and seventy men in all, illtrained and poorly mounted; and although they were ably handled by Herennianus, a dashing and skillful young officer Aurelian had brought with him from Gaul, they were capable of little more than scouting duties. Their attempts to harass the Gothic rear guard were easily warded off.

Fort Quintilian was reoccupied without a fight, but it stood empty, its stores of food and equipment swept clean. Of Lucius Prudens, its commander, no trace could be discovered.

Astonished to find the formidable Goths continuously giving ground, the legionaries grew elated. But Aurelian rode thoughtfully among the marching files, revolving the thousand and one possibilities. Most disquieting of all was a report of powerful bands moving swiftly along the opposite shore of the Danube, through war-desolated Dacia; if they crossed the river, the horde he was pursuing might turn to confront him with double strength.

28

Every instinct, every calculation, told him that, reinforced or not, the Goths would, sooner or later, turn savagely on him. He would have to stand and fight, no matter what the odds; retreat had become inadmissible. For despite the strict orders he had given to Demaratus, whom he had left in charge at Sirmium, the peasants, impatient to get back to their fields, were pouring out of the city, with the active encouragement of the Council.

The Gothic withdrawal continued through the fourth day, but now it was almost leisurely, with a menacing assurance about it, as though the barbarians felt themselves masters of the situation. Frequent skirmishes exploded in which too-eager Roman patrols were bloodily repelled. That evening from the Gothic position could be heard wild cheering and the clash of thousands of swords on shields; and campfires began to pierce the falling dark over an area much wider than formerly. It was clear that very substantial reinforcements had arrived.

There would be a battle the following day; every Roman soldier knew, even before orders were issued to prepare for one, and gloom replaced the easy exhilaration of the past. The officers gathered round Aurelian for instructions. They stood in a silent half-circle, while in a brisk matter-of-fact way he described his dispositions, pointing to landmarks just visible in the fading light. Nobody interrupted; his voice went on for fifteen or twenty minutes, never faltering, never raised.

When the briefing was over and the officers dispersed, one of the Centurions hurried to the nearest bivouac and called the Fourth Cohort on parade. Grumbling darkly, about two hundred and fifty legionaries formed up in the open space at the center of the encampment.

Aurelian nodded to the Centurion, who turned toward the men and bawled, "All Christians—one pace forward!"

The men stared dumbly in front of them; no one stirred.

"All Christians one step forward—march!" repeated the Centurion, exasperation in his tone. Aurelian groaned inwardly. The soldiers obviously scented punishment for some of their number; both their instinct to stay out of trouble and their loyalty to their comrades were at work. He would never learn anything from those deliberately blank faces. He motioned the Centurion aside and himself came forward. "Soldiers!" he rapped out. "I want to find one Christian. He shall come to no harm—on the word of a Roman General. Now, quick, where is he?"

In one section of the front rank there was an almost imperceptible tremor, as though a strong impulse to glance in a certain direction had been instantaneously checked. Aurelian walked toward the center of this fleeting agitation. "Come along!" His voice was commanding, but not unkindly. "Step forward—no one will harm you!" This time the stir was evident and indicated one man as clearly as if a dozen fingers had pointed.

"You there!" ordered Aurelian. "One pace forward!"

The soldier stood a moment irresolute, swaying slightly; then he obeyed.

"Your name?"

"Damasius, sir." It was a Pannonian rustic voice—slow, with a burr, stubborn.

"You're a Christian, aren't you?"

There was a moment's pause, while Aurelian could sense the heightened tension in the ranks. Then, "Yes, General," the soldier answered quietly.

He was a rangy, muscular fellow, sallow-skinned, with a knobbly face disfigured on one cheek by an oblique scar from ear to chin. His gray eyes, deep-set under shaggy brows, had a fanatical gleam; his clean-shaven, aggressive jaw was set. All ready for martyrdom, Aurelian thought, surveying him.

"Dismiss the parade," he directed the Centurion. He waited till the men were streaming away. "Damasius," he began, "I want you to do a service for the Army, for Rome. . . ." The man's eyebrows went up; he shot a suspicious glance at Aurelian. "It's simple enough," Aurelian went on, "I want you to pray for our victory over the Goths."

Damasius frowned and glared to either side, both confused and affronted. Then he looked Aurelian in the eyes, without flinching.

"I can't do that!" he said.

Up strode the Centurion, arm raised to grasp his shoulder. "Do as you're told, you swine!" he shouted.

30

"I can't pray," Damasius repeated, doggedly.

"Keep away!" Aurelian curtly bade the outraged Centurion. "Now, Damasius, why can't you pray?"

Damasius shuffled, clearly at a loss for an acceptable answer, but as clearly obstinate in his resolve.

"Well . . . you see, sir . . . I'm not ordained," he brought out finally.

"What's that got to do with it? You've got a tongue, haven't you?" Aurelian tried to keep a patient manner, but already there was the grind of exasperation in his tone.

"Only an ordained priest should make a request like that to God," Damasius muttered.

"Pray! D'you hear? That's an order!" snapped Aurelian. At once, he realized his mistake. Damasius stiffened; his face became rigid. In a voice that did not falter, he answered, "I haven't the right to offer such a prayer."

Aurelian made an effort to bring his anger under control. "Not for our victory over the barbarians?"

"No!"

"Why on earth not?"

"They're God's creatures, just like us," Damasius said stonily. As Aurelian stared, he swallowed and went on, "My God does not . . . approve . . . the shedding of blood."

"Then why are you a soldier?" Aurelian retorted, more and more perplexed.

"It's my trade," Damasius replied, unhappily. "I became a Christian after I enlisted. I can't get my release . . . I don't want to desert. . . ."

The two baffled men, the General and the soldier, stared at each other.

Aurelian put his hand on Damasius' shoulder. "Look," he said reasonably. "I respect your convictions. But tomorrow there's going to be a battle—against these Goths. Your unit, your mates, your closest chums, will be in it. Surely, you don't want to see them slaughtered?"

Damasius seemed at a loss. Aurelian glanced at the Centurion. "Is he married?"

"Yes, sir. Two youngsters, both girls—growing up now. Family 'vacuated to Sirmium."

Aurelian bent his gaze again on Damasius. "You may not care if your own comrades are killed. All right, forget about them. Think of your children. Do you know what those Goths would do if they beat us? They'd march on Sirmium—and take it. They'd plunder and they'd burn and they'd go for the women, the younger the better. Think of a mob of filthy savages lining up to rape your daughters. That kind of thing's happening all the time—and you know it!"

Damasius gulped; his mouth opened; his eyes roamed.

"Why don't you say a few words of prayer—something very simple?" urged Aurelian, profiting by his advantage.

Damasius gave him a piteous look. "All right, I'll pray," he muttered.

Aurelian stepped back. "Go ahead," he encouraged. "Silence there!" he rapped, as the Centurion growled, "About time!"

With head bowed and hands clasped, Damasius mumbled inaudibly for a few moments. Then he licked his lips. "I've prayed!" he announced with evident relief.

"That won't do!" said Aurelian sharply. "Let's hear what you're praying!"

Damasius had now gone too far to withdraw. Unwillingly he returned to his former posture and articulated in a vibrant, disturbing voice that suggested genuine contact with some supernatural Being, "Give us victory over the Goths, Father of Mankind, for the sake of Christ our Redeemer!" Aurelian was impressed by the simple force of these words, but felt doubtful about the efficacy of such a prayer, so brief and compelled. "Pray some more, man!" he exclaimed. "Plead with your god!"

"I can't!" said Damasius glumly. "I'm not ordained."

Aurelian contemplated him a few moments. Clearly he was ashamed of his extorted prayer and unlikely to talk about it. No need to caution him to hold his tongue.

"Right," said Aurelian. "You can go."

Thoughtfully he watched the retreating figure of Damasius. There was an obvious power in this Christ—and, by Mithras, they had need of it! But even if, angered by the persecutions of Valerian, He refused them help, the prayer of Damasius should have neutralized Him. Aurelian felt reassured that in tomorrow's battle they need not fear the malevolence with which the Christian god may well have pursued Decius on the day of his great disaster.

Before dawn the soldiers in morose silence drew a hot meal, which only the veterans ate with relish and of which many found difficulty in swallowing a few mouthfuls. They sat around, leaning against the wheels of wagons or corded bundles of equipment, barely exchanging a word as—at the Centurions' urgent reminder—they checked over the weapons and armor they had already checked the night before. When the last breastplate strap and the last sword belt had been adjusted, they waited while the oppressive minutes passed, rarely looking at one another.

At the first glimmer eastward a raucous, far-traveling call from Mucapor sent a tremor through the figures on the ground. It was answered from different points by shouts equally harsh and urgent —soon the whole camp rang to a concerted clamor of command from the Centurions. Everywhere the men, still silent with their own somber thoughts, struggled up and shuffled through the semi-gloom to form in ranks. Soon column after column was setting out to occupy the positions Aurelian had indicated to their officers at last night's conference.

Already scouts had brought in word that the Goths were stirring; it was vital to forestall any move on their part to seize this favorable ground.

In the chill dimness, after their restless night, the legionaries felt, not sharp and vivid fear, but a numbing depression. Still, mechanically, their legs obeyed. And with every stride across the damp grass toward the Goths, unseen but close at hand, they abandoned themselves more completely to the one force whose brutal assurance not cold, nor dark, nor the nearness of the enemy seemed in the slightest to diminish, the voices of the Centurions.

The sky slowly revealing itself, as veil after veil drew away, was overcast and the breeze that kept the clouds in motion bore with it countless droplets.

A widespread vague trampling sound confirmed the reports that the Goths, too, were early getting ready to engage. With their new superiority in numbers, no doubt they were impatient to sweep the little Roman army aside and help themselves to the rich plunder of the province.

Time wore on. In the gray dawn light a faint, low, spreading bulk began to take shape. Peering painfully, the Romans, with quickened heartbeats, saw it very gradually sharpen, deepen, solidify, identify itself as a hostile army stretched right across their front and threatening to overlap their left flank once set in motion.

Aurelian gave a curt order. His left wing, the extreme end of which was formed by the runaway Cohort from Fort Quintilian, fell back a little, though still hinged to the main body; and was thus better placed to resist an outflanking movement.

Thanks to his foresight, such advantage of position as existed rested with the Romans. They stood at the top of some gently rising ground, about one hundred yards before their center being a shallow dip—a step scooped roughly out of the slope—which was certain to drain some of the impetus from an uphill charge. On a low knoll at the very summit, Aurelian sat his horse, surveying the whole theater of battle. Beyond his right flank the ground fell away to a streamlet with swampy margins; approach would be difficult on that side. His left wing was easier of access.

His scouts had served Aurelian well. The calculations on which he had based this morning's dispositions seemed reasonably accurate. Unless the Goths were keeping substantial reserves out of sight, they comprised between five and six thousand men, as against his own total of somewhat under four thousand. They had a dangerous but not decisive superiority.

It was not his lack of numbers that filled Aurelian with disquiet. With dependable troops he would have fought a battle of swift maneuver, concentrating at the critical places, baffling the expectations of the barbarian chiefs, giving them no time to redeploy. But he dare not engage in intricate tactics on the battlefield with men of doubtful morale, whose training had grown rusty; they simply could not combine steadiness with the necessary mobility. He hated to fight a purely static battle, but with troops such as these he had no choice.

Against the headlong fury of the Goths he could ask no more of them than to stand firm—even then it would be touch and go.

His handful of light troops, North Syrian archers, would make no impression on a host as dense as that arrayed opposite; they were dispersed in patrols to give timely warning of any attempt to work widely round to his rear. Immediately behind his center, where Mucapor's Cohort was stationed, was drawn up his infantry reserve, a composite force of about three hundred of his staunchest soldiers. A few score paces to his left hand the cavalry were concentrated, now little more than one hundred and fifty poorly mounted troopers. Their instructions were to charge only if the Goths drove clean through the Roman line, or if the Fort Quintilian men, who were sure to come under fierce pressure, looked like breaking.

Aurelian's searching gaze could detect no movement in the ominous shadowy bulk that was the Gothic host; but this, he knew, was an illusion born of distance. It was easy for him to picture those seething thousands, shouting, jostling, stamping, waving their arms, impatient to begin the killing. Their faces would be twitching, they would be breathing hard, not from fear or fatigue, but from mounting battle frenzy. Their leaders would not be able to hold them much longer.

Perhaps half would be genuine Goths, big and powerful warriors with drooping yellow mustaches and blue eyes glazed with excitement; the rest, rugged adventurers from neighboring tribes, drawn to the Goths by their renown as fighting men and by the prospect of loot in their company. They carried round, tough hide shields and long swords, as well as spears. Most wore only a pelt or simple woolen kilt around their muscular bronzed bodies; but the numerous chiefs and their picked bodyguards were conspicuous for their shirts of scale armor, as well as their splendid weapons and the gold rings on their arms.

The wide mass seemed to vibrate and along its whole front noise, distant but menacing, was incessantly flung from it. Yes, it was on the move—the leaders, no doubt straining to maintain some rough

35

alignment as the warriors trudged on with heads bent truculently forward and eyes glaring. But battle intoxication was taking grip; individuals would leap ahead, screaming toward the Romans and gesticulating frantically; sudden clusters of men spilled forward, spread and thinned and were caught up again in the plodding mass.

They grew . . . and grew . . . and grew. An endless, swelling, inhuman clamor rolled before them. They were no longer a grim shadow slowly skimming over the ground . . . no longer an immense swarm of stunted, baleful creatures, like the trolls and gnomes of their own tribal lays. They had become a dark multitude of armed men, dwarfish still but rapidly gaining stature, surging on in a great tidal flow. And now the eye could plainly discern, as the hammering heart acknowledged, the tall warriors in the forefront of this onpouring host, their shields, their naked swords, the spears bristling before and above them.

From the center of their vanguard a gigantic figure with winged helmet and flame-red beard streaming bounded forward a dozen paces, then turned and swung his sword in a wild onward-beckoning gesture. At once dozens of ensigns shot up, the horrible, wildbeast heads the barbarians carried on poles, and an appalling roar burst out, in which the shuddering blare of many war horns was distinguishable; it prolonged itself into unceasing thunder.

With one vast convulsive movement the Gothic host launched itself into a charge.

Still the ranks of the Romans stood motionless and silent. Aurelian, impassive-faced on his horse, thought: They have started their run too soon—the older men will be winded. But the impact will be terrible.

"Mithras," he murmured. "Guardian, Savior, Soldier of Light, stand with us now . . . fight for us!"

He felt a swarm of needles swim from within against the fleshy part of his forearm as it rested against his thigh; his legs tingled, and he was aware of the rhythmic thud against his ribs. After all, there were only a few ranks of undependable troops between himself and the howling fury driving nearer and nearer. But only a small part of his mind was concerned with the man, Aurelian. With steady gaze and cold judgment he continued to measure the onslaught's weight and swiftness against the courage and resolution his commanders might be able to extract from their men.

Now the Goths were streaming into the shallow depression, their legs suddenly sliced away—they were emerging, with speed hardly slackened, and were racing onward. The space between them and the silent lines of legionaries was shrinking fast . . . eighty paces . . . sixty . . . forty. A few moments more and that raging sea would smash against the slender Roman wall of steel.

Trumpets resonated, feeble against the uproar. The wall of steel seemed to dissolve, momentarily, as the legionaries twisted round in massive unison, reaching far back with their weighty javelins; then again into line they swung and the javelins flew forward. At such close range, against such a tight-packed target, the volley was shattering. The rim of the Gothic vanguard crumpled. Aurelian felt a tremor communicate itself to the whole onrushing host. Their impetus faltered—but only briefly. On they came, in headlong fury, bellowing their war cries.

Again the trumpets thinly penetrated the din. The Romans drew their swords and paced deliberately forward. The march met the rush—and halted it. Now the two armies grappled; and along the entire line of their contact shield collided with shield, spears flickered, swords thrust or rose and rang on helm or shield, bodies sagged and slumped and were trampled, while fresh men pressed forward, shouting, to maintain the desperate struggle.

The Roman ranks did not waver; it was as if they felt at their backs the presence of Aurelian, the Decimator.

Only their extreme left wing, reduced as it was, had not yet engaged. The Goths were wheeling round on it in great numbers, though not with quite the same élan as everywhere else; the maneuver had disconcerted them. But for this very reason their onset proved more dangerous. They were headed not in a compact mass which would have presented an ideal target for a javelin volley, but by loosely strung-out clusters of men, who did not wilt under the hail of missiles. Unchecked, they flung themselves on the Roman shields and a savage hand-to-hand battle began.

The tumult was ear-splitting: the innumerable clangs and crashes of murderous blows; the yells, the screams of the maddened fighters;

the piercing cries and howls of thousands of men straining to reach the zone of combat, the bray of the Gothic war horns and the vibrant peal of Roman trumpets.

Aurelian could smell his own sharp sweat. But to his staff the stern, composed figure of their General seemed to emit unyielding strength. He sat there, inclining slightly forward in the saddle, slowly sweeping the battle with eyes that seemed to penetrate both contending armies. He seldom spoke. He gave no orders. Last night, he had given the sufficient order: Stand and fight!

After a while, Aurelian's stiff posture relaxed a little. The first deadly charge had been checked—that ocean heave and thrust that might have battered clean through the Roman lines. They were settling down to a long-drawn-out struggle, the frenzied tribal warrior against the scientific legionary, the shapeless horde against the supple Roman formation. The longer it lasted, the better the outlook for the Romans, for they were trained to persist, coolly warding and thrusting, while the minutes fled and the hours accumulated to sap the untutored fury of barbarians who rarely curbed their fighting instinct in order to husband their strength.

Abruptly, he grew rigid; the crisis had come on the left wing. The men from Fort Quintilian who, since the decimation had behaved with an extreme docility, uncommon nowadays in Roman soldiers, had been resisting stoutly, but at last some Gothic chieftain and his stalwart retainers, grouped round their uplifted wild beast's head, were cutting a way into the Roman ranks. Suddenly the two ensigns confronted each other, swinging in the confusion, the gaunt, withered wolf's muzzle and dead, staring eyes, and the simple bronze laurel wreath above a column of medallions inscribed with Latin letters; around them the melee boiled.

Herennianus urged his horse alongside Aurelian. "General!" His tone made the name an urgent plea, as he indicated the quivering rear rank of the extreme Roman left. Aurelian stilled him with a gesture and continued to watch, through narrowed eyes, the frantic struggle round the standards. He was thinking: if we charge to their rescue, they will incur fresh blame. No, let them fight it out, themselves. They were Illyrians, men capable of a peculiar bitter obstinacy in battle. He had the firm conviction that they would never relinquish their standard, newly dedicated, to replace the one abandoned at Fort Quintilian. "Wait!" he said evenly to Herennianus. The Tribune obediently composed himself in the saddle, but when several minutes passed and still Aurelian had neither spoken nor changed expression, he saluted and trotted back to his post at the head of his squadron.

As though the men had sensed Aurelian's confidence in them, as though something of his indomitable spirit had poured into their hearts, their ranks no longer gave ground. There was a heaving and jerking as their formation expelled or ground to pieces the intruders; suddenly the wolf's head was gone and the Roman ensign rode unchallenged aloft as the legionaries pressed hard on the reeling Goths.

For some while longer, the fighting elsewhere, though ferocious in the extreme, had remained static. Now a slow shudder seemed to travel through the Gothic masses; Aurelian could see figures detach themselves from their rear, turn irresolutely back toward the battle and then continue to waver down the slope. More and more of these withdrawals took place, until there was a widespread scampering downward. Gradually the Goths still entangled with the Romans tore themselves loose. The Romans adjusted their ranks and began to move forward, but the Gothic recoil was faster than their advance. Open ground was showing between the two armies and Aurelian could see his men stumbling over the strewn bodies as, still keeping formation, they maintained the pursuit.

He dispatched one of his staff to the reserve infantry Cohort with orders to harass the retreat; then turned toward Herennianus, who was beating with his right fist on the palm of his left hand. "Now!" he shouted.

Only as the fighting ebbed down the slope did Aurelian become aware that the pall overhead was breaking up. Random patches of gold were glinting among the heaped dead where the two armies had collided and swayed together. He looked up. Stately, a radiant Conqueror emerging in triumph, the Sun was riding free of the cloud wrack; full and refulgent, its orb swam on to a tatter of pallid blue and the battlefield blazed with a thousand fires. The clouds closed in again, but one broad beam persisted, stretching far over the ground, probing, until it fell across Aurelian. He felt draped in light, his own heart an earthly sun, kindled by the shining Ruler of the Heavens. Now he knew whose hand had vanquished the Goths. Not the senile Olympians, so cold and remote from the Roman soldier's battles; not that meager Christian god; but the Bright One who Himself eternally warred against Darkness. Light flowed through him and a consciousness of the God within and around.

"Hail to Thee!" he whispered. "Savior Mithras, giver of victory. Hail Unconquered Sun!"

After an hour of slow and grueling pursuit, for the Goths now were falling back with steadiness behind an organized and strongly resisting rear guard, Aurelian recalled his main forces, which were showing signs of exhaustion. Herennianus, with the cavalry and the light troops, backed at need by the still fresh reserve Cohort, continued to shepherd the barbarians toward the Danube. On Aurelian's order, while ceaselessly harassing the Goths, he did not press home an attack, for there were no more dangerous Germans than those over whom one had gained a partial advantage.

While the cooks were scrambling some warm food and the men, overcome by weariness and their reaction to the intense strain, were sitting numbly or sprawling on the ground, Aurelian was surrounded by Officers making their reports. About a thousand barbarians had fallen, while among the Romans only a fraction of that number were casualties. Not a crushing victory, but the Goths had undoubtedly suffered a bloody repulse.

"Now," said Aurelian briskly. "A mounted messenger to Sirmium —top speed. They're to requisition a couple of big houses . . . clear them . . . install beds. The barracks hospital won't hold all the wounded. Instruct the Chief Magistrate to set free the barbarian slaves they've locked up. They're to give them a meal first—not too much, for they must be half-dead with hunger.

"Next, the men executed at Sirmium. . . . Enter their names as fallen in action. They were unlucky—no reason why their families should lose by it. Remember to praise your men. They all did well. Later, when they're rested, we'll have a parade and I'll thank them myself."

The officers saluted and turned to go. Aurelian recalled one Centurion. "That man, Damasius—the Christian. How did he fight?"

The Centurion shook his head admiringly. "Terrific, he was! Captured one of their wolf-heads, Sir. Laid out three men to do it!"

Aurelian reflected. A first-class soldier. But promotion? . . . No, it was unwise to have Christians in posts of command. They had queer notions—and they weren't really loyal to the Empire.

"Here," he said, finally. "Give him this gold piece. Tell him to buy something for those kids of his in Sirmium."

Afterward, Aurelian stood anxiously by, while his interpreter questioned the few wounded Goths who, through some miracle, had escaped having their throats cut by the vengeful legionaries. They struggled to lift their heads from the stretchers and answered through ashen lips in guttural whispers. None could throw light on the question that concerned Aurelian most, the fate of Lucius Prudens at Fort Quintilian; he would have to be posted, "Missing —believed dead."

Aurelian walked across the field. The soldiers were now standing round or squatting, with bowls of steaming gruel in their hands. Their energies were reviving. Some were already singing; others set their food down to show with vivid mimicry how they had warded off shrewd blows and struck deadly ones in return. Flasks were circulating with the local spirit, a raw concoction from fermented plums. One young soldier, drunk less with the potent liquor than with fatigue, elation, and downright astonishment at having shared in a victory over the dreaded Goths, lurched to his feet, pointed toward Aurelian and yelled, "Good old Hand-on-Hilt!" There was an instant's silence; then a hoarse cheer rose from his companions. It was taken up by neighboring groups and rolled right across the field. The Centurions looked on, grinning.

4

IN THE middle of one morning a small company of people wound their way in a straggling procession from the fashionable Esquiline quarter through some of Rome's busiest thoroughfares in the direction of the Palatine Hill. First came Severinus himself, walking with dignified gait at the head of a throng of clients and servants, and acknowledging with distant politeness the salutations of many of the passersby. Behind, also accompanied by attendants of various kinds, was the litter of Drusilla, followed by that of Severina, both swaying aloft on the shoulders of robust household slaves.

The spring sunshine already had the power to make an enclosed litter uncomfortably warm and Severina parted the curtains to admit more air—and also to enjoy more freely the endlessly varied pageant of the streets. A prisoner of her own high position, restricted for weeks and months at a stretch to her own house and those of the family's wealthy friends, she was virtually a stranger to the city where she lived. An excursion such as this was like visiting a foreign town, colorful, teeming, noisy, and continuously exciting.

The litter twisted through the crowds, sometimes so entangled among the unhurried pedestrians that it seemed in danger of being finally separated from the rest of the company. Its elegant woodwork and the smart turnout of its well fed bearers did not ensure it an easy passage. On the pavements of Rome lingered the last of her democracy; there a ragamuffin could jostle a millionaire and, if a wrangle ensued, could find a score of disrespectful tongues wagging vigorously on his side.

On they went at their uneven pace, skirting the miles of slums whose swarming tenements rose several storeys above narrow, winding streets; past shops, booths, and stalls with every kind of ware for sale and vendors uttering their shrill cries; along broad

42

avenues flanked by nobly proportioned temples and other civic buildings. Everywhere people were sauntering; all Rome's hundreds of thousands seemed abroad enjoying the sunshine. At last the litter tilted slightly; they had begun to climb from that never-resting sea of humanity toward the great bronze gates of the Imperial Palace.

Inside the wide enclosure Severina's litter was expertly eased on to the flagstones and Porphyry, one of her father's understewards, who had preceded the bearers, solicitously helped her to alight. A squad of rigid guardsmen marched briskly by, some twenty paces off, to the barked commands of an officer in loftily plumed helmet and showy breastplate. Behind a complex of low brick buildings—barracks, stables, and stores—there soared and stretched to the summit of the hill the gleaming main structures of the Palace, a sprawling marble city.

Though here were wonders to make an envoy from the luxurious Court of Persia gape, Severina looked round without enthusiasm. Her mood had changed. She was no longer the secluded girl enjoying the spectacle of the Roman streets. Here she herself was to be inspected—coldly. Everyone knew that they were attending the Emperor's levee because he had expressed a wish to see Aurelian's future bride. This visit was part of the extraordinary business whereby her marriage was being arranged as an affair of state, a kind of government operation, efficient and completely heartless.

Valerian's sudden urgency to have her presented to him showed what concern he felt about the matter. Yet nobody troubled sufficiently about what she herself felt even to supply a painting of this stranger to whom her body (and with it a good portion of her father's property, no doubt) would soon belong. If now indeed she carried a portrait of him in her imagination, it was one largely shaped and colored by hearsay.

Having broached the marriage and so aroused her boundless curiosity, her parents had obviously decided to be reticent. They meant to give her time to get used to the idea. She had been deeply chagrined by this diplomatic silence, but she could not bring herself to pester her stepmother (much less her father) with questions about Aurelian.

Her parents had proved right; she had, in a sense, grown used to the idea. The barely-known, vague-featured Aurelian had become an inhabitant of her thoughts, almost to the exclusion of everyone else. He occupied the whole horizon of the future. And he had ceased to be repellent. It was strange how something in prospect could at first appear horrifying, then grow tolerable, and finally be awaited with a feeling not far from eagerness.

These reflections engaged her as she followed her father and step-mother through the interminable Palace, recording its splendors with a preoccupied mind. There were long, silent corridors lined with pedestaled statues taller than the passerby, whose insignificance their stony gaze seemed to emphasize. They crossed vast halls glimmering with rich mosaic on walls and floors, where it needed little imagination to picture the illustrious rulers of the past and the infamous, the Trajans and the Caracallas, holding audience. They traversed a gallery, paneled in polished cedar, where a succession of stone-balustraded balconies gave breathtaking views of Rome's tumbled landscape of roofs with here and there streets cutting through like rivers that had worn themselves deep ravines. Before long Severina became aware that the Palace was something more than an Imperial residence; it was also the headquarters of the Empire's administration. Every now and then, clerks would hurry by with documents and one whole suite of rooms, whose interiors they glimpsed through the occasional door left open, were unmistakably offices.

Severina also could not help noticing that her father, so coldly dignified in the streets, was here almost preening himself; he was looking round with an air of profound self-satisfaction. Her step-mother, on the contrary, gave the impression of being overawed. She seemed to goggle at the magnitude of the place and its endless opulence. Once when a clerk turned suddenly out of a doorway in her direction, she jumped and obviously checked herself in the act of giving him a respectful bow.

At last double doors were thrown open at their approach and an imposing footman announced Severinus by all his long-winded titles of rank and office. They entered a pleasant reception chamber of modest size, bright with charmingly colored frescoes of country scenes. Perhaps a dozen men, all elderly and of distinguished ap-

44

pearance, stood in little groups by the walls, while several more clustered round two figures in purple togas at the center of the floor. These wearers of the Purple could only be the Co-Emperors, the senior Augustus, Valerian, and Gallienus, his eldest son and colleague. Severina guessed that the mixed bag of courtiers and petitioners who would attend an Imperial levee must already have been dismissed; as was seemly, Valerian would be receiving a noble Roman matron and her daughter only in the presence of his Councillors and confidants.

"Wait!" commanded Severinus, in a low voice. He approached Valerian and made a deep obeisance. The Emperor's other companions drew back and left the two together: soon there was a murmur of talk between them. Severina saw Valerian turn and direct a look toward her for a moment, keenly. Uncertain what to do, she lowered her eyes.

When shyly she began to study them again, she was puzzled why her father was looking with such transport into Valerian's face: there was nothing in the Emperor's demeanor or his tone, as it faintly reached her, to suggest matter for such a worshipful expression on a listener. Two or three times Severinus turned his head and looked round the room with a smile of such rapture that it seemed to invite everyone present to join him in relishing the Emperor's words.

Severina began to feel painfully embarrassed. She was making the first discovery of an unsophisticated visitor to a Court; that the more brazen the flattery by word, look, or gesture, the more acceptable it seems to be.

Her first impression of Valerian was disappointing. She had seen him once before, when he was still a Senator, but she found herself innocently surprised that elevation to the Throne had not made him six feet tall and majestic of person. The elderly Augustus was a short, stocky man with a trim gray beard, who was without the natural stateliness to wear the toga really well. He had an amiable, rather worried face; indeed he had the air, incongruous in an Emperor, of lacking self-confidence, almost of trying to ingratiate himself. A couple of paces behind him, Gallienus, a youngish, lanky man, whose height was accentuated by his father's lack of inches,

45

stood wearing a broad grin as he chatted animatedly. An onlooker could not fail to be struck by the contrast between the solemnity of the one Emperor and the other's ease, not to say lightness, of manner.

Severina had been a gawky child when Valerian, accompanied by several other Senators, had unexpectedly called one afternoon at the house to consult her father; with them was Gallienus, who already was widely known as a brilliant and unconventional young man. They had conferred with some agitation in the garden, nobody appearing to notice the little girl sitting quietly at the other end, except Gallienus. His eyes fell on her, he pulled a comical face and then turned his back. Severina later gathered that the trouble had been a threat by the reigning Emperor to curtail some privilege of the Senate. Her father, who set greater store on the privilege of remaining alive, had counselled extreme caution. As the others had, in any case, been too afraid to do anything beyond complain among their intimates, they agreed his advice was statesmanlike. Shortly after, the Emperor had perished and the threat had blown over.

After a while Severinus nodded toward his wife and daughter; interpreting the look, they approached. Drusilla's face was flushed and tiny globules of sweat glistened on her brow. She looked far more the born plebeian here in her formal robe than in her more casual and comfortable clothes at home. She almost sank over the hand which Valerian graciously extended, looked up dumbly when he said a few polite words and then, with a little stumble, drew back.

Severina took her place, making a graceful obeisance. Strangely she was not nervous, but—feeling at a loss—kept her head inclined while the Sovereign of Mankind regarded her for a few moments.

When he spoke, it was in a benevolent voice. "I have told your father, my dear, how pleased I am at your marriage."

She looked up; he was nodding paternally, but with that slightly uneasy air she had noted on her entrance. Valerian's words suggested she must play her part in the pretense that this marriage, which he himself had ordained without her knowledge, was in accordance with her own fondest wishes.

"Your Majesty is very gracious," she murmured.

46

He leaned toward her confidentially. "I myself must soon return to the Army in Asia. But the Emperor Gallienus will be seeing a good deal of Aurelian when he is in Rome—the staff meetings are being held here in the Palace."

Severina did not know what this meant and judged it best to say nothing.

"You know there has been a battle—near the Danube?" Valerian went on, looking into her face. Startled and a little frightened what he might say next, Severina stared back at him.

"Your future husband distinguished himself again," the Emperor continued with a sudden, simple warmth that touched Severina. "He won a fine victory—and very economical." He seemed pleased with the term and repeated it, "Yes, very economical!"

She was struck with his evident desire to win her goodwill. This impression was confirmed by the attention she sensed she was drawing from everybody in the room; even Gallienus, she saw from the corner of her eye, kept a searching gaze upon her. It was not the cool, even cynical, assessment she had expected. There was a seriousness in the looks fixed on her that went beyond mere curiosity and suggested that these exalted persons regarded her as someone of importance to themselves.

She understood now that Valerian had been indirectly complimenting her on Aurelian's victory. Appropriate words came to her lips.

"May I offer Your Majesty congratulations on the success of your Army!"

Valerian beamed and nodded, as though he had achieved what he sought. He gently touched her arm and turned toward Gallienus. "It is time to present you to my son."

Gallienus gave her a charming, lazy smile, as if they were already well acquainted. He said a word to his two companions, disengaged himself, and came directly toward her. Placing his hand—a long, finely shaped one, on the fingers of which sparkled two handsome jeweled rings—with easy familiarity on her elbow, he drew her away from Valerian.

"So you're the bride of Aurelian—the economical Aurelian!" he said in a musical voice, with an undertone of raillery.

Half-scandalized, half-amused, she glanced toward Valerian, who apparently had not heard.

"Where have you been hiding yourself, all this time?" continued Gallienus. "One doesn't often see a real beauty in this Court!"

There was such an extraordinary blend of admiration with banter in his tone that she could not feel offended.

She looked at him, twinkling. "The last time Your Majesty saw me, you didn't even give me a second glance!"

He laughed, delighted to be scored over in this fashion. "They do say mine was a misspent youth! Still, I shall enjoy making amends in your case!"

To see ready smiles and read frank amusement in a man's eyes was refreshing. Despite his frivolous air, there was undoubtedly something engaging about Gallienus, she thought, though she divined that he turned his charm on and off as the whim took him. They said he was a versatile man, accomplished in many arts; certainly he had talents as a flatterer.

"There was no offense, so there need be no amends," she answered.

"Oh, I insist," he said lightly. "I hear, dear young lady, that you are quite the scholar."

She found it natural to answer in the same vein of pleasantry. "Well, I can read, Your Majesty."

"You do read, you mean," he said with an unexpected emphasis. "That makes you a rarity. Nobody reads nowadays. Rome is a city of boors. . . ." His glance traveled round the room and came to rest, momentarily, on her father—"and pretentious pedants."

She glanced at him sharply, but he looked so guileless that she decided he was probably uttering airy generalities. Still, the comment had been a warning, recalling her to herself. Gallienus had begun again, with a seductive air of intimacy as if, at last, he had found someone who shared his slighted dreams, "Why shouldn't we make Rome a City of the Arts—a second Athens? It's a question of finding people of taste and sensibility and bringing them together."

Severina did not answer or meet his look. She felt a movement beside her and with some relief heard Valerian's voice. "We must hand you back now, my dear, to your father." She bowed very low to Gallienus, certain that he was gazing down at her with mockery in his smile. Then, without looking up, she turned and repeated this farewell obeisance to Valerian.

When she rejoined her father near the door, he was radiant and she noticed her stepmother gazing at her with respect.

"You did very well," he whispered. "Perfect breeding! The Emperor (presumably he meant Valerian) is enchanted!"

Severina followed them out, also feeling—though it was hard to give reasons—that the interview had been a success. She tried to sort her series of brief but powerful impressions. This had been her first excursion into the world of great affairs and she found it full of interest and not without both comedy and pathos. The first revelation had been her father's behavior. She had never imagined that he could play the sycophant. Curiously enough she had no impulse to condemn him for these facile public ecstasies which contrasted so strongly with his professions of philosophic principle and the biting irony of many of his private allusions to Valerian. She began to appreciate that the same Necessity which had made her submit, with hardly a murmur, to an imposed marriage also swayed the conduct of Senators and nobles, closely and cruelly.

Her stepmother, too—dazzled by a show, tongue-tied before a purple robe! Poor Drusilla—who could blame her? After all, it was natural enough to be overwhelmed at the Roman Court, for the Emperor was virtually a god, even amiable, uncertain, undersized Valerian, and his Palace the most stupendous place of its kind on earth.

With a flash of illumination she understood why she was being so cheerfully tolerant. The whole episode had abruptly altered not only the relationship between her parents and herself (she had obviously become an important personality in her own right), but also the relationship in her mind between them and Aurelian. Unconsciously, she had been fearing for him, assuming that he would suffer by comparison with her father. Now she realized that an honest, unschooled soldier need not cut such an ignoble figure beside the patrician, the public dignitary, the famous orator.

It was as if Aurelian, the victor by the Danube, had scored another, more subtle, victory here in Rome—and she took pleasure in it, although it was over her own family.

As, silently, she walked behind her parents along the endless corridors of the Palace, she forced herself to go, moment by moment, through her interviews with the co-Emperors—the ordinary man who seemed weighed down and wearied with the Purple and the extraordinary man who, in the highest station of the land, coupled brilliant gifts with levity.

Though her conversation with each had been very brief, she must have been in a receptive mood, for their diverse personalities had made a sharp impact upon her.

Valerian's demeanour had made it plain that Aurelian was a man of such consequence that, by reflection, his wife-to-be was considered worth the courtesies, the flattering attentions of a Roman Emperor. Probably what was true of Aurelian applied broadly to all those her father called "the Illyrians," the small group of hard-fighting generals of Illyrian origin. Either the Roman State was indebted to them for invaluable services or they held such power in their hands (the control of Rome's most formidable legions) that they— and anyone likely to wield strong influence with them—must be courted and conciliated.

Far above mankind, at the dizzy summit of the Absolute State which embraced the civilized world, the Emperor was enthroned. But all the time he was vulnerable; the swords of the Legions could reach swiftly up and tip him ignominiously into the abyss.

That was why Valerian had talked so solicitously in her ear, virtually wooing her to be his friend and keep her husband loyal. Poor Emperor! Poor Autocrat! Vividly she recalled his tired eyes with a little discolored pus at the inside corners, his gray beard agitating as he spoke, his old man's body oppressed by the toga's weight and the strain of the long reception.

He, too, must be finding Necessity an unrelenting master.

Gallienus was obviously a more complex character. She found an undeniable fascination in him. His lack of the gravity proper to a Roman Emperor did not leave his personality weak or negative; far from it. Behind his lightness of manner was something positive, aggressive, challenging. His flattery had been so facile that it

50

seemed to advertise its own insincerity. He cultivated a mocking—perhaps self-mocking—affectation that must puzzle and provoke those who had not the freakish taste to find it rather enjoyable. Yet in spite of this affectation, he had given a glimpse of genuine feeling when he spoke of Rome as a city of boors.

By now they had emerged from the Palace buildings and, espying them, her father's head steward motioned to the litter-bearers, lounging in the sun against one wall of the huge courtyard. Drusilla who, conscious of her failure in the Emperor's presence, had stayed subdued ever since they left the reception chamber, turned to Severina almost diffidently. "Wasn't it wonderful!" she said.

Before Severina could answer, her father moved between them. "Your litter is ready," he said coldly to Drusilla, who gave Severina a pathetic look and went obediently away.

"Now," he murmured, taking Severina's arm in a grip that startled her, "what did Gallienus say to you?" Though at his side, she could barely catch the words. He looked round, as if by compulsion, to reassure himself that nobody was within earshot.

It seemed impossible that he should be interested in the trivialities of Gallienus. "You mean Valerian, don't you, Father?" she observed, smiling.

"No! No!" he answered impatiently. "Valerian is well disposed to us—up to a point. I mean that sneering young devil of a junior Augustus."

Severina stared at him. "But, Father, I don't understand . . ."

"Gallienus!" he repeated, almost hissing the name. "He's a sinister man, I tell you. He's got dangerous ideas, as well as a nasty tongue. He hates us Senators. It will be an evil day for us all if ever he becomes sole Augustus. It's bad enough Valerian is soon going back to the war in Asia."

A look she had never seen before passed over his face, the gray, haggard look of a man mortally afraid. Then he recovered himself and glanced round with an appearance of casualness. No one seemed to be watching them.

"Severina, please think—think!" he said, his apparently relaxed manner contrasting with the urgency in the words. "He didn't try to pump you about me?"

Deeply disturbed, she searched through everything she could recollect of her exchanges with Gallienus.

"No, Father," she said decidedly, after a little while. "Nothing of that sort—he talked a little about culture . . ."

"Culture!" He gave a derisive laugh. "That playboy!"

Her litter was approaching and they walked to meet it. Severina was relieved to draw the curtains and shut out the imposing facade of the Palace; suddenly it had grown ominous. Her petty triumph of the morning had lost its savor.

For the first time, she thought of Aurelian with longing. He was a famous, fearless soldier; with him she could feel secure. Then a kind of panic took hold of her. What if he were unhappy about this marriage and had consented only because it was the Emperor's express command? Strangely, it had never occurred to her that Aurelian, too, could have had his strong objections.

She found herself hoping desperately that he would not dislike her.

5

WHILE all around her the household was astir with preparations for the afternoon's reception and dinner party, Severina grew increasingly restless. She drifted about her room studying herself with dissatisfaction in the mirror, where her image seemed to betray fresh imperfections every time she looked at it. More than once she sat down with a book, only to find herself in a few minutes on her feet and moving about again, unaware of what she had been reading. She felt at once on edge and half-numb with weariness, for she had enjoyed little sound sleep in the last few nights.

Drusilla, bustling between the kitchens, the dining hall and the guestchambers, had found her wandering aimlessly about the garden and persuaded her to return to her room and try to rest—as though rest were possible when Aurelian was in Rome and she would, in a couple of hours, be meeting him!

She had long ago abandoned her fears that he would prove repellent. Partly because of the esteem in which he was held by the most exalted personages in the Empire, but mainly because time had reconciled her to the notion that he, and none other, was to be her husband, she had come to accept him trustingly. She still knew very little of him and that at secondhand. But the absence of solid fact gave more scope to her wishful fantasies and she had ended by endowing him with a personality rich in attractions. By now she was obsessed with the thought that it was he who would find her lacking, too plain, too dull, too ignorant of the world, perhaps disappointing in many other respects. With a humility that surprised herself, she hoped she would find favor in his eyes.

The door opened and Drusilla came in, smiling but looking rather tired after strenuous hours of closely supervising her domestics, who were stupid when they were zealous and idle if the gods had granted them intelligence. She passed her fingertips across her brow and announced in a cheerful voice, "I'm getting a headache!" All the same she came over briskly to Severina, put an arm round her and said, "Everything's going very nicely, darling. We're practically ready—it'll soon be time for you to start dressing."

She looked with disapproval at the plain table by the mirror with its neglected pot or two of cosmetics, and thought of carrying Severina off to her own well stocked boudoir. At once, she decided against it. The girl was looking so strung up, it would be best to talk to her calmly for a little while.

"I'll have to get rid of Aglaia," she said. "It was a mistake to promote that clumsy creature to lady's maid. The kitchen's her place. She nearly ruined my best robe. . . ." The small talk flowed placidly on and on and though Severina did not bother to listen she found its pleasant murmur soothing. Suddenly she said, "I'll be all right, Mother, don't you worry." She went across to the mirror, laughed, and said, "Well, let's get it over. I think I'll wear some jewelry. Help me choose."

The guests had been carefully chosen, Senators of good standing and their wives, but none of the men was distinguished, wealthy or influential enough to challenge the easy preeminence of Severinus. Their womenfolk, looking both uniform and oddly barbaric in the towering coiffures which were the rage, were obviously flattered at the rare invitation to this august house. They eyed Severina curiously, but when they spoke to her it was with deference.

By the time her father was summoned to the entrance hall to receive the guest of the evening, Severina was tolerably calm, though every now and then she had to exert herself to control a tendency to shiver. Her suppressed excitement showed itself in the brightness of her eyes and the color in her cheeks, which gave an unusual and becoming warmth to her rather austere beauty; it had been no mere phrase when Drusilla, after helping her to dress, had exclaimed, "Oh, you're looking lovely!" Her white robe, of costly silk, cut with exquisite simplicity by the most skilled craftswomen of Rome, had drawn a compliment even from her preoccupied father. Round her neck was a simple row of small but flawless diamonds and rubies, set in gold. Two rubies hung from her ears. Her only other ornament was a thin gold band round one wrist. She sat upright with her head proudly held, not because she sought nobility of deportment, but because she found it impossible to relax.

Outside, her father's voice was becoming plainer, rising above the tones of two or three other persons—all men as far as she could judge. Her heartbeats grew more violent— One of them must be Aurelian!

As the arrivals reached the door, she became aware of Drusilla's anxious eyes upon her and nodded slightly with apparent composure. Drusilla smiled, with a little shake of the head, as if she understood what an effort this self-command must cost.

There was a murmur just outside, her father saying something indistinguishable . . . the murmur, louder now, was in the room. She gave only the briefest glance in that direction, for it was necessary to preserve the calm demeanor of a Roman lady. Her father, accompanied by two stalwart men, one of whom, standing beside him, outtopped him by a head, while the other stood a pace behind, was already presenting these newcomers to Drusilla.

Her tense ear caught the name, "Aurelian." Drusilla's voice was answered by a man's deep voice, quiet but suggesting authority. A slight pause; then her father's voice and her mother's, once more: the second visitor was being introduced.

Now, without daring to look, she could sense that they were moving toward her. A group of togas arranged themselves before her in the same pattern they had made before Drusilla: her father's alongside Aurelian's; his companion a little way behind.

Her first impression was of Aurelian's size. Try as she would to look him evenly in the face, for a moment or two she could not lift her eyes above his chest: he seemed enormous, a headless Hercules. The thought that his gaze must be resting critically on her confusion jerked her chin up. Her cheeks were burning as their eyes met.

Her father was speaking: "Severina, my dear. Here is the General Lucius Domitius Aurelianus come all the way from Illyricum to see you!"

Aurelian's features were large and regular. His expression was proud and virile. He was smiling in a pleasant way, but without intimacy; she could not sustain his gaze.

She swallowed, then murmured the carefully rehearsed formula of greeting. "Welcome to Rome and our house!"

Above her slightly inclined head, a voice replied, low-pitched but vibrating through her. "I am happy to meet the Lady Severina." He had an unfamiliar but agreeable accent.

She forced herself to look up and to smile, briefly. This time her vision lingered and was precise. Aurelian had small gray eyes, set well apart under a brow that was narrow but unusually wide; his head was massive; the gray was already vagrant in his thick, coarse brown hair.

Their looks met and held together; this and not their exchange of formal phrases was their first true encounter. She felt herself tremble, trying to bear the weight of his gaze, in which she could read candid interest. But her eyes fell away and she had a strange sensation as if his own were traveling to the back of her skull, searching her thoughts and emotions. It was a relief to see her father indicate Aurelian's companion, who came forward, bowing. He was, she gathered, for her father's words somehow had not registered quite clearly, Aurelian's adjutant, a Tribune called Probus; he struck her as good-looking in a fresh, wholesome, boyish way.

55

This time she was able to smile spontaneously and to say with unforced warmth. "You are very welcome, sir!" But she was thinking; he looks much younger than they said, "he" being not Probus but Aurelian.

Her father had placed a hand on either visitor's elbow, preparing to move them on; he had been warned by Drusilla not to prolong this delicate first meeting. Aurelian, who seemed perfectly self-assured, disengaged himself from Severina with a slight inclination and a smile that was friendly without suggesting any special bond or claim. With a flash of insight she divined that he was pleased to find her so personable, but that had she been ugly and awkward, he would have agreed to marry her just the same.

Her eyes followed him as they moved off—a tall, broad-shouldered man, handsome in a mature way. He held himself erect, the soldier even in his civilian toga. There was command in his bearing, as in his voice. His stride was slow, deliberate, and powerful beside her father's quick, light paces.

So this man was to be her husband. . . . It was impossible to define what she felt—his impact on her was too new and overpowering. She was aware only that since she had set eyes on him the other people in the room seemed curiously diminished.

Dinner was announced and she took her place beside Drusilla on the first of the women's couches, opposite that where her father reclined next to the guest of honor. On Aurelian's other side was Maximus Balbus, the most eminent of the Senators invited. The dishes, prepared with consummate artistry by masters of their profession, repelled Severina. She swallowed only a few mouthfuls, and those with difficulty. The talk was as little to her inclination as the food. She soon realized she was something of a barrier between Drusilla, on one hand, and the wife of Balbus on the other, a heavily rouged lady of reluctant middle age, whose plump, simple face was eager with gossip.

To avoid obstructing the exchanges between her neighbors, she leaned back a little, studying alternately the untasted water in the bottom of the silver goblet with which she was toying and the occupants of her father's couch, a little distance away.

Aurelian, she noticed, was eating steadily, without being absorbed

56

in his food. Her father was making most of the conversation but, at intervals, Aurelian would say something in his quiet, firm way: each time it set Balbus nodding vigorously, as though he were impelled to advertise his agreement with whatever such a famous soldier said.

Once or twice Aurelian caught her glance and gave her that friendly smile that had no intimacy, no springing cordiality in it, the smile he might have given to any of his new-made acquaintances in that room.

Yet in that smile, restrained though it was, some emanation from the depths of his personality reached out to her so strongly that she wondered why everyone else did not feel her own compulsion to keep staring at him. Her impressions were steadily growing sharper. His speech was terse and emphatic; he handled the Latin words as no doubt he handled his men, masterfully. His face, his form, his glance, even in this social gathering, were dominating, even in this festive room, amid flowers and heaped fruits and gleaming glassware and costly delicacies served on silver plate. He brought with him an air of the wide frontier. Beside that head of bronze her father's skull seemed small and fragile and his aristocratic features refined to the point of weakness; while the full-fleshed face of Balbus looked gross and flabby.

The meal dragged on and on, and before long Severina was automatically waving away the servants as they approached with new courses. Occasionally she murmured a few words in reply to some comment by one of the older women to either side, but for the most part they were content to leave her out of a conversation of the kind to which she was too young, innocent, and charitable to make an interesting contribution. When she did say something, it was hesitant and not exactly to the point; at this evidence that she had not been listening properly, they would give her a tolerant smile, which made Severina blush but did not prevent her eyes straying back to Aurelian's table.

She knew she was behaving like a moonstruck country girl, but she was powerless to resist the imperative need to rivet her whole attention on this one disturbing man.

Suddenly she noticed her father's gaze turn toward her; no—it had shifted to Drusilla. Her parents exchanged the briefest look, made significant by a tiny lift of the eyebrows.

Drusilla rose; it was the signal for the women to retire and leave the men to their drinking. Severina felt a rush of resentment against both her parents; her urge to absorb herself in watching Aurelian was still unappeased. They had barely met and had exchanged only a few formal, meaningless words. Still, etiquette must be observed. She stood up, to feel her legs go suddenly weak. The room had become a blur through which the figure of Aurelian wavered in a sickening motion.

She knew at once that too much excitement, too little sleep, too little food, were making her body protest. For a moment she had a dreadful fear that she was going to faint—faint before the eyes of Aurelian, the very first time they had met! This won't do, she told herself firmly, and bit her lip till the intense local pain made her less conscious of her general weakness.

Slowly, in a half-daze, she made her way across the unsteady floor behind Drusilla, the other women following on according to order of precedence. Outside, she stood a few moments, trying to collect herself, while Drusilla gave sharp orders to the slaves about carrying in the wine. Then, feeling she could endure no more, she smiled wanly and nodded to their guests—it was all the farewell she could manage—and walked with precise steps, on each of which she had to concentrate, to her own room. She sat down on the bed, trembling.

There her stepmother found her later on, sitting with an abstracted expression, hands clasped on her lap. Drusilla sat down beside her, rather heavily, for she too was feeling the strain, and put an arm around her. "Well, darling," she said, "what do you think of him?"

Severina looked round absently, though she had heard the question, which indeed she had been pondering ever since she returned to her room. She knew that by now the guests, their function fulfilled, had gone home; that Aurelian and her father must have settled down to the practical details of the business transaction, in which she was the commodity changing hands. Curiously, she felt no anger. Perhaps because she was so tired and it seemed pointless to make a fuss about what, anyway, was inevitable, she was content to be handed over, no matter how many gold pieces and acres and slaves were considered a suitable dowry.

She saw Drusilla's look grow anxious at her long silence and she smiled, painfully. "I like him, Mother," she whispered. "He seems very kind."

It was lame—and it was misleading. She could not understand what prompted her to describe Aurelian as kind. She could have said that he was handsome, in a virile, exciting, frightening way, in a way that was utterly new in her experience. She could have said that there was something about him that drew her, whether she willed it or not. She could have said that he looked far younger than she had anticipated, far stronger, more masterful. But she had said he was very kind and Drusilla, taking the meek words as a sign of consent, bent forward and kissed her on the brow with a warmth that showed her relief.

"I'm so glad," she said—then added briskly, "But you'll have to have lots of new things for the wedding!"

6

AFTER that, it seemed the gates of the house were thrown open wide and all Rome roared in. Dressmakers and hairdressers, shoe-makers, jewelers, perfumers, provision merchants, wine merchants, dealers and suppliers of many kinds, were for ever coming and go-ing. Most of the matrons of Roman high society called at various times; often two or three were present together. They would hold up fabrics against Severina's figure and grow absorbed in arguments about quality, cut and color, trimming and ornaments. As the debate prolonged itself Severina, whose view was rarely asked, would begin to droop, while Drusilla waited anxiously for the final verdict.

With these august ladies were their unmarried daughters who, too overcome to chatter, stared at Severina with silent envy, for everybody agreed that one of "the Illyrians," whatever his age and disposition, was a catch!

There were stranger visitors. One afternoon a slave brought Severina an urgent request. "Hurry, please, Mistress says!" the girl kept repeating. Severina hastened to Drusilla's room—to be confronted by an extraordinary tableau. A swarthy, eagle-nosed old woman, with a yellow kerchief round her straggling gray hair, was bending over Drusilla's upturned palm, on which her clawlike finger was apparently tracing some pattern. Drusilla herself was leaning forward from her chair, her neck twisted to bring her ear closer to the woman's moving lips. She wore a foolish, deliciously scared expression.

"Come in! Come in!" she cried, as soon as she saw Severina. "Here's that Lucilla I told you about—the best fortuneteller in Rome—she's from Phrygia."

The old woman painfully straightened up and turned to Severina. Her predatory profile and bold, intensely black eyes gave a grotesque and malevolent liveliness to her crone's face, with its sunken cheeks, bony jaw and sallow, puckered skin. Shapeless on her stooped body hung a faded white gown, embroidered in gold, black, and purple thread with mystic symbols, among which Severina could detect some of the Signs of the Zodiac.

She gave Severina a swift, appraising glance; then smiled with insolent frankness, as though to say: this one looks too clever to be taken in by my hocus-pocus.

"Let her read your hand—she knows about the wedding. Everybody goes to her," called Drusilla, greatly excited by the promise of happiness for herself and feeling, no doubt, that this was an auspicious moment, with the Gods in giving mood and Lucilla, the dispenser of their bounty, so encouraging.

Severina started and instinctively put her hands behind her back.

"Never mind!" cackled Lucilla. She fingered the shining jet beads hanging from her scraggy neck. "Leave the young lady alone—she thinks it all stuff and nonsense, don't you, m'dear?" She

60

had a neighing voice, unpleasant but strangely retentive to the ear. From her accent Severina judged her origin was nearer the slums of Rome than Phrygia.

"I just don't feel like having my fortune told today," said Severina mildly.

Lucilla chuckled: her mocking gaze rested on Severina, who felt more and more uncomfortable. She realized the fortune teller, with absolute confidence in the invincible credulity of her dupes, was enjoying a moment of calculated frankness, was—as it were—saying: you know, of course, that I'm a fraud, but try telling your mother—and see what happens!

"All right, then, Severina," said Drusilla, good-humoredly. "I expect she's a bit excited—the wedding, you understand," she added, addressing Lucilla. "You'll come and read her hand some other time, won't you?"

Lucilla's eyelid twitched. "Any time the young lady wants me," she answered with a grin; then she turned and took between her choppy fingers the hand Drusilla had again tremulously lifted toward her.

Severina walked out, surprised how deeply agitated she was by this absurd, distasteful episode; she had a feeling that her marriage had been defiled.

A few days after her encounter with Lucilla, another urgent summons came for Severina—this time from her father, bidding her join him in the garden. On arriving there, she was startled to find, seated lazily on a low wall or lounging nearby, about a dozen bored-looking Praetorians in their gaudy armor. They brightened up as she approached and she felt their eyes travel all over her. Then she forgot them, for at the opposite end of the garden she caught sight of Gallienus gracefully at ease on a marble seat, in the act of taking a silver wine goblet from the tray held out by a bowing servant, behind whom hovered her father.

Severina stared at this unexpected scene. Despite the presence of the soldiers, there appeared no cause for alarm. Gallienus looked so relaxed, was smiling so affably, that her recollection of what her father had confided to her during those painful minutes in the

Palace courtyard seemed quite unreal. She walked toward them with a little stir of pleasurable excitement, surprised that she was glad to see Gallienus once more.

The servant was retiring with his tray. Her father's back was turned. Gallienus glanced in her direction. "My dear Senator," he said coolly, "oblige me by sending to warn my rascals outside that I shall be leaving soon. They had better start forming up." He turned to watch Severina, while her father hastened with dignified steps in pursuit of the servant, whom he overtook some distance away.

Gallienus regarded Severina with a beaming smile as she came up. "Ah, the beautiful bride!" he exclaimed. She gave him a little bow. "The tired bride, Your Majesty," she answered, unable to resist the infection of his bantering tone.

Her father, having dispatched the servant to the Emperor's retinue waiting in the roadway outside the house, had started back.

"Of course—well, it won't be long now," Gallienus said, looking at Severina with sympathy. "Still," he added with a change of manner, "tired or not, I'm sure you'll make a radiant picture at the ceremony. You really ought be painted while you still have that rapt, virginal look!"

Even more than the playful familiarity of these words the candid admiration of his eyes put her out of countenance. He smiled broadly, enjoying her confusion. Just then her father came bustling up. "There you are, Severina," he began self-importantly. "His Majesty is doing our house a great honor. He was on State business in the neighborhood and was gracious enough to look in and inquire how the wedding preparations were going."

"A temple dedication!" explained Gallienus with a grimace which flattered by implying that his audience shared his distaste for such ceremonies. "Really Rome is chock-a-block with gods—and pretty odd some of them are! There was a great crowd of the devout—rather smelly in this warm weather. And, of course, we had to have a sacrifice, with the Priest sticking his nose right into the poor beast's entrails. My good Senator, the fervor—and the flies! I simply felt I must have a few minutes' conversation with a genuine philosopher before I returned to the Palace!"

Severina gave Gallienus a quick, searching glance—he had reeled off this compliment so glibly. Her father apparently found no irony in it. He bowed, looking pleased.

Gallienus rose. "Thank you, Senator, both for your hospitality and your conversation—I feel quite restored." He smiled at Severina with such effortless charm that her resentment was disarmed. "You must not neglect us in your happiness, dear young lady. I shall look forward to seeing you—with your husband—at Court."

He patted her arm twice, with that easy familiarity which in anyone else would have been offensive, and sauntered toward the garden entrance, her father in attendance. The guardsmen fell in with a clatter and followed in single file.

Severina waited, conscious of the place just above her elbow where his hand had made its light, swift, double contact. It was a considerable time before her father returned. He still looked pleased, though rather puzzled.

"Quite a success, don't you think?" he said. "Everything went off well. Polite of him to ask to see you—and he stood chatting quite a time by his litter. Yes, he was on his best behavior!" He paused and regarded her fixedly. "Still, I wonder what he was really driving at, coming here like this." She did not venture a comment. After a few moments he shrugged. "I suppose Valerian left instructions I was to be kept sweet. I won't flatter myself it was entirely for my own sake. The Illyrians are gaining more and more influence. It's Aurelian's goodwill they want!"

He smiled complacently, for his expectations from her marriage were being realized. Severina stayed silent. She suspected that a clever man of affairs must be specially liable to the folly of assuming that people always acted from carefully calculated motives. An instinct she did not doubt assured her that Gallienus in paying his unconventional call had been prompted by nothing more significant than a whim—the whim to pass a few agreeable moments in bantering talk with her.

So the days flew and her wedding drew nearer. Though all manner of strangers demanded time of her, the one man she longed to converse with, freely and in quiet, was rarely in the house. Aurelian had spent the night there after his first visit; but had left early next morning. He returned a few times, but only for an hour or so and on each occasion her parents both contrived to be present.

Throughout the period of her betrothal they did not relax this strict regard for decorum. And even when she met Aurelian, try as she would, she could not manage to exchange more than a few banal words with him. In his proximity her inspiration dried up. She could think of nothing to set the conversation flowing. As for Aurelian, he was polite, friendly in a formal way, laconic. Perhaps, she told herself, he felt there was nothing much to say to an inexperienced girl less than half his age—after all he was a famous man of great personal achievement, while her only claim to interest lay in being her father's daughter.

Only once—and then by chance and very briefly—did she find herself moving with him toward a mood of greater intimacy.

With a book in her hand she had entered one of the big reception rooms on her way to her father's library. At once she stopped. At the opposite door was Aurelian: with him were two men, one of them the pleasant-looking young adjutant, Probus, whom she had already met. The other, also an Illyrian, she felt sure, was gracefully made, and had an air of melancholy charm. He was virtually of a height with Aurelian, and their faces were close together; the stranger's showed an aristocratic refinement while, by contrast, Aurelian's suggested almost harsh power.

Her footfalls, slow and light, had not reached them and they continued absorbed in their conversation.

For some reason, she assumed that she herself was being discussed and her heart went leaden when she saw Aurelian frown. A moment later the distinguished-looking stranger set her fears at rest.

"Brilliant, yes—but too unstable. If only he'd learn to stick to the point!"

"At least, Claudius, he spared you his gush," Aurelian said, smiling grimly. "Did you hear about my first audience?"

Probus laughed. Severina had already gathered that the subject of this uncensored talk was Gallienus.

"He put his hands on my shoulders and looked into my face. 'The famous Aurelian!' he said. 'What men Illyricum breeds!' "

64

He himself joined in the laughter, but made a grimace as he resumed. "The next moment he was dragging me over to see a statue of Valerian. By somebody called Diocles of Corinth, I think. He kept insisting it was a masterpiece—look at the grain of the marble, look how it took the light. Then he started to say this Diocles must do a statue of me!"

"How did you cope with that one?" asked Claudius chuckling.

"I just grunted—and he changed the subject. And yet I agree with you, the man's no featherbrain. Look how he smashed the Alemanni when they broke into Italy last year. It was first-class, though the bulletins exaggerated wildly. And he's got some remarkable ideas about the Army reforms. The trouble is pinning him down to a practical scheme."

The others nodded. These were the longest speeches Severina had ever heard Aurelian make and the only ones in which he had given evidence of warm feeling. Suddenly she felt an intruder. Without consciously willing it, she made a slight scraping noise with her foot. At once, all three turned in her direction, Claudius and Probus alert, Aurelian angrily.

His face cleared when he saw her. "Come here, Severina," he said quite pleasantly. "I want you to meet another friend from Illyricum—Marcus Aurelius Claudius."

She took an instant liking to Claudius, who bowed a moment over her hand, smiling with a grave and gentle charm that put her at her ease. "This is indeed a pleasure, Severina," he said, "if an old friend of Aurelian's may call you so."

"Oh, go ahead!" put in Aurelian cheerfully.

The courteous and sympathetic manner of Claudius gave back to Severina that command of her tongue of which Aurelian's presence had always deprived her.

"You know, General," she said, returning his smile, "a few months ago I'd hardly heard of the Illyrians. Now I know that you're one of our most distinguished commanders. It was you—wasn't it?—who won a big victory against the Sarmatians? And wait—recently you were cited for throwing back an invasion of the Hercules—or was it the Vandals?"

All three Illyrians laughed. "Bravo!" said Claudius, both touched

65

and amused. "You'll make a splendid general's wife—it was the Vandals."

"General's wife." The phrase gave Severina a secret thrill of pleasure and she glanced at Aurelian.

Claudius caught the look. He placed a hand on the arm of Probus and said, "Do excuse us, Severina. They'll be expecting us at the Palace pretty soon. I look forward to seeing you again. Come along, Probus."

With some agitation, which she hoped she did not betray, she bade them farewell. She watched them disappear through the doorway—and then, for the very first time, she was alone with Aurelian.

He looked at her steadily for a few moments, then asked: "You heard what I said—about Gallienus, I mean?"

She nodded, once again tongue-tied.

"You won't repeat any of it, will you?" The form of his words was a polite request; his tone made them an emphatic command. "I won't repeat it," she answered quietly, a little chilled.

"Rome is a city of politics, you understand," he went on with a frown, assuming correctly that this was a sufficient explanation.

"Yes," she said, feeling helpless. Politics was the last subject she wanted to discuss in these precious, fleeting moments.

His air grew more relaxed. "What is that book you've got there, Severina?"

She glanced down; she had quite forgotten the book. "Oh, this? It's a play—*The Trojan Women,* by Euripides."

"Let me see it," he said, reaching out. His strong fingers brushed her palm. She felt an impulse to raise her hand and look at the place. Aurelian examined the book. "Greek," he said. "I don't know Greek, though I picked up a few words from a Tribune called Demaratus. A clever chap, keen on philosophy."

He gazed at her curiously until she blushed. "You know, Severina, when I was your age, I could neither read nor write."

There was no self-pity in his manner for the ignorance of his youth, nor self-congratulation on having overcome it. No, what he implied was only admiration for what he seemed to consider her own remarkable scholarship.

"Oh, there are lots of books here," she said softly, leaning a little

66

toward him. "We could read some of them together—later on." She had wanted to say, "When we are married."

"A good idea!" He sounded almost enthusiastic. There was a surge of feeling in her; she longed to know if there was an answering warmth in him. She did sense that the distance between them had begun to diminish, that she was drawing nearer the strange, disturbing essence of this man.

"Oh, there you are, Aurelian!" It was her father's voice. She became aware, suddenly, how overprecise and complacent it was. "Here is the map of Rome you wanted—it shows the chief thoroughfares. Severina, my dear, where have you come from?"

He meant: how long have you been here? Before she could think of a reply, Aurelian said, rather stiffly: "Severina has been telling me about your library. I must see it one day." He nodded politely to them both, once more withdrawn behind the barrier of formality. "It's time I was off to the Palace. Thank you for the map."

He turned away and walked out of the room, out of the eager embrace of her heart and mind. Her father muttered something, but she paid no attention. She stood there unmoving, still seeing Aurelian's broad, indifferent back.

And that was all. They met twice more before their wedding, but only for a short time and amid a swirl of company. That mood of dawning intimacy did not, could not, recur. Their betrothal had made her familiar only with his name, his appearance, his reputation, as countless others must have known them. His thoughts remained secret, his personality baffling. He was still a stranger when they stood before a great crowd of guests watching the Augur take the auspices of their marriage from the entrails of a sacrificed ewe; Severina, in a bride's traditional saffron cloak and sandals, pale and tense behind her orange-colored veil; Aurelian, at her side, the stately soldier even in his civilian robe. He was still a stranger when, in tremulous answer to his deep and confident tones, she repeated the words, derived from the rustic infancy of Rome, which made them man and wife: *"Ubi tu caius ego Gaia."* Still a stranger when he shut the bedroom door on the broadly smiling bridesmaid, leaned against it for a moment and then turned toward where she waited, silent and afraid.

67

7

EVEN up here in the Alban Hills the morning was already growing very warm. Severina thought of Rome down there in the plain,
crowded and smelly and airless Rome sweltering in heat that
heralded the dog days. No wonder Aurelian came back from the
daily staff talks at the Palace tired and with poor appetite; though
she was certain it was not fatigue alone that often made him so
morose and taciturn.

She sighed. If only he would discuss things with her. Yet though
she always eagerly awaited his return and the ring of hooves on the
courtyard stones brought her hurrying into the porch, she knew he
might greet her with a preoccupied look and would be sparing of
conversation through the evening.

Not only was he uncommunicative about what he did in Rome;
he showed no interest in the small events of her own day, which it
would have given her so much pleasure to recount to him.

A brief current of air from the porch agitated the skirt of her simple, girdled linen gown and coolly caressed her bare throat and arms
and ankles. While she stood waiting for Porphyry, her steward, she
looked with a critical eye round the atrium, the main living room
of modest size, where he reported early each day for his instructions.
And, as every morning during the past two months, when she had
made the same instinctive survey, she was pleased with what she
saw. She had done well to persuade her father to give Aurelian and
herself the smallest and least pretentious of his three villas, set in a
fold of the hills which seemed to banish neighboring Rome a hundred miles away.

The house, an irregular single-storey building, stood well back
from the winding country road by which it was approached and its
grounds were enclosed by a high wall of weathered brick. None of

its rooms was large and all were furnished simply. The gardens at this time of year were specially inviting. Although small by comparison with those of the sumptuous country houses scattered among the slopes of the district, they offered an agreeably varied prospect of lawns and flower beds, fountains, pools, and shady walks. Their only statue was a naked, chubby Eros in weather-dulled bronze, his poised stringless bow like a toy in some game of make-believe. A pleasant, tranquil home, comfortable without being luxurious, secluded yet accessible to friends, had been what she sought for and achieved.

It should have been the setting for an easy and trustful relationship, an attachment growing stronger as time passing brought them into deeper and deeper harmony. Yet they had made no progress toward such an intimacy of hearts and minds. To her the villa was home, as her father's mansion had never been, something peculiarly and intensely hers—just because Aurelian shared it. But Aurelian, she felt, saw the villa as a billet, the latest in a long succession he had occupied from the Euphrates to the Rhine. She had discarded her girlhood, those eighteen shadowy years before the sharp reality of the last two months. Her life now revolved round the fact that she was Aurelian's wife; everything was oriented to him. But she suspected that for Aurelian nothing had radically changed. He had taken on some extra commitments, that was all. He had simply added a wife to his routine.

The steward came in, mopping his plump, solemn face, while the gray tufts round his bald, sweating brow trembled in the draught that had again begun to play through the room. They greeted each other formally, but the smiles they exchanged were affectionate. Porphyry had been the husband of her nurse, now dead these five years, and among the entertainments of her infancy had been to ride astride his knee and be hoisted to the dizzy height of a seat upon his shoulder.

It was due to her that her father—who, while firmly holding that all men were equal, was reluctant to part with valuable human property—had recently manumitted Porphyry. She had insisted on having him as her steward and, equally, had insisted that her steward must be free.

Severina gave him his instructions for the day. He listened gravely, sometimes repeating them in his own words, the better to impress them on his memory.

"The room is ready, in case your Uncle Crinitus arrives today," he said. "He isn't hard to please." A childlike smile momentarily smoothed the anxious creases from his forehead. "How well I remember his last visit—I had just been made an understeward. His first words were—begging your pardon—'I want a bowl of wine and a pretty girl to bring it!'"

Severina laughed and Porphyry looked delighted that his reminiscence had pleased her.

"Well, you bring his refreshments yourself this time," she said smiling. "Something light—traveling up from Rome in this weather doesn't give one much of an appetite," she added, thinking of Aurelian.

"Yes, Lady—we shall do our best—we shall do our best." It was his ritual formula of farewell. He inclined his head, lower than a freeborn steward would have done, and hurried out, brimming with zeal to perform her wishes.

"Oh, send Prudentius in!" she called after him. It always put the testy, half-deaf old gardener in good humor to be consulted about the flowers she cut for the house—and just now she wanted a few choice blooms for her uncle's room.

She was still surprised how much she enjoyed this ordinary, everyday business of running her own home. At first the responsibility of being mistress of a household had rather scared her. But soon she had found her domestic duties easy enough, especially as Porphyry, for all his fussy ways, was a shrewd and efficient steward and he had handpicked for her a capable little staff from among her father's servants.

Suddenly it occurred to her how pleased her uncle would be, when he arrived, to find her wearing her Scythian gold brooch. It was months since she had put on this gift of his and she had a moment of mild panic lest she had mislaid it. Forgetful that she had sent for Prudentius, she left the atrium and with hurried steps walked toward her bedroom.

By the door, Pervica, one of the maids, was scouring the floor

70

with a mop. She straightened up when she saw Severina and drew her bucket out of the way. Severina replied somewhat absently to her respectful greeting and entered the room. Except for the big double bed, it was sparely furnished and with its high ceiling and unadorned walls had a bare look. Its single window faced the garden.

Instead of going directly across to the closest where she kept her jewel box, she stood a few moments by the bed, staring down at it. Under its smooth white coverlet it looked by daylight something innocent, without memories. Yet at night, by the dim lamp or in the sultry dark, it had been a place of anguish for her, of physical pain, of frustration. No doubt her own inexperience was in part to blame. All the same, Aurelian's lovemaking was too rough and impatient for a delicately nurtured girl. A few perfunctory caresses to rouse himself and he took his pleasure simply from her unawakened body, indifferent to her own needs.

Perhaps he was used to the paid-for services of the women of the camps or to helpless barbarian captives. Even after his moments of utmost sensual gratification he showed no tenderness.

With a sigh she turned and walked over to the closet; taking a key from the purse at her girdle, she unlocked it and drew out the jewel box.

Her fingers searched of their own through the costly little heap; her thoughts were still engaged with Aurelian. There was something impersonal about his claims on her. All he required of her was to discharge the official obligations of marriage; any other woman might have satisfied him in her place. If only he had said, even in a revealing look: "I need you—you, personally." If only she were admitted through that outer zone where his personality expressed itself in eating and drinking and sharing a bed with her in the same spirit as he shared her meals. She felt that one tender word, one foolish endearing name, would have swept away all her restraint, and the instinctive tautness that kept her numb in his arms would melt in rapt surrender.

A tiny shock of recognition traveled up from her fingertips as they touched the antlers and glided over the cold proud neck and elongated body of the golden stag. She lifted out the brooch and, absorbed as she was, gave its glinting perfection an admiring glance. Then she replaced it on top of the other jewelry, put the box away, and locked the closet. With a glance at the bed she had turned to the door, when she gave a start. Prudentius! The poor old man must be waiting for her in the atrium, muttering to himself and itching to kick off the sandals he was obliged to put on whenever he was summoned into the house. She hurried out, but stopped with her hand still upon the door. Pervica was standing there with an anxious expression, evidently waiting to speak to her. The mop was leaning against the wall, beside the bucket.

"You want me, Pervica?" asked Severina.

Pervica's hands came together and she took an uncertain step forward. She was a dark-browed girl, plain but intelligent-looking, in her middle twenties, with an air of reserve that gave her a dignity uncommon in slaves. Severina knew her to be sober and hard-working and had heard from Porphyry that she kept herself aloof from the menservants.

As Pervica still hesitated, Severina said kindly, "Yes, what is it?"

Pervica swallowed and answered carefully, "Lady, I beg a favor of you . . ."

"It's all right, Pervica," Severina said, smiling. "Don't be afraid to ask. I won't be angry."

"I want . . . I'd like to be excused duty . . . for three hours this evening. I'll make them up tomorrow—without fail!"

It struck Severina as odd that this modest request should occasion so much nervousness in a normally self-possessed girl. Pervica must have noted the shade of perplexity in her mistress's face, for she fixed her honest brown eyes on Severina and spoke firmly, with no hint of her former hesitation, "I want to attend Divine Service. You see, Lady, I'm a Christian."

"A Christian!" murmured Severina, touched by the girl's trust. She tried to recall what she knew of Pervica's past. Practically nothing, except that she came from somewhere in the East. "You want then to pray to Christ?"

"And to His Mother," the girl amended quickly.

Though half the Roman world worshiped maternal deities, it seemed strange to Severina, reared as she was on philosophical

72

rationalism, that a god should be begotten like mortal man. "Has Christ then a Mother?"

The girl's rugged face softened and she leaned forward, her eyes shining. "Yes, Lady. She brings the prayers of women before the Throne of God!"

"Go on!" said Severina.

Pervica spoke with growing confidence. "Our congregation—we're mostly slaves and freedmen from the villas here—has a new preacher, the Deacon Paul. When he speaks, you can feel the burden of sorrow lifting." Her hand went to her breast. "The Grace of God enters your heart. He is leading many to Christ."

Severina looked hard at Pervica, reflecting for the first time that this reserved and seemingly self-sufficient girl must have had much suffering to endure and little joy in compensation. Except in her religion, which gave her this assurance, this simple eloquence.

That was a specially moving phrase about Christ's Mother bringing the prayers of women before God's Throne. Immeasurably different in their stations, she and Pervica were equal in that they both were women who needed help. An audacious thought occurred to her.

"Do you think your Deacon Paul would come here to talk with me?"

The girl regarded her in silence for a few moments. "You know, Lady, it would be dangerous," she said soberly.

"For the Deacon?" asked Severina, already feeling she had been precipitate.

"And for you, Lady. The authorities have been arresting Christians. In Rome and in other towns there has been the worst persecution for years. Many have been put to death. Still, things are not so bad now that the old Emperor has gone away to the war."

Severina grew uncomfortable under Pervica's steady gaze. She was conscious that this slave of hers was appraising her courage.

To herself she owned that she was considerably shaken. She had been aware, vaguely, of the hunt for Christians and of numerous martyrdoms, but it had all been too remote from her own life to have reality. Now the danger had drawn close to her—at her own invitation. Her eyes fell away from Pervica's. She was angry with

73

herself for an apprehension she could not master and with the girl for perceiving it.

As she stood there biting her lip, she caught a hurried footfall. She glanced round guiltily, unable to avoid the thought that it might be incautious to let herself be seen in private conversation with Pervica.

It was Porphyry, to her relief. He looked quite flustered. He came up, motioned sharply to Pervica to stand well back, waited a few moments and then said in a low, agitated voice, "Lady, the Emperor Gallienus is here. He is asking for the Master. He didn't say who he was, but I recognized him at once—I've seen him in processions."

Porphyry's hands were making little nervous movements. He dropped his voice almost to a whisper. "There's a whole squadron of cavalry out in the road—and some horse litters in the middle of them —covered litters!"

Soldiers—covered litters. They could have a sinister purpose! Porphyry was so obviously scared that she could not help feeling a little frightened herself. "The General has left for Rome," she said. "Didn't you tell him?"

He shook his head slightly, with a wary expression. "I showed him into the atrium and said I would go and see. Then I came straight to you."

Frowning, she reflected. But soon an explanation suggested itself that made her feel less anxious. There was an Imperial summer villa a few miles away; Gallienus was said to have crammed it with artistic treasures. No doubt he had been staying there and had made this characteristically unconventional call on the way back to Rome.

"I'll see him at once," she said and was moving past Porphyry when she became aware of Pervica standing patiently out of ear-shot, with beseeching eyes still fixed in her direction. Really, she thought, with a shade of vexation, this girl is persistent! However, she nodded and called out, as pleasantly as she could, "You can go tonight." She felt relieved that her hurry and Porphyry's presence absolved her from referring to the Deacon Paul.

In the atrium, she found Gallienus conversing with Prudentius. An uncouth figure in his tattered cassock, the old gardener, who smelt of earth and sunburn, obviously had no idea who the visitor

74

was. Gallienus wore a plain military-style tunic, though the clasp of his leather belt was silver and the hilt of his light parade sword was also of silver, finely enchased. He was laughing merrily, evidently enjoying a joke with Prudentus, whose grizzled, knobbly face wore an unaccustomed broad grin.

"Ha, Severina," said Gallienus, turning to her with his charming smile. She made a deep inclination. "Your gardener and I have been having the most interesting conversation," he went on. "All about manure . . ." He leaned toward Prudentius' ear and shouted, "You're quite an expert on manure, eh?" Prudentius nodded vigorously, beaming at the compliment.

"Welcome to this house, Your Majesty," said Severina. "I'll send for you, later, Prudentius," she added, much more loudly. He lifted one finger to his scruffy, iron-gray scalp and went out, still cheerfully nodding.

The easy, engaging manner of Gallienus had set Severina's last fears at rest. "Please forgive my delay in coming," she said. "I was not prepared for a visit so early in the morning."

"Yes, it is early, isn't it!" he answered, with a comically rueful look. "These staff conferences, you know. They're run military-style —everyone punctually on parade! . . . Well, I thought I'd pick your husband up—give him a lift. There's room in one of my horse litters. He'd find it broiling hot riding to the Camp."

"The Camp?"

"Yes, the Praetorian Camp." He gave her a swift, penetrating look. "We're seeing another parade in the new cavalry armor—we were there yesterday, too. Surely Aurelian told you!"

She was unable to restrain a momentary pursing of the lips. Aurelian had not told her—and Gallienus instantly was aware of it. His smile had a facile sympathy not far removed from mockery.

There was a brief pause. "I am sorry, Your Majesty," she said. "Aurelian has left already." She spoke calmly, but she felt she had betrayed to those keen eyes watching her how much she was hurt. To go off like that, without a word—for two days in succession. To let her assume he was still spending the time at the Palace! It would not occur to him to tell her where he went—or that she had a right to know!

"Ah, well," said Gallienus easily, not looking in the least disappointed. "I may catch up with him on the road. Nice room, this. My compliments on your taste!" He gave the "your" the merest flicker of emphasis, which seemed to imply: Your husband's a boor—this elegance must be due to you!

"Your Majesty is very kind," she said with a rather strained smile. "May I offer you some refreshment?"

"Oh, I've been greatly refreshed already," he answered, his eyes holding hers for a few disconcerting moments. "You've some choice things here," he added with a light pretense of transferring the compliment from her to the room. "That goblet—it's old Alexandrian, I'll warrant. They don't give their glass that lovely soft glow any longer."

He lifted the slender, fragile vessel from the simple elm-wood platter on which it stood and held it to the pale-golden light slanting into the room. "Come and look at this, my dear!" The light melted on the faintly incised surface of the glass, to be diffused with a gentle amber radiance. "Superb! . . . What do you do with your time, Severina?"

Watching him set the goblet back on its stand with reverent fingers, she had a suspicion that his query was not as innocent as it sounded—he meant that for someone like herself her husband was an unsatisfactory companion, with whom her days must be wearisome.

"Running the house keeps me occupied, Your Majesty," she replied shortly.

"So you get no time for reading?"

His mock sympathy nettled her. "Oh, I read a good deal," she said, making an effort to keep the tartness from her tone.

Her answer seemed to amuse him. "Anything special?" he pursued mildly.

Pervica came into Severina's mind. Without reflecting, she answered, "Religion." The moment the word escaped, her instinct told her she had been unwise.

"Now isn't that interesting!" said Gallienus with a bright smile. "Religion is a favorite study of mine. It's practically a duty—the Empire swarms with divinities. The Olympians, to start with . . .

76

The Great Mother . . . and Isis and Serapis . . . and Mithras . . . and the God of the Jews—a curious stern old fellow, that—and the Christian God. . . ."

He must have detected some slight unconscious movement or faint change of expression on her part, for his eyes narrowed and he continued in a voice unwontedly serious, "My dear Severina. I shouldn't trouble to study the Christian doctrine if I were you. These people are the dregs of society and their beliefs are so much gibberish."

She stood there troubled, thinking again of Pervica, her quiet strength, her simple, moving way of speech.

Gallienus came over and clasped her hand with a reassuring pressure. "I must go now. All those distinguished generals mustn't be kept waiting! But I'm glad we have this interest in common . . . I know a most singular Egyptian, a Priest of Isis. He has had great success with the ladies of Rome—and not only as a practitioner of religion, I believe. I must see that you meet him one day."

His hand lingered on hers. She was aware of his nearness, of his long, elegant, easily held body stooping slightly toward her, of the faint, astringent perfume from his clothes.

He walked out and Severina followed. In the porch he turned. "No farther, my dear. Thank you for your charming reception. It was such a pity I was too late for Aurelian." He took a step away, then looked round. "Oh, by the way, Severina," he said, smiling blandly, "we shall be holding another of those displays at the Praetorian Camp tomorrow."

With agitation she watched his graceful figure move across the courtyard in the direction of the gate. He was a trifler—and impertinent. One searching glance, a light question or two, and he had uncovered a hidden area of her relations with Aurelian which she herself could not contemplate without humiliation. And yet. . . . He had been obviously glad to see her. He had lingered to chat with her of interesting things. When your own husband cannot be bothered even to mention where he is going for the day, it is some consolation to find that the Emperor himself, a young, gifted, fascinating man, actually enjoys your company!

No, it was not against the prying eyes and smooth, intrusive tongue of Gallienus that her resentment burned, but against the careless indifference of Aurelian. To learn from Gallienus what Aurelian himself should have told her; to be hurt this way and to know that she had not been able to disguise her hurt—that, indeed, was mortifying.

Her anger soon gave way to something like despair. Slowly she walked through the house toward the guest room which had been got ready for Crinitus. Near her own bedroom she saw Pervica busy again with her mop. She stopped and the girl paused in her work, waiting for her to speak. "Tell your Deacon that I should like to see him, Pervica," she said quietly.

8

CRINITUS arrived in the middle of the afternoon. The weather had grown stifling and after her simple midday meal of bread and fruit, Severina's eyelids began to droop; even the muted grumble of thunder in the distance seemed to have a soporific effect.

A hubbub awoke her. She shook herself and went out to the porch. There was Crinitus in the courtyard, standing by his grounded litter, loudly berating a couple of ragged, swarthy muleteers, who were answering sullenly. The four bearers, dispirited-looking slaves fagged by the burden they had shouldered through the wilting heat, stood in a knot, with glistening, vacant faces.

"Uncle!" she exclaimed.

"Well, we got here at last, Severina!" he called. "These fools have gone and dropped your presents." He pointed to a large corded bundle at his feet. "They may have broken something!"

"Never mind, Uncle," she said, going over and clasping his hand. "Come in, out of the sun. I'll call Porphyry to take your men to the kitchen and get them some food."

The noise had already disturbed Porphyry's siesta. He emerged from the house startled and sleepy-eyed, but at a word from Severina was soon fussing about, getting the litter moved into a shed and the baggage—several bales of it—carried indoors.

With a smile for Severina, but still mechanically grumbling, Crinitus flung a couple of coins at the muleteers, whose leathery countenances split in huge grins at the sight. They poured out hoarse thanks together, gave their animals a few enthusiastic thwacks across the rump and made for the gateway.

Dragging his right leg slightly, Crinitus followed Severina to the atrium. There they embraced. She was astonished by her intense pleasure at seeing him and kissed him with fervor. He hugged her, then stood back, holding her hands and surveying her fondly. "My dear!" he murmured, "my dear!"

Crinitus had changed, there was no doubt of it. He had aged far more than she had expected. His hair, though still thick, was mostly white, and his massive body, much more gross than she remembered, was no longer held with the same firmness. Only his little eyes, at the center of their network of wrinkles, were as bright as ever, twinkling with humor.

"Uncle dear, your leg—have you been wounded?"

"My limp? Oh, it's not what you'd call an honorable wound—far from it." His chins trembled as he chuckled. "Just a husband returning home inconveniently early. I had to jump for it—from an upstairs window—and I daren't even groan!"

She managed a smile, to please him, but her expression showed how troubled she was by his appearance. His look grew more serious; he sat down, heavily, and fanned himself with one fleshy hand.

"I'm sorry I couldn't get to Rome for the wedding, Severina," he said. "My doctor had packed me off to the baths at Aquae Sulis— it's in Britain, a poky little provincial place trying to ape the big spas of Gaul and Italy. The truth, my dear, is that my health isn't what it used to be."

"What is the matter, Uncle?" she asked anxiously.

He shrugged. "Don't exactly know. Pains here . . ." he patted his abdomen, high up . . . "pretty nasty at times . . . nausea, too. I used to be strong as an ox," he added, with the resentment of a man unaccustomed to illness.

"Don't look so worried, Severina," he went on. "Did you know I lost a battle? That may have something to do with it. Last autumn, against the Franks. They'd crossed the Rhine; we caught them retreating with their plunder. My cursed troops just ran—they were Regulars, too! The officers tried to stop them—then they also ran. In the end I had to run myself—as fast as any. I'm told the Frankish minstrels made a ballad out of it—they sing about the fat coward of a Roman General in the forests of Germany."

Severina seized his hand and pressed it. "Poor Uncle!" she said softly.

"That sort of thing you can't get over," he said, smiling wryly and patting her hand with his free one. "They never really accept explanations for a defeat. People try to be tactful—and that makes it worse!"

He made a grimace. "Ah, well," he said, dismissing the subject, "and what about you, my dear? Let me have a proper look at you." He gazed at her with an affectionate smile, but searchingly.

"More beautiful than ever," he pronounced after a few moments. "But, oh, so serious! Can it be that the siege of Troy is still distressing you?"

She dropped her eyes; then looked at him frankly. "Not Troy, Uncle," she murmured. "The siege of Aurelian."

His eyes narrowed as he studied her. "The inconstant husband?" His slight shrug conveyed that a woman was capable of making much out of trifles.

"Say the indifferent husband," she amended. "No, he's not quite that—he's just not particularly interested. He does everything a husband's supposed to do . . ." Crinitus chuckled and she felt herself go scarlet at her unfortunate choice of words . . . "only he's not really interested in me as a person—any girl would do just as well."

"Would she?" He stroked one chin with his thumb tip, then the other—two distinct movements.

He continued to gaze at her shrewdly and the curious sense of sympathy she felt with this rarely seen, battered old rake of a relative emboldened her to confide in him further.

"I want to be a good wife, to make him happy. But he doesn't need me. Why should he? He's a famous soldier; I just happen to be a rich Senator's heiress. Oh, he's kind enough as a rule—perhaps I ought to say polite. It would fit our relations better," she added bitterly.

"Boys?" said Crinitus.

The abrupt question startled her. She frowned over it for a few moments, but then rejected the possibility. Aurelian's appetites were normal enough, if rather indelicately satisfied.

"Oh, no!" she exclaimed. "I'm sure of that."

"I thought not," said Crinitus. "Listen to me, Severina. One can be in too deadly earnest, even about a marriage. Yours is still very new. Aurelian will come to know you better and to value you, not only for your beauty, but for your character and your brains. You're the only woman I've met a man can talk to without feeling he's talking to an inferior. Aurelian will get very fond of you in the end. It isn't hard, you know," he concluded, smiling.

"In the end?" she repeated drily. "A wife wants something in the beginning, too. We seem to be so incompatible. I wonder what made you think of bringing us together in the first place."

"So you know I started it," he said, looking a little sheepish. "Well, I suppose it was bound to come out. Just why did I think of you in connection with Aurelian? There you were, a beautiful, talented girl, wasting your years in that museum of a house. Who was there to appreciate you? Your father—no, don't interrupt me, Severina—I suppose he regarded you like one of his precious bronzes or his manuscripts, rare and beautiful, but with no feelings of your own. Drusilla?" He shrugged away any claim she might have to serious consideration. "Your place is in the great world of affairs—give you a little time and you'd make a far better Senator than your father . . . I wonder if one day there will be women Senators! . . ."

He chuckled at the grotesque fancy, while she stared at him astounded by the extraordinary impression he had given of herself. The staggering thing was that he had spoken with a cheerful assurance, as though no one would dispute that she had conspicuous gifts for public affairs, a subject about which she knew herself to be profoundly ignorant.

"When I met Aurelian," Crinitus resumed, "I saw at once that he was marked out for great things. Now you're my favorite relative, the only one I've really got any time for. I hated the thought that they might throw you away on some blue-blooded fool. I thought: Why not pair them off? One day, Aurelian might even become— you know what, Severina. . . ." He winked and lifted a waggish finger to his lips. "It's time we had one in the family—or should I say, 'another,' if we count Trajan?"

This incredible conversation had now become so fantastic that Severina felt quite at a loss. She would have been sure her uncle was merely joking, recklessly joking, but for a certain emphasis in his tone which told her he was in earnest despite his jesting manner. He looked so pleased with himself that she was afraid he might enlarge on his dangerous theme; she decided to change the subject.

"What are you going to do now, Uncle?" she asked with a rather strained smile.

"Have a holiday," he said. "Travel here and there, digging up old comrades. You know, Severina, I sometimes think it's a pity I never married. Too restless, I suppose. Besides, no woman could stand me long. I've always taken my pleasure where I fancied—other men's wives for the most part. Funny thing, I could have had any number of slave girls, but I never wanted to. Perhaps it's because my mother was a slave girl, as no doubt your father told you." For the first time, there was malice in his voice.

Why do men like Crinitus and Gallienus dislike my father so? she thought. As a matter of fact, it had been Drusilla who told her, as a simple item of gossip, without spite or gloating.

As if to make amends for his unkind remark, he leaned forward and patted her hand. "When shall I be seeing your husband?"

Severina sighed. "Not till this evening, I'm afraid. He's mostly away all day at the staff conference—I can't imagine what they find to talk about all this time."

He gave her the same quick and penetrating glance as had Gallienus; he too seemed to say, "Does Aurelian never talk to you?" Then, looking unwontedly solemn, he said, "The Army's being overhauled, my dear—it's this crisis of the Empire."

"What crisis?" asked Severina absently. She was thinking of Aurelian's long ride back through the heat to the villa. "Is there some crisis on?"

82

"By Jupiter, there is! The biggest that the Empire's ever had—and it's growing!"

"Forgive me, Uncle," she said, disturbed by his serious manner. "Do you mean there's danger again of civil war?"

"There's chronic civil war in the Empire—interrupted by truces," he answered deliberately. "The Army has no loyalty to its head. Who's its head, anyway? That flabby windbag, Valerian! Discipline's gone to hell. The Germans are stirring—they've learned to combine—we're fighting not clans but whole nations. And in Persia we've got an enemy who's capable of smashing right through to the Mediterranean."

Somehow, the thought of the frontiers collapsing did not touch her imagination. They were too far away; she had never seen a Persian—or even a German, except as a slave or a Roman auxiliary. Still, her uncle's somber look impressed her.

"We're getting poorer, too," Crinitus went on. "Nowadays nobody wants to serve on the local councils—it's too expensive. We squeeze the provincials without mercy; if they had any spirit left, they'd be at our throats. Why, in Gaul whole villages are taking to the woods and hills to get away from the tax collectors."

"Uncle," said Severina, now deeply alarmed, "just how bad is this crisis?"

"Very bad—it could be fatal. The truth, Severina, is that unless someone pulls the whole fabric together, we're going to get the biggest smash of all history. I used to think the Empire would last my time—I'm not so sure now!"

"Someone?" queried Severina, who perceived a significance in the deliberately neutral word.

He smiled at her without levity, appreciating her discernment. "The Illyrians," he replied. "One or all of them. If only they stick together and don't start fighting!"

Crinitus fell silent. Porphyry had come bustling in with a tray on which stood a bowl of fruit, a heavy cut-glass decanter, ruby-red with wine, a water jug and a couple of slender-stemmed glass goblets. Severina pushed a little table forward. "Here, Porphyry," she said, anxious for him to go quickly and for her uncle to resume.

Porphyry beamed at her; set the tray down; moved it fussily a

83

fraction of an inch first one way, then another, so that it rested squarely on the table; bowed very low to Crinitus and, with a motion toward the little bronze gong by the wall, said, "If the General wants anything . . ." He carefully adjusted the positions of the vessels on the tray and only then withdrew, facing them and inclining his head several times. For once his unrestrained zeal jarred on Severina.

She raised the decanter and looked at Crinitus. "You said the Illyrians, Uncle . . ."

"Neat, please," he said. He listened to the tiny clink of glass on glass and the faint plash of wine. "Yes, I said the Illyrians. It's like this . . ." He took the overfull goblet from her, grimacing as his nostrils caught an unfamiliar aroma. He looked at the wine without enthusiasm and continued, "They're the last of the provincials to come to the front. First there were Gauls and Spaniards, like our kinsmen, Trajan and Hadrian. Then the Africans and Orientals—you know, Septimius Severus, Severus Alexander, Philip the Arabian. We're all burned out now. Only the Illyrians are capable of taking over and keeping the Empire alive. Nobody else is nearly equal to the challenge."

He glanced down at the goblet but made no move to drink.

"Just look at them," he went on. "Their brows are craggy; their noses are aggressive; their jaws jut. They're rough and they're tough. They're ready to knock you down at a word. They've got 'fighter' written all over them!"

Severina reflected. Her uncle's words were giving sharp definition to the vague impressions that had accumulated in her own mind. She had met several of the Illyrians and it was a fact that something harshly virile distinguished them; even Claudius had it, though in his case it was overlaid with aristocratic charm.

Crinitus was watching her absorbed face. "That's true, Uncle," she said, nodding. "Please go on."

"The trouble, my dear, is that we Romans of Rome no longer really care. We know the challenge is too big for us. We've accepted defeat in our hearts. But the Illyrians do care, passionately. They're peasants, most of them, and they've not been corrupted like ourselves. They're concerned about the crisis with all the force of their unsophisticated natures. That's why they're hurt and angered by the sickly spirit they meet everywhere, the way people are resigned to their fate like cowed slaves. The Illyrians can't understand such weakness, such total surrender. As I've said, they're natural fighters —the only men left to confront the appalling dangers that are closing in on Rome!"

He stopped, to recover breath. Severina's eyes did not leave his face, in whose loose skin the furrows seemed to have deepened. "Why, Uncle?" she asked in a low voice. "Why should they be so different? Not just because they're of peasant stock, surely. There are peasants all over the Empire." She awaited his answer tensely, for she felt it would shed light not only on the crisis of the world, but also on the strains in her own marriage.

Crinitus shifted in his seat; the goblet he held vibrated, but there was no overspill of the wine lipping its brim. "I could give you several reasons," he said, "but there's one to which I'd attach most importance. There's no secret about it. What drives these Illyrians, your Aurelian included, is their religion. They're Mithraists to a man!"

Religion! The moment the word was uttered she understood why so much of Aurelian had been inaccessible to her. He was a believer; she had been bred a skeptic. Apart from their marriage ceremony— and that was traditional, rather than religious in any elevated sense —religion had hardly touched their lives together. The ways of their household were entirely secular, like those of her father's home, from which they derived.

Suddenly, she saw deep into Aurelian. In the heart of this man, who so intimately shared her life, a fire blazed—and she had not been aware of its existence!

She thrust these thoughts aside and concentrated on listening, for Crinitus had resumed and she felt he was pronouncing on her personal destiny and Aurelian's.

"The trouble with our family—yes, I'm just the same as your father in this, anyway—is that we haven't got religion. Everyone else has nowadays—the Illyrians in particular. Their Mithraism is a soldier's creed; it's intense, but stern and disciplined. They have initiation rites—very impressive ones, I believe—purifications and a state of mystic communion with the Sun God. Add the impulse that comes from such a faith to the tough, stubborn, truculent spirit of men raised in a near-primitive land on an exposed frontier and you begin to understand the Illyrians; you begin to understand why they're in such deadly earnest; why they're so formidable. There are plenty of ambitious men from other parts of the Empire and clever generals, even from Rome . . ." he paused to enjoy her responsive smile . . . "but none of us cares a damn about anything larger than ourselves. The Illyrians are different. They're determined to save the Empire, clean it up, set it on a new political and moral basis. They've a kind of collective sense of mission. It makes them very effective leaders, but rather taxing in off-duty hours. An Illyrian is seldom off duty in his mind!"

Uncle and niece regarded each other soberly. "You make it sound convincing," Severina said slowly. "But I can't look at it your way. I didn't marry this dedicated band of Illyrians. I married one man—called Aurelian."

"All right, my dear, we'll consider your husband. Some people would write Aurelian off as a Centurion of genius, an iron-hearted soldier with a voice like a trumpet, who sees the Empire as a barracks round a parade ground. That's a bad mistake, though a natural one. A Centurion doesn't have dreams that involve all mankind. He doesn't see life as a struggle of Light against Dark. A Centurion feels no mission, except to carry out orders, fill his purse, and get his due share of booze and women."

Crinitus looked thoughtfully at the wine in his hand, pursed his lips and then, with a critical air, took a sip. Severina saw him grimace and set the goblet down, withdrawing his hand sharply, as if even the touch of it were distasteful.

"Don't you like it, Uncle?" she asked, dismayed.

"It's not bad," he said, with a shrug. "Bit syrupy, that's all. Haven't you any Gallic wines?"

"No—I don't think so," answered Severina, after a moment. "I don't know much about wine," she added, rather guiltily. "Aurelian never expresses any preference. He's very temperate."

"Temperate, eh?" His face, which had been rather glum, not to say peevish, recovered a humorous look and he broke into a frankly

86

lascivious chuckle. She felt herself go red under his satyr's eyes. With this amiable old sensualist even the most innocent term seemed to take on an erotic significance.

"Well," he said, "one can't expect a properly brought up young lady to know much about wine; but I must say I'm surprised at Aurelian. I should have thought anyone who's served on the Rhine would have acquired a taste for Gallic wines; some of them are superb. If you want my opinion—and I've sampled the lot—the best of them come from the Burdigala district, on the Atlantic. Now I mention it, there's a wine merchant from Burdigala in Rome at the moment. Name of Matthaias—he's a Jew. I'll send him along, if you like. He'll charge you top prices, I warn you, but you'll get top quality."

"Please do, Uncle," she said quickly. Obviously with men the quality of wine could be a question of prime importance. Perhaps Aurelian really did prefer Gallic wines, but had not wished to put her to trouble.

"What were we talking about?" demanded Crinitus, his good humor fully restored. "Ah, yes—the Illyrians. It's easy to see, they're coming right to the top, Severina. Who could keep them under? Valerian? Pouf! He couldn't even if he wanted to; in point of fact he's trying to win them over, to make them his prop. Gallienus? . . . H'mm. He's got the brains, certainly. But he's too inconstant, too much the poseur, too much the jester. My guess is that the Illyrians will grow tired of him and pull him down—you mark my words. And then we shall see. . . ."

Severina studied the rejected wine, feeling an odd sort of kinship with it. But for the moment her personal problems did not seem very important. The summary way in which Crinitus had emptied the Throne of the Caesars, condemning the reigning Emperors with a contemptuous word, gave her a glimpse of the realities of power in Rome—below the pinnacle lay the abyss. Nor could she be happy in the thought that the dynasty might founder, no matter what opportunities this might bring for Aurelian's advancement. There would, no doubt, be a disputed succession, as on previous occasions, with another of those dreadful civil wars which injured the Empire more than a barbarian invasion.

"Now you can see your marriage in true perspective, Severina," resumed Crinitus. "You've a handsome husband, a magnificent specimen of a man, brave as a hero of antiquity. You want him all to yourself, to make love to you, to dance attendance on you, to say the pretty things that women love to hear. You want a snug domestic idyll. But outside Rome is tottering; our world is in collapse. There are only a few men who can stave off ruin—Aurelian's one of them. You don't expect him to have time for the silly little attentions and phrases of courtship, do you?"

"They're not silly to a woman!" she retorted, her eyes suddenly filling, not at the derisory note in her uncle's question but at the sharp sense it gave her of isolation from Aurelian. She was wedded, wholly, to him; he was almost wholly involved in an unending crisis, which reduced his home to a refectory and bedroom, and his wife to one member, and not the most important, of his staff.

There was a little silence, which she was the first to break. "Very well, Uncle. Rome's in decline. Aurelian and the other Illyrians are dedicated men trying to stop the rot. Where do I come in? After all, it was you who proposed this marriage. Well, you've succeeded. I've been Aurelian's wife for the last two months. And now you blandly tell me that you knew all along he would not have time to be a normal husband—the kind every ordinary woman wants."

"He's not a normal husband and you, my spirited little niece— that angry color really becomes you—are not in the least an ordinary wife. You're not interested in trivialities. You're not a chatterbox, a gossip monger. You can see beyond the next meal. You've a mind that's capable of appreciating our modern problems. You can share Aurelian's life, in very great measure: though, frankly, you can't expect him to concern himself very much with yours."

"Did you really think of my marriage as a kind of sacrifice, Uncle?"

"As a matter of fact, I did. Only men like Aurelian can save us— shouldn't we give him what help we can? After all, is it a worse fate for a gifted young woman like you to be Aurelian's helpmate in great events than that you should be just a kind of stewardess and bed companion, something that a well trained slave girl could do as well or even better?"

"I can't say I agree with you, Uncle. I don't particularly want to play a part in great events—I understand too little, to start with. But you're right in this sense: I've got no choice. Aurelian is what he is and—it's not a pleasant thing for a woman to admit about her husband—he isn't going to change for me, not in any real way. So I've got to change for him."

As she spoke, she was conscious of relief that she had put her problems frankly to Crinitus. His answers had been painful, but they seemed to have opened a path that brought her nearer to her husband. He was no longer so remote; she felt that eventually she would reach him. And to begin with, she must school herself to be patient. Two months were an absurdly short time to create a happy relationship that could endure for the years.

Crinitus placed his hand lightly on hers. Looking at her with a gentle and affectionate expression, against which she could not hold out, he said, "It's your destiny, Severina! I know I played my part. But, girl, it's your own character and your own brains that are the decisive factors. Don't you really want to stand beside Aurelian up there on the heights, rather than be just another wealthy, pampered, idle young wife?"

"Let me put it like this, Uncle," she said, smiling not without a certain bitterness. "Aurelian's up there on the heights. If that's the only way I can be beside him, I shall have to climb up on the heights, too. But I still feel I'd rather be down in the valley; it's where I really belong. And it seems to me not such a bad thing to be obscure when the world is falling to pieces. You see, Uncle, I'm not an Illyrian myself—I'm only married to one."

9

ON THE outskirts of Rome lay the Praetorian Camp, protected by ramparts, a fortress whose unruly garrison in former days had made and unmade Emperors, on one occasion even putting the Throne of the Caesars up for auction and knocking it down to the highest bidder. Nowadays the Praetorians played a diminished role. It was the suffrage of the frontier Legions which was decisive; their swords conferred the Divine Right of supreme military power, against which no claim of personal merit or seniority in descent from earlier sovereigns could prevail. Still the Camp remained an important base, with its rows upon rows of uniform barracks, its immense parade grounds, its sheds for winter training, its stores and administrative buildings, its stables and baths. It was a soldiers' city, created by a superb military science, displaying in conspicuous form those qualities of method, discipline, efficiency, which had spread the Roman dominion from the moors of Scotland to the caravan routes of the Syrian desert.

If the Camp itself demonstrated warlike severity and order, the guardsmen who occupied it conveyed an impression of martial pride and splendor. Here was the elite force of an Empire still, in appearance, mighty; picked detachments of tall, sturdy men from the Danube and the Rhine, who marched with easy, fluent precision and wore their ornate armor with a swagger that, in their case, did not seem absurd.

Round the fringe of the main barrack square, where several squads were at strenuous drill, a loosely strung-out party of about fifteen officers was walking in the direction of the Praetorium, the headquarters building. Suddenly the Centurion handling the nearest squad barked agitatedly; the men snapped to attention and, wheeling round, he jerked his arm up in salute. The foremost member of the party, a lanky, youngish man, elegant in gilded armor, responded rather languidly. As one squad after another stamped to attention and their commanders saluted, his answering salutes grew more perfunctory. At the foot of the short stone stairway which led to the open double doors of the Praetorium the officers saw his back lift and droop, as if he were breathing a hearty sigh of relief to leave behind that arena of tiresome ceremonial. He ignored the sentry, who with a clash of steel froze to a statue, and disappeared inside. The officers followed.

Gallienus, for it was he who headed the little procession, led the way directly into a sizeable room which had the utilitarian air of a council chamber. In the center was an oblong table, with a high-backed chair at one end and about a score of leather-topped stools along the sides. A faint gleam caught the eye in one corner, where an hourglass stood on a tiny shelf supported by a bracket. On the walls, otherwise bare, were nailed a number of maps showing the disposition of forts and camps in various frontier regions. The single wide window looked across the barrack square, from which the crisp commands and the crash in unison of heavy-shod feet on the paving stones came muted into an appropriate background noise for a military discussion.

Sinking into the seat of honor, Gallienus doffed his light, ornamental helmet and set it on the table; then he drew a limp hand across his damp brow. "Jupiter, it's warm!" he exclaimed peevishly. "Sit down, everyone. Helmets off. Let's be informal, for goodness' sake. Ah, that's better!" The last remark was occasioned by the brisk entry of two orderlies, each with a tray containing a wine jug and a number of drinking pots. Gallienus poured himself a drink, took a long gulp, muttered, "Vile!" and went on to drain the pot. He waited while the orderlies carried the trays round and the officers helped themselves. Then, with a sharp glance at the hourglass, he called, "To business! Who's going to speak first?"

Nobody answered. The silence stretched out awkwardly for a couple of minutes, while the gaze of Gallienus traveled slowly from face to face round the table and back again, lingering longest where the five or six Illyrians sat together. With an impatient movement, he turned toward a burly, florid man, with placid blue eyes and tiny spikes of ginger hair all over a broad scalp, close cropped for the hot weather. "You, Gundobald. Come on, let's hear from you!"

Everyone looked at Gundobald, whose brow furrowed and whose full cheeks went red. He was a German, once chief of a small tribe which—harried by its neighbors out of its fields and hunting grounds somewhere north of the Danube—had been granted asylum in the Empire, in return for providing recruits to the Roman Army. After twenty years of loyal service to the Eagles, he had risen to high command, having fought with courage and equal zest against his fellow Germans and in the civil wars which these cultured Romans waged with a ferocity that never ceased to astonish the simple barbarian.

He looked round pathetically, but remained tongue-tied. Gallienus' eyes flickered to the hourglass and back. "Well, come on, Gundobald!" he said irritably. "You've seen the men; you've seen the horses; you've seen the armor. What do you think? Out with it!"

"One must have time to r-r-reflect," answered Gundobald haltingly in guttural Latin.

"You've had plenty of time to r-r-reflect," snapped back Gallienus with a precise reproduction of Gundobald's accent. "I asked you: what do you think?"

Gundobald shifted on his stool. "I think this cavalry . . . it is not good for forests . . . marshes, like on frontier. To run after invasion . . . maybe. To smash invasion . . . maybe. Also in East, where is open country. But over there . . ." he gestured "against Franks, Alemanni, Juthungi—the country no good!"

There was a murmur round the table. The point, though it had to be extorted from Gundobald, was a sound one. Conditions in Germany and in most of the northern frontier zone were unsuitable for the new-style cavalry which they had seen demonstrated that morning. Gallienus looked malevolently at Gundobald; then he shrugged. "Anyone else?" he invited.

Claudius raised a hand. "Oh, good!" said Gallienus, his tone of relief obviously intended to show his respect for the new speaker's understanding and his contempt for Gundobald's.

"We've seen only a few horsemen," began Claudius, his pleasant but authoritative manner creating an intent stillness in the room, "but it's easy to imagine whole squadrons of such cavalry and, as you, Sire, promise us, whole armies of them. Who can doubt that they would represent a striking force of tremendous power? Rome has never produced their like!"

Gallienus permitted himself a little smile. His eyes swiveled to Gundobald, enjoying his evident discomfiture; then they went, briefly, to the hourglass.

"Still," resumed Claudius, "there's one serious drawback—it might even be a fatal one." Some of the officers stole a glance at Gallienus. He sat more stiffly now, looking down, with the air of a man sorely tried but determined to be patient.

"And this—er—drawback?" he asked, studying his fingertips.

"Too heavy, Sire," answered Claudius courteously. "All that armor calls for a big, beefy soldier and a charger capable of carrying a heavy load in field conditions. You would have to impose the most rigorous standards of selection for the men; and you would have virtually to start a new breed of horses. It would cost a great deal; and for years you would probably have to make do with a cavalry force too small to operate in more than one place at a time."

"It might be the decisive place, though!" retorted Gallienus. His fingers drummed lightly on the helmet resting before him on the table. "Well," he called finally, "anyone else?"

Two other officers, neither Illyrian, commented favorably in turn on the new cavalry prototype. But both expressed their approval in somewhat guarded terms, which hinted at unspoken reservations.

After this no one seemed willing to voice an opinion. Gallienus shot another glance at the hourglass, then gazed directly at Aurelian, who had so far listened impassively. Aurelian, if he were aware of the invitation, the appeal or the command in this look, ignored it. After a perceptible interval, Gallienus transferred his gaze to the young, good-looking officer next to Aurelian. "You there," he said sourly. "That's right—you. Let's hear what you've got to say!"

"My name is Probus, Adjutant to the General here, if Your Majesty has forgotten," the young officer rejoined in a quiet but firm tone which startled everyone. He met the Emperor's angry look unmoved.

"All right, the name's Probus. And would it be too much trouble for Probus to favor us with his views?"

Probus appeared to weigh this petulance for a few moments. Then, quite calmly, he said, "My view is that this cavalry could ride down any infantry. That is, except the most obstinate pikeman—whom they're not likely to meet. They'd scatter any light horse that awaits their charge. But a question is: what would happen if they came up against other heavily armored cavalry, like the Persian Cataphracts. I fancy both sides would get worn out quickly by the weight of all that armor—they would cancel each other out."

Gallienus made an impatient noise. "Look here," he said, addressing the whole table. "Heavy cavalry must be the core of the new Army, everyone sees that." He thumped the table. "Heavy cavalry.

93

Cavalry that can smash the enemy at a charge. Once we've got them, we can start on the other reforms."

He spoke rapidly and with evident enthusiasm, sketching a multiform Army of immense strength and unprecedented versatility. It would dispose of every arm in abundance; armored infantry for garrison duty and to support the shock cavalry on the battlefield; masses of archers trained to hail down concentrations of arrows of great penetrating power, even at extreme ranges; swarms of light horse, as the scouts, foragers, and sometimes the fatal sting of the Army; artillery deadly and mobile beyond anything the past had known. He envisaged battles fought mainly by field artillery showering missiles on an enemy maneuvered into a compressed position on exposed ground.

Whatever personal feeling his audience harbored against him, whatever their secret hopes and ambitions, they were professional soldiers, with Rome's martial glory at heart. The revolutionary Army taking shadowy shape as Gallienus proceeded laid their imaginations under a spell. Only Claudius began to stroke his chin and Aurelian openly scowled. Gallienus, finger uplifted, was in the middle of an eloquent passage, when an extraneous thought seemed to strike him; he darted a glance at the hourglass—and looked horrified. Recollecting himself, he brought his discourse hurriedly to an end. "There it is, in outline. But it all depends on the new cavalry. They are phase number one." Then, briskly and brightly, he addressed himself to Aurelian: "What do you think, General?"

In his deep and vibrant voice, that seemed to have a kinship with those of the Centurions outside on the barrack square, subdued but still sonorous as they came through the window, Aurelian answered, "Not mobile enough!" Everybody understood that he had deliberately ignored the picture of the New Model Army which Gallienus had sketched and was referring to the prototype heavy cavalry.

There was a general shifting and scraping as the officers all focused on Aurelian; he alone had led large forces of cavalry in person and he had done so with conspicuous skill.

"We must have horses that move faster and farther than infantry —and still be fit to charge," he went on. "Cavalry that can live off the country, if need be." He looked round, as if challenging his col-

94

leagues to question these basic principles, and then turned back to Gallienus and resumed with the same daunting emphasis, "In war, the problem's to catch the enemy when you want—and where. Weight at the cost of speed is useless. One mile a day slower than the enemy—and he's your master! These horsemen of yours would not even keep up with the legionaries. We'd have to transport mountains of fodder. They'd slow everything down!"

Gallienus reflected, eyelids drooping; then he glanced at the hour-glass, smiled rather bleakly and said, in an affable tone: "No doubt they are a bit on the heavy side. Thank you, General. We'll have to do something about it. Victor!" He bawled the last name toward the door. One of the two orderlies appeared. "A message to the Palace," ordered Gallienus. "Tell Nicias the Painter I'll be half-an-hour late for the sitting—and give him my apologies for keeping an artist waiting. Ask him to be my guest at dinner."

He looked round at the officers. "These artists are so temperamental!" he complained. "Last time I was late, Nicias threw his brush down and swore that inspiration had deserted him for the day!"

He stood up stretching. All the officers rose. He smiled at them with good humor, but a little absently. "That's all for today. To-morrow here in the Camp—at the same time." He nodded cheerfully in reply to the chorus of dutiful farewells and walked out with a hurried step.

The officers stood silent for a few moments, then broke up into little knots, from each of which soon came a murmur of conversation.

Claudius put a hand on Aurelian's elbow, gave Probus a nod and the three walked away from their seats to the wall opposite, where they were out of earshot of the others. The two senior Illyrians faced each other with somber expressions, while Probus took up his position a little apart, but closer to Aurelian. "Well?" asked Claudius quietly.

"We stressed that the armor shouldn't be too heavy," Aurelian said frowning but making an effort to keep his voice subdued. "That man always flies to extremes."

"That's not the worst of it," commented Claudius. "The real trouble is that he won't persist; he starts a dozen things, but he can't bother to finish any one of them. This cavalry, for instance—we might get somewhere if we cut the armor down, but by next week—mark my words—he'll be working up enthusiasm about something else."

"Still," put in Probus diffidently, "he's got some marvelous ideas. Massed artillery on the battlefield—it's never been heard of!"

"Brilliant, but just not practical," growled Aurelian. "It's no use dreaming about fancy armies we'll never be able to produce. We've got a military crisis here and now. There's this confounded Persian campaign that seems to be going worse even than last year's. Who's doing all the fighting? The Legions, of course! Some good cavalry would make all the difference. But even a cavalry corps would take years to build up. And the gods alone know where the money would come from—the pay of half the Army's in arrears, as it is!"

For a while there was a baffled silence. The problem appeared insoluble. Infantry were too slow; cavalry too expensive. In the past, Rome, for all her vast military establishment, had combined power with parsimony. The Legions cost heavily, yet not more than the Treasury could bear. But the New Model Army projected during their debates would cost infinitely more and the means would have to be extracted from an Empire of dwindling population, shrinking resources.

Aurelian leaned a little toward Claudius, his face unrevealing. A brief murmur came from him and his eyes were intent on Claudius as he spoke. Probus could not catch the guarded words, but he saw Claudius at once stiffen and give Aurelian a quelling look.

"Gallienus is one of our Co-Emperors," said Claudius in a low voice, but with decision. "Let's not forget that. The stability of the State comes first. We can't afford trouble. Besides, he's very clever, even if he wants to do too much at once. He's got ideas—and militarily Rome hasn't had a fresh idea for hundreds of years. He's our one hope for the Army reforms!"

Grimly the two Illyrian commanders regarded each other. Probus watched the silent conflict of their eyes. Aurelian's face grew slowly less harsh. He shrugged. "I'm afraid you're right, Claudius!" he said glumly.

Claudius smiled and took Aurelian's arm. "Come and dine with me. We've finished early today. You, too, Probus."

"Thank you, General," said Probus, obviously pleased.

On the point of accepting, Aurelian hesitated. The slight figure and rather wistful face of Severina had come into his mind. His mood was dispirited. He had an unaccustomed feeling that he would like to be with her. "No, thank you, Claudius—I think I'll go home," he said, with a friendly smile to convey that his refusal was not prompted by resentment.

They exchanged farewells. With a word and a gesture of leave-taking to the officers still chatting around the table—he got a ceremonious salute, accompanied by an almost awed look, from Gundobald—Aurelian walked out. He decided not to send an orderly for his horse, but to go to the stables himself.

His depression persisted and, with it, the image of Severina, which amid the gloom of his mind seemed to have taken on a comforting glow. Still musing about her, he left the Praetorium, acknowledging automatically the sentinel's double stamp into rigid attention.

She was a gentle girl. Very pretty, too, in her own way. Once he had come across her absorbed in a book; as she became aware that she was being watched, she had raised her head with a rather dreamy smile. For some reason it was just so that he now pictured her.

He found himself wondering whether she were really happy, although it did not occur to him that he might ask her.

As he walked along, he noted that the paths were properly metalled; the huts freshly whitewashed and innocent of the stains of urine; the occasional soldier he met sprucely turned out and smart in saluting. Mechanically, he contrasted this luxury camp of model soldiers with what he had left behind in Pannonia.

These reflections did not interrupt the main drift of his thoughts. When he had obeyed the Emperor's summons to Rome he had felt strong curiosity not only about the bride who awaited him, but about his future father-in-law, a distinguished Senator of great wealth and—it was said—of influence at Court. As it turned out, Severinus was little to his taste, a rather sour politician with an obvious self-conceit and a tendency to parade his breeding. A rather foolish man, too, in spite of all his worldly shrewdness, for he seemed to think he could use his son-in-law to further his own ambitions. Aurelian knew Severinus was a little afraid of him—and the thought gave him pleasure.

Severina, on the other hand, had proved an agreeable surprise. Gradually, for there was nothing assertive or challenging about her to assist prompt conclusions, he had made several gratifying discoveries. She was exceptionally intelligent. Her mind was quick, penetrating, and retentive, and she had the gift of explaining things simply and lucidly; listening to her he sometimes forgot she was so young. She managed their household efficiently and gave the place a quiet, restful atmosphere. She did not fuss and never complained—not even about the servants!

He tried to define the feeling she inspired in him. Eventually, with some astonishment, he decided it was one of respect. He had never known such a feeling for any woman before—except, of course, his mother.

Yes, he thought, it would be pleasant, after his waste of time with that glib weathercock of a Junior Augustus, to be again with Severina.

Putting the subject aside he strode through the open wicket gate of the stables.

It still lacked an hour or so to dusk when Aurelian reached the Villa. Tired by their long journey through the stifling heat of the plains, his horse—a sturdy pony placed at his disposal by the Army—came along the path from the gate to the house at a walk, with head drooping.

A bend in the path brought the porch in sight. Severina, fresh and charming in a simple linen gown, was with a bulky man who outtopped her by a head. He was waving his hands in animated talk. Something about him was decidedly familiar.

At the sound of Aurelian's approach they turned. In the same moment old Prudentius began stumping over from the garden to take the horse. Aurelian dismounted. Severina came hurrying to meet him, followed a step or two behind by her companion, who was delayed by a slight limp.

A broad smile broke out on Aurelian's face. "Why," he exclaimed, "if it isn't Crinitus!" He moved forward quickly, greeted Severina with a couple of words and strode past her to grasp the outstretched hand of Crinitus. The two soldiers pumped each other's arms.

When they had exchanged hearty greetings, Crinitus gave a significant twitch of his eyebrows. Aurelian looked round. Severina was watching them with a rather wan smile. "This is a grand surprise, Severina," he said. "I didn't expect Crinitus till tomorrow!"

At his smile and warm tone, her face brightened. "You don't know my uncle, Aurelian," she said. "No one can ever be sure when he's going to arrive."

Both men laughed. Still, as Severina walked between them into the house, she felt her pleasure in her uncle's visit a little dampened. She could not help contrasting Aurelian's curt greeting to herself with the enthusiasm he had shown Crinitus.

Over their meal, Aurelian and Crinitus talked jocularly for a time about experiences they had shared and common acquaintances and touched on events after their separation; their talk was interlarded with military terms and camp slang that left Severina rather puzzled. But gradually their conversation took a more serious turn; they spoke more deliberately and did not eagerly interrupt each other any more. Two main themes now blended in their talk: the Army reforms and the political situation.

Crinitus continued to expound his views with his customary freedom. Aurelian was more guarded. Once or twice he shot a glance at Severina, as though to ask: is this really for her ears? Crinitus cheerfully ignored these signals. Indeed, more than once, he looked round at Severina, as if embracing her in his audience and appealing to her judgment.

Since Crinitus had spoken to her that afternoon, many things were illuminated for Severina, if only in part, that before lay in darkness. She followed their discussion with great interest, but did not venture any comment. After a while, she stood up and said: "I'll leave you two to your wine. By the way, Aurelian, I'm going to order some Gallic—this Falernian's rather syrupy, don't you think?"

Aurelian's eyebrows rose and he looked quizzically at Crinitus, who responded with the flicker of a smile. "Of course," Aurelian answered gravely, "Gallic would be very nice." Severina was turning away, when Crinitus said, "Come here, my dear." She went round to him and he took both her hands in his. "I'm still sober," he said, "so you can believe me when I say how happy I am to be in your house and"—he paused a moment, surveying her fondly—"to see you looking so beautiful. Your husband is a very lucky man!"

The color in her cheeks gave a sudden warmth to her beauty. She glanced shyly at Aurelian, who said nothing. Then she stooped, with a murmured word of thanks, to kiss her uncle and turned again to the door.

10

VERY early the next morning, to avoid traveling in the heat, Aurelian left for Rome. He was accompanied by Crinitus, who had a variety of business to transact there, including an interview at the Palace, which he looked forward to with distaste, for since his defeat by the Franks it had come to his ears that Gallienus had often publicly made him the butt of malevolent witticisms.

They were almost ready to leave when Severina, wrapped in a woolen cloak against the rawness of the hour, came out of the house. For a minute or two she watched them silently. The enthusiasm with which they had greeted each other on their meeting was not apparent now; they both showed the dour matter-of-factness of veteran soldiers roused in the dark to get ready for some bleak dawn parade. But even in their grunted monosyllables there was a suggestion of old comradeship. More strongly than last night, when Crinitus, at any rate, had exerted himself to please her, she felt herself excluded.

When she had left them to their drinking, she lay awake a long time, reflecting with pain how much more convivial the meal had been than when Aurelian dined with her alone. It was absurd, she knew, to be jealous of Crinitus, especially when she was fond of him and he, so obviously, of her. But there was in the pleasure Aurelian took in her uncle's company an unreserve he had never shown toward herself. In masculine society, among his fellow soldiers, Aurelian really could unbend. Despite their very different origins and temperaments, he and Crinitus were drawn together by a sense of fellowship. What had Aurelian in common with her—except a roof and table and a bed?

Hugging herself under the cloak as the chill air fingered her flesh, she saw Prudentius, moroseness in every slow step, move through the twilight, leading Aurelian's horse. The four bearers were already standing, without animation, by her uncle's litter. She had barely glanced at them, on their arrival yesterday; now she noticed that they were all of a height, hollow-faced men with powerful shoulders. One, who was bald and gray-tufted above the ears, seemed rather elderly for the grueling work of supporting a weighty litter's cornerpole over long distances. Two others, with seamed expressionless faces, might have been any age. The fourth was a dark young man on whose left cheek showed faintly the curving white ridge of a scar. He stood, with eyes downcast, on feet planted well apart; his posture, though motionless, was alert and resilient; his weight was not dead weight. In his stillness something sullen and dangerous contrasted with the lifeless passivity of the others. Perhaps he was a recent prisoner of war, his barbarian soul still untamed by the fetters and whips of the slave compounds.

But the others. . . . Half in pity, half in revulsion, she studied their unresponsive faces. They seemed creatures of another order, manlike beasts of burden, grown numb and dumb in the horror of their condition.

Had they really gone beyond all hope? Suddenly, she wondered if any of them were Christians.

Aurelian mounted, uttered his laconic farewell, and began to walk his horse toward the gate. Crinitus turned to Severina. "I'll bring you something from Rome," he called, and waved his hand. He entered the litter. A few moments later, with the smooth motion of a machine having four bodies as its parts, the slaves had swung it aloft; in another moment they were pacing soft-footed with the same mechanical unison in Aurelian's wake.

Prudentius went off, muttering to himself. The courtyard was empty. But though the air still had a bite, Severina stood pensively for a few minutes more in the porch. It was with a feeling of dejection that she turned, at last, back into the house. She dressed absently, listened with a preoccupied air to Porphyry, who looked at her anxiously, and approved all his suggestions for the day without bothering to consider them.

It was in this unsettled mood that, later in the morning, Pervica found Severina. "Lady," she began, her manner implying that she had something private to communicate. Severina nodded and the girl said, "If you please, Paul is here." At Severina's puzzled expression, she repeated, "Paul—the Deacon. . . . You told me to ask him round."

Severina stared. The Deacon Paul. . . . It was true; she had asked Pervica to invite him. But that was only yesterday. Pervica had lost no time. These Christians were ardent in anything that concerned their faith!

Abruptly the question recurred to her: were any of the bearers Christians? She could not understand why these figures from the abyss should haunt her so. Well, she was glad Paul had come. She would enjoy a talk with him. Aurelian had his staff meetings, and who knew what else that he would never trouble to discuss with her. Why shouldn't she fill her time with interests of which he had no knowledge?

She reflected: a shady seat in the garden would be pleasant now that the sun was growing warm, but it was too public. She must receive Paul where a visitor's presence would be normal enough, but where they could converse quietly without being overheard.

"Show him into the atrium," she directed Pervica.

The Deacon Paul was a broad-shouldered man of middle height, who looked little more than forty, square-faced with strong features and a calm, intelligent air. He had a good head of straight black hair in which the gray was making inroads. Not a particularly spiritual man, was her first impression, and certainly not the fanatic. He suggested the headmaster of an important school or an enlightened magistrate. Her preconceptions and vague prejudices seemed absurd at the sight of him. This man obviously was not from the dregs of the slums and could have no traffic with conspiracies and obscene rites such as people attributed to the Christians.

He advanced toward her, slightly inclining his head. "You sent for me, Lady." His manner was courteous, but not in the least obsequious. His voice was unexpectedly deep and there was authority latent in it; his accent was that of one who had studied in the schools of rhetoric.

"Sit down, please," said Severina, seating herself. He waited politely for her to begin. "Are you from Rome?" she asked, curious about the origins and background of this man, so out of character with what she had expected of a Christian priest.

"No—I'm from Smyrna."

"Smyrna? You're a Greek then?"

"Say a Greek by environment." His shrug was faintly self-deprecating. "My family are from Bithynia," he added.

"Landowners?" she asked, prompted by some insight.

"Yes." His brief reply conveyed a disinclination to pursue this theme.

"I wanted to see you," resumed Severina, feeling more at ease at the certainty that she was speaking to a cultivated man, "because I would like to know more about Christ and His Mother."

He smiled gravely. "There is also God the Father and the Holy Ghost . . ."

Severina knitted her brows and set herself to listen carefully. It was an altogether extraordinary, yet strangely compelling case that Paul began, quietly and methodically, to expound. She asked several questions; to her they seemed natural enough, but he must have considered them searching, for each time he hesitated a little and answered slowly, obviously seeking his words with great care.

Absorbing as his exposition was, she could not forget the need for caution. Paul seemed at once to sense when she felt they had been in private session long enough. He had, even in the short time they spent together, made a profound impression on her, yet it could not have been exactly of the kind he had sought. She had been moved profoundly, but as an onlooker. Paul's account of Mary Magdalene and the women round the Cross wrung her heart; her mind kept its distance. The nature of the Christian Godhead, as Paul described it, imposed no conviction. She could make nothing intelligible out of a Trinity of Divine Persons, who, Paul insisted, were not a Trio but a Unity. She found it hard to reconcile this celestial geometry, these tortured equations, with such a direct and burning creed of the salvation of a sinful race of men by a God first martyred and then self-resurrected.

Paul she liked very much. There was a simple earnestness, an un-affected sincerity, about these Christians, no doubt of it. Pervica had it, too, but not coupled with a strong, persuasive personality, such as Paul's. He had spoken in a direct and vivid way, far more eloquent and arresting than her father's contrived images and rounded pe-riods. Severina could understand what Pervica meant when she spoke of the effect of his preaching.

They rose together. Her hand went to the purse dangling at her girdle and she took out some gold pieces. "You have many poor among you, I am told," she said. He accepted the money without any show either of effusiveness or reluctance, merely thanking her with a simple word or two. "You must come again," she said. "I'll let Pervica know when it . . . it is convenient." The phrase in her mind had been "When it is safe." Though she was sure Paul had guessed her timorous thought and hasty self-correction, and the term she had substituted had some flavor of condescension, he only smiled in his pleasant way and said, "Most assuredly."

As she watched Paul go, she was glad that Aurelian never troubled to ask how she passed her day; glad, too, in a scared way, that now she was engaging on something she would need to keep from him, something forbidden, even dangerous.

Late in the afternoon, Severina had another visitor. Porphyry ap-peared in the little orchard, the foliage of whose dozen, regularly spaced apple trees afforded a pleasant screen against the sun; behind him came a small, neatly made, brisk man, with a trim, gingerish beard. Severina was sitting rather drowsily on a stool, her back against a trunk, in her hands a book she was making no pretense of reading. She stirred, conscious of the newcomer's shrewd and humorous eyes upon her.

He introduced himself in a Gallic accent as Matthaias, the wine merchant of whom her uncle had spoken. He had received a note from Crinitus, a most peremptory one, he added with a twinkle, bidding him wait without delay on the Lady Severina. As it chanced, he had already arranged a number of calls among the villas in her neighborhood—and, well, here he was at her service.

"It's all right, Porphyry," said Severina. He bustled off, after exchanging an affable smile with Matthaias. She was a little surprised, for Porphyry tended to assume a rather comic watchdog air whenever he brought in a stranger.

There was indeed, she soon perceived, something agreeable and disarming about Matthaias. He must have been about sixty, but was hale and active. The rosy face above the beard was keen, but its smile was kindly.

"There's another stool over there," she said. "You must be tired after your journey from Rome."

"Thank you, I'll stand. I've been sitting for hours—on a mule," he explained with a little grimace.

She told him frankly what Crinitus had said about her Falernian and, encouraged by the sympathy with which he listened, admitted in the next breath that she knew nothing about Gallic wines and precious little about Italian.

He nodded over this thoughtfully. She saw that he did not regard her inexperience as a matter for amusement. "It's simply this, my dear young lady," he said. "Soldiers like to drink what they are used to. Gaul is a garrison province; Italy has only the Praetorians. So far, more soldiers are accustomed to Gallic wines than to Italian. That's all there is to it—a vintage Falernian is a drink for Emperors. I keep some for my most honored guests. Gallic is a bit dearer, too—there is the transport in the price. But if it makes your husband happy. . . ." He gestured with a little backward wave of his hands and gave her an understanding smile.

She warmed to him. Your husband may be a bit unreasonable

about his wine, he seemed to imply, but you are right to humor him. I respect you for it. These details are important in a marriage.

"What shall I have?" she asked.

He smiled at her eager innocence. "That's not the way to do business, my dear young lady," he said with mock severity. He went into a rapid technical explanation about vintages, strengths and degrees of dryness, with his head slightly turned and tilted up, as though he were reflecting aloud. Finally, he pronounced gravely three or four names of which she had never heard.

"Very well," she said. "Send me a dozen jars—no, a score—of each. I'd like them as soon as possible," she added, thinking of Crinitus.

Matthaias opened his eyes wide. "Don't you want to know the prices?" He sounded a little shocked. "They're all expensive wines, you know."

"My uncle—Crinitus—said that I could trust you," she replied, smiling. "The truth is I wouldn't know if you charged me double the usual price."

For a few moments he gazed at her, obviously touched. Then he said, "Your uncle was right, dear young lady. You can trust me."

Before he left he had impressed on her a whole series of instructions about the storage of his precious liquors and had promised to send his foreman over with the main consignment the following afternoon. A score of the superb vintage of five years ago from his personal vineyards near Burdigala would be delivered in perhaps a week, when his eldest son arrived in Rome with another mule train.

"Bring them yourself—and ask to see me," said Severina on an impulse, holding out her hand. "I should like very much to talk to you again."

He took her hand and patted it. "I shall bring them myself and make a point of asking to see you," he assured her.

The day's two encounters, with the Deacon and the wine merchant, the Christian and the Jew, so stimulating in their very different ways, left her feeling much more cheerful. Both were men of experience, yet of a simple, warm humanity—and both had spoken to her as a person of understanding. She was sitting in the atrium, smiling to herself at the almost parental concern of Matthaias about

106

the way to store his wares, when she heard heavy, rapid footsteps. Aurelian strode in.

She got up, startled. "You're early!" she exclaimed, uncomfortable at the memory of her session, not many hours ago, with Paul.

"Yes, I'm early," he replied, not volunteering an explanation. "Here, Crinitus sent you this." He thrust a little package into her hands. "He'll have to spend the night in Rome. Gallienus is keeping him waiting at the Palace."

Aurelian's voice had an edge to it. He did not look directly at her as he spoke. His face was harsh and daunting with ugly temper barely held in check.

Without more words he went to cleanse himself of the dust of the journey.

Severina could tell that his feeling was not directed against her; yet her brightness of mood had faded. She looked forlornly down at Crinitus' gift—it was wrapped in costly red silk secured with ribbon whose ends were tied in a pretty bow. Mechanically she opened the package; it contained a dainty pair of sandals in choice red leather, delicately patterned in gold thread on the toe caps and bands.

"Thank you, Uncle," she said softly. Still deeply troubled, she summoned Porphyry to give instructions for dinner.

At the meal, Aurelian sat darkly brooding. Under his curt replies Severina's timid attempts at conversation died away. Never more than a moderate eater, he seemed on this occasion to have no appetite at all; Severina, on her side, felt the food choke her. Porphyry's face gradually took on an anguished look as he removed, first from his master and then his mistress, dish after dish that was barely tasted. So unnerved was he by this continued rejection of food on which he had spent much loving thought and much time, visiting the kitchen frequently to harass the cook, that when carrying the roast fowl he stumbled, and some of the hot juice shot from the platter across Aurelian's bare, brawny forearm.

"Be careful!" There was such a clang of concentrated fury in Aurelian's voice that Porphyry, white-faced, set the platter hurriedly down for fear of dropping it. Severina started, appalled. Aurelian waited until Porphyry had with trembling hands clumsily carved the bird and placed a portion before him. Then he pushed it back.

"Take this away!" he snapped. "Bring some wine!"

Severina said nothing until Porphyry had gone. Then she rose and said in a low voice, "I think I'll go to bed."

He regarded her somberly and seemed about to speak, but contented himself with silently nodding.

She had not been long in the bedroom and had made no move to undress, when the door opened; there stood Aurelian with a peculiar, tense expression. After a moment, he came over to where she sat on the bed and looked down at her fixedly. She had a spasm of panic, for such a burden of distress weighed on her that she never was less in the mood for his rough lovemaking.

But whatever his strange look betokened, it was not amorousness. He did not touch her; all of a sudden he said in a voice that was harsh with the vehemence of his feeling, "You're a clever girl, Severina—though you're so young. I want to talk to you." The bed creaked as he sat down. They were not in contact, but his set face was close to hers and he did not smell of wine.

"A clever girl"—it was more like a father's praise than a husband's but her heart had bounded at the compliment, the first he had ever paid her.

She could feel herself tremble as she looked up into his face. "What is it, Aurelian?" she murmured.

"I'm worried," he answered slowly. "My heart is heavy today."

He saw her fingers clench and her cheeks go pale. "No! No!" he said impatiently. "I'm not in any danger!" He got up and began to walk with long, lithe strides about the room. Still anxiously, though a little relieved, she followed him with her eyes.

"I'm listening, Aurelian," she said quietly, after a while. She realized that the glare he turned toward her was directed at somebody or something very vivid in his thoughts.

"I never liked this Persian war," he said abruptly. "Valerian's mismanaged it from the start. I've warned him, we've all warned him. But he's withdrawing more of our best troops from the Danube. He's leaving the frontier wide open."

More to himself than to her, he added frowning, "I wonder if Gallienus passed our warnings on . . ."

He paused, looking at her as though he expected some natural comment at this point. Severina, guided by intuition, made it.

"Can no troops be found—anywhere—to reinforce the Danube?"

"None—none worth having, anyway. They don't even seem to appreciate the danger. I tell you, Severina, we've wasted weeks listening to that brilliant, maddening young Augustus with his fancy schemes—and we're still where we started. We'd be more use back at our posts on the frontier."

He resumed that long-paced prowl about the room, a fighting animal caged.

"Sit down, Aurelian," Severina urged gently. "Isn't there anything that can be done?"

He came over and sat down heavily. They were closer than before. His knee bored into her and it was as though through the contact she could feel the torment of his unhappiness, his baffled anger. "Something must be done!" he muttered. "There's trouble coming. Worse than ever before. It's rushing down on us. The whole frontier will crack. What will become of the Empire?"

She had never seen him suffering like this, indeed had never guessed that this iron man could be so hurt. An instinct warned her not to place her hand on his; the gesture would only irritate him. He shifted once or twice, with a jerky movement. Suddenly he stood up. For a few moments he seemed to struggle with himself; then in a low voice he began to speak.

He was so close to her and so tall that, sitting, she could not see his face. His words came painfully, in starts, so violent was the feeling behind them.

"Sometimes I think . . . A river Danube flows through every man's soul . . . One side's civilized . . . As though it had a government . . . and laws . . . and cities and roads . . . There's discipline . . . and order. The other side . . . it's in darkness . . . a savage land . . . no law, no order . . . just wild confusion, just barbarism. . . ."

He moved a little, the physical action helping his search for words.

"Sometimes the barbarian side invades the civilized side. Everything goes smash. There's chaos . . . You can't see clearly any

109

more . . . That's how I feel today . . . Something is surging up here . . ."—he struck his chest—"I want to hit out . . . to kick down everything. I want to tell that slick, frothy young Augustus to go hang himself!"

He breathed gustily several times, but presently grew quieter. "Mithras, Saviour," he murmured. "Be with us. Help us. Show us our way. Make us strong to save Rome. . . ." The sounds lost their outline and merged into a faint vibration persisting in the ear. He seemed unconscious of Severina now and no longer struggling for words. Laden moments passed; a few inches from his body, she could feel, like a physical impact, the terrible intensity of his prayer.

Severina sat rigid; she dared not disturb him. Awe mingled with her pity. She had no experience of the anguish of prayer and could only partly comprehend this reaching out through mortal barriers to clutch at the hand of a God. But she knew that something vehement beyond anything she could have imagined was breaking out in agony from the depths of her husband's being.

Yet as she waited tensely a sense of elation came to her. A new situation had arisen between Aurelian and herself. Though her heart ached for him, there was joy with her grief, for his ordeal had brought him close to her, it was to her that he had turned in his pain. Even if he did not demand love from her, it was much—for the moment it was enough—that he felt some need for her sympathy, her understanding. Whatever he wanted, she was willing, eager, to give. Her one desire was that he should ask of her.

After a while—it might have been a minute or two—Aurelian stirred, stretched himself, and looked round the room slowly, as if he had only just become aware of the enclosing walls. "It's getting dark," he said in his normal tones, indicating with a nod the pale, narrow window.

"Yes," said Severina. It cost her an effort to speak. She stood up, close to him. He looked down at her, soberly enough, but with more of comradeship in his eyes than she had ever noted there before. If only he had bent and kissed her, her happiness would have been too great to endure. But he merely said, "I must give Prudentius his orders for the morning," smiled briefly at her and went out.

She sat down again on the bed, hands clasped, moved in the

depths of her being, happier than she could have believed possible, a little disappointed.

11

LYING awake that night beside Aurelian, whose sleeping face was sculptured by the dark into a stern composure, as if the antique Roman discipline in him had reasserted its mastery over his elemental feeling, Severina reflected on the new relationship between them. She sensed that she must not presume too much on it; it was still untried and a false step on her part might jeopardize everything.

In those shattering moments of revelation the initiative had come from Aurelian. She had done nothing more than listen and utter a few appropriate words—and with this he had been content. That would be her cue. She would demand nothing, never intrude. Only, when he set his reserve aside—or it suddenly forsook him—and he voluntarily opened his heart and mind, she would respond with all her sympathy and understanding, but her words would be sparing and careful, lest she jar him back into silence.

A passive role, a patient role—perhaps some women might consider it humiliating in the bargain. No matter, she would play it to the best of her ability.

She turned her cheek against Aurelian's arm, a pillow of stone but somehow comforting; lulled by his warmth and the calm, slow, powerful rhythm of his breathing, she drifted off to sleep.

A few hours later Aurelian, in whose ear reveille seemed regularly to sound about this time, began to stir and, as usual, she awoke. Her body was lethargic with sleep too soon broken, but her mind was tranquil and bright. As soon as he had gone, quietly, from the room, she got out of bed and dressed. When she went into the porch he was methodically checking over the straps of his pony's harness. In the chill dawn light Prudentius, hunched and sullen in his shapeless robe, at the horse's head, looked scarcely more human than the beast. Intent on his task, Aurelian had not heard her light-footed approach.

"Aurelian," she began. He swung round. "I've been thinking. Wouldn't it be nice to invite a few of your friends to dinner?" she went on eagerly.

He gazed at her, weighing the proposal.

"It wouldn't be hard to manage a few of them—Claudius—and that adjutant of yours, Probus—and any other Illyrians you like."

"A dinner party for the Illyrians!" he said, obviously taken with the notion.

She was delighted that he looked pleased. "Oh, yes!" she exclaimed. "Let's give a dinner party for the Illyrians!"

"I warn you," he said, with a boyish grin. "They're pretty hard drinkers."

"Well, why not?" she answered boldly. "I've ordered plenty of wine—good Gallic wine—from Matthaias. We'll have ample for half-a-dozen guests."

"Matthaias?" repeated Aurelian.

"He's the Jewish wine merchant Uncle recommended. A very interesting man."

"As long as his wares are interesting," said Aurelian, approval in his smile.

About the middle of the afternoon Crinitus was back, looking worn out and dejected. His limbs moved stiffly as he descended from the litter, where Severina guessed he had been uncomfortably dozing. He made no attempt at pleasantry when she greeted him and he spoke with half-hearted peevishness to the bearers, as though the malice were there but he could not summon up the energy to be downright nasty. Accompanying her into the house, he rested one hand, warm but inert, on her shoulder; his limp was more pronounced, and they walked slowly.

Once in the atrium he slumped on a couch and gazed at her dully, an aging man whose bulky, indulged body had become a burden.

Severina waited a little; then, very gently, said, "What happened, Uncle?"

He roused himself with an effort. "I've had a terrible time, Sever-

112

ina," he answered, "a terrible time! The journey from Rome half-killed me."

"Let me get you something," said Severina, rising.

"Nothing, nothing, my dear!" he said, much more briskly. "Let me speak—I'm feeling better now. You know I had an interview at the Palace. Well, that damned young swine, Gallienus, kept me waiting all the afternoon—it must have been nearly five hours! When he sent for me at last, I was sick with weariness and irritation and the pains"—he passed a hand between his ribs and over a wide area of his stomach—"had started up. He kept me standing, though he could see I was groggy—he seemed to enjoy it—and he made a lot of clever, sneering references to my defeat. He kept a straight face, himself, the devil, but there were half-a-dozen of his hangers-on—young men, you know, of doubtful sex—who were giggling openly. Then, I suppose, he must have got tired of the sport, for he told me in his most silky voice that, in spite of everything, he would see I was allowed to resign from the Army with a general's full gratuity. 'In spite of everything,' he said, the insolent young fop! You wouldn't think, Severina, that I'd done thirty years and more of soldiering, and commanded in seven battles, big and small, and had only one defeat, one single defeat!"

Crinitus seemed to choke on the words. There was a little pause before he continued, "Then he just turned his back and walked away. I went out of that Palace like a leper. Not a soul had the guts to come up and greet me!"

"At any rate, Uncle dear, your ordeal's over," remarked Severina soothingly.

He gave her a mournful look. "I wish it were. Last night I saw a doctor. He's an Asiatic Greek, Philip of Ephesus—the best in Rome. Make a note of his name; you may need him one of these days"—he made a significant gesture toward her abdomen. "He went over me very thoroughly and he was wearing an awful long face when he finished. He asked me if he could speak frankly. If a doctor ever asks you if he can be frank, shut his damned mouth, Severina. Like a fool, I said: 'Go ahead, blast you!' He put that 'blast you' in the bill, no doubt. Well, he warned me to stop gadding about—'give up this nomad life' were his words. Rest! he said. It's essential. And a very careful diet—I must get my weight down. Wine three parts diluted and very little at that!"

Severina stared at him, with deep concern. "Three parts water!" he muttered. "I'll become a proper hermit!"

"Stay here, Uncle," she broke out. "Let me look after you!"

"Thank you, my dear girl, thank you, but I won't. A testy old invalid's no house guest for a young newlywed. Besides, Philip says Baiae's the best place for me—sea air, plenty of winter sunshine. I've given my agent instructions to rent or buy a small villa there—I'll be setting out in a couple of days . . . And Severina . . ."

He looked very anxious. Hastily, she answered, "Yes, Uncle?"

"You'll come and see me, won't you? Come and stay with me for a while." He paused; then added, less eagerly, "Bring Aurelian."

"Of course I will, Uncle dear," she assured him.

At this point Porphyry came bustling in and, all solicitude, took Crinitus off to his room. Severina gave orders that her uncle's rest was not to be disturbed, but toward evening, feeling that he had fasted long enough and mindful of his need to diet, had a light meal of bread, milk, and salad carried in. Crinitus sent the dishes back with a message that he would rather starve.

When Aurelian returned there was no sign of the scowling mood in which he had arrived the previous evening, although he was fatigued after his journey and, as usual, laconic. He showed no surprise when Severina worriedly told him about Crinitus; hearing of the rejected meal, he said calmly, "He'll be in to dinner."

Surely enough Crinitus joined them punctually when the meal was announced. He was spruced up, his hair carefully brushed, and his bulk imposing in a spotless white gown, a gesture of defiance at his infirmities. But his step was heavy and a little uncertain; his eyes, which always dominated their nests of wrinkles, were lusterless and the folds of his cheeks and jaws limp and waxen in the lamplight.

He greeted them with a show of heartiness. But as the meal proceeded, his gusto flagged. He made only a pretense of eating; more than once Severina noticed his eyes stray pathetically to the tall wine jar standing against the wall.

All the time she wavered between concern for her uncle, whose silences grew longer and more morose, and a kind of compulsion to lean toward her husband with a fond and intimate smile. From a source deep within her, newly unsealed, affection for him came welling up incessantly. Her eyes shone whenever they rested on him.

It was a display that went beyond the program of reticence that she had set herself, but at the moment she did not care. Looking at him she saw, projected into the brightly lit chamber, a shadowy bedroom and in it Aurelian and herself, very close, her heart opened to the cry of his heart. It was too rare, too exquisite, a pleasure, this of being esteemed and needed by him, of being invited to share his innermost secrets—how could she coldly curb her gratitude and mask her happiness?

Crinitus observed all this sourly. It struck Severina that he was jealous of her interest in Aurelian, as before she had been jealous of Aurelian's interest in him. At one point he looked at her with a sly, lascivious smile, as if to say: I know why you're so happy tonight, why your eyes go soft and luminous when you turn to Aurelian. Much more quickly attuned to her uncle than to her husband, she could tell that Crinitus, too, pictured a bedroom scene with Aurelian and herself close together, but in a nakedness of bodies, not of hearts.

Porphyry came in, carried the wine jar across to the table and began, with extreme care, to pour some for Aurelian, of whom after yesterday's scene he was plainly still very nervous. Crinitus stood up. "I must be getting off to bed—doctor's orders," he said gruffly, his eyes avoiding the wine.

Aurelian half rose, but Crinitus waved him back. When Severina solicitously came over, however, he grasped her arm. Only with an effort was she able to sustain the weight he placed on it; slowly they walked out together.

Outside, Crinitus stopped and looked at her fixedly. "You *will* come and see me at Baiae?" The emphasis he gave the "will" was a plea that moved her.

"Most certainly I'll come," she said.

Even that did not seem to satisfy him; his head jerked back slightly toward the door, as if he were calculating the rival attractions that lay beyond.

"You'll be my heiress," he said abruptly. His face, unfamiliar with its intent, almost beseeching expression, bent towards hers. "I'm leaving you everything!"

"Uncle!" she exclaimed. "Don't talk like that. You'll feel better at Baiae—you'll see."

He took no notice of her words, but continued to regard her with that disquieting look.

"Everything!" he repeated.

With a pang of fear, she wondered what the doctor had really told him.

Now the days had a new quality for Severina. She was using them, not merely, as before, passively waiting for something she could not guess at to draw Aurelian closer to her. Even the departure of Crinitus, though it left her deeply upset, contributed to this feeling of being actively involved, more intensely alive. Repeating her promise to visit him at Baiae, she walked beside the litter to the road. Crinitus leaned out and took her hand, while he solemnly said good-bye, an ill, dispirited man who, obliged to abandon the self-indulgencies of his prime, clung to the comfort of her affection.

There were tears in her eyes as she watched the litter move away down the road.

That week Paul came twice to see her; the first time at her invitation; the second, calling—after Pervica had asked permission on his behalf—with a work of Christian apologetics by someone called Tertullian, whom he had mentioned in the earlier interview. She welcomed him, for although it had been mainly an impulse of resentment against Aurelian that had made her send for him in the first place, she was attracted strongly by the fusion in him of simple integrity with a massive and subtle intelligence. On both occasions she kept him conversing with her in private longer than she would originally have considered prudent.

The debate between them continued. She was powerfully drawn to the human personality of Christ, as Paul presented it; but her mind still resisted the apparatus of doctrine, so cunningly—too cunningly, she felt—constructed round the great central theme of Mankind's Redemption by a God Himself become Man and martyred.

Her mind resisted—but no longer with the first instantaneous recoil and rejection. The absolute assurance of Paul was making its impression; the faintest of erosions was taking place along the edges of her unbelief.

Still, what chiefly dominated her waking hours and even confused her dreams with landscapes of war was Aurelian's return to her with fresh, or rather more detailed, revelations of his anxieties. He came now without the compulsion of an emotional crisis, but freely, as to a natural confidante. It was as though she had passed her examination with credit and he could now feel trust in her discretion and judgment. Three times in eight days—how could she fail to make an exact registration of such almost painfully happy experiences?—he discussed with her the problems of high policy which agitated the Illyrian officers. Perhaps "discussed" was the wrong word, for she contributed little beyond her capacity for sympathetic listening and her quick grasp, while he walked about the room, throwing off a trenchant commentary on the transactions and personalities at the staff talks.

Severina soon discovered that the shift in her relations with Aurelian was a limited one. He seemed incapable as ever of tenderness and the little considerations that women prize; he still showed little interest in her personal concerns. It was as an audience for his frank and somber reflections that she had been admitted through the barrier—but here the gain was unqualified.

Her presence, she came to see, acted as a release—it enabled him to vent, cogently and clearly, the thoughts that oppressed him. She would marvel as he ranged with a kind of cold passion over the map, pausing on threatened frontiers; throwing beams of light along the great highways, now revealed in their essential character of military roads; probing at the endless, formless, sinister forests where the German tribes might be gathering unperceived for a thrust. He spoke of arsenals and depots, of armor and weapons, of recruits, training, length of service, soldier's pay. She learned, with silent surprise, that a cavalryman cost twice as much as an infantryman and that the survival of Rome was bound up with this elementary proposition.

Perhaps the Mithraist in him, conceiving of human life as a

struggle between Light and Dark, found it natural to picture Rome beset by Barbarism in terms of a similar contrast. Listening to him, she had a sense of the flood lapping against the thousands of miles of frail defenses the Empire had erected along the frontier zones; she seemed to catch the measured footfalls of sentinels pacing on high parapet walks on the rim of the lands where Rome was the Defender and sweeping with uneasy gaze the silent hills and woods and swamps where Rome was the Enemy.

But only as she listened; when he stopped speaking, her thoughts went back to him. The things that deeply stirred him were really alien to her. He could make her understand their vital importance, but it was on him, personally, that the force of her feeling was concentrated.

She sat and watched him, conscious even in her sensation of his nearness how much his nature turned him away from her. Theirs was a marriage of Alpha and Omega, uniting extremes. Aurelian stood for primal power, action, mastery over material things; no wonder his was a passionate religion which ignored the mind and answered the heart's fierce impulse. He was the soldier, the intense worshiper, the leader in mortal conflicts. She was the passive woman, sufficiently far from the crisis to view it with detachment, unable to take the threatened ruin of a world as seriously as a husband's lack of tenderness.

Severina was nervous but outwardly composed when her first dinner party began. Four Illyrian officers arrived punctually, on horseback, virile-looking men in undress uniform, who brought a warlike atmosphere into her quiet courtyard and automatically fell into step when they dismounted and walked toward the porch. She felt dwarfed by so much masculine bulk advancing on her.

Claudius led the way. Tall and harmoniously made, maturely handsome with gray at the temples and a rather pensive air, he had a natural distinction that would have told Severina he was superior to the others, even if she had not known he was their senior in rank. He took both her hands, pressed them, and, regarding her with his grave and winning smile, said, "We are happy to be your guests, Severina."

"Welcome, Claudius," she answered, a little shy at exercising her right, as Aurelian's wife, to address his friend, though such a famous soldier, in this familiar fashion.

Aurelian and Claudius grasped hands; they grinned at each other and said, "Hullo!" Then Claudius turned to the trio of junior officers formed up in a row behind him and drew a stalward, good-looking young man forward. "You know Probus, don't you, Severina?" "Of course," she replied, smiling warmly at Probus. "You came twice to my father's house with Aurelian and you were at the wedding." In his candid, faintly freckled face, she could read his pleasure at being remembered with such particularity.

"I am happy to be your guest," he answered, making use of Claudius' phrase.

"And now Herennianus, our dashing cavalryman," resumed Claudius.

"When there's cavalry to be led," Herennianus said, laughing. "My salutations, Lady Severina." He was a dark, lithe man, with a suggestion of swagger and devil-may-care about him, a trifle shorter and (Severina judged) younger than Probus. His bright, impudent eyes surveyed her with frank approval. In spite of herself, her look went to his forehead, where a fresh scar, inches long, just missed the corner of one eye. His smile gleamed. "I got it in the battle," he explained cheerfully, nodding toward Aurelian. "We all expect hard knocks when we serve under the General!"

Everyone laughed. "Diocletian," announced Claudius. The burly man with the heavy, aquiline nose and the big jowl saluted her solemnly and said, "Thank you for inviting me, Lady." His voice was harsh and emphatic, as if he were forestalling some objection, his accent uncouth to Severina's ear. He had a cold, impressive calm, and his little gray eyes, deep-set in fleshy hollows, were shrewd and penetrating. Probably he was younger than he looked.

"Diocletian's one of our best organizers," Claudius added, completing the introduction.

"That's to say he's even more flint-hearted than other Quartermasters," commented Herennianus.

"There's something in that," put in Aurelian, smiling with a kind of grudging admiration. "He supplied the Army during this last campaign and not one extra item of stores could we get out of him. Still, I must admit the rations came in without fail."

Diocletian smiled grimly.

"And not only rations," Herennianus added. "Why, Lady Severina, I tell you that man's got a passion for demanding returns. You can lie, dead-beat, under a bivouac, in the pouring rain—and someone drags you out because Diocletian wants to know—top priority—the exact number of trusses of hay consumed between New Year's Day and a week after Midsummer. He expects you to keep accounts in the middle of a battle!"

"In your case it's necessary," said Diocletian calmly. He turned to Severina. "You should see his accounts—they look as if they were drawn up in the middle of a battle!"

Severina and Herennianus himself joined in the laugh provoked by this prompt rejoinder.

The dinner party went very cheerfully. All the Illyrians soon relaxed and applied themselves with zest to the appetizing roasts which Severina had agreed in advance with Porphyry would best suit these martial guests, unaccustomed to subtle and exotic dishes. Aurelian and Claudius were obviously in comradely good humor; Probus looked boyishly pleased with everything; while the meal was enlivened by the battle of repartee between the irrepressible Herennianus and Diocletian, in which the stream of darts launched by the one was more than requited by the heavy lance thrusts of the other's sarcasm.

Aurelian did not exert himself as a host, perhaps because he appreciated how much his guests preferred an absence of ceremony. Indeed, their attitude made it clear that it was Severina they regarded as the dispenser of hospitality. Much of their conversation, though really directed at one another, was formally addressed to her in the first place. She felt warmed by their consideration and their evident regard for her. For the first time in her life, she was savoring the profound pleasure of the successful hostess.

The moment came when she judged it advisable to leave the men to their drinking. She got up, but was startled and infinitely flattered when a chorus of protests rose from her guests. "Please, Severina, not so soon," said Claudius. "You don't have to stand on etiquette with

us. Why, it's you we've come to see—we've seen plenty of Aurelian!"
When the chuckle died away, Probus stood up, with a smile of
youthful sincerity and charm. "Please stay, Lady Severina. If you go,
it will be just another drinking party. With you"—he hesitated, then
went on boldly—"it will be a banquet!"

Everyone applauded. She looked round. On those strong Illyrian
faces, reddened a little by the substantial meal, there shone a goodwill that went far beyond gratitude for hospitality, that disconcerted
—and delighted—her. For some reason these tough men of war liked
her, not merely for the entertainment she had provided, but for her
own sake. They did not consider her a nonentity whom Aurelian
had happened to marry. They were glad that she was his wife.

Her eyeballs prickled; her lips parted, but she found herself unable
to speak. She sank down on the couch and smiled at them steadily. Then Claudius, who perhaps divined what was passing in her
heart, said very gently, "Thank you, my dear! And now," he added,
more briskly, "you'll pardon us if we talk a little shop."

After that, to Severina's relief, nobody paid much attention to her.
They simply accepted her and it was wonderful to hear them talk
with such freedom about their professional concerns. Porphyry came
round with a jar, filling the goblets; he could not quite exclude from
his expression his shock at her presence among the men at this stage
of the party. Drinking went on, but quite temperately—it merely
lubricated the conversation. She herself took an occasional sip, for
form's sake, though she did not care for this Gallic wine—it was
harsh and biting to her palate.

Severina made no attempt to intervene in their talk. At first it was
about technical matters she did not understand; a charger's diet and
harness; the disposition of a trooper's weapons on its back; the
marching rates of different types of cavalry. But, gradually, by a
natural drift and under the influence of the wine, which was bringing to the surface thoughts about which they were normally more
reticent, the company began to touch on themes related to the military situation and the general malaise—what her uncle had called
the crisis of the Empire.

The Army's condition was poor—and getting worse. New equipment, when it could be got, was shoddy. Volunteering had fallen off

alarmingly; recruits were being accepted who were of an unsatisfactory standard. Soldier's pay needed to be increased, substantially, for money was buying less and less—the Empire was in the grip of an inflation.

In all this wide-ranging discussion, which shifted ground at times with bewildering suddenness, Severina could see that Aurelian was regarded as the final arbiter. Until he had pronounced upon a question, the others, even Claudius, seemed to consider it as still open. Yes, even Claudius, that self-assured aristocrat with his penetrating mind and obvious authority, seemed to concede that Aurelian supremely had the practical genius that matched the idea against the facts.

After a time, the tone of the conversation had grown decidedly pessimistic. Though nobody made a direct attack on the Co-Emperors, to Severina the brutal implication was clear; the wrong persons were ruling Rome.

Absorbed as she was in the discussion, she was startled when the latest speaker—Claudius, as it chanced—halted in the middle of a sentence. She became aware that Porphyry had entered the room and was making directly for her.

"The wine merchant, Matthaias, is here, Lady," he announced in a loud whisper, conscious of the eyes of the Illyrians on him in the sudden stillness. "I told him you were engaged, but he said you particularly wanted to speak to him."

She rose and addressed the company. "Please excuse me. There is someone I must see."

As she was going, Aurelian called, "It was Matthaias, Porphyry said—that Jewish wine merchant?"

"That's right," she answered, over her shoulder.

Outside she became aware how much of a strain it had been sitting there among the men at the time of drinking when women were traditionally excluded. She was proud of their insistence that she stay and glad she had yielded to it. But it was a relief to be herself again, without any constraint, free to feel and think as a woman.

Matthaias was in the atrium, standing with a connoisseur's air of concentration before the finest of her bronze miniatures, a youthful athlete, nude. His reflective "Hmm," was not altogether approving. He turned as she approached and greeted her with respect, but there was a fatherly warmth in his smile.

She returned his greeting cordially and said, "My guests are already enjoying your wine."

He looked pleased. "My dear young lady," he said, "as you wished, I have myself brought you the balance of your order—and, besides this, a half-dozen jars of a true nectar which I press in my own vineyards. It would give me great pleasure if you accepted them for yourself and the General." Before she could thank him, he added, "I hope to call on you again when I visit Rome next year."

"So you're leaving—oh, I am sorry!"

"In two or three days. My sons are already on the road home." Smiling, he explained that the eldest of his four sons, all of whom assisted him in the business, was to be married shortly. It was to attend the wedding that they were all returning to Gaul.

They stood chatting pleasantly for a while. Matthaias, it was easy to see, enjoyed talking about his family and she was interested by the impression she got of a close-knit Jewish clan, sustained by a warm mutual affection, which contrasted with the formal and rather frigid relationships existing within her own family.

Porphyry came in, looking rather agitated. "Ah, Lady!" he exclaimed. "So the wine merchant is still here. The Master wants you to bring him in. He was—er—very emphatic!"

Puzzled, she glanced at Matthaias. He shrugged. Customers must be humored, the gesture conveyed.

"Please come with me," she said, feeling uneasy.

When she returned to the dining room, followed quietly by Matthaias, she at once noticed a change of atmosphere. The faces of the Illyrians were flushed; wine had been spilt on the tables and its smell was sharp in the air. There had evidently been some hard drinking in her absence.

Claudius had a look of gloomy resignation, as if he had abandoned the hopeless defense of a viewpoint he knew to be right. His gaze rested somberly on Severina for a few moments and then traveled past her to comprehend the puzzling vision of the slender, gingerish-bearded tradesman. Herennianus gaped; he seemed to have difficulty in focusing. Probus smiled rather foolishly. Drink had given a solemn, stiff dignity to Diocletian and in his heavy, strong-hewn face the proconsul seemed to mingle with the plebeian. At the sight of Severina he set his goblet down with exaggerated firmness; it rang on the little table and some of the wine splashed out.

Only Aurelian looked fully composed, but there was a cold gleam in his eye that disturbed Severina. When he spoke, it was with a rasping, jeering note that suggested the Centurion prodding awkward recruits at drill.

"Sit down, merchant!" he said.

Matthaias raised his eyebrows a little, but he silently went over to the couch Severina indicated. With a faintly ironic smile he stared at Aurelian.

"Have some of your own wine—it's good!" went on Aurelian, his words amiable, but the goading note becoming sharper. "Porphyry!"

At this parade-ground bark, Porphyry hastened over to Matthaias with a jar and goblet. His hand trembled so much in pouring that the Jew, removing his calm gaze from Aurelian for a few moments, placed a light, steadying hand on his wrist until the operation was safely over.

"Drink up!" said Aurelian. "What are you waiting for?"

Matthaias looked down at the goblet; then he raised it with deliberation, rebuking by his unhurried manner the importunity of Aurelian. "Your health, General!" he said coolly.

All the Illyrians had now fixed their eyes on Matthaias. He might have seemed a prisoner confronting an unfriendly tribunal, but for the relaxed way he sat and his good-humored expression.

"You're a Jew, aren't you?" asked Aurelian.

"Yes, General," replied Matthaias equably.

"My wife tells me you're an intelligent man." Aurelian contrived to make the compliment almost derisory.

Matthaias met his overbearing gaze quite unperturbed. "Your Lady is too kind," he said.

"Drink up—you're just trifling with it!" Matthaias raised the goblet to his lips. "Porphyry!" snapped Aurelian. "More wine for the merchant." With a pitiful look the steward shook a splash or two from the jar to make good the few sips Matthaias had taken.

"Now," resumed Aurelian, "keep drinking. I want to ask you a few questions."

"Questions?" repeated Matthaias mildly. "I hope you will permit me to ask you one first."

"As you like," answered Aurelian indifferently.

"Why are you plying me with drink?"

"To loosen your tongue," replied Aurelian with brutal candor. "I want the truth." Suspiciously his eye rested on the goblet at Matthaias' lips. He made a peremptory gesture, indicating that it should be tilted for a copious draught.

"Tell me," he continued, as soon as Matthaias had lowered the vessel and held it out, reluctantly, for Porphyry to fill, "are there many Jews in the Empire?"

Matthaias shrugged. "Not many. Just small communities here and there."

"And outside the Empire?"

Matthaias raised the goblet and smiled at him with a hint of mockery across the faintly trembling brim. "There are many of us in Mesopotamia."

Claudius frowned and for the first time joined in this strange interrogation, pronouncing his words with the unnatural distinctness of one who tries to prevent himself from slurring them. "Mesopotamia—then you are pro-Persian!" He glanced significantly at Aurelian, who said sharply to Matthaias, "Well?"

Matthaias looked quizzically first at Aurelian and then at Claudius. He was taking his time, but there was no suggestion of hesitancy in this manner. Severina began to suspect that he was enjoying himself at the expense of his tormentors. "My dear Generals," he said suavely, "Mesopotamia is a frontier region. It is the first to suffer in any war. We are therefore pro-peace!"

Claudius wrinkled his brow; then nodded slowly. His attention seemed to wander from Matthaias, but Aurelian bent his gaze more ominously at the Jew.

"Your people have been against Rome," said Aurelian. "They had to be driven from Palestine!"

Matthaias stiffened a little. Perhaps the wine, of which he had now drunk quantities, had broken down his self-control; perhaps the sting in Aurelian's deliberately provocative words had at last penetrated. But he eyed Aurelian coolly enough. "We had to be driven from Palestine, yes. It wasn't exactly easy, though—was it, General? We broke a Legion, you may remember."

Feet scraped and couches creaked. The continuity between the Legions of the Empire's brilliant days and the disintegrating Legions of the present had grown largely fictitious, but in most headquarters and senior messes there persisted some memory of the savage wars in Palestine, which had brought ruin upon the Jewish people and dispersed their survivors, at the cost of terrible losses to Rome.

Aurelian's smile was bleak. "Yet you were driven out. You lost everything. Your God went down before the Gods of Rome!"

Matthaias fingered his gingerish beard leisurely; in the mood of the moment it was almost a contemptuous gesture. "We survived," he said evenly. "Who knows—we may yet survive Rome!"

The shock of these words not only took the power of speech from the Illyrians; it froze their postures. In the loaded hush, Matthaias looked round the tableau of consternation and realized his grave mistake: he had contemplated aloud, almost with relish, a future in which the Empire did not exist. But the potent wine had released his tongue and his resentment was clamoring to appease itself with fanged words.

"There was a before-Rome," he went on, helpless against his own rashness. "Why shouldn't there be an after-Rome?"

The half-circle of rigid, narrow-eyed men continued to stare at him. From their appalled stillness he understood that he had touched upon some superstitious fear in their pagan hearts. Uneasiness prompted him to speak again. "Well, you asked for frankness, didn't you?"

Even Aurelian had been quelled by the enormity he had provoked, but of all the Illyrians he was first to recover. His voice seemed to clatter with fury barely controlled. "What have you to complain about? You've managed to do pretty well for yourself— thanks to Rome! Who else protects you and your wine cellars? It's for the likes of you that we're trying to save the Empire!"

Unbidden, Matthaias took a long swig; the rhythm of drinking in the intervals of speaking had become compulsive. He tilted his head aggressively at Aurelian. "It is worth saving?"

Aurelian stared at him. Again there was a deathly hush in the room.

Matthaias studied his glass with concentration, as if seeking there an answer to his question. "Perhaps," he murmured, "perhaps not . . ."

"What do you mean?" Bewilderment, as well as anger, sounded in Aurelian's voice.

"Remember, you asked for the truth," Matthaias said with an insolent smile. "Anyway, I've said enough to earn a halter round my neck—I might as well deserve scourging first. Now, General, hear me out. For every free man in the Empire, there is probably one slave. If you were a slave in the mines or in one of the chain gangs on the plantations, would you think the Empire worth saving? Take a stroll round the slave quarters on some of your big estates— you'll find the graves of many, many babies. If you were a slave woman whose baby had been strangled by the overseer because it is uneconomic to rear slave children, would you think the Empire worth saving? Over there in Gaul we export wine to Britain—the exchange rate is one jar of wine, common wine, for one slave. If you were priced at a jar of wine, would you want to save the Empire that values you so highly?"

"You've slaves yourself," growled Aurelian. The browbeating note was gone. "I've seem them humping your wine jars into the cellar."

"Your eyes are keen, General," acknowledged Matthaias, with a mocking smile. "Yes, I have slaves. But my Law bids me treat them humanely and free them every seven years."

"All of them?" It was Claudius again intervening. "Surely you don't obey such a law!"

Matthaias made a wry face. "I groan—but I obey. Still, I must admit there is no particular merit in my action. Plenty of Romans manumit their slaves."

He could sense that his stricture on slavery had made a strong impression on all the Illyrians, except Claudius, who obviously was an aristocrat, his ears insensitive to the cries of despair from far below. The others—in that way more typical soldiers—came no doubt from a level of the population close enough to slavery to hate and fear it, if not to pity it.

"Slavery apart," began Claudius. He paused, seeking in his rather fuddled mind for words to convey his argument.

"Slavery apart," echoed Matthaias, making of the repetition a deadly retort. He glanced knowingly at the other Illyrians, who listened withdrawn into a silence that no longer was quite hostile.

"Yes, slavery apart," resumed Claudius with some exasperation, "what have you to grumble at? As Aurelian—as the General here—pointed out, you live and prosper under the protection of our Legions."

"I don't grumble," rejoined Matthaias. "But my business takes me out and about and I see much that no humane or sensible man could approve of. These great estates, for instance, which you find everywhere—they've swallowed up the free peasant proprietors who ought to be the backbone of the Empire."

There was a little movement among the Illyrians. Claudius frowned, but said nothing, although Matthaias, with eyebrows raised, was obviously awaiting his answer.

"Correct me if I'm wrong," persisted the Jew, "but I've always imagined that the best recruits for the Army came from the free peasants. Wouldn't you agree that whoever crushes the peasants undermines the Army?"

Still Claudius stayed glumly silent.

"Now take taxation," went on Matthaias. "It's merciless. Even we merchants are nearly crippled by it—and we are used to being the milch cows of the Empire. But how can the small owner-farmer or the free tenant hold out? The peasant has come to dread the tax gatherer more than the barbarian. Why, in Gaul the peasants are taking wholesale to the woods and hills—they find it easier to live as outlaws."

Matthaias had been unable to check the flow of his words, but he had become conscious of growing difficulty with pronunciation. Cloud drifts were swirling through his brain and closing in on the protruding rock where he felt the last of his reason precariously perched. He ceased to search those rugged, puzzled, intent Illyrian faces before him and looked down. "Outlaws . . ." he muttered. Then, with a final effort, he addressed Aurelian, thickly. "General, I must thank you for your kind hospitality—even though I fear I

128

have abused it to some extent. It is getting late and I have important business early tomorrow. May I request your permission to leave?"

"You can leave," Aurelian growled.

Matthaias rose. He bowed, audibly gulping as the movement compressed his stomach. Then he turned and walked with slow, very careful steps, pausing at intervals to steady himself, toward the door that seemed so far away.

Severina, without a word to Aurelian, followed him.

Outside, she clutched his arm. For the first time since she had met Aurelian, she felt contempt for him and even a spurt of hatred. "Believe me," she faltered, "I had no idea—I am so ashamed . . . !"

He looked at her whimsically, swaying slightly. "My dear young . . . lady, do not . . . distress yourself." He spoke in gushes of words, with odd intervals between. "Soldiers . . . you know . . . they're rather masterful people . . . they don't go in for tact . . . I hope . . . they don't mind a little . . . bluntness in return." His mouth opened and his face contorted. With a wavering smile he said, "Besides, dear young lady . . . your husband's conduct is really a . . . testimonial to the quality of my wine!"

He shook his head dazedly, two or three times. "May I ask you to tell me where I can be sick?" he said deliberately. "Please hurry, dear young lady!"

12

TOO distressed to sleep, Severina much later heard Aurelian seeing off his guests. To her surprise there was not much noise; certainly not enough to suggest a little company of horsemen departing at the end of a revel. Almost directly after, Aurelian entered the bedroom. He stood looking at her, she knew, though she pretended to be fast asleep. She heard light movements as he undressed swiftly;

then was aware of him slipping in beside her, carefully, so as not to disturb her. He smelled strongly of wine, but did not breathe stertorously when he fell asleep, which was within a few minutes.

Wakeful though she had lain for hours, the warmth of her contact with him gradually lulled her and she drifted among confused and exhausting dreams.

It was still dark when she awoke, her head aching, and realized at once that Aurelian was no longer there. Thinking he might be ill from his recent debauch, she sat up, torn between revulsion and concern. She listened intently; in all the house no one appeared to be stirring. Growing worried, she was trying to decide what to do, when the door opened very quietly and Aurelian was in the room. Despite the gloom, he at once saw her. "What are you doing?" he asked in a low voice, but instead of approaching the bed he crossed to his clothes chest and bent over it.

"I wondered where you were," she addressed his back, speaking with an effort, for she was still sluggish with her dreams. "Has anything happened?"

He stood up, a tunic dangling from his hand. "Orders came from Rome last night," he said. "I must report early today. The others left about midnight. You had better get back to sleep."

She was still bitterly offended by his behavior last night. But dulled as her wits seemed, she knew this was no moment for recriminations. "Food?" she said. "You'll be hungry . . . and it's cold riding out at this hour."

He laughed softly, pleased at her practical turn of mind. "I've breakfasted in the kitchen—on last night's leavings. And I've got a thick cloak here." Cold surged over her thin shift and bare arms as he swung the garment round his shoulders. "No, don't disturb yourself," he added, as she made to get up. "There's nothing you can do. I'll send word from Rome if I'm delayed."

"Aurelian," she called, shaken now. "Is it—trouble?"

He turned in the doorway and looked at her silently for a few moments. "Yes," he said abruptly and walked out.

Severina spent a restless day, contending with anxiety about the trouble that had called Aurelian so urgently to Rome; but at intervals she felt an uprush of hot resentment against his boorishness the night before. She knew they had arrived at a crisis—the more acute because he seemed unaware of it—and that if she let the matter pass without protest, she would never again find the firmness to complain, however outrageous his conduct.

In the morning she had summoned Porphyry and heard his account of what followed at the drinking party, after she retired.

At first there had been an animated discussion, he said, the murmur of which, though not the words, had been audible through the door. ("I was on hand, in case I was wanted," explained Porphyry blandly.) Then the messenger had arrived, a Praetorian officer in loftily plumed helmet and vivid scarlet cloak, dust-spattered by furious riding. When Porphyry announced him, Aurelian and Claudius had exchanged looks. All the Illyrians sat up, smoothing their clothes and assuming a serious demeanor. "Bring him in," Aurelian directed. Porphyry, back at his station outside the door, indistinctly heard the officer's voice for a couple of minutes and then those of Aurelian and Claudius at intervals, with the officer responding.

Soon after the officer left, the party broke up. The leave-taking of the Illyrians had none of the high spirits of their arrival. Aurelian and Claudius had a few minutes' quiet talk in the garden, apart from the others, who waited in silence. When the two Generals returned, the guests exchanged a brief handshake with Aurelian and a murmured word or two. Then they filed away into the darkness.

"It must have been serious news that officer brought," declared Porphyry with some satisfaction.

"We don't know," said Severina shortly. "Still, keep all this strictly to yourself. There's another thing. . . ." She had made the decision to send a special messenger to Rome with a gift for Matthaias—or rather his eldest son's bride—as some atonement for the insults he had suffered in her house. Her choice had fallen on a beautiful antique bracelet in filigree, of great value. To accompany it she had written a few simple words expressing her good wishes to the young couple.

Curiously, she felt less resentful against Aurelian once the present had been dispatched, although he himself had done nothing to make amends.

He returned from Rome earlier than she had expected. Though obviously tired and a little withdrawn in manner, he greeted her calmly. At the sight of him thus apparently undisturbed, it struck her that the trouble which had recalled the Illyrians to Rome must have been happily settled. Her relief reawoke her anger. Cost what it may, she resolved to speak her mind about last night's shameful occurrence.

As soon as dinner was over and Porphyry had left them to themselves, she broached the matter.

"Aurelian, I was shocked last night . . ."

He looked at her sharply, though she had an impression that he was giving her only part of his attention. Quailing inwardly but in a firm voice, she pressed on. "How could you treat a man like Matthaias so?"

His brow cleared. "Oh, Matthaias," he said, almost as if he had expected some other name. "Don't worry about him. He gave as good as he got—and better. I must say you were right, Severina. He's a very clever man." Aurelian's smile was unpleasant as he continued, "So he's feeling injured, is he? Well, I suppose you'd better give him another order for wine!"

This brutal comment took Severina's breath away. Before the bitterly indignant words could burst from her, she saw Aurelian's expression grow stern. "There's something *I* want to talk about to *you*," he said, giving a chilling emphasis to the two personal pronouns. "This is serious. You've been seeing a Christian priest. Three times!"

Panic swamped her anger. "How do you know?" she managed to bring out. Even to her own ears, her voice was a confession of guilt.

"Never mind. I do know—that's all that matters. You must stop it!" His eyes were hard and steady on hers. She had an impulse to shrink away from them, but they seemed to pin her down.

Having issued his command and witnessed her confusion, he

looked at her more tolerantly. "I know some gods have a special appeal for women. And I don't want to interfere in your private life." She winced at this large-mindedness, knowing it was born of indifference. He was speaking with a deliberate patience which showed he ascribed this folly of hers to youth and inexperience. But behind his reasonableness she could sense a decision so firm that there could be no question in his mind (nor, indeed, in hers) of any defiance.

"Still, try to understand that a woman in your position should not associate with Christians. Decent people have no use for them. They're tricky customers—no loyalty to the State—too many shirkers and pacifists among them."

Every phrase hurt, less for the meaning it bore than for the way he said it.

"There's a lot of good in them, too," she said helplessly. How could she explain to this harsh, overbearing soldier the simple strength and courage of someone like Pervica, the deep earnestness, the fine, strong, honest intelligence of somebody like Paul?

A furrow appeared between his brows, but he spoke with the same maddening calm as before. "Of course. But face facts. They've always been unpopular. Both the government and the people are against them. You know hundred and hundreds were rounded up by Valerian—and they got no mercy. Just use your common sense—it won't help me if my wife is known to mix with Christians!"

"Mixing with Christians isn't the same as being one— All right," she added hastily as his eyebrows rose. "Next time the Deacon comes, I'll tell Porphyry to send him away. I'll let him have some money for alms—that will make it easier."

His frown showed that he did not like this—it was modifying his order. "Very well," he said after a moment, with a little shrug. He got up and went quietly out.

She sat silent, thinking with pain that it was the first time they had clashed and that her will hardly seemed to exist in collision with his. Their married life was totally on his terms. Her protest against his brutal conduct toward Matthaias he had simply brushed aside; but when he disapproved of her behavior he expressed himself with a natural masterfulness so overpowering that he did not even have to raise his voice. She just had to obey, like one of his soldiers.

After a while, she got up, feeling in her wretchedness that the shadowed quiet of the bedroom would be preferable; she shrank from the thought of Porphyry bursting in on her, all agitated over some trifle. But, to her astonishment, Aurelian was already in the bedroom, stooping over his clothes chest; on the bed lay a small pile of garments compactly folded.

Her heart gave a sickening thump. Aurelian was leaving her! But no—the face he turned was quite friendly; he was even smiling in a preoccupied way.

"What is the matter?" she stammered. "I'm posted," he said. "To Pannonia." He looked critically at a faded gray woolen cloak he had fished up from the box. She took the cloak from him, noted with a glance its threadbare patches and threw it aside. "Why?" she asked. "What has happened?"

"What I expected." He spoke very soberly. "Tell nobody—we don't want alarm spreading. The barbarians are flooding into the Balkans. Goths mostly—and Vandals. First reports are coming in. No big invasion yet, just raiding parties. But they've broken through at many points all along the frontier. The defenses just don't seem to be functioning."

Her feeling against him was forgotten. Unable to restrain herself, she moved closer and seized his hand, as if to say that whatever little strength she had was his to dispose of. He left his heavy, sinewy hand in her nervous grip; perhaps he was hardly aware of it, for in the same grave voice he continued his laconic commentary. "There's this cursed Persian war—we simply haven't the troops for every sector. I know the Balkans well—that's why I'm being sent there. The Gods know where my base will be. Sirmium perhaps— if it's not too far forward."

Severina understood just enough to sense the magnitude of the threat, the possibility of disaster sweeping on a wide front over the Empire.

"Trouble's brewing on the Upper Danube, too," Aurelian went on. "These barbarians have a sixth sense—it tells them when to strike. To make matters worse, there's a mutiny in Gaul. Gallienus has been making light of it—but it's spreading. He ought to be there himself, to stamp it out. We can't afford to lose the Gallic Legions!"

She had room only for the thought that he was going far away from her.

"What am I to do?" she asked. From his expression, it was plain that he had not even considered the problem. After a few moments he answered, "Stay here till I send for you. No doubt I'll settle down somewhere before long."

She looked so stricken that he added in a tone not unkindly, "Why don't you go and stay with your father?" Slowly she shook her head. Somehow Drusilla's gossip and routine of trivialities would be impossible to endure with Aurelian far away, fighting a difficult war against fierce savages and herself on tenterhooks for news of him. "Or you could visit your Uncle in Baiae," Aurelian suggested. "Yes, that's a good idea. He's very fond of you."

Severina went to the window. She gazed a little while abstractedly at the garden. It lay so tranquil in the mellow evening sunshine; there was hardly a breath of air to set the foliage trembling in the trees whose lengthening shadows slanted black across the lawn. She felt an autumn gale should be howling. Turning, she said, "Let me help you pack."

"That's all right," he answered. "I've practically finished. I don't need much from here. The Praetorians are giving me a full new issue."

Even in this he had failed her. Her one small consolation now would have been to busy herself with what he needed.

"When will you be leaving Rome?" she asked, taking a firm grip on herself, but almost sick with fear that he would say, "At once!"

"I can't be sure. If I know Gallienus, he'll dawdle for days—then he'll send urgent orders and there won't be a minute to spare!"

His simple preparations completed, he came over to her and said, "Don't take it hard, Severina. Find yourself something to do." She looked at him ironically and he seemed a little embarrassed, as though he, too, recalled his recent ban on her association with the Christians. "I'm a soldier—and there's a bad time coming for the Empire."

135

"I want to be with you!" she answered, desolation in her heart.
"I'll send for you as soon as possible," he repeated patiently. The
phrase was no comfort. She could tell that their reunion did not
figure very high in his list of priorities. Once he quitted Rome, who
knew what months—or even years—would pass before she again set
eyes on her husband?

13

SEVERINA stood outside her father's room, trying to remember
the emotions with which she had answered his summons—those
short months ago, that whole existence ago—when he first announced the name of the husband the Emperor had chosen for her.
No, that green, scared, resentful girl had become a stranger. Today
she could not call those emotions back. The same house, the same
door, another summons, the same father waiting—but she herself
was utterly changed.

Her father may have heard her quiet approach or he may simply
have been impatient for her coming. At any rate, the door opened
and he said with relief, "Oh, Severina—there you are. Come in!
Come in!" He led her to a couch and sat down opposite.

During the two days she had spent in her father's house—she had
followed Aurelian to Rome the morning after his own departure—
she had found Severinus fretful and apprehensive. His skin looked
grayer, his cheekbones sharper. His appetite was poor and he complained of frequent nausea. She had soon discovered what was prey-
ing on his mind. Owing to the situation on the Eastern front, where
the Persians were pressing the Emperor Valerian very hard, the
Junior Augustus had been vested with full sovereignty; Gallienus
had become, in effect, sole Emperor.

Severinus had spoken to his daughter of little else since her arrival
and now he lost no time in returning to the theme. "The playboy!

The poseur!" he said bitterly. "We sent a deputation with a loyal address to him this morning. He took the scroll from me. Then he looked at Fabricius—you know him, Severina? That big, pompous, prosy man with a huge villa in Campania—very old family, very rich. Well, he looked at Fabricius with that chilly, mocking smile of his and said: 'What are you doing here?' He pronounced that 'you' like a death sentence. The truth, Severina, is that Fabricius has been behaving like a fool. He let himself be overheard making some jest about Gallienus as a patron of the arts—not that the matter isn't one for jesting, of course. Then Gallienus turned toward the Guard Commander. Fabricius went white—I thought he was going to faint."

Severina listened without close attention. In the upshot she had not been able to catch even a glimpse of Aurelian. Occupied with last-minute conferences, he had not emerged from the Praetorian Camp. Nor had he sent word, until this morning, when Claudius had stopped by with a terse note from him, written late last night, to say that at dawn he would be on his way to Pannonia with a detail of infantry. By now, he was probably twelve or fifteen miles away on the Via Flaminia, the great road northward.

"Gallienus looked down at the scroll with a nasty sneer," her father was saying. "Do you know, Severina, he had the effrontery to criticize the composition—he actually pointed out several faulty Latin constructions, so he called them. He also said the sentiments were stilted and the whole thing obviously insincere!" Severinus paused, struggling with his indignation.

"But was it so very sincere?" she inquired mildly, still thinking of Aurelian. She did not feel acute distress as yet, but rather a vague sense of loss and an expectancy that as the days passed and his absence became more real, a grief would take hold of her that would be beyond bearing.

Her father smiled sarcastically. Too distrustful to talk freely to any of his colleagues about Gallienus, he enjoyed opening his mind to Severina. He had always recognized unusual intelligence in her, and because of her marriage she had come of age in his eyes.

"Of course, it wasn't sincere," he said. "It was one of those traditional pretenses that both sides affect to take at their face value. But not Gallienus, oh, no! He's full of shams, himself. He's always playing a part—I grant the man has a certain perverted talent as a low comedian—but now he chooses to insist on sincerity, if you please! It's only his way of humiliating the Senate—and there's worse to come."

They had been married less than three months, Severina reflected. He had not come to love her as she hoped and he showed little consideration for her feelings. He had placed his heavy foot on her association with the Christian Deacon and ground it out of existence. Yet in the short time of their marriage, he had taken possession of her—and not only physically. He filled her thoughts, her deepest feelings drew her to him. She did not know how she could endure it if their separation were long.

Her father's petulant tones flowed on, maintaining a grip on a segment of her mind. Suddenly she became aware that these words she was listening to so absently were taking on a very serious import. With an effort she focused her attention on her father. He was leaning toward her, in a wary, confidential posture, and speaking with solemnity. ". . . A man like Gallienus is unpredictable. Some of us he'll send to the executioner, I have no doubt. But I fancy I shall find myself providing him with even better entertainment. He will keep me in suspense as long as possible—and get an exquisite pleasure out of it!"

He looked so haggard, there was such bitterness in his voice, that Severina took alarm. "You don't mean you yourself are in real danger?"

"Who knows? I doubt whether Gallienus himself, if he were frank—which, of course, he never is—could tell you at this moment what he means to do where I'm concerned. But I don't mind admitting, my dear, that I felt much easier when Aurelian was here. Valerian and his precious son are nervous of the Illyrians. But now they are being packed off. Aurelian's gone; Claudius is going. Soon Gallienus will have a free hand."

He got up and, going to the closet in one corner where his most precious manuscripts were locked away, he inserted a key. A minute later, he came back with a document closely written in his own small and delicate hand.

"Look after this, my dear," he said. "It particularly concerns you." He sat down and, inclining toward her, went on, "I'm taking no chances. What with the war and Gallienus' own extravagance, we are going to have plenty of confiscations—if nothing worse. Well, he's not going to get as much out of me as he anticipates! You may have wondered why your mother is away all this time. I can tell you, if you haven't guessed already, that this old aunt she has been visiting is not so very sick after all. The fact is, your mother is doing some quiet business on my behalf. Nobody would suspect her."

He paused to recover breath; then continued, "I am dispersing as many of my most valuable effects as I can . . . books, works of art . . . even currency. Here is a list of my agents—it's the only one in existence. That's so much out of Gallienus' reach. And if anything happens to me"—he grimaced painfully and flicked the document—"it's yours, all of it. Don't worry about your mother," he added. "She can go back to her own family."

It still seemed hardly credible to Severina that the baleful figure haunting his mind was the same man as the affable, bantering Gallienus she knew. Yet her father's obsessive fears troubled her deeply. "Why not leave Rome?" she urged. "Retire from politics for the time being. Your health is not too good—there is your excuse!"

He gave her a sickly smile. "Can't you imagine how Gallienus would love me to run away—so that he could have me brought back! He would like nothing better than to humiliate me—before he robbed me. Don't forget that he has a sense of inferiority toward us. Who are his family? Where do they come from? What distinguished men have they produced? But we are kinsmen of Trajan himself—don't smile, Severina, we are his distant kin. And in every generation we've produced outstanding men—right up to the present. Take soldiers alone. There's Crinitus—what other Roman family could show someone with a record as brilliant? And, of course, there's Aurelian, who is one of us by marriage."

Severina did not reply. She was thinking how her father's hatred of Gallienus had made him forget his old antipathy for Crinitus, who had now been promoted to one of the family's ornaments!

"It's easy to understand," Severinus went on, "how he would like to strip me of all dignity, to shame me before Rome and the world.

Well, I am not going to give him the chance. If he means to destroy me, I shall just have to face it with what composure I can command. I shall not gratify him by running away—or by begging for mercy!"

Despite her anxiety, Severina was impressed by this nervous, desperate courage. Under the tyranny of earlier Emperors, her father had shown more suppleness than independent spirit; but there was an intense personal antagonism between Gallienus and himself that made the Emperor and the Senator contend, in a way, as equals.

"As for you, Severina," he said, "now that Aurelian's gone, I think it advisable for you to leave this house and Rome—both for your own sake and because I want that list away from here. All the same," he added rather wistfully, "I should have been glad if you had been able to stay . . . I . . . I shall miss you."

Severina had never seen her father look so forlorn. She placed her hand on his; then leaned forward and kissed his cheek. It was cold to her lips. He seemed a little startled at her display of feeling.

Heavy-hearted for Aurelian, filled with foreboding about her father, Severina returned the following day to her villa in the Alban Hills.

The gusts of terrible grief which she had anticipated, almost with eagerness, never materialized; she was incapable of these extremes of primitive release. Instead, a dull ache, a heavy blankness, persisted. She felt at once without energy and unable to rest. The house seemed inexpressibly empty; their bedroom huge and unfamiliar. She wandered from room to room, knowing that the curious glances of the slaves were following her and that Porphyry was in a flutter of distress.

One thing she did with decision: she manumitted Pervica. The presence of this Christian slave was too painful a reminder, both of her own weakness and of a dissension between herself and Aurelian. Reluctant to face the strong-willed girl, who no doubt despised her, looking on her sudden repudiation of the Deacon Paul as a kind of feeble apostasy, she bade Porphyry arrange everything. He came in one morning to say that Pervica would be leaving within the hour and wished to thank her mistress for her freedom. It would have been cowardly and ungracious beyond pardon to refuse such a natural request. "Send her in," she said, after a moment's hesitation.

Pervica the freedwoman was already different from Pervica the slave. She entered with grave composure, inclined a little and stood with her brown eyes steady on Severina's face. It was Severina who looked uncomfortable. "I wish to thank you from my heart," Pervica said quietly. This girl always had an inner dignity, Severina thought. Now it is outward, too; it governs her bearing and the modulations of her voice. To Severina she seemed a couple of inches taller.

"Don't thank me," Severina answered rather guiltily. "I want you to be happy." Pervica smiled faintly and her plain, coarse-skinned, rather masculine face was transfigured. "I shall pray for you, Lady," she said in a low voice that was charged with feeling, "and for your husband in the war."

"What are your plans?" Severina inquired. She had presented her with a sum sufficient for her immediate needs, but of course Pervica was the kind of person who looked beyond the present. "I shall work among our poor in Rome," Pervica said and once more that subdued glow gave her face a rapt and moving beauty. "Since the persecution, many families are without their breadwinners. A small group of women are already helping these distressed people—I shall join them." Severina gazed at her in wonder. How little this girl had had; how much she wanted to give!

She bade her former slave farewell with a sigh and saw her go almost with envy.

The next day she was sitting listlessly in the garden with a book, when Porphyry came up. Even the abstracted glance she gave him told her something extraordinary was elating him. She looked at him more sharply. "Lady, there is a visitor for you!" he announced with an affected wariness which did not conceal the swelling of his self-importance.

This tiresome mystification irritated her. "What visitor?" she said. "Hasn't he got a name?"

Porphyry came closer. His eyes opened wide, his air of exaggerated caution suggested a bad actor miming a conspiracy. "The

Emperor is here!" he breathed and he drew back to relish the effect on her.

"The—Emperor!" she stammered.

"Yes, the Emperor Gallienus!" Porphyry nodded with a complacent smile. "He has come without a retinue this time and he is wearing ordinary dress. When I bowed very low and greeted him humbly, he waved his hand and said, 'No ceremony, please. Just tell your mistress that I'm here.' I conducted him to the atrium. Oh, he was most pleasant, I assure you!"

"Is he alone, then?" Severina's lethargy was gone. Curiously mixed emotions agitated her at the thought of Gallienus in her house. The alarm and perplexity with which she had heard her father's bitter diatribe against him; indignation at his heartless treatment of Crinitus; a certain disquiet at the impropriety of this visit, now that her husband was far away—and, stronger than these, a shamefaced but lively pleasure.

"Just half-a-dozen soldiers waiting in the road and one man he left in the courtyard—a foreigner, I should say, by the look of him."

"What does the Emperor want here?" she could not help reflecting aloud. Porphyry answered with a beaming look, so revealing that she realized with angry astonishment that he not only placed an obvious construction on the visit, but thoroughly approved as well. In the same moment she divined how much he must have feared and hated Aurelian, so harsh and uncivil a master to a senior domestic accustomed to the polished manners of a great Roman house and a measure of polite consideration even from his superiors.

Resolving that when the time came, she must do something to curb Porphyry's presumption, she calculated swiftly. It seemed impossible that anything relating to her father should occasion a call on her by Gallienus. Aurelian? He was still on the march, probably somewhere in Northern Italy—and if there were news of him, it would surely reach her by a normal channel. Gallienus had come informally and virtually unattended. Porphyry's demeanour reflected an easy and affable manner in him. She could only conclude that nothing affecting the safety of her father or her husband was in question. Gallienus' visit was concerned with herself alone.

With a quickened heartbeat she entered the atrium. Gallienus, his back to her, was looking down at the Alexandrian goblet he had admired so much before. He turned at once, with a brilliant smile. "Severina!" he exclaimed. "What a pleasure!" He had an air of cool elegance, though he wore a simple gray woolen tunic, plainly belted, and his only ornament was a thin gold ring.

Severina bowed and murmured a formal welcome. As she spoke, he came sauntering toward her; she found herself measuring the distance between them. "Please be seated, Your Majesty," she said, resisting the impulse to retreat a few steps.

He stopped by the couch at which she had motioned, but he did not sit down. Watching her quizzically, he said, "You have such an eloquent face, Severina. I can read your thoughts. You're asking yourself what brings me here."

His tone was playful—and intimate. With a few words and the inflections of his voice he had established a relationship that flattered her and made her nervous.

She spoke calmly, however. "That is only natural, Your Majesty."

"Of course. Well, one of the reasons"—he said this lightly but deliberately—"was that I wanted you to meet that Priest of Isis I told you about. Come, come, Severina—surely you remember. Or has anything happened to make you lose your interest in the study of religion?"

His question might well be innocent raillery—perhaps it was because she had a feeling of guilt that she sensed in it a sly and disturbing mockery. She forced herself to meet his gaze, trying to fathom this strange man with his engaging smile and subtle, unsettling charm. Even in his simple dress he had the air of a rather dandified trifler. And yet she could not quench the suspicion that his bantering words contained some barbed allusion.

"I remember quite well, Your Majesty," she answered. "Won't you sit down?"

"Just a moment, my dear," said Gallienus pleasantly. He went to the door, opened it and called, "Porphyry!" Then he returned and made himself comfortable on the couch, stretching his long legs. "Your steward will be getting the priest," he explained. "He'll also see that we're not disturbed. I must say I find him a very understanding man."

143

Almost everything Gallienus said seemed to have some implication that troubled her, yet he smiled with such apparent candor that she felt at a loss. Within a minute, Porphyry, his face solemn with gratified self-importance, led in a massively built man, whose stately pace contrasted with the fussiness of his own quick movements.

"This is Mena-Ra," said Gallienus, not bothering to look round. "Offer him a seat, Severina."

Porphyry withdrew. Standing there motionless in his ankle-length girdled gown of white Egyptian linen, the Priest of Isis made an imposing figure. His skin, almost Negroid, was smooth and glistening. The high, shaven dome of his skull helped to give him a grotesque and baleful look, as though he were some warrior insect magnified to human stature. His jet-black, heavy-lidded eyes were large, slightly protuberant, and compelling.

Moving with a solemn dignity, he sat down at Severina's invitation. There was no deference in his manner, nor did he thank her. His weighty look rested on her. Even his silence had authority; behind it she could feel his physical bulk and the force of a forbidding personality. He had a trick, every now and then, of closing his eyes for some moments. Then his face, so charged with power, seemed to go cold and lifeless; but as soon as the eyes reopened the frozen mask came alive again.

"Tell the Lady all about it," said Gallienus easily. Severina had the impression that he was inviting a precocious child to recite. Mena-Ra fixed a quelling look on him, but Gallienus merely smiled and added, "Come on, now. We mustn't keep the Lady waiting!"

Compressing his lips, Mena-Ra switched his heavy regard back to Severina; then in a strong, measured voice which imparted an alien singsong to the expressive Latin, began to expound the essentials of his faith.

At first Severina found his discourse hard to follow; there were so many esoteric terms and allusions she could not understand. But Gallienus, she noticed, for all his casual air, was listening closely, nodding and at times smiling or grimacing to himself. To her Mena-Ra was fully intelligible only when he forsook theology and points of ritual for more general observations. Multitudes in every land, he declared, were turning to Isis. Miracles were being wrought, sinners redeemed, by the grace of this tender, loving Mother. Her religion was born many thousands of years ago. It was older than the Pyramids. For uncounted generations it had brought the Faithful consolation in the trials of this life and bliss beyond the grave. Yet what it was in the beginning, so in all essentials it remained. And this, asserted Mena-Ra in conclusion, established its truth beyond all challenge. For how could it survive the test of whole millennia unless it were absolutely true?

This confident claim and the hypnotic near-chant in which it was delivered made a deep impression on Severina. Gallienus stirred lazily. "Now here we have a most interesting proposition—that whatever is old is right!" he remarked. He gave Severina a quick, pleased glance, which had the significance of a nudge: Mena-Ra had laid himself open! "Would you say the same," continued Gallienus smoothly, "of other religions that have lasted unchanged for ages?"

Mena-Ra's head did not move, but his eyes gleamed a moment on Gallienus; then the lids fell.

"Other religions?" he repeated warily.

"Yes," intervened Severina, for whom the spell of Mena-Ra was now shattered. "We— I have a friend called Matthaias. He is a Jew. His people hold that their God gave them a body of laws in the desert of Sinai far back in the past and they have preserved it without change up to the present day."

Mena-Ra gave a brief, grating laugh. "The Jews—look at them now!"

Severina was silent. A debating point to the Priest of Isis.

"And the Egyptians?" inquired Gallienus. At once Severina perceived how Mena-Ra's argument could recoil on himself. His protuberant gaze rested forbiddingly on Gallienus, who met it with a malicious smile. "Why, man," he resumed—at this irreverent mode of address, the portentous solemnity of Mena-Ra seemed to puncture and sag and a sullen perplexity to take its place—"the Egyptians have been a subject race for centuries, despite their Isis, despite all their tribe of peculiar gods. Assyrians, Persians, Greeks, Romans— we've all lorded it among the Pyramids. Your people have just had to obey. Whatever benefits they enjoy in that queer Egyptian heaven of yours, you must admit that Isis has done precious little to protect them down here on earth!"

Mena-Ra scowled, licked his full lips and finally said, "Your Majesty has a notable sense of humor."

"A sense of the ridiculous would suit this case better," said Gallienus coolly. "Be off with you now—we've finished with you. Here!" He detached his purse from his belt and carelessly threw it in Mena-Ra's direction. The Priest, with incongruous agility, snapped an arm out and clutched it. He closed his eyes, raised one hand in an attitude of blessing, pronounced some sonorous phrases in a strange tongue and went out.

Gallienus turned to Severina. "Find the fellow interesting? He's nine parts fraud, of course—but what an actor!" he added with enthusiasm.

Severina did not answer. She was uneasily aware that the episode with Mena-Ra had involved her deeper in this dangerous familiarity with Gallienus and that they were alone in the room together.

Gallienus was watching her keenly, with a slight smile. "Wouldn't you say that all religions have an element of fraud in them, that they are a mixture, which varies from case to case, of fraud with inspiration?"

"It may be, Your Majesty," she murmured, after a pause. "I don't know."

"You'd agree, at least, that it's true of, say, the Christian religion?" he pursued. "Or haven't your studies gone far enough?"

He was smiling broadly now. Severina felt her cheeks go hot and could not meet his gaze. She struggled to master her agitation.

"What does Your Majesty mean?" she said in a voice that was not quite steady.

"Call me Gallienus," he said, a little impatiently. "Drop this Your Majesty nonsense. You're the only woman in Rome—or out of it— with whom I can really be myself. And you, Severina—own up, don't you feel at home with me?"

He seemed to be speaking in earnest. There was no doubt; despite her father's revelations about him—if, indeed, these were not the fantasies of unreasonable fear—there was a natural communion between Gallienus and herself. They shared interests; they understood each other readily; their minds met.

Something compelled her to revert to his previous topic. "What did Your— What did you mean . . . about the Christian religion?"

"Come, Severina, you mustn't keep up these little pretenses! It was I who told Aurelian—in private, of course—that you were seeing rather a lot of a certain Christian priest. He looked pretty grim about it, I don't mind telling you. Yes, it's my business to find out these things," he added calmly, answering the indignant comment of her look. "You'd be surprised how much I know about the personal lives of many Roman notables. But you've no need to worry. I've every reason to think warmly of this house!"

His eyes, suddenly wide and luminous, moved over her. She caught her breath. He stood up, stretching luxuriously. "By the way, Severina, I saw Aurelian the day he left."

He spoke so casually that eagerness on her part would have seemed out of place. "How was he?" she faltered. "How did he look?"

"Oh, well, very well," Gallienus answered. "These big, beefy men—they always look their best in uniform."

She could not take offense at these slighting words, for he gave her a smile full of his insidious charm. He came toward her slowly, with long, springy strides that made his progress a kind of deliberate demonstration. She stood up, wanting to back away, but unable to compel her legs.

"People like us should get to know each other better, Severina." Gallienus was looking down at her; his voice was smooth, his smile caressing. "We're both sensitive persons—and we're both lonely. I'm a man as well as an Emperor. To me all these fawning courtiers are not worth one true friend. And you, too, need someone. Your husband . . . Now wait, Severina," he reproved her, as she made a gesture and opened her mouth. "I'm a friend of his and I admire his talents as a soldier. But what is he, after all, but a Centurion of genius—oh, do be patient!" he added, with a little irritation, as Severina started at this remembered phrase.

"I'm his wife," she said. Under the ironic gaze of Gallienus the statement sounded intolerably priggish.

147

He grinned. "Of that I'm only too painfully aware. Still, here I am, Severina. And here you are. Aurelian's away—for a good long time. Why should you waste your youth regretting him? Life can still be full of delights for you!"

Her eyes, despite herself, went to the door. "It's all right," he said softly. "No one will come in. I told you I found your steward an understanding man." His right hand lightly slapped his belt where his purse had hung.

His nearness, the ardor in his voice, made her tense. Her limbs faintly tingled. The aura of his masculinity encompassed her—that predatory and shameless masculinity that can disarm even a self-possessed woman at the seducer's approach. Feverishly, her reason assailed her with warnings. This complex man was not swayed by straightforward, if illicit, desire. He wanted her so that he could make Aurelian a private laughingstock and, even more, to inflict the most wounding of insults on her father. He wanted her because he was, for the moment, bored with other women; because she was a reserved, intellectual girl and it would be interesting to see her succumb to passion; because he was so constituted that what he had seemed tame, but what belonged to another was irresistibly attractive.

All this she told herself, but that part of the mind which governs the actions was scarcely paying heed.

Obviously he knew his power and could calculate his effect on her. Still unhurried, he came closer and placed his right hand lightly on her shoulder. He must have felt her trembling. For a few moments, his hand stayed passive; she wanted to shrink away, but that hardly perceptible contact drained from her the strength to move. Then his fingers began to probe gently through the fine, woolen fabric of her dress, making long, fiery grooves in her flesh. He stooped and the warmth of his breath poured over her face.

As if in final, desperate protest, her reason invoked again the thought of her husband and her father. But even the figure of Aurelian, present so painfully in her heart, could not now interpose a veto; indeed, the hurt of his absence pleaded harshly for consolation. As for the possibility that this man before her, who could dispense death at his whim, was planning to destroy her own father, it simply gave his fascination for her an element of perversity and corruption that made it more poignantly demoralizing.

His left hand was now on her other shoulder. She leaned toward him. If only he had murmured some endearment, some tender word, however facile, she would have abandoned herself to those subduing hands. On the point of closing her eyes, she looked up at him, supplicating some sign of the tenderness for which she starved. His fine nostrils, with a cluster of clipped dark hairs in each, were dilating. A foolishly complacent smile hovered on his moist lips; his eyes were gloating.

She closed her eyes, not in surrender of her body to his, but to shut out his image and to think more clearly. To him, this was good sport, nothing more. Aurelian still on the march to the frontier and already his wife . . . ! What laughter there would be—and envious congratulations—when Gallienus bragged about it to his friends!

Severina had a spasm of icy self-disgust. Her shoulders jerked to detach his fingers and she squirmed away from him with such vigor that she almost overbalanced.

Even now, she could see, he was enjoying his fun untroubled, confident that he could at will reestablish his mastery over her. He raised his eyebrows and said with soft reproof, "Why, Severina!"

His look, his voice, were so coaxing that she had to beat down the impulse to smile at him reassuringly. He advanced toward her again; she stood hesitant, then backed away in an awkward, wavering motion that placed the couch between them. At first she could think of nothing to say across this barrier. Feeling the smart of her disappointed flesh and ashamed of it, she stood there, scarlet-cheeked, enduring the amusement in his eyes. Then, falteringly, she began, "Why do you behave—like this? You're not really—interested in me."

He shook his head slightly, as though in admiration. "A nymph disconcerted," he murmured. "What a delightful picture!"

The conceit jarred on her. Even at such a moment, artifice came slickly to his tongue. She wondered if he could ever be sincere. Struggling to find more adequate and persuasive words, she said, "Isn't it . . . unwise . . . to come and see me? People will think— They'll start talking. . . ."

He waited until her speech dried up under his quizzical gaze. But she had made her point and he answered without evasion. "I like people to talk," he said with a sharp grin. "It gives life a relish. Anyway, my dear, you have nothing to worry about. This is a secluded place. And your steward is discreet. Now come here, Severina!"

His change of tone from the wheedling to the masterful was another mistake. The command provoked defiance. "No!" she breathed. "No! Please go away, Gallienus!"

Abruptly, his grin vanished. His brows came together. For a moment he presented an unknown visage to her, hostile, angry, cruel. She was glad of it and felt no fear.

However, it was best to use diplomatic phrases. "I'm very tired," she said. "I've a bad headache. I—I'm feeling out of sorts today."

His expression changed. He gave an indulgent laugh. "Oh, it's like that, is it?" he said with a knowing look. "I've come at the wrong time. How unlucky!"

It took her a moment to grasp his meaning. She was about to answer tartly, "No, it isn't like that!" but thought it better to leave him to his conclusions.

"Well," he said with cheerful resignation. "I must call again—when you haven't got a—headache! Good-bye, dear Severina. I have greatly enjoyed our little conversation and look forward to renewing it under—shall I say?—happier auspices."

He raised one hand in graceful farewell and went to the door. There he turned with his charming smile and called, "Let's say—in a week from now?" He must have taken her assent for granted, for with another wave he walked out.

She dared not follow, whatever etiquette prescribed, but stood motionless, listening till the light noises of his movements died away. Once he had gone an enervating warmth went from the room. Still shaken, but much more in command of herself, she tried to think calmly. How quickly he had brought her to the verge of yielding! She would have ranked among his easiest conquests. No doubt the series of severe shocks she had undergone—over Matthaias, over the Deacon Paul, over Aurelian's departure, over her father's tormenting fears—and the lassitude of the mode of life

150

into which she had drifted had sapped her self-control and made her pliant to his arts.

This time she had evaded him—but he might return. At the thought, frightening yet not altogether unwelcome, the subtle, penetrating flavor of his personality, with its strong element of sensual attraction, began to steal on her again. She felt that if he swung now on his heel and reentered the room, her willpower would melt and he would swiftly reassert his domination over her.

There must not be a next time. It was not a question of fidelity to Aurelian—that aspect of the matter hardly troubled her. It was something more primitive, the instinct to flee from a situation she felt herself helpless to cope with, one in which she contended not merely against Gallienus but also against herself.

First, however, there was Porphyry. . . . She struck the gong such a vicious blow that the resonance traveled up her arm and the clamor swelled through the house. Porphyry came hurrying in, looking quite discomfited. She could imagine how his jaw must have dropped when Gallienus emerged so soon and, no doubt, signaled his frustration with an expressive gesture.

There was guilt in Porphyry's red cheeks and an almost pathetic dismay in his eyes. Severina guessed that he had been counting on a series of prolonged visits by Gallienus, all highly profitable to himself as watchdog for the Emperor's pleasures.

She fixed a steely gaze on him and with keen satisfaction saw him shrinking. "The next time the Emperor comes, you will tell him I am not at home!" she said. "But—" he began. "Don't answer!" she snapped. "Don't argue! Do as I tell you!"

He goggled at her fury. She waited some moments, till he had recovered a little. Then she went on in a peremptory tone: "I want a messenger to leave at once. He's to go first to Rome with a note for my father; then to push on to my uncle's villa at Baiae. As soon as you give him his instructions, start packing. I'm leaving for Baiae tomorrow or the next day, at latest—and for a long stay!"

Her uncle's house, in the midst of a scandal-loving resort, frequented by Roman society, would be a suitable refuge. Even Gallienus would not have the effrontery to lay public siege to her there.

Porphyry opened his mouth; then closed it. At last he said timidly, "How many of the servants are we taking, Lady?"

"We," she said brutally, "are not going. I'm leaving you behind. I shall take only Flavia and the new little girl, Plautilla. You will be in charge here. Keep only Prudentius and one of the kitchen girls. The others send back to my father."

He looked stricken to the point of tears. But remembering how close she had come to irreparable folly, she had no pity for him. "Remember, in future, that you are the steward of a little country villa, not an intriguer in high Court circles," she continued. "See that the house is kept in good order. I'm considering offering it for sale."

His consternation at being thus cast out from her favor touched her, but only fleetingly. The next instant, anger at his presumption and his venality, shame at her own weakness and, lingering still, the ache in her body of instincts roused and unappeased, combined to give malevolence to her voice as she dismissed him. "You can go now. The next time I find you taking bribes, no matter from whom, I shall turn you out of my service!"

Bowed, he walked slowly out. She watched him, thinking: Aurelian must never know anything of this. But, after all, what is there for him to know? Nothing—except that Gallienus put his hands on my shoulders.

With the thought, her shoulders seemed to burn where the hands of Gallienus had rested on them.

14

FOR Severina, who had led a sheltered life in the women's quarters of an old-fashioned Roman household and whose months of marriage had been spent as mistress of a secluded country villa, Baiae was an uncomfortably public place in which to live. Everyone pried into everyone else's business. Crinitus described it as a scandal emporium. "The Empire's tittle-tattle is our chief import," he declared with something of his old gusto, "and the main local industry is embroidering it!"

There was an intense social life among the circle of wealthy Senators, retired officials grown rich by corruption, financiers, war contractors, and the like, for whose self-indulgence the resort really existed. Every night somebody gave another luxurious entertainment.

Though the infirmities of Crinitus, Severina noticed, were gaining on him, his satyr's eyes still followed the lilting carriage of pretty young women. It was understood that he was in no state of health to attend banquets, but he had a stream of callers, some like himself veteran officers, with whom the staple of conversation seemed to be indecent jokes. Much guffawing and rib-poking would take place and there would be wary looks in Severina's direction, if she were anywhere in sight.

Crinitus had welcomed her with undisguised exultation. "So you came! You came!" he exclaimed, pressing her hands. Then he started bawling at the slaves—unnecessarily, since everything had been ready for her reception for at least twenty-four hours.

Naturally, by the evening all Baiae knew of her arrival; by the weekend all Baiae was pleasurably debating the import of such an uncle's doting affection for such a niece. Reports—authenticated by several credible witnesses—that Severina was an eccentric who every day spent whole hours reading were universally taken to confirm the worst suspicions.

Severina felt herself so little committed to Baiae as a home, so restless with longing for Aurelian, so worried over his safety and his health now, it was plain, the military situation was fast deteriorating, that she troubled very little about the delicious scandal to which she had innocently given rise. If she thought of the matter at all, it was with relief and some amusement that the gossips were unaware of a far choicer tidbit—one that would have set all Baiae breathlessly babbling—the episode between the Emperor and herself at her villa in the Alban Hills.

Of the brief infatuation that had made her then so susceptible

153

to his spell only the troubled memory remained. It had passed like a strange sickness, the recollection of which brings back a certain languor.

As for Gallienus, he appeared to have forgotten her existence. Perhaps that visit with Mena-Ra had been the result of a short-lived caprice; but in Severina's heart the conviction persisted that if she gave him fresh opportunity, he would renew his attentions. She did not stir from Baiae.

Once the excitement of her arrival had died down and she was accepted as a member of the household, Crinitus revealed an understanding and a tact of which she had hardly thought him capable. He never disguised his pleasure in her company and seemed twice as animated when she was with him. They dined together, abstemiously, for he was on a rigorous diet and her own appetite was poor. But he carefully restricted his demands on her and saw to it that she had long, regular spells of freedom. During these she generally read in the quiet of her room or sat in the portico overlooking the blue, sunlit bay, lost in her thoughts of Aurelian. She made it part of her routine to supervise the administration of her uncle's medicines, of which he had a variety, all—according to himself—revolting. While he grumbled blasphemously, her presence and her voice and her touch made him submissive in a way that never ceased to amaze his servants.

After some weeks, Crinitus even sent an invitation to her father, less from any spirit of goodwill than because he hoped that a visit from Severinus would help to allay her restlessness. To her surprise, her father accepted with alacrity. He came within the week, Drusilla with him, and he was almost cordial in his greeting to Crinitus.

The decline in her father's health and spirits, which had already made Severina anxious, had become more marked. All his life he had been fastidious about his appearance to the point of fussiness; now he seemed deserted even by the normal vanity that puts the elderly to pains to conceal the ravages of the years. His hair straggled; white stubble showed in the hollows of his cheeks. His expression was irritable. His step had lost its briskness. In company his conversation was guarded, but in private he talked freely and with

much bitterness, tending always to the one theme—not the gloomy
military situation, but the domestic war Gallienus was waging
against the Senate. Several Senators had been arrested—seized by
the Praetorians in the dead of night. A couple, brought to trial, had
been almost beggared by enormous fines; another had been summarily banished to Africa; and a fourth, faced with a charge of
treason, had committed suicide in prison. Everyone was worried
about what these victims of Gallienus might have said under interrogation. More arrests were expected daily.

Severinus himself had been deprived of a couple of minor but
honorific and lucrative posts and, to make the dismissal more gall-
ing, two utterly obscure officials, mere Palace clerks, had been appointed in his place. Only his family tie with Aurelian protected
Severinus now; and with a capricious ruler such as Gallienus,
whose impulses might take odd and violent forms, one could not
depend too confidently on the protection afforded by the prestige of
an eminent but absent son-in-law.

The unhappiness of Severinus was reflected in Drusilla. Her hair,
still intricately set in architectural piles, appeared grotesquely frivolous above her troubled face, whose raddled cheeks had lost some of
their firm amplitude. She no longer had that relaxed and comfortable look indicative of a placid nature and tranquil mind. The
loud voice and fruity laughter of Crinitus seemed to make her
nervous and the glances she turned on Severina had a timid appeal,
as if their former roles were reversed and she now were the child
seeking to be reassured.

After a while, Severina said, "Come on, Mother. Let me show
you my room." Drusilla eagerly rose and, taking her arm, Severina
led her out.

The wide window of Severina's room, which was secluded in an
annex on the garden side of the house, gave on a grove of stately
trees in their full pomp of foliage; their lofty, trembling screen
reduced the sun's glare to fitful bursts of gold and cast a grateful
coolness. Drusilla sat down with a sigh of satisfaction, fanning her
glistening face with her hand. "Now this is what I call a charming
room," she said. "That bedroom in your little villa was like a cubicle
in a barracks." Her glance traveled with approval over the hand-

some bed, snowy-white between its polished walnut endpieces, the low, luxurious couches with thick gold and royal-blue thread picking out a sumptuous design on their coverings, the walls whose fresh colors depicted a somewhat languid Diana pursuing through dappled glades a deer too graceful to be genuinely in flight. Severina smiled. The annex had been built by an amorous banker for a Lydian courtesan. "Tell me, dear," went on Drusilla, her gaze now directed at Severina's robe where it covered her abdomen, "is anything happening?"

Severina felt herself go red. "No, Mother," she answered quietly. "I'm afraid nothing is happening."

Drusilla looked disappointed. "Hasn't Aurelian?" She broke off, leaving the question to complete itself.

The topic was painful to Severina. She could not bear her stepmother's clumsy fingers probing at the complex and equivocal relationship—intimacy coexisting with reserve—between Aurelian and herself. Rather brusquely, she replied, "Aurelian's done his duty. In time, Mother—in time!" Seeing Drusilla's pained expression, she made her tone more gentle and said, "Tell me about that visit to your aunt. Father confided to me how you were helping him."

"It wasn't much of a success," answered Drusilla wryly. "Word had got around—I don't know how—that your father was in disfavor and people were unwilling to discuss business. My aunt's an old dear who lives in the past and still thinks of me as a young girl —she was very sweet. But her sons seemed nervous about my being in the house." She looked at Severina dolefully. "Do you know, Severina—I got the feeling I was being followed! Anyway, I tried to be very careful. I made contact with two agents, but I wouldn't be surprised if that dreadful Gallienus knew about it all the time. Your father was very upset when I got back to Rome."

Suddenly, her eyes filled. Two tears hung at the corners of her lids; first one, then the other splashed over and soon she was weeping noisily.

Severina came over and sat beside her, pressing her hand. "Don't, Mother, don't!" she whispered, her own eyes smarting. She could not recollect ever having seen Drusilla cry thus before. In her heart there was a surge of hatred against Gallienus, although she still could not reconcile the dandified philanderer she knew with this crafty and sinister tyrant whose terror pervaded the Senatorial class.

Drusilla gulped and with the forefinger of her free hand flicked alternately at either wet cheek. "I'm so worried about your father," she stammered. "He's a sick man—he's gone right off his food."

She fixed her imploring eyes on Severina, who again recognized with a pang that the burden of giving comfort and courage was now laid on her. Strange what a difference her few months of marriage had made. Though Aurelian was far away and she herself felt weak and spiritless without him, they all turned to her for support—Crinitus, her father, even the once strong and equable Drusilla.

Facile words came and she uttered them with a bright conviction of manner. "Don't worry so, Mother darling. Father's given no offense—and he's very well connected. Gallienus wouldn't be fool enough to make enemies of Aurelian and his friends."

"You really think so?" cried Drusilla, willing to be reassured. "That's what I keep on telling your father!" Severina did not withdraw her hand and the two women sat quietly together for a while, a little comforted.

They were startled by a quick tapping on the door; it opened and Severinus came in. Taking one of the carved chairs, he addressed Severina. "Your uncle has had a couple of unexpected visitors— old Army officers, by the look of them. They seemed highly agitated. Whatever they wanted to say, they wouldn't say it in front of me; they glared at me so fiercely that I took the hint and excused myself. Severina," he added, pettishly, "whoever was responsible for this ghastly room? Couldn't you have thrown the furniture out and had the walls redecorated?"

"It was like this when Uncle bought the villa," explained Severina mildly. "I just don't feel like bothering about such things any more."

Her father shrugged and they began to talk desultorily about the weather and the lamentable state of the roads. The topic of roads led back to Rome, where social life was drooping under the invisible influence of an army of informers. People more and more shunned conspicuous gatherings; they tended to visit and entertain only intimate friends. Even these could not always be trusted. More than once, so rumor said, giving names and places, some guest to whom an unwary host had freely unburdened himself had sought to curry favor at the Palace by passing on a damning version of these confidences. People watched their words and were particularly guarded in front of servants. An evil exhalation had spread through the city, seeping into every aristocratic home. Gloomy old men, enjoying the novel attention they now commanded, were recalling the terrible years of the Thracian peasant-Emperor, Maximin, whose natural bloodthirstiness allied with the rancor of a low-born usurper against the Senatorial nobility had taken a terrible toll of lives.

Severina caught the approaching tread of Crinitus, heavy and halting with his bulk and his infirmity. She looked toward the door; observing her, the others followed suit, falling silent. The door slowly opened; Crinitus stood in the doorway, gray-faced, his shoulders hunched. He tried to speak, gulped and gestured awkwardly with his right hand. Severina, horrified lest he was going to have a fit, jumped up, but before she could reach him his voice emerged, hoarsely, in jerky phrases.

"A disaster—that fool, Valerian!"

She grasped his arm and he followed her, stumbling, to a couch. There was a choked silence, while they all stared at him. Severinus broke it. His face was pinched and bloodless. "The Army—and the Emperor?" he stammered. "The Emperor—what has become of him?"

An unnerving yelp, as from an animal convulsed with rage and pain, escaped Crinitus. He made an abrupt outward motion with his arms, indicative of dissolution. "Capitulated—six Legions! Our best! Valerian is a prisoner."

Severinus bowed his head. "So Gallienus is sole Emperor!" he said huskily.

"Uncle!" Severina implored, clasping her hands. "Aurelian—what is going to happen?"

Crinitus looked at her drearily. "There's nothing to stop the Persians now," he answered in a voice that was still harsh and unfamiliar, but again under control. "Sapor can ride down to the Mediterranean if he likes. But Aurelian's in the Balkans, on the

Danube—he's not involved—so far." Then he turned to Severinus, as the only other present who could understand the enormity of the blow. "He threw the Army away! He walked into a trap—the fool, the damned fool!"

"How do you know this? Are you sure? Is the news official?" demanded Severinus with the asperity of shattered nerves.

Crinitus made an angry gesture. "D'you think I'm joking?" he growled. "Rufus Celer—he was a Tribune with me in the Eighth—lives here in Baiae. His son's a Guard Commander at the Palace and he sent word today. It's all over Headquarters, he says. Rufus came right away with his brother. Well," added Crinitus, glaring at Severinus, "satisfied?"

"Uncle! Father!" entreated Severina, realizing that the two dismayed men, whose mutual antagonism was always close to the surface, would be glad to vent their emotion on each other in a furious quarrel.

The scowl slowly ebbed from Crinitus' face and he went on less aggressively, "When they brought Gallienus word of the disaster, he took it very coolly. He just said, 'So my father's a prisoner—well, Rome has one fool less and Persia one fool more!' That's what they're saying at the Palace!"

It was hearsay, of course—and quite probably invented by some enemy of Gallienus. Yet Severina had to admit that it was just the kind of slick, showy, heartless levity of which he was capable.

Her father snorted, "The actor! But all this will shake the dynasty, won't it? The soldiers would be ashamed to follow Gallienus now!" Hope illuminated his haggard face.

"No such luck," said Crinitus. "Gallienus is a monster, but he's got his wits about him. He's giving the troops a donative—both the Praetorians and those he's massing up north against Gaul. Yes, he knows how to look after himself. All reinforcements for Asia have been stopped. The East can go hang, but he'll fight for the West. Above all, you can trust him not to relax his grip on Italy!"

"A donative!" repeated Severinus sourly. "I wonder whose estates will pay for that!"

Severina went to the window. Sun gold was exploding here and there as the sea breeze probed among the foliage. Dread gripped

159

her in a spell. Where was Aurelian? A picture, ghostly at first but becoming more vivid, seemed to flow over the familiar garden, reducing it to a faintly apprehended background. Before her tranced eyes swarms of mailed Persian cavalry were pouring westwards, in their midst the towering palanquin of the Great King Sapor, surrounded by the arrogant black-bearded nobles of his bodyguard in glittering panoplies. Their hooves rang on vast plains from which the people had fled; towns and villages blazed in their wake. Wider and wider they spread, long tongues of them curling ahead of the main body. Now Severina perceived a tall, lonely figure in Roman armor on the banks of a great river whose choppy waters were cold silver in the slanting rays of a pale northern sun. He was straining his eyes toward the dim contours of the farther shore, unsuspecting that behind him was a swift, inexorable swirl of Persian horsemen threatening to cut him off from her. "Aurelian!" she struggled to scream in warning, but only a light moan came.

Sirmium, she thought in panic—where is Sirmium? If she saw a map of Pannonia and Moesia, the northern provinces of the Balkans, she could guess which river was the Danube. But she would not know exactly where to look for Sirmium, nor the river on which it stood, some tributary—she believed—of the Danube. It was shameful. Far away her husband was fighting for his life and she had only the vaguest notion where the town lay that he hoped to make his headquarters. In that anguished moment, deep below her conscious understanding a daring resolve began to articulate itself, but she was aware only of the fearful question: shall I ever see Aurelian again?

Three days later Severinus left for Rome with Drusilla. He was obviously reluctant to go, yet on the morning of their departure he fretted till the litters were brought round and chided the bearers for delay. He said farewell to Severina with a mournful air. As she made him comfortable in the litter, he looked an old man, ailing and dispirited. Drusilla, on the other hand, had recovered some of her former cheerfulness during the visit. While she was at Baiae, Rome and the menace it held seemed far away. The catastrophe in Asia was beyond her powers of imagination; in spite of her husband's nervous depression and the blasphemous gloom of Crinitus, it appeared to her something too remote to impinge on their lives in Italy.

There were many like Drusilla; many for whom the crisis was still too distant to have much meaning. Life went on pretty normally at Baiae and for the majority, Severina had no doubt, in Rome itself, although fighting now raged over immense areas and barbarians were pillaging within the frontiers less than a month's march away.

No word came from Aurelian. At first, in spite of her impatience to hear from him, she had not worried deeply. On his hurried march to the war zone, he might have had little opportunity to write and, once arrived, he might find himself involved in military operations. But the continuing absence of letters was ominous. It could only signify a widespread collapse in the Balkans, with the posts disrupted. She knew at least that Aurelian was alive and in health, for—urged by her—Crinitus made inquiries at Rome and learned that he was in active command of the Sirmium region. But Crinitus had been able to discover little more. It gave Severina a measure of the Empire's disintegration that even at the Palace nobody seemed clear about the situation on the Lower Danube.

Such news as reached Baiae from the war zones was uniformly bad. By watching Crinitus, whose circle of embittered ex-officer cronies picked up a good deal of information and had the experience to assess it shrewdly, Severina could judge how calamities without pause were assailing the Empire. Though he had once insisted, airily, that he did not care about the fate of Rome, contrasting himself in this respect with the earnest and fully committed Illyrians, it was obvious how hard he was taking the reports. Anxiety and exasperation wore away his flesh faster than his diet had done; his loose wrinkled skin and angry eyes gave him a ravaged and aggressive look. His tongue was biting. His discussions of the war situation with his friends tended to develop into loud altercations. The servants went in fear of his temper.

As his stomach gave him increasing pain, his doctors ordered him to cut out wine altogether. He obeyed, but with grumbling that would have seemed peevish in a personality less overbearing with a voice less masterful. Only in Severina's presence did he recover a little of his old, good humor. She saw how he suffered and was patient with him. He needed her affection and she gave it in generous measure.

At last a letter came from Aurelian, a short one whose terse phrases implied that others had preceded it. Fighting had been continuous, but he was now establishing headquarters at Sirmium. The letter closed with a brief sentence that moved her deeply: "I think of you often." There was something brutal about the firm, inelegant strokes of his writing, the hand of a peasant who had learned the alphabet after growing up.

She read the dozen lines again and again, feeling a traitress, hating herself for living in luxury, sleeping in a comfortable bed, while hundreds of miles away Aurelian was marching and fighting in a province given over to incessant war. She seized her pen and eagerly wrote her answer. She was ready to come to him—let him send her word, she begged. Then she added a budget of news about herself, her parents, and Crinitus, not too long, lest it bore Aurelian, and not too melancholy, lest it depress him. She restrained herself from urging him not to run into danger and with deliberate moderation signed herself, "Your affectionate wife."

By now the war had begun to affect them in Baiae—in the form of soaring prices. The currency was steadily losing value. Food, even the simple provisions of the poor, was becoming very dear and knots of hungry people gathered, murmuring, at street corners. But their murmuring was ignored and their discontent never found more dangerous expression. The lower classes in Italy had lost the instinct for rebellion; they accepted it as part of nature that they should starve in rags while a wealthy few flaunted a gross excess. Still there was a vague menace in the air; violence did not seem so very far away.

One day a rumor brought shaken crowds into the streets. An immense host of Alemanni, from their forest settlements between the Rhine and the Danube, were said to be pouring into Italy. The Emperor Gallienus was marching to meet them on the River Po where he had, not so long ago, crushed a similar invasion. A week of acute suspense followed. Then it became apparent that the alarm was false—but not before it had destroyed the last illusion of security.

The excitement passed—for Baiae. Elsewhere, alarms did not prove false, nor did rumor exaggerate the approach of danger. Blow on overwhelming blow crashed down. Before men's eyes the huge, majestic structure of the Empire split wide open and lurched over in ruin. Every enemy of Rome set himself in motion against her; every frontier was breached; every horror—invasion, defeat, devastation, civil war, famine, pestilence—afflicted her helpless population.

The military system, already in decay, broke under the endless battering, the intolerable strain of savage and simultaneous war in a dozen theaters. In the general breakdown anything like a centralized direction of defense had become impossible. Whole provinces were overrun by the enemy or seceded from their allegiance to Gallienus, setting up local Caesars to rescue them from barbarian inroads and weltering anarchy.

At Baiae a gray apathy settled on people, an acquiescence in disaster—as long as it struck somewhere else. The fall of a populous city, the looting of famous shrines, massacres, conflagrations, no longer registered on the consciousness as things exceptional and tragic. One was simply relieved, in a dull, primitive way, at not being involved oneself.

Meanwhile summer's torrid climax was over and its splendor waned. Autumn painted the leaves and loosened them and set them drifting across the garden before freshening winds. As the season wore slowly on, the coolness grew sharper and the nights were chill. But winter arrived in clement mood, dispensing on most days a few hours of tempered sunshine; though there were several storms, with downpours lashing the deserted streets and an endless succession of white-topped waves pounding the shore.

Severina rarely stirred from the house, not to avoid the weather but because of her mood of feverish uncertainty. Aurelian's letter might come any moment; it might come after days, or weeks or even months; it might never come. She lived poised between expectancy and despair.

Still she wrote every week to Aurelian and automatically went about her domestic routine. Outwardly calm, she nursed and soothed her uncle, whose medicines seemed at last to be checking the progress of his malady, and listened half-absently to his grumbles, but with sharp concern whenever he retailed the latest news, meager though it was and largely meaningless to her, from the Danube war zone.

Time dragged on and on. But the only letters which arrived were the regular messages from her father, their fretful tone contrasting with the cold, impeccable Latin in which they were couched. One day she yielded to the urging of Crinitus and, escorted by his steward, walked to the Forum to look at the shops. There were few people about in the gusty streets and dispirited shopkeepers stood at their doors, shrilly soliciting any prosperously dressed passerby. Their wares were fantastically expensive. Severina made a few small purchases. She was examining a warm woolen cloak, asking herself if its dark-gray shade would please Aurelian, when her heart began to beat violently and she felt herself tremble. What am I doing here? she thought, in panic. The letter may come. She spun round, then—recollecting herself—thrust her purse into the steward's hands and said, "Here, buy it." At her words, she was aware of the dismay on the shopkeeper's face changing to delight. With a gesture of farewell to him, she rushed out.

She hurried homeward almost at a trot, ignoring the startled looks of other pedestrians. In the courtyard, she nearly collided with Crinitus; he had been awaiting her and came stumping out at her approach. He waved a letter. "From Aurelian!" he announced, beaming. She felt the texture of coarse parchment in her hand and, closing her eyes, leaned against him.

After a moment she looked up at him, but her vision was blurred. "Excuse me, Uncle," she managed to say and, on legs suddenly shaky, made her way to her bedroom. Without haste, enjoying the exquisite pleasure of anticipation, she opened the letter.

It proved, to her bitter disappointment, brief. Aurelian acknowledged several of her letters, which had arrived together, although there were gaps in the sequence. He hoped she and her kinsfolk were well. He himself was in good health. Now that winter was closing in—the phrase was a measure of how long the letter had been on its travels—fighting was dying down. On her request to join him, he made a terse but sufficient comment. Conditions were too bad for a winter journey; in spring the roads would be unsafe for a woman.

Still holding the letter, she went out to the portico and seated herself on the bench out of the wind, though the pale sunshine reached in to her knees. She looked over the bay, where a few squat fishing boats rocked on the furrowed water. From the house came the deep voice of an overseer calling—and then the lighter voices of women slaves answering. There was a whirr as somebody frightened the pigeons who came daily to the kitchen for stale bread.

She sat musing, conscious of a faint, obscure excitement, as though there were a little stir, still not clearly perceived, in the depths of her mind. Revived by the letter, the pain of Aurelian's absence pierced her through. How strange, she thought, that she should love someone like Aurelian—a man without tenderness, harsh and overbearing, his great intelligence concentrated on interests alien to her. Yet love him she did, in her own fashion, deeply, without illusion, with compassion, with an aching need for his presence, for the sound of his voice.

His presence, his voice—from hidden layers of her mind a decision came surging up. Instantly, with overwhelming conviction, she knew she must obey this inner command. She would go to join Aurelian! Whether he gave permission or not, she would go to join him!

For a little while she was filled with elation, but then her mood began to change. Others now were silently urging their claims on her, their powerful claims, against those of Aurelian. Her uncle was virtually an invalid. True, in the past two or three weeks he had been a trifle better, but this improvement might well be only temporary. She was the slave to his pain, the solace of his embittered retirement when, an impotent onlooker, he saw the Empire he had served go down in ruin. Her father was a sick, fearful man, querulous and fast aging. She knew what relief he found in unburdening himself to her. In this time of sharpening stress, Drusilla would be increasingly inadequate to his need. Only his daughter was sufficiently close to him in mind to understand his self-torments and, in part, to alleviate them.

There was no doubt that Aurelian's need for her was less, far less, than theirs. Still, she had to obey the imperative of her nature. Perhaps she would never set eyes on them again . . . a dreadful pang assailed her at the thought. Well, she would accept the risk. If it must be so, let them die, alone, uncomforted. This was war. Many had died already; many more would die. Her father and Crinitus could not be exempt. They had had their lives, years of happiness, of success, years of fulfillment. Now she must make her choice between them and her husband—and there was no choice to make. She would let her father die and Crinitus, too, rather than forfeit her chance of being again with Aurelian. He supremely mattered. They—they would have to be sacrificed.

But though there was no doubt in her mind and she was not tortured by indecision, there was deep grief in her heart. She stood up, her eyes following the triangular red sail of a fishing craft, dipping and thrusting up with the boat's uneven motion. With her father and Crinitus something in herself would die. That she knew, but it did not shake her bitter resolution.

She went into the house and confronted Crinitus. He eyed her as though something in her expression disturbed him. Severina came directly to the point. "Uncle, I want your help. I'm going to Aurelian!"

His head jerked back, as from a blow; his brows came sharply together. For long moments of silence, his scared eyes measured her will. "Oh, no, Severina!" he said at last, breathing heavily. "The Balkans are infested. It might be a year before the roads are clear—even more!" He spoke with the vehemence of his dismay, but with a curious lack of conviction, as if he sensed that his words would be unavailing.

Beyond her ache for his distress, she felt the Olympian calm of one who has taken an irrevocable decision. "You told me yourself that I must stand at his side," she answered quietly.

He winced. "I'm a selfish old man, Severina, I know. Stay with me a little longer—a few months more. I need you, my dear. The house"—he motioned at the walls—"wouldn't seem the same without you." His hands, when their gesture was over, were trembling.

Her eyes filled, but she did not waver. Her resolution was adamant—and he knew it. Crinitus' own exhortation to her at the Alban villa gave the answer to his present despairing plea. She must stand at Aurelian's side—above all, now, in this time of disaster.

"I didn't marry Aurelian to live in safety and comfort where I don't even know from day to day whether he's still alive. I couldn't bear it any longer. You were right, Uncle—my place is with him. And you must help me. You must show me the way."

"When do you want to start? Can't you stay a few weeks longer?"

"As soon as possible," she said, answering both questions with the phrase and noting with satisfaction that he had already acquiesced. "I shall go to Rome tomorrow to get some things for the journey."

"But how are you to travel? What about the route?"

"That," she said smiling, "I'm leaving to you, Uncle."

His eyes, though sad, were no longer reproachful. "You're a brave girl, Severina," he said heavily. "A Roman of the old breed!"

Severina shook her head. Brave? An antique Roman? These were the high-flown words you could expect of a man. A woman would have understood instantly. Her courage—if you could call it such—came from her complete selfishness. Her decision had no large ends in view. No, all she wanted was to be with her husband, who was out there battling with the tempest.

Crinitus sat down, brooding. When he spoke, it was evident he had espoused her cause without reservation. "Well, since go you must, travel light—and travel fast. You're right about starting early. You don't want to be on the Balkan roads too late in the spring. Better weather is going to bring the raiders out."

His brow wrinkled. "Your route—here, I'll write it down." He went to a shelf and came back with stylus and wax tablet. He began to write, frowning and muttering place-names. As the stylus scratched away, he spoke at intervals to Severina in abrupt phrases. "Take a small party. Escort? . . . Six. Rugged fellows, used to discipline. Ex-soldiers under a first-class man who can drive them anywhere. A litter . . . not a horse-litter, you'll be going through the mountains. Don't be silly, my dear!" he reproved Severina at her gesture of protest. "You can't march or ride a mule all that way. Face it—you're just not hardened. It would kill you! Now a litter means four bearers plus two replacements—trained, absolutely hand-picked slaves. I must see to it myself—you can't afford trouble. You'll also need two mules . . . the escort will look after them. Army men are used to mules.

"There—your route," he added, throwing down the stylus. He began to read a succession of names but, pausing to observe her reactions, noted her blank expression and burst into one of his old guffaws. "Of course. I forgot. It doesn't mean anything to you. Well, Severina, this is what it comes to. You'll cross the Adriatic, instead of going round the north of Italy; then through the Dalmatian Mountains. It will be very rough going, but reasonably safe. Then the foothills bordering the Pannonian plain. You might run into raiders there, but they're likely to be small, isolated bands, not an army. If you do, just scuttle. Don't stop even to reconnoiter. Once barbarians are reported in the neighborhood, make yourself scarce. When you reach the plains, you're right in the war zone—never forget that for an instant! Go like the wind. Your men's legs will be dropping off and every bone in your own body will be aching. But keep moving, keep moving until you're inside the strong walls of a Roman town. On no account pass the night in a village. Better get off the road and bivouac in a wood. And don't light fires where they can be seen."

She was staring at him, astonished by such precautions. "Understand this, Severina," he said, very soberly. "You mustn't fall into their hands. The men they'd butcher, but you—I'm talking frankly, so that you should know what they're capable of. They're brutes, murderous brutes. They'll rape a woman, a dozen, twenty of them —and then cut her throat for the fun of it!"

She stood silent, white-faced and shuddering. It had never occurred to her that she might fall living into the hands of savages.

"That's the kind of thing a woman's up against in wartime. Of course, you can still change your mind, Severina," he suggested sardonically. At that she came out of her stupor and shook her head, whispering, "Oh, no, Uncle!"

"While we're on the subject," resumed Crinitus, "don't attach

168

yourself to any stray Roman soldiers, either! They're not always to be trusted. Only if they're a sizeable force, properly officered—bear that in mind!"

She sat down. It was harder to absorb these shocking revelations standing.

"Now, your personal requirements," he pursued briskly. "Take essentials only; as few clothes as possible, but hard-wearing. I'll send your wardrobe on later, if I can. A small medical kit. And a maid. Not one of those flighty bits here, made out of porcelain. A tough, capable girl, a village wench, you know, who'll be willing to oblige the men of your bodyguard. That will make them less likely to go wandering off. I'll get my agent looking . . ."

"And the slaves," interrupted Severina tartly. "Is she to oblige them, too?"

"Slaves arrange these things among themselves," he answered indifferently. "Come to think of it, I know just the man to put in charge. What the devil's his name?—He's a Berber, an old Centurion of the Eighth—that was a Legion! Hanno? . . . Hann . . . Hannibal, that's it! A real old sweat. Must have done ten, twelve years in the Balkans . . . He'll know the route pretty well—and he'll get you to Sirmium, if anyone else can! Look here, Severina. I'll come with you to Rome tomorrow and hunt him out."

"But, Uncle, that's not necessary. You'll make yourself ill again!"

He grimaced. "Now don't you bully me, Severina. Once you're off to the Balkans, who knows when I'll see you again? I'm coming with you to Rome tomorrow—if I didn't have this accursed stomach, I'd come with you all the way to Sirmium!"

15

ALL the morning and well into the afternoon they had been traveling through a somber Balkan landscape, not yet softened by the early spring, along a path that wound slowly upward. Fatigued by the endless vista of shaggy woods that clung to the slopes and seemed to exhale the winter's dampness, Severina secured the litter curtains which had been flapping noisily in the breeze. She closed her eyes and abandoned herself to the lulling influence of the litter's smoothly rhythmic motion. No matter how rough or slippery the going, those silent, unsmiling bearers, on whose padded shoulders she rode, paced on steadily, without a stumble.

Soon it would be time for a halt (only a brief one, for they must reach the day's destination, a little mountain village, before nightfall) and the two expressionless slaves now trudging with the mules would relieve a couple of men at the litter. It had been quite a time before Severina could readily distinguish between the bearers, they so resembled each other, built like oxen and, like oxen, impassive and dumb. Crinitus had paid a handsome price for the sextet; he had insisted on thoroughly trained bearers, accustomed to work as a team, docile, tireless, and strong.

Drowsily she listened for the noises of the little convoy's progress, the slap and drag of sandals on the moist earth, a mule's occasional slither and the cries it evoked from the men, the laconic exchanges (for idle chatter was forbidden on the march) between the half-dozen members of the escort and—most frequently—the coarse, rasping speech of Hannibal, their commander, and his jeering laughter. Hannibal laughed a great deal, but there was nothing lighthearted about the almost military discipline he maintained.

He was a jovial, beak-nosed African, with pitted, leathery skin and a short, intensely black beard; of middle height, thickset, muscular, and restlessly energetic. His humor was of the aggressive kind and his speech pungent with an old soldier's blasphemies delivered in a rich, guttural Punic accent that suggested a special relish in abuse. Crinitus had dug him up from a Roman slum, where he helped to run a disreputable tavern, the haunt of thieves and pimps and rowdies, enjoying there a fearsome reputation for his summary way with drunken brawlers. He boasted of having once broken a leading gladiator's arm.

But he had his domestic troubles. His wife, an angular, careworn, shrewish woman, had brought him the inn as dowry. Though ruthless and hardheaded in business matters, she had all the infatuated woman's capacity for self-deception and had persuaded herself that it was her charms, not her property, which made Hannibal so ardent (if rough-spoken) a wooer. She had expected him to be faithful. He had not troubled even to be discreet. Within a week of their marriage he had deceived her—if a term suggestive of forethought and design could be applied to so casual, instinctive, and virtually public an operation—with one of the tavern's serving wenches.

He went on giving similar cause for complaint. His wife's voice, whining and accusing, pursued him all day long and he had to deny himself the relief of thrashing her, since this only made her recriminations more shrill and tearful.

Above all, a man of his masterful disposition, accustomed to bossing and bullying scores of soldiers, found inadequate scope in assisting a woman to conduct a tavern, even in a notoriously tough quarter of Rome. When Crinitus offered him, at a generous rate of pay, command of Severina's little expedition, he had first, out of habit, made a show of hesitation in order to force the price up, but had then accepted gladly. On his separation from his wife he had made the heartfelt comment, "That bitch won't be able to nag me when I'm in the Balkans!"

At first, he had repelled Severina. His breath smelled of garlic and on the march the acid odor of sweat from him was sharper than from any of the others. He refused to let any of the men approach her and discouraged her from speaking to them. "Your uncle's orders," he explained, adding with a brutal smile, "They wouldn't understand—they're scum, Lady!"

Once she had seen a member of the escort, a lean man, with a wizened face and sour expression, thrust under Hannibal's nose a platter of beans, complaining of their quality. Hannibal knocked him down, sending the beans flying. As, groaning, the man slowly lifted himself, Hannibal addressed a stream of obscenities at him and lifted a rocky fist again. Severina called out fiercely and he checked himself, turned round and went up to her. "Don't look, if you don't like seeing blood," he said, quite solicitously, "but it's the only way with these dogs!"

As time passed, however, and they maintained a remarkable rate of progress across the Apennines towards the Adriatic, she began to appreciate that there was value in his ruthlessness and to respect her uncle's judgment in placing him in charge of the convoy. He stood no nonsense from men or mules; but while he drove them, he saw efficiently to their needs. Men and mules responded by marching well and staying healthy. He saw to it, too, that they got good service, promptly, at the inns—and at a reasonable price. Himself a landlord, he was alert to all the wiles and dodges of other innkeepers. Two or three times there were altercations over the reckoning, which ended abruptly in Hannibal's favor when his grin changed into a scowl.

Still Severina was obliged to accept a life of virtual isolation. She seldom spoke to any member of their party other than Hannibal and her maid, Antonia.

When they had set out from the little village north of Rome where the convoy had assembled, Severina had felt conscience-stricken and weighted down by grief. The farewells had been so final; they were like dismissals clean out of her life. Crinitus, overcome by his exertions on her behalf, had suffered a relapse and had been ordered to bed without delay by his doctor. He could not come to see her off. She was obliged to say good-bye to him in Rome, where he lay obviously in pain, though to spare her further distress he restrained his habitual grumbling. The parting was tearful on her side; subdued on his, as if he could not trust himself to say much. "Thank you, Uncle dear, for everything—oh, Uncle!" she sobbed, bending over his hand. She felt his other hand, unwontedly gentle, on her hair and heard his murmur, "Take care—and come back, Severina!"

At the door she turned. Her last sight of him, through a blur, was of a bulk leaning from the bed with a white smudge moving slowly to and fro, his hand painfully waving.

Even sharper was the pang she endured at her last meeting with her father. To her astonishment he had readily approved her plan of joining Aurelian; obsessed with the danger from Gallienus, he judged it wise for her to remove herself far from Rome and, unlike Crinitus, he had no vivid personal experience of a theater of war to appreciate the terrible risks she would be braving. Nevertheless his face, in which the bones were always prominent, looked gaunt and his eyes were sorrowful as he made his brief, consciously stoical farewell. Severina had a moment of bitter clarity as she looked at this cold, clever, limited man, disappointed in his worldly ambition and without the capacity to love generously which redeemed more vulgar and foolish men. Pity wrung her heart, but she could not feel for him the warm, compulsive affection of a daughter. Part of her searing emotion was shame—and guilt. She had a presentiment that she would never see him again and, in a confused way, felt that she was pronouncing sentence of death on her own father.

It was easier to bid Drusilla good-bye; the tears came more readily and they expressed a purer, less complex emotion, though one far less intense. Drusilla herself wept without restraint and, with a gesture that recalled the distant, secure, and happy days of childhood, took Severina's head to her breast. It was she alone who came to see the convoy start, though on this occasion she sat decorously in her ornate litter, mindful of a Roman matron's dignity in public.

For the first few miles of their journey, Severina preferred to stay hidden behind the curtains of her litter. Gradually, however, her heart grew less heavy and she began to feel curious about the world flowing past. Leaning out, she beckoned; Hannibal and Antonia came hurrying up. "I want to walk," she said to Hannibal. He looked startled, but promptly gave an order and the litter sank gently to the ground.

She stepped out onto a country road sunken between steep banks. Now that she was on foot, Severina was surprised at their pace; it was the legionaries' marching rate. A brown, bare field was visible to one side and, beyond it, a vineyard, above which rose the gable end of a cottage roof. The day glittered. The air was cool and invigorating; convoys of white clouds sailed with steady motion across the sky's washed blue.

Ahead strode three men of the bodyguard, stalwart fellows all; the slaves trudged in rhythmic unison, shouldering the empty litter. Behind her were Hannibal, fingering his black beard as he watched her, and Antonia. The mules, the relief bearers and the remaining three members of the escort, who brought up the rear, were out of sight round a bend in the road.

It was a better introduction to the rigors of wartime travel than Severina had expected. She had an urge to talk—but not to Hannibal, from whom she still felt a strong revulsion. "Antonia, come and walk with me," she invited.

A week before, Crinitus had sent for Severina. "Here's your maid," he announced, jerking a thumb over his shoulder. "She's never been in a town before, so you'll find her a bit shy. Comes from the hills somewhere, a genuine creature of the wilds. Name's Antonia. Strong as a horse, but ignorant of everything except the facts of life."

"Welcome, Antonia," Severina said with a reassuring smile. "How old are you? Have you any brothers and sisters?" The girl, short and thickset, with a strong, swarthy, intelligent face, broadnosed and full-lipped, weighed Severina's words, as if she had difficulty in following. Then she answered, in a not unmusical voice, in a kind of decomposing, liquid Latin which Severina, in her turn, found hard to understand.

In the course of time, Severina grew accustomed to Antonia's odd dialect and pieced together her simple history. Her father, a colonus or half-serf tenant of some absentee landlord, had a small hill farm, rough grazing mostly. It lay in the former Samnite country, which had been depopulated in the civil wars of the declining Republic and partially revived later by the establishment of latifundia, giant ranches or plantations worked by gangs of slaves swept in by war and piracy from all the corners of the Mediterranean. Where the sturdy Samnite yeomen and shepherds had once dwelt, there emerged a new race, servile in origin, tough and enduring, because their pitiless exploitation killed off all but the tough and enduring. Gradually their condition and their status improved. Antonia's father, part Syrian, part Greek, part Punic and part Gaul—and now wholly Italian—was the legally free occupant of his primitive farm, where amid his animals and in much the same natural state his children grew up.

When Crinitus' agent had explained his mission, Antonia's father had sent for his five daughters, the least valued part of his eleven children. Their ages were from twelve to seventeen and only one was born in what approximated wedlock; three mothers, all living, were responsible for them. Antonia's father made a gesture, as though to say: help yourself—and the agent, running his eye over the sturdy, unkempt, brown-skinned girls giggling and shuffling before him, took the easiest course and chose the eldest.

Antonia's finest features were her jet-black eyes, which were seductive without coquetry. Her teeth were large, white, and flawless. She had never been seriously ill; could do a man's work without the expectation of a man's wages—or, indeed, of any wages at all. As soon as she was of an age to lose her virginity, she had lost it. She coupled with men with the same simplicity as she ate. She could handle a mule expertly, could cook the kind of camp fare on which they had to subsist when no inns were available and had no fear of falling into barbarian hands, having been reared in a world that had reverted to the primitive. She had no nerves and her body endured with ease the periodic discomforts of womanhood.

Severina found her completely illiterate and unused to urban ways, but quick to learn and good-humored. Her favorite reaction was a wide grin. There was an ineradicable tang about her of ripe female flesh. It took the fastidious Severina some time to get used to it, but—if anything—it attracted the men.

From the start, their eyes had been drawn by the magnificent swell of the breasts under her artlessly worn gown, the provocation of her haunches as she strode along firmly and freely. Hannibal permitted no liberties on the march, but often at night she would slip away to spend an hour or so with one or other of them. As far as Severina knew, she had no particular favorite.

Altogether they took nearly three weeks of steady plodding to cross the Apennines and reach the little port high up the Adriatic, which Crinitus had chosen for their embarkation. Part of the distance they traveled by the Highway and Severina was surprised at the neglected state of this great artery; the crumbling surface with its frequent potholes made their progress toilsome. On the secondary roads which they were obliged to follow for much of their route no maintenance had been done for years. Only the decline of wheeled traffic slowed the course of deterioration. Peninsular Italy,

175

though still spared the irruption of war, was in the grip of economic decay and the farther they journeyed from Rome the emptier grew the roads.

By the end of the first few days Severina had evolved a sensible routine, escaping from the litter at fixed intervals to enjoy the keen air and tempered sunshine of the season. Her southern skin took kindly to the pigmentation of sun and wind. The exercise and the timetable regularity of each day's program gave her a feeling of physical well-being and, in spite of each evening's weariness, a tingling vitality such as she had not experienced since childhood. Within a week, thoughts of her parents and Crinitus occupied her mind infrequently and did not leave her heavily troubled. Though she resented the uncomfortably close surveillance which Hannibal maintained at her uncle's orders, she felt herself expanding in a freedom undreamed of before. The sense of constant movement toward Aurelian, of aiming beyond the horizon, even beyond the sea, was exhilarating. From her hand mirror there looked back at her a thin, tanned, animated face, the eyes bright, the cheeks glowing, the hair often wind-blown.

Italy, even wartime Italy, with a stagnating economy, was a civilized and relatively populous country where the day's march ended in the courtyard of a comfortable inn, whose proprietor, assessing the promise of profit in the handsome litter and the party's size, would come hurrying up with obsequious smiles. Tolerably clean beds and good food were never lacking to a well filled purse. Once they had embarked, however, their real hardships began. The sea for the whole of their crossing was choppy. Their boat, a battered old trader, skippered by a taciturn, gray-haired islander from the Balkan side, lumbered before a stiff breeze, its single discolored leather sail bellying out. Cargo was lashed on the deck and among the bales and boxes over twoscore green-looking passengers had ensconced themselves. As the ship lurched along her ancient timbers creaked protest all over; adults groaned and children wailed. Tethered to the mast amid these unhappy travelers were the mules of Severina's party. Barefooted Dalmatian sailors, dark, lithe, smiling men with brass earrings, clambered indifferently over cargo and bodies in their comings and goings.

Severina knew little of what was happening. She lay below on the bunk of the ship's only cabin, a cramped, airless hole which the captain had vacated after some obstinate bargaining with Hannibal. Her stomach moved in queasy sympathy with the hull's erratic motion; the waves seemed to slap against her ear. Antonia, just as stricken, but managing a wan smile of encouragement for her mistress, sat beside her or, when the ship's drunken jig grew unendurable, lay on the floor, retching.

Severina awoke from an exhausted doze to feel the vessel sliding smoothly through calm water. After a while, as she lay feeling too weak to stir, she heard Hannibal bawling at the men to get ready. At this she made an effort and staggered to her feet. In the door Antonia met her with a flask of wine; she took a couple of long sips and felt warmth coursing through her numbed body. Assisted by Antonia she stumbled up the ladder to the deck. They were sailing amid a panorama of green islets toward a little cluster of roofs, above which the flanks of towering hills showed dimly through drifts of vapor. The sky was lowering.

Before long the sailors were tying up at a rickety landing stage. Beyond the wide but almost deserted quay was a sprawl of ramshackle houses, a little town with a forlorn, half-derelict air. The rain on the slopes was moving seaward; as Severina looked a drizzle began to spatter the planks of the jetty.

Hannibal pushed aside the motley passengers crowding at the gangway and led the convoy ashore. He formed up the men and mules—equally dispirited after that dismal voyage—in a military-style parade and walked up and down checking that packs were properly in position, the bales securely fastened and the provisions for the day easily accessible. Still a little lightheaded, Severina—who with Antonia was looking on and savoring the feel of solid, immovable earth underfoot—knew that a more dangerous and much rougher phase of their march was opening. However, Hannibal seemed cheerful enough; his jovial curses obviously put heart into the men, as his voice boomed over the quay, attracting a few wide-eyed but silent urchins. After a little he signaled to Severina, who entered the litter. It swung up and came to rest on four sturdy shoulders; within a few moments she was riding smoothly through

177

the air. Hannibal himself led the way along the delapidated main street of the port—an ancient colony from the Greek island of Corcyra, but long ago gone to seed. Some of the houses were empty and tumbledown. There were only a few citizens about, shabby and depressed-looking folk, who stood and watched them listlessly. Soon they were in the outskirts, earthen hovels and flimsy wooden cabins dotted among vegetable plots; then the road dwindled into a hill track and they were pressing on between bare, windy slopes strewn with boulders.

Ahead of them the summits of wooded ranges showed dimly. Before long the wind dropped and the rain became a steady downpour; underfoot was slippery mud. Hannibal's voice prodded them on; as the hills closed in, his cheerful obscenities rolled back oddly magnified and distorted. The men pushed forward dourly, enduring without complaint the wet and the penetrating cold and the drawn-out strain of climbing. At last the litter checked in midair and sank slowly to the ground. A grinning Antonia, face glistening with raindrops, helped Severina out and under the shelter of a leather awning slung from the convenient branch of a young oak. Already acrid smoke was streaming from wet twigs fed to a little fire and a couple of slaves, bearing iron pots, were forcing their way through the thickets to a stream gurgling along the valley floor. Everyone looked tired and gave off a blended odour of damp and sweat. But there was no slackness; all went about their business purposefully.

They spent their first night in the Balkans in a poor village, a single, irregular street of windowless huts, within sight and ceaseless sound of a far-plunging waterfall. It did not boast an inn. The menfolk, shockheaded, rangy fellows, with a proud, irascible look, supported their families by felling trees and floating them in rafts down the swift rivers; in lean seasons they supplemented their earnings by a little discreet brigandage. They eyed the convoy with surly suspicion. It might have quickened into active hostility, but Hannibal jabbered at them in some strange lingo which they understood, although his accent obviously amused them. He was soon poking the headman in the ribs and cracking a joke, a bawdy one, no doubt, which set them roaring. All was good humor now. Half the village had joined in the palaver and at some word from Hannibal there was a vigorous wagging of heads. Severina, drooping with sleepiness, found herself installed in the headman's hut. She nibbled at some bread which Antonia put into her hand and was aware of an unfamiliar, tangy wine on her lips and scalding her throat. The headman's wife led her to a bench against the wall, on which she lay down; someone spread furs over her. As she drifted off, she was dimly conscious of Hannibal briskly settling the men for the night. That hoarse, jeering voice which had accompanied her all the way from Rome gave her a sense of security; it blended with the first of her dreams, and she slept untroubled.

In the morning Antonia told her that Hannibal had concentrated the whole company in the two huts adjoining the headman's and that two of the escort at a time, arms handy, had maintained a watch throughout the night.

16

NOW they went warily, at a slower pace, with a couple of men moving well in advance of the main body to search the landscape with alert eyes. They were deep in the mountain zone of the Western Balkans, but Hannibal was taking no chances. For Severina there was something dreamlike about their travels amid this remote, sparsely peopled Alpine world. It was austerely beautiful. Immense slopes heaved to meet wide skies across which frozen foam of cloud drifted on the biting wind, although sometimes they were arched by a leaden pall and rain beat down pitilessly.

Severina would rise very early from her comfortless and often grubby bed in a village inn, where the usual callers were uncouth shepherds and goatherds, as shaggy as their animals. Completing her simple toilet, at which Antonia was a spectator rather than an assistant, she would tread between the puddles of the unswept yard to the single public room for a spare meal of bread and cheese with a pitcher of milk warm from the byre on the other side of the wall. She and Antonia would eat together, the men breakfasting outside.

Then, while milky vapor still swathed the upland pastures, they would be off, the men stamping, flailing their arms, and blowing into their fingers. As the sun rose, a stupendous vista would unveil itself, of mountains with peaks still lost among the clouds, walls of sheer rock, steep valleys where an occasional far-off gleam suggested the course of some rushing river, precipitous forests whose miles of treetops wre furiously agitated by the wind.

By rough and little used trails, they labored on. All the men were bearded now. Severina herself felt unkempt and grimy. For days on end she could not wash properly, let alone take a bath. Bread and cheese were her staple diet; a slice of greasy mutton a luxury. Sometimes the men cooked and Antonia brought her the gruel which had been their fare in the Legions. She ate it with relish, because it was also Aurelian's food, and she found it wonderfully sustaining.

Gradually the landscape changed, softened, drew them downward. The great rampart of peaks was at their backs, slowly, slowly receding. They were emerging from the high mountains—and safety. One day, suddenly, they walked into the war.

It was midafternoon, sunny and windless. They had been following a narrow trail twisting between bare hills, a faint scar on the brown earth. New precautions had become part of their routine. Besides the men scouting ahead, one trailed behind, continually turning to scan the country in their rear. At the distant sight of any likely spot for an ambush, Hannibal would detach another man or even two to join in a cautious reconnaissance.

This time Severina was walking with Hannibal at her side. He was trying to estimate for her the distance still separating them from Sirmium. Gradually, through a gap on their left the white buildings of what seemed a pleasant little town rose into view. The forward patrol, veering with the track, moved steadily in its direction. In the middle of a phrase Hannibal broke off and stood staring toward the gap with a frown that grew deeper. Suddenly he flung up his arm, bringing the convoy to a standstill; then, with another brusque gesture, he motioned everyone close to the hillside. In a low but peremptory voice he called to one of the escort, who immediately doubled after the men ahead. He came up with them near the summit of a low ridge; they turned, and, after a few moments' colloquy, all three moved crouching toward the skyline. They crawled the last few yards and peered over.

A knot twisted itself in Severina's stomach. She said quietly to Hannibal, "What is it?" He studied her face, calculating her power to withstand alarming news. As if reassured, he muttered, "The place is dead. Nothing's moving." He turned and his intent gaze once more searched the distant town. "The barbarians have been—or they're expected."

They nibbled some dry rations—Hannibal would permit no fire—and waited restless and apprehensive till, a couple of hours later, the patrol came trudging back. Hannibal heard their brief report. Then he swung round and barked an order. The slaves hastened up with the litter and the convoy moved on.

It must have been a comely little place. A few streets of simple whitewashed houses and, at their center, a cluster of more imposing residences round a miniature Forum with a graceful Ionic temple and a Basilica entered by an impressive stairway. Presumably its inhabitants must have fled in time, for there were no corpses. The town itself was a corpse, mangled and decomposing. Every building had been looted, many set on fire. Rain streaming down the walls had added to the marks of scorching a dismal pattern of dark-brown stains. The shops of the Forum gaped empty. In the temple, the image of the local goddess stood on its square base, with marble breasts hacked off and gashes marring the severe folds of its robe, but the mutilated figure retained a pathetic nobility. The altar was overturned and lay among the fragments of the sacred vessels. The roofless Basilica, whose stout stone walls had resisted the conflagration, must have been the billet of the raiders; the brand of their fires was black on the tessellated floor and their excrement fouled the hall where Roman magistrates had dispensed justice.

Severina felt sick and shaken. It was her first view of the desolation war leaves in its wake. Though she was to become familiar enough with such horrors, the sight and touch and smell of that murdered town persisted in her memory and many times disturbed her dreams—the caved-in, blackened ruins—random wreckage on the road—shattered pottery sharp against the sandal sole—odor of charred wood made acid by rain.

It was here that Hannibal's quality as a leader showed itself, again conspicuously.

To Severina everyone else looked oppressed by the spectacle of havoc. The men of the bodyguard were scowling. The eyes of the normally impassive slaves flickered among the debris and their lowered heads suggested not so much humility as fear. Even Antonia no longer grinned, but stared round her, wide-eyed.

Severina wondered what impression she herself made as, dry-throated and conscious of a weakness at the knees, she watched the convoy dispiritedly forming up in the littered roadway. A resounding curse from Hannibal made them all start. "Jump to it, you lazy slut!" he bawled at Antonia, his teeth gleaming in a ferocious smile. "Help your mistress in, d'you hear? Let's see your fat bum wriggle!" The men guffawed, Antonia giggled. Severina found it hard to repress a shrill laugh, so acute was the relief to her overstretched nerves.

A more purposeful stir began. But just then an emaciated dog, apparently drawn by the reverberations of Hannibal's voice among the ruins, came loping round a corner. At sight of the party, it drew back, with teeth bared. Its hair bristled; its eyes burned with fury and fear; an unearthly prolonged howling issued from its slavering jaws.

The apparition froze everyone—except Hannibal. He picked up a jagged splinter of masonry and flung it. A terrifying yelp escaped the cur as the missile almost scraped its protruding ribs and crashed on the paving just beyond its tail. When Hannibal stooped again, it tore round and bounded into the shell of a gutted house.

"Get moving, scum!" shouted Hannibal. "Come on, what d'you think you're paid for?" The patrol men darted forward. After a few minutes the rest of the convoy followed, Hannibal leading at a steady pace.

Though the plains were still far off, they were now unmistakably in the war zone. The hilly region across which they were pressing—at a pace that to Severina seemed agonizingly slow—had once been populous, but parts of it had been indescribably ravaged. Village after village had been plundered and burned; others simply abandoned at the approach of raiders. Where they could, they made a circuit round the pillaged settlements, chiefly from fear that barbarians might still be lurking there, but also because it was unnerving to be surrounded by devastation. Most eerie of all it was to pass through some deserted village which still stood intact; however gingerly they instinctively trod, their footfalls made the silence of those empty streets and lifeless houses more uncanny.

Once, for a mile or so, from behind the screen of a wooded summit, they had a view of the famous Highway that ran straight as an arrow in the Sirmium direction. Not a single vehicle, not a solitary pedestrian, was in sight. Even on the secondary roads, there was only scanty and furtive traffic.

Life was shrinking toward the fortified towns. Only in their neighborhood was there much movement by day, and one could expect to see a wide expanse of cultivated fields.

Every evening when the march was over and often during their brief and vigilant wayside halts, Hannibal would unroll his worn map and con their route. From day to day he adjusted their itinerary, to make wide detours round areas where barbarian war bands were rumored and, if possible, to bring the convoy by nightfall to the shelter of strong walls, even though this might mean a spell of cruel forced marching.

Across a countryside increasingly empty the little expedition pushed doggedly on. Slowly the miles were flowing away under their feet; slowly Sirmium, their haven, their golden city, was drawing toward them, though still beyond many days' horizons. By this time Severina's nerves were growing ragged. Danger was the close companion of their march. From the moment the convoy issued from the gate of the town in which they had passed the night, the tension came alive, growing stronger as the walls dwindled and sank from view. Then each felt exposed naked to a host of perils. The men spoke in whispers, as if normal conversation might betray their presence to a ferocious enemy. They dared not light fires. They rested briefly, without relaxing. Unexpected noises froze them, but quiet was no reassurance, for cunning savages might be lying motionless in waiting until the little company came within striking distance.

Only when the walled town came in sight, toward which they had all day been straining, did the tension begin to ease its grip. To hear the rough tones of the sentries on gate guard was to hear music: the clanging-to of the gate behind them and the feel of city cobbles under their feet brought an almost giddy relief.

The town would give them a night's safety in conditions that seemed, by comparison with their wayfaring, luxurious. But, as often as not, word would get around that the wife of the General Aurelian had arrived and Severina would be obliged to defer her rest in order to receive one of the civic magistrates. He would ask for news of Rome, from which his Council had long been completely cut off. As clearly as her weariness permitted she would answer. Then he might go on to impress upon her how dangerous it was to proceed with her journey. War bands had made terrible forays into the district and had only recently withdrawn; others were reported not far away.

Severina would politely put such warnings aside. Shortly before dawn she would wake from confused and frightening dreams to hear Hannibal hoarsely hurrying the men through their preparations. A couple of yawning, blue-jowled sentries, haggard from their long vigil in the dark, would indifferently watch the little procession defile through the gateway. The great door would slam behind them; the massive bolts slide home—and they were once more defenseless in an abandoned land from which murderous enemies might materialize at any moment.

Steadily the frightfulness of the war increased. Though they had not set eyes on any raiders, the dreadful evidences of their passage multiplied. Severina now understood the true nature of barbarians. They butchered and smashed and burned even in places where all was yielded to them, yielded without a struggle that might have roused their fury and left them with fallen to avenge. They did not simply plunder; they effaced settled life.

Corpses with shattered skulls or fearful body wounds lay in the village streets or on the roads nearby. There were none to render the last simple rites or even to push them into a ditch. Severina grew familiar with the stench, the chilling pallor, the manifold postures of death. Looking, she thought: one unlucky meeting—and this might happen to us. Yet in some respects the enemy's invisibility was hardest of all to bear. It meant that the terror of their image grew in the mind unchecked, until they appeared not fiercely destructive men but demons.

Severina felt that she could not stand any more days of it. So she was startled when Hannibal once casually mentioned that her composure had helped to keep the men in good heart. "You're a cool 'un, Lady, no mistake!" he declared, looking at her with approval. "None of these swine have made trouble. D'you know why? There's this . . ." He raised a huge, knobbly fist. "There's that bitch . . ." He jerked a thumb at Antonia, who caught the gesture and giggled. "But seeing you not giving a damn, walking around so calm and dignified, it's also kept their pecker up, believe me!"

By now, both mules were in very poor condition. Hannibal sold them at one stopping place and of their greatly diminished burdens what could not be discarded was distributed among the men; fresh mules were impossible to obtain in the war zone.

The garrison commander at this town, concerned perhaps lest the wife of a famous general come to grief in his territory, spared a half-dozen horsemen to ride with the convoy for the morning. When she thanked him for his offer, Severina asked where the nearest barbarians were known to be and what their number was. He replied that latest reports were of an attack on a place about twenty miles to the south. As to their number—it might be a couple of hundred.

Severina stared at him incredulously, but he smiled sourly and said, "We'd need ten thousand troops to hunt them down. Besides we never know when a new band might join them." He made a wide, swimming motion with his hands. "They're . . . they're fluid. If you'd believe the rumors, the whole Balkans are swarming with hundreds of thousands of them!"

Later that day, as they were struggling across the fields to bypass some devastated village, Severina recalled the officer's words. A couple of hundred barbarians! If there were a militia to harass them, to kill them off one by one, handful by handful, the region would soon be rid of them. But no, the Empire's population would not fight. Even these rugged Illyrians, these gnarled, stubborn peasants, would not take pitchforks and hammers and stakes and go out to assail the destroyers of their homes.

As they drew nearer Sirmium, the town officials grew more solemn in their warnings, more urgent that they should wait the indefinite time until some Roman column came their way in one of the sweeps launched now and then. Severina took the decision to conceal her identity. To press on had become an imperative emotional need; keyed up as she was, she felt that delay would precipitate her into a nervous crisis. Yet magistrates and military officers in Aurelian's own command, fearful of his anger, might insist on detaining her in safety. At her request, therefore, Hannibal sternly impressed on the men that they were on no account to give any information about the convoy. Henceforth it was assumed, wherever they went, that she was a wealthy lady of somewhat eccentric disposition, who had taken it into her head to go visiting in the province at this most inappropriate time.

One evening, on the fringe of the plains, they reached a small town after a grueling march along country lanes and cart tracks to avoid the main road, where marauders were reported to be firing settlements. Their approach had been watched, with some mystification, from the walls; and the magistrate, a youngish man, but gray-headed, with a thin, irritable face, was at the gate to inspect them.

The strain of the long day's journey through an area where war bands were on the prowl had been severe. Even though they had reached safety, Severina remained on edge. From her grounded litter, she saw the magistrate come toward her, pause and bend his shoulders in a painful seizure of coughing, straighten up and come on again. As he drew close, she was astonished to hear her own voice, gone shrill and rasping, fling words at him. "Why do you lock yourself up, like this? Why haven't you patrols out? The Goths could be a mile away—you wouldn't know a thing!"

He sucked his lip in annoyance, but her obvious authority impressed him. For a few moments he stood there weighing up her patrician face, tanned like a nomad's, the purity of her diction, her woolen robe, plain but of fine material and worn with unconscious distinction. Significant too were the workmanship of her litter and the size of her retinue, in particular the armed retainers, powerful fellows all, under a grinning bully who had ex-Centurion written all over him.

"We know where the Goths are, Lady," he answered, both respect and resentment in his tone. "They have set fire to a couple of villages."

"And the villagers?" she demanded. "Have you bothered to find out what has become of them?"

He flushed, but decided to reply civilly. "Some of them got away in time—they are here."

What had befallen Rome? Was there no defense against invasion but stone walls? Give the Goths a few battering-rams and everything would be at their mercy! She was furious at the craven passivity of this magistrate, who now was coughing again, twisting his neck in the paroxysm. Conscious of her unwisdom in thus drawing attention to herself, but unable to curb her tongue, she broke out, "Why didn't you send a force to defend those villages? Why don't you try to keep the main road open?"

"That is the military's job," he answered in a surly tone. "In any case, there is only a bare handful of troops in the town."

Severina stepped toward him, her eyes glittering, but he seemed to recede and waver in a mist, though she was aware at the same time that he was bending toward her with an expression of concern. She felt herself swaying; then an arm powerful under its smooth young flesh was supporting her and she let herself sink against Antonia.

The magistrate was speaking; only with an effort could she follow. ". . . There is an inn, but it is a filthy place, quite unsuitable for a lady . . . a lady of your rank. May I offer you the hospitality of my own house? A whole wing is unoccupied."

Hannibal was now at her other side and she heard him growl, "Wants to watch us!" But she was too spent even to discuss the offer; she merely nodded.

Less than an hour later, she was drowsing over a steaming bowl of porridge which Antonia had brought in from the magistrate's kitchen. Two or three spoonfuls of the thick, scalding stuff and a few sips of an amber local spirit, raw and nutty-flavored, turned her limp exhaustion to a more pleasant torpor. She was aware of Antonia peeling off her clothes and leading her to a couch.

She awoke much recovered. Antonia put some bread and stew on the little plain table and went out to get her own more substantial breakfast; almost immediately she returned to say that the magistrate was asking to come in.

He greeted Severina deferentially, expressing the hope that she had passed a comfortable night, but he did not meet her eyes. She answered with a few courteous words, which were interrupted by another of his violent coughing spells. As soon as he found his voice again, he said, politely enough, but with unmistakable firmness:

"You will forgive my being frank, Lady, but obviously you are the wife of some Senator or high government official. If anything happens to you in these parts, he will have my head. I am sorry, deeply sorry, but I must ask you to remain here until the region is cleared. Probably the roads will be safe again by the summer. Everything will be done for your comfort."

Severina looked at him mildly. He meant well, no doubt. It was a pity about that nasty cough.

"I'm going on," she said with a little shrug. "I haven't come all this way to give up now."

He could hardly have expected instant compliance, but Severina's almost casual rejection of his request stung him. He straightened up, frowning. A couple of times he coughed, but he compressed his lips and managed to resist the irritation, although his face went sickly. After a few moments, he said in a strained voice, but with emphasis, "I am in authority here, as the Emperor's representative. It is my duty to prevent your leaving!"

"Antonia," said Severina calmly, "call Hannibal—at once." Whatever this summons portended, the magistrate perceived that he had made no impression on her attitude, which remained one less of defiance than indifference. He opened his mouth, but first one cough exploded, then another and another, till his whole body shook with the vehemence of the spasm. His eyes bulged; droplets flew from his pale lips.

Antonia went to the door and beckoned; Hannibal, suspicious of the magistrate's early call on Severina, was already awaiting a summons. He came barging in, past Antonia. Besides the scrawny magistrate, whose face was still contorted, he looked a powerful animal.

"Our host here forbids us to leave," announced Severina with perfect composure.

"Oh, he forbids us to leave, does he?" Baring his teeth in a sardonic smile, Hannibal approached the magistrate. In one deft movement he slipped the knife from his waist and flicked in onto the table, so that the point embedded itself beside the platter of bread and the long, wicked blade quivered almost upright. The magistrate gazed at it spellbound. His coughs gradually died away.

Crouching over the table, his face close to the magistrate's, Hannibal went on jeeringly, "So he forbids us to go. Now isn't that a pity! Because we're going whether he likes it or not. We'll have to tie him up, that's all. And he'd better not make a noise—oh, no, or we shall have to be rough with him!" At this Hannibal roared a command, making the magistrate jump; two men of the bodyguard hurried in.

"Tie him up!" ordered Hannibal. The magistrate gulped, tried to speak, thought better of it and with a lowering brow permitted the men to gag and truss him.

"Not too tight!" cautioned Severina, as the magistrate began to splutter and choke in a new paroxysm of coughing.

"Tight enough!" growled Hannibal. "Stick him in the end room, along the corridor—it's empty. Don't worry, Lady. We'll tell 'em at the gate where to find him." The magistrate's face was purple, till the cough subsided. Then, his brow still damp, he glared at Hannibal.

"I regret this," declared Severina with feeling, "but you made it necessary. I'll send a written apology and a gift, once I reach . . . my destination . . . Now, Hannibal." She walked out.

Hannibal drew the knife from the table and followed.

189

Outside the walls, Severina put her head from the litter and motioned Hannibal.

"Nothing to worry about," he assured her. "They won't come after us."

"It's that magistrate's cough," she said. "He may have suffocated in the gag!"

Hannibal grinned. "Can't see why you should worry—he tried to stop us, didn't he?"

Though Severina's anxiety remained acute until the walls had faded into the distant hill on which they stood, Hannibal proved right. There was no pursuit. They were trudging now along a rutted country road, which like the fields it traversed was utterly deserted. Their loneliness was complete as that of a crew far out at sea, but here the absence of human beings hour after hour was unnatural and sinister. Severina noticed Hannibal raise his heavy nose and tilt his head slightly, as if he were straining to hear something. At once they all stopped and listened with him, intently. Nothing . . . except the harsh repeated call of a bird, invisible in one of the nearby copses. Then everybody caught it—the unmistakable bark of a dog.

One of the forward patrol came doubling back. He said a few words to Hannibal, who swung round on the others. "Get moving, you scum!" he roared. "Who told you to stop! It's only some cattle." They stepped out more eagerly now and within a few minutes came in sight of a small herd of cows being driven at a sharp pace in their direction. Soon they could plainly make out the meager beasts with their swinging dugs, the dog frisking round their legs and the drovers, five ragged peasants armed with staves, the sinewy, dour-faced Illyrians of these frontier regions.

As soon as they had approached within parleying distance, both groups instinctively halted. Hannibal strode forward and from among the distressed-looking cattle there emerged a stocky, dark man in a tattered leather jerkin, the grimness of whose lined, weather-beaten face was redeemed by small but bright and shrewd gray eyes. His age might have been anything between forty and sixty.

He shrugged when Hannibal asked for news of raiders and motioned roughly over his own shoulder. "Everywhere!" He and his mates were driving the cattle off to the mountains. The village women and children had already fled. He spoke Latin as though it were a foreign language, poorly learned.

Severina walked over and tried to follow the replies of the drover —whose name, he said, was Aglon—to Hannibal's urgent interrogation. "Sirmium—not go—this way!" he insisted, awkwardly. It became apparent that the route they were pursuing would lead them directly toward several war bands who appeared to be closing in on Sirmium. Aglon pointed with a gnarled thumb, whose nail was long and grimed. "East," he said gruffly. "That way . . . over the river . . . Savus . . . go round." He made a gesture indicative of a wide circuit.

Hannibal turned to Severina. "It's a long way—rough country, most of it. We'll need a guide. I'll ask him. The brute's got his wits about him." He clapped his broad hand on Aglon's shoulder and, trying to look benevolent, made his proposal. The drover listened stolidly, but cast a brief, calculating glance at Severina. "How much?" he demanded.

Hannibal read the consent in Severina's expression and settled with him at once, though swearing under his breath at the price. Aglon collected his scrip, patted the dog, exchanged some terse remarks with his companions in a virile-sounding dialect—presumably fixing a rendezvous—and transferred to the convoy.

At once he led them swerving sharply eastward across the forsaken fields into some extensive scrub; at his heels they burst through this onto a narrow track, almost obliterated by undergrowth.

For more than an hour they trampled, sweating, in his wake. It was murderous going, though Aglon himself showed no distress, and the determined pace he set did not flag. Toward noon, the sky began to darken. The swollen clouds, with smaller and smaller intervals between, bore such a burden of rain that Hannibal and Aglon held an anxious conference. Severina could see Aglon point several times to their right in the direction of the plains.

Hannibal approached the litter and explained. A terrific storm was going to break. The light scrub through which they were struggling afforded a screen against observation, but no shelter. Yet get under cover they must as soon as possible—and the only roof within fairly quick reach was the villa of a magnate called Egerius. He and his household had evacuated it, leaving behind a steward and two or three slaves as caretakers. It lay about three miles off in the plains below—at least one hour's forced march. As far as Aglon knew, no barbarians had reached the neighborhood.

Severina glanced up. The sullen cloud masses were piling, spreading; the gaps between disappearing. An ominous hush had fallen on the earth. Her nerves were taut with the expectation of shattering violence. Notwithstanding the risk of raiders, a roof on the plains was just now infinitely preferable to exposure here among the shelterless slopes. "The villa!" she assented quietly.

Behind Aglon's raking stride, the convoy swung right at something like a trot; their course led gradually downhill. Hannibal called in his outlying scouts. In this failing light, among the scrub and pathless fields through which they were breaking, patrols unfamiliar with the country would certainly lose themselves.

The leaden canopy which now stretched unbroken across the sky seemed to be sagging with its own weight; the landscape steadily faded. They strained on, panting behind the tireless Aglon, the litter jerking and plunging as the bearers hastened over the broken ground in the unnatural dusk. They splashed into a wide but shallow stream, water slapping cold against their calves, mud and weeds clutching their feet. In midstream the storm struck. Gusts of wind exploded. A spatter of stinging drops flung down. Then the floor of the reservoir overhead disintegrated and an endless torrent crashed onto them. In a moment they were soaked. The wind tore the litter curtains aside and Severina's clothes, the cushions and the covers were soon wringing wet. There was a spell of confusion; only Hannibal's furious herding kept the party together—anyone who strayed would have vanished in a trice. They crossed the stream obliquely and dragged themselves with squelching steps up the slippery bank. There was a brief halt, the men standing miserably with hunched backs and chattering teeth in a drowning world, while Aglon prowled around to find some trustworthy indication of their position. Soon he bawled and gestured; they surged toward him in a body. Hannibal got them into some semblance of order and they followed Aglon at a run.

At last they struggled up to a low, freestone wall. They groped along it until they came to a narrow gateway between ornamental stone posts. Stumbling through, they found themselves in the wreckage of a garden. One of the men tripped over some trailing plant and fell, face downward, into a pond. Hannibal lugged him out and yanked him to his feet with curses that sounded a magnificent defiance of the weather. They wandered a little until, in the gloom, a solid structure showed across a sanded yard. They dashed toward it at a pace that flung Severina from side to side of the litter.

Abruptly, her forward motion stopped; the litter sank to the ground. Hannibal seized her arms and pushed her through a door held open by Antonia. A little dazed, Severina was aware that the lash of the rain had ceased and the uproar had slackened to a steady drumming. Hannibal kindled a lamp. They were in a wide, lofty room, with a couple of stools by a little table and tiers of empty wooden racks along the walls. Pools gathered at their feet on the stone floor. At once the men began to smash the stools and table for kindling.

After a short while, Hannibal with a second lamp came up to the trembling Severina, took her limp hand and led her into a smaller room. This was also bare—except for some empty grain sacks lying on the floor amid mice droppings. Its single window was shuttered. A door stood ajar opposite that by which they had entered. Hannibal left Severina with the lamp, but came back promptly with Antonia, both bearing blazing faggots.

"Get the litter things," he growled to Antonia. He had the alert and menacing look he wore when something made him uneasy. "We're in the stores," he addressed Severina. "There's at least half-a-dozen rooms, Aglon says—big and small. I'm going to have a look round. Don't you move from here!" He crossed to the door they had found ajar. Severina saw him check that the knife was loose in the sheath at his belt; then he disappeared.

Antonia soon built up a crackling fire. Severina crouched near it, feeling the warmth invade her chilled body. The front of her robe began to dry. She kicked off her wet sandals and squeezed the water from her hair, squirming as cold trickles inched down her back. Meanwhile Antonia spread out the cushions and covers from the litter as near the flames as she dared. There was a smell of smoke blended with steam and sweat.

Severina had forgotten Hannibal's exploration and she was startled when he quietly reentered, shutting the door behind him. His face was grim. "Get out—quick!" he shot at the half-undressed Antonia. "And send the guide in. He's with the men. Hurry! Hurry!"

Flustered, Antonia pulled her garments around her and stumbled out.

"What's wrong?" demanded Severina. He indicated the door from which he had just emerged. "We're in trouble!" Almost immediately Aglon hastened in. "Now, listen," said Hannibal. "Those Gothic bastards have been here. They must have been mad when they found old Egerius had hopped it and all these storerooms were empty. But they caught up with the steward and his men— in there!"

Severina went pale. There was the faintest flicker across Aglon's harsh face, but he kept his sharp little eyes fixed on Hannibal. "When?" he said.

"Couple of hours ago—not more," answered Hannibal deliberately. "I know—I've seen plenty of corpses in my time."

"Then they are . . ." Severina's voice failed as the implication of his words reverberated through her.

"Nearby," he completed. "With the storm brewing, they must have made themselves snug in the main building." His glance questioned Aglon, who reflected a few moments and said, "Three— four hundred yards."

"We can't go on till the storm eases off a bit," Hannibal resumed. "Our mother's darlings couldn't stand it. They were nearly in a panic before. Some might get lost and wander round till they ran into those bloody savages."

Aglon went to the shutters and pulled them apart. Noise boomed into the room. A deluge slanted between the clapping shutters, till Aglon forced them back and secured the catch. "One hour—at least," he declared.

194

It was an eerie wait. Bodies hardly cold lay hacked and bloody, somewhere beyond that door. In the mansion of Egerius, four or five minutes' walk from these outbuildings, perhaps scores of ferocious barbarians would be sprawling in the empty rooms. The storm was the convoy's only protection. But Severina's appalled imagination made little impression on her jaded nerves. She felt a heightened tension and was aware of her heartbeats, yet she mechanically accepted a hunk of bread from Antonia and took a few bites. She even helped Antonia gather up the rumpled and still damp litter equipment.

Eventually Hannibal came in, followed by a couple of men. "Get the fire out," he directed them. To Severina he said, "Come quickly, Lady. We're ready to start."

The wind had dropped and the cataracts it had buffeted into their faces had diminished to a heavy vertical downpour. Just before they issued into the rain, one of the men let slip his pack; attached to it was a metal mug which rang on the stone floor. Hannibal rushed up, seized his shoulder in a grip which made him wince. "Quiet, you clumsy swine!" he hissed, his snarling face close to the man's. "Quiet—or I'll strangle you!" He released the man, who sullenly rubbed his shoulder and retrieved his pack with care. "Now out, everyone," ordered Hannibal. "And if anyone makes a sound, I'll stick my dagger in his throat!" He and Antonia held a cloth as canopy over Severina, while she scrambled into the litter. Their light movements were drowned by the crash of rain and the gurgle of water boiling from the pipes which drained the gutters of the roof. They trod gingerly among the shallow lakes that lay everywhere over the vegetable plots and flower beds. It seemed an eternity before they reached the gateway by which they had first entered the villa grounds.

Then, less apprehensive of being overheard, they quickened their pace, making for some still invisible broken ground which, Aglon said, began about half a mile away. Soon the perimeter wall of the villa had been swallowed up in the rain. The downpour continued, chill and penetrating. They slithered on thick mire. In the occasional copses, every branch someone brushed against brought down a drenching shower. It must have been almost two hours before the sky began to lighten. Gradually the sting went out of the rain. When Hannibal permitted their first grudging halt, it had dwindled to a drizzle they barely noticed in their saturated state.

The rain eventually ceased, but the nightmare journey went on and on. Was it eight days or ten or even twelve? Severina afterward could never be sure. Several times the patrols brought in some terrified wretch of a peasant, who had lingered unwisely on his little holding and had only escaped the marauders by a hairbreadth. The information such fugitives yielded under Hannibal's questioning always had the same purport. War bands were on the move between the convoy and Sirmium. It appeared that the bulk of the city's garrison had been summoned to the neighboring province of Moesia, which was contending with a large-scale invasion; hence the impunity with which the raiders were pressing their forays almost up to the walls.

Dully Severina reflected that Aurelian was certain to be in personal command of the column which had gone to the aid of Moesia —the husband she had come so far to join, through endless dangers, would be absent when she arrived! It was the final irony, but she was now too spent to react deeply. For the cruel strain of their journey had reached a climax, long-drawn-out. They seemed forever to be stumbling forward, doubling on their tracks, twisting frantically off course, then crawling back again. Daytime halts were short and tense; the night substituted the torment of broken and haunted sleep for the ordeal of the day. At dusk they would settle themselves in some dank wood or in some hollow, with sentries peering over the rim in all directions. The newborn moon was an enemy; they sought to flee her into impenetrable shadow. Once they were on the march in the open, they dared not linger; fear flogged on their weary bodies. They had gone back to the primitive. Everyone was filthy. The men relieved themselves in Severina's presence without shame and Antonia squatted within sight of the indifferent bodyguard.

Evening was coming on when they saw through the edge of some straggling woodland a level expanse of cultivated land, forlorn in its emptiness. As they gazed, a curl of dense black smoke shot up behind the fading skyline to the east; it tossed and dispersed on the breeze; then more smoke streamed up, thick and frothy, a sinister, flowing column that marked the funeral pyre of some Roman village.

Hannibal, followed by Aglon, came over to Severina. "They're on the main road—the murdering swine! We should be able to slip by, cross-country, when it gets a bit darker. It's only eight miles to Sirmium—we'll make a dash for it!"

Minute by lagging minute, the light ebbed; the wet, deserted land shrouded itself in dusk. Abruptly, Hannibal gave the order, "Now! Quiet as you can!" When the scouts were about fifty yards ahead, each bent and solidified into the shape of some odd, scurrying animal, he himself followed, crouching. Behind him came Severina on foot, with the bearers holding the poles of the litter knee-high, for its broad silhouette riding aloft might be observed at a distance. The remainder of the convoy pressed on in their rear.

The clay sucked at Severina's feet; every step was a struggle. She felt crushed by fatigue of body and mind. Several times she became aware that her knees were buckling and only by a prodigious effort of will managed to make her legs rigid. She bit her lip to stop herself from crying out hysterically.

Suddenly she was conscious of Hannibal lifting her, of Antonia propping cushions behind her. Then, in a half-trance, she was sliding forward—as during so many marches—on the shoulders of the bearers. Once she realized what was happening, she was stricken with guilt. Because she could not drag herself a few miles, Hannibal had placed her in the litter, though its presence at a man's height above the ground might betray the whole party, even in the deepening gloom, to a watchful enemy.

The pace Hannibal maintained was grueling; the bearers tripped and floundered again and again, only their instinctive cohesion averting a spill. Severina clung to the side of the litter as she listened fearfully to the ragged padding of their feet on the damp soil. Once she caught a fleeting glimpse of a roofless cabin with disintegrating walls, long abandoned to the weather, at the edge of a field already lost in the night. It was a mournful scene, voiceless save for the soughing wind. She resisted the impulse to call out, "Hurry!" The bearers needed no lash of whip or words to urge them on.

As darkness closed in, the reflection of the burning village flickered on the clouds more and more plainly, an evil eye blinking on them, spying out their course for the Goths. Without warning, a naked fire erupted somewhere on their right, long yellow tongues discharging smoke which coiled upward, sank and again spurted furiously. Severina gazed appalled; it could hardly have been three miles away. She could imagine the savages roaring with laughter at their handiwork and the blaze ruddy on their armor and weapons. Surely, this bonfire they had made of Roman homes must illuminate for them the convoy's scamper across the fields.

She dragged her eyes away. In the drear light diffused by the near and distant flames and their reflections on the banked clouds, she searched the distance ahead for a glimpse of Sirmium approaching. Their progress seemed an agonizing crawl. Her temples throbbed; it was painful to breathe deeply. Now she dared not turn her head, for the fancy grew stronger that just beyond the convoy's vision, to either side and closing stealthily upon its rear, were bloodthirsty enemies; at any moment they would bound from the shadows, huge figures, yelling, with axe and longsword uplifted.

Her gaze detached itself from the gloom ahead and came to rest on the forward right-hand bearer. His full neck glistened with sweat and she could make out his soft, regular panting. Twice she saw his foot slip a little on the moist, uneven ground, but he recovered himself instantly and plodded doggedly on and on, in unison with the others.

When they reached Sirmium—if they reached Sirmium, for at the moment its certainty seemed a foolish challenge to the Powers of Chance—she would grant all the bearers their freedom. Once, in the mountains, she had mentioned this thought to Hannibal, but he had laughed with good-natured derision, for he had seen no point in holding out to them the prospect of liberty, when he could get the same results from rougher and cheaper methods.

Withdrawing her head, she leaned it wearily on a cushion. Minutes stretched on, one and then another, until significant time accumulated, time stolen from the death that pressed them close. Still the litter surged forward; still the only noises outside were those of a small band of urgent men plunging across muddy fields in the dark. Now, surely, Sirmium could not be far away. A little reassured, she closed her eyes. She fell into an unquiet doze, waking —it seemed—almost immediately. But, looking out, she saw a lofty wall looming; the convoy was already curving in Aglon's wake toward the Highroad. The feet of the bearers struck on stone. She listened raptly, with an inexpressible, piercing relief, an anguished exultation. Suddenly intenser gloom around announced that they were at the great gate of Sirmium, deep in the massive wall.

Slowly, it seemed unwillingly, one half of the gate moved back. Soldiers surrounded them, exchanging words of startled comment in an accent reminiscent of Aurelian's. The litter glided forward. Behind them the gate creaked to, shutting out danger. They were inside Sirmium!

This was Aurelian's town. Here was their home. It did not matter so greatly that he was away. When he returned he would find her waiting for him.

Only slowly could she grasp that there was no longer cause to feel afraid. City noises were about her . . . carts trundling . . . clip-clop of hooves on cobbles. She heard a man's drunken tones . . . a woman's sharply answering . . . laughter, as from a crowd of onlookers. Then children's cries at play (vaguely she wondered why they were not in bed). All these sounds were a single voice in her ears: "You are safe, Severina, safe—you are inside Sirmium!" A great stone wall, secure, impregnable, stretched in a circle between her and the Goths. Dimly in her dazed mind there glimmered a realization of what the wall, though it were only a rampart of turf, had meant in human history.

Now that the tension which for so long had kept them straining onward was suddenly, totally, withdrawn, the whole convoy seemed to have experienced a sagging of the spirit. They moved at a tired, hesitant pace between shabby buildings, their dark facades pricked with occasional lights. Gradually the houses grew less crowded together and more imposing, the streets wider. They stopped before a courtyard wall. The litter eased to the roadway. Hannibal parted the curtains and helped Severina out. His face, gaunt and sweat-grimed, was more predatory than ever, but he grinned at her with weary triumph. She stood unsteadily, concentrating to follow his words. "The General's gone to Moesia . . . mother's at home. . . ."

A gate opened. A man's voice, mingling with Hannibal's—the porter, evidently. She entered the house, shivering in spite of the unaccustomed warmth and wrinkling her eyes against the light. Curious glances from strange women . . . exclamations. A hand pushed open a door, an excited voice spoke behind her. Severina found herself in a pleasant room, lamplit, with a brazier close to one wall. Confronting her was an elderly woman of middle height. Severina had a strange sensation, as though two personalities blurred together in the woman; someone of authority, firm of carriage, with a penetrating and commanding gaze—and an aging peasant wife, with withered apple cheeks, capable and kindly. She strongly resembled Aurelian.

Severina blinked. She felt herself swaying a little. "You must be . . . Aurelian's mother," she said with an effort.

With wonder and dawning recognition the woman took in the overwrought girl, her dark eyes huge in a thin, tanned face, hair damp, brow and cheeks scratched as though by twigs, stains and ragged tears all over her simple woolen dress.

"Yes, I am Aurelian's mother." Her voice was unexpectedly deep and warm.

"I . . . I'm Severina."

The woman's gaze widened at the faint, stammered words. Her compassionate look seemed to divine the long, weary trek across the desolated land, the pelting rains, the alarms, the scenes of horror, that last frantic stumbling on and on past imagined ambushes in the fearfilled dark.

"Severina!" she repeated softly. "Oh . . . my dear!" She opened her arms and Severina sank toward her, laying her head on the older woman's strong shoulder. In that comforting embrace, her body began to shake with uncontrollable spasms; hot tears forced themselves through her closed lids and on to the robe of Aurelian's mother.

They were happy tears. Severina had come home.

17

DROWSILY Severina propped herself on one elbow and looked round the clean and sparely furnished little bedroom. Whitewashed walls and ceiling, bare of decoration and suggesting a peasant's cottage; a clothes chest, a small closet, a tiny mirror, slightly chipped, which no woman would have found sufficient. The bed itself was long and hard. It must be Aurelian's, and she had lain there many hours, drowned in sleep.

With the first of her dreams she had found herself trapped in a fantastic world recalling that of her journey. Weird processions, luridly lit, struggled through gloom. Jumbled and distorted, there reappeared the retainers of her bodyguard, the mules, the broad-faced, oxlike slaves who bore her litter, Hannibal grotesquely laughing, huge teeth bared, Antonia with her guileless smile, a bound magistrate with twisted face and eyes bulging, coughing into a gag. Still, panic was not strident in these visions. She awoke sluggishly, with aching limbs, but more relaxed in mind than for many a day.

Somebody was at the door, a homely, elderly woman, who stared at her, smiled shyly, and disappeared. Severina began to recollect something of the previous night . . . how she had stood in a torpor, while this woman and another had sponged her down with warm water. . . . Aurelian's mother (should she call her "Mother" or Mammaea, her proper name?) lifting a hot drink to her lips. She did not recall this room, this bed. . . .

The door opened and Mammaea entered, bearing a small tray with cakes and a bowl of milk. She wore a simple robe and her gray hair, neatly parted, was arranged without artifice. Again Severina was struck by her resemblance to Aurelian. In particular, she had his high, rather narrow brow. She would have appeared a not untypical elderly countrywoman, of sturdy build and comfortable air, but for the dignity of her carriage and a curious calm strength in her face, with its clear and steady gray eyes, that suggested an altogether different range of experience.

Mammaea came over to the bed. "Try to eat something, my dear," she said, pronouncing the words firmly in an accent more marked than that of Aurelian. Severina had the feeling that this was their first true meeting; last night's encounter had been an episode in a waking dream. The two women regarded each other in silence for a few moments; Severina, the patrician, with anxiety lest she make an unfavorable impression on her peasant mother-in-law, Mammaea with curiosity and concern about this refined but willful girl who had staggered into her home out of the night. Then the grave composure of Mammaea's look softened and her face grew warm. She propped the cushions behind Severina, settled her against them gently, and sat down on the bed. "Aurelian said you were beautiful," she murmured, nodding to confirm his judgment.

Impulsively Severina reached out and took her hand. "Thank you, Mother," she said. She could see how the name and the gesture pleased Mammaea. They smiled together; the beginning of intimacy was established.

More to please Mammaea than because she had any appetite, Severina made an effort to eat. Mammaea did not press the food on her, but insisted that she remain in bed. "None of your clothes are fit to wear, anyway . . . and that girl of yours!" She touched her hair with a grimace.

After a little while, she said, "Now get some more sleep, my dear." Severina watched the broad, compact figure move with dignity to the door. Closing her eyes, she wondered how it was that Mammaea should have in her bearing, her expression, even in the quality of her voice, something so impressive. With sleepiness gaining on her, she recalled that Aurelian had briefly mentioned that his mother had been a priestess . . . once . . . of the Sun . . . a minor priestess. . . .

In the midst of these reflections, Severina dozed off.

She slept fitfully, half-awakening several times, while the ache and weariness ebbed slowly from her bones. At one point her eyes opened sharply. It seemed that in that quiet room she had caught a man's voice not far away, pitched low but penetrating—and familiar.

She was still frowning over this improbable sound when there was a faint movement at the door . . . and Aurelian was in the room. Her mouth opened. She sat up, trembling. Her cheeks burned. It was difficult to breathe. Aurelian came closer. He was much thinner. His cheekbones were more prominent. There were deeper lines on his forehead and his thick brown hair was more copiously veined with silver. But his face shone. She had never evoked such a look from him before—with admiration and pride in it and eagerness at the sight of her.

For a moment she had a sense of embarrassment, for their separation had been a long one after their short time together and all she now wore was some bigger woman's roomy shift. But her thin bare arms stretched out to him. He took her hands and sat down close to her, gazing with wonder into her face. "Severina!" he said hoarsely, shaken by so much devotion and courage.

She buried her face in his chest. He smelt of horses and ancient leather and masculine sweat—and no perfume could have been sweeter. "Aurelian!" she sobbed. "Oh, Aurelian—my love!" She lifted his two heavy hands and pressed them against her breasts.

Well before dawn had begun to drain the darkness from the window, Aurelian swung his legs on to the floor and stood up. Severina felt herself lifted as the bed was released from his weight. Sleepily she watched him kindle a tiny lamp and dress with rapid, decisive movements by its glimmer. Her body felt light and relaxed, its tensions all discharged, and it was lapped in a delicious warmth. Aurelian was speaking and she listened with a pleasure unrelated to the content of his words, for she lay there thinking: this is the voice of my husband again, my husband who is now my lover!

In terse phrases he explained that the barbarian host ravaging Moesia had broken up as the Roman columns converged against it. Instead of the swift battle he had hoped for, he found himself involved in the pursuit of elusive, fast-moving bands. Still, he now disposed of a nucleus of efficient cavalry and these were giving a good account of themselves when the grave developments around Sirmium obliged him to turn for home at full speed.

He was speaking with sharp emphasis now. Severina shook off her languor and gave him all her attention. "We've got to keep the neighborhood clear," he said. "Otherwise the peasants will run away. Sirmium will starve." He had allowed his weary troops a night's rest after their forced march back from Moesia, but in the early morning they would muster to begin a sweep against the raiders.

Aurelian took his departure as a matter of course; she must learn the same attitude to their separations. Their idyll had lasted a few hours only. It was not yet dawn and already he was marching away. Full morning would see him well beyond the walls. Tonight he would sleep under the stars, wrapped in his cloak against the cold and dew.

She slipped out of bed and began to look for a robe. "I'm coming to see you off." She spoke with calm, her emotions disciplined, for Sirmium was a city under siege and she was a soldier's wife. Aurelian smiled down at her, as she fumbled with the unfamiliar clasp of his sword belt.

It was Severina's introduction to the shifting and intermittent but deadly warfare of Roman and barbarian in the Sirmium area, the odd spluttering and flare of fighting here and there; the first of countless dawns when Aurelian was gone from her side and she had no notion when he would return and could not quite still the whisper of fear that he would never come home again.

On that same day, Hannibal came to say good-bye. His burly frame was spruce in a clean woolen tunic which left his bulging calf muscles bare; his glistening black hair and beard, newly trimmed, reeked of perfume. He grinned rather sheepishly and said, "The General was in a state, Lady. He said he'd have the hide off my back for taking you into all those dangers. Then he kind of poked me in the ribs and offered me command of a garrison."

"You refused?" asked Severina, puzzled by his expression.

"Well," answered Hannibal cautiously, "between ourselves . . .

that magistrate . . . you remember, the one I had to tie up. They found him dead—choked himself. A mounted messenger brought the news this morning—some of the routes are open already. One of my old chums quartered here showed me the report. Now don't take on so, Lady. It was just unlucky. Anyway, you had nothing to do with it. Still, it's a bit awkward. A magistrate, you know, he's somebody, even up here on the frontier. So I'm going home. There's a convoy leaving first thing tomorrow for the coast with a strong escort. Don't fret yourself about that report, though. I shouldn't be surprised if it gets . . . mislaid."

Severina was deeply shocked. That poor magistrate! His only crime had been excess of zeal in his duty. With bitter remorse she told herself that she had acquiesced too readily in his rough handling by Hannibal. Suddenly it occurred to her that Hannibal had deliberately drawn upon himself the whole burden of responsibility for the incident. His prompt departure from Sirmium would be interpreted as a confession of guilt—and nobody would think of blaming her. She gave him a searching look. His grin betrayed nothing; yet she was sure he was protecting her. All along he had shielded her from harm. No wonder she was grieved at their parting. This coarse, foul-tongued Berger was a man of courage, relentless drive, and unfailing resource—a born leader. And he had proved faithful to the trust placed in him. He had watched over her like a father and brought her safe through many perils to Aurelian.

To her astonishment, he refused a gift. "No!" he said firmly. "Your uncle paid me well. I drove a hard bargain—and I'm satisfied. So it's back to serving good-for-nothing drunks," he added with a sigh. "Wonder how the wife is." He rose and said awkwardly, "I won't forget you, Lady. It was a privilege. The General's a lucky man." Severina held out her hand and he pressed it gently in his huge paw. He mumbled, "Good-bye, Lady," and walked out.

A little later, Mammaea came in. "Forgive me, Severina," she said, "but that girl of yours—don't you think it better if she went home? Aurelian didn't like the look of her—she is too free and easy for a garrison town."

Mammaea, too, Severina could see, regarded poor Antonia as a slut. Though she had grown attached to her simple, smiling, eagerly willing maid, she had to admit that such a girl would hardly fit into this sober and decorous household. Not disguising her regret, she promised to send Antonia back to Italy under Hannibal's charge.

Antonia wept bitterly, but soon forgot her grief and clapped her hands when Severina produced her parting gifts, including a silver brooch and a couple of dresses already cleaned by Mammaea's efficient servants. Mindful of Antonia's inexperience and easy-going disposition, Severina gave her only a modest sum of money, sufficient for the journey. She had already decided to write to Crinitus, asking him to provide Antonia with a dowry.

The litter-bearers were hurriedly manumitted and each presented with a well filled purse. Bewildered by their sudden freedom, they left Sirmium with the convoy. Its departure cut her off from her past. Italy had become a distant land from which she felt increasingly detached as her new life in Sirmium more and more absorbed her.

On the second day after her arrival, Severina did not resist Mammaea's suggestion that she stay quietly indoors. But sitting inactive on a couch soon made her restless. She sought Mammaea out and asked to help with her household duties, only to be told, smilingly, that there would be plenty of time for that later on. Still, Severina passed much of the day in Mammaea's company and could not fail to admire the firm and brisk though good-natured way in which she managed her little establishment of two elderly women and a porter who was also general handyman.

The single-storey house proved to be larger than Severina had expected and was simply furnished but comfortable; everywhere it was scrupulously clean.

By next morning, Severina felt ready to make the acquaintance of the town, whose shadowed nocturnal streets had gone reeling past when she had glimpsed them from her litter. At first Mammaea demurred. But Severina insisted that she was perfectly well again and, a little doubtfully, Mammaea gave her consent. She impressed on Severina not to walk too far and assigned as her guide Phoebe, one of the servants.

However, Severina found she had a further escort. Once outside,

Phoebe, a slight but active little woman, with gentle dark eyes and a tuft of gray hair springing from a mole below one corner of her drooping, meager mouth, asked her to wait a little. Soon they were joined by a sturdy, open-faced youth who was dangling a stout cudgel. "My nephew," Phoebe announced, evidently not deeming it necessary to account for his weapon. We can start now, my dear."

Severina felt a compulsive urge to go as far as she could in Aurelian's direction. "Take me to the main gate, please," she said shyly. Phoebe, who must have had her private instructions, considered a moment; then, as if she divined Severina's motive, a sweet smile brightened her tired and patient face and she nodded. They set out, with Severina restraining her eager feet to the older woman's gait. A little behind came the nephew, cheerfully swinging his cudgel.

Phoebe led the way through some quiet streets with few passers-by; and then along a more frequented road flanked by low, monotonous, almost windowless buildings of drab gray stone, which Phoebe said were military depots, though now mostly empty. Their route must have been a shortcut; much sooner than Severina expected they came within sight of the imposing gateway, with its guard-rooms to either side. Severina stopped, her eyes riveted to the massive, iron-bound timbers; somewhere beyond them was Aurelian.

After a little she relaxed and looked around. Aurelian was far beyond that gate, but his imprint was plainly to be seen here in Sirmium. The smartly turned-out guards over there; the sentinel up on the rampart, deliberately pacing his regulation number of steps, to halt and wheel precisely with a triple stamp—they struck her as more alert, brisker, more purposeful, than the legionaries she had seen elsewhere. Her eyes followed the wall's slow curve; at intervals rose the menacing bulk of what must be powerful artillery, canvas-draped against the weather.

The gate swung open. Severina noticed that the roadway was emptying. People took up their station alongside her on the sidewalk verge, their heads turned in the direction of the town. Phoebe's nephew planted himself directly behind Severina, cudgel restless in the crook of his left arm; his amiable smile had given place to a hard and watchful expression.

Soon a rhythmic tramping caught her ear . . . steadily it grew.

Round a corner swung a compact body of legionaries, fifty—eighty —perhaps a hundred strong. With its powerful fluent motion the column seemed to swim along the road. Striding rigid-backed at the rear was a stocky, bull-necked Centurion; every now and then words of command crackled from him, unintelligible to Severina. The formation surged past her and dwindled through the gateway.

The great portal remained open. Now a clattering sounded on the cobbles, rapidly drawing nearer. A troop of Horse trotted into view; there was a stir and murmur among the onlookers as they jogged past—burly, hard-bitten fellows they looked on their sturdy mounts, equipped with lances, slashing swords, and bucklers.

It was Severina's first glimpse of the new-model cavalry being raised in the Illyrian provinces, "Aurelian's Own," people already called them.

By now she was conscious of some fatigue. To Phoebe's obvious relief she expressed a wish to return home, although she asked to be conducted by another route, so as to observe more of the town. With Phoebe's nephew still in close attendance, cudgel at the ready, they began to traverse a crowded quarter of narrow streets. Though the cleanliness of these was an indication of good civic morale, the buildings, with paintwork faded, plaster peeling, and masonry in poor repair, had a down-at-heel appearance. Like their homes, the people were shabby. The strident youngsters chasing each other in the road looked badly undernourished. At street corners little groups of roughtly clad men stood dejectedly—refugees, Phoebe said, from the countryside, waiting till the war should move away and they could return to their ruined farms. They conversed without animation and watched Severina pass with incurious eyes.

Even for a city in the war zone Sirmium had a terrifying number of beggars. Hollow-cheeked, tattered like caricatures of poverty, they loitered in doorways or squatted against walls. Phoebe slipped an arm through Severina's and drew her away when she might otherwise have passed too close to some of these scarecrows. Once Phoebe was too slow. An emaciated arm shot from behind a buttress and grimy, clawlike fingers scrabbled at the hem of Severina's dress. She looked down, with mingled pity and revulsion, at the grimacing features of an old woman with an idiot grin, who was sitting on the stones beside a filthy bundle. Her gray hair straggled over her withered face; she was whining some beggar's incantation. Severina was feeling in the purse at her belt, when there was a brisk step behind and down with a thwack came a cudgel on the creature's wrist. She yelped and jerked her hand back and, whimpering, began to rub the injured place with her other hand. Severina turned fiercely round on Phoebe's nephew. His cheerful look showed such expectancy of approval that she realized he had only done the duty laid on him; a rebuke would have been beyond his comprehension. She said quietly, "Don't do that again!" Then she dropped a coin at the woman's feet and walked on, sickened by sight of her, the stench of unwashed flesh wrapped in decaying rags, the savagery of the blow so zealously given, so meekly accepted.

The way now seemed long and wearisome. Even in the better quarters her imagination was haunted by the slime of human decomposition she had seen deposited on the streets of Sirmium. It was an intense relief to be home again. When Mammaea saw her white, drawn face, she made her sit down, but did not ply her with questions. Instead, after a little while, she began a pleasant rambling tale about Aurelian's youth. Calm and measured, her voice held the attention. Gradually Severina relaxed as she grew absorbed in the picture which emerged of a gangling, stubborn, silent boy assisting his father on a little tenant farm in the Sirmium region.

Phoebe interrupted to announce visitors. These proved to be two City Councillors, fully Romanized Pannonians of good family, who had come to pay their own and their colleagues' respects to the garrison commander's wife. Caius Sempronius was a tall, forceful-looking man, iron-gray at the temples, with an aquiline nose and thin lips. He carried himself rather stiffly and his expression was cold. His colleague, Metellus, was shorter and plump, with brown eyes that protruded a little and a fair skin whose hectic tinge suggested that the slightest access of temper would make him apoplectic.

Sempronius was evidently the senior; he greeted Severina first. She could see that her youthfulness surprised him. There was a hint of condescension in his manner as though he were exerting himself to be polite to someone he considered an immature girl. Metellus, on the other hand, was plainly gratified to be meeting a Lady of genuine Senatorial family and he spoke his formula of welcome with great earnestness.

For Mammaea both showed an obvious respect. Even the coldly self-important Sempronius addressed her with deference.

Severina was struck with her deep and tranquil dignity in the presence of these urban patricians. Her dress was plain, her speech simple. Yet gazing on her and listening, Severina thought not of this morning's homely and frugal housewife but of the woman ministrant in the Sun God's shrines.

The Councillors—in particular, Metellus—appeared in buoyant spirits. Aurelian's return had caused an immedaite upsurge of confidence in the town. After a few inquiries about Severina's journey, which she described briefly as "tiring," Sempronius asked in a somewhat complacent tone what her impressions were of Sirmium. This time Severina answered with strong feeling. "I was appalled at the number of beggars."

She caught the affronted stare of Metellus; his cheeks had gone purple. "I hope you realize," he said, "that most of these people are not from Sirmium at all—they are Dacians from across the river!"

"And surely Rome, too, is infested with beggars," observed Sempronius with an acidulous smile which stung Severina. She met his look angrily. "That is no reason for doing nothing!" she retorted.

"I must remind you, dear Lady, that we are not in Italy," Sempronius said in his faintly disdainful manner. "Pannonia is a war zone. The Council is hard-pressed even to maintain the most essential services—let alone look after a horde of useless paupers. Besides, we have only to wait. Last winter they died like flies. In time the problem will solve itself."

Severina's shocked silence lasted so long that Metellus threw his colleague a reproving glance and said, reasonably, "We would do anything possible. But our finances are in a desperate state. We simply have no resources."

"I could find resources!" said Severina bitterly.

The Councillors looked at each other. They recalled rumors that this importunate young woman was heiress to a great fortune. Sempronius was already smiling more amiably when, for the first time, Mammaea intervened. "You should reflect, Severina. You can have no idea how many of these unhappy people there are." She shook her head at the quick dismay in Severina's face and went on, "But perhaps something can be done for the more urgent cases—mothers with young children and pregnant women."

"And the old!" eagerly amended Severina, seeing again the wizened face of the beggar woman who had clutched her dress.

Metellus gave a snort. The compressed lips of Sempronius made the same comment. Despairing, Severina turned to Mammaea. For a few moments she looked in the older woman's compassionate eyes. Then she bowed her head, almost ashamed at having struggled for the right of aged beggars to survive in this crowded and hungry frontier fortress.

Even if the Councillors regarded Severina as an impetuous busybody, she was Aurelian's wife and they had no desire to antagonize her. "Naturally, the Council would be most happy if anything could be done out of private resources," said Sempronius with facile goodwill. "We should be pleased to give what help we can. There are several empty warehouses on our hands—we could put one at your disposal where you could open a soup kitchen."

"On the understanding," added Metellus promptly, "that it would be only for special categories of paupers!"

This episode together with Aurelian's continued absence weighed on Severina's mood. The following morning, observing her lack of spirits, Mammaea suggested that they go together to the market. "Shopping is so hard nowadays," she remarked with a sigh. "There's so little worth buying and everything is impossibly dear."

There were plenty of people about, sauntering among the booths and stalls and gossiping on the sidewalks, but business appeared slack. Shopkeepers stood glumly at their own doors, hope brightening their faces as Severina's elegant figure came in sight. Many of them had a warm though respectful greeting for Mammaea.

Beggars in their hideous rags were everywhere, but they did not importune the two women, thanks to the close proximity of Phoebe's nephew, his eyes alert and cudgel swinging.

After a while, Severina became aware of a commotion some distance down the street. She spoke of it to Mammaea, who listened for a moment and said matter-of-factly, "They must have caught a thief."

Soon one of the burly market policemen appeared, lugging by the scruff of the neck a weedy beggar, a wispy tatterdemalion, with frightened eyes wide in his hollow, scrubby face; he was protesting his innocence in a thin singsong that had no hope or conviction in it. If Despair had a voice, it must be like this, thought Severina. A leather-aproned stall-holder, brawny and bare-armed, was jabbing a finger at the beggar and bawling abuse. The onlookers showed little interest; evidently this was a familiar scene. Before long the beggar's protestations subsided and he went quietly in the policeman's clutch, with a hangdog look.

Severina watched till they were out of sight. Then she turned to join Mammaea who was inspecting some woolen cloth at the open front of a shop. She waited until Mammaea had made a purchase; then asked in a low voice, "What punishment will he get—the thief, I mean?"

Perceiving how the incident had impressed Severina, Mammaea patiently explained that petty stealing had become so rife that penalties were extremely severe, although no penalties had been able to check it. Once a confirmed offender would have been sent to the Dacian mines, but these had long been abandoned. Today's thief would probably get a whipping; if he had been in trouble before he might lose a hand.

Severina listened unhappily. I must do something for these poor people, she told herself.

However, the project for opening a soup kitchen for "special categories" of paupers made very slow progress. Costs appeared staggering when she began to go into them with the aid of a clerk from the Town Council's financial department. He was a scraggy, sharp-featured, elderly man, whose sardonic expression conveyed that he was wasting his time to gratify a senseless whim. After one particularly discouraging session, Severina went to Mammaea.

"The Council obviously think I'm making a fool of myself," she said with painful candor. "I'm beginning to suspect they may be right."

Mammaea did not answer for some moments. Her calm gaze rested on Severina. Before a word was spoken Severina felt the other woman's quiet strength sustain her; somehow the problems of relief work among the paupers of Sirmium appeared less daunting.

"It is you who are right," Mammaea answered. "You can help many poor women and children nobody else cares about. Also you can help yourself, my dear. You were not meant to be just a house-wife!

"Only don't try to do too much," she added with a little smile. "You will wear yourself out—for nothing. And you will make it easier for those who oppose you."

Mammaea said no more on the subject and Severina herself no longer had the inclination to pursue it. She saw the way ahead clearly.

The next day, the clerk found Severina, who previously had been uncertain and inclined to look to him for decisions, full of a new confidence. When he resumed his obstructive tactics, she overruled him sharply. Still wearing a sour expression, he set to work and produced a budget of more reasonable dimensions. The scheme began to take on practical shape.

So, in the first rather blundering phase of adjustment to her new life, Severina found the quiet understanding and sympathy of Mammaea her mainstay. Herself highly strung and reserved, though liable at times to give vent to feeling with unreasonable heat, she was attracted by the tranquil disposition and easy, outgoing vitality of her mother-in-law. Their common concern with Aurelian mani-fested itself not—as it might have done—in rivalry and friction, but as a happy bond. Their relations had from the first been pleasant; soon they had grown deeply affectionate.

Early one evening, the door of the main living room opened and in walked Aurelian.

He gave Severina a weary but cheerful grin. Instinctively she knew she must not show too much emotion, but emulate Mammaea's calm and behave as though she regarded his departures and returns as matters of routine. Yawning, and in the jerky phrases of extreme fatigue, he told her briefly that the sweep had been successful in that the raiders had been cleared from a wide area round the town; unsuccessful in that they had slipped away between the Roman columns, except for one small band cut off by his cavalry and exterminated in a bitter fight. More raiding parties were reported across the Danube and one or two might move in the direction of Sirmium.

The ardor of their first reunion naturally could not be revived. This tired man, already thinking of fresh sorties and skirmishes, could not play the lover. He smiled down at her sleepily as she helped unfasten his armor, pulled off his weighty cavalry boots, collected his soiled and sweaty clothes and with the bowl of warm water Phoebe hurriedly brought in, washed the caked mud from his legs. Mammaea entered with a salve which Severina applied to his saddle sores and an aromatic concoction for cleansing his cuts and bruises.

Sitting naked on the bed, Aurelian swallowed a simple meal of bread and cold meat with diluted wine; then he rolled himself over and closed his eyes. Severina covered him to the brawny chest with a blanket. In a minute, as she stood watching at the bedside, he was fast asleep.

He was off early next morning to the barracks, where he was delayed until long past nightfall. He slipped quietly into their bed, so as not to awaken her, but she had been lying sleepless and turned into his arms.

Two days later he marched to the relief of a township threatened by the new incursions from across the Danube. And so he came and went. In such a continually interrupted married life, her love could not sustain a high note of romance. It became less exalted and more sensible and utilitarian; it took on more the quality of a tender but practical service, which included the service of her body when Aurelian required. He responded with a silent affection and complete trust; his scant leisure was unreservedly hers.

At the first convenient opportunity Severina explained to him her plan for a soup kitchen. Conscious that she had committed herself without his knowledge, she began rather nervously. Aurelian frowned and her heart sank; but he glanced at Mammaea who was present and, evidently reassured by what he read in her look, gave a little nod.

"Can't see any harm in it," he said. "But watch your purse among all those women, Severina. Some of them are cleverer thieves than the men. The place ought to be policed—I'll talk to the Council."

After that, he inquired occasionally about the progress of the work, but at no time showed particular interest in it.

It was primarily because of the impact of the war on her marriage that Severina for the first time felt herself profoundly involved outside her home. Her training, which was that of a member of a small elite, had never encouraged broad sympathies. Now something unsuspected in her came to life; she developed a feeling of strong kinship with the men and women of Sirmium. Though people showed her deference, she was nevertheless one of a threatened community whose solidarity in the face of danger was more important than distinctions of rank. Let the soldiers waver, let the peasants now venturing out again refuse to till their fields, and it would avail her little that she was the garrison commander's wife and daughter of a Senator who claimed forebears in common with the Emperor Trajan.

Most people were supported by this sense of community. Only the beggars in their underworld of misery and squalor were excluded. Severina's attempt to organize welfare work among them found no sympathizers and advanced very slowly. The attitude of the dozen or so wealthy families remaining in Sirmium was that it would only further demoralize worthless paupers. The other citizens were simply indifferent. Still, the Town Council, mindful of Aurelian, assigned her a derelict warehouse. A number of unemployed were engaged to scour the place and a battery of huge cauldrons was installed. The Council even acceded to Severina's request that wooden benches be provided where the women and children could rest while waiting to draw their ration.

However, the Council insisted on detailing four policemen to be present while the food was served; two of them, handpicked men, were to be Severina's personal escort, in close attendance on her until she was safely home again.

Eventually a proclamation was made that the doors were opening. The news sped along the alleys, through the doss houses, into the cellars, wherever these outcasts maintained a semblance of home; and crowds of shrill, excited women, many dragging along bewildered children, came surging toward the soup kitchen. By no means all the women belonged to the classes designated as alone eligible for the food distribution, and among the throngs skulked a few vainly hopeful men. The police used their truncheons with zest until the uproarious mob resolved itself into an orderly queue, from which most of those disqualified for the dole were—not without tearful protests—soon ejected.

The routine of service worked out in advance proved smooth and expeditious. The paupers filed steadily past the row of cauldrons, each having drawn on the way a wooden bowl; into this one of Severina's assistants, sturdy hired women of trustworthy character, ladled a generous helping of thick appetizing porridge, scalding hot; the older children were issued smaller portions at a separate table. The meal was eaten on the spot with noisy appreciation and the bowls were returned under the grimly watchful eyes of the police, to be scoured by a small squad of women and reissued.

Severina attended daily at the cold, cheerless building, with its enormous, lofty, stone-floored rooms, from which the mustiness was never quite banished. Though most of the women settled themselves on the rough wooden benches to wait their turn with patience, the scene was animated enough. Steam poured from the bubbling cauldrons; the staff of helpers moved brisky about their preparations. From the doorway of the hall, where a policeman lounged, there was a constant shuffle of feet toward the benches. A babble of gossip rose on every side. Youngsters at their games dodged among the legs of the adults. Infants wailed; older children squabbled; mothers shrieked to rebuke their offspring or recall them as the moment approached for drawing their ration.

At first, Severina had a struggle before she could overcome her revulsion at the proximity of so much grimy and malodorous flesh, scabby faces with matted hair and almost feral expressions, eyes rimmed with pus, skeletal and rickety limbs, hands gnarled with rheumatism. She took up a ladle and, gritting her teeth, did a long and wearying stint beside the other servers.

Eventually her nerves ceased to twitch, her nostrils no longer

216

registered the stench of this human wreckage. She even began to recognize many and to greet them with smiles and friendly words, which were often received with titters, for her Roman accent was unintelligible to women who spoke only the argot of the Sirmium slums.

Custom stilled her physical revulsion; her mind never grew reconciled. She never ceased to wonder why these emaciated wretches, these scarecrows of the gutter and the cellars, never railed against the malevolence of their fate and the society that rejected them and callously saw them dying of hunger and disease.

Only when drunk were they dangerous. Occasionally, they would get hold of a quantity of raw liquor, presumably by stealing, and in and around their haunts a wild carousal would begin. Severina's bodyguard would close in on her as, appalled and fascinated, she walked past a rout of tattered starvelings with flushed faces screeching out some ribald chorus or reeling about in a tipsy jig. Their potions usually ended in savage brawling, with men drawing knives on each other or foul-mouthed viragoes clawing at each other's cheeks and clothing amid the jeering laughter of the onlookers. Sometimes a collective rut would seize on them and their howlings would gradually die away to grunts and moans as they lay about the street, coupling.

A rudimentary family life persisted among them, but most lived promiscuously, and slatternly girls, scarcely more than children themselves, would grow gross-bellied and, when their time came, would whelp like animals in some outhouse corner. On the benches of the soup kitchen it was a common sight for some unkept slut to pull aside a shred of clothing, lift a skinny, blotchy breast and put the nipple to the mouth of a babe so tiny that even in its wrapping of rags it seemed more like a puny doll than a living creature.

In that infernal world, where the graces and disciplines and even the pretenses of normal society had collapsed, there came to Severina moments when she could have cried out in agony. This dreadful war would continue without end. There was no limit to the misery it spread. The Gods, if Gods there were, had turned their faces away and humanity was abandoned to sorrows past counting.

One day at the warehouse had been particularly trying. A cauldron

217

overturned, inflicting dangerous scalds on two of her helpers. There had been a few minutes of terrifying mass hysteria as screaming women dashed to snatch their children from the clouds of steam and the lavalike surge of the boiling porridge. The outburst had been quelled by the police with their truncheons; Severina, attending to her servers' wounds, had been unable to check them. The food issue was delayed long past the usual hour. The hall was strangely quiet; the women were subdued and the children, many of whom looked badly shaken, clung to their mothers. Severina's assistants were sullen and even the police wore scowls instead of their normal bored expressions.

Chilled to the heart and weary, Severina set out for home. On the way she was jostled several times, despite her muscular escorts, by people hurrying to the roadside. More and more people came pouring out of houses, shops, side streets. Severina stood and waited with the rest, although her view of the road was restricted to a gap between two heads. Soon the crowd grew quiet. Harsh cries could be heard approaching. Then there was a murmur among the spectators as along the road appeared a company of about thirty men of towering stature, naked but for a short kilt or pelt around the middle. Their long fair hair gave them a youthful look, though many wore golden beards; their ruddy faces glistened with sweat. At the rear were some who walked feebly, as if injured. The wrists of all were tightly roped. They were followed by half a dozen guards, tough, heavily built fellows, who, loudly cursing, prodded the laggards on with the butts of lances.

For once barbarians had permitted themselves to be taken prisoner; for once the legionaries had permitted their captives to live. They looked bewildered, their blue eyes roaming over the crowds that hedged the road. But even in captivity, even in bonds, they appeared to Severina twice the men that the Romans were. Life had not systematically crushed them. Their rude society had not stripped them of self-respect. No tax gatherer had stood, ominous, in the doorway of their huts. They tilled no man's land and paid no man rent. They were fanatically loyal to their kings and chiefs, but with the unforced devotion of freemen.

Stumbling along with goads in their ribs, they had more essential human dignity than the crowds that gaped at them. Severina gazed at their open, virile faces and thought: We Romans have done some irreparable injury to life; we have lost forever something these savages have—and have abundantly.

For two days a storm had been blowing over the town, with torrents of rain that scourged even the beggars from the streets. Aurelian was out with his flying columns, hot in pursuit of raiders. Severina knew by now that he pressed on vigorously with military operations in weather that would have daunted most commanders. She stood behind one of the huge cauldrons, which was coming slowly to the boil, her eye absently on the wisps of vapor, while visions of Aurelian marching and bivouacking in the sodden fields made inroads into her mind. Troubled on his account, she was also conscious of a physical unease. Of recent days she had been fretful and vaguely out of sorts.

Through the gathering steam a face persisted, a woman's thin face, with a timid and patient smile. Severina threw off her reverie. She became aware that the first of a long file of women stood beyond the cauldron, waiting for her to give the signal for service to begin.

Gazing on the hollow-cheeked, pitiful creature, in whose thin hand the bowl was trembling a little, Severina saw that she was young and had a pathetic, already wasted beauty and that she was advanced some months in pregnancy.

Her heart missed a beat. She felt the motion of nausea up into her throat; its taste was on her tongue. What is the matter with me? she wondered. In the next instant she knew, with absolute certainty, that she herself was going to be a mother. She looked dazedly around, recollected herself, and made an abrupt sign; at once the servers' ladles dipped into the cauldrons. Then unable to endure the stale human odor and the wails of the frail babies so many of the women carried in their arms, Severina fled from the hall.

All the way home Severina walked as though stunned. She was neither happy nor afraid. Simply she was overcome, as by some prodigy. Dismissing her puzzled bodyguard at the gate, she entered and stammered out her news to Mammaea. She saw Mammaea's face glow, felt her warm embrace, heard the rare excitement in her voice as she asked her experienced questions. Only then did Severina awaken from her stupor and a radiant joy and wonder filled her at the thought that she was bearing Aurelian's child.

Strangely, her approaching motherhood made her nervous not for herself but for Aurelian. She thought far less often of the babe safe within her womb than of its father endlessly in danger out there beyond the walls. Mammaea watched the tense and jumpy girl, divined her worries and set about distracting her. Already she had discovered that what most quickly absorbed and tranquilized Severina was some anecdote about Aurelian's childhood. The theme was one on which she herself loved to dwell. So, although Severina still spent part of each day queasily directing operations amid the odors of the soup kitchen, in the evenings she permitted Mammaea to take charge of her. After their meal and before their early bedtime, the two women would sit for an hour or so in the softly amber light of the lamp; Mammaea placidly talking, while Severina said little but listened relaxed, hands clasped on her lap.

Gradually the random episodes shaped themselves into the story of Aurelian's youth before he left home to join the Eagles. From the depths of the famous general's personality emerged the boy buried there by the turbulent years. For the boy thus resurrected, so strange yet in certain ways so familiar, Severina felt something of a mother's love, for she saw him with the eyes of his mother's memory.

18

IN MAMMAEA'S narrative one figure at once emerged and for long maintained itself in the foreground—lantern-jawed, with angry gray eyes under shaggy brows, an aggressively protruding lower lip, and powerful lean limbs longer than most, even in that region of well grown men. Bato, to whom Mammaea was given in marriage when she was an illiterate village girl of sixteen, came of the untainted Pannonian stock. That is, he was stubborn, cantankerous, afraid of no one, suspicious, ready to quarrel, and a dangerous man to quarrel with. But he was hard-working, thrifty, and sober. He beat her only occasionally, though the mark of his bony knuckles was slow in fading. Even these rare spells of violence toward her did not outlast the early years of their marriage. Gradually, she established an ascendancy over him and he tended more and more to defer to her judgment—if in a surly, grumbling fashion.

Of the five children Mammaea bore him, only Aurelian and the youngest, Julia, survived their first year. Bato loved them with the force of his harsh nature and a dumb yearning to be loved in return. But he was too clumsy and irascible to win this answering affection. Both the boy and the girl, as they grew older, showed him an antagonism that puzzled and exasperated him and made him deeply unhappy. In spite of the fear he inspired, particularly during his bouts of savage temper, his authority over his wife and children continued to diminish.

To some extent, his loss of standing with his family was due to the fact that he was unlucky. The parcel of soil he rented was his passion. His ancestors had been peasant proprietors and it was his overmastering dream to become absolute owner of these few acres into which he poured his sweat. But no matter how he planned, labored, sacrificed, they proved unprofitable. One summer, there was drought; another year, hailstones flattened his barley. Blight repeatedly attacked his crops. His yoke of oxen was requisitioned by the Army during an invasion scare that coincided with harvest. His best cow mysteriously sickened and died.

With each setback to his hopes of accumulating enough to make an offer for the freehold of his farm, he grew more sullen, more resentful of the fate that condemned him, a free Pannonian, to be the tenant of a stranger from Rome. Actually, Aurelius, the local landowner, was of Gallic extraction. His grandfather, a First Centurion, who was born at Lyons, had been demobilized at Sirmium and had bought an estate in the neighborhood with his gratuity.

Bato's hatred of Rome tended to isolate him from the other villagers. In particular it made the younger peasants regard him as an eccentric; and this, had he known it, was a powerful factor in his children's hostility toward him. In that prolific countryside, flourishing in the peace established with a Pannonian army by the fierce African Emperor, Septimius Severus, younger sons abounded—and it had become a tradition for them to join the Legions. Pannonia, though bloodily conquered six or seven generations before and still a half-barbarous frontier province, was being steadily Romanized. Only Bato and a few other irreconcilables gloomily cherished the legend-enshrined memories of an older day before Rome planted her Eagles on the Danube. At home he spoke the ancient Pannonian tongue, an uncouth dialect everywhere in retreat before a bastardized but vigorous and expressive Latin; and in his rare expansive moods he would chant in an angry-sounding bass the lays of his warlike people in the epoch of their freedom and anarchy. Still, he commanded enough scraps of broken Latin to chaffer suspiciously with the foreign traders at their booths and stalls in the annual local fair.

The old Aurelius, an aloof, tight-fisted landlord, died and his son Lucius broke off his study of Rhetoric at Rome to occupy the manorial villa. He proved a young man of unusual cultivation for those parts, handsome in a ratser smooth and pallid way, easy-mannered with an agreeable disposition; and he was at pains to ingratiate himself with his surly tenants. Rumor maintained that he had treatises on agriculture in his library. Certainly he showed himself a considerate landlord, prepared to wait if the harvest were bad and loaning his peasants money at rates other landowners would have thought foolishly generous. He visited his properties at intervals, sauntered into the huts, shrewdly discussed crops and cattle with the men in his faintly silky voice, shot dazzling smiles at their gaping womenfolk and patted their snotty, unkempt brats on the behind.

If the dour Pannonian peasants were indifferent to his rather facile charm, their wives and sisters were his ardent partisans. On Mammaea, accustomed as she was to oafish men, he made the liveliest of impressions.

It was the time of her third pregnancy. She had gone on pilgrimage, carrying a lamb from their exiguous flock, to the local temple of the Sun. The long-bearded priest in his impressive vestments lit a candle and stood bowed in silent prayer before the crudely gilded image of the rural Apollo. He turned to assure her that the God had accepted her offering and that, though her first two children had been girls and both had been carried off in early infancy by fever, she would now give birth to a son, who would grow to robust manhood.

Bato had wished to name the boy after a legendary Pannonian hero, celebrated for the slaughter he had wreaked among his people's enemies. It was Mammaea's suggestion that they call him instead after their Master, whom this overt flattery would be bound to dispose in his favor. Though sourly, Bato had finally acquiesced. So it came about that the sturdy infant began his life in their humble cottage with a majestic trio of names derived from Imperial Rome, Lucius Domitius Aurelianus.

The young Aurelian had no education and no illnesses. As his years increased, he developed into an active, strong-willed, rather silent lad, rarely involved in a fight, but of a furious temper once roused. He was endowed with exceptional physical strength and with some more intangible power of personality, so that he exercised a natural leadership among the boys of the neighborhood. He was devoted to his mother, even if she did not always find him easy to manage; toward his father he early showed himself intractable.

Lucius took only a distant interest in his young namesake, though his occasional careless inquiries never failed to excite soaring hopes in Mammaea. But his interest grew as Aurelian grew. He was almost forty, rather gross of body and with a white, puffy face, though still affable and smooth-mannered, when he proposed that Aurelian, then a fine-looking if angular lad of thirteen, come to the villa to serve him as a page. Bato shouted at Mammaea that no son of his was going to be a servant. However, confident that Aurelian's fortune was about to be made, she argued and wheedled until, in the end, Bato growled that she could do as she liked.

Mammaea even made a special journey to Sirmium, where her pitiful savings were invested in a decent coat and pair of shoes for Aurelian. He resentfully endured a scrubbing from head to foot at her hands; his moroseness over this indignity did not wear off until, a couple of hours later, the cart from the villa creaked into the yard and a plump and haughty domestic bawled his name. Then Aurelian's face grew taut. He disliked Lucius and had given way only because his mother was so enthusiastic. She followed the cart a hundred yards or so along the path that led to the Sirmium Road. Aurelian turned to wave, self-consciously, several times. Mammaea wiped away a few unobserved tears, but comforted herself that Aurelian now had something far better to look forward to than the endless, unrewarding drudgery of the farm.

The cottage was a bleak place when she returned. Neither her younger child nor her husband could assuage the ache for her son. Julia, at eight, was a pretty girl, but with too much of Bato's surliness to evoke from Mammaea the deep, painful, self-recognizing love she felt for Aurelian, so peculiarly her own. As for Bato, although his relationship with his son had been the reverse of cordial, he went about gloomily, too dispirited even to grumble.

After some dreary days, Mammaea persuaded him that his periodic business with the steward of Lucius had suddenly become urgent. Wearing her only good dress, so that Aurelian need not be ashamed of his mother, she accompanied Bato to the villa. They waited uneasily in the huge kitchen with its gleaming pans, neat rows of colored pots along the shelves and a rank of ponderous jars against one wall. Mammaea tried to look unconscious of the smirks of the scullions. Aurelian appeared, greeting them shyly before these strangers. To his mother he seemed fuller in the face; his hair was trimly cut; he was resplendent in a pale-blue tunic that left most of his wiry legs bare—it was of some smooth and glinting fabric whose like Mammaea had never seen on a man. In one respect only he disappointed her: he was not yet in attendance on the Master. Still, he was happier than she had expected, knowing his unaccountable antipathy for Lucius. "Demetrius—he's a Greek slave here—is teaching me to read!" Aurelian confided. He spoke gravely, for he was a serious boy, but Mammaea understood him well enough to perceive how pleased he was and proud.

Toward the end of a wet, cheerless afternoon, about a week later, when glancing through the cottage window, she was staggered to see Aurelian. With glowering face, he was tramping barefoot straight across the miry yard. The soaking coat which clung to his body was that in which she had sent him off to the villa. In one hand he carried his shoes; a shapeless bundle dangled from the other. There was a purpling bruise on his forehead; his lower lip was swollen. His legs were mud-splashed to the calves.

He stalked in, scowled round, dropped his sopping bundle, which contained his few belongings, in a corner and announced in a tone of absolute finality, "I'm not going back!" To her questions he opposed a glum, unshakable silence. He dried himself, changed into his ragged old shirt and drawers and, leaving her baffled and dismayed, squelched across the field to join his father in the orchard.

Nor did he ever offer Mammaea an explanation why he had thus abruptly renounced the villa. Finding his silence impenetrable and that persistent questions only drove him to avoid her, she forced a curb upon her tongue. But a curious woman will contrive to find sources of information; before long she discovered what had happened.

Following an early afternoon repast, Lucius had summoned Aurelian, who found him reclining on a divan, scented and clad only in a wide-sleeved, silken oriental robe. It was loosely-girdled so that glimpses could be caught of his sleek, white body and plump legs. The gawky boy had stood tongue-tied. Smiling languorously and with amused eyes on Aurelian's downcast head, as if deriving an extra relish from his troubled innocence, Lucius had begun with sly, lingering fingers to explore inside his tunic. After a few moments, Aurelian looked up. His puzzled frown had given way to a thunderous scowl. His brows contracted over a jutting nose; his lower lip protruded. Just then his face was a younger version of Bato's gone brutish with anger. He closed a thin, wiry, quivering hand round the wrist of Lucius and wrenched the intruding hand away; the tunic ripped to the waist. Lucius recoiled, clasping his wrist where the rough nails had scored it. Aurelian bounded across the room to a bronze statuette of Eros, snatched it up with its weighty pedestal and flung it at Lucius. Just in time Lucius rolled over behind the divan; the missile hurtled past and crashed into the wall. Amid splinters of plaster, it clanged on the mosaic floor and ended its career a few inches from the terrified eyes of Lucius.

Aurelian looked wildly round, then darted towards a small table on whose marble top were arranged a tall decanter, ruby with wine, and several slender-stemmed goblets. The back of his hand swept the glassware away. He gripped the table by one of its spindly legs of polished walnut and was swinging it up, when two servants rushed in and hurled themselves upon him. Fortunately for their Master, they had been spying on his sport from a corner of the window and had seen his discomfiture and danger.

Lucius bolted. Other domestics came hurrying in. The room was in a state of wreckage before the frenzied boy was overpowered.

They did not beat him; they simply thrust his clothes into his arms and let him go.

The episode had lasting effects. In Aurelian it confirmed a tendency to dour self-sufficiency; he grew less and less communicative. He developed a frostiness of will, so that he did very much as he chose, vouchsafing no explanation. However, from this time his relations with his father grew somewhat less unfriendly.

Bato's rage against Lucius was bitter and implacable. It was with the utmost difficulty that Mammaea prevailed on him not to go storming to the villa with a scythe. The need to contain the compulsion for revenge seemed temporarily to unhinge him. He muttered as he went about; the intensity of his angry stare was unnerving; he bared his teeth in fury at the slightest provocation.

One night a barn of the villa home farm went up in flames. Bato had gone about wild-eyed that day. Twice pedigreed cattle of Lucius were found maimed. The name of the perpetrator was an open secret in the countryside, but Lucius took no action. Public opinion, which could be formidable to a landlord isolated without armed retainers among a notoriously quick-tempered peasantry, had been aroused. In the village stones and clods were thrown at his servants and insulting names shouted after them. Lucius himself met with lowering looks when he went among his tenants. Rumors circulated that Bato was going to lead a crowd of demonstrators in a march against the villa. Before long the situation had grown so threatening that Lucius moved stealthily away by night to a distant property.

The steward he left in charge, a native of Sirmium, was a typically rough-tongued and overbearing Pannonian, with whom the peasants felt at home.

After Lucius flitted, Bato grew calmer. Aurelian helped him on the farm, acquiring his breadth of shoulder and long, sinewy frame. The village girls showed more than a passing interest in the handsome though taciturn youth; but Aurelian remained absorbed in his private thoughts.

What these were at last became evident. One damp autumn evening, when patches of mist clung to the copses, he trudged back from the fields. Mammaea and the already shapely thirteen-year-old Julia brought him hot water and a towel. "Mother," he said directly, "I'm going to Sirmium—to enlist."

Mammaea hurriedly set the trembling bowl at his feet. Julia put her hand to her mouth. She did not understand this self-sufficient, undemonstrative brother of hers and had no strong affection for him, but she sensed that his words portended an upheaval in their lives. Aurelian bent to scrape the encrusted soil from his legs. Mammaea watched him with silent anguish. Her heart cried out to him not to go away and leave her desolate, but all she said, eventually, in a faltering voice, was: "What will become of the farm without you? How will we pay the rent?"

Aurelian looked up. "Don't worry, Mother. I'll send you money." She could see that he had thought the matter out in all its implications. "I'll get on—you'll see. I mean to be a Centurion. They get good pay!"

Mammaea handed him the towel; he rubbed his legs vigorously. "Look at Father," he went on. "He's as bad off as a slave, drudging year in, year out—just to pay the rent. And you yourself, Mother—without a good dress to your back." He stood up, suddenly a grown man, more impressive in stature and carriage and speech than his father. "I want to be someone," he said. "I want to see the Empire. I want to fight the barbarians. It's a big world, Mother. There must be a place in it for me!"

"Very well," she said, in two words resigning herself to a future in which she might never see her son again. "I'll explain to your father."

When Mammaea had haltingly told her news, Bato made no comment. He sat down, awkwardly. His shoulders were bowed a little. In the grooves of his bony, weather-beaten face, the fatigue and frustration of the hard years showed plainly.

Next morning, the two of them, with Julia, stood wordlessly watching Aurelian's tall form diminish along the path that led to the Sirmium Road. At his shoulder was a scrip with a few belongings and some goodies Mammaea had baked for him—and burned. Later that day, Mammaea entered the byre and came across her husband. His forehead was pressed against one of the rough beams and terrible dry sobs were shaking his body.

Aurelian was true to his word. A proportion of his pay reached them at intervals, meager enough to begin with, but increasing steadily as he won promotion. Bato and Mammaea were enabled to carry on, despite a collapse one year in grain prices. He also remitted part of the proceeds from his booty in victorious campaigns and of three donatives he received, thanks to the quick succession of Emperors, each of whom strove to buy the loyalty of the troops with a lavish distribution of gold.

With this more substantial aid, the farm at last began to prosper.

Another factor contributed to Bato's change of fortune. The steady worsening of the Empire's military position and constant civil wars between pretenders to the Throne gave a powerful impetus to the general inflation; and, at first, the peasants enjoyed some benefit. Even grain prices, long depressed, began to soar; and although rents also rose rapidly, Bato and Mammaea could not recall such a period of relative abundance. They acquired first one slave, then another. Julia was provided with a dowry and gladly left her parents to live with her husband's family in a neighboring village.

Late one fresh afternoon in spring, Bato was hammering nails into the timbers of the big new cowshed he was building, when a flash low down across the fields caught his eye. As he stared, his heart sank. The declining sun was reflected from armor and weapons, in regular formation, steadily approaching along the path from the Sirmium Road. Roman soldiers! It could only mean billeting or requisitions—and these, he knew, could half ruin a small farmer. He was already cursing his luck, when the words died on his lips. His eyes bulged; his cheeks grew red. "Mother! Mother!" he rumbled, unwilling to turn his gaze from the path. Mammaea put her alarmed face out of the cottage door and heard his half-choked shout, "Aurelian's coming!"

The soldiers stood grinning while the two elderly peasants (as they seemed with their toil-worn faces and rough working garb) embraced their Centurion. Bato wrung his hand speechlessly; Mammaea kissed him and cried till he looked embarrassed. Their first effusion of feeling spent, they stood back and regarded him with pride and with joy inexpressible. It was their Aurelian, yes, but a stranger too; his face no longer lean though still strongly molded, across his powerful chest a splendid breastplate in which their pale reflections wavered. Topping as he did by inches the tallest of the twenty-odd soldiers he was conducting to the legionary camp which the Emperor Decius was forming for the war against the Goths, he appeared to Mammaea like the Sun God in arms.

That night Aurelian's men, installed in the aromatic hay of the barn, were regaled on fresh and ample farm fare. Unaware that their feast was in the nature of a thanksgiving, they gorged themselves on chickens and geese and suckling pig, washed down by the fiery plum spirit of the district which they quaffed as freely as though it were the diluted wine of the barracks. Long after they were snoring, Aurelian sat by the fire of the snug, familiar cottage, struggling to find words in which to tell his parents of the great world beyond their horizon; the vast, swarming marble cities of the Empire's richer provinces, making even Sirmium seem puny; his campaigns and battles; the scar on his cheek, souvenir of a partly warded-off slash from a broadsword when the Emperor Maximin cleared Gaul of a German invasion. Bato and Mammaea marveled at his assurance and authority and at what they considered the fluency and eloquence of his speech.

Bato's face grew most animated when Aurelian spoke of his warfare, the fierce charges, the fields heaped with dead, the towns taken by storm. For Mammaea the greatest wonder was how her son had made himself scholar enough to write his own letters. She had taken them to the villa for Demetrius (Aurelian's tutor for a few days when he was a page there) to read and reread until she had committed the dozen or so lines of terse soldier's Latin to memory.

"At first I used to get one of the Headquarters clerks to write for me," Aurelian said. In Gaul, his commanding officer had nominated him for a vacancy at the Legionary School at Treves, where potential Centurions were put through a short course of elementary education. Afterward he had practiced his writing as best he could. He grinned with boyish complacency. "A letter doesn't take long now. And I read quite a bit. I've bought two books—they're about tactics."

He marched away at dawn. About ten weeks later an alarm set the whole countryside in motion. A powerful band had broken through the net which the Emperor Decius had drawn close round the Goths and was heading in the direction of Sirmium across a province denuded of its garrisons, now absorbed in the field army. Raging, Bato drove the cattle into the woods, while the slaves helped Mammaea stow the most essential gear in the cart. Then it trundled behind its yoke of oxen toward the Sirmium Road; Mammaea had virtually to drag Bato after it. Their little procession merged into the swelling flood of countryfolk that poured toward Sirmium.

On the way, a sudden rumor spread panic through the throngs of refugees. There had been a great battle somewhere to the east— and the Romans had been defeated!

Settling in the squares and public gardens and a few requisitioned buildings, the peasants discussed in subdued tones an unprecedented disaster, which the authorities had found impossible to hide. The Emperor and an entire great Roman Army, trapped in a bog, had perished at the hands of the Goths. Mammaea sat apart, for a long time stonily refusing food. Aurelian might be lying there, under the stinking slime that had engulfed the legions. Only later did word come that, though wounded in the shoulder by a spear, he had escaped. A force of Pannonian soldiers, Aurelian at their head, had cut their way to firmer ground and there had beaten off attack after attack, until tardy night had fallen and the battered, exhausted barbarians had been glad to withdraw, leaving the indomitable handful to make an unmolested retreat to a Roman fortress.

So Aurelian's fortunes grew brighter as the Empire moved inexorably into eclipse; amid the defeats he fought his way forward. Centurion; then First Centurion; then Prefect of a Legion, of a Legion that—it was grudgingly conceded in the camps—he had made the finest in the Service. But Mammaea had been left alone to rejoice in his success and share its growing rewards. For against

230

her tearful appeals and the warnings of the authorities, Bato had refused to wait for confirmation that the district was clear, but had insisted on going back to see whether the farm had been plundered. A week later, a patrol from Sirmium found him with skull split to the jaws in a copse not far from his ransacked cottage. The cattle were roaming unharmed in the woods.

In one piercing day Mammaea heard that her son was alive and her husband dead. She gave Bato decent burial in the village cemetery and decided to dispose of the farm. The stock and surviving implements were sold; the land reverted to the absentee Lucius.

Mammaea returned to Sirmium and, after the necessary tests and a prolonged initiation, was consecrated a minor Priestess of the Sun. But of this spiritual preparation and her part in the rites which took her from shrine to rustic shrine in the region, she would say nothing to Severina.

19

BY HIGH summer, when the anarchy had prevailed for a full calamitous year, it seemed to have lasted a decade. The past receded; there appeared no continuity between its happiness, its security, and the present of unending misery and disaster.

Now Rome endured a Promethean agony, sprawled impotent, while the steel beaks and talons of the northern eagles tore at her vitals.

Over the Balkan provinces the defensive system had been disrupted, so that wandering bands of a few hundred barbarians could spread terror through wide regions by the mere threat of their approach. In the plains agriculture was coming to an end, except in the immediate neighborhood of fortress walls. Famine and plague and the ceaseless sapping by privation slew in places where the sword had spared. Many of the wealthier inhabitants fled to the south, only to find themselves preceded there by the Goths who, launching themselves with careless confidence on the water, had broken through to the Aegean. On both sides of the sea, burning cities marked the unchecked progress of the barbarians, the weakness and abasement of Rome.

Round Sirmium the fighting dragged on and on, a war not of dramatic strokes but of slow, grim attrition. There was no encounter big enough to dignify with the name of battle; but instead groping marches of small Roman columns, with aging equipment impossible to replace, in search of swift-moving raiding parties; contact meant a brief though often bitter skirmish. Among the Romans there was seldom more than a trickle of killed and wounded, but losses through sickness and desertion were heavy. Discipline grew slacker, despite all the vigilance and rigor of Aurelian, for to punish one made hundreds of disaffected; and, in any case, when pay was suspended for months and bare rations subject to interruption, the most dutiful soldier felt a strain on his loyalty.

Still, thanks to Aurelian, Sirmium maintained itself energetically, amid a province steadily growing depopulated. Raiders who ventured too near took little plunder and were lucky to make off without a bloody clash. Aurelian, the saying went, had tied wings to the legionaries' ankles. Assisted by his overworked cavalry, he closed in so rapidly that marauders were often prudent enough to turn elsewhere in search of booty. The fields round Sirmium were tended daily—though most peasants sheltered by night within the walls— and they kept the city alive with their harvests.

When Aurelian returned from the protracted operations on which he was engaged at the time Severina became aware of her condition, Mammaea greeted him and then left the two of them together. Severina at once told him her news. A smile of deep pleasure made his tired face boyish and touching, and with a rare demonstrative gesture he put an arm round her shoulder. Her head resting against him, they talked about the child. Severina did not ask whether he preferred a boy or girl—the question would have been superfluous.

Their reunion was a short one. The military situation was grave in the extreme and the following morning Aurelian was back at the barracks to prepare another drive to free the city's communications with the south. A few days later he was in the field again.

The time of his return was uncertain, but Severina knew that his stay with her would be brief. She schooled herself to pass the greater part of her pregnancy without the comfort of his presence. Except for phases of acute anxiety when his absences were prolonged and no word came from him, she awaited her confinement with the fortitude of a soldier's wife. Her swollen stomach, particularly ungainly and oppressive on a woman with her slight frame, obliged her to hand over the supervision of the soup kitchen to her chief assistant, a Centurion's stalwart widow with a no-nonsense attitude toward their charges; but she resolved to resume her duties there as soon as she recovered from childbed. From her own past self she felt utterly sundered. She could recognize no kinship with the skeptical, self-doubting, barrenly intellectual onlooker she had been, devoid of practical experience, isolated among ancient books. Now she had the quivering contact with reality of a woman whose husband's days were spent in ceaseless danger. Through Aurelian, through his baby kicking in her womb, through Mammaea, through the people with whom she daily mingled, she was completely involved with Sirmium and its struggle to survive.

A new self emerged, patient, disciplined, resourceful, equal to the emergency and more intensely alive because of it. She learned to emulate Mammaea's self-possession. The future loomed uncertain and sinister; it was enough for her if the day promised to be uneventful. She was thankful for any interlude in the fighting. When Aurelian came home unwounded, she knew unqualified bliss. When he was away, she hid her apprehension—except, perhaps, from Mammaea's discerning eyes—and her face and speech were calm. She did not fuss. She did not rasp on taut nerves. To be harassed, to be in constant demand, to cope with shortages, to improvise, did not shake her equanimity. The absence of ceremony, the direct speech natural to resolute or hard-pressed men suited her disposition.

In all this she was sustained by the example and companionship of Mammaea. Diverse though they were in age, background and temperament, the association of these two women whose lives were

233

focused on Aurelian was a happy one. Theirs was a household remarkably free from bickering. Even the vexations of an ever more straitened siege economy did not disturb its harmony.

In spite of her condition, Severina did not seek privacy, as she would have done in the polite and artificial society of Rome. Aurelian's colleagues and subordinates and civilians engaged in the urban and regional administrations were often in the house and she did not withhold herself from them. Once, too briefly, Claudius called; he had left his Command Headquarters at Carnuntum, higher up the Danube, to spend a night at Sirmium concerting some operation with Aurelian. Though he appeared tired and a little preoccupied, he greeted her with charming courtesy and his smile was warm. He inquired with obvious concern about her health and asked a number of questions which, while not intrusive, showed understanding of the difficulties she must have experienced in her translation from the sheltered luxury of Rome and Baiae to a harried frontier province. She was sorry to bid him good-bye, for there was in Claudius a sympathetic and endearing quality which did not take in any degree from his manliness. The war had made him older, not harsher.

Probus, Aurelian's former adjutant, was another hurried visitor. He had been promoted to an independent command in the neighboring province of Moesia, which was suffering from ravages worse even than Pannonia. There he had demonstrated brilliant leadership and he was now looked upon as one of the foremost generals on the Danube. Severina found him pale from a recent wound and much thinner. It was hard to recognize in this spare, authoritative soldier, with his incisive speech, the fresh-faced, rather shy and boyish-looking young aide she had first met less than two years ago. He greeted her a little formally, but there was feeling in his strong handclasp.

At long intervals, Diocletian, another of the Illyrians she had entertained at the Alban villa, came to the house to be closeted with Aurelian. On these occasions he had little leisure to converse with Severina, but he always inquired politely after her health. With his ponderous build and strong, heavy-jowled face, in which the small shrewd eyes seemed to miss little, he had an air of alert and masterful calm. He spoke shortly and to the point, with a touch of sardonic humor. Severina knew that his abilities were highly esteemed. On her he made the impression of an ambitious and guarded man, prepared to bide his time but likely to be extremely formidable when the moment came to assert himself.

Most frequent visitors of all, because of their constant attendance on Aurelian, were Herennianus, his ablest cavalry commander, and the tough infantry veteran, Mucapor.

Herennianus became something of a favorite with Severina. Not even the incessant campaigning which hollowed his cheeks could subdue his jauntiness and his buoyancy of speech. He was always animated in Severina's company, unashamedly enjoyed a gossip, displayed keen interest in topics as domestic as recipes and the behavior of servants, showed enthusiasm about Severina's clothes and a cheerful mock-despondency about his own. In his vivacity there was something almost feminine, especially when contrasted with the rather drably masculine personalities of other officers frequenting the house, but Severina was aware of his reputation as a daring and dynamic leader, almost worshiped by his rugged cavalrymen.

He was fond of poking fun at Mucapor, who stolidly shrugged it off. Few others ventured to make fun of Mucapor. As a former First Centurion, he came of a heavy-fisted, iron-throated breed. He was broadly built, though surprisingly quick of movement, with a massive head, now graying, on a bull neck. His prominent nose was somewhat flattened, his mouth wide and brutal. He had nothing in the way of boudoir conversation. For all his crudeness, Severina felt goodwill toward him, because of his dogged devotion to Aurelian. According to Herennianus who, once Mucapor's back was turned, spoke of him with considerable respect, he was a stark fighter, unsurpassed in rough-and-tumble warfare.

Among the civilians Sempronius and Metellus were the most assiduous callers. Severina was amused to find them exhibiting pride at having been the first of the urban patricians to make her acquaintance. The stiffness of their first encounter was forgotten and she could not help feeling flattered by the freedom with which they discussed Council problems in her presence and the attention they showed when she hazarded an opinion.

235

Severina's baby was born just before morning, during a January gale, which brought snowflakes swirling down hour after hour through the dark to cover with untrodden white the dirty slush of the streets. She was sitting alone in her room, the brazier's warmth and the subdued lamplight making her drowsy, when the pains began. They soon subsided and she determined not to tell Mammaea yet. Instead she tried to concentrate her thoughts on Aurelian, who in the dreary twilight of yesterday's dawn had ridden away, with a dozen troopers for escort, to a conference of regional commanders at the headquarters of Claudius.

Soon the barbed prodding began again, more and more viciously. She was aware of the sharp intake of her breath and the soft, quick drumming of her feet, every now and then, on the floor. Mammaea appeared, spoke to her a little, soothingly, and went, returning soon with Phoebe. Interminable hours dragged on, while the pains ebbed and flowed, more savagely fanged at each return. Then they became incessant, tearing her apart. She clenched her teeth, but all at once she gasped and the screams went traveling out of her. She saw the concern in Mammaea's face and heard her quiet voice; then she closed her eyes and sank into a stupor from which the consciousness of everything but agony was banished.

Much later Severina awoke from a numbed sleep. She lay limp and drained, beginning slowly to recollect. When her head moved slightly, Mammaea came over and moistened her lips with a warm drink that had the tang of herbs. "A lovely baby, darling," she whispered. Severina's eyes opened wide. Mammaea stroked her damp brow. "The sweetest little girl!" she added softly.

Severina managed a tremulous smile. But she was thinking: A girl—Aurelian will be disappointed!

The years passed. Years of siege, of formless warfare, of shortages of every kind. Years in which people saw with distress, but without surprise, many of their family and friends grow peaked and wan and die slowly of privation. Years in which few babies, even among those whose parents tried to rear them, lived out their first twelve months; while only the exceptionally hardy and resistant of the older children grew to maturity.

But Severina's baby, the younger Julia, thrived. She waxed plump and rosy, despite Severina's lack of mothercraft. Perhaps it was the tough peasant strain in the child; perhaps it was Mammaea's experienced nursing. Severina's milk failed early—the wrong diet, Mammaea said—but a cow was found and later a goat, as well. It mattered little what they poured into the infant's gullet. She swallowed it all cheerfully, digested it calmly, punctually produced sound teeth and, as soon as she could toddle, spent much of her time unsteadily following her grandmother. Severina interfered as little as possible, conscious of her own inadequacy and fearful of disturbing a regimen that kept her daughter in vigorous health while all around children sickened and died with hardly a struggle.

Aurelian grew fond of little Julia. He was clumsy in handling her and more than once rode her so roughly on his knee that Severina snatched her away, although Mammaea had looked on laughing. It was not often, however, that Aurelian found time for such family play; even when he was at home he had many callers and no lack of urgent problems demanding his personal attention.

Still, each year brought a phase, all the more precious because it was so brief, when he could relax. Far into the autumn, sometimes into early winter, the raids persisted and Aurelian could seldom count confidently on a few days undisturbed. The depth of winter enforced a respite. Nature shrouded the land with her hundreds of leagues of ice and snow, over which the glacial winds patrolled. In Sirmium, whose lofty walls rose from a white desert, a kind of spring kindled in people's hearts; for a few months war had been banished. Except for a skeleton stand-by force, the soldiers could unstrap their armor and enjoy such diversions as their hard-pressed frontier fortress offered.

Aurelian, too, rested between his still long and strenuous spells of duty. There was a snug domesticity about those days snatched from war, the gift of merciless winter. Mammaea, with a sensitiveness and a magnanimity Severina had not encountered in her own sophisticated family, would as a rule withdraw early to her room, leaving them to spend the evening alone together. Then Severina and Aurelian were just a wife and husband relaxed in each other's company, secure for a while against separation. They sat in peace, enjoying the brazier's warmth, perhaps talking a little, often with Aurelian drowsing over his mulled wine and Severina reading, without concentration.

She had been at Sirmium over three years when word came from Crinitus that her father had died. Many of the letters between her family and herself had gone astray; of the remainder, most were delayed en route. This one arrived promptly.

Though in the universal calamity even a father's death could not make such a tragic impact, the news filled Severina with bitter sorrow. Her uncle wrote with unwonted seriousness, disclosing facts she might well have guessed before, had her thoughts turned more often and with greater concern to Rome. The letters that had reached her from Severinus, himself, had contained sufficient clues; she had read them and dismissed them, not troubling to probe for the feeling behind the pedantic words. Now, as she weighed each phrase of her uncle's, she knew that in her self-absorption she had shut her eyes and heart to her father's distress.

While members of the Senate had been suffering disgrace, imprisonment and even execution—such penalties often being accompanied by sweeping confiscations of property—Severinus had remained unmolested. Everyone had expected him to be among the earliest victims. His survival, unscathed, caused vicious tongues to wag. This Severinus had to endure, when for all he knew the fatal blow might fall on him at any moment. What with the suspense, the mistrust with which he knew himself to be widely regarded, and his increasing isolation from his former colleagues, he had felt the strain acutely.

As time passed, he stirred less and less from the house. Once the activities of the Senate had provided him with opportunity to exercise his undoubted talents; the applause of his fellow Senators had gratified a deep craving. Now all this was denied him. In any case the functions of the Senate had become quite empty. Gallienus treated it with open contempt. He did not bother even to render it the formal reports which maintained the pretense that it was a vital part of the apparatus of government. He was a despot—and a ruthless and unpredictable despot at that.

In the end, Severinus had taken to his bed. There he had been scared almost out of his wits by a surprise visit from the Emperor. Gallienus, however, had shown himself extremely affable. Indeed, he had been so glibly solicitous that it soon became apparent how much he was enjoying himself. He chided Severinus with not having taken good care of his health. "We can't afford to lose men like you, my dear Senator," he said reproachfully. Poor Severinus had been obliged to play his part in this comedy, in which each was fully aware of the other's real sentiments, and to express fervent and loyal gratitude for the Emperor's sham concern.

Perhaps Gallienus also had a hand in the rumors that immediately afterward began to circulate. It was said—and, according to Crinitus, commonly believed—that at this sickbed interview Severinus had saved his property by denouncing to Gallienus many of his former associates. Confirmation was found in the spate of arrests that accompanied the closing stage of his illness.

For whatever reason her father's property had been spared, it passed intact to Severina. She could not credit the injurious rumors that had pursued him even on his deathbed. To her it was plain that fear of Aurelian alone had restrained Gallienus from laying violent hands on her father and his possessions.

Drusilla had suffered much during her husband's ordeal, helplessly watching his decline. As he grew weaker, he became more testy and unreasonable, and in the last stage of his illness she herself was near collapse. Now a nervous and ailing woman, prematurely aged, she had gone back to her family.

At the end of his lengthy letter, Crinitus for the first time lapsed into flippancy. "My doctor has died and my health has improved tremendously. He used to complain that having me as patient would be the death of him. Still, he turned me into an anchorite. It's no good the wives of my friends casting languishing looks at me—no man could meet their requirements on my diet. Do you know, Severina, I never taste wine, no matter how diluted. What a waste of the most refined palate in the Empire!"

Crinitus had forwarded a sheaf of documents bearing on her inheritance. Into them had strayed a brief, reproachful note from Porphyry, whom she had left as steward in her Alban villa. As she had apparently forgotten him, he wrote, he had decided to leave her employment. After a lifetime spent in the service of her family, this was a painful step. However, he was a free man and could choose a more considerate employer. He had accepted the post of steward to an elderly merchant who was retiring from business to an estate in Africa.

At this time Africa was the most tranquil of the provinces. Severina never heard from Porphyry again.

It was with a feeling of detachment that she looked rapidly through the inventory which set out in summary form the enormous estate bequeathed to her—the sumptuous mansion in Rome, and two luxurious villas beside; a small army of slaves; one of the finest private libraries in the Empire; statuary including works by ancient masters; a superb collection of jewels; gold and silver plate in profusion; furniture and costly hangings; kitchen equipment; wine cellars stocked by connoisseurs—the list was endless. Much of this property she determined to sell—she would send her agent in Italy instructions. If this war ever finished and they returned to Italy, the villa in the Alban Hills was all the home she wanted. In particular, the thought of settling in the huge Roman mansion was abhorrent. Perhaps some war profiteer would be willing to buy it.

Except for the elderly, she decided to manumit the slaves, although this, in a time of general impoverishment, with so many artisans unemployed, might not prove an unqualified boon to them.

She put the inventory down and thought of her father. All his possessions had not saved him from bitterness of spirit. The closing phase of his life had been without honor, his death without dignity.

Severina's grief was desolating, but she knew that it was essentially the grief of remorse—not of love deeply stricken—and that it would not last. An elderly man, unloved, defeated, had been interred in the ornate sepulchre of her family near Rome. Here there were war, hunger, and sickness. A single far-off death could not hold the attention long. Soon the hundred problems, great and small, which she had thrust aside, would press themselves on her again and she would be too occupied to go on mourning.

She had hoped to have made her father happy with news of a grandson. However, after her daughter's birth, her womb never quickened again. She assumed—as she sensed everyone else did— that the failure was hers. Aurelian was a famous soldier, valiant, virile. The wife of such a man should have borne him sons. She felt her lack of fecundity a conspicuous blemish. At times she wished herself under the sway of some belief, however absurd, which would have sent her on pilgrimage to one of those shrines where women sought, with tearful prayers and offerings, the blessing of fertility. But the skies were empty for her. There had been a moment when she might have been capable of faith. But Aurelian had intervened and the mood had passed beyond recall. Her reason would never again renounce its sovereignty.

As her hopes of a son had to be abandoned, Severina began to feel resentment that even her daughter seemed less her own than Mammaea's. When Julia entered the room, it was to her grandmother that she trotted first for a hug and kiss; it was by her grandmother's chair that she squatted on the floor with her toys. Now Severina became more sharply conscious of these things and of the ease with which a word, a smile, a touch of Mammaea's would soothe or persuade the child, when all her own earnest efforts had been unavailing.

Young Julia continued to prosper amid the shortages and the sickness. She was a sturdy little girl, active and strong of body, rather than quick of brain, serious, calm, stubborn. Severina felt she had contributed little to her daughter's makeup; Julia was almost all Aurelian's.

Although Severina chafed at the child's obvious preference for her grandmother, she too was deeply attached to Mammaea and she tried hard to restrain her impulses of jealousy. In the course of time these were diminished and then altogether ousted by an increasingly poignant sense of loss. For Mammaea had begun to show signs of aging. She tired more easily, took less interest in the day's events and appeared content to let more and more of the household management slip into Severina's now fully competent hands. She would sit dozing for long spells, particularly after meals and in the evenings; and as her head began to nod, her sleeping face shed its strong, mature composure—it was worn and simple, the face of a wrinkled old peasant wife who had never stirred beyond the next village.

Severina too was showing the impress of the years, harsh, unsparing years in a community concentrated on survival. Her body, especially after Julia's birth, grew fuller; she lost the nervous grace of her walk. Her face was broader, less mobile, more commanding. Her complexion suffered from the stodgy siege rations.

She hardly bothered to resist this process of physical coarsening, but she strove to keep her intellect vigorous and keen. Books still occasionally came through on the convoys and over a period of years she accumulated a substantial library. She was reading one day when Aurelian strode in, having broken off a routine inspection of the city's defenses. He was splashed with mud and looked uncommonly grim and harassed. She put her book on a table and hurriedly set about arranging a bath and meal for him; she had long schooled herself not to trouble him at such times with questions.

Aurelian countermanded the bath and ate the meal standing, between mouthfuls grunting out instructions about clothes he wanted sent within the hour to the barracks. "Bad news from the south. I'll be away some time," was all the explanation he offered.

He was on the point of finishing his bread and meat, when his eye fell on the book. Still chewing, he picked it up absently. "Greek," he said. "What's it about?"

She could see that his thoughts were elsewhere. "Oh—it's *The Eumenides*," she answered with an effort. "It's about Orestes. He's mad, but recovers his sanity when he finds sanctuary in Athens."

Aurelian gave her the book. "Athens," he repeated heavily. "We heard today—it's been burned."

Pale, shaking, she stared at him. His words scorched her brain.

"The Herules sacked it and burned it down. They're a Gothic people. I've a friend who settled there. A Greek called Demaratus. He was on my staff. . . . Wonder if he's still alive."

Severina found her voice, the ghost of it. "Athens burned!" Her grasp tightened on the book, relic of a lost civilization. "The Parthenon?"

242

He flicked the crumbs from his fingers. "You mean the big temple on the Acropolis? No, that's all right. It was the town center. They made a mess of it!"

It was obvious that his concern was with the military situation. Another big town captured and sacked, that was all he saw. He had no notion that he had given utterance to an earthquake. Athens laid waste! True, the august marbles of the Parthenon had escaped destruction, but they had looked down on a gulf of flame into which the Stoa, the Odeon, all the buildings of the ancient and hallowed Agora, must have crumbled to the yells of bloodthirsty savages.

Without a word she watched him go, but something within her was screaming out to him, "Kill them! Kill them! Kill them!"

After this darkest of disasters, a mood of despair weighed Severina down. It was as though the fires of Athens illuminated in her mind the ravages of the war far and wide in the Balkans, and the spectacle crushed her. The life of the province had waned to a point where extinction threatened. It was hard to believe that the parents of these fearful, harassed, half-starved folk had been born into a world where nobody had seriously challenged the majesty of the Roman Peace, when all over the Plains the farms crowded. Now, desolation. Now, emptiness and silence, charred timbers, abandoned plows, boundary walls disintegrating, weeds rioting everywhere. Even the roads, by which civilization had entered the land and maintained itself, were breaking up.

Sometimes an ordeal roused the vitality of a people, evoking unprecedented powers of resistance, a spirit of daring and high endeavor. The people of the Roman Empire were incapable of such a response. For them the ordeal had been too great, lasted too long. Slowly they were being sapped, exhausted of energy and hope, overwhelmed.

Fortunately, the untamed ferocity that made the barbarians so formidable also placed a limit on their effectiveness. They had no concerted plan. They irrupted, destroyed with zest and without mercy, amassed plunder—and were off. Had a single, overmastering will imposed a strategic design on their raids, they would soon have brought the Empire to the last extremity.

243

Often in her mood of defeat Severina wondered how Aurelian could continue resolutely to go out on operation after operation. In the end, she was convinced, he would fail. Civilization would fade out. In its place would be barbarism, or perhaps not even that— only an unpeopled wilderness.

But Aurelian himself did not falter. If there was doubt, as obviously at times there was immense weariness in him, he never betrayed it in word or action.

He never spoke of yielding, never of retreat. Only he grew more grim, more taciturn. Thanks to him, resistance continued, fiercely. The ordeal was so constant, the pressure on muscle and nerve and will so intense and prolonged, that it was incredible to Severina how men could sustain it. Yet Aurelian himself, she knew, would not give way. Death might take him, perhaps in one of those innumerable obscure skirmishes, but he would not, while living, withdraw from or even relax the struggle.

Never yield, never flinch. If the sky falls, hold it. If the earth rocks, stay fast. Confront each danger. Seek out and grapple with each invader. Fight and fight and fight while men from beyond the frontier stand upon the Empire's soil.

Nor was he alone. A whole company, though small compared with the vast populations supinely watching their struggle, small indeed measured against their colossal task, stood with Aurelian and Claudius, battling with the tempest. Most were Illyrians. Their inspiration was the Soldier Mithras; their emblem, the Unconquered Sun, the burning God of the wide skies riding out undimmed after each reign of darkness.

They, too, were unquenchable. Wearied, beset, endlessly pounded, they would not cease to defend themselves and the land entrusted to their protection.

Sirmium stood. Its weathered, unbreached walls were a symbol of the gaunt, unyielding strength of these defenders of the Danube frontier. Severina could not feel their unquestioning faith, their adamantine sense of duty, but their constancy was a rebuke to her phase of weakness. From them she drew courage to hope again.

Slowly, against immense difficulties, Aurelian made progress with the development of a cavalry striking force. The plan, modified though it was from the soaring projects of Gallienus, could be realized only in part. Mounts had to be found, equipped, trained, fed. The right type of trooper had to be created from soldiers whose immemorial tradition was of fighting on foot. Tactics had to be evolved, commanders discovered and given the opportunity to acquire experience.

But once in being, the cavalry, however meager their number, proved their value. In this vague, shifting, intermittent warfare, this groping for and then hot pursuit of a nimble enemy, the horseman gradually restored some of the advantage to Rome. If only Aurelian could have built up the great and varied cavalry corps Gallienus had so lightly envisaged, the war in the Balkans would have been swiftly over. He could have probed relentlessly for the raiders, cramped their movement, pinned them down, crushed them.

As it was, after years of superhuman effort, he was able to maintain in the field, despite heavy wastage, about two thousand medium cavalry, although even these were scattered far and wide in small detachments, so that he could never dispose of more than a few hundred at one time and place, no matter how pressing the emergency.

Over the years, painfully, with many setbacks, Aurelian and the other Illyrian generals gained the upper hand. Wider and wider areas of the Balkans were for longer and longer periods free from incursions. The neighborhood of certain fortresses, Sirmium prominent among them, had acquired a bad reputation with the barbarians; little plunder and hard knocks in plenty were to be found there. Though fighting continued, the time came when the Illyrians could lift their eyes from their own horizons and take in the vista of the shattered Empire. Tyrants and Pretenders all over the scene . . . Britain and Gaul under one usurper . . . Zenobia, the widowed Queen of Palmyra, enthroned over the eastern provinces which she and her husband, Odenathus, had rescued from the Persians . . . the great province of Dacia foundered in darkness.

Amid the anarchy, the sentiment had always prevailed with the Illyrians that the true Sovereign of the Roman world was the

Augustus established in Italy. It had been in the name of Gallienus that they had fought on and to him that they had addressed their reports and their usually futile appeals for supplies and reinforcements. Now the gravest challenge of all appeared to Gallienus. His senior general, Aureolus, rebelled and led an army south through the Alps into Italy. Gallienus roused himself to one of his brilliant bursts of energy. He drove straight at Aureolus, routed him, chased him into Milan, blockaded him there.

For Gallienus it was imperative to stamp out quickly the last vestiges of this threat to his authority so near Rome. To the Balkans came urgent orders. The Emperor bestowed honors and promotions on Claudius, Aurelian, and several of their colleagues, at the same time commanding them to join him speedily, with what armament they could muster, at the siege of Milan.

The Illyrians consulted together. Year after year they had faithfully served Gallienus. They had not taken advantage of his difficulties, nor called him to account for his failures. Now he had summoned them—away from the Balkans—to waste their strength in beating down the latest of the endless series of Pretenders whose emergence was due largely to his own inadequacies as Emperor.

They looked at one another, and a thought that had grown, unspoken, in the mind of each presently found its way to their lips.

20

IN THE middle of one morning, a soldier brought a laconic note from Aurelian at the barracks bidding Severina prepare for guests that afternoon. There would be Claudius, Mucapor, and Herennianus; all would leave by the evening.

Severina assumed that this meant another of those urgent conferences on scraping together the contingent that Claudius and Aurelian were very soon to lead into Italy to reinforce the siege of

Milan. She sighed over Aurelian's characteristically brief notice and, in the calm, brisk manner she had acquired from Mammaea, set about the arrangements for a meal. But the phrases of the message kept coming back. All Aurelian's letters were concise in the extreme. A stranger would have found this one not a whit different from the others. To Severina, however, sensitive to even the slightest change of his mood, the faintest shift of emphasis in his words, there sounded something more than usually purposive and peremptory in that note. She had a feeling that this was not to be a routine conference.

Mucapor accompanied Aurelian from the barracks. To Severina's astonishment, two Centurions followed them past the porter's little shelter. One remained in the courtyard, loitering by the outer wall where he was invisible from the street but able to keep the gate under observation; the other, a chunky man, with broad nostrils and the lowering brow and aggressive jaw of the parade-ground bully, entered the house behind Aurelian.

After a brief greeting to Severina, Aurelian led the way to a small room isolated at the end of the corridor, where from time to time he conferred with callers in privacy. Its walls and floors were bare, and the only furniture was a plain oblong table and half a dozen stools. He went in with Mucapor; the Centurion attending him pulled the door to and planted himself in front of it.

Severina's other guests arrived singly. First came Herennianus. For once he was in sober mood, without his bright, provocative smile. To Severina's cordial welcome he returned only formal phrases and he walked beside her mutely while she conducted him to the conference room. She had hardly returned when Claudius was announced. With a warm smile, he pressed her hands and inquired after her health and little Julia's; but from the way he listened to her answer she could see that he was occupied with thoughts of his own. Like Herennianus, he fell silent as they approached the conference room.

In due course the meal was ready, but Phoebe, whom she sent to inform Aurelian, hurried in to declare indignantly that the Centurion had turned her back. Severina went along herself to investigate. At her approach the Centurion shifted his feet a little, so as

247

to interpose his forbidding bulk more squarely between her and the room. "Nobody to go in, Lady," he said gruffly. "Gen'ral's orders!" There was no arguing with his tone. Not so much humiliated as disturbed by what might be going on behind that dumb door, she went away, resigning herself to wait.

So long did she wait that mingled with her unease about the conference was a housewife's vexation over a spoiled meal. She sent refreshments out to the Centurion in the courtyard. He munched his bread and meat and took frequent swigs of wine without once removing his sharp eyes from the gate. A similar tray, carried by Phoebe to the Centurion outside Aurelian's door, came back at once, untouched. "On duty!" was all he had said, with a dismissive gesture.

At last, Severina heard a heavy, measured tread from the direction of the conference room and the Centurion entered. "Gen'ral says in five minutes," he announced.

They filed in, Claudius at their head, looking tired and depressed. Aurelian, who followed, had an air of bleak composure, which did not reassure Severina. Mucapor's tough, solid face gave nothing away. Quietly she observed Herennianus. He was just keeping his excitement under control, but the way his eyes darted from one to another of his companions gave him the appearance of a rather juvenile conspirator not quite equal to the strain of secrecy.

Conspirator! As the word inscribed itself in her mind, she gazed intently at the four silent men standing at the laden tables, where Mucapor alone was eating steadily while the others seemed to find relish chiefly in the wine.

They stood revealed. It had been no combing out of garrisons, no troop movements, that they had planned in their withdrawn and guarded conference. They were engaged in a plot—a deadly plot that could have only one possible victim!

At the surge of these thoughts, incandescent, into her brain, her eyes happened to meet Aurelian's. He must have read her horror, for he frowned and gave her a sharp little nod that was both confirmation and warning.

There could be small doubt who had been reluctant, who urgent, in these fatal counsels. Claudius must have given only tardy and grudging assent, while Aurelian's was the decisive will, the driving power behind the conspiracy. As for Mucapor and Herennianus, they were subordinates; they could only have been there to receive instructions.

Hurriedly, Severina lowered her eyes, for the tears stung them. She felt sick with shock and the sense of mighty and bloody events impending. Gallienus who once had placed caressing hands on her shoulders and had wooed her lightly with bantering words, the gay, frivolous, mocking, indolent, brilliant, brave, and resourceful Gallienus was doomed. The Illyrians had turned against him!

Long afterward, Severina, for whom the subject had an appalled fascination, set herself to discover all she could about the last tragic phase in the camp before Milan. Her instinctive sympathy for this strange and complex man, which had been inactive for years, sharply revived, so that she could divine something of his feelings and the atmosphere around him as his reign and life drew inexorably to their close.

Gallienus had aged—a gray-haired man, with a lined, irascible face, though he could still speak honeyed words to those he feared or needed. His humor had usually a bitter flavor. He had proved himself the ultimate cynic. His corrosive tongue had reduced all values but one to emptiness; power was the only thing he respected.

As long as the Illyrians stayed loyal, Gallienus had just strength enough to hold Italy and the Balkans. His energy was intermittent but when, at intervals, under the stress of deadly danger, he roused himself, it was as though he blazed with vitality. His generalship, at its best, was inspired. He could snatch the initiative from an enemy, pounce on him, smash him on the battlefield by daring maneuvers and swift attacks carried out with fiery courage.

When the Balkan Legions marched into the camp before Milan, they made the impression of a hostile army, rather than of reinforcements. The sullen faces of these rough frontier veterans showed their resentment at having been dragged far from home on an unpopular campaign. The troops of Gallienus, who lined the road, watched them without a cheer.

Gallienus welcomed the Illyrian commanders effusively, but there were no answering smiles; they looked at him dourly. That such blunt fighting men, fatigued by years of war, should feel no enthusiasm for the siege was natural enough. But this was something more. Gallienus, the most subtle and penetrating man in his army, could not mistake the signs. Death was in their demeanor.

The liberality of Gallienus had kept him popular with his own troops. He could still make a fight for it—if he chose. But most of his senior commanders, even the Prefect of his Guard, were Illyrians; they would stand together with their countrymen. He was in the toils; to struggle on was really pointless. After all, a man can fight only so long for an endlessly disputed throne. A day comes when discouragement begins to master him.

He shrugged his shoulders, dismissing hope. There was no escaping the Illyrians.

Gallienus had made a mockery of too much to feel self-pity; but he felt afraid. As he walked back to the Praetorian Tent through the falling dusk from his conference with the newly arrived commanders, the expressionless sentries of the Imperial Guard observed him two or three times hesitate and then cast a quick glance over his shoulder.

That night Gallienus, still wearing his breastplate, sat a long time in the tent, a miniature pavilion, in which the purple silk coverlet of the camp bed struck the only note of luxury among the studied simplicity of the furnishings. At last he called his body-servant, "Hey—come and help me unbuckle." To the uncomprehending slave he said with a twisted smile, "I've a fancy they won't murder a sleeping man!"

Several days passed uneventfully, except that Claudius left to take command of an outlying force a few hours' ride away. Then, in the dead of night, a trumpet shrilled somewhere on the camp perimeter nearest to the town; answering clamor of trumpets from other points set the night shuddering.

The entrance fold of the Emperor's tent was snatched aside. Gallienus emerged, fumbling with the clasp of his cloak. His eyes were bloodshot and a stale odor of wine was thick in his breath. From the agitated gloom nearby, Mucapor materialized. "A sally, Augus-

tus," he announced gruffly. "The rebels have broken into the camp!"
Gallienus listened, shivering in the night air. The tumult was growing; more and more lights kindled in the distance. A soldier led one
of the Emperor's charger forward. "This way, Your Majesty," he
said in a strong Illyrian accent and he helped the Emperor to mount.

Mucapor turned and made a vehement gesture. A vague bulk advanced with a multiplied clatter and shaped itself into half a dozen
troopers of one of Herennianus' squadrons. Mucapor indicated the
Emperor's tall form already receding into the dark and they set
off in pursuit, surrounding him rapidly.

Dawn was paling the torches in the Praetorian Tent when
Claudius walked in on legs stiff from his long ride through the
night. His face was strained and grim. At once a group of Illyrian
officers with Aurelian at their head saluted him as Emperor. Their
voices were subdued and their eyes avoided the bed on whose purple
coverlet lay motionless a long figure under the cloak Gallienus had
snatched up when the alarm sounded.

Claudius acknowledged the salute, unsmiling; he kept his back to
the bed. "Is the war chest safe?" he demanded with unwonted
harshness. "Good! Then get the troops on parade in an hour. I
shall announce a donative!"

With Aurelian absent and on such grievous business, a burden of
melancholy weighed on Severina's heart. Whatever powerful reasons of state actuated the Illyrians, they had gone to strike down a
man to whom they had pledged faithful service, a man whose image
was vivid and—despite all she knew about him—still attractive in
her mind. It seemed to her that a pall of evil lay over the world.
Loyalty and the trust of man in man were extinguished and the
killing would go on without end.

The days passed in dreary procession, with no word from Aurelian.

One morning Mammaea did not appear from her room. A
presentiment turned Severina cold, but she forced herself to speak
calmly as she asked Phoebe to see if her mistress wanted anything.
Phoebe came tottering back, her old, bent body shaken by sobs.
Severina gazed at her wildly, then clutched her bony hand.

251

Through a blur of tears she saw Phoebe raise her gray head and nod as though dazed, while the drops ran down her wrinkled cheeks. Severina walked on unsteady legs toward Mammaea's room. She had a nightmare sensation, as though the corridor walls were bulging inward to crush her.

A waxen replica of Aurelian's mother lay upon the bed. Death had no reticence, no decent regard. Mammaea's mouth had sagged open. Her staring eyeballs were a murky yellow. White hair straggled over her face. Moving the cover, Severina saw that the hands were clenched tight, as though death had come in a sharp spasm.

"Good-bye, Mother!" she sobbed and leaned over to close Mammaea's eyelids, shuddering at the contact with the chill, dead flesh. She drew the cover over the rigid face and stood debating with herself whether or not to send the news at once to Aurelian. Quickly she decided to inform him; delay would not make the blow any lighter. With deepened anguish she wondered for a moment whether it could be only chance that his mother had died while he was gone on a treacherous and bloody errand; then, with a feeling of guilt toward him, she thrust the thought away.

Numbed inwardly, though still the active mistress of a household, Severina waited for Aurelian's return. The rooms, even when Julia played noisily in them and the servants bustled around, seemed empty and cheerless. Mammaea had stamped them with her individuality, filled them with her warmth. She was gone now, leaving them mournful.

Early one afternoon, Aurelian walked in, haggard and mudsplashed after days of furious riding through foul weather. His grief was silent and enclosed and terrible. He asked only where his mother was buried. Severina did not accompany him to the neglected cemetery outside the city wall. When he came back his face was stony and, for once, his soldierly erectness had forsaken him and he was a little bowed. Severina approached, but his bleak look forbade her comfort. This was pain that he had to endure alone.

After Milan and his tragic homecoming, Aurelian was grimmer than ever, more taciturn and withdrawn into himself. He was absent a good deal and this made the barrier of silence behind which his sorrow hid more difficult to breach. Yet while Severina suffered with him almost unbearably in this voiceless, masculine grief, it was hard to dismiss the image of Gallienus, hacked by the swords of men who had sworn obedience to him. The dead Emperor still pursued her, his wounds more insidious than his charms had been.

Only little Julia could coax her father, if briefly, from his heavy mood. With her bestriding his knee, artlessly chattering, he would forget for a while his somber reflections. Julia was eight when Mammaea died. She had been very fond of her grandmother, but she was a stable child who soon adjusted herself to her bereavement. Severina was her tutor and found her without much subtlety or invention, but with a quick, strong grasp of practical points and a retentive memory. A soldier's daughter rather than a philosopher's granddaughter.

Meanwhile the war against the barbarians had rekindled. Burying his sorrow deeper within him, Aurelian went out to fight at the new Emperor's side.

The relations between Claudius and Aurelian, two commanding men, though disparate in character, had long been those of sturdy comradeship, but had now grown delicate and uneasy—the relations between a king and a kingmaker. Aurelian, regarded everywhere as second man in the Empire, had become too powerful for a subject. Claudius owed him too much for gratitude.

Happily no open antagonism developed out of the implicit challenge of Aurelian's eminence. Their old mutual goodwill was for the present stronger than the strain upon it; their common Mithraism also exerted its effect. Above all, new dangers pressing upon the torn and enfeebled Empire gave them no choice but to stand together.

Their dissension would have split the Army and completed the Empire's disintegration; their cooperation was bound to be fruitful of good. Rome now could benefit from a leadership at once cool and judicious, prompt, daring, and decisive.

And, as never before, the Empire had need of such supreme leadership. A day of fiery trial, transcending any during all the foregoing years of anarchy, was at hand.

At last the chiefs of the Goths and their confederates resolved to abandon the dispersed raids that had become productive more of casualties than plunder and to throw the whole of their energies into a concerted onslaught that would bring the Empire down in ruin. In turf cabins and leather tents on the wide plains, in smoky timber huts in forest clearings, in warrior assemblies at the tribal meeting places, where the clash of swords on shields acclaimed the fierce oratory of the advocates of war, the new master plan was elaborated and explained.

Through vast regions of barbarism sped the call to arms and the tribes mustered, tens of thousands strong. Forests were felled; a huge fleet of light galleys built. The warrior multitudes, of which the Goths were the core and the command, were to launch themselves toward the straits dividing Europe from Asia, burst into the Aegean and take the Balkan defenses in flank and rear. No army that Rome could conceivably put into the field, they felt assured, could withstand their numbers.

Such was the confidence in success that the wives and concubines of many of the chiefs and more important warriors embarked with them on the galleys. Once the seaborne invasion had begun, the women and children in the tribal settlements awaited word to load their domestic gear in their leather-roofed wagons and travel to the new homes the swords of the men had carved out for them beyond the Danube.

The swarming Gothic flotillas issued from the rivers of Sarmatia and pointed their prows south. Hundreds of leather sails swelled out; thousands of oars churned the sea. Before long the host made its first landfall and fighting rapidly spread toward the Aegean. Here and there a powerful fortress beat off attack. But few places could long resist the battering-ram thrust of the great horde. News came that the Roman Army was on the march. The Goths decided to meet it. They abandoned the fleet and, doubly unwieldy now with their burden of loot and long trains of miserable captives, moved slowly inland. In their wake briefly flamed the funeral pyres of Roman towns that had resisted a day or two, until the scaling-ladders tilted against the walls and files of warriors spurted irresistibly up onto the ramparts.

Calm amid the mounting crisis, Claudius had energetically mobilized. Cities were stripped of their garrisons, outlying detachments called in to strengthen the field army. Still, his forces, shaky in morale and poorly equipped, were decidedly inferior to the Goths in numbers. When Aurelian would join him from Sirmium, he could reckon on perhaps twenty-five thousand men, mainly infantry, the remnants of a dozen battered and dispirited legions, to meet over forty thousand barbarians.

In Sirmium the troops of Aurelian's command paraded. Silent crowds waited on the sidewalks to see them march away. Severina stood with a group of anxious-looking City Councillors watching the muster. She had never thought to count the garrison of Sirmium; now, concentrated before her, it appeared a frighteningly inadequate reinforcement for an Emperor striving to stem a great invasion—one undermanned legion in all. Gazing on the soldiers' sullen faces, Severina appreciated for the first time the full gravity of the crisis. Defeat meant irretrievable disaster, and defeat was in the air. These were men who could see Death beckoning, who felt themselves marching into her embrace. They passed between the frozen crowds, their step mechanically precise, but with no zest, no pride in their bearing.

Only the cavalry squadrons clattered by with the dash and swagger of soldiers spoiling for a fight.

A skeleton force was left behind, a mere shadow of a garrison, to occupy the guardhouses and post lookouts on the towers.

After the march away, all that people could do was wait. Long and empty days dragged by, stretching out into weeks—and still no news came. There was even a dearth of rumor, as if invention were appalled at the possibilities and waited, paralyzed, on events.

Every day the temples of Sirmium were busy. Worldly citizens, accustomed to think of the Gods as somewhat unreliable business associates, now paid zealously for sacrifices. Skeptics prayed; the devout multiplied their supplications. Pale and tense, the mothers and wives of soldiers crowded the services. As before in time of

255

crisis, there were murmurs against the Christians, of whom a handful were known to exist in the slums. Once the Town Council even approached Severina—whom, in Aurelian's absence, they regarded as his representative—with a proposal to arrest the heads of the Christian congregation in order to allay popular feeling. Severina forgot her poise and treated the startled Councillors to one of her old outbursts of indignation. Out there Claudius and Aurelian, with Rome's only army, were engaged on their forlorn hope, ready to go down fighting, to maul the enemy with their last flicker of strength; here grave City Fathers could find no better occupation than to harass poor and inoffensive folk who worshiped differently from their neighbors.

All this time apprehension was a throbbing wound in Severina's side. She knew the temperament of the two great Roman commanders and foresaw with certainty what their strategy would be. As soon as they had marshaled strength enough for reasonable prospects of success, that is when the odds against them ceased to be overwhelming, they would seek the enemy out. They would not waste time in intricate maneuvering; instead, they would choose their point, advance upon it swiftly, and strike with all their strength. The clash of host on host would be tremendous.

One night sleep eluded Severina even longer than usual; hour after hour she lay restless with an aching head, while the familiar worries scuttled through her mind. Eventually a dazed sleep sealed her eyes but, instead of muffling these cares, plunged her into a world of tumult lighted by a deathly sun. Tight files of men with rigid faces under Roman helmets, all Illyrians in plain and battered armor, plodded in silence toward a vast swirling sea of barbarians, from which a monstrous clamor burst endlessly. On and on marched the grim ranks, never varying their pace, until with a convulsive motion they merged with the dense enemy masses. The conjoined armies writhed and heaved amid howls and piercing screams and a shattering clangor of metal.

Countless bodies cumbered the ground, the glint of armor marking the Roman dead amid the pallid white skins and leather accoutrements of the Goths.

At last her eyes, frantically searching the miles of chaos, caught hold of Aurelian. Her heart lunged against her ribs and she moaned. The thickest press of battle was round him; he towered above the melee. A thousand arrows shivered on his shield; swords glanced from his helm; spearpoints blunted on his breastplate. A twisted smile made his face strange and cruel as he drove deeper and deeper among the Goths, exultant with the terrible joy of battle.

Shuddering, she started awake. The vision still blazed before her eyes. A half-stupefied glance at the window told her the hour was already well past dawn. The servants, finding her asleep, had been careful not to disturb her. As her mind cleared, an intolerable sense of expectancy took hold of her. She dragged herself from the disordered bed, sluiced her face with cold water, dressed hurriedly, and threw a warm cloak about her; then, not troubling to summon an escort, she went out in the cool morning toward the main gate, where from an early hour little groups of women were accustomed to wait patiently for the arrival of a messenger from the Army.

There were several on the way to join the vigil. They recognized Severina and came timidly round, gazing at her in speechless interrogation. She shook her head, smiled wanly, and walked on in their midst, a little comforted by their company.

They halted, transfixed. The universe shattered. Smashing through the air came a trumpet's jubilant pealing. Everything reeled round Severina. She braced herself and followed with her ear that breaking voice of triumph . . . it arose from the gate, piercing a faint swell of cheering. Severina sprang forward. Her cloak flew out as she ran, outpacing her more heavily built companions. Soon she could see the guards with glistening faces clustered round a dusty dispatch rider, who was bowed in fatigue over his horse's neck. High on the wall above the trumpet smote the heart again with its strident crowing; she saw the wild gesticulations of soldiers signaling from tower to tower.

The women poured round the messenger, grasped his legs, his saddle, his cloak, his bridle. Before he could speak, one of them, overcome by an agony of relief, collapsed almost under the hooves. A rushing noise in her ears almost deafened Severina; there was a confusion of bodies, faces, smells. But she gritted her teeth and caught the messenger's words. "Victory!" he cried and a savage grin divided the streaked grime of his face. "A terrific victory! At Naissus—in Dardania." A long sigh came from the crowd. The soldier lifted himself in the saddle and raised his gruff, parched voice to reach the limit of his audience, which was growing every moment. Curt, racy phrases came jerking out of him. The Illyrians had saved the Empire. They had cut the Goths to pieces. Scores of chiefs, thousands on thousands of tribesmen had fallen.

The messenger shook his dark, curly head. His white teeth gleamed. He looked strangely young to bear such momentous tidings. "You should'a' been there!" he called, gloating. "Miles of 'em—all dead!"

Severina tugged at his leg. "Aurelian—the General?" she implored, forgetting all reserve, just one among a multitude of women filled with terrible anxiety for their menfolk. "Safe!" the messenger croaked. "By the Sun, Lady—tell 'em to fetch me some wine. I'm dying o' thirst!" An eddy ran through the crowd; somebody thrust a slopping tankard into his grasp. Drops splashed over Severina's upturned face as he lifted the vessel to his lips, and she exulted, for this was the stinging savor of victory!

Once he had drained the wine, the messenger's demeanor changed. "Look, Lady," he said, addressing Severina as obviously a person of consequence. "I've got to see the Council." He slapped his pouch. "The Army needs supplies."

But still the women obstructed him, pressing round, babbling, crying out to each other, weeping noisily, one or two holding children up to look at the man who had brought them news of the great deliverance. In vain the soldier waved his arms and shouted hoarsely. By now the crowd's last self-restraint had been swept away by the explosive ecstasy of release from weeks of nightmare.

A thousand loosened tongues maintained a deafening uproar, which went on and on, drowning all his appeals. Severina herself was shaken by such a tumult of emotion that she found herself laughing and crying together. But somehow the soldier's plea—which she, at least, could make out—and his indication of a letter from the Army struck through to her understanding. With an intense effort, she mastered her hysteria. The Army needed help. Aurelian needed help. She must do something!

Thrusting herself alongside the neck of the horse, she seized the bridle and tugged it. "Make way there!" she called in a high, strained, imperious voice. She drove with her shoulder at two women directly in front of her and pushed and twisted between them. At once they grasped her purpose and struggled to make room for her; the horse followed its taut bridle into the gap. "Make way!" repeated Severina shrilly, caring nothing for dignity, nothing for decorum. A dozen voices on both sides took up the cry and, slowly, an irregular lane opened through the crowd down which the First Lady of Sirmium led the stumbling horse with its grinning rider.

Prompted by some irresistible mass impulse, the women fell in behind the horseman and followed. Soon there was a long, noisy, gesticulating procession at the head of which strode Severina with the bridle in her hand. As in a dream she was conscious of the multitude with waving arms innumerable that lined the sidewalks and from which endlessly rolled a storm of cheering.

21

LEAVING Aurelian in command of mopping-up operations against the Goths, Claudius shifted his headquarters to Sirmium. Severina was not there to greet the new Emperor. For with the Army came the plague, which had often before traveled with the Legions along the great arterial roads. Warned by an urgent letter from Aurelian, who wrote bitterly that the plague was killing his men faster than the Goths had done, Severina hurriedly moved with Julia and her little household to a villa that Claudius had placed at her disposal some nineteen or twenty miles from the town.

She had lived so many years in a fortress that a circuit of walls had become necessary to her sense of security. Her first days and, more particularly, nights on the open plains proved an ordeal. It was some time before she ceased to listen for the stealthy tread of raiders and to feel a stab of apprehension when she approached a corner. Very slowly country quiet and solitude exerted their healing effect; her nerves relaxed, her sleep grew more tranquil. The villa, whose owner had abandoned it years ago, had been ransacked by the Goths and left in a ruinous state. Now one wing had been hastily restored and workmen were busy elsewhere in the rambling group of buildings. But they were invisible most of the time and their hammering muffled by distance. There was nothing to mar the rather limp calm in which Severina passed the days.

In particular, the huge, neglected gardens suited her mood. She would wander absently along the grass-cloven paths, where last year's leaves rustled and crackled underfoot. Barbarian axemen had had much sport with the florid statuary, but the headless torsos and hacked limbs did not affront one's eyes. To Severina it seemed that these mutilated marbles had had time to grow accustomed to their injuries and were at peace; they were in harmony with their setting of unkempt bushes and towering weeds.

The weeks slipped by in a gentle, recuperative melancholy, their only excitement an occasional brief note from Aurelian. He wrote that there were practically no more cases of plague among the field army, but that in Sirmium the death roll remained heavy.

Out of habit, though rather inattentively, Severina still followed events, mainly through the medium of letters from acquaintances in Sirmium. Claudius, she could perceive, was a beloved Emperor, one of those rare sovereigns whose goodness makes itself felt by whole populations although they are mostly invisible in palace or camp. Indeed the moment had need for a ruler of his mild and amiable genius. Everywhere there was a state of lassitude. Naissus had been a supreme effort wrung from men worn down by a decade of grueling warfare; the Army was at the end of its tether. The civil administration had undergone an equivalent strain. In the war zones it had virtually disappeared and elsewhere it functioned primarily as a clumsy and oppressive engine of taxation.

Yet—though at this stage only faintly—Severina had a sense of a slow reflux of Roman energies; the weakness of the moment was that of convalescence, no longer of decline. For the first time in many weary years there was inspiration from the Throne and firm leadership. Illyrian valor and warcraft had dealt the Goths a resounding rebuff and won the reeling Empire a respite.

One morning a steady downpour kept Severina restlessly indoors; early in the afternoon, when the rain had ceased and a watery sun blinked on the sodden world, she went into the garden and walked about, inhaling the cool, washed air with pleasure. She halted a little while before a beech which stood near the intersection of two paths and watched in a preoccupied way the drops falling as the wind shook the sleek leaves. The swish of brisk feet through the puddles startled her. She turned and saw Herennianus impatiently striding ahead of the woman servant who was conducting him to her.

It was their first meeting since, months before, the garrison of Sirmium had marched to join the Emperor for the impending battle with the Goths. Even at a distance his keen face looked worn. In his gait was still something of his cavalry captain's swagger, but as he drew near she saw that his demeanor was solemn and intent, as though he bore news of grave import. Her heart beat painfully while she waited. He came up and saluted her. "Welcome, Herennianus," she said, forcing a little smile.

"By your leave," he answered and gestured sharply to the servant to go away. He appeared to be measuring the time until he judged she would be out of sight and earshot. Then he dropped on one knee on the wet gravel of the path, took Severina's hand and raised it gently to his lips. "I bring you greetings from the Emperor, your husband, Augusta." He recited the words like a rehearsed formula.

She drew back a little, disengaging her hand. Herennianus remained kneeling. Unable to find her voice, she motioned him to rise.

For a full minute she stared at him, saying nothing, though two or three times her dry mouth worked and she was on the point of speech. Well, it had come—as Crinitus had predicted in his jesting manner so long ago. In an odd way she had always known. It had to be, she could see that. Now Aurelian was alone on the heights—except for her standing beside him. Her mind could grasp the fact coldly and clearly, but her emotions had not yet stirred. The transition had been too sudden, across too wide a gulf—for an immeasurable distance separated the absolute ruler of millions from even the most exalted of his subjects.

"Come and sit down," she said at last, indicating a stone bench not far away. "Tell me what happened. The Emperor—Claudius, I mean?"

He spread his cloak over the cold, discolored slab, but did not sit down beside her. "Dead of plague," he answered briefly. "We proclaimed Aurelian, the obvious successor."

"Did Claudius—did he nominate anyone? He has a brother . . ."

"Oh yes, Quintillus." Herennianus frowned. "A nobody—but he may give some trouble. As to nominating anyone— They say Claudius sent a personal message from his deathbed to your husband, urging him to assume the Purple."

She looked at him sharply. He met her scrutiny with steady eyes. "I can't vouch for the message. I just don't know. But Claudius died of the plague—of the plague!" he repeated with emphasis. "We heard of it two days later. Still it wasn't altogether a surprise. He couldn't have put up much resistance. He was a sick man, already . . . ever since . . . since Milan. You know, Severina—Augusta—he took it very hard."

Herennianus began to walk a few paces up and down, swiveling in a parade-ground movement. "Anyone else would have taken to his bed. But Claudius was a hero of antiquity—he led us against the Goths. Things were in the balance a long time, I can tell you! Our infantry were being forced back. Then Aurelian—Your Majesty's husband, I mean—launched us cavalry at their right wing. We smashed through and swung round on their center, where the Gothic chiefs had their ensigns. Even then they held us off until some of our men got round their rear. Mithras! That was fighting, Severina!" He laughed, his eyes kindling. "Aurelian went straight for their standards and the infantry closed in again. I've seen some battles but, by all the Gods, this one dwarfed the lot! The uproar—well, you just couldn't describe it. Men were screaming and sob-

262

bing with rage as we cut through to their ensigns. I grabbed one—three javelins whacked onto my shield together. Spears were coming at me from all directions. My horse went down. When I picked myself up, the cavalry had gone twenty yards on and Aurelian was still in front—he's so tall, I could see him plainly."

Herennianus ceased his restless prowl and stood before Severina with ardent face. "Claudius died," he said in a low, intense voice. "We lost one hero—but now we have another on the Throne. Severina, dear Augusta, we are going to rescue the Empire! Mithras has heard our prayer. With all my heart I believe it!"

He came closer, still agitated by the mighty events he had described and the future, tremendous with strife and hope, into which Aurelian would lead them.

She smiled at his faith, simple and noble; at his brave heart that welcomed great perils in a great enterprise. "I believe it, too, Herennianus," she said softly.

He appeared to hesitate. "Augusta!" he brought out compulsively. "You can depend on me . . . always . . . to the death!"

"I know!" she answered, touching his arm, moved by his concern, so close to tenderness, at the dangers to which the pinnacled Throne would expose her. "I shall be all right," she added. "Guard my husband well!"

He nodded soberly; then he said, "I have his orders for you, Augusta. He wishes you to report to him. I've brought your escort. The Army is marching this way, so you won't have far to go. You will not be returning here. A party will arrive tomorrow to begin stripping the villa."

Severina smiled faintly. She could recognize the decisive tone, the prompt command of necessary detail—and the disregard of ordinary comfort and convenience. Reading her thoughts, Herennianus smiled, too, and shrugged, as if to say: That's the way things are going to be done henceforward!

Her expression grew serious again. Fixing her eyes on Herennianus, she asked, "What did Aurelian say when you proclaimed him Emperor?"

A shadow flitted across his face. He did not answer. "Herennianus —I beg you," she stammered, feeling it vital to know.

263

"You could command me," he said.

"I prefer to ask you, as an old friend."

"Well," he began uncomfortably. "We were all there. Probus—Diocletian—Mucapor—several others—and we decided at once. We were absolutely convinced the Army would accept no one else. Aurelian said nothing for a while; he just stared at us in a strange, fixed way, as though he were looking through us. Then he spoke very quietly—or, rather, murmured something . . ."

"What was that?"

Herennianus shifted under her gaze. "I just caught it," he answered slowly. "The Gladiator's Salute, you know—one who is about to die salutes you."

". . . Who is about to die . . . ," she repeated under her breath. "Go into the house, Herennianus," she added aloud. "Say that I want a meal prepared for your men. You will dine with me. I will join you shortly."

Already, though she did not know it, she spoke in the mandatory manner of an Empress. Herennianus studied her face anxiously. "Don't reproach yourself," she said gently. "I had to know. Just go into the house."

He saluted her and went.

Now pain had awoken in her heart and an exaltation that had no joy in it. Yes, this had to be. Herennianus and the others were right. With Claudius dead, the Empire needed Aurelian. The times demanded a giant; he alone was equal to the task. He would be unsparing to himself and to others, for such was his nature; he would be unsparing to her. He would offer himself, an incessant sacrifice, upon the altar of his dream of Rome regenerate. He would lay those puissant hands of his upon the battered Empire and with terrible exertions bend it to the shape of his desire.

As for herself, an Empress against her will, she would do whatever he required of her, as best she could. At his side; wherever he sent her. She would serve his dream, without his faith, without his courage, but she would not fail him.

Stern times lay ahead. Aurelian was a dedicated man engaged upon a task that would absorb him wholly. She could see little prospect of the companionship, the simple satisfactions of marriage, which a woman cherishes. But what right had an Empress of Rome in these evil days to expect otherwise? With all her strength she would help Aurelian. In that there might be for her a fulfillment beyond the vulgar categories of pleasure and happiness.

". . . One who is about to die. . . ." She understood what had prompted the words, but she wished he had not said them.

After two days on their journey, at the laborious pace of a man-borne litter, they encountered the first signs of the Army. A rider, crouched in the saddle with his face almost against his horse's neck, came at a gallop in their direction. "Imperial courier—priority on the road," Herennianus explained hurriedly to Severina; and he shouted to the cavalrymen of her escort to clear the way. With a clatter, the man flew past.

A couple of hours later, a second courier sped by. Before long, another brought the litter and its escort to a standstill on a crumbling section of road, while he brushed past at reckless speed, dust and tiny stone fragments spurting from his horse's hooves.

Severina watched his furious course for a little while, before settling back in the litter. An Imperial courier at full gallop. . . . It suggested the character of the reign. Aurelian would govern on the march; the camp would be his capital, his tent the center of a pulsating web that reached to the limits of the Empire.

By late afternoon, the countryside was swarming with soldiers preparing to bivouac. They looked very weary—as well they might, for Aurelian marched heavy infantry faster than any Roman commander had done before. Those nearest the road glanced indifferently at the litter and its escort of smart troopers. Herennianus trotted to Severina's side. "Here we are," he announced, pointing to a straggle of poor little houses that marked the outskirts of some village.

It proved a mean-looking place, consisting mainly of wooden hovels, which the barbarians had not thought worth plundering. Severina at once picked out Aurelian's headquarters—the only house of any consequence, a spacious though dilapidated one-story structure with a wooden verandah. No doubt it had belonged to the village headman. Two tough legionaries paced up and down before it with pike and shield.

The litter eased to the ground. Herennianus helped Severina alight and conducted her up the single creaking step onto the verandah. She was startled by a synchronized triple clash from the soldiers; it took some moments to realize that they had presented arms to their Empress.

Aurelian's voice, brisk, curt, forceful, could plainly be heard from one room. Herennianus rapped on the door, then threw it open. Severina saw Aurelian slowly turn, still talking in that commanding way to a couple of officers; they were Probus and Mucapor.

"Ah, Severina, you already!" said Aurelian. "Probus, Mucapor," he added over his shoulder, "I want five minutes. Order some food. Just five minutes—then come back. Well," he addressed Severina as soon as they had gone, "what's it like to be an Empress, eh?"

She took both his hands and searched his face with her eyes. "My dear Severina," he said with a little smile, "I'm just the same. Nothing's changed, except that I've got ten thousand problems to settle all at once, instead of only five hundred."

Still holding one of his hands, she sat down. "Now, Severina," he continued, "I want you to go to Rome."

She let his hand go. "Rome?" she repeated, puzzled and deeply disappointed. "Can't I stay with you?"

He gestured toward the window. "This is my place—with the Army. Listen, Severina. The tribes are still restless. We knocked them about at Naissus, but they'll argue that with Claudius dead, we'll have civil war—or at least disagreement among ourselves. They know the plague cost us thousands of men. They'll be back at us soon, I'm afraid. Another thing . . ."

There was a rather crude map of the Balkan provinces hanging from a nail on the wall; it was a trifle askew. Aurelian went over and rammed his right forefinger against the name, "Dacia," slanting northeastward from the river Danube. "I'm going across. No Emperor's been there for years. It's in an unholy mess. Goths—Vandals—Sarmatians—they've all been running wild. I'm going to see for myself. Maybe we can clear them out—reorganize the province—re-

266

group the population nearer the Danube. Otherwise . . ." His shrug conveyed not indifference or uncertainty but a stark decision.

Severina nodded, but did not interrupt. He had set a five-minute limit on their private conversation and she was anxious not to waste precious time with unnecessary words of her own.

"You never met Claudius' brother, did you, Severina?" Aurelian went on. "We're likely to have some trouble with him. It shouldn't last long. He's of no account, really. Still, what with one thing and another, I've got to stick with the Army. You are free. That's why I want you to go to Italy. It must be kept quiet—and I must have money and supplies as soon as possible. Write to your uncle, Crinitus. Tell him that you want him at the Palace, as your private adviser. Set up a Council of Regency. You in the chair; a few senior officials; perhaps a Senator or two . . ."

"Do you really think I'm capable of all that?" asked Severina in astonishment. "It needs someone of authority—experience . . ."

"Of course you are!" he said with emphasis. "You're the obvious choice. I've plenty of good soldiers, but nobody with your understanding. You've a first-class brain, Severina. Why, you can interpret what I think so that I myself understand it better! Take charge in Rome. Follow your uncle's advice when you're worried, but don't be afraid to made your own decisions. Be firm. Never show those Senators you're afraid of them or uncertain what to do!"

"Very well," she answered. "I'll go to Rome. My instructions?"

"As I've said. Keep Italy quiet. Get supplies and money moving to me. And stand no nonsense from the Senate."

Severina nodded. So she was not to be an idle, merely decorative consort, but something like a co-ruler. It should have been a daunting prospect, but she no longer felt those first doubts of her capacity to shoulder the responsibilities Aurelian was laying upon her. Nor was it hard to understand this quick assertion of her self-confidence. She was a woman of the frontier now. Ten strenuous and testing years in Sirmium had taught her to confront any problem with calm, to trust her own judgment, to make prompt decisions. She had learned to impose her will upon uncooperative people. Above all, she had come to share the instinctive scorn of the self-reliant frontier folk for the inhabitants of the safer and softer interior.

Besides, she was a Senator's daughter. She had seen behind the imposing ceremonial front. Those grave dignitaries of the Senate she knew to be, for the most part, shallow and timid prattlers disguised as statesmen by their official togas. She felt increasingly certain she could master them; if need be, bully them, drive them. After all, she would have the power. Speaking in Aurelian's name, she need not anticipate open defiance. It was slipperiness, evasion, the stratagems of shifty men, sycophants in the open and malicious grumblers in private, with which she would have to contend.

In these latter years she had seldom given thought to revisiting Italy. Sirmium had been her home; Aurelian's whereabouts her horizon. Now suddenly she had a picture of her uncle worn by many years of painful illness. A longing welled up in her to set eyes on him again and on Drusilla, growing old in widowhood, before they too were swallowed, like her father, into the irrecoverable past.

She thought: There will be compensations for me in Italy. But for Aurelian? Listening to him, studying his rough-hewn soldier's face, with its deep-furrowed brow under hair predominantly gray, she told herself: If mine will be a heavy burden in Rome, how much greater will his be!

The tribes were stirring again, he had said. Would these Germans never cease their restlessness? There was the obsessive ambition of Persia also to reckon with. The whole North, the whole East, were in agitation against this one man. In the Roman provinces were tyrants, usurpers, rebels—challenging, threatening this one man. And in those places where his authority was acknowledged, everything depended on him alone, everyone looked to him; his spirit must infuse itself into millions, his strength must shore up, clamp together the fabric of the decayed and disintegrating Empire.

She knew Aurelian. A dozen wars impended. He would shrink from none, but exert himself to the utmost in all of them. He would rule as Commander-in-Chief, rarely quitting his army. He would set himself to master the whole vast and varied realm his predecessors had ruled, never pausing until Rome's mandate was obeyed from the towers on Hadrian's Wall, on those far northern moors of Britain, to the parched land where the great fortresses watched

268

Persia across the Euphrates. It was a long way to march, but Aurelian would set the Legions marching it.

In that effort he would grudge nothing and it would exact all or almost all from him. It was useless to remind him that he was a man no longer young confronting a superhuman task, and that he needed to husband his energies; he simply would not listen to her pleas. She could only hope that he himself was mindful of the drain to come on his vitality, the ceaseless sapping at his bodily and mental powers, the pressures that might warp his judgment and break down his self-control.

Aurelian was looking at her, rubbing his chin. "There was a representative of the Senate—Eutropius, he's called—with Claudius at Sirmium. I'm told he's an honest man. He will travel back with you to Italy. Find out from him as much as you can about the situation there. He'll join you outside Sirmium. You're not to enter it, yourself. The plague is still killing people."

"When shall I see you again?" she asked quietly.

He reflected a moment. "When the position clears up. Perhaps when I'm back from Dacia. I may come to Rome. Maybe you'll visit the Army again." He grinned. "We'll proclaim you Mother of the Camps!" Then, without turning round, he called, "Yes, come in, Probus."

"Dinner, Augustus," Probus announced. He smiled at Severina. "A place is laid for the Augusta."

"Come and sample our rations," Aurelian said, taking Severina's elbow. "They're chiefly porridge—in various disguises."

A small convoy, with a string of packhorses, met Severina about ten miles from Sirmium. It carried in neatly docketed bales and cases everything she had designated to Aurelian's clerks as required on her journey. Miniature though the assemblage was, it did not spare Severina the ceremonial that attends the travels of an Empress. The whole retinue was drawn up for inspection; dismounted cavalrymen standing motionless with fists clenched round their upright lances; seven or eight officials, conscious of their dignity, in the robes appropriate to their rank; a dozen women—maids, laundresses, cooks—and half as many grooms, all looking awe-struck as though lightning might fly quivering at them from the litter.

A smiling, obsequious Greek secretary and the hefty Captain of Horse in command of the escort came forward to salute her and ask instructions. As she answered, Severina was very much aware that her manner lacked the aloof authority no doubt expected from her rank; she was a little surprised by the close and respectful attention with which both listened.

Her first order was for the dispatch of a messenger to inform the balance of her little household, with whom she had left Julia, where to meet the convoy. The question of her daughter was already troubling Severina deeply. Her new duties made the old routine impossible; when they got to Rome, the supervision of Julia would have to be handed over to a governess.

Such was the penalty of ascending the Throne. Aurelian would have no time to be a husband; she would have little time to be a mother.

The convoy plodded on its way and soon the walls of Sirmium rose into sight. Brave, haggard, shabby Sirmium; she would always think of it as home. Pacing along the potholed road came a deputation of Town Councillors to present congratulations and homage, Sempronius and Metellus, obviously proud of their long association with her, in the lead. With them was Eutropius, the emissary of the Senate, of whom Aurelian had spoken, a man of about fifty, with plump, rosy cheeks, a comfortable paunch, and an air of placid good nature.

Contrasting his sleek visage with the lined, nervous faces of the Town Councillors, she appreciated how much they—and she—had aged in their all-but-beleagured city.

Not much more than a decade had passed since she had made that journey from Baiae through the war zone to her husband's side. She felt as though in that time she had lived through five brutal decades. Yet in spite of her bereavements, the mortal dangers, the ever-harsher privations, those years at Sirmium had a glow as she looked back on them; they had brought her a happiness deep and strong enough to offset the personal loss and all the pain of war. Now she had a superstitious feeling that her happiness was rooted in one place; she would not be able to take it with her. Slowly, slowly, the walls curved in the distance round her right shoulder and dwindled. The past claimed Sirmium and the unforeseeable future beckoned her. To ease her heavy mood she summoned Eutropius and began with him the first of many conversations.

There was an odd innocence about Eutropius, and a warm simplicity of feeling that made it easy to like him. He was transparently surprised to find among all these uncouth Illyrian soldiers an Empress who was a woman of breeding and culture; and he soon became deeply attached to her. Something of a glutton, he could not help showing his distress at Severina's meager appetite. After a time, he began respectfully but earnestly to urge her to drink milk. "It is our mothers' food, Augusta!" he would say, fixing on her a regard full of concern. "Easy to digest—the best food there is!"

From his discursive and uncritical talk, Severina was able to learn much about the unreal politics, the personal feuds, the petty feverish bickerings, in which the Senate employed the energies denied outlet by its loss of effective power. At first she wondered why such an essentially naïve man had been entrusted with his delicate mission at the camps of the formidable Illyrian Emperors; later she decided it must be because he was not identified with any of the factions and cliques—Nature had made him too kindly and tolerant to be anything but a neutral.

Steadily, although slowed by the appalling conditions of the roads, the convoy pushed west and south. From her litter Severina watched the countryside painfully returning to life. Peasants were trickling back to the villages. Often she would look down on a family group pushed off the road by the procession. There might be an occasional graybeard or bent crone leaning on a stick; a thin wailing might be heard from a tiny bundle in some woman's arms. But as a rule she observed few old persons and even fewer children of tender years. For the most part, just ragged, bony-figured men and women of the more vigorous age groups, bowed under the weight of nondescript belongings, their faces inscrutable as the well appointed convoy defiled past. The only animals Severina saw with them were a few skinny and cruelly overloaded donkeys.

There was a bustle in the wrecked villages. People were rummaging in the ruins, fixing up ramshackle shelters, hauling in felled timber from the woods. Yet Severina could detect little zest in all this activity. Most of the peasants wore a dispirited look, which she attributed not only to the severity of their losses and the magnitude of the work of reconstruction, but also to lack of confidence in the future. It was as though their hearts told them that next year, or in five years' time, or in ten, the barbarians would come streaming back; that the rebuilt huts would go up in flames, the herds and flocks be driven off or slaughtered, the harvest trampled or left to rot unreaped.

Repeatedly Severina sent ahead instructions to the magistrates of the towns along her route, emphasizing that she was to be received without extravagance. But once the convoy had left behind the plains, littered with the debris of war, she found that the habit of sycophantic ostentation persisted strongly. Outside one town, the litter with its retinue entered a lane formed by white-clad boys and girls, who sang some adulatory chorus composed for the occasion. From the gate advanced a train of notables, including the Councillors, the Priests of the local cult, the leading merchants and the heads of the craft guilds. Severina alighted. The Chief Magistrate made an almost groveling obeisance; then, in florid and servile phrases, invited her to preside at games arranged in her honor and, afterward, to grace a grand banquet. The soldiers and servants of her retinue would also be feasted.

Severina was on the point of reminding him curtly that the province was near starvation. However, she checked herself. All were inclining toward her with looks of such eager anticipation that she decided it would be wrong to hurt their feelings as, evidently, they were determined to hurt their purses. Perhaps in this display was an upwelling of goodwill toward the wife of a hero—one of their own Illyrian heroes. In any case, her primary duty was to bind these people in loyalty to Aurelian. At her word of assent, there was an enthusiastic murmur and every face shone.

So, anxious though she was to press on, she sat through the morning watching the local youths contend in footraces and wrestling; heard fresh choruses in praise of her beauty and graciousness and Aurelian's valor; presented prizes; made an effort to swallow a little of the expensive viands set before her in nine elaborate courses; answered the fulsome address of the professional orator with a simple little speech, in which she spoke chiefly of the skill and charm of the boys and girls who had competed in sports and sun before her. She was astonished at the effect of her unpretentious words. The whole company stood up, applauding wildly. For the first time she heard the full-throated cry that never failed to shake her with a gust of answering emotion, "Long live our Augusta!"

From town to town, serving in this way a kind of apprenticeship as Empress, it was evident she was succeeding. The concourse lining the streets in the places they traversed grew more and more demonstrative. Severina made a point of walking a little distance on these occasions, restricting the scandalized civic officials to a minimum of ceremony. The crowds beheld a youngish woman of dignified bearing, simply dressed, with a pale, thoughtful, rather tired face. Her unaffected interest in everything she saw, the gentleness of the looks she turned toward the aged, the sudden warmth of her smile for the children, spoke to their hearts. They sensed that this Augusta loved her people and felt with them in their trials and sorrows. Their affection vented itself in endless hand-waving and thunderous cheers.

Outside Salonae, on the Dalmatian coast, an Imperial courier overtook the convoy. The brother of Claudius had committed suicide. All Italy had submitted to Aurelian and a deputation of leading Senators would be waiting to accompany Severina to Rome as soon as she had crossed the Adriatic. "Make all speed," Aurelian wrote. "We need supplies of every kind—and money. Another campaign may open soon. New forces of Goths are massing over the Danube."

22

TO THE Gothic chiefs pursuing their slow and sullen retreat through Dacia came word that the Emperor Claudius had died of plague. Their primitive mentality saw the world as an arena where mighty champions contended in personal combat and victory in pitched battle primarily as the epic achievement of some hero. It was easy to persuade themselves that, with Claudius dead, Rome would be incapable of wielding the sword that had vanquished them at Naissus.

They halted and conferred. News that the succession to the Roman Throne was being disputed confirmed them in their sanguine views. They were aware that Rome, destitute of reserves, could not maintain a field army in immediate readiness for operations, but only a nucleus of mobile fighting formations round which troops drawn from garrisons and other scattered forces would have laboriously to be assembled. A heavy blow falling on the frontier defenses could not be instantly countered.

The chiefs reminded themselves that the Balkans were far from having been picked clean; rich and still unravaged areas within it invited attack. All of them burned to efface the stain of defeat upon their renown and to avenge the thousands of their fallen. Their mood thus matched the apparent situation. It was decided to renew the invasion of the Empire.

From the camp messengers sped with fresh appeals to the martial spirit and the cupidity of the neighboring tribes. Reinforcements poured in. The Goths swung south; surged across the Danube; brushed aside the flimsy Roman forces stationed on its shore; absorbed many of the broken bands of their countrymen who in the wilds had eluded the great hunt after Naissus. Before long, a host almost as formidable as that which Claudius had bloodily repelled was bearing down again deep into the Balkans.

At this critical juncture, a mutiny broke out in the camp where Aurelian was swiftly concentrating his tired and depleted Legions. It was a routine explosion of restlessness and discontent among Illyrian soldiers of unruly temperament, worn out with marching and fighting, resentful of discipline, interrupted pay, monotonous rations. Ostensibly the grievance this time was Aurelian's failure to issue the donative customary on an Emperor's accession. The men recalled the generosity of Claudius—unaware that he had profited by the lucky seizure of Gallienus' war chest—and contrasted this with the tight-fistedness, as they saw it, of Aurelian.

First there were grumbles here and there among the more surly and the habitual troublemakers; then murmurs spread and mingled and became a gale. The voices of the Centurions announcing a parade were drowned by derisive shouts. Scowling, the men hung round their tents, retailing to each other with the monotonous foul language of angry soldiers the many wrongs they had endured since they had been fools enough to enlist. If that miserly old bastard wouldn't brass up, he could go and fight those flaming Goths himself! Loud, uneasy laughter greeted these sallies.

Mutiny was the reversal of the established order and, thanks to the frequency with which it occurred, had its own topsy-turvy conventions. The dreaded Centurions became the first target of the mutineers. It was their turn to be afraid, to hang back, to stay mute under threats and insults. One who was rash enough to try and hustle a soldier in the direction of the parade ground had his head laid open by a spear shaft and was kicked in the ribs as he lay bleeding on the ground.

In the Praetorian Tent Aurelian, on his feet before a little audience of senior officers, was reviewing with the aid of a map his proposed operations against the Goths. Everyone turned at the sound of feet pounding toward the entrance. The Guard Commander pushed in, red-faced and breathing heavily. He saluted Aurelian and hurriedly reported the sedition; before he had finished, there came a swell of indistinct but menacing noise from the distance to add urgency to his words.

Among the officers was Demaratus, who years before had been a Tribune on Aurelian's staff. Recently summoned by his old Commander from the studies for which he had abandoned military service, he was now gray-haired, and on his keen Greek face lines of suffering were graven, for he had lived through the sack of Athens. During the worst of the anarchy, he had resumed his armor several times to help repel or harass raiders.

Like some of the others, but with a more sensitive eye, he watched Aurelian as the Guard Commander announced the mutiny. An expression of stony coldness came over the Emperor's face, that front of bleak and rigorous self-control which disturbs rather than reassures the beholder. His voice was composed but a little harsher than usual, as he ordered Mucapor to call out the Praetorian de-

tachment of picked troops and post them to guard the Headquarters lines.

Then, deliberately, he looked at each officer in turn, as if to
observe if any were jumpy; sardonic and probing, his gaze rested
on Demaratus a trifle longer than on the others. This chilling survey
over, he turned to the unrolled map on the little table at his side
and, moving a steady forefinger over it in correspondence with his
comments, he continued calmly to detail marches and maneuvers,
just as if no mutiny were raging.

Demaratus found it impossible to keep his attention on this businesslike discourse. His ear was cocked for noises in the distance,
while his imagination distracted him with pictures of masses of
soldiers aimlessly drifting round the camp—armed groups brawling
—barrack politicians inflaming with their oratory crowds who bayed
back applause. . . .

At last Demaratus, who could see his own anxieties reflected in
the faces of other officers, could no longer stand the Emperor's unnatural indifference to the mutterings of a tempest that at any
moment might veer toward the Headquarters lines. He interrupted
Aurelian. "Augustus, the men are defying orders. How can you
assume that they will march and fight?"

Aurelian fixed a sarcastic stare on him. "Don't look so worried,
Philosopher!" he jeered. "The men will march. The men will fight.
Just try and be patient. I'm giving those fools out there a little time
to cool off. You understand, do you? Good! And now, with your
permission, we'll carry on. . . ."

He continued methodically to expound his plan of campaign, but
with a grating note that warned any faint-hearts to stay dumb.
Rather ruefully, Demaratus reflected that Aurelian was right. This
was a situation where any active course might add just sufficiently
to the soldiers' exasperation to turn them into a murderous mob,
quite beyond the power of the loyal troops to repel. Anything might
happen then; everyone's life was in jeopardy. These men were
capable of butchering their Commander-in-Chief and the Empire's
best generals, with the Goths only a week's march away!

Yet inaction was itself a course fraught with danger. Demaratus
could divine the almost unbearable tensions in Aurelian and pitied

him. Take action and draw upon himself the frenzy of these reckless soldiers; stay passive while his prestige and authority were brought into contempt and the mutiny might grow into a major revolt—such appeared his alternatives.

With a start Demaratus became aware of the Emperor's malevolent gaze directed at him; Aurelian's voice jarred on his ear. "Any questions so far?" He shook his head slightly; the little half-circle of officers stayed silent. "Very well," said the Emperor with a sharp little smile, "we'll move on to the next stage. . . ."

The morning drifted by and the mutineers, keyed up for action and in the mood which seizes on almost anything as a provocation, began to grow bewildered. They had not reckoned on being simply ignored. Their noise gradually subsided, they stopped milling around, and regarded each other with uncertain looks.

Now the afternoon had begun and still they were left alone by their commanders. Not even the precautions normal during a mutiny were taken; no loyal troops marched in to seal the stores and the armories. When, prompted by hunger, they belatedly went to draw their dinner, they found the cooks waiting patiently to ladle out a hot, substantial meal.

It was almost a relief when a few men of the Headquarters detachment appeared and, keeping at a safe distance, called out that the Emperor wished to address all ranks on the parade ground. There were some catcalls and a few clods were flung, but two or three soldiers began to move shamefacedly toward the huge field on the camp boundary where mass parades were held. Several others followed; soon there was a general drift in that direction. The lines emptied; the parade ground filled.

Demarcated from the rolling plain beyond by a brook lined with trees in full pride of foliage, the wide and empty expanse of the parade ground in the bright sunshine, under its blue canopy of sky, had presented a peaceful scene, with only its areas of trampled grass to suggest the presence of an army. Now, as the mutineers came slowly spilling in and spreading—thousands of sullen, childlike men with swords loose in their scabbards—the atmosphere grew ominous. They still refused to fall into proper ranks, but as men took up their station among comrades and acquaintances, they bunched in shapeless aggregations roughly corresponding to their units. There was no great noise; just a continuous murmur and the multiplied shuffle of feet.

Suspiciously the men watched four soldiers of the Praetorian detachment carry in two sturdy tables and set them together at the far end of the field as a kind of dais, with a stout, low stool as step. Then a ripple traveled through their restless masses, leaving quiet behind. The Emperor, taller than almost all his little retinue of officers, was striding onto the parade ground. Without a glance to right or left, he made for the improvised platform and mounted it.

A charged, quivering attention concentrated from all parts of the field on his powerful figure, elongated by the men's angle of vision and silhouetted against the dreamy azure.

His first gesture, as it were, legalized the men's disarray, so that the way each stood no longer was an insolent defiance. With both hands he motioned them toward himself. "Come closer, boys!" he called in that pealing, far-carrying voice of his.

Not too close, though. The tidal movement of this huge gathering could hurl the tables backward and trample him and the officers drawn up behind into bloody pulp. Eyes slightly narrowed, he measured the slow surge forward; the nearest men were five or six yards off when he shot up both his arms, palms toward them, imperiously. The multitudinous flow instantly halted, save for a few of the foremost soldiers who were carried two or three paces onward by the impetus of the masses behind. Aurelian bent an intense, coercive look on them and they shrank back against their comrades.

Long moments passed, while the men stared up at the Emperor's towering form and he gazed back, unwavering.

Time now to speak. No pleading, for this they would meet with scorn. No threats, for these would enrage them. Speak their own crude language. Offer what—money apart—their rough, simple natures craved. Aurelian raised his head and sent his voice ringing across the field, reaching to the most distant of his audience.

"You want a donative—eh? Well, it's no good beating about the bush. The Treasury's broke. You can't have one!"

This was blunt, final. The menace in the air grew sharper. But as yet there was no outcry. Aurelian sensed that at a single howl from somebody's throat, the immense, hushed wolf pack at his feet would break into murderous fury. He spoke quickly, to forestall that fatal voice.

"Still, do your duty, boys. Follow me like true Illyrians—I'm an Illyrian myself and proud of it" (at this the faintest of murmurs played over the dense throng of heads) "and I'll see you get something every bit as good as a donative!"

The men were very still now. He could feel their thousands of eyes intent on him. "Over there"—Aurelian's thumb jerked toward the east—"are the Goths. A big army, but not so big as the lot we smashed at Naissus. They've got rich plunder, whole wagon-loads— all of it Roman property. And don't forget their own ornaments and horses and weapons. Now listen, boys. Give them a whipping and all that loot will be yours! I mean every word. What you take, you keep—gold, silver, jewels, coin—everything! Only the Roman prisoners will go free."

Briefly he enumerated the regions the invaders had swept clean, the towns they had stormed and pillaged or which had bought off attack with heavy ransoms.

Excited little sounds were leaping up here and there among the men. The list was a formidable one. A soldier's share of such plunder recovered might well be equal to a lavish donative.

"Later, you'll get a proper donative—hard cash. That's a promise! Only we've got to clear out the Goths first and our other enemies. But here's something to start with. The Goths took it from our people—we'll take it from them. It's their turn to be looted. And nobody can teach us Illyrians anything when it comes to looting!

"That's not all . . ." Aurelian leaned forward with a cold, lewd smile. "The Goths have women with them. Very pretty, too. Blue eyes and flaxen hair. Big, floppy wenches, plump in the right places" (his hands coarsely molded the air). "Let's show them the stuff Illyrians are made of! We'll make a bargain, boys. Give me a victory—you can have the women. Pay them back for what our people suffered. Make them squeal for mercy—or for more!"

The snigger which ran across the field was an unmistakable release of tension.

279

"Well," called Aurelian, still with that cold smile. "A victory with plenty of loot and a night's fun to celebrate—what d'you say, boys?"

During the last minute or so he had noticed out of the corner of his eye a few men of the Praetorian detachment insinuate themselves into the edge of the crowd; he knew they had been hand-picked by Mucapor. With an effort he restrained himself from peering in their direction. But he was aware that one hulking man among them would at this instant be leaning back a little, his hands a trumpet against his lips. Aurelian's challenge had hardly died on the air when the man's stentorian answer exploded. It made the eardrums vibrate, set the blood pounding. "Lead us against those bastards, Caesar—we'll give you your victory!" Immediately after, a second voice of staggering power resounded over the thousands of heads. "You pick a woman for yourself, Caesar—then pass her on to us!"

Gales of laughter burst from end to end of the parade ground; they merged into a storm of cheering—and the rush came. The tables were swept away. A dozen hands grabbed Aurelian and hoisted him onto two men's muscular shoulders. Round him swirled a great throng of wildly excited soldiers, red-faced, bawling, stamping, struggling to thump their approval on his buttocks and legs. A measured chant of "Good old Hand-on-Hilt" swelled again and again over the field.

At last the tumult began, of its own, to subside. "Right, now—boys. Get fell in!" a grizzled Centurion could be heard calling good-humoredly. Other robust voices broke through the fading din, repeating the command. Sluggishly at first, but with ever smoother momentum, the crowd flowed into ranks that stretched, stiffened, multiplied themselves and cohered into complex formations and took on the semblance of a formidable army.

Aurelian, on the ground again, stood a little while stiff and pale; then he began not quite steadily to walk away. Demaratus started toward him, but Mucapor snatched his arm. "You bloody Greek fool!" he hissed. "Don't touch him—he'll murder you!"

Even a week's grueling marches did not abate the men's ardor to fight. Their mood precluded standing on the defensive. The numerically superior Gothic army in a position difficult of access was thrown off balance by the speed with which the Romans approached and deployed for battle and the élan with which they charged. The barbarian left wing collapsed. Roman cavalry after a wide sweep stormed their camp, cut down the guards and seized a train of wagons laden with plunder, as well as whole droves of women. Wan Roman captives by the hundred streamed from the enclosures where they had been penned to grasp their liberators' hands.

Meanwhile the struggle on the battlefield had grown more even as the dogged courage of the Goths and their still massive numbers slowed down the Roman advance; not till dusk was falling were they finally evicted from their positions. Aurelian was left master of the field and the barbarian camp; but though their allies had disintegrated and they themselves were badly mauled, the Gothic contingents were still unbroken as they staggered north into the night.

This was no second Naissus, but it was decisive. The chastened Gothic chiefs, as they rode through the dark among the plodding swarms of weary tribesmen, talked together dejectedly. In place of the dead Claudius, another hero, favored by the Gods, stood as champion of Rome. While he confronted them, there would be no easy spoils—let alone conquests—in the Empire. One of them proposed that they send emissaries to Aurelian the following day to offer peace in return for an unmolested withdrawal across the Danube. The others nodded gloomy approval. They were confident that Aurelian would accept; the Roman Army was as much in need of a respite as their own.

Behind them, the exhausted legionaries, reanimated by the prospect of loot and women, broke ranks and rushed in disorderly crowds toward the Gothic camp. It was one of those occasions when the sternest commander takes the leash off. Some of the men made for the many scattered tents, prizes of earlier Gothic victories over the Romans, and slashed open the leather walls in their eagerness to rummage inside. The biggest mobs, however, poured shouting toward the lines of wagons, round which were strewn in scores the corpses of the barbarian guards who had made there a last desperate stand against the storming Roman cavalry. Torches were kindled and lashed to poles; by their wavering flames, under smoke wildly spiraling in the gusty night, soldiers clambered onto the wagons and began to throw the contents out. There was a clamor of yells and cheers as hairy muscular arms reached out to snatch at enchased plate, goblets, gold rings, bracelets, necklaces, silver-buckled belts, purses filled with a medley of coins, furs, silks, bolts of cloth, fine garments, leather shoes—the pillage of countless Roman homes. Amid heated arguments, the more precious objects were assigned to groups of varying size; several times costly vessels were hacked into sections and shared out on the spot. A rough and ready equality was enforced. Any man who, having received his portion, lingered for more was driven away by the curses and blows of his own comrades. The aggrieved resisted, drawing their swords, and brawls raged as the distribution went on.

Meanwhile wine jars and skins and a multitude of bottles of assorted liquor, much of it rough and potent, from ransacked Balkan towns and villages, were being emptied. The men gulped recklessly, slaking in a few minutes the raging thirst of the day's forced march and fiercely contested battle. Then, having secured their booty, they ran to a clearing at the camp center where soon a dense ring of soldiers, with loud bawdy jesting and boisterous laughter, were waiting impatiently for another distribution to begin.

Huddled here under guard of men from the Praetorian detachment were crowds of women, conspicuous among them the robust, flaxen-haired wives and concubines of Gothic warriors, standing in little knots; but the majority listless and bedraggled camp followers.

As more and more soldiers pressed round the enclosure, an increasing stream of curses and jeers and whistles warned that further delay was dangerous. The guard commander gave a signal. His men seized several women, hustled them forward and shoved each into the outstretched arms of a number of soldiers, who lifted her bodily and carried her away among the shadows. The clearing emptied so rapidly that later comers were enraged to find the distribution ended and came to furious blows with the guards.

Shouts and shrieks and drunken songs made a hideous uproar in the darkness.

Only within one sector of the camp quiet prevailed, although there was constant movement of torches. Here were arranged the cluster of taller tents where the principal Gothic chief had lodged with his retinue of nobles; armed pickets had now been posted on every side. Before the roomiest tent, which stood at a little distance from the others, a stalwart sentry, pike at shoulder, was pacing up and down. Mucapor appeared, waved the man aside and pushed through the entrance. His face was lined with fatigue, but brutally exultant. "Augustus!" he exclaimed, "we've sorted out the women of the chiefs. Come and see—there's some real beauties among 'em!"

Aurelian, who was seated on a stool in an attitude of weariness, looked slowly round. He was struggling with an oppressive and turbulent feeling born of exhaustion after the efforts and tensions of a week spanning a mutiny and major battle, elation at his victory over the Goths, shame at the vileness of the revenge he was exacting from their helpless womenfolk. He caught Mucapor's leer and the shame grew keener. He was on the point of refusing curtly, when an intense paroxysm of hatred took away his power of speech; he felt himself go weak with sick desire to see Goths suffer. He pulled himself to his feet and stared at Mucapor. "I'm coming," he said at last, thickly.

He walked out, a little shakily, and saw drawn up for his inspection an uneven rank of perhaps a score of women, ranging from a nubile fifteen or sixteen to weather-beaten middle age. A dozen torches flooded the scene.

Some of the captives were weeping noisily; most stared numbly before them. They were pale and disheveled and their dresses, generally of rich Roman fabric, were rumpled and torn as if they had fought their captors or been dragged from hiding.

At sight of Aurelian making for them, they seemed to shrink together without moving from their places. With a gratification that made him tremble, though marred a little by a sour self-disgust, he saw the row of heads—occasionally a gray one among the flaxen and the gold—droop as his glance traveled along them. He was turning away, when one of the faces he had skimmed over grew strangely vivid in his mind. Round he swung; then pointed to one of the women, a strapping beauty of twenty or so, with high cheekbones, full pouting lips, and a proud carriage. Her head was erect now and her wide dark-blue eyes met his with naked hatred and horror. His interest quickened. "That one to my tent!" he ordered hoarsely. "The others—to the soldiers!"

At once Mucapor's gnarled forefinger curled in a cruel, mocking gesture at the woman, who with a stricken look stumbled forward. As Aurelian turned toward the tent, Demaratus stood in his way. "Is this well done for a Roman Emperor?" he demanded firmly.

Aurelian surveyed him with a taunting grin. "Why the fuss? You're always talking about Justice—well, here you are, Philosopher. You know how the Goths treated thousands of our women. She's going to get exactly the same from me! That's Justice— isn't it?"

He brushed past Demaratus and went into the tent.

Now at last the Balkans were at peace. The Goths had pledged their word and the best guarantee that they would keep it was that their wounds would smart for many a year. Till the youngsters grew to manhood who had never met the Illyrians face to face, there was small danger of a new Gothic invasion, although no doubt minor raids would come.

Next year's harvest in Illyricum would be reaped undisturbed.

Aurelian was anxious to visit Rome, where he knew Severina was contending with heavy problems. But, first, things must be left in order along the Lower Danube and that meant crossing into Rome's derelict province, Dacia, where for years now the population, overrun by Goths, Vandals, Sarmatians and other ferocious tribes, had been left to fend for themselves.

With a powerful cavalry force, he struck north. This time he had the leisure, the freedom from pressing military preoccupations, to look at the land with concern for its condition. The squadrons clattered on through a devastated region which for many of the men was their birthplace. In their own brief lifetime, even in the twenty years or so of the youngest troopers, it had changed enormously for the worse. Roads and bridges, the apparatus of Empire, were in shocking disrepair. An aqueduct they passed stood breached and empty; the town it once had supplied was a fire-blackened shell. Over wide areas the inhabitants had just faded out; there were only the ruins of villages in untended fields. The desolation had its grave military significance. The source of the superb Illyrian soldiery, the world's finest fighting men, was drying up.

Their spirits depressed, they launched themselves on the Danube crowded together on rafts and a few leaky fishing boats they had found abandoned. The current bore them past dense reeds on the northern bank to an uninviting mud beach. Mutely they watched it approach and they splashed ashore with foreboding.

They left a guard over their transports and moved inland, at the alert, with patrols probing ahead and covering their flanks. A silent, deserted country spread before them, its settlements so long scooped away by war that the traces of them were hard to detect. South of the Danube, the wounds were recent and raw; here the scars had faded and the soil seemed to have little memory of the folk who formerly had dwelt upon it.

Across wide, monotonous plains the column trotted, guided by the crumbling milestones of a road almost foundered under the drifting earth. Hour after hour the sun beat down, its beams glistering aslant the dust clouds that enveloped them; their jingling sounded mournful in the great hostile emptiness. No one greeted them; no one disputed their passage. Only, at intervals, they would spy a few fur-clad riders, who stared as the Roman scouts drew near, then wheeled, dug bare heels into the flanks of their shaggy ponies and scampered off. Even the stolid Roman troopers looked glum; even they felt ill at ease in this alien, depopulated land. Dacia had gone irrevocably back to barbarism.

Once they came across two square gateposts standing forlornly alone, surmounted by stone lions deeply pitted by the weather. No gates stretched between them; even the hinges were gone. Behind, where formerly an imposing villa must once have hummed with life, was a dreary tangle of scrub and coarse undergrowth and weeds climbing a broad low hillock and several isolated mounds. No masonry was anywhere visible. It was no doubt fire—with the gales of a generation—that had obliterated the house and its outbuildings. They could only guess the wild scenes in which the place had perished.

Not till full three days had passed did they strike upon the first occupied settlement, a wretched village which had survived by paying tribute to the chief of a Vandal war band. He had discreetly retired with his followers as the formidable cavalry column entered the neighborhood. Only three old men, bowed and cadaverous, with straggling gray beards and rheumy eyes, and perhaps twoscore women and naked, rickety children stood gaping as the Romans rode along the rutted path that wound between the shacks. The able-bodied men had decamped, fearing—it turned out—some kind of impressment.

After that, fragments of the old Roman population became more numerous, although they were never plentiful and always nearly destitute. A tiny hamlet, which somehow had escaped the attention of the barbarians . . . a few families squatting in the ruined buildings of what had been a prosperous market town . . . a little community living in a mine, whose complex disused workings provided shelter more secure than fortress walls . . . one palisaded village whose half-starved and dwindling inhabitants had managed to beat off several light attacks by wandering bands. Here and there some fields were still cultivated, but for the most part scrawny cattle, sheep, and goats were the people's only means of subsistence.

Aurelian was aware that his men were growing restive. They felt no kinship with these tattered and emaciated folk who spoke some weird gibberish of a dialect. Day by day, the atmosphere of this strange, forbidding land oppressed them more. They would not be easy until the Danube again rolled north of them.

He decided to halt for a time and send a picked detachment under a trusted young officer on a sweep into Northern Dacia to contact what remained there of the Roman population.

The men stood moodily at the camp verge, watching the little troop's plume of dust move far over the heat-shimmering plain until it faded. Then the emptiness closed in. They watered the horses at the shrunken stream in the bed of the broad river along whose bank the tents were pitched; did their rigorous daily drills; held contests in riding, javelin-throwing, tilting at the gallop against dummies hung from the extended arms of tall posts—but always without zest. Their brooding air disturbed Aurelian. Though his flying column had long distances to traverse in regions that had reverted to wilderness, he awaited its return with impatience.

On the twenty-fourth day after their departure the string of mounts and riders could be descried moving over the sun-baked levels like a slow arrow feathered with dust.

Aurelian sent word for the commander to report immediately. The dust-blanched young officer, who was followed by half a dozen of his men into the Emperor's presence, stepped up, saluted stiffly, and with parched lips told his tale.

Occasionally they had observed people, but these had fled, despite the conspicuously displayed Roman ensign. The few bigger settlements were in ruins. One puzzling feature was the number of villages with no mark of a human destroyer on them, which appeared to have been deliberately abandoned; their emptied houses still stood, though far gone in decay. The troopers had worn strained looks as they searched these places; they had felt ghosts watching them.

At last they seized a couple of herdsmen in charge of a dozen scraggy cattle. One, whose speech they could barely understand, promised to report their mission to his village in the hills nearby. They had let him go, but detained his companion and the cattle as sureties.

The next day a deputation of agitated scarecrows presented themselves, led by a shriveled old man who, by contrast with his followers, stayed cheerfully calm. This aged spokesman had coolly told the officer that the people of Northern Dacia refused to quit their refuge in the foothills of the wild mountains. They had renounced Rome, preferring to live in freedom, however precariously. His people had no quarrel with the Emperor Aurelian, the graybeard added, and they were delighted to hear that he had given the Goths such a drubbing. But if the cavalry detachment did not withdraw from that territory, there would be trouble. "You're a long way from the Danube!" he had insolently reminded the officer.

Reluctant to return with an uncorroborated tale which the Emperor might regard as an invention to excuse the failure of their mission, the officer had insisted that the old man should accompany the detachment back to camp. There had been a vehement colloquy between the hillmen in their barbarous jargon, with the ancient apparently trying to soothe his excited followers. Finally, he had turned to the officer and said with his cheeky grin, "Here I am!"

They had hoisted him behind a trooper and set out on the long ride back.

At this point of his tale, the officer said, "With your permission, Augustus," and half-turning he signaled his troopers. Flanked by two of them, a beggarly-looking little graybeard trotted forward.

He made no obeisance. "Hail, Augustus!" he piped in a villainous accent. Aurelian stared. The envoy had a puckered, impudent face. His mouth was sunk over almost toothless gums. One eye was covered by some horny excrescence; the other, a gray, twinkling pinpoint between wrinkled skin, was shrewd and humorous. His scalp, its baldness accentuated by a few straggling gray hairs and the white tufts above his protruding ears, was smooth and rosy, in contrast with his creased brow. He was clad in a faded, tunic-like garment which reached to his knees; it had a fraying cord for girdle. His bare forearms and calves were lean and wiry. He must have weighed little more than half of either of his burly escorts.

"Who are you?" curtly demanded Aurelian, affronted by the spectacle of this aged ragamuffin. Mentally he made a note to reprimand the officer for involving him in such a farcical situation.

"My name is Georgius, Senator of the Free Dacians," chirped the envoy, not without an odd dignity. Aurelian frowned at the self-styled Senator. "May I sit? The journey's tired me." Georgius, not waiting for permission, squatted on the ground before Aurelian's camp stool. "I'm a very old man, you know."

Aurelian reddened at this bland disregard of propriety and at the reproach, which found an echo in the simple countenances of the troopers. He looked down wrathfully at the uptilted old face, so fragile yet animated, almost at his knees. Quite unruffled, Georgius met his gaze with a friendly smile. Aurelian could not maintain his anger. In spite of himself, he began to feel a little amused.

"Who are the Free Dacians?" he asked ironically. "Who made you their Senator?"

The network of corrugations in Georgius' face split in a wide grin. "Natural choice!" he chuckled, ignoring the first question.

"You see, Augustus, I was Headman of our village when the Goths came. We couldn't fight—Rome had kept us disarmed. So we trekked to the hills."

An attitude of severe aloofness was impossible with this cheerful old chatterer. Aurelian leaned forward, his interest aroused. "The Goths—did they come after you?"

Georgius nodded, with a crafty look. "We dodged them. When they came back, we dodged them again. We're hillmen now. It was hard at first, but we learned to manage. And we run our own affairs. We're poor—but we're free. That's really why I came to see you. Leave us alone. We've no quarrel with you, but we're not going to let strangers rule us—not Rome, not the Goths. Go home, Augustus. You'll never reestablish Roman rule in Dacia. You're a generation too late!"

Aurelian's aides, the young officer who had made his report, the escort, all within earshot, were listening to the thin, insistent, curiously persuasive voice. Every face confirmed its wisdom. Georgius paused, with a sly, insinuating smile, as if to say: "You know I'm telling the truth. It's no use pretending, Emperor!"

Of course it was true. Behind his unrevealing mask, Aurelian confronted with pain a conclusion no longer to be avoided. Dacia would have to be abandoned, written off. It would be madness to risk Rome's last Legions to recover the desert left by forty years' ravaging. Even if, with his scanty resources, he could evict the Goth, the Vandal, the Sarmatian, where would he find the men to garrison the open frontiers of this vast region, embedded among ferocious tribes, and the money to rebuild the ruined cities?

He felt a hand, light but firm, on his knee. "That's right, Augustus," said Georgius gently. "You're a wise Emperor. Go home. Send us a few convoys of arms, steel-tipped arrows mostly—we fight from ambush—and we'll get word across to you whenever the tribes get restless. Otherwise, leave us alone!"

Aurelian stood up. "The Senator will dine with us," he said to his staff with a faint smile. "Tomorrow we'll send him back to his Free Dacians."

So, at last, Rome turned her back and retraced her steps. Aurelian withdrew from Dacia. The free communities of the North, such as the one on whose behalf Georgius had spoken, were left undisturbed; only the scattered remnants of the population in the South were rounded up by the Roman cavalry and herded across the Danube, to be settled in a new province along the river, to which—in a pretense that no surrender had been made—the name of Dacia was given.

Iron-visaged, Aurelian watched for a while the little groups of men and women, with their pitifully few and puny children and their miserable bundles of belongings, scramble ashore from the boats and stare round at their new homeland, until the troopers briskly shepherded them along the road southward. As a soldier who had witnessed the carnage of twenty battlefields, he had no pity for the wretchedness of these exiles. But his spirit was heavy with the humiliation of Rome and with what it augured.

He had no illusions that the Danube, even when reinforced, would prove a secure barrier against the barbarians. They would return to the assault again and again. Once across and victorious, they could split the Empire in two, threatening Italy on the one hand; on the other, the rich, soft cities of Asia Minor, an easy prey.

Absorbed in these grim reflections, he was walking back to his tent, when a noise made him turn. The Guard Commander was hurrying toward him, leading by the bridle a horse on whose back sat wearily a man in the uniform of an Imperial courier. "Dispatch from the Empress, Your Majesty," announced the Guard Commander. The messenger dismounted jerkily and with a stiff movement saluted. His face was sweaty and grimed; there was stubble on his cheeks and his parched lips were sore.

"Augustus," he croaked, fumbling in his pouch. "The Alemanni are in Italy!"

23

WITH its only adequate field army positioned in the Balkans, the diminished Empire over which Aurelian ruled, though still precariously, simply did not have sufficient strength to withstand a heavy blow at the Upper Danube. The irruption of the Alemanni penetrated deep and swiftly. Making light of the Alpine barrier guarding Northern Italy, they poured in a destroying torrent into the valley of the River Po. The rich plains, on whose corn Rome more than ever depended since the granary of Egypt was in Zenobia's hands, were torn mercilessly by the harrow of war. While the walled cities shut their gates and waited for succor, the Germans swept far and wide over the countryside, leaving the familiar trails of trampled harvests, wrecked villages, mangled corpses.

Worse even than the bloody ruin of a populous and wealthy region was the threat to the City of Rome, only a few days' march away by the undefended roads along which the Legions had tramped north long ago to plant the Eagles on the Rhine and Danube. Already rumors of warrior hordes driving toward it set countryfolk along their imagined route stampeding for the shelter of town walls or the recesses of the Apennines.

Soon, however, another rumor blew with the winds across the agonized land: The Illyrians were coming!

The fugitives heard it, cowering in woods and marshes. The barbarians heard it, too, and assured each other uneasily that it was absurd—Aurelian was known to have plunged far into Dacia—but their wild career of rapine and slaughter began to lose impetus. Just then two Illyrian dispatch riders stumbled into a marauding band of Alemanni. That night they were dragged before the huge, red-bearded High King Vadomar and his principal chiefs for questioning. Stripped to the waist, they watched an iron being heated. One of them moaned and struggled frenziedly in his bonds as the glowing end was pressed against him; but no word passed his lips. He still had not spoken when an impatient sword cut his torment short. The other writhed away from the brand and muttered disjointed phrases that made the burly, hairy chiefs glance at one another in disquiet. Already their ears could catch the far-off rhythmic thunder of the famed Illyrian Legions pressing relentlessly westward.

A spear thrust through the heart was the Illyrian's fee for information. Vadomar now began to speak, chestily. Their inroad had been richly rewarded. They had swept aside all who dared oppose them. The bards would long celebrate their prowess and their victories. Still, Aurelian was known to be a stark, grim fighter. They could crush him, of course. But the price in blood was bound to be heavy—and was it wise to jeopardize the bountiful plunder they had gathered? The time surely had come to march north again to the welcome that awaited them in their homeland.

The chiefs rumbled applause. They enjoyed the braggart words and shared the fear behind them. Aurelian's name was terrible even to their ferocious hearts.

At dawn, the Alemanni reduced their cumbrous train of captives by slitting the throats of the young and aged. The prick of spear points kept the remainder trotting, with hammering hearts, to match the pace set by the tall, long-striding tribesmen. Roman bodies marked the course of the rapid retreat as the host quitted Italy, traversed the white silence of the Alps by valleys emptied of their inhabitants and approached the Danube.

In one vital respect, however, Vadomar had drawn the wrong conclusion. Though it was true that the bulk of the dreaded Illyrian Legions were fiercely straining toward Northern Italy, the Emperor himself was not with them.

Aurelian had closely questioned Severina's messenger (the second she had dispatched with news of the invasion, but the first to locate the constantly shifting Imperial camp). Then, urgently, he had summoned his senior commanders to the Praetorian Tent. At Aurelian's bidding, Mucapor unrolled a map and pinned it on the table. Aurelian motioned the officers nearer. They saw him measure with his eye and then with the span of his muscular right hand sections of the empty space north of the Danube which they knew was occupied by hundreds of leagues of primeval forest stretching from Dacia toward the territory of the Alemanni. He turned to the officers. "The Alemanni won't stay and fight—not with all that plunder. They're no fools. They'll make for home at top speed, once they hear we're on the way. Now here's my plan. Probus, you take command of the army. Chase them hard. Follow them out of Italy right to the Danube. In the meantime. . . ." He continued in the same terse fashion for a little while, three or four times stabbing the map with stiff forefinger. Astonishment was depicted on the officers—and, on some faces, alarm. "That's all," added Aurelian. "Diocletian, you stay. I want to go into supply and transport."

The Army mustered without delay. Briskly but methodically, the Centurions moved along the ranks, pulling out the toughest, the most resolute, the tireless marchers. Two thousand legionaries so selected were ordered to draw forty-eight hours' hard rations and to parade again in light marching order.

This composite force was the first of the columns shortly streaming from the camp; but while the others bore south and west, they soon veered in a northerly direction. On they tramped at a cracking pace, swinging from the Highway into a side road that wound through rough, monotonous pastureland, completely deserted. Striding alongside unfamiliar neighbors, the soldiers wondered to themselves on what strange maneuver they were racing thus. A few hours later, a little cavalcade came pounding across country to overtake them. The soldiers looked at one another and muttered blasphemous dismay.

It was the Emperor himself, towering on his pony even among the strapping Illyrian troopers of his personal Guard. Everyone now understood that they were engaged upon a dangerous mission. Old Hand-on-Hilt's presence certainly meant terrific marching and bloody fighting at the end of it!

In glum silence the men tramped on.

For over a week they drove by little known roads across the ravaged, almost depopulated Danubian borderlands, their only baggage train a couple of dozen sturdy packhorses. Three times little food convoys met them; with these they left behind their few sick. Late one afternoon, when the men were already looking forward to the day's final halt, the column's head twisted from the metaled road onto a corduroy track through the marshes. The stars were out when the vanguard caught the gleam of a broad river. Wearily they stumbled onto the creaking planks of a little jetty emerging from a cluster of abandoned fishermen's cabins. Oars whispered in the dark; a boat came alongside and embarked as many as could crowd aboard. It slid away; another took its place immediately.

The expeditionary force slept or lay awake shivering that night under swirling mist on the Danube's northern bank.

In an eerie white dawn they ate a comfortless meal and were off on a westerly course, squelching over the boggy ground. They soon broke out of the mist, but the going continued cruel. The extended, supple column, with its scouts and flanking patrols, was like some monstrous insect with nervous feelers out, dragging its way across the mournful riverside wastes. On their right hand, sometimes distant, sometimes thrusting close to the bank, stretched the unbroken wall of an immense forest.

One grueling day passed; then another. On the third, they were still pushing through the stiff, tall grasses, floundering in the soggy margins of innumerable streamlets, splashing through the swift, cold water; but in the early afternoon the column's head slanted toward the somber rim of the forest that had followed and hemmed in their march. As they approached, the trunks appeared close-set like a palisade overhung with a dense canopy of green. Nearer and nearer they trudged; the trees rose taller still, but stood apart, as though to bid them enter. Splitting into files, the column insinuated itself into the forest. Now they were in lofty, gloomy aisles, treading a slippery, yielding floor. In those enclosed spaces, the trampling and shuffle and jingle of their movement were magnified startlingly; but it was local, imprisoned noise. To the outside world they knew they were invisible and unsuspected, soundlessly swimming through the depths of an opaque green ocean.

By now they had practically none of the impedimenta of a Roman army; only a few led ponies with reserves of hardtack. Though it cost them heavy exertions they made rapid progress through this uncanny world where the sun—the normal measure of their marches —was only an occasional burst of fire high among the tiers of branches. Sometimes they followed discernible tracks, trodden by hunters and the rare trader, but even these were obstructed with tangled roots and spiny undergrowth. They could not keep step nor maintain column of route. The expeditionary force articulated itself as a loose series of clusters, each never quite out of sight of the ones before and behind. Perhaps a fifth of their number were even farther dispersed in the far van or rear or on the flanks, as scouts and patrols. There was no question of surprise by an enemy. In fact it was the irruption of this powerful, swift-moving force in the depths of their own forest retreats that surprised the Germans. There would be an insistent murmur, growing steadily into a rushing sound, as if a gale were tearing through the trees; then, with a crackle of snapped stems and twigs, sweating legionaries would burst into one of the forest clearings. They might be received with a squealing of pigs, whose herder—often enough a Roman captive—would wait frozen till these gaunt soldiers surrounded him. Here and there the expedition closed so rapidly on a little stockaded settlement of wooden cabins that the unkempt, fur-clad population of hunting folk had no time to flee into the dark forest recesses.

Where they could, the Romans impressed one of the barbarians as guide. He would be some tall, muscular fellow, his splendid chest bare, his long, naked legs grimed. Mopping his brow with a white forearm, on which golden hairs glinted, he would growl to himself in guttural dialect, as he stepped out with the points of two or three javelins never more than a few inches from his unprotected back. At night his guard was doubled; there was no possibility of escape. Nor could there have been a vengeful muster of forest folk against this alien army, as when the tribes rose against Varus. Before the little communities of hunters and trappers, their women and young, had fairly rubbed the astonishment from their eyes, Aurelian was gone from their neighborhood, a westward-flaming meteor, and silence settled again on the forest.

The Romans had a nightmare illusion of struggling onward yet being rooted to one place. Their dank, chill world of trees whose light, diluted by plumes of foliage in never-ceasing motion, brought only a dim mockery of the day's brilliance, seemed just the same at every dawn's reveille, every noontide halt. Their routine of a day-long march, briefly broken for food and rest, did not vary. Slogging through undergrowth, slipping on spongy moss, bleeding from innumerable scratches, panting, swearing, the legionaries pressed on until dusk seeped down to thicken the forest gloom.

The men muttered, but they did not flag. Aurelian strode tirelessly among them, his equerry leading his horse, his terrible glance forbidding men's hearts to acknowledge the weakness of their limbs. Gradually a fever took possession of the soldiers. At no matter what cost, they meant to get there—wherever "there" might be. Then they would make those bastards of Alemanni pay bitterly, bloodily, for all they had undergone.

One night, a faint breeze rumpled the lofty foliage and pallid shafts of moonlight filtered through and flickered along the trunks. The air was cool and aromatic. Blue-black shadows shivered in the depths between the trees. An occasional silvery flash showed where a fleeting moonshaft had struck on armor. It was a night to stir and trouble the imagination. There was a hushed and haunting beauty about the moon-pierced forest that banished sleep even from the eyes of rough, worn-out legionaries. A murmur of conversation began among the dark, cloak-wrapped figures on the ground. One of the soldiers, a swarthy, good-looking, wiry youth, stood up and—leaning with a faraway smile against the corrugated black trunk of a giant oak—started to sing.

His song was one of those sentimental ballads of parting and regret such as soldiers love. The vapor gushed from his mouth as he uttered the melancholy notes. He had a light, sweet tenor and the words, banal but made so poignant by the moment that the heart ached at them and eyes grew wet, seemed to hang themselves, a lingering vapor, among the branches. The men stilled their talk; the silence spread and deepened until all within earshot hung upon the slender, plaintive voice. There was a faint crunch; the singer slowly, dreamily, turned in its direction. Then he started and drawled a couple of notes as his gaze met the glittering eyes of the Emperor, standing haggard in the dimness. The soldier's jaw dropped. Incredulously, he thought: The Emperor is a lonely man! But the tall, spectral figure made an abrupt gesture that he was to continue and withdrew into the shadows.

After days more, the trees at last thinned; light advanced on the Romans. They paused at the forest edge and, shaken, saw an almost level, sunlit expanse, with an arc of woods to the north; but to the south, where the terrain sloped gently to the Danube, the way was open. They reeled out, drunken with the sun, the vault of sky, the broad landscape. That night they lay down to sleep under the stars, cursing because the Emperor had forbidden fires. The forest march, which veterans long years after were to recall with garrulous pride, speaking with disdain even of the other prodigious marches of Aurelian's winged infantry, was over. But for days the clinging odor of forest decay was in their nostrils; while in their dreams the trees closed on them in dense ranks and, lost amid shadows, they stumbled on and on, sobbing for breath, through myriad-pointed undergrowth.

It was a wet and gusty afternoon. The sentinel on the high platform of a Roman signal tower saw through a swinging curtain of rain a small boat bobbing over the leaden wavelets of the Danube. Two men were straining at the oars; the third, cloaked to the chin, crouched forward almost into the face of the nearest rower, urging them on. As soon as the boat grated in the shallows, the three splashed ashore toward the tower gate. The cloaked man curved his hands before his mouth and with head back-tilted yelled to the half-dozen soldiers now watching from the parapet. To give his words authority, he threw back his cloak, revealing the badges of a Roman First Centurion.

A minute later, smoke streamed up from the platform's heaped faggots to alert the tower's parent fort with the first of a series of messages that, relayed by beacon-blaze and couriers furiously riding, set the whole frontier zone in motion. The Emperor Aurelian was moving into position to cut the retreating Alemanni from their homeland—all available troops must be rushed to join him!

The vanguard of the Alemanni poured from their boats and rafts onto the Danube's northern bank and pushed forward with careless confidence. Already they were picturing their noisy welcome in the tribal settlements. Suddenly, they stood frozen. From the broken ground before them ordered ranks of men-at-arms had appeared and were closing on them with measured tread. Superstitious awe took hold of the tribesmen when they beheld a Roman army advance from the direction of their own country. Most of them fell back in confusion. The tardy were cut down and, before long, the stupefied survivors found themselves hemmed against the river's swampy shore.

Split in two by the Danube, the Alemanni were for the moment completely immobilized. Their leaders, who were with the main body, on the southern bank, were at a loss what course to pursue. When a sleepless night had dragged by, scouts brought in word that Roman forces were arriving almost at the double from different directions. All day the legionaries, whose numbers continuously grew, toiled feverishly over wider and wider areas, setting up road-blocks, piling ramparts of turf surmounted with stakes across level stretches, felling trees across woodland trails, and generally establishing a powerful blockade. Among the Alemanni the warriors passed the hours in scowling inaction, while the chiefs, awoken from their stupor, conferred with bitter words, each blaming the others for their plight. Their wrangling grew so fierce that they forgot the enemy gathering on every side and reached for their swords. At this point Goderich rose, a graybeard famed for his sagacity and more than forty years of profitable warfare. His first words quelled the incipient brawl. Sternly he reminded the chiefs how the Romans would rejoice if they destroyed one another. Their urgent need was to extricate the host, sprawled for miles among marshy meadows and woods, and get it into posture for fighting. A stout swimmer should cross the Danube at dusk with orders for the remnant of the vanguard to return to the southern bank unobserved in the dark. Meanwhile the whole extent of the Roman lines should be closely reconnoitered; if any weak spot were found a picked force should be quietly concentrated against it. The captives and the plunder would have to be abandoned, he added gloomily.

The circle of beards wagged mournful assent. In the hearts of the chiefs resentment was hot against the tribal gods who could suffer such masses of lovely loot to slip out of their hands.

By the time the host was reunited and brought into semblance of order, its situation was plainly becoming hopeless. A cordon of strong points, buttressed at intervals by fortlets and with strong mobile forces to call on, compressed them into a narrow, irregular space along the river; every avenue of escape was blocked. The second council of the Alemannic chiefs was subdued and brief. After a few frank observations by Goderich, from which nobody dissented, the High King Vadomar nominated him and three others to bargain for terms with the Emperor Aurelian.

A tall Roman officer, stern-visaged, with a few phrases of German at his command, received the envoys. He conducted them to an extensive level area where, to their astonishment, thousands of Roman soldiers were paraded. "Present yourselves to the Emperor!" he ordered curtly. The chiefs followed the direction of his gesture and found themselves walking down a wide corridor whose walls were formed by legionaries in perfect alignment massed behind their uplifted ensigns. The silence was so profound that the shuffle of feet on the grass could be heard as the chiefs slowly drew near the low platform where Aurelian waited on a gilded chair. To each side his senior officers sat their horses rigidly upright, while on either flank of these were ranged the stalwart Illyrians of his bodyguard. Behind him stood a row of picked standard-bearers, high above whose heads gleamed with sinister brilliance the golden Eagles of five Legions.

On the Alemanni came, big, bulky men with a natural swagger, not in the least like suppliants. From time to time they turned a contemptuous glance over the heads of the far shorter legionaries.

Their unabashed eyes met those of the Emperor. He gazed down at them with a cold aloofness that was more disturbing than open anger. The chiefs halted and the three others looked rather irresolutely at Goderich, who drew himself up, an imposing figure in his winged golden helmet. He began to address the Emperor slowly in a guttural tongue; after a few words he paused for the interpreter to render them into Latin. Aurelian forestalled the interpreter. Waving a peremptory hand, he said without raising his voice, "Tell them to kneel."

A look of anger swept over the faces of the chiefs as the interpreter's harsh voice repeated the command. They glared at Aurelian, but after a few moments Goderich shrugged and lowered himself on to his knees. The others awkwardly followed.

"That's better!" said Aurelian calmly. "Now tell the brute in front to speak."

Still with an air of cool detachment, he listened while Goderich began meekly to explain how wrong it was for the Romans and Alemanni to wear themselves out in futile warfare. It was time to make a pact, declared the old chieftain, warming to his theme as he savored his own crafty eloquence. The winged helms behind him nodded as he denounced the follies of war. In earnest of their love of peace, he declared, they were ready to leave Roman territory without delay—yes, even to restore their captives! All they asked was a substantial annual payment—not tribute, of course, but simply a token that the Empire genuinely returned their goodwill. The kneeling chiefs behind nodded again, enjoying the felicities of his oratory and expressing admiration of his willingness to make sacrifices in the cause of peace.

The Emperor heard him in silence, without the least change of expression. After a while Goderich, having said all he wished in his own resonant and half-poetic way, was disconcerted to find that his words, so persuasive to his own ears, had dissipated themselves into vacancy, without impact, without echo. The stately figure seated above continued to gaze down impassively and, suddenly, amid the unbroken silence, Goderich felt thousands of other eyes boring into him and his fellow envoys.

It was the pitiless gaze, the massive, unnerving silence of a hostile and victorious army, beyond the reach of argument or entreaty, full of menace.

The old chief smiled pathetically up at the cold, unmoved face of the Emperor. For the first time he felt the anguish of the utterly conquered. "Be gracious, Emperor," he faltered. "Have mercy!"

At last Aurelian answered. His tone was calm, and his direct and pithy phrases struck more implacably because of it. "What mercy did they show? Say there will be no mercy—unless the whole army lays down its arms. It must be unconditional surrender. We are not bargaining."

There was a little pause after the interpreter had finished. Then Goderich began another appeal. "No more talk!" interrupted Aurelian. "Tell them to be off. They're not to come back—except to surrender!"

Breathing audibly, the envoys scrambled up. For a few moments, all four, red-faced and shaken, muttered together; then they bowed their heads to the Emperor, growling farewell. Slowly and raggedly they walked from his presence; this time they did not survey the ranks of the stocky legionaries with scorn.

At this juncture word arrived from the Balkans that a powerful force of Vandals was assembling for an inroad across the lower Danube. The first intelligence had come by runner from Georgius in the hills—orally, of course, since the Free Dacians had no scribes. The threat appeared very serious. Aurelian pondered how far the original message of Georgius might have been modified by various persons transmitting it. With some misgivings, he came to the conclusion that his own presence was advisable at the point of danger. After all, the Alemanni were now pinned down in country that made it very difficult for them to mass for a breakthrough. A zone of improvised but stout fortifications enclosed them tightly. There could be no escape for them, providing the Romans remained vigilant.

Aurelian sent for his senior officers and impressed on them the imperative need for alertness, by night even more than by day. Then, after appointing Marcian, the best of Gallienus' generals, to take over command, he set off eastward with a strong mobile column, at the fantastic pace that was becoming routine in the armies he personally led.

On arrival, he found that the Vandal threat had been greatly exaggerated. The danger lay less in the number of the invaders than in the absence of the normal garrisons, who had been embodied in the field army campaigning against the Alemanni. All but a few of the war bands scuttled back over the Danube at his approach; the others, across whose line of retreat he directed his march, sent heralds offering to take service with the Eagles.

The situation was thus rapidly being cleared up, when a messenger, the first of a series with tidings of disaster, lashed his horse into the Imperial camp. He bore a dispatch from Marcian, which he himself amplified by word of mouth. The Alemanni, on the point of perishing from hunger or surrendering at the mercy of the Romans, had managed to escape.

In the dead of night they had surprised one of the Roman forts blocking the road southward. Crude scaling ladders glided up from the gloom against the parapet; barefoot, almost naked knife-men had swarmed up and butchered the garrison with virtually no resistance. A neighboring fort, taken from the rear, was overrun with ease; the troops manning the strong points between had been seized by panic and fled. Even before the brief fighting had died down, the Alemanni, abandoning their baggage train, booty, and captives, were surging through the gap in thousands. Marcian had not anticipated that any determined attempt to break out would be aimed due south, directly away from the Danube. A couple of feint attacks diverted his attention from the critical point; his misjudgment was aggravated by faulty communication within the Roman lines. The Alemanni brushed aside the nearest Roman mobile column, which threw itself across their path, and before a powerful striking force could be assembled and launched in chase, they were a full furious half-day's march away. Unimpeded as they were, with every hour they drew farther ahead of their confused, half-hearted pursuers.

Before Marcian had grasped their intention, they were clear away —heading toward the Rhaetian passes back to Italy. The bulk of the Roman army, gathered with such prodigious effort, was left in the air, dispersed among its fieldworks around the vacancy which once the trapped Alemanni had occupied. Worst of all, the soldiers had been demoralized by the abrupt reversal of fortune; an audacious stratagem had in a single night nullified all their hard-won advantages. Officers and men alike were convinced that they would never catch up again with the Alemanni.

Most of this Marcian's messenger hurriedly detailed. The blow was so severe that the staff saw the Emperor go livid. For a brief while he sat a little bowed, teeth clenched and fists doubled, as though seized by some spasm. Nobody dared address him. Soon, however, he mastered himself and began hoarsely to question the messenger. This interrogation over, he pulled himself up from his campstool, glared round, and walked heavily into his tent.

Not many minutes later he came out. His color was less sickly, but his expression remained grim. Immediately he began to issue a stream of orders. The first dismissed Marcian from his command; the second nominated Probus to succeed him.

One of the dispatch riders hurtling from the camp, in which the tents were already being struck, bore directions to the Vandals who had sued for enrollment in the Legions where to rendezvous with the Emperor. Their initiation into the Roman service was to be a march at a speed of which they had never dreamed armored forces capable.

Aurelian caught up with Probus when the main Roman army was descending from the mountains in the wake of the now-distant Alemanni. He at once took over command and extorted another two or three labored miles a day from the jaded troops. Except for the relatively few who had made the already fabulous forest march, none of the soldiers, not the oldest veterans, could recall such cruel footslogging. The men had long ago stopped singing. Their weary legs automatically obeyed the Centurions' bawling. When the final halt was ordered, they felt they could not have marched another step. They sank numbly down. So exhausted were some that they had to be helped to their feet to draw their evening ration of gruel. There was little talk. The meal over, the men just stretched themselves on the ground and closed their eyes.

The swift-moving campaign in rugged country had been very wasteful of horses; remounts were unobtainable without long delays, so that Aurelian's fine cavalry brigades were dwindling from shock formations into a source of mobile scouts. The hunters, like the hunted now, were almost entirely infantry.

To the soldiers it was a slow, interminable agony; to a spectator hovering over the mountains and the wide plains it would have seemed a rapid, inexorable pursuit. The unthinkable was happening; a Roman army was catching up with a fleeing host of barbarians.

One midday, when the troops had fallen out to munch their bread and bacon, the Centurions threaded their way among the squatting figures, calling out news that electrified them. Patrols had made contact with the Alemanni; their main body was only twenty miles ahead.

The legionaries scrambled up. Their eyes were burning. A fierce excitement gripped them as they felt this bitter contest of endurance drawing near its bloody conclusion. No longer was there need to urge them on. The spur of revenge had become more potent than the drag of weariness. Though a terrible battle lay at the end of their marching, they stepped out, stiff-legged but with zest.

Every night the distance between the campfires of the two possessed armies had grown a little smaller. Day after day, the Romans were heartened by passing through or close to the site whose hundreds of blackened circles strewn with ash and charred kindling showed where the Alemanni had spent their brief and anxious rest.

It was characteristic of the Germans that the more desperate their situation, the more savage their atrocities. Naturally there was no scope now for wide-range marauding; only foraging parties scoured the land in advance of the host. But even these pounced upon the occasional unlucky fugitive, the unwary, the blunderer, the misdirected. They would have some noisy sport with him in the night; then, growing sleepy after a while, would slit his throat and leave the mutilated body where the Romans would be sure to find it. The sight goaded the legionaries as they plodded past, hours later, not because their rough hearts felt any sorrow for the frozen agony of the dead face, but because they understood and resented the mockery of the gesture.

As the late afternoon of one hot day wore on, the legionaries were visibly flagging. They trudged jerkily, eyes on the ground, forced on by a will which annulled their own, stronger than their weariness. The whole army, extended in column of route with its supply train of mule-drawn wagons, stretched over several miles. Aurelian sat erect in the saddle, raking the landscape with narrowed eyes in a wide arc in front of him. He was sensitive to the soldiers' mood and worried by their fagged condition. These two factors he weighed with a third which troubled him more deeply. The light was beginning to fade and in this countryside retreating into shadow, among these woods and undulating fields, with here and there an abandoned hamlet, even a numerous enemy, craftily hidden, might escape detection.

Still, the army traveled inside a screen of scouts who would give the alarm even at the distant approach of danger; and it was too early to call a halt. The men had another half-hour's marching in them; if they camped now, the Alemanni would gain a mile and a half, perhaps a mile and three-quarters, in this terrible reckoning of flight and pursuit. A few deficiencies of that order and he would probably lose for good his chance of overtaking them.

Twenty minutes passed. The day was steadily ebbing; the shadowy rim of the visible world drew closer and closer. Beyond the tramp and shuffle and jingle, the creaking and rattle of a weary Roman army on the march, evening silence waited to take possession of the land.

There was a sudden flurry; startled soldiers threw themselves out of the way, as three horsemen of the vanguard drove straight through the Emperor's personal retinue, hauling after them by a rope a haggard giant in the leather accouterments of an Alemannic warrior, though he wore a battered Roman helmet. His face was wetly streaked with blood from a gash across one cheek; he panted with lolling tongue, as he trotted and stumbled in the wake of his captors, but his eyes gleamed with animal ferocity and defiance.

"We spotted three behind a fence," announced the leading horseman unceremoniously. "Killed one; one got away; we nabbed this brute." He flicked a gauntleted hand toward the German and his companions twitched the rope and sent their prisoner sprawling in front of the Emperor. As he picked himself up with an awkward weaving motion, Aurelian snapped to one of his staff, "Question him—quick!"

He bent forward, face taut with concentration, nose raised as if to smell out what lay behind the presence of that trio of Alemanni surprised by his patrol while peering at the Roman army from their fence. The interpreter shot a guttural stream at the prisoner, who with a wordless snarl shook his head deliberately. "Jog his memory!" rapped Aurelian.

Two of the bodyguard seized the man's arms, tugged them free from the rope's tight embrace and twisted them back and up with such violence that he was almost lifted from the ground; his head sagged forward, his shoulders grotesquely tilted from his neck. "Harder!" Aurelian grated. Sweat stood on the man's grimy brow, his clenched lips twisted wide open, showing irregular rows of blackened teeth. Now he appeared no longer human, but some demoniac spirit, evil and suffering. "Well?" demanded Aurelian, inclining farther toward him from the saddle. The interpreter barked a questioning syllable in the barbarian dialect. Closing his eyes, the man groaned some almost inaudible reply.

The interpreter whistled. "An ambush, Augustus!" he exclaimed.

"Halt the army! Form the wagons round that hillock back there!" Aurelian shouted. The staff spurred their horses in several directions. "Where?" Aurelian addressed the interpreter. Already shattering trumpet woke trumpet, spreading the alarm.

Again the barked question; again the maddeningly slow answer jerked in slurred guttural sounds between those distended, ashen lips.

Before the voice lapsed into silence, Aurelian saw the interpreter turn toward a wood curving dense and dark in the early twilight, its nearest bulge within a mile of the road along which the Roman columns were strung out. He shouted more terse orders; paused a couple of moments to hear the interpreter confirm what he had already divined; then with desperate haste resumed his directions to the extended army to close up into line of battle.

It was easy to guess why the ambush had not been discovered. The Roman scouts, exhausted by the day's strenuous searching among rough ground and momently expecting the army's halt and the distant trumpets of their own recall, had simply not troubled to beat the wood beyond its open fringes. The Alemanni had withdrawn well back, posting a few carefully hidden observers to report the Roman army's movements.

A confusion of scurrying, above whose medley of noises rose the bellows of the Centurions; then distinct ranks began to waver, one behind the other, in the milling mass, to close up and congeal. The formations rapidly elongated themselves and merged into a continuous front, still uneven, facing the direction of the ambush. But there was simply not time enough for the whole Roman army to compose itself for the shock of battle. A roar swelled along the margin of the wood; loose clusters of running figures, diminished by distance, came oozing out; the wood was still oozing men when the forefront of the wild, screaming Alemannic charge was already bearing down on the Romans.

It was not a massive, tightly marshaled onslaught, such as might have gone crashing clean through the Roman ranks at the first impact; the Alemanni, too, had no time to form up in close array, for this would have cost them the decisive advantage of surprise. But their charge impinged on the line of Roman shields, spread along it, pressed it back. A fighting madness gripped both armies so nearly at the end of their tether. Hunger for revenge against these destroying, mocking savages and the almost frantic desire to put an end to their own intolerable exertions drove the Romans on; the Alemanni were animated by despair, for if they were defeated they could not escape utter destruction. The contention within each soldier of ardor with weariness produced a kind of delirium. Science was cast aside and men stumbled toward each other and yelled and stabbed and hacked and grappled in a galvanic stupor. This mode of berserk fighting accorded ill with the instincts of the Romans, whose training aimed to produce the cold and tireless mechanical killer. Gradually the Alemannic fury prevailed. Sensing even through the blood-red glaze of their battle-frenzy that the Romans were at the breaking point, the barbarians extorted from themselves one supreme effort. There was a scatter toward the rear of legionaries from the center; then a wide streaming back. The Roman front had been riven through.

Panic was in the air, about to swoop upon this overdriven, outfought, stupefied army. Aurelian with the reserve cohorts of Praetorians flung up his arm and shouted; his words were swept away by the savage booming roar that answered his gesture. Straight at the emerging head of the Alemannic battering-ram the Praetorians charged; a volley of javelins flew before them. Even the raging barbarian fighters momentarily recoiled. The breach in the Roman line closed with a band of iron.

However, the picked Praetorians themselves no longer had the stamina to exploit their advantage. They strove to press forward, but fresh masses of Alemanni, lurching against them, brought them to a standstill. As night gently deepened, the monotonous carnage continued all along the swaying lines, with the Romans gradually giving ground, until at last, unbidden by their trumpets, they reeled off that battlefield strewn with thousands of their dead.

From the darkness behind resounded the triumphant baying of the Alemanni.

Crowded within their laager of wagons, the soldiers of the defeated army lay slumped on the ground in exhausted sleep. Only the sentinels could be seen on the move, pacing heavily with nodding heads between the wagons. Somehow, amid the darkness and confusion, the bodyguard had cleared a space and got the Praetorian Tent erected. There Aurelian waited, confronting his defeat alone, until his chief officers could join him for a Council of War, after taking a rough tale of the fearful casualties.

His body ached as though battered all over; the flame of the single torch above troubled his eyes. For a while he sat with shoulders bowed. Then he walked slowly over to his camp bed and lowered himself onto it. His drooping eyelids closed, but the yellow light still pounded through them on his eyeballs.

Around the tent the ground was strewn with thousands of sleeping soldiers. Yet here in the midst of his broken army, an immense solitude surrounded him. In all that camp there was no man to whom he could say, "I am afraid. This defeat has been too heavy for us. Can we ever recover from such a blow?"

That was the penalty of his supreme position. He must never confess his fear, never ask comfort of another man, however desperate the hour.

Often during that terrible forced march through the German forest, his aging, hard-driven body had protested, and at night his mind, exploring the morrow's chances, had tormented him with fears he dared not voice. But then hope was strong; he was hastening, unvanquished, to an encounter. Now the encounter had taken place and he had been hurled back—he and Rome's last army.

No one would approach to share his burden. He was alone in the vast wilderness of his defeat. Oppressed with thoughts he could not utter, he brooded over the battle and his ruined hopes; and his weariness grew and a darkness he had never known before invaded his soul.

It was as though a voice that was his own, yet strange and mocking, spoke to him.

This was downfall, the ultimate defeat. There could be no recovery. The soldiers' will to fight had been shattered. The Alemanni had been left masters not only of the field but of Italy. At the news of their triumph all the enemies of the Empire would rise and pour over the frontiers and they would find nobody to resist them.

Despair, Aurelian! The day of disaster has come. Rome is falling —and it is you who have lost her last battle!

He wrenched himself on to his side and opened his eyes. The torch above flared, then sank, in a draught. For moments there was semigloom. Aurelian's ear could catch no noises from outside. A silence deep as the night had swallowed the camp.

Help could not come from mortal men. But there was One who would sustain Rome's failing soldiers, because He, too, fought against Darkness—endlessly. High above the world He shone, but when men called on His Name in their sore need, He drew near to them.

Even in the privacy of his heart, Aurelian had always found it hard to pray. Yet now something more primitive than conscious thought strained from the depths of his being toward the Radiant God, the Sun-enthroned, sole hope of the stricken Roman Army.

No words formed on his tongue, but an agony of supplications went streaming out of him. Come to our aid, Lord God Mithras. Give us back courage and strength. Light our road. Terrible perils weigh on us. A barbarian army, victorious, is at the gates of Rome!

After his brief and silent passion of prayer, Aurelian grew less agitated. The saw-toothed blade of despair was disengaging itself from his breast. Through the murk of night and defeat, he knew,

Mithras was riding the gulfs of air to the help of His faithful soldiers. Behind closed lids, Aurelian felt a luster fill the tent. Already the noble face below the Phrygian cap was bending over him and the smile of the stern yet compassionate Warrior God shone upon his heart.

The harsh lines of Aurelian's face relaxed. On the shadowy frontier of sleep his thought was: We shall fight again—and conquer!

It seemed a few minutes later when a man's hand moved on his shoulder. Probus, haggard but calm, was looking down at him. "Time for the Council, Augustus," he said and helped Aurelian to rise. Other generals were already entering—soon nine, including Mucapor and Diocletian, had assembled in the Praetorian Tent. The look of most showed weariness and dismay; Aurelian's, only weariness. His expression did not change as briefly he studied the casualty estimates they handed him. Then, firm and challenging, his gaze rested on each of them in turn. Instinctively they came closer, already reassured, ashamed of having faltered because of a repulse, Roman commanders gathered round their dauntless Emperor.

"The Alemanni fought better than I expected." The cool and deliberate voice which owned to this error of judgment took the consternation out of its theme and set a reasonable limit to the consequences of their defeat. "But they'll soon find out they haven't finished with us!

"Tomorrow, we must let the men rest . . . clean themselves up. Get the units properly sorted out. Combine the weak ones. That's a day lost. . . ." He paused. Some of the generals reflected that a single day was precious little time to get the battered army back into fighting trim, but nobody commented.

"I'm certain the Alemanni won't attack. They'll make off somewhere—that's my guess. Probably they'll wander about a bit and then decide to march on Rome. But they won't get there—we shall see to that!"

He glanced round the absorbed little group. "Long before they're anywhere near Rome, we'll catch up with them. One day's rest; then we're going to follow. As hard as ever. Hang on their tails. Hustle them. Make it awkward for them to forage. We've got food" —he nodded at Diocletian—"they must look for theirs. When they can't stand any more of it, they'll turn and fight. This time we'll be ready for them."

His voice, brisk and confident, took on the familiar mandatory ring. "Those are my orders. Tomorrow: rest and reorganize. Next day: Reveille one hour before dawn. Parade at dawn—full marching order."

There was a few minutes' businesslike discussion before the officers dispersed. Aurelian settled again on his blanket. The soldiers of his bodyguard found him still quietly asleep when the whole camp was rousing. One of them stooped and touched him gently. Aurelian opened his eyes, blinked, then sat up. He rubbed his cheeks and grimaced. "Get the barber, boys—I need a shave!" he called cheerfully.

24

LISTENING to Crinitus, Severina marveled once more how such a stream of pungent comment could issue from a man so enfeebled.

Her uncle sat propped up on a bed in the little suite adjoining her own apartments, from which a private door gave unobserved access to him. Years of illness had wasted the flesh from his broad frame. Almost bald now, his massive head overhung a sunken face which, with nose sharp and cheekbones jutting, would have suggested the fanatical ascetic, but for the bitter humor of his eyes and the arrogant set of his bloodless lips.

An urgent plea to Crinitus at his seaside villa had preceded her return from the Balkans and by her arrival in Rome he was already installed at the Palace. He hobbled on two sticks to the inner courtyard and stood shakily waving one in his right hand while the great ornamented Imperial litter grounded and two liveried Palace servants drew back the gold-threaded purple curtains. The assembled domestics prostrated themselves as the Empress emerged. Crinitus toed aside a woman slave and limped slowly toward Severina with a grin that made his hollow face deathly.

Careless of etiquette, she hastened to meet him, threw her arms round his neck and almost sobbed, "Dear Uncle!" His breath was sickly sour as she kissed him. "You look older!" had been his first words, in a voice gone thin and sharp. But the brusqueness of this greeting had been redeemed by his next remark. "I didn't think I'd live to see you again—I should never have let you go!"

On Julia, who stood timidly a little behind her mother, he had gazed for a while in cold silence. Then he said, as in dismissal, "Aurelian's child!" After that he had shown no further interest in Julia.

Severina could now study her uncle with the discernment of a mature and experienced woman. She soon discovered that the deterioration of his body had not been accompanied by any decline in the trenchant vigor of his mind or the force of his masterful will. Indeed, the effect of prolonged ill-health had been to render still more salient the less agreeable aspects of his personality and make him more caustic, derisive, and domineering than ever. His outlook was cynical, his tongue unsparing. He even grumbled ferociously at his doctors though, she noticed, he was almost fussily careful to observe their instructions. Only toward herself he showed good-humored affection. She cherished this genuine fondness and tried to make allowances for his bouts of severe pain, but his aggressive contempt for people jarred on her.

Yet she recognized that his judgments, while altogether lacking in charity, were shrewd and penetrating and his knowledge of politics and the personalities of the Capital remarkable in someone who had lived for years in retirement. In this vast, frightening Palace, filled with a still faceless multitude of officials and servants, it was deeply reassuring to have as personal adviser so forceful, acute and well informed a man, on whose devotion to her interests she could depend absolutely.

Now, three days after her arrival, Crinitus was giving his views on the composition of the Regency Council which Aurelian had instructed her to form.

"Four officials, to start with—heads of departments," he recommended incisively. "They'll be routine-minded, glorified bookkeepers really. But they'll have the facts at their fingertips. It's for you to make the decisions, but you can't govern without a grasp of the details—they'll supply it.

"As Secretary, Eros. He's that long-nosed fellow, with freedman written all over him. Very clever, though corrupt of course. I could suggest some honest blockhead, but the job needs a smart brain and lots of initiative. Otherwise you'll find yourself endlessly tangled up with petty problems."

To the officials on the Regency Council Crinitus advised Severina to add a couple of Senators.

"One must exploit one's gifts, my dear," he observed. "Gallienus had the gift of making people hate him. He used it to the full and derived great satisfaction from it. Your gift is to make people like you. Even a Senator might do something unselfish on your behalf!

"Of course, they're a worthless crew—timeserving, venal, malicious. But you'd make a mistake to ignore them. They're just like eunuchs, impotent but shrill. They've got nasty tongues—and they love wagging them! They can make things harder for you, if only by grumbling and spreading disaffection. Most of them will hate the idea of an Empress exercising authority over them. Old women detest being ruled by a young one! Aurelian they're afraid of, but he's far away; the Gods alone know when he'll be back. Your best course is to cow them right from the start!"

"Cow them?" she repeated, disturbed by the brutal term.

He mistook the reason for her concern. "Never mind that you haven't got the force. Bluff them. We had a golden rule in the Army: never show hesitation. If you make a mistake on the parade ground, you bawl all the louder at the recruits."

"But you can't treat Senators like raw, ignorant recruits!"

"Can't you!" he chuckled. "They'll react in exactly the same way. All men do. You rule an Empire by shouting. A raised voice strikes fear—that's why you yell in battle. Let those gentry of the Senate sneer at you behind your back, provided they obey in a hurry. Remember, my dear, good manners have nothing to do with good government. Septimius Severus was a Berber brute; when he barked, how the Senators jumped to it! And he was a great Emperor. He

313

gave the Empire victory and peace and founded a dynasty. You yourself told me Aurelian's briefing was: Keep Italy quiet. Well, you won't keep Italy quiet by staying quiet yourself!"

Crinitus eyed her narrowly and his voice, usually so sharp and positive, took on an insinuating note. "I don't suppose you could have two or three really prominent Senators arrested on a capital charge? . . . There's always some clause in the law books that can be made to fit. No? Not even one? Hmm . . . a pity! An execution or two would do a power of good, you know. Well, in that case you'd better appoint a couple of Senators to the Council. Then the Senate can pretend it's helping to govern the State. But remember—show them who's boss! Look them straight in the eye. If anyone presumes to meet your look for more than a moment, clap him in irons on the spot!"

In accordance with the advice of Crinitus, four senior civil servants were nominated to the Regency Council. They were Salvian of the Treasury; Philip the Epirot, Controller of the Corn Supply; Longinus, in charge of the maintenance of ports, roads, and bridges; Milo, whose office handled petitions to the Palace.

All were standardized products of the Imperial bureaucracy. It took Severina some time to distinguish between their personalities. Eros, on the other hand, at once made a strongly individual impression. Lanky and drab-skinned, he was an Asiatic Greek or Hellenized Asiatic, with a bald, narrow head, curiously elongated, dim brown hair, alert brown eyes, almost without lashes, and a thin, drooping, slightly twisted nose. He spoke nasally, to the accompaniment of an agitated Adam's apple.

In charge of the personnel of the Imperial Household, he was one of a bewildering succession of dignitaries and officeholders presented to the new Empress. He had stood before her a very little time, repeated the same formula as the others, pledging humble duty, thanked the Augusta for her gracious words—and then moved on. But when the long and wearisome ceremony was over, Eros stood out from the blur of figures in Severina's recollection as someone whose physiognomy and manner of speaking had compelled her to look at him keenly—with a faint stir of distaste.

Mindful of Aurelian's pressing need for money to pay the troops, she sent for him the following day. "I am surprised at the size of the Palace establishment." she told him. "I find it hard to believe that all these hundreds and hundreds of domestics are really necessary."

He listened gravely, though she had a sense of wary eyes assessing her. "I can assure Your Majesty that the Palace staff is a very modest one, bearing in mind the duties it has to perform. Every man and woman in it has some useful function. However," he went on, smoothly, "if the Augusta so wishes, we can prepare a roll of those we might be able to dispense with. I am sure Your Majesty will pardon me for pointing out that in the present time there would be no possibility of other employment for most of them. Some of the younger men might perhaps find work. The women . . ." His faint shrug, as he broke off, implied a world of tragedy with which the Empress could hardly be expected to concern herself.

Severina frowned, recognizing in this bland reply an impudent maneuver to baffle her intrusion into his province. Really, the fellow fancied he had summed her up already and knew exactly how to play on her feelings! Still she had to acknowledge that he had shown a good deal of perception. Aloud she said coldly, "I intend to go into the matter later on."

Eros lowered his eyes, made an obeisance, and withdrew.

After some thought, Severina decided not to let this encounter weigh against her uncle's recommendation of Eros to serve as Secretary to the Council. It was less easy to follow his advice regarding the nomination of two Senators as members. Of the dozen or so whose names were submitted for her consideration, none appeared eminently qualified, while several were clearly unfitted on grounds of ill health or extreme age. In the end, her choice fell on two Senators who enjoyed some reputation for sound judgment and integrity. The senior was Corvinus, an elderly, pigeon-breasted man with a distressing sniffle; his colleague, Drusus, was corpulent and black-bearded, with suspicious bright eyes under bushy brows. To theirs she added of her own initiative the name of Eutropius, the emissary of the Senate who had accompanied her from the Balkans. He was no statesman, of course, but he was an honest and kindly man who had shown himself attached to her; and she felt that, at the outset,

315

it was important to have one familiar and friendly face at the Council table.

The first session was occupied mainly with settling procedure and a brief review of the situation in the Empire. Severina welcomed the members and directed that Eros take up his duties as Secretary. This time there was no hint of the effrontery he had displayed at their recent interview. He did not assert himself in any way, but quietly busied himself with note-taking and the circulation of documents. Even so, it was not long before he gave evidence of outstanding ability. Several awkward procedural questions were referred to him. He answered with such promptness and clarity that Severina could see he was a master of the subject and that, further, he had the rare gift of making a complicated matter appear simple. Though her instinctive dislike of him persisted, she acknowledged to herself that he had talents well suited to his key post.

Apart from this Severina's first impressions of the Council at work were not particularly encouraging. The four departmental heads were able administrators, conscientious but limited; they were unaccustomed to framing policy and timid in the face of issues beyond the scope of civil service rules. Once they had reported briefly on conditions in their own sectors, they had little to say. Of the trio of Senators only Eutropius revealed much animation. He beamed at Severina and was quick to support her point of view. The other Senators contributed hardly anything to the discussion. They were transparently on their guard, taking stock of the Empress and their civil-service colleagues. Their wary attitude disturbed Severina. She had a foreboding that this excessive caution would continue and prove a serious hindrance to the Council's work.

The occasion had naturally been an ordeal for Severina; it was with relief that, after an uneventful hour and a half, she saw the close of the agenda approaching. She judged now that the time had come to raise a matter of vital interest to herself. Pointing out that the tribes along the Lower Danube were still in a state of unrest and that the Army, after its recent heavy losses, was urgently in need of reinforcements, she announced that a first draft of five hundred Praetorian Guardsmen must be dispatched without delay to the Balkans.

316

At once concern showed plainly in the faces before her; there was an unmistakable atmosphere of anxiety in the room. Severina looked round the table, inviting comment. The lips of Drusus molded the phrase, "first draft," but he remained silent. She had a feeling that each member of the Council was waiting for somebody else to voice his own objections. To her surprise, it was Eutropius who overcame the unspoken doubts or opposition of the others. Speaking with an earnestness that moved her, he declared, "I have seen our brave Army in the field and—even though it means some reduction in the city's garrison, which is already weak—I can assure my colleagues that the Augusta's proposal is a necessary one."

A unanimous vote endorsed the immediate dispatch of five hundred Praetorians to the Danube.

Severina found herself, in effect, a prisoner in the Palace, doubly fettered by long, exacting hours of duty and the consequent draining of her energy. She slept badly and was reluctant to rise, but forced herself from bed with the thought of the crowded day's program. Her appetite, never robust, wilted under the strain; she was the despair of the consummate Palace cooks, whose exquisite dishes went back to the kitchens barely tasted. Bread, cheese, fruit, salad, vegetables—on these she chiefly subsisted.

Her manner became nervy, her temper irritable. Curiously, this proved an asset. Tenseness gave a peremptory edge to her voice; when she spoke with the asperity due to a restless night, she appeared to threaten—and was obeyed the more promptly on account of it.

Daily she consulted with Crinitus, not hesitating to disclose to him the most confidential information laid before the Regency Council. His guidance and the example of his self-assurance were invaluable. Without him, she would have groped and wavered; with him, she was able to maintain a firm and effective course. At the same time, his personality was anything but restful. More and more she longed for a woman companion in whose society she could relax, as she had been accustomed to in the home of Aurelian's mother. She often wondered why Drusilla had not come hastening to the Palace. A letter did arrive, after a puzzling interval, from her rural villa; it was affectionate in tone, but Drusilla excused herself from visiting Rome on account of illness. She did not specify the illness and Severina grew anxious. Within the hour a courier was on the way with a message that she herself would take the earliest opportunity to go and see Drusilla.

It had been a particularly tiring day for Severina and her head was aching. In the afternoon she was trying to rest a little, when Eros entered bearing two neatly tied rolls of documents. With an inclination he laid them on a little table near Severina and made to withdraw. "What are these?" she asked, picking them up in turn. In astonishment, she answered herself, "Private reports on the Lady Drusilla and the retired General Ulpius Crinitus!"

At her question Eros had halted. "It is the practice, Your Majesty," he said with a guileless little smile. "You wrote today to the Lady Drusilla and you honor the General Crinitus by taking counsel with him."

Severina went hot with anger. But she forced a check on her tongue, for this apparently deliberate provocation puzzled her. The Imperial government, she knew, employed agents to spy on persons it suspected of disloyalty (a category which under some Emperors broadened to include almost anyone of eminence in the Capital). She was less surprised at the existence of Secret Police reports on members of her family, which in the days of Gallienus was known to be disaffected toward the regime, than at the presumption of Eros in producing them. Not for a moment did she believe that he had done so because it was standard procedure. And he must be well aware that the mere sight of them would arouse her revulsion. What, then, was his motive? His face revealed nothing to her sharp scrutiny; it bore the same expression of untroubled candor as before.

Eros was a man who calculated his words and actions, of that she had no doubt. Was his aim now a subtle persecution—to lodge in her mind the thought that everything she did was known to him? Or was this reminder that her family were among yesterday's suspected traitors meant to imply that she was an upstart? Whatever his precise intention might be she was sure that animosity had prompted him. It was easy to account for such ill will. She had hardly reached Rome before she had criticized the numbers on the

Palace payroll, an affront to him—and a threat to his influence—as officer in charge of personnel.

With a guilty feeling she recalled that, having complained, she had taken no further action. Contempt for her weakness and lack of purpose must now color his resentment.

Yet an intuition told her that there was something more basic in his antagonism. Perhaps it mortified him to take orders from a woman. Perhaps his motivation was more fundamental still and he had simply reacted to her personality with hatred, as she instinctively had felt dislike for him.

It was the second time that, in a private interview, he had with a demeanor of respect and dutifulness shown her a cool insolence. Perhaps, on this occasion he was presuming on his position in the Council, where her growing dependence on him had become obvious. Nevertheless, she was surprised at his boldness. He must be one of those extremely clever men whose sense of superiority impels them to take risks in the confidence that they can extricate themselves from any danger.

He misunderstood—or chose to misunderstand—her evident anger. "Of course, Your Majesty, you should have seen these much earlier—but you have been so busy since your arrival."

"It is the practice, is it?" she said. "Was it so under the Emperor Claudius?"

He still wore that odious look of innocence. "The Deified Emperor Claudius stayed only a very short time in Rome," he said evenly. "From the point of view of the administration, his reign was something like an interregnum. But it was certainly the practice under the late Emperor Gallienus. He insisted on full reports—kept strictly up to date—on everyone, Your Majesty—everyone."

She curbed her wrath at this last impertinence. "You regret Gallienus, don't you?" she remarked, eying him ironically. "The Augusta is very understanding," he answered with a little bow. Yes, she could understand a natural sympathy between these two subtle and devious men. Eros, she felt sure, must have admired the artistry of Gallienus in those accomplishments in which he himself appeared something of a master—the insinuation, the smile while infusing malice, the bland voice for the wounding word.

319

I must get rid of him! she thought. He stood there with a perfect simulation of deference, awaiting her permission to leave. For some moments, she reflected how intolerable the burden of the Council's work would grow, once the special talents of Eros were lost to her— and, involuntarily, she shook her head.

"Leave the documents!" she bade him abruptly. "Tell the woman in attendance I want a kindled brazier as soon as possible." She picked up one of the sheets and ostentatiously tore it to shreds, averting her eyes as she did so from the lines of writing.

"As Your Majesty pleases." Eros drew back, inclining his head. It struck her suddenly that she had done exactly what he had anticipated, that he was smiling to himself at her childish exhibition of temper.

I must get rid of that man! she told herself again with vehemence. As soon as he had gone, she pushed the documents away and wearily closed her eyes.

The noise of someone entering aroused her. It was one of her women who announced a messenger with dispatches from the Emperor.

These proved to be Aurelian's final instructions before he crossed the Danube for his indefinite absence in Dacia; they were unusually long and complicated. Severina soon grew absorbed in them. The appearance of a manservant with a glowing brazier startled her. She knitted her brows before she could recollect her order to Eros and told the puzzled domestic to take the brazier away. Then she picked up the two confidential reports and thrust them into a drawer. She turned again to Aurelian's communication; some moments later, everything else was banished from her mind.

Severina did not have to pay her projected visit to Drusilla. Three days after she had written by special courier, her stepmother presented herself at the Palace.

Returning to her apartment from a Council session, Severina found Drusilla standing rather forlornly by the tall window that overlooked the inner courtyard. Drusilla gave a nervous start at Severina's quick footstep, turned round and looked at her a little uncertainly. Then she opened her arms with a warm smile as Severina almost ran to her. "Mother!" exclaimed Severina. "How are you? How . . . oh, we have so much to tell each other!"

Though Drusilla's hug could only have been spontaneous affection, she seemed relieved to draw away and sit down. "I keep feeling I ought to say, 'Your Majesty,'" she admitted in a voice less firm and brisk than when Severina had last heard it.

"Oh, forget that nonsense!" Severina said huskily. "Mother, tell me everything—that illness—how are you feeling?"

"Oh, yes—my illness. . . ." Drusilla looked uncomfortable. "It's all right—I'm much better now."

"What was the matter?" asked Severina.

"It wasn't anything much, really," answered Drusilla. "Just pains here." She indicated her abdomen. "Anyway, they're gone now."

"Couldn't I send you a doctor?" suggested Severina, puzzled by her stepmother's vagueness, but still worried. "In the country you must find it hard to get anyone good."

"Oh, no—I assure you! I have a good doctor. He comes from Rome—it's not far really. Thank you, Severina, but I don't need anyone."

This reluctant and evasive manner of hers persisted. It was quite unlike the old Drusilla, from whom talk would have flowed—random and inconsequential talk, perhaps, but certainly without reserve. More and more it appeared that she was on her guard. Though she listened with evident interest to what Severina said, particularly about Julia, she volunteered little information about herself. She answered Severina's eager inquiries briefly, at times with signs of confusion, and asked few questions of her own.

Could it be that Drusilla remained excessively conscious of the gulf in rank between them? Severina studied her with perplexity. In some ways the portrait was that of a rather pathetic aging woman, of much vanity and little taste, struggling with an uncertain hand to obscure the traces of the years. Her hair was lighter than Severina remembered it; from its uneven color it had passed through several transformations. The paint was too conspicuous on her cheeks, and glistening eyebrows, darker than her hair, rose in exaggerated curves above her anxious eyes. Yet despite her raddled dowager appearance, she did somehow look younger than her age;

despite her embarrassment she suggested a freshness and warmth of feeling which Severina sensed was not due to this family reunion. Once or twice, losing herself in some reminiscence conjured up by Severina, Drusilla forgot whatever it was that made her ill at ease and her face shone, her voice brightened. At those times she made on Severina the impression of a woman not only recalling the past with pleasure but also with a lively source of happiness in the present.

At length Severina rose. "I have to discuss one or two things with Crinitus. Won't you come along for a few minutes, Mother? He'll be glad to see you. Then, if you'll wait till I finish my business with him—it shouldn't take very long—we'll both go and find Julia."

At the mention of Crinitus, Drusilla looked positively alarmed. "Not now, Severina," she said, in a low, troubled voice. "Perhaps I'd better leave.—I'm rather tired. You know I haven't been very well. . . ." She stood up, eying Severina nervously.

"Then, dear Mother," Severina said, "please forgive me, but I must go to Uncle at once. He hates to be kept waiting. But you'll come again soon, won't you? If you don't feel well enough, I'll come to see you myself—and I'll bring Julia—at the very first opportunity."

Drusilla did not answer, except with a half-hearted smile. They kissed good-bye with some constraint.

Much disturbed, Severina lingered in the room, although she knew that Crinitus would be awaiting her impatiently. Finally, exerting compulsion on herself, she walked to the window and, standing to one side where she would be unobserved from below, glanced down into the courtyard.

A little time passed; then Drusilla emerged. With a feeling that this was more or less what she had expected, Severina saw the plump, shortish man, richly dressed, who had been lounging against one of the uprights of the grounded litter, turn swiftly round. His vivid face wore an expression of artificial ecstasy. He even wagged his head in playful reproach at Drusilla's delay; she lifted her hand in an intimate signal. He had liquid black eyes, full red lips, rounded cheeks. Drusilla's step quickened and she reached out to grasp his elbow.

It was a painful tableau to Severina. The man looked sensual, un-scrupulous, and glib; Drusilla, foolishly enamored. He helped her into the litter solicitously and leaned inside, evidently making her comfortable.

Severina was late for her appointment with Crinitus. She entered a little apprehensively, for his afternoon rest was nearly due and, although he cursed his doctors, he was almost obsessively careful to obey their orders. "Get out!" he snapped at the young woman who was handing him some strong-smelling concoction in a glass. She made an obeisance to Severina, shot Crinitus a sidelong look from her lively dark eyes, and went out; she was finely built and had a provocative carriage.

"You're late, Severina!" Crinitus said sharply, as soon as she had gone. "I can only give you ten minutes—I've been thinking about that militia."

Long ago at Sirmium, Severina had once put it to Aurelian that women could play an active part in the city's defense. Why not a women's militia? They could patrol the walls, learn to load and aim the great catapults. All manner of administrative and routine base duties could be handed over to them, setting free numbers of men for service in the field.

Aurelian had listened at first with some surprise, but before she had finished his faint smile told her that he had already dismissed all she said as a piece of whimsical nonsense. He had made some uninterested comment—and begun to talk of other things.

Afterward, reflecting on her suggestion, she came to the conclu-sion that he was right to shrug it off. In their brutal masculine world women were abject creatures, spiritless household drudges for the most part, incapable of facing the same dangers, discharging the same responsibilities, as men.

Still, the idea of a militia—if not of women, then of men—per-sisted with her. No part-trained troops, she was well aware, could stand in line of battle against German barbarians who were, so to speak, full-time soldiers from their boyhood. But a militia could de-fend a town, even against heavy attack, even in the absence of a regular garrison.

323

All this had hitherto represented little more than a fanciful exercise of her imagination, a kind of daydreaming on a practical theme. Since her return to Rome, however, she had given a good deal of earnest thought to the subject. She had a strong personal motive, which she had decided to disclose to no one for the present. Even when broaching the question of a militia to Crinitus, she had done so in general terms, not revealing to him why the notion had come to occupy a place in the forefront of her mind. Severina, too, was learning to be devious.

Her private reason apart, an ominous new factor had emerged that gave cogency to any sound project for strengthening the armed forces in Italy. Just now, when Aurelian was somewhere deep in Dacia and the field army, already partly dispersed, was positioned in the Balkans, intelligence reports from the Upper Danube, due north of the Alps, had begun to indicate suspicious movements among the tribes that composed the powerful and warlike confederacy of the Alemanni.

Severina paid close attention as with characteristic vigor Crinitus propounded his view. "In principle, you're right—a militia could help stiffen our defenses, appreciably. Naturally, I'm referring only to Rome. You haven't the means to control militia units at a distance from here—and control is the vital consideration. Which brings us to the next question. Whom are you going to recruit? The riffraff? D'you think they'd meekly keep their place once they had weapons in their hands? They'd be more danger to the State than to an enemy! Then, you'd have to exclude the whole Senatorial class— give those gentry arms and they'd fancy themselves back in the days of the Republic! It boils down to some carefully selected middle-class elements—shopkeepers—small merchants—property owners in a modest way—and the like. You might raise four or five thousand —not many, but there's a desperate shortage of equipment. Commanders and drill instructors? I suppose we could dig up enough discharged soldiers of the right type—we don't want boozy, decrepit old veterans. But on no account use the Praetorians—there are far too few of them already and they should be kept concentrated. . . . What are you making a face for, Severina?"

He did not wait for an answer. "And now," he said, "time to lie down." He smiled at her as she assisted him to the couch. "Come and see me tonight, my dear."

During the next days Severina, preoccupied though she was with weighty affairs, several times found herself reenacting in her thoughts the scene below her window between Drusilla and that man who had so much the appearance of a plausible adventurer. More than once she glanced irresolutely toward the drawer where she had locked away the two confidential reports. Was it possible that the one on Drusilla could throw light on this unpleasant-looking relationship?

She was in the midst of these reflections one afternoon, when Eros was announced. He bore a batch of drafted decrees for her signature. She picked the topmost up and began methodically to go through it. At one point she turned to make some observation and although Eros met her gaze with his usual composure, she had a lightning impression that his face had just changed, that a moment before his look had been anxious.

"All these decrees have been fully discussed by the Council," he reminded her, with a little smile for her unnecessary thoroughness.

"Just wait," she said curtly.

After examining the first decree, a relatively simple one, Severina signed it. The second, more complicated, made her wonder at the intricacy of official phraseology; she knitted her brows before she could unravel some of its passages. It was duly signed and she began to peruse the third. After a few moments she glanced at Eros again. "What does this mean?" she demanded.

This time she definitely caught a flicker of uneasiness over his face. "The reduction of taxes for the Campanian municipalities in districts where the harvest was ruined by drought last year, Your Majesty," he replied, a shade too glibly.

"Eight municipalities were granted reductions," Severina said, emphasizing the number. "This list shows nine."

"Oh, that!" Eros said, as if at last comprehending her. He spoke with an air of perfect frankness. "The harvest failure was widespread, as Your Majesty knows. It seemed advisable to add."

"Whatever seemed advisable," interrupted Severina, "should have

325

been brought up by you at the Council. You know well enough that each claim was gone into carefully and that you have no authority to amend the Council's decisions." Her look probed his unrevealing face. What was that phrase of Crinitus? "Clever though corrupt."

"It couldn't be," she said deliberately, "that you are doing this for —some private reason?" An instant later, she wondered why she had not said, "bribe"—then realized it was because this would have been conclusive. It was a word from whose consequences she could not have drawn back.

No one could have portrayed more convincingly the mute re-proach of a faithful servant wronged. After a little, he said, "If the Augusta has any doubts in the matter, may I respectfully ask for an inquiry?"

Of course he did not fear an inquiry. It would reveal nothing—he was too clever to leave a trail. She would have no proof of anything, except that he had exceeded his instructions. But of that he was plainly guilty. I have my pretext now, she told herself. She would be justified in dismissing him out of hand.

Still, the truth had to be faced—she did not wish to dismiss him. After all, she could have got rid of him, had she so desired, without awaiting formal justification. The fact was that for the time being his usefulness to her on the Council outweighed her doubts of his integrity. Efficiency was her first requirement. An honest blockhead —as her uncle had put it—would be no substitute for Eros.

For the present she must hold her hand. For the present only. The time would come when she would deal drastically with him! Mean-while he had had a bad fright—he would hardly dare to practice these deceptions on her in the future.

"I have seen fit to entrust you with certain duties," she said. "You will be held strictly to account for the way you carry them out. I shall not waste time on an inquiry. Take this away"—she pushed the document toward him—"and have it redrafted precisely according to your instructions. Don't let this kind of thing happen again. If it does, I shall dismiss you instantly from all your offices. However much you regret the fact, you will do well to remember that there is no longer a virtual interregnum, as in the reign of the Deified Emperor Claudius."

Her tone was biting but she knew that she was being deplorably weak. The sternest words were inadequate if they stopped short of actual dismissal.

Eros picked up the decree. His face was expressionless as he waited for Severina to finish with the remaining documents. For the next ten minutes she gave these her attention, scrutinizing each before she signed it. Finally she motioned him to take them. Watching him, as unhurriedly he collected the documents and arranged them in order, she could tell that he had already begun to recover from his discomfiture.

The episode left her deeply vexed with herself and irritable. She found herself staring once again towards the drawer where lay the confidential reports. Contact with a man of Eros' stamp had the effect of making her scruples seem childish. She went across, unlocked the drawer and took out the two reports. Rather gingerly, she opened that on Drusilla.

She was staggered to discover how careful a watch had been set on this harmless, aging woman living in retirement. The bulk of the entries related to the first years following her husband's death; afterward they tailed off. By its nature the information must have come from a member or members of Drusilla's own household. It was easy to suborn domestics or plant spies in the swarming establishments of the rich.

There could only be one explanation: Gallienus must have transferred to Drusilla much of the suspicion with which earlier he had regarded her husband. Possibly he had made the mistake of an overcunning man and credited poor Drusilla with a capacity for intrigue of which she was destitute. More probably he had assumed that she had some knowledge of treasonable secrets and hoped for an indiscretion on her part that would lead him to her husband's former accomplices. So close was the surveillance over her at first that, although aimed at detecting evidence of political activity, it could hardly fail to register many facts pertaining to private life. Severina flicked the sheets over—Drusilla's robemaker, her hairdresser, the fortunetellers who exploited her gullibility—even these rated a mention. There it all was, preserved in the dreary Latin of the Imperial clerks, the self-indulgences, the pathetic little follies of a wealthy, middle-aged widow, afraid of loneliness, afraid of growing old, whose nerves had never recovered from the strain she had undergone as wife of one of Gallienus' victims.

Only close to the end was her love affair mentioned, in matter-of-fact terms—it might have been the record of an operation on the corn market. The steward, Marcellus, had been receiving her intimate favors for over two years. Eldest son of a Sicilian freedman and unmarried, he was in his early forties, considerably younger than his Mistress.

Vividly, Severina recalled his face, his gestures, his attentions to Drusilla. His domination over her was obvious—and he looked the type to take shameless advantage of it. In control of her very considerable property, he would have abundant opportunities to enrich himself. Severina reflected that he would also find it easy to abuse her trust in another way, for the large household of which he was in charge included numbers of women slaves, among them no doubt some who were young and pretty. Yet, clearly, it would be futile (as well as cruel) to try and warn her against him.

With the death of Gallienus, the authorities appeared to have lost any remaining interest in Drusilla and the entries ceased.

There had been some excuse for Severina's intrusion into her stepmother's personal affairs. But now her hand was drawn irresistibly to the dossier on Crinitus. She had a few moments' struggle with herself before she opened it. This keyhole witness, this tabulation of the unguarded word, the furtive act, both repelled and fascinated her.

The dossier began with her uncle's retirement from the Army—which coincided with the accession of Gallienus to sole power. It was a substantial one. For years these creatures had dogged him with their peering and eavesdropping. Some of his recorded conversation was so reckless that Severina wondered why no action had been taken against him. There were no more entries after his arrival at the Palace, when—presumably—it was recognized that he stood high in favor with the new regime.

As Severina read cursorily here and there, her self-disgust grew. She had no right to scrabble among the secrets of her uncle's life;

to look at this record degraded her to the level of its compilers. But she could not resist one more glance at the final entries. Their source was the dark, bold-eyed girl, Agrippina, whom Severina had seen a number of times in her uncle's rooms. He had brought her with him from Baiae and described her as his nurse, though obviously she was much too pretty for a man of his nature to have engaged her solely for handling medicines. She, too, was a spy, a particularly vile one, who took full advantage of the fact that she was placed to overhear the extremely intemperate talk to which he was liable during his bouts of pain.

Severina's first angry impulse was to have the girl removed without delay; but soon she had misgivings. She would have to offer some explanation. It would be humiliating for her uncle—nor would he thank her for her interference. His routine, on which he set such store, would be upset. The girl, evidently, was useful as a nurse, as well as in other ways. In any case, the mischief was done. Nothing was to be lost by letting her stay on for the present.

Perhaps later—perhaps when Aurelian came home.

Sickened, ashamed, Severina set down the report beside that on Drusilla. It was likely that she and Aurelian, while they lived in the neighborhood of Rome, had similarly been shadowed, observed, painstakingly recorded. Eros had hinted as much; and she recalled that Gallienus had been aware even of her cautious dealings with the Christian Deacon. She had small doubt that, at that moment, many Roman notables harbored informers in their households. It was a painful reflection that, Empress though she was, there was very little she could do about it.

The normally full-blooded face of Marcellus wore a distinct pallor, as with uncertain steps he entered the ornate room behind one of the Palace servants. At sight of the Empress sternly upright in a gilded chair, he prostrated himself. "Get up!" she commanded. He scrambled to his feet, looking as though he would be far happier on the cold marble floor.

"Does your Lady know you are here?" she demanded, not hiding her contempt.

"Your Majesty—oh, no!" He clasped his hands in almost feminine distress; his plump red lower lip quivered. "I obeyed your order. I told nobody—nobody at all!"

"Now listen," said Severina. "And stop twitching—stand still! I know exactly what your relations are with the Lady Drusilla. I will not interfere with any arrangements she chooses to make for her private life—even if she has given her trust to a despicable creature like you." He brightened considerably, although at her last words he did his best to assume a pained expression.

"On the other hand," Severina went on icily, "I will not tolerate any attempt to take advantage of—her kindness."

He looked comically hurt. "To leave you in no doubt of my meaning," she continued, "if you are guilty of any frauds in administering her property, if you persuade her to give you large sums of money or costly presents of other kinds, if you influence her in making a will—in fact, if she has arranged to leave you anything beyond a token legacy—I shall have you arrested and fitly punished."

She had spoken with the impetus of anger, not waiting to consider the nature of this fit punishment. But obviously he made his own prompt and precise interpretation, for he gasped and with a shudder looked down at his own person.

"Oh, no, Your Majesty! I would never—never—take advantage—of my Lady," he stammered. "In any way— Believe me."

"Further," she continued pitilessly, "since you are an unmarried man, you owe the Lady Drusilla your first and absolute loyalty. I am warning you that if you betray her confidence by taking your pleasure with anyone else"—she paused here with a cruel smile—"with some pretty slave of the household, for example, you will suffer for it!

"Since the Lady Drusilla has the misfortune to depend on you for her happiness, you will have to devote yourself exclusively to her—at a steward's normal wages! Now go—and if ever you are brought back here, you will have plenty of cause to regret it!"

"Your Majesty!" he whimpered. He went out like a man on the verge of collapse.

Severina felt certain that before long, with a beating heart and many a glance over his shoulder, he would go back to his plundering and his casual amours—but he would not dare to abuse her stepmother's favor brazenly and wholesale.

He was gone, but the taint of corruption remained. In anguish, she thought: life in this horrible place is poisoning me. Wherever she turned, to Drusilla, to Crinitus, to Eros, there was something to make the heart sicken. She herself had become degraded, nosing in the depositions of loathsome spies. A woman could not make headway against so much that was evil. Where was Aurelian now? She longed for him to come trampling into this abominable Palace, bringing with him a blast of the cleansing air of the wide frontier.

There was a time when, engulfed in unfamiliar and taxing duties, Severina felt that she had virtually lost not only her husband but also her child. Hundreds of hands were outstretched to snatch her away from Julia. For days on end she saw little of her; and of an evening when, shortly before Julia's bedtime, the nurse brought in the grave-eyed, unnaturally quiet girl, Severina was generally too exhausted to do much more than inquire if she were well and how she had passed the day.

Yet she knew that Julia must be quite bewildered by her transition to this enormous complex of buildings—a whole Imperial city which consumed the upkeep of an army and some of whose pillared marble halls were each more spacious than their entire house in Sirmium.

Lying awake one night, her thoughts feverish, Severina forced herself to concentrate upon the problem of her daughter, abandoned to servants (among them who knew what scheming and depraved characters?) in the huge Imperial Household. Before long an idea emerged. Anxiously she revolved it. It grew and answered her doubts and became more and more persuasive. Yes, she had the solution! Sitting up, she reached for the tablets she kept at her bedside and scribbled unseen notes in the dark to unburden her mind of the details.

Here in the Palace she would open a little school—under a senior tutor or headmaster—for the young daughters of Senators. Julia would be enrolled among them. Her supervision would be in qualified hands. As one of a number of pupils of roughly the same age, she would be in a much more wholesome environment than the Palace itself could provide and have suitable companions.

First, then, the right kind of tutor-in-charge. A humane, gentle man, for he would be instructing girls. Not one of the fashionable teachers of Rhetoric. Even for men Rhetoric was largely a barren study; for girls it was entirely sterile. But some knowledge of the great writers of antiquity Julia ought to have; and it would not be easy to find someone who could make such knowledge attractive to her stolid and rather pedestrian mind.

Who . . . who . . . who? Though she was Empress of Rome the circumstances were such that there was nobody to whom she could turn in this vital matter, confident of counsel that was both well informed and disinterested. Crinitus had no contact with scholars. Eros would probably recommend someone who had promised him a commission on the salary. Eutropius? No, he was a thoroughly conventional man—and, moreover, childless. He would not understand what she required.

She thought of her father and his genuine love of the great literature of the past. It was in his library that she recalled him, bent a little with a characteristic expression over one of his books. Her memory stirred. Into her mental picture there intruded an image, slight of shape and with features blurred; deferentially it approached the keenly envisaged figure of her father. She knitted her brows. The image sharpened, grew precise. Plainly now she recollected the underfed, hollow-chested, shabbily gowned young man who used to call, long ago, at her father's house to give her lessons in reading and recitation. What was his name? They used to send him to the kitchens for a meal, so needy he was, but he had the enthusiast's kindled eye when he declaimed from the Aeneid. Crassus . . . was it? Cassius? No, it was Cornelius—Cornelius the Grammarian!

Rapidly Severina completed her outline plan for Julia's education. All the dozen or so pupils must be treated as of equal standing; she must have friends and playmates, not a retinue of inferiors. Beside her grounding in literature, she must learn to sew, to spin, to understand the preparation of food and the elements of domestic management. These were women's accomplishments, best taught by women. Cornelius, if he could be found, would have to be supplemented by two or three tutoresses.

Cornelius was found. By the following afternoon he had been located in the attic of a slum tenement where he lived with his childlike crone of a mother. The spirit of Severina's instruction to have him traced had been misinterpreted. A squad of Praetorians surrounded the building and a detail clumped, cursing, up the rickety stairs. While the neighbors on the landing listened terrified, they thundered with gauntleted fists on the door. The panel had already split when he appeared, still tousled from his siesta. They haled him off without explanation to the Palace.

He was badly flustered, but soon recovered when Severina greeted him. Yes, of course he remembered her. His face bore a sweet, absent smile, as if he contemplated not the Empress before him, but the responsive adolescent girl he once had taught. "Your Majesty was an excellent pupil—one of the best, one of the best!" he recalled. Severina felt a flush of pure pleasure at this praise she had merited so many years ago.

Cornelius, whom she had remembered as a skinny young man with a faraway expression and a sacred enthusiasm for the Classics, was now middle-aged and almost cadaverous. He had a scholar's stoop and his gown was tattered and not very clean. But he still had the simplicity of the dedicated teacher. He nodded to himself, as Severina explained her project. Gradually his face kindled; his mild eye beamed. To teach literature to a whole class, including the child of a former pupil of his—why, it would give him great happiness!

This starveling scholar, Severina noticed, said nothing about salary. He simply answered, "Thank you, Your Majesty," when she mentioned a sum probably far more than ten times his current earnings. He would no doubt have assented just as readily had she proposed a fraction of the figure.

Cornelius showed some surprise when Severina detailed the curriculum she had in mind; it had never occurred to him that the feminine crafts, cooking, sewing, and the like, should be taught formally in the classroom and by paid instructresses. He demurred, however, only when Severina suggested that he take up residence

333

in the Palace. "Oh, no, Your Majesty!" he said quite firmly, "I couldn't leave my old mother by herself!"

"Bring your mother here," invited Severina. He looked at her, distressed. "Your pardon, Augusta, but my mother could never be happy away from home."

This man, Severina thought, had the noble innocence of the Golden Age. She saw him leave for his slum almost with envy.

When, later that day, she explained the arrangement to Crinitus, he at first listened indifferently. He had never bothered to disguise his lack of interest in Julia. But as Severina described her plan for enrolling the daughters of Senators in the school, he looked thoughtful. "So they'll be living here in the Palace!" he said. "That's a clever stroke, Severina—we'll have hostages from some of the leading Senatorial families!"

25

GRADUALLY Severina emerged from the first phase of her Regency, when she had felt almost overwhelmed by the endless onset of unfamiliar problems. Her duties, however, continued to tax her to the utmost. The worst ordeal, one that revisited her in disorderly dreams, was the daily session of the Regency Council. In this, loath as she was, she was still obliged on many occasions to let herself be guided by Eros, the keenest brain and most widely knowledgeable among the members. Instance after instance confirmed his analytical power and his ability to state a complicated case briefly and clearly. It troubled Severina a good deal that this venal and rather sinister man had become virtually indispensable to her.

He had no serious rival on the Council. The four departmental heads—whom privately she labeled, "the bureaucrats"—had executive talent, but lacked breadth of vision; they were more useful in implementing a policy decision than in reaching one. Eutropius was honest and eager to be of help. But his mind was just not penetrating enough; often he floundered. As for the other two Senators, they almost maddened Severina by their circumspection. They demurred to everything with a kind of weighty wariness, and owing to them many problems were needlessly slow and troublesome to resolve. She forced herself, however, to show them forbearance for the sake of the goodwill of the Senate.

Severina continued her regular consultations with Crinitus, her counsellor in the shadows, though now she knew enough to weigh his views with some detachment. For his cynical outlook and sharp, unsparing tongue she felt a growing distaste. She appreciated that his advice was conceived entirely in her interests, but she had begun to recognize that some of the measures he so vigorously urged on her required a brusque and overbearing personality, such as his own, to impose them on the Council. They simply were inappropriate to a woman Regent.

Little by little, she acquired a knowledge of the administration and an understanding of the basic principles and problems of government. As her insight developed, her quick mind, equal in penetration to any there and free from the self-seeking that might have deflected it from a judicious course, prompted her now and then to some conclusion opposed to that of the majority of the Council. The first time she openly expressed dissent from the unanimous voiced opinion of the others, she was conscious of a quickened heartbeat. Their reaction could not be mistaken. Eros frowned a little and stared at the table. Corvinus and Drusus exchanged a hasty, revealing glance. Eutropius looked pained. The bureaucrats sat impassive. The announcement of her views, to which her nervousness gave a challenging emphasis, had the effect of overruling earlier arguments and was accepted rather than approved, nobody venturing to contradict her.

To some extent this stronger tendency to assert herself was due to the progress of her scheme for Julia's education. Here, where she had acted entirely of her own initiative, not consulting Eros and with Crinitus shrugging the matter off, her unsupported judgment had been vindicated.

She had personally received the dozen solemn little girls who were to be Julia's fellow pupils, all obviously distressed, all trying hard—no doubt after earnest parental warnings—to keep the tears back. She spoke gently to each in turn, asked their names, strained to hear the whispered replies. One adorable little nymph with jet ringlets was called Julia. "My own daughter's name," said Severina, smiling warmly, "is also Julia. I shall have to call you Julia Black and Julia Brown!" She stroked the two heads, the dainty, dark-shining Roman one and the sturdy chestnut head of her own half-Illyrian child; and then placed a hand on their young, thin shoulders. There was a stir among the children and a faint giggle. They followed readily enough when she led the way to a table of refreshments and fell with appetite upon the cakes and fruit. By the time she quietly withdrew, they were much more relaxed and the bolder ones were already talking freely to the others.

Like Crinitus, the Senators regarded the enrollment of their daughters in the Palace school primarily as the taking of hostages. They felt some degree of relief, however, that the Empress had contented herself with the girls, when she might as easily have laid hold of their sons. Even though the children returned home at frequent intervals and Severina invited the others to visit them at the Palace as often as they pleased—out of school hours—the opinion persisted that she had found a diabolically clever way of detaining the offspring of leading Roman notables in her power. Her prestige was enhanced on account of it.

One day, not long after Cornelius and his women assistants had taken up their duties, Severina stole unattended from her apartment to the group of rooms assigned for the school. In the antechamber to the classroom there was a table, on which was set out a little exhibition of sewing: cloth purses neatly stitched in gay scarlet and blue; handkerchiefs with varied hems; a simple cap; a miniature apron. None of this handiwork was of outstanding quality, none bad. Against each item lay a slip with the name of the pupil responsible. It gave her a little thrill of maternal pride to find that one of the most workmanlike of the purses was the product of her own daughter's fingers.

Faintly voices were penetrating the classroom's double doors. She tiptoed up and laid her ear against the meeting line of the two decorated panels. Cornelius was declaiming familiar lines from the Aeneid, with loving precision following the swell and cadence of the majestic rhythms. Strange words to address to an audience of little girls; but either the sound of those nobly molded phrases or their meaning or, perhaps, the grave and reverent quality in the voice of their teacher kept them hushed. Severina heard Cornelius revert to conversational pitch as he called the name of one of the children. Her sweet pipe recited a few lines from the epic, imparting a tremulous, childish fragility to the splendid, sonorous words. Next, Cornelius called on Julia and, holding her breath, Severina heard her daughter's clear, rather hard voice repeat unfalteringly, though without the other child's fidelity to their music, the same few lines.

Again, the deep male voice. Again, the higher, sweeter tones of one of the children responding. Severina listened a little longer, with eyes moist. Then, as quietly as she had entered, she left.

Aurelian's victory over the Goths and the tranquilizing of the Balkans, although to the Romans they appeared distant events, had strengthened Severina's authority. The irruption of the Alemanni shook it; the military crisis brought crisis to the Council.

The breach of the frontier, the penetration in depth, the advent of a barbarian host in the North Italian plain and its unchecked ravages there—these disasters in rapid sequence laid bare the basic difference of viewpoint between Severina and the majority of the Council. She thought of Aurelian, the Army, the Empire; their concern was primarily for themselves.

During one session, the deliberations of the Council were uncommonly agitated and inconclusive. For the first time Severina could detect the note of resentful feeling against herself. In particular she sensed in the attitude of the two Senators, Corvinus and Drusus, the accusation that it was the Emperor's failure which had exposed Rome to this grave and growing danger. Indignation kindled in Severina against these mean-spirited men. There was now almost a cut-and-thrust quality about the discussion; had the Senators been able to overcome their habitual caution, they might have fallen to open wrangling with the Empress.

At this juncture, a courier was announced with dispatches from

337

the Army. Severina broke the seal, conscious of the intent eyes upon her, glanced through Aurelian's characteristically brief message and then read it aloud: The Illyrian Legions were on their way, by forced marches, to Italy!

Its effect was electrical. The surly faces wore smiles, the voices so recently raised in querulous complaint and carping argument now chorused congratulation. Severina coldly assessed the Council's reaction. She made a quick decision. This unfeigned enthusiasm, these transports of relief, had brought the mood and the moment for a proposal long maturing in her mind.

With curt phrases, unconsciously reproducing the peremptory style of Aurelian, she pointed out that there were still four thousand Praetorian guardsmen stationed in or near Rome. Though picked troops, better trained, equipped, paid, than men of the frontier Legions, they were engaged chiefly on ornamental functions—at a time when the striking power of the field army ought to be increased to the utmost. Two thousand of them must be dispatched north without delay to reinforce the Emperor on his arrival.

Her tone hardened as the consternation showed itself more and more plainly on the faces round the table. "In any case, the Praetorians are the Emperor's personal guard. The Emperor is on campaign—their place is with him!" she concluded.

The silence that followed was charged with such bitterness that Severina knew that at any moment determined opposition would confront her. Their fears, briefly quieted, were now thoroughly rearoused. To them her proposal was reckless folly, nothing more, endangering Rome, their lives, their property. She caught the quick, expressive glances directed at Eros; he was being tacitly nominated their spokesman. He licked his lips; then got reluctantly to his feet. Keeping his eyes on the table, he began to marshal his arguments, obviously seeking phrases that would state a case firmly, without drawing on himself the anger of the Empress.

The bulk of the Praetorians, he pointed out, were already with the Emperor; all that was left was a skeleton force, inadequate to a real emergency. The Augusta herself, against the feeling of the Council, had recently reduced this insufficient garrison by dispatching five hundred guardsmen to the front. A high sense of patriotism had kept the Council silent on that occasion, however dubious they had felt. The same high sense of patriotism obliged them now, respectfully but with deep conviction, to urge the Augusta not to weaken the defense of Rome any further. Of course, none could appreciate more warmly than themselves her concern for the field army; they shared it to the full. But now Rome, the Empire's capital, was in danger. So was the Empress herself. The Praetorians were responsible for safeguarding her, as well as the person of the Emperor. Besides, it was his duty to remind the Augusta that the city contained lawless elements always ready for violence. The police were under strength and in any case were by themselves no guarantee against mob rule. Order could only be ensured by the presence of a powerful body of dependable troops. The Council begged the Augusta to reconsider her proposal.

Eros sat down, still keeping his look averted, although the Empress had not stirred during his careful speech. He was followed by Corvinus, the oldest of the Senators, whose chronic sniffle now seemed eloquent of indignation and alarm. Breathing heavily between the phrases, he spoke of the rabble, idle, depraved, easily excited, in the city's swarming slums. The Augusta should understand the effect on men of property and position if the troops were moved. No one would feel safe. Shopkeepers would put their shutters up. Respectable people would flee.

His jowls trembling, he looked round; there was a murmur of sympathy that was tantamount to a burst of applause. Corvinus sat down with a little complacent smile and Drusus, his younger colleague and an altogether more formidable debater, slowly rose.

Bolder than the others, he looked directly at Severina as he spoke. His voice, with its undertones of sarcasm, grated on her. "The crux of the matter is: will two thousand Praetorians add sufficiently to the strength of the field army to justify leaving the capital of the Roman Empire defenseless when the barbarians are a few days' march away?" He paused weightily. Encouraged by the overt approval in the expressions of his fellow members, he was about to proceed, when Severina snapped, "That's enough!" and waved him to his seat. She knew now that the discussion would go wholly against her; even the loyal Eutropius looked dismayed. "We are

339

wasting time!" she said. "Whether Rome has a garrison of four thousand or two thousand, her safety depends on the field army. Our business is to ensure that the field army is as strong as possible when it meets the Alemanni—that is the crux of the matter! Eros, take this down: 'To Ventidius, Commander of the Praetorian Guard. Two thousand men will set out as early as possible tomorrow to rendezvous with the field army.'" Eros hesitated, his Adam's apple fidgety. "I have given you an order, Eros," she said viciously. "In the Emperor's name!"

Her voice had risen; her cheeks burned. A solid front of defiance had formed against her in the Council. It was the first critical test of her authority as Regent, but that hardly troubled her. Aurelian needed reinforcements—only that mattered. She was going to send them. She would let nothing stop her!

"Any more delay," she said deliberately, looking first to Corvinus and then at Drusus, who glowered but did not sustain her gaze, "and I will call the Guard Commander!"

The Guards were mostly Illyrians. They were certain to obey the Empress—who clearly was in an ugly mood. Eros hastily adjusted his tablets and began writing. All eyes followed the lines flowing from his hand.

Severina almost snatched the order from him. "I shall give this myself to the Guard Commander," she said. "The session is adjourned for three hours. You will all remain in the Palace. Eros, see that the Senators have somewhere to rest and are given a meal."

She rose; all stood up. Eutropius hurried to open the door for her, his normally good-humored face showing pain and bewilderment. She gave him a brief smile and walked out.

Crinitus, to whom she went directly, twitched his lips as she described the incident. "Proper Illyrian, aren't you!" he observed with a sour grin. "Bullying the Councillors as if they were children! Still, they were right, Severina—you've been foolish. You know I've a fancy you've had this cunning stroke in that pretty little head of yours for quite a time. That's why you've been so keen on a militia! Anyway, you've acted like Aurelian's wife, not his Empress. He entrusted Rome to you. Her safety is your first responsibility. But all you could think of is that he needs reinforcements. You didn't stop to reflect that Rome couldn't spare them."

Severina reddened. "He's in the field, fighting; we've not seen an enemy yet," she said indignantly.

His smile was caustic. "We might—and very soon. A flying column might come our way, with precious little notice. Those barbarians move fast. Four thousand men, picked men like the Praetorians, might hold up a strong attack. Two thousand—that's all you've left us—are hardly enough to mount the ceremonial guards and protect your person."

"Protect my person?" she repeated, struck now by the argument she had disregarded from the lips of Eros.

"Literally that!" he said with emphasis. "Not only the rabble might get out of hand. People—higher up—might think their opportunity's come. An Emperor has many enemies. Now thanks to your womanly intuition, you've exposed yourself, personally, to all manner of danger!"

His tone and even more his look, somber and censorious, deeply disquieted her. She repressed a shudder. It was all too easy to imagine assassins hurrying in search of her along the corridors of this ill-omened Palace which had seen so much violent death already.

He eyed her in silence for a little while. "Still, you can't possibly countermand that order," he resumed, less harshly. "To show weakness now would be fatal. As you'll no longer have the armed force, which is the reality behind all government, you'll just have to bluff the more brazenly.

"Your first step must be to give the remaining Praetorians a donative—a big one. Never mind where it's to come from. Get it and give it to them. Order Ventidius to put his Guards in state of alert. Bring one thousand into the precincts of the Palace. Station detachments at key points in the city.

"And start recruiting for that militia of yours. Place it under direct command of Ventidius.

"Be ready to round up at least fifty of the more influential Senators. In the meantime, why not take hostages?" He grimaced as she vigorously shook her head. "Very well, then," he went on with a grunt of resignation, "those little girls will have to do—they're all from leading families."

Again he paused, while his shrewd eyes studied her. "And Severina," he added, in a changed tone, "do try and eat more—and get some sound sleep! You're fading to a shadow. I shall have to get my doctor to look at you."

His fleeting reference to the little girls had awoken in her the longing to rest her eyes on them. At the school her heart would cease to ache, her overstrung nerves would relax; the very atmosphere was healing. She half-smiled at her mental picture of the children standing up to greet her in unison, making the formality charming, while their teacher beamed on them and her. Rising, she took Crinitus' hand. "You're a wise old uncle," she said, "even if you do bite my head off. But don't think I'm one bit sorry for what I did. If I had my way, I'd send the last two thousand Praetorians as well to Aurelian!"

He looked at her wryly. "I really believe you would!" he said with grudging admiration.

By the time the Council resumed its session Severina had regained her composure.

Her visit to the school happened to coincide with a break in lessons; bright-eyed and high-spirited, the children clustered about her, chattering. One by one they thanked her with quaint politeness for the brooch or the necklace or other little gift she had sent them. Cornelius assured her they were all making good progress. Julia studied and played very happily with the others. His pride was selfless and touching; speaking with this undernourished scholar, whose simplicity would have seemed absurd to worldy eyes, Severina felt herself in contact with something pure and noble. That and the sight and sound of these delightful children refreshed her heart, diminished her mind's burden.

Ventidius, the Praetorian Commander, arrived while she was eating a light and hurried meal, more because Crinitus had admonished her than because she had any appetite. He was instantly admitted. Close to forty and already graying, he was a tall, rangy man, with quick decisive movements and a mobile face that sug-

342

gested temperament. He reported preparations for the departure early tomorrow of four Praetorian cohorts, none of them far short of full strength—some two thousand men altogether. The remainder would have to be redeployed. What were the Augusta's orders?

While he spoke, she watched his keen, virile face. She decided to trust him. As frankly as she dared, she described the situation. His eloquent expression showed that he was promptly taking note of all the implications.

"Augusta," he said with the vibrancy of strong feeling, "I'm an Illyrian. Matter of fact, I was born only a few miles away from His Majesty" (indeed, his manner of speech closely reproduced Aurelian's, though in a lighter, brisker fashion). "Nine out of ten of my guardsmen are Illyrians. We'd let ourselves be cut to pieces for you and the Emperor!"

"I know that, Ventidius," she said quietly. "But thank you for saying it."

"Don't you worry about the Senate, Augusta," he resumed. "If they make trouble, we'll soon shut their mouths for them! The Emperor Gallienus—he was an odd fish, Your Majesty, but no fool —gave us a list of Senators to be rounded up in an emergency—a pretty comprehensive list, I can tell you! We'll just bring it up to date and wait the word from you. As for the mob . . ." He gave a short, derisory laugh.

"My aim," she pointed out carefully, "is to avoid a situation that calls for drastic measures. But there must be no disorders of any kind here in Rome. I will personally give you your instructions if an emergency arises. But if it happens that I am—not available—you are empowered to take any necessary action to keep the city loyal to the Emperor."

His look had gone fierce before she finished speaking. There was a glint in his gray eyes. "Let anyone dare. You can depend on the Praetorians, Augusta—absolutely!"

Yes, she could depend on the Praetorians, she could see that. Still, she must make doubly sure; the stakes were so high. "I also have a secret list," she said smiling. "I shall hand it to the Emperor on his return. It contains the names of those I am strongly recommending for promotion. Your name is at the top, Ventidius."

343

From that evening's renewed session of the Regency Council, Severina established a moral ascendancy over the members. Though Rome was almost denuded of troops and her authority lacked the substance of armed force, it grew rather than diminished. She had the advantage of being accustomed to the proximity of danger; to the others war had usually meant unpleasant happenings in remote places. Now with the Alemanni ravaging a few days' march from Rome, the resolute woman dominated the apprehensive men.

When the Council finally broke up that night, Eutropius approached her and said, with every appearance of sincerity, "You have been an inspiration to us, Augusta!" He paused and added, "But you are so pale and tired! Dear Lady, I beg you. Try to eat properly and take warm milk last thing at night—it will help you sleep!"

She smiled a moment, wearily. Food and rest. . . . First Crinitus and now here was Eutropius exhorting her on the same subject. "I have never eaten properly all my life," she said. "Still, I promise to take a cup of milk when I go to bed—just because you ask me, Eutropius."

The following morning, a deputation of Senators, headed by Tacitus, the senior member of the House, came to protest at the latest sweeping reduction in the city's garrison. Tacitus was a tall, hoary-bearded man of majestic presence, with an inner uncertainty that betrayed itself in nervous movements as he spoke or listened. The half-dozen others all deferred to him. In an aged voice, dignified in spite of its quaver, he conveyed the Senate's perturbation.

Look them in the eyes, Crinitus had once impressed on her. Steadily she looked into the old, faded brown eyes of Tacitus, gentle and tired eyes that could not sustain her bleak gaze. He blinked, lost the thread of his discourse, found it again, stammered a few more sentences, wavered to a halt. "It is a pity . . . a great pity . . . that the Praetorian cohorts were sent away. We assure the Emperor of our loyal and heartfelt support in this hard campaign, but it can only add to his anxieties to leave the city of Rome defenseless."

All this she had heard at yesterday's Council; it left her quite unmoved. She continued to eye him sternly. Behind him the little

344

group of Senators shuffled and coughed. Through them she could catch the throb of fear in this great, soft city, crammed with the world's plunder, now in its turn menaced by a fierce and greedy conqueror. "Rome is not defenseless," she said cuttingly. "We have a first-class Army in the field—that is our sure defense!"

Tacitus leaned a little forward and turned his head, to bring one ear nearer to Severina. She made her voice louder, sharper, more mandatory. "But we should not be content to sit here and wait, while others do the fighting. No, we too must play our part! Now listen. . . ." The Senators stared at this slight, pale, intellectual-looking woman whose eyes flashed and whose voice rang, as in curt, almost military style she detailed her plan for a militia.

Armed citizens in the streets of Rome! Impressed, troubled, the Senators exchanged glances. "Only men with a property qualification," Severina added—and relief was plain in their expressions. "They will support the regular troops. If any flying column of the barbarians comes south, we shall stop it far short of the Forum!"

They nodded, swayed by her resolute spirit, infected with her confidence. Severina was quick to exploit their change of mood. It was by a kind of coercion that she had overcome their opposition to the dispatch of the Praetorians from Rome. Now she set herself to win a more positive goodwill from them, for at this moment of acute danger, in Aurelian's absence, the zealous cooperation of the Senate would be invaluable.

"Only persons with a property qualification will be enrolled," she reiterated. "And then only if known to be of good character. There are not arms for large numbers, in any case. At the same time other steps must be taken. We must check the food supply and the routes by which it enters the city. Stocks of essential food must be built up. All doctors must be registered and warned to be ready for a summons."

She paused in this catalog of preparations. The Senators waited, expectant; they had resigned the initiative to her. "For these and other necessary measures, I want the Senate's assistance. You will nominate a small committee—six, eight at most—of your best men; men with experience of big-scale organization. They will work under the Regency Council and meet here at the Palace."

It might have been patriotic ardor that excited them; or perhaps they were flattered by the vital and conspicuous role they had been assigned. They all looked extremely pleased. "We will do our utmost to be of service to Your Majesty," Tacitus said simply.

One final appeal. For a fleeting moment she sought the right note. "If the barbarians reach the neighborhood of Rome," she said firmly, "I expect the Senate to set an example of courage and composure. You inherit a great name—I am sure you will show yourselves worthy of it!"

It occurred to her that she was a woman exhorting men; that these men were among the most eminent in an assembly of august reputation; that one of them, Tacitus, was nearer three times than twice her own age. But they showed no sign of resentment; their looks suggested pride in her high expectation of them. Gravely Tacitus answered, "The Senate will not fail the State, Your Majesty!"

With gathering momentum the city prepared itself for an attack. A sense of purpose pervaded the administration. Public morale, badly shaken by the lightning inroad of the Alemanni, improved as the signs manifested themselves of a vigorous and provident leadership. Stocks of grain and other foodstuffs were rapidly built up. There was an embarrassing rush of volunteers for the new militia. The first squads started drill and their route marches drew enthusiastic crowds to the roadside.

The encouragement Severina derived from this was offset, however, by growing doubts whether the Senate was capable of equal staunchness, notwithstanding the earnest assurance of Tacitus that it would not fail in its duty. Like the Regency Council, the Senatorial Committee met daily at the Palace and she came to respect two or three Senators, especially Tacitus himself who attended regularly in spite of advanced years and uncertain health. Others on the Committee and among those who frequented the Palace on business connected with the city's defense filled her with aversion and helped her understand why the Senate had faded to a phantom assembly. They were gross-looking, voluble men, fussily self-important, although obsequious to the point of cringing when they addressed the

346

Empress. She could feel little confidence that such men would set an example of resolution if the city had to fight for survival.

It was at this time that Eutropius warned her of increasing criticism of the conduct of the war and defeatist talk among Senatorial circles. The disclosure came as no surprise, yet it caused her much bitterness.

At Sirmium she had endured grim years, with the enemy prowling over the neighboring fields and frequent bloody clashes part of the season's routine. But a dour courage then sustained people. There was no exaltation, yet little or no flinching; nobody whined. Here at Rome, while from beyond the Apennines rumor blew in black clouds, many whined. These paunchy cravens, who sat comfortably at home, far from the battlefield, could only complain in the hour of their country's danger. They blamed Aurelian for Italy's plight— Aurelian who with a remnant of weary soldiers was struggling against a great host of ferocious invaders!

However, in the supreme organ of State, the Regency Council, and in the Senatorial Committee which it closely supervised, no symptoms of war nerves were permitted. Severina had assumed a personality that kept weakness dumb. She seemed to draw a fiercer intensity of will from the increasing fatigue of her frail body. Seeing the taut and masterful calm of this still young woman with lines of strain on her face and shadows under her eyes, the Councillors and Committee members kept their heads and labored conscientiously. The government of Rome under the Empress-Regent functioned with energy and decision as the crisis continued.

When the Alemanni retreated, there was inevitably a slackening off. Senators remembered their ailments and their estates. The Committee could no longer be relied on to complete their daily agenda; arrears of business accumulated. Disturbing reports came in of the disappearance of arms from the militia depots and the culprits could not be traced. There were fears that efficient weapons in some quantity might be finding their way into the hands of disaffected elements.

On the day news arrived that the Emperor had trapped the Alemanni on the Danube, the Senatorial Committee set aside their work as superfluous and spent a garrulous session drawing up a memorial of congratulation to the Empress-Regent. They were dumbfounded when Severina tossed their address on to a table and sharply ordered them back to their duties until the Emperor had reported final success. Back they went sheepishly, but now their discussions were desultory and as much concerned with market prices, condition of crops, shipping freights, and such accustomed peaceable topics as measures connected with the war.

The ascendancy which Severina had for a time maintained without challenge in the Regency Council could not survive a steep decline in Aurelian's fortunes. The return of the Alemanni to Italy brought an immediate change of attitude among the members. Once more a front of defiance hardened against her; once more she found herself fighting what would have been a lone battle, but for some uneasy support from Eutropius.

It was his fellow Senators, Corvinus and Drusus, who constituted the nucleus of a party of opposition or, more precisely, of determined obstruction. They now seemed actuated by a personal malice that made them seek to thwart her at every turn. The contention was no longer disguised, although it had not yet taken an extreme form. Severina on her side could not bring herself to make the slightest concession. As the war surged again across the North Italian plain toward the Apennines and her hold on the Council weakened, she grew more and more intolerant of views that challenged her own. In particular, she listened to Drusus, the more outspoken of the two hostile Senators, with visible anger and she more than once cut him short.

She would have dismissed both out of hand but that, at this juncture, it would have been too damaging an admission of disunity at the highest level of government; and, further, she despaired of finding among the Senators—with the possible exception of Tacitus—successors of ability who would be more cooperative.

To make matters worse, the Senatorial Committee, on whose efficiency so much depended, had been unnerved by the abrupt alternation of success with disaster, violent relief with violent alarm. Muddle ensued over a wide area. The provisioning of Rome, their most vital function, was bungled; the issue of foodstuffs began to exceed their inflow and stocks in the magazines fell.

Tension rapidly increased in the City, where the ear of panic could already catch the trampling of a mighty barbarian host drawing nearer and nearer.

For Severina the time was wearing in the extreme. To beat down the obstructive and animate the limp spirits of the others, to prevent inertia spreading through the machinery of defense, drained each day's vitality. She could no longer find a regular half-hour to visit Julia and the school. At her consultations with Crinitus, the need to maintain her poise being temporarily over, she drooped and yawned, without the energy even to give a coherent account of the Regency Council's discussions.

She was closeted with her uncle, almost overcome with lassitude but striving to follow his trenchant analysis of the military situation, when one of her women hurried in. Ventidius was in her apartment, demanding urgently to see her. At once aroused, she exchanged an anxious glance with Crinitus. "Bring him in," she directed.

The face of Ventidius was grim. "A messenger from the Army. Bad news, I'm afraid, Augusta!"

She opened Aurelian's letter with fingers gone rigid. "We have had a defeat. Losses are heavy. The Army is still capable of fighting. Be ready for an attack. The Alemanni may march on Rome."

If Aurelian called it defeat, it must be almost catastrophic. For a few moments the battering of her heart prevented thought and it was painful to breathe. The face of Crinitus, gaunt and gray, approached her own. Her mind grew clear. "A defeat, Uncle," she said levelly. She clung to that saving phrase about the Army's ability to continue fighting.

Poor Aurelian, how tired he must be! If only she herself were not so tired. "Ventidius," she said, surprised at the firmness of her voice, "have the members of the Council warned—we shall meet in two hours. Then come back immediately. You must be ready to act. This is the emergency we spoke of."

The Councillors, with the exception of Eutropius, greeted her with sullen looks. The spell finally was broken. No bluff, no exertion of the force of personality, could blind them now; they were convinced that the fortune of war had abandoned Aurelian. A bitter anger filled Severina against these ignominious men whose sole concern with the agony of the Roman Army was because their own skins were endangered. The time was past for tact—it would be an acute relief to drop pretenses and to indulge the passionate impulse to wound them!

"The news is very serious," she said coolly. "The Emperor bids us see to the defense of Rome. We must now put into full operation our plans for an emergency."

For a little there was silence, in which Severina could sense mockery as well as hostility. "Who are you to give orders?" those cold eyes, those compressed lips seemed to say.

Then Drusus placed both plump hands on the table edge and hoisted himself slowly up. His bulk loomed in opposition to the slight form of the Empress; his eyes glistened, as though he were savoring a long-delayed revenge.

"For my part, I can see no point in trying to defend Rome by arms," he said. "It is a wide-open city. We had a more adequate garrison once, but"—he looked round with ponderous irony, while the gray beard of Corvinus wagged emphasis—"those soldiers are probably all dead—their lives just thrown away. Still, time presses. We must face the crisis—even though it could easily have been avoided—in a practical spirit. I propose a motion, namely, that an embassy be sent to the camp of the barbarians to offer a big sum of gold on condition that they retire from Italy. Since the Emperor," he paused here, shot a defiant glance at the motionless Severina, then added deliberately, "and the Empress have failed to protect Rome, we must take what steps remain for the city's safety."

There was a murmur from the others which needed only the slightest indication of weakness or confusion on Severina's part to articulate itself as clear approval.

For some moments Severina could not speak; the fury boiled and choked her. Then a name came hoarsely from her constricted throat, "Ventidius!" The Praetorian Commander must have been listening ear against the panel, for on the instant the door flung open. In full

350

armor he stood there, giving the astounded Councillors a view of armed men behind him crowding the antechamber.

He clanked in. Severina pointed at Drusus. "Arrest him!" Her voice was shrill and trembling; her hand shook. "The charge is—high treason—attempting to treat with the enemy!" Ventidius turned a terrible stare on the shrinking Drusus and opened his mouth. Commands unintelligible to the Councillors clattered against the walls. A half-dozen grim-faced Praetorians tramped up to Drusus. Hands shot out to his neck, his shoulders, his arms. He blanched, moaning, and sagged away from them; but they yanked him from his chair and dragged him, his face contorted with pain, across the floor and pushed him into the arms of their comrades in the antechamber.

There was a deathly stillness in the Council room, while Severina sat with a smile of vicious satisfaction and everyone else listened petrified to the noise of Drusus being manhandled into the corridor.

Severina's gaze traveled slowly round the table; then she turned to the door. "Ventidius, stand by!" she called. "I may need you again!" "Augusta!" he snapped, and saluted stiffly. The door closed on him; the Councillors could feel his menacing presence an inch beyond the panel.

"Now," said Severina. "I have prepared an edict bearing on the situation. Eros, you will read it. It is quite short. You will all sign it. I would advise no one—no one, I said—to refuse!"

She pushed the document toward Eros. He rose and picked it up, the tip of his tongue moistening his lips, while he scanned it for a few moments amid the stricken hush. Then he began to read:

"Any Roman, of whatever status, who spreads alarm, either by retailing rumors or by cowardly talk of surrender or flight; any person who, whether deliberately or not, by word or action disheartens the defenders and populace of Rome, will be arrested and summarily tried by court-martial, the Commander of the Praetorian Guard presiding. For lighter offenses in this respect, the penalty will be confiscation of all property and goods; for graver offenses, death."

Severina held out her hand. Soft-footed, Eros came over and laid the edict before her. She wrote her name obliquely, with brutal

351

emphasis, below the single short paragraph. "Now, everybody sign. Confiscation," she repeated with relish, as she noted their eyes fall away from hers, except those of the open-mouthed Eutropius, "or death!"

That night Severina could not sleep at all. The following day she felt numb as though from a severe concussion. When Eros called at an early hour to go into a mass of urgent business with her, she at first looked at him vacantly; only with a painful effort could she jolt her mind into motion. Hour after hour passed and the pressure did not slacken. Somehow she struggled on, though at times she became aware of the bubbling irritability in her voice.

It was shortly before noon when the Senatorial Committee, reinforced by about a dozen other prominent members of the House, sent to beg an audience. Admitted without delay, they noted with apprehension Severina's tense rigidity of posture and the steely glint of her eyes, while in a voice strained but quiet, she gave them polite greeting. She looked fully capable of dealing out to others the fate that had befallen Drusus.

The Senators glanced at Tacitus. He studied the ground, stroking his white beard. Some moments passed; then Severina asked with a sharpness she could not restrain, "Well, what is it?" The tremor of irascibility in her voice galvanized Tacitus. He looked up and began, "The news from the Army is very grave . . ."

"It is," she confirmed curtly. She could divine that mingled with alarm there was a certain satisfaction among these worthies, themselves long dispossessed of real power, at the discomfiture of one of the plebeian Emperors who had usurped their authority.

"The Senate," Tacitus resumed with some hesitation, "has received a message this morning from the Emperor. It was at once read out and discussed. His Majesty approves our consultation of the Sibylline Books and will provide in full for such sacrifices as the danger to the State requires." At this point, Tacitus made a grimace of worry or distaste and his shaky hand went again to his beard; he appeared to be screwing himself to something unpalatable. "There is a strong feeling that the situation calls for something quite extraordinary in the way of sacrifices. The customary services and intercessions have proved unavailing and it is this, no doubt, which has prompted His Majesty's generous offer. Nevertheless"— here he shot a glance at Severina under his shaggy white eyebrows— "the course being demanded by many of our members represents a departure of magnitude from more recent practice."

He glanced at her again, almost beseechingly, but her brain was too sluggish to catch his drift. She simply felt exasperated by his rotund and allusive style and found herself wishing desperately that he would come to the point.

"Continue," she said.

"It is felt that something must be done," he resumed uncomfortably, "something of—ahem—a striking nature—which would restore the people's confidence in the successful outcome of the war. Once the Gods were consistently on the side of the Roman State; but now, obviously, They are angered. We must do whatever is necessary to placate them. It was an ancient custom—and no doubt it ensured the favor of the Heavenly Ones—in a time of supreme crisis to offer a supreme sacrifice—something more likely to turn away the Divine wrath than even an unblemished beast."

He paused as Severina's face darkened. "But others among us feel . . ." he began again.

One of the Senators pushed himself forward. He was a dark, bony, intense-looking man, with glittering eyes, and his jaw was slowly and rhythmically working. As soon as he spoke, tumbling the words out in a distinctive provincial accent, Severina recognized him as someone who had once made a deposition before the Regency Council on a taxation complaint and startled everyone by his needless vehemence. His name was Laetus.

"I beg the Augusta's permission to speak." She nodded slightly. "Your Majesty, Tacitus, whom we all respect, is not a suitable spokesman for us in this matter. His personal view differs from that of the majority of the Senate. He has not made our opinion clear. He has given the wrong impression altogether. Dear Augusta, we have in mind as sacrifice, not some innocent person, a chaste maiden, a virtuous youth—no, no, Your Majesty! Just a prisoner of war or a condemned criminal!" He laughed a soft, fanatical laugh, with the assurance of having disposed of the only possible objection. Then he looked puzzled, for a grimace had made Severina's face ugly.

"Why not, Your Majesty?" he pursued with ardor. "It's a little unusual, of course. But in the extremity of the State anything is justified!"

"Not that!" Severina almost spat the words.

He seemed unable to comprehend her. His face twitched. "It will be so good for morale!" he said excitedly. "It will capture the imagination of the people. And it comes within the terms of the Emperor's offer. The blood of animals"—he made a dismissive gesture—"it's of little account. The Gods are gorged with it. But human blood—ah, there's real power in that! What objection can there be, Your Majesty? Some man whose life is already forfeit."

"Cheating the Gods, eh?" she queried bitingly.

Laetus glared. Above his angular jaw his mouth was a little twisted. "I do not follow the Augusta," he muttered.

Obviously he was not the only Senator present stung by her comment. "Then I will make my meaning clear," she said. "There will be no human sacrifice. I will not permit it. Not even some condemned wretch, so that you can buy over the Gods on the cheap!"

Severina checked herself with an extreme effort which, she could see, frightened them with memories of Drusus. She realized the folly of maintaining an aggressive tone—with her nerves screaming out for relief, it could lead to some reckless outburst. In any case, irony about the State religion was dangerous; she must not give these fanatics and cowards an opportunity to spread allegations that the Empire's disasters were a punishment incurred by her blasphemies.

Inclining toward the distressed-looking Tacitus, she forced herself to speak in a conciliatory manner. "I am sure enlightened noblemen, such as you and your colleagues here, must agree with me: we are not barbarians to think an altar reeking with human blood a sight pleasing to the Gods. Rome has higher traditions—of which the Senate has always been the guardian. It is by them that we should be guided. Let us ask ourselves how our great ancestors would have acted in this crisis—and we shall recall that they had a truly inspiring way of entreating the Heavenly Powers when the city was in danger!"

354

She had struck the right note—their expressions showed it. These gentry of obscure pedigree liked nothing better than to hear their forebears identified with the Conscript Fathers of early Rome.

"I am absolutely confident that a victory, a decisive victory, is a matter only of time. Meanwhile, nothing would so hearten the people as a procession of all that is most pure and venerable in our city. In all respects we should follow the ancient custom—maidens and boys, dressed in white, chanting hymns—priests in their cere-monial robes—the Senate on foot, headed by its most august mem-bers"—her glance embraced the now intent delegation—"men famous for a lifetime of service to the State. I myself will be present with my ministers—all of us humbly walking around the city's boundaries. I cannot believe the Heavenly Ones will reject our prayer!"

Her eyelids drooped. These words, which she had struggled to utter with enthusiasm, had drained the last of her strength. Now they seemed to have had no force. She had failed to win the Sena-tors over. For a moment she had a feeling of helplessness and total isolation. Then she thought of Aurelian and, angry at her weakness, opened her eyes. But instead of beginning another plea, she stared. The face of Tacitus shone; behind him several heads were solemnly nodding.

She bit her lip, fighting a sensation of dizziness. Her voice was fainter when she resumed, but she held the hushed attention of her audience. "Let us deserve Their Help—by helping ourselves. Our brave Army is still facing the enemy. We, for our part, must ease its task by putting the city in strict order of defense."

Tacitus tugged at his beard. "But the walls," he said. "The city has long outgrown them. It sprawls in every direction . . ."

"Our plans are ready." Severina clenched her fists. "We are going to build barricades in the suburbs—a whole system of barricades, so that any"—she sought a confident, derogatory word—"any intruders would have to fight every fifty yards. But it may not come to that. The Emperor will do his utmost to prevent the barbarians approach-ing Rome. So let us send our loyal greetings to encourage him and the soldiers. It will double their strength to feel that we are with them in the struggle!"

Only Laetus maintained a surly silence; from the others came a deep, continuous murmur, unmistakably enthusiastic, a decorous old men's version of a cheer. Tacitus did not go through the formality of consulting his colleagues.

"With all our hearts we are with you, dear Augusta!" he said in his tremulous, aged voice. Tears glistened on his white lashes.

For Severina it was a moment of almost unbearable emotion.

Tacitus leaned toward her. "Pray, Your Majesty, do not mar the sacred concord of this day by having Drusus put to death! So many Senators have been done to death in the past!"

Severina gazed at his reverend visage; then at the more calculating faces of the others who, although they had not heard, must clearly have guessed what plea Tacitus was making. She choked back her generous and compassionate impulse. She must strike a balance; concede something—but not too much.

"Drusus will not be put to death—for the present," she said levelly.

For once Crinitus had deviated from his strict routine. That evening, on her return from a prolonged session of the Regency Council, Severina found him waiting in her apartment. With him, contrasting with his gaunt, formidable presence, was a delicately-made man of middle age and height, with fine Hebraic features. He turned his penetrating black eyes on Severina with more than a subject's curiosity.

"I've brought my quack," Crinitus said. He waved at the man, who shrugged with a humorous spread of his hands, his shrewd gaze still appraising Severina.

She sank onto a chair. "You can't carry on like this," continued Crinitus. "You're looking ghastly. Better take something to make you sleep. Benjamin here really knows his business. Go on!" he added impatiently. "Take a look at her!"

Benjamin was beside her, a peaceful presence; a faint musky odor came from his robe. Smiling gently, he passed a cool hand over her forehead; she felt the touch of sensitive fingers on her wrist and heard murmured words whose sound had a strangely soothing effect. Benjamin meditatively sucked his lip. "Bad overstrain—lack of sleep—I'll get a potion ready in a few minutes." More words traveled across the room between the two men—whom now she apprehended through a kind of fog—but she did not have the energy to apply them to herself. She drowsed for an indeterminate while and then felt her chin lifted and was aware of an aromatic cup at her lips, a warm, agreeable trickle on her tongue and down her throat. It seemed to her that Crinitus was shouting to her women, "Come and put the Augusta to bed!"

A woman's face bent close to hers; a woman's whisper, intense and persistent. "Your Majesty, wake up! A courier from the Army." Severina recoiled from the gross, intrusive noise and snuggled deeper into the pillow. But some words had broken into her mind and were racing round it, maddeningly: "The Army . . . the Army . . . the Army . . . courier from the Army. . . ." She struggled up from the comforting cloudiness and warmth. "Yes?" she muttered. "What is it?"

The tiny glimmer from the lamp made the woman's face darkly sleek and lit a gleam in her eyes. Severina sat up. "What time is it?" A half-hour to dawn! She had slept her drugged sleep almost the night through!

The woman assisted her from the bed and found a woolen robe to wrap round her plain thin shift. Still sluggish, Severina went through the door the woman opened. In the dazzle from two giant pendant lamps of glass she saw Ventidius; he looked worn but cheerful.

"Message from the Emperor, Augusta," he said briskly, pulling forward a chair for her. "Better news!" He waited silently while she broke the seal of Aurelian's dispatch. It was the shortest note she had ever received, even from his economical pen. "We are marching after the Alemanni. You have done well."

To what did his praise refer? The reinforcement of Praetorians? The Militia? The fact that Rome under her administration stayed apparently tranquil? No matter, the four brief words intoxicated her. She had not failed him. Even in the agony of rising from defeat, this dour man, so sparing of words, had been moved to praise her!

So he was marching after the Alemanni again—there would be another battle. Half her life, it seemed, she had been waiting for the

357

result of one battle or another. But henceforward she would not be afraid. Obscurely she divined that the fortune of war had forsaken the Alemanni and passed to Aurelian.

The procession on the following day proved a great success. Even the faint-hearted and the habitual doubters felt, as they viewed it, that the Gods owed Rome some goodwill in return for so rare and impressive a spectacle.

Severina, who was borne in a litter preceded by Ventidius with a powerful detachment of Praetorians and followed by a stately train of matrons, felt the multitude of eyes seeking her out. She turned her head a little from time to time with a faint smile which did not take from the solemnity of the occasion. Between the noble, long-sustained anthems from the deep-voiced priests and the white-robed choirs of youths and maidens there were intervals when a chant broke from the crowds massed along the Processional Way, "Augusta! Augusta! Augusta!" She recognized at once that these were no hired claques strategically stationed by Eros. Thousands of throats contributed; all Rome's heart was in that cry.

It was her first real contact with the populace, the hundreds of thousands of humble folk so remote from the Palace that rose in their midst. The only Rome she knew as a personal reality was that of the Imperial Household and the restricted circle of aristocratic Senatorial families. But today the People's Rome clamored to her. Again and again along the route, the cry swelled from the embanked faces—"Augusta! Augusta! Augusta!" Rome had one mouth and it was gushing thunder. Surging up, beating upon her, came the prolonged, tremendous bursts of enthusiasm and affection and her whole being quivered to the sound. She could no longer smile, for to relax the fixity of her face would have set hot tears uncontrollably welling. Instead, she bowed her head slightly, first to one side, then to the other, gripped by the intolerable ache of an answering love and of compassion for all these vast multitudes who could find in a single frail woman the symbol of their hope for deliverance.

On the Capitol the noise died away; an awe-inspiring hush prevailed. Only the Colleges of Priests, the Senators in their white togas with the broad purple stripe and the chief dignitaries of the government were present with Severina, her personal attendants, and faithful escort of Praetorians. She had a struggle not to avert her gaze as the knife flickered in the hand of the Sacrificial Priest. The white bull seemed the most beautiful creature there and the whole gory, archaic ritual filled her with revulsion. But she knew what an unfortunate impression it would make to betray her feeling. Setting herself to think with intensity of Aurelian, she gazed steadily at the slaughter and the examination of the entrails; while her brain refused admission to the images imprinted on her eyes. A triumphant shout told her that the auspices were favorable and she forced herself to nod graciously at the red-handed Augur.

The day ended on a note of anticlimax. In the Palace courtyard, Eutropius made his way through the soldiers and the drooping, leg-weary women. Peering anxiously into Severina's white face, he asked, "Have you taken your milk today, Augusta?" When faintly she answered, "No," he stared at her so reproachfully that she called an attendant and bade her go at once and have some milk warmed.

Back in her apartment she swallowed a few mouthfuls and felt much better for them.

26

CLOAKED against the drizzle which had persisted since the evening's downpour, the Roman sentinels peered into the gloom. The night was pitch-dark with raincloud and the watchfires of the Alemanni, only a few miles away, were hidden from them. Behind them, in their own sleeping camp, they were aware of unusual light and movement. From time to time they would turn to follow for a few moments the sloping tongues of flame that indicated small parties picking their way from several directions toward the Praetorian Tent.

So old Hand-on-Hilt had called a Council of War. That confirmed what everyone had guessed already. The sentinels cursed the luck which had brought their turn of guard duty on the night before a battle.

They shrugged and resumed their slow pacing over the soft, clinging earth. Dead or alive, by tomorrow night they would at any rate have finished with all these killing forced marches.

After they had ravaged the Romans in the tremendous battle of the ambush, the Alemanni had felt no desire to complete their victory with further bloody fighting. Badly mauled themselves, they were still dominated by the impulse to get clear away from Aurelian. At first light, they dragged themselves to their feet and, turning their backs on the still shrouded battlefield, set out toward the emerging sun, convinced that the Romans, in state of wreck or at least grievous disarray, were incapable of following.

For hours the host, now hampered by a train of walking wounded, trudged rather aimlessly eastward. By early evening, however, when they encamped, the chiefs had thrown off the fixity of idea imposed on them by Aurelian's long and bitter pursuit and were adjusting themselves to the new situation, in which they could march where they pleased, with nobody opposing.

The canny veteran, Goderich, rose and harangued the campfire council. They had come very far, across wide rivers and lofty mountains. They had broken through every obstacle. The Emperor Aurelian himself, the famous conqueror of the Goths, had sought to bar their way. They had routed him and a numberless Roman army. The whole world would ring with the prowess of the Alemanni. Everywhere men would speak their name with trembling. Yet their losses had been heavy. The host was worn out. They were deep in a hostile country, where their own distant gods had little power. It would be wise to tempt Fate no further. Content with the glory they had won, they should turn for home, there to gather strength for a new inroad, perhaps in the year after next.

His eloquence was heard in resentful silence. A huge, shaggy figure with winged helmet and fiery red beard, the High King Vadomar heaved himself up and his guttural rumble propounded a

360

more adventurous plan. He lacked Goderich's command of cunning words, but he spoke directly from his own greedy and ferocious heart to those of his tributary chiefs.

They had invaded Italy not to lose thousands of their warriors, but to strip the country bare. Now all roads were open. Further south was a region bursting with riches, where no one had ever raided. South, then, should be the direction of their march. They should press right on to Rome—with none to hinder them, they would be there before many days. It was the greatest city in the world and full of treasure, so they were sure to find it strongly garrisoned. But even if an assault stood no chance, they would have the entire surrounding countryside at their mercy. They would be the first to plunder there—the haul would be beyond precedent!

The chiefs grunted applause of this naked appeal to their rapacity. At the moment they were empty-handed. It was pitiful to think of those masses of beautiful loot they had been forced to abandon by the Danube. Glory was all very well, but sour would be their welcome in the tribal settlements if they returned with nothing to show for all their wandering and fighting but cruel gaps in their ranks. Let them make a foray into the wealthy South. Laden with plunder, they would swagger home. Gold, silver, jewels, silks and other costly fabrics, droves of slaves—those were the arguments with which to silence the reproaches of the widows and orphans!

Even Goderich's caution forsook him at the dazzling prospect. It was decided to make a sweep toward the Adriatic, into Umbria, where nobody would expect their approach; then to cross the Apennines to the overflowing booty afforded by the luxurious villas and well stocked farms in the neighborhood of Rome. They would probe the defenses of the great city and, if these proved too strong, they would defile contemptuously past, daring the garrison to come out and fight. They might even pillage and burn some of the suburbs.

The host swung southeast, no longer a loose horde shambling, but an ordered, fast-moving army, each tribal contingent tightly grouped round the standard of its chief. Scouts and foraging parties were active far ahead and on their flanks. Before long, the unexpected direction of their thrust and the mobility of the raiding bands

361

had begun to bring rewards. They burst into a rich region where the population was still in flight and ample stores of food had been abandoned in the manor houses and farms.

Toward evening word came in from the rear that Roman scouts—regular cavalry they seemed—were following in the track of the host, though at a respectful distance. Vadomar chuckled throatily and called for wine, now again abundant; but Goderich and two or three of the older chiefs looked thoughtful.

The scouts were still there in the morning, keeping their position. In the early afternoon, they began warily to close in. Uneasy at this development, the chief commanding the Alemannic rear guard rode with a few followers to a hillock surmounted by a clump of trees. A young warrior was hoisted into the branches; he scrambled his way near the top and leaned out in the direction of the Romans. Those below jumped when his agitated shout reached them. At once a mounted messenger went racing away to overtake the main host.

Vadomar stood dumbstruck at the news that a formidable Roman vanguard was in sight and that column after column of dust showed the Emperor Aurelian's army in orderly formation toiling in its wake. Then he bellowed, gesturing vehemently, and retainers sped to alert the chiefs and call in distant detachments. Almost immediately, the motion of the host quickened. But when sunset illuminated the west, the scouts were still there and beyond them the level rays sparkled on the helms and lances of many soldiers.

The nightmare chase had begun again.

With a Roman arc overhanging their rear, the Alemannic host, pointed southeast, continued the march in the direction of Umbria. Raiding, except for the bare necessities, had ceased; everything was concentrated on increasing their lead over the Romans. But press on as they did through all the hours of daylight, desperately, they could not increase their lead; they could only maintain it. The two armies seemed invisibly tangled, one wearily dragging, the other wearily dragged.

Day succeeded day. Still the Romans hung on the Alemannic rear, so that the barbarians dared not break the march save for the shortest breathing space and, when night compelled a halt, sank

362

spent and sweat-drenched to the ground for sleep too brief and troubled to be reinvigorating.

Most of the day and more than once well into the dark there was a crackle of skirmishes, with the Roman van heartened by the knowledge that powerful reinforcements were driving forward at their heels and the Alemannic rear guard discouraged because their own main body was racing away from them. It was a grim Marathon of thousands of fatigued but dogged men pounding on through walls of dust which excited a thirst they had no time to slake; or slipping and butting through lashing rain that turned the ground to gluey mud and made each step a labor.

Beyond the eastern horizon the Adriatic was drawing near. Aurelian's pursuit threatened to pin the Alemanni against it.

Vadomar called on his men for a tremendous effort, of which only rugged and lightly equipped barbarians were capable—a forced march virtually at the double, sustained for many hours. Behind a dense screen of warriors with orders to delay the Roman advance at any cost, the Alemanni, guided by captured peasants, drove in a gradual curve along field tracks and woodland paths and emerged at last at a point to the north of the pursuing Romans.

It was in vain that now they faced the direction of escape; they could not shake the Romans off. The prodding at their rear became, if anything, more vicious. In this conflict of endurance and willpower, the High King Vadomar gave up first. A magnificent fighting man, he was no Aurelian to keep a weary army slogging along an endless road; nor did he dispose of anything like the Roman corps of brutal, iron-hard Centurions, who could transform men sick and sluggish with the accumulated fatigue of weeks by bullying them back each dawn into the relentless organism of the mustered Legion.

One day the Alemanni halted some two or three hours before sunset. Torrents of rain were falling as, in the gathering dusk, the Romans established their camp at the opposite edge of what was to be tomorrow's fatal battlefield; it was pitch dark before their last, sodden units limped in.

Aurelian consulted briefly with his generals; then sent to summon all Centurions not on essential duty. He stood before the Praetorian Tent, towering in his plumed helmet; the generals formed a motionless rank immediately behind. Slowly his gaze traversed the hundred and fifty-odd Centurions drawn up in a double line, according to their units, a little distance away. Torchlight washed over his armor as he moved; rain glistened on his strong-hewn features.

"Attention, everyone!" His voice rang far in the night stillness; the sentries, well beyond the range of his words, could hear masterful tones plucking at the dark.

"Tomorrow we're going to smash the Alemanni. I want them wiped out—not a man left alive! There's only one way to do that. Get your orders clear—and carry them out!"

He paused, then added with harsh emphasis: "I'll take no excuses. Any man who fails me I'll break!"

Again an interval, while the rigid figures ranged there in the dark mutely pondered this warning.

"The Alemanni will start off by charging," Aurelian resumed. "There's a bit of a slope in their favor—it's bound to tempt them. The first job will be to beat them back.

"Our battle order will be just as you are. Praetorians on the right"—he motioned as he spoke—"left wing, you two Legions. Center, five Legions—three in the front line, two in close reserve. Archers and javelin-men will support the center. Now get this absolutely clear. Most of the time, the wings will fight a defensive battle. It's the center that's going to counterattack—that's why I'm making it so strong.

"Even if the sun comes out hot, the ground should be sticky in the morning. That will take some weight out of their charge. We'll soon bring it to a stop. Then, right and left—stay where you are. The center goes after them as hard as possible. As their center falls back it exposes both their wings on the inside; the reserve Legions close in and wheel onto them. Our own left and right—wait for the massed trumpets. I don't want a general retreat by the enemy too soon. But when you hear the trumpets—forward! No quarter, remember! They've given Italy hell—and tomorrow we're going to make them pay for it!

"Cavalry will move well over to the left, near those farm buildings where we've got an outpost. They're not to take part in the battle. I want them fresh when the barbarians start running. Then they're to follow and kill them—kill them—till there's not a man left!

"One last thing. You Centurions there, of the Thunderers. Your Legion wasn't at Naissus. Now you can win equal glory with those that were. You'll be right at our center, opposite their High King and his bodyguard. Here are your orders: Destroy his bodyguard to the last man. Bring his head to me. I want to see it dripping from a lance! I'm giving you my personal standard—I wish I could be there with it. Tell me, you Thunderers: Will you cut a way for your Emperor's standard—right through the Alemanni?"

A stocky First Centurion, with a face worn to wrinkled rock by wars and weather, stamped forward. His square jaw thrust out and the far-carrying rasp of his pugnacious voice made the distant sentries turn, wondering.

"Give us your standard, Emperor. We'll bring you the High King's head. We'll rip those bastards to pieces for you—we promise!"

A bloodthirsty growl broke all along the line, associating every Centurion with this pledge of victory.

As Aurelian had predicted, so it proved when, in the middle of next morning, battle was joined.

The Alemanni, slithering in wild career down the drying slope, lurched like an avalanche against the steadfast Roman line and were halted after a desperate struggle. The slender Roman wings were almost jolted back at the first tremendous shock, but they soon recovered; not the most violent onslaught could dislodge them. In the center, the Romans, more densely massed, repelled the charge more bloodily and, as the Alemanni recoiled, followed them up the slope, fighting like demons. The Thunderers surged against Vadomar's retinue of stalwart young nobles, equipped by him with splendid helms and weapons; even the heroism of this devoted bodyguard could not stem their overwhelming fury. Soon Vadomar on his giant warhorse was almost surrounded. For a little he kept his assailants at bay with a hail of strokes from his broadsword. Roman after Roman was cut down before one young legionary turned a ringing blow with his shield, dropped his sword, grabbed the High King's foot and jerked it fiercely upward. Vadomar flung out his arms; his bulky form sloped from the saddle, wobbled—while the hilt slipped from his loosened fingers—and then sank among the swords of the Romans. Half a dozen blades slashed or stabbed at him as he slumped to the ground. Maddened legionaries stooped to hack at his still twitching body. A pike was wrenched from the clutch of a dead barbarian—and a few moments later it swung aloft. On it was impaled a huge head in a dented winged helmet; above the shaggy red beard was frozen a ferociously snarling expression.

Mockingly the trophy was lowered before Aurelian's stern effigy on the tall Imperial ensign; then, deliriously cheering, the Thunderers tore open the remnant of the Alemannic center.

Behind them a brazen clangor rode through the uproar of battle. The whole Roman army stormed forward; both Alemannic wings were clenched in a contracting grip of iron and slowly dissolved. A few thousand men, with them the cunning Goderich, who alone of the barbarian chiefs had not sought to fight among the foremost, stumbled from the battlefield.

The Roman cavalry launched themselves in pitiless pursuit.

Aurelian walked with a halting tread, staring down at the bodies thickly strewing the battlefield. So savage had the struggle been that even the mortally wounded seemed to have twisted themselves in impotent frenzy to arise from the ground into which their lifeblood was soaking; while in many places Romans and Alemanni lay literally in heaps, with the later fallen sprawled across the earlier dead. Drying pools of blood everywhere; swords and broken lances; battered shields on arms gone limp; javelins and arrows bristling— and the Thunderers' drive that broke the Alemanni's center and their army's heart traced by a continuous pathway of corpses.

With an expressionless face Aurelian gazed on the dead. He had walked thus over many a gruesome field, with stirred though silent emotions, sometimes exulting, sometimes with stoical grief for comrades fallen. This time he looked around dully. His glance seemed to glide over things, not grip them. He stumbled among the corpses like a man half-tranced.

366

The campaign had lasted too long, exacted too much. The force that had sustained him was drained away. His will, exerted with such extreme concentration for so many weeks against hostile Fortune, against the weary limbs and failing spirits of twenty thousand legionaries, against the wild courage and cunning of the Alemanni, had gone suddenly slack. Inwardly he sagged. It was beyond his strength to raise his head and survey the scene of his triumph with the proud regard of a conqueror.

With hunched shoulders, an aging man borne down by too great burdens, he walked painfully back to the Praetorian Tent. Soldiers came in, bearing food and drink. He looked blankly at the steaming bowl of porridge they set before him on the table, but reached out for the flask and splashed red, tangy liquor into a mug, spilling half. As the undiluted wine flowed down his throat, he could feel the contact of its descending fire with his parched, sluggish body. Warmth glowed through him; his eyes brightened. Abruptly, he called in a creaking voice, "A message for Rome—hurry!"

One of the soldiers ran out, to return within the minute, followed by the chief clerk of the Headquarters section, tablets in hand. The clerk, a lean, brisk man gone gray in the service, approached Aurelian. With a mixture of awe and pity he gazed at the commander who had crushed so terrible a foe at so terrible an expenditure of his own life's energy. "Yes, Augustus?" he asked, troubled as the weary, weighty look of the Emperor rested on him.

"To the Senate and People of Rome," dictated Aurelian, bringing out the familiar terms with the effort of one laboriously improvising. "The Gods have granted us a complete victory. The barbarians have been destroyed. Their High King is dead." He struggled to compose a phrase or two more, but the words eluded his feeble search. "That's all," he muttered, gesturing toward the entrance. "Copy to the Empress—with my greetings."

He pushed the flask back, stretched his arms on the table and let his heavy head sink onto them. His eyelids glued themselves together. He snorted and a grinding sound came from his throat. For some moments a tenuous causeway held him to the shore of consciousness. It crumbled and, panting, he was in the midst of the battle, while the swords of his bodyguard flickered toward the dis-

367

torted faces of huge warriors, an endless swirl of faces, from which rose incessantly the dreadful battle roar of the Germans.

A few minutes later the soldiers found him helplessly asleep, mumbling, moaning, shaking all over. They dragged him, without rousing him, to the camp bed, hoisted up his heavy, inert legs, and covered him with a military cloak.

Gradually he grew calmer and lay almost motionless, no longer staggering amid tumult but drowned in heaving seas.

After about four hours he awoke, haggard but master of himself, and called for his horse. While a Praetorian held the reins, he stood by, spooning hot porridge into his mouth with relish. Then the soldier helped him into the saddle. As he rode to visit his generals and observe the Army's condition, legionaries were still methodically quartering the battlefield, sword in hand. Every now and then one of them, after poking with foot or blade at some sprawled form, would stoop to deliver the deathblow.

27

AS THE tramping drew near, Severina went to the window, the only one in the inn's upper storey. Through the open gate of the untidy yard and over the low roofs of neighboring cabins, she commanded a stretch of the village's single, winding street. She stayed at her place for a long time, watching the Army defile past.

The men marched raggedly, staring straight ahead. Their sole motive power seemed the voices of the Centurions. Whenever the hoarse, automatic curses, the compulsive, rhythmic bark of "Left— Right! Left—Right!" ceased for a while, they began to falter, their shoulders to droop, their feet to drag and muddle the step.

These soldiers had reached the stage of exhaustion that even victory cannot exhilarate. It was as well, thought Severina, that the Alemanni had suffered such a crushing disaster. The report would reverberate through the forests of Germany, paralyzing the tribes, and the spent Legions would have an interval in which to recover.

She had traveled several days to meet Aurelian, for once the military crisis was over, her presence at the Palace was no longer essential. A hundred miles behind, Rome was preparing a hero's welcome for her savior. But Severina knew that there was also widespread apprehension, particularly among the Senatorial Order, at Aurelian's approach, accompanied by a large and victorious Army devoted to himself. The image that preceded him was of a stark fighter, of the humblest origin, product of the barracks and the battlefield. How would such a ruler comport himself in a great capital completely at his mercy? Why, when the troops so desperately needed rest, was he dragging them to Rome—thousands of fierce, semi-barbarous Illyrians?

A tall horseman wheeled through the gate; hooves clattered on the paving stones. Aurelian was in the yard, seeming to fill it. He looked up, a piercing glance that was recognition rather than greeting. He dismounted, a little heavily, handed the reins to a soldier and walked into the public taproom directly underneath her. The stairs creaked to a slow, weighty tread; the door opened. He looked at her unsmiling and said, almost formally, "I hope you are well, Severina." She was shocked by his haggard appearance; victory does not erase from a face the grooves driven by defeat. His hand, as she clasped it, was hot; the cheek against which she pressed her own was burning.

"Are you ill, my dear?" she asked softly, trying not to show too much concern. In all their married life he had never been sick, to speak of, and had needed medical attention only once—after a minor wound in a skirmish near Sirmium.

He took a stool from beside the trestle table. "A touch of fever—those Danube marshes," he grunted. "I'll shake it off." Catching her anxious look, he put on a more cheerful expression. "We came through—eh, Empress?" he said. "The rest won't be so hard."

She smiled down at his face which was now indistinct through her tears. "How's the girl?" he asked heartily, although still with some suggestion of strain.

"Flourishing!" said Severina. "She's grown inches."

"And your uncle? He wrote me, you know. About those Praetorians you ordered to the front. You gambled there, Severina.
Lucky it came off." He gave her something like a comradely grin.
"I was glad enough to have them—first-class men, though not so
good at forced marches."

"It wasn't a gamble," answered Severina. "I didn't bother about
the risks. You needed troops—that was all I cared about!"

He chuckled. Still, despite the cordiality now emerging, there
remained a hint of reserve in his manner. She put it down to the
odd, shamefaced constraint this iron man would feel because she
knew of his illness. Feminine fuss would only irritate him. Sitting
beside him, she began quietly to talk about Julia and Crinitus and
the Regency Council, whose last act had been to prepare an announcement of its own dissolution, to be issued on the Emperor's
entry into Rome.

"This Eros sounds like a valuable man," Aurelian remarked
thoughtfully.

"I wouldn't exactly recommend him," observed Severina with
some hesitation. "He's the sly kind—tricky—not too scrupulous . . ."

"He wouldn't try any nonsense with me! Anyway, I'll look him
over when we get to Rome. Ah, here's the food. Join me, Severina."

Grinning sheepishly, the red-faced, stocky innkeeper set the table,
tucked his wooden tray under his arm and bowed himself out. Severina could hardly force herself to swallow anything, but Aurelian
attacked the broiled kid with zest. After a little, however, his appetite began to flag. He pushed the platter away and reached for the
flagon.

When he held it up, she shook her head. He helped himself,
liberally. "The dust gives you the devil of a thirst!" He emptied the
tankard and set it down. But he made no move to refill it. A change
had come over him. His face was kindled and intense. His eyes had
fixed themselves on hers in an almost oppressive stare.

"Severina—listen to me. It was not I who won the battle!" He
spoke deliberately, with a resonance that suggested the pulse of a
strong and urgent emotion.

She shifted uneasily under his concentrated gaze. What he hoped
or feared to read in her face she could not guess. His words—though

370

hardly his strained manner—suggested some tribute to the skill of his lieutenants or the valor of his legionaries.

"No," he said solemnly. "No! It was my Lord. . . . It was Mithras Himself. He appeared to me!"

Severina drew back.

"I saw Him, I tell you. He was close to me—in my tent. It was the night we were defeated. When all was lost, He came to save the Army! I heard Him speak—His Words sounded in my heart. It has happened before—but never so plainly!"

Aurelian rose awkwardly and walked a few paces; then he swung round and again his look bored into her. "Severina," he said in a low, vibrant, exulting voice, "I have had a Revelation. I am one of His Elect. He is here!" Aurelian struck his chest a blow that jarred Severina, although it did not seem to hurt him.

He thrust his head forward. His eyes glittered as they searched her face. "You understand, don't you?" he demanded, almost menacingly.

A painful few moments passed before she found her tongue. "I'm trying to," she murmured. He had never mentioned mystical experience before. Among the rites of Mithraism, she knew, was a sacramental meal which brought the initiated into collective communion with their god. But what Aurelian had asserted with such frightening conviction went far beyond this. He had met Mithras face to face, alone, in the night, in his tent. And he had spoken of other, earlier, visitations.

Severina took a grip on herself, for he was speaking again.

"It stands to reason, doesn't it?" he said with a smile that chilled her. "A Roman Emperor rules over millions—he's their absolute Master. He can't be just an ordinary man. There's something special about him—he's been Chosen. Oh, not every Emperor, of course. I don't mean a trifler, like Gallienus. But Claudius and, in his day, Marcus Aurelius—and Trajan—the Emperors who served their people. They must stand in a special relation to God—share in the Divine Nature—somehow."

There was a pause. "We ourselves held a Procession to invoke the help of the High Gods," she said, hoping to recall him to sober reality without incensing him.

371

"The Olympians?" His tone was derisory. "What could they do? They're senile. They've lost their power. Why else has the Empire fallen into such a plight? You know, Severina, sometimes I doubt whether they exist at all!"

Quite at a loss and by now deeply afraid, she did not answer. Soon she became aware that Aurelian's heavy, intent gaze was relaxing. He looked round the room and frowned at the window, evidently measuring the passage of time. "I must go now," he said, to all appearance normal again. "Tell the landlord I'm spending the night here. The Army will bivouac round the village. We'll billet Headquarters in some of the better houses. By the way, Severina, my officers want to pay their respects to the Empress-Regent." He grinned, incredibly changed from the man who a minute ago had asserted himself something more than human. "You've shaken them, you know—a woman defending Rome with a militia of shopkeepers!"

He went out. Some residue of his presence, formidable, disquieting, a little eerie, persisted in the room. She did not go to the window, but sat motionless, trying to understand in what aberrations he had lost himself.

It was no use. Her mind was too rational and earthbound. She groped in a darkness faintly tinged by the far-off glare of something Unearthly.

She realized now that right from the start something had gone amiss with their reunion. They had never really made contact. They were not the same husband and wife who had parted in the Balkans. Their separation had interposed some distorting medium between them; the old harmony, the old mutual understanding were broken.

Absently, she had been aware of noises below, then on the stairs. A gentle tap at the door; it opened and there stood Probus, rather shyly smiling. "Augusta!" he said with evident pleasure.

"How wonderful to see you safe—oh, do come in!" she cried, extending her hand.

Like Aurelian's, his face had become hollow and its skin burned brown; the flesh seemed to have been scorched away. He came in, still very handsome, his gauntness giving him a spiritual aspect lacking before, and bowed over her hand with words of formal

372

greeting. But after some polite preliminaries, he leaned a little closer and asked earnestly, "May I speak to you in confidence, Augusta?"

"Of course," she answered, encouraging him with her smile, though something in his expression made her a little uneasy.

"It's about Marcian," Probus said directly. "He made a bad blunder in letting the Alemanni escape. Nobody is defending him. But he's been sentenced to death—to death, Augusta!" Probus drew back, his eyes snapping, a level-headed man angered to the point of danger. "He's been an able and loyal soldier all his life—wounded half a dozen times—won many actions, even a couple of sizeable battles. Death—it's monstrously unfair! Forgive my bluntness, Augusta. I've tried to make the Emperor understand what the Army feels. The trouble is, he's too busy, too tired, to listen."

Severina could easily envisage Probus broaching the subject, at first diffidently, and then with respectful insistence, while Aurelian heard him in bleak silence, preoccupied with matters of weightier concern than the justice of the death sentence on an old officer who had failed at a critical juncture.

"What do you want me to do?" she asked quietly. "I have never interfered in military matters—I understand so little about them."

"You're the wisest woman I know," he answered with unaffected conviction. "We—all of us—the chief commanders—we're absolutely devoted to you. We're certain you would hate a wrong like this to be done. Augusta, talk to the Emperor. Point out the unfairness of executing Marcian and the—yes, folly—of outraging his most loyal officers. After all, anyone might make a mistake."

The manner of Probus was firm and authoritative, but without the harshness so marked in that of Aurelian, from whom some emanation of aggressive will seemed to press tangibly upon people. Here was a temperate but resolute man, prompted to speak out by a deeply felt sense of injustice. She studied his grave face for a few moments. "Very well, I'll talk to the Emperor," she said with an inward sigh.

As he answered, smiling boyishly, "Thank you, dear Augusta," a medley of masculine steps ascended the stairs. She raised a cautioning finger; she had no wish for her intervention to become known and herself to be regarded as an instrument for thwarting the Emperor's will. Probus nodded. The next moment, Mucapor bulked in the narrow doorway; behind him she could see Diocletian and, last, the face of Herennianus, eagerly smiling.

"Greetings, Augusta!" came their cheerful chorus. "Oh, come in, come in!" she exclaimed. She took each in turn by the hand and said, addressing all three, "I'm so happy to see you!" Her smile became tender as it rested on Herennianus, the youngest and her favorite. "Please pour some wine," she said to him. "And do sit down, everybody. You all look worn out!"

In fact, Mucapor and Diocletian seemed better than the others to have withstood the rigors of the campaign; there was such a bulk of frame to them that no exertions and no privations could wear them down to insubstantiality. Herennianus looked more peaked than any, though as usual he was the most animated. He rose, tankard uplifted, and called gaily, "To our brave Empress—the defender of Rome!" They drank with great enthusiasm, Mucapor gulping noisily. Their looks saluted her. There could be no doubt of their affectionate esteem.

Before long the banter was bubbling out, with Diocletian as the far from passive victim. Severina was glad that they were so much at ease in her company and sensed how the strains and dangers they had undergone had long inhibited such laughter. At one point she herself set the badinage sparkling by observing, innocently enough, that they must sometimes have been half-starved.

Probus, to whom the others naturally accorded priority in speaking, said, "As a matter of fact, Augusta, apart from the Emperor's wonderful leadership"—he looked admiringly at Severina as if the brilliance of Aurelian's warcraft and his greatness of soul were due to her inspiration—"the reason why we beat the Alemanni was that we ate and they didn't."

He motioned at Diocletian, who permitted himself a little smile of self-satisfaction. Herennianus set his tankard down; this topic was more to his taste than wine. "Do you want the truth, Augusta?" he asked twinkling. "Well, Diocletian was afraid in case we got too weak to render daily returns. That's the only reason he kept us fed!"

"Which reminds me," Diocletian rejoined with a tart smile. "If

374

we had enough to eat, you cavalry had far more than the rest. It was amazing, Augusta—their fighting strength went down, but their eating strength remained steady. They never remembered to deduct one day's casualties when indenting for the next day's rations."

"Too busy," said Herennianus coolly. "I know you'll find this hard to credit, Augusta, but it's rumored he wanted to call off the pursuit to check our nominal rolls—and hold kit inspections!"

"Pity I didn't," remarked Diocletian. "No doubt I'd have found enough undeclared loot to pay for the campaign. Plus a good deal of Army issue the Quartermaster never dreamed had left his stores!"

"You can't grudge trifles like that to the Cavalry," retorted Herennianus. There was genuine pride in his voice, though his grin was mischievous. "We're the elite of the Army. Most of you infantry sat down and nursed your corns after the battle—we chased them all the way to Pavia."

Again Probus, who had kept aloof from the chaffing, though he smiled at the quick exchanges, intervened with a word of praise, this time for Herennianus.

"Truly, Augusta, the Cavalry did a magnificent job. A few thousand barbarians got away—they went off north like the wind. Herennianus followed and headed them off near Pavia; then Mucapor's legion caught up with them. They were slaughtered to a man"—Severina shivered a little at the undisguised exultation on every face—"but they fought bravely. It was Herennianus who killed their one surviving chief, a foxy old brigand called Goderich—and got wounded himself for his trouble."

Severina's eyes swung to Herennianus. He touched his left shoulder carefully. "A graze, Augusta, nothing serious, I assure you," he answered her distressed look.

Though not reassured, she did not wish to embarrass him by showing her concern before the others. But her feeling made her voice very gentle as she asked, "What are you going to do when you get to Rome, Herennianus?"

His eyes opened wide to contemplate the heavenly prospect. "Leave!" he said in an ecstatic voice. "I'm going to spend the first forty-eight hours in a bath, soaking!"

375

There was a hoarse guffaw from Mucapor. "And the next forty-eight in the brothels!" Grinning he looked round for appreciation of his wit. Herennianus colored and shot a glance at Severina. Diocletian made a grimace. Probus, his face impassive, leaned slightly toward Mucapor; Severina just caught his voice, low but peremptory, "Remember where you are, man!" Mucapor drew away scowling, but as Severina seemed neither to have taken umbrage at his remark nor to have heard the reprimand, his face gradually cleared, although for a time he did not join in the conversation.

The banter between Herennianus and Diocletian resumed, with Probus contributing an occasional word of explanation when one of the allusions might have been obscure to her. She smiled impartially on jester and victim and, after a time, was startled to hear herself laughing, a gay, spontaneous laugh, untouched by care. But these brave men gathered round her, with their affection shining through their respect, touched deeper chords in her. Particularly when Probus illuminated the repartee with some little anecdote of the campaign—Diocletian walking into an ambush and fighting for his life; Mucapor falsely reported wounded and rough, bloodstained legionaries with stricken faces seeking news of him—she felt moved to gratitude for their attachment to her and their survival of so many perils.

Listening to this quartet of Aurelian's commanders, Severina was struck again and again by the difference in their personalities. Sane, clear-sighted, quietly authoritative, Probus obviously dominated the others; he was second in their regard only to Aurelian. Mucapor was the tough, aggressive, coarse-humored fighting soldier, popular with his men though he drove them brutally. For Severina his most amiable characteristic was his utter devotion to Aurelian, in whose shadow he had grown great. The sardonic Diocletian had emerged from the campaign with his reputation established as the Army's best organizer; his administrative talent and drive had kept the Roman war machine efficient through the most adverse conditions. By contrast with Mucapor, who seemed granite from the surface down, he suggested to Severina a man of many layers. He gave an impression of powers deliberately held in reserve. An observer, wary, shrewd, calculating—and patient—sat in that broad skull, noting all things with a detachment that was far from being disinterested.

Compared with these formidable men Herennianus was really a lightweight—but she liked him all the better for that.

After a time they begged leave to go, pleading their duties. Herennianus brought up the rear as they filed out; softly she called his name.

He turned back into the room. "Herennianus," she said, "tell me the truth about your wound!"

She had spoken with a fond severity. "It's not much, I assure you," he replied. "Just a glancing blow—see!" He lifted his left arm and swung it; then, more carefully, brought it down. He had grown pale and breathed more sharply. "All right! All right! I believe you!" she said hastily.

There was a moment's pause. "How has the Emperor been?" she asked.

He gave her an enigmatic look. "Frankly?"

The question was itself a disturbing answer, but she replied without hesitation, "Yes, of course—frankly."

She had the definite feeling that he was debating with himself, that he had snatched back into guarded silence words about to issue uncensored from his lips. When he spoke, it was a quite commonplace phrase, "Oh, pretty well."

"That's not very revealing," observed Severina drily. "He did not seem very well to me."

Again that hesitancy, as though he weighed the effect on her of a candid answer. "He's been under a heavy strain," was all he said, in a rather lame way.

His evasive manner puzzled and disquieted her. Still, she could not go on interrogating him about Aurelian. "Herennianus," she said with a change of tone, "why don't you get married?"

He frowned. "That remark of Mucapor's—is that why you called me back?" There was no resentment in his voice; he seemed rather shamefaced.

"Well, perhaps," she conceded, smiling a little. "As a friend, my dear, you won't mind my talking."

"No, Augusta," he said slowly, his glance not meeting hers. "I don't mind anything you say." He gave the "you" a faint but eloquent emphasis.

"Well, then," she urged, "why don't you get married? You could make some girl very happy. I could help you find her—I wish you'd let me."

He flushed and looked at her with a curious sad expression. "I don't know," he said, shrugging. "Perhaps I'm not the marrying sort."

"Personally, I think you are, Herennianus," she said, smiling affectionately.

"What's the use?" he said abruptly. "You understand me, Severina. I'd find it easy to get fond of someone—someone more like yourself—you know, with a brain and a civilized heart—a real equal, a mate for any man." He looked at her and added soberly, "There's no one like you, Severina—not for me. There never will be. Though it's presumptuous to say that to an Empress in the way I mean—I don't really want to get married. Don't worry about me. I'm not worth it. Mucapor was right. Still, I'd be very grateful if you'd let me go on being your friend."

Severina flushed. For the moment she was put out of countenance. She had never dreamed of such feelings in him. But though his words had come as a shock, she was also touched to pity. This accent of sadness, almost of bitterness, was something new in Herennianus. Deeply she regretted the clumsy matchmaking offer that had goaded him into declaring himself. Yet he had been presumptuous. Far better if neither had spoken. She met his look firmly. "I will always be your friend—if you let me, Herennianus," she said, aware that their former easy and pleasant relationship had already given place to one of constraint. "Now you had better go!"

He nodded. "Forgive me! I said too much. You, too, need friends, Severina. You can count on me to the end."

He raised her hand gently to his lips; then went out, leaving her distressed on his account and even more deeply troubled by the implication in his words and manner—plain to her woman's sensibilities—that all was far from well with Aurelian.

So long after dark was Aurelian's return delayed that Severina began to yawn and her eyelids to droop. The table was removed

378

and the dismantled bed which had traveled with her from Rome was brought in and assembled against one wall; against the opposite wall the inn's best couch, narrow and hardly more comfortable than a camp bed, was installed for Aurelian.

It was luxury to sink back in the cool sheets of Egyptian linen and to rest the weight of her head on the pillow. But tired though she was, her thoughts were agitated and sleep evaded her. She found herself listening to the unaccustomed sounds of a great army, never silent, even when at rest. Faraway bugle calls floated on the air; insubstantial voices to order the hours of twenty thousand soldiers. From the darkness which had swallowed the village street came an occasional pounding of hooves or a brisk challenge and a measured tramp as some patrol marched by. Beyond the hushed cabins, though invisible to her, the night was pricked by the circling campfires of the Legions. Somewhere out there, eluding her searching heart, Aurelian moved among the shadows.

Severina was dozing when he came in, stepping lightly for so heavy a man. She caught the faint scrape as he crossed the room, the rustle of his swift undressing, the creak of protest from the bed. There was a straggle of little noises as he fidgeted and cleared his throat of some impediment; slowly he subsided into sleep.

But his slumber was unquiet. He snorted several times and made a grinding noise that ended in a gulp. Broken muttering came from him. Severina lay there motionless, alert for every sound, picturing with painful vividness his dream-tormented face. Suddenly a low continuous moaning started. She sat up. His nightmare was giving her, too, the sensation of nightmare. She debated with herself a few moments; then slipped out of bed and went over to him. His head hung back and his mouth was open; the rise and fall of his muscular chest, bare above the crumpled blanket, showed how he labored for breath. She placed a tremulous hand on his forehead; it was damp and feverishly hot. He stirred at her touch. His eyes gradually opened wide and his movements ceased.

"Severina?" he said in a thick voice. Then, after an interval, more clearly, "Light the lamp. On that shelf by the window."

When she returned, he was sitting upright with a sickly appearance, his eyes screwed against the light.

379

She sat down on the couch near his feet and studied him anxiously. "I'm sorry I was late," he said, speaking with an effort. "It couldn't be helped."

"Aurelian, my dear," she said tenderly, "you're really ill. Have you seen the doctor?" In spite of her deep concern, she was aware of relief that nothing in his manner or words recalled the frightening fantasies of their earlier meeting.

He shrugged. "Yes, he's given me something. I'll be all right." His tone discouraged further reference to the subject, so she changed her approach. "There's so much I want to talk over with you. Couldn't you travel back to Rome with me in the litter and let Probus bring the Army in?"

Aurelian gave a brief, sarcastic smile. "People are going to cheer the Army and its commander," he answered harshly. "Whom d'you want them to cheer—Probus?" Seeing she was taken aback, he went on more amicably, "He's loyal all right. I made him—and he's grateful. But I've got to be there for the people to cheer." As he continued, his voice again grew irritable. "Don't forget I'm not descended from Trajan, or whoever it was. My father was a rough Illyrian peasant, who couldn't read or write!"

The point he had made was reasonable enough and even his irascible manner could be excused in a man mortally weary and sick into the bargain. Nevertheless, she felt rebuffed, humiliated. Quietly, controlling her distress, she said, "Very well. I shall make my own way back to Rome." He frowned heavily, giving this simple question far more weight than it seemed to warrant. "No," he said finally. "You travel back with the Army. You've done as well as any of my soldiers—let the people cheer you, too!"

A great gust of love and thankfulness to him glowed through her; she had not been turned away. "Back to bed with you, Severina," he said, his tone not unkindly. "Have a good rest. Don't get up too early. I've ordered a late start—the troops are tired. We'll have a talk about things in the morning."

"Right!" said Aurelian. "I'll give Ventidius a command in the field. He certainly behaved well. Besides, you as good as promised him promotion." His voice was again incisive, his color better. He

380

was obviously much recovered after his night's rest, short and broken though it had been.

His manner appeared normal. Severina's quiet scrutiny could discern no trace in him of yesterday's dark exaltation.

A little before dawn, careful footsteps on the floorboards had awoken her just in time to see him slipping through the door. She closed her eyes and slept again for about an hour; then rose and dressed. Soldiers entered with the landlord. Swiftly the beds were removed, the table restored and set with fruit, milk still warm, and a fragrant loaf fresh from the oven. She was breakfasting sparingly when Aurelian entered, invigorated by his early morning ride among the lines. "I've eaten," he answered her invitation to the table. "We march in an hour—better do our talking now."

He stood by the window without stirring, except for an occasional nod, as she described the session in which she had over-awed the Regency Council by calling in the Praetorians. Once he had agreed to honor her virtual pledge to Ventidius, an awkward silence followed. He waited, frowning a little, as if aware that some unwelcome request was on the way. "There's something else I want to discuss with you," she said at last, more firmly than she felt. His look grew sharper, but he merely said, "Yes?"

"You've won a great victory—one of the greatest in our history. And you've beaten the Goths into the bargain. Don't you think you should mark the occasion in some fitting way when you enter Rome?"

His curt nod bade her continue. "I mean," she went on uncomfortably, "one of the things you ought to do, surely, is proclaim an amnesty."

He stared at her until she felt herself redden. "Come to the point," he said. "Whom d'you want amnestied?"

She swallowed, but replied steadily enough, "Marcian—and Drusus. I had him arrested mainly to scare the others—and now the crisis is over."

"Hmmm." His reflective noise, she tried to persuade herself, did not suggest anger. "Somebody's been getting at you, Severina," he said abruptly. "Who was it—Probus?"

She did not answer the question. After a pause, during which she sought for tactful phrases in vain, she said a little breathlessly, "I know he let you down—Marcian, that is. He simply wasn't clever enough for the Alemanni. They're wily fighters; you told me so yourself. But," she went on, forcing herself to meet his gaze levelly, "you appointed him. You could have appointed a better man. Didn't you make the real mistake? Aren't you punishing him because you misjudged him?"

Aurelian's face stiffened. Under his stony regard her tongue suddenly lost all power. But though beaten into silence, she had not yielded. Her words still quivered in the room, accusing him.

Slowly his expression changed. His stare was no longer so cold and daunting. He made a curious sucking noise and scratched his chin; the fingernail rasped along Severina's nerves. When he began to speak, it was in a manner unexpectedly moderate. "I owe you amends, Severina." She gave him a puzzled look, but did not interrupt. "Very well, have your way. I'll pardon him—restore his rank. But no more commands. I'll make him an Inspector of Recruiting—something like that. What about this Drusus?" His tone had become harsher. "The man's a traitor. Worse than Marcian— he was only a fool."

"I hope you'll pardon him, too!"

"No, no pardon!" Aurelian spoke with vehemence. "Treat with the enemy, eh? Well, I'll spare his life—only because you ask. I'll make it confiscation instead. Half his property to the State. And I'll see there's a strict assessment. He's getting off lightly, as it is."

He looked at her, frowning a little. "There, you've changed my mind. But just this once, Severina. I've paid my debt. Don't try it again!"

"Not unless it's necessary," she answered with a wan smile. Now that the struggle was over she realized how intense had been her effort, how much this encounter of their wills had cost her.

"Another thing," resumed Aurelian. "The sentence on Drusus will be announced as the last act of the Regency Council. Then it can dissolve. I don't want my name associated with clemency to Senators—not just now."

"Just now? Surely you are in a stronger position than ever. Your victory . . ."

382

He made an impatient gesture. "You don't understand. It's the Mint. The coin from Rome is poor stuff—worse than from other mints. One unit nearly had a riot on pay parade—the men slung the money away. You had your hands full, so I started investigations myself. I've had reports—I tell you, Severina, they've been stealing bullion—silver, anyway—on a big scale. It's a regular conspiracy—all sorts of people are mixed up in it."

"What are you going to do?" she asked with foreboding.

"I've not decided yet—close the Mint, perhaps."

"But that would throw hundreds and hundreds out of work!"

He smiled coldly. "I'm going to clean things up, cost what it may. Nobody will be spared—the small fry or their protectors. I've reason to think that Senators are in the racket, too. A dirty business with fat profits—you couldn't expect them to keep their fingers out of it! Well," he added, with a savage relish, "I shall choke their loot out of them. Drusus—they'll think him lucky by comparison."

There was an intemperance behind the deliberate words, a zest in severity that went far beyond his former habit and seemed almost unbalanced. A distant bugle interrupted her thoughts; it set others close at hand imperiously resonating. Aurelian rose. "Not a word to anyone!" he cautioned. "It must be a complete surprise."

A brisk knock sounded. At Aurelian's growl the door opened. A handsome young Tribune glittering in Praetorian armor stamped to rigid attention. "The Augusta's litter is ready, Your Majesty!" he rapped.

"Good!" said Aurelian. "Now listen. No horsemen are to ride alongside the litter. I want the people to see the Augusta. Another thing. There are many persons on foot in the Augusta's retinue. Some elderly men are among them. If the pace tires them, put them in the carts. I'll hold you responsible for their condition."

He nodded to Severina and strode out.

"It's a great honor to be Your Majesty's escort," said the Tribune as he held the door open for Severina. "Everyone in the Army knows how you defended Rome!"

Two squads of Praetorian Guards stood waiting in the street, with the ornate Imperial litter and its burly team of bearers between them. There was a cry, "The Augusta!" At once the men broke into a deep-throated cheer and, drawing their swords, began to beat with the flat of the blades upon their bucklers. To this martial clamor of welcome, Severina was helped by the Tribune into the litter and hoisted above the rows of burnished helmets.

More bugle calls singing vibrantly far ahead, beyond the village. The clamor stilled. Men shifted a moment, then froze in their places. The stillness shivered at a shouted command. The curt thunderclap of the first step—the answering crash of the second. Then the litter itself slid forward, to the majestic pace of Praetorians marching.

So the Emperor Aurelian's victorious army resumed its march on Rome; at its center the Empress Severina in a litter with curtains drawn back, riding above the streaming plumes of the tall Praetorians of her bodyguard.

28

FOR the Army, encamped outside Rome, there were rest and recuperation, later reveilles, remission of drills, generous leaves, disbursement of arrears of pay and, for combatant troops, a handsome donative. Small parties at a time were permitted into the city. The rugged Illyrian infantrymen wasted no time gaping at the historic sites and marble monuments of Rome. As a popular witticism put it, they came in swaggering and went off staggering. Their bulging purses were emptied with reckless haste in riotous enjoyments, accompanied by much drunken brawling among themselves, with the police, and with various unlucky civilians. The tavern keepers, the proprietors of the stews, the pimps and whores of Rome were the last beneficiaries of the spoils of the Alemanni.

For Aurelian there was no rest. At once he assumed a stringent control of the administration and set in train a number of great new enterprises. To assist him he took over the officials who had served on the former Regency Council. Of their two remaining Senatorial colleagues, he released Eutropius from further duties with a few words of formal thanks; Corvinus he dismissed contemptuously.

Severina relinquished all her functions as Empress-Regent. Still, in the period immediately following Aurelian's return her knowledge of many problems of government was too great an asset to be wasted and from time to time he invited her to be present at the new Council of State.

Here she found no regard for the principle of free debate and compromise decision which she had generally sought to follow when presiding over the Regency Council. Essentially, the new Council was Aurelian himself. His manner was that of a brusque military autocrat. He would sit morosely withdrawn, saying little, but blasting irrelevancies with a word or two, withering rhetoric with a look. A strict timetable was enforced. Severina had the impression that Aurelian expected thinking to be done by timed parade-ground movements. She was staggered by the speed and thoroughness with which they got through their formidable agenda, but she always found the process exhausting. So, from their appearance, did the officials.

Whatever the malady that had troubled Aurelian on the march to Rome, he had thrown it off soon after his arrival. A morbid change, however, persisted. In place of his former sturdy and unforced vigor, Severina now observed a ruthless drive that bore down on all problems with the same vibrating intensity. His decisions were prompt, although not arbitrary. He would hear out—sometimes with visible impatience—those versed in the facts and question them in his peculiarly laconic and peremptory fashion. When necessary, he did not hesitate to consult the select few—Severina included—whose judgment he respected. This done, he gave his ruling with the least delay.

Once his mind was made up, opposition became dangerous. To announce a decision was with him tantamount to issuing an order; he expected it to be carried out, military style, without questioning.

At night, when not engaged in further conferences, he would sit in their apartment opposite Severina, silently revolving his problems and projects or enlarging on them in a forceful monologue. He

385

spoke his mind openly, but she had the feeling that he was addressing her as an Imperial Consort, not as the wife with whom he had
lived in warm and easy comradeship. In some intangible way he
kept his distance; the intimacy of their years at Sirmium did not
revive.

Nor did Aurelian reestablish his former bond with Julia, for
whom he used to show his fondness rather boisterously. When she
greeted him, he looked so fixedly at the tall, maturing girl, whose
features strongly recalled his mother, that involuntarily she drew
back. It was over a year since they had met and both were greatly
changed. Severina tried to picture her daughter's reaction to this
gaunt-faced man from the battlefields, with his intent and disconcerting gaze. It was hard to believe that they had ever been playmates. The two had become strangers and Julia, at an age when her
own femininity was growing more conscious and sensitive, must have
been baffled and repelled by her father's harshly masculine front.

At Severina's suggestion, Aurelian went with her to visit the
school. The children, who had risen eagerly at the sight of her, were
petrified by the bleak aspect of the Emperor. He stared down at
them rather helplessly, jerking out a gruff comment or two that was
meant to be affable. Cornelius plainly was awestruck. Aurelian,
meaning to put him at his ease, asked several questions about the
school, but they shot out in such brisk military style that the children looked alarmed and Cornelius could only stammer confused
replies.

Forty-eight hours after Aurelian's entry into the Palace, Crinitus
was on the way back to his villa at Baiae. He went of his own
accord; indeed, when Severina brought Aurelian along to see him,
servants were already bustling around, stripping the place of his
effects.

Dismissing them with a wave and a word, he waited in his chair
to receive his visitors. He surveyed Aurelian without a smile as he
approached, extended his hand briefly and said, "I am glad to see
you safe." There was no cordiality in his tone. It struck Severina as
an unaccountably cold welcome, after so many years, for an old

comrade and kinsman by marriage, who was also Rome's brilliantly victorious Emperor.

When Aurelian inquired about his health, Crinitus merely grunted, "Could be better!" His ill-humor could not be mistaken.

Severina was the more puzzled by this incivility because it appeared to her deliberate; there was no sign that he was speaking under the influence of one of his bouts of pain. She began to feel a little apprehensive of the effect on Aurelian, whose own temper was hardly patient.

As soothingly as she could, she addressed Crinitus. "Why are you going, Uncle? What is the hurry?"

"Doctor's orders, my dear." The smile he gave her and his bland tone were in marked contrast with his tetchy manner toward Aurelian. "He let me come here only on the understanding that I would go home at the first opportunity. I need quiet and fresh air—sea air. Anyway, I don't like Rome. It stinks!"

"I'm sorry you're set on going," Aurelian said calmly. "But first let me thank you for the help you gave Severina—and the whole Roman State."

"It's to Severina that you should be grateful—remember that, Aurelian!" replied Crinitus with a sharpness that startled her. He gave Aurelian a look she could not comprehend and added drily, "You did very well yourself. You'll go down in the history books as one of the great Emperors!"

He contrived to make the compliment almost derisory. Severina wondered at Aurelian's self-control. She judged it best to intervene. "Are you taking your doctor with you, Uncle? I understand he has quite a few patients now in the Palace."

"Can't do without him!" answered Crinitus. "I'm leaving the girl who mixes my medicines, though. You must have seen her, Severina—a dark-eyed baggage. Matter of fact"—he spoke with a trace of embarrassment odd in so domineering a man—"she turned out a police spy. I must say I congratulate them on their taste! She confessed to me last night in floods of tears. Her conscience had given her no rest, she said!"

"More likely someone's tipped her off there's to be an edict against informers," put in Aurelian. "I hate the breed! Give me her name, Crinitus. I'll have her whipped."

Crinitus shrugged. "Thank you—I can deal with her myself." He paused, as if to emphasize the rebuff, and then went on, "I'm letting her go. She'll soon find herself another protector—she's pretty enough. I've nothing against her. Truth to tell," he added, with a lascivious grin, "I'm heavily in her debt for—well, services rendered."

Severina found the subject distasteful. "I still don't understand why you are rushing away like this, Uncle," she said. "Surely you could have stayed a few days longer."

"Out of the question," he answered, looking not at her but Aurelian.

"I wish you'd let Severina persuade you to stay," said Aurelian in a friendly tone. "There's a lot I would like to talk over with you. I was hoping to consult you from time to time."

Crinitus met this overture with a sour smile. "You'd find me too blunt, I'm afraid. But if you really want my advice, Aurelian, here's one vital point—don't try to do things too quickly. Rome has lasted a thousand years—you're not going to cure all her troubles overnight."

At last Aurelian, whose restraint so far had amazed Severina, betrayed that he was stung. "I have to be in a hurry," he said harshly. "There's so much to do—I can't waste time!"

"Well, you've been warned," retorted Crinitus. "Go easy, Aurelian. Don't just draw the sword and charge! Otherwise you'll head straight into trouble. It won't be long before you'll be asking the Senate again to consult Sibylline Books!"

Aurelian's brows drew together. "I don't think the Sibylline Books a matter for jesting."

"I do," said Crinitus.

Severina stared at him in alarm. Some moments passed, while Aurelian weighed this latest provocation. "Let us part friends, Crinitus," he said at last, pacifically. "And let not the parting be a final one. I have need of good counsel. I want to ask your advice as an experienced old soldier. The wars aren't over yet—not by a long way!"

For the first time Crinitus appeared a little mollified. "Very well.

388

Send as often as you like. I'll do my best. But there's one thing I must ask in return. Be . . . kind . . . to Severina. You understand me, Aurelian?" His manner had become less hostile, but to these last words he gave a strange, almost threatening inflection.

By now deeply troubled, Severina watched the two men eying each other. She was baffled equally by her uncle's attitude toward Aurelian and by Aurelian's determined forbearance. Nor could she make head or tail of the allusion to herself. It was time, she decided, to bring this trying interview to an end. She rose. "We must go now, Uncle—we're seeing Julia. I'll come again this evening."

Outside, they walked in silence for a little while; Aurelian's expression showed the anger he had curbed before. Quietly, Severina asked, "What did all that mean? Why was he so—so aggressive— toward you? Why did he refer to me in that peculiar way? It was almost as though he were trying to protect me!"

Aurelian looked straight ahead. "I don't think your uncle's ever forgiven me for taking you away from him," he said, after an interval.

"But he himself promoted our marriage!"

"That's how people are!" Aurelian answered with a curtness that dismissed the subject.

Before long Severina herself had an open clash with Aurelian, the first since she had interceded for the lives of Marcian and Drusus. It confirmed that a profound change had taken place in their relationship, in which hitherto his had been unquestioningly the dominant will. Now again she found that she could persist with a viewpoint directly opposed to his—and not be brushed aside.

The cause of their contention this time was Eros.

Aurelian was greatly pleased with his efficiency and, in particular, with that aspect of it lacking in the other extremely able members of the Council—promptitude. Eros had the capacity for quick and accurate thinking and for carrying out instructions with dispatch. Here was an assistant with talents exactly suited to an Emperor in a hurry.

As time passed, Aurelian entrusted to Eros more and more work that called for initiative and independent judgment, while tending to confine the others to predictable routine tasks. Though all decisions of importance were made by Aurelian himself and his was the only will that counted, Eros was on the way to acquiring a position of considerable personal influence.

Severina watched this development with anxiety. She made up her mind to warn Aurelian again of her doubts about Eros, but with graver emphasis than before.

One evening in their apartment, when Aurelian was showing himself a little more agreeable than usual, she broached the matter.

"Aurelian, there's something I've been meaning to talk to you about—I'm really worried. It's this man, Eros . . ." Immediately, Aurelian's frown put her on the defensive. "I've a right to speak. I know him well."

"Go on," he said.

Resolutely she continued, "He's not to be trusted. Listen to me, Aurelian. He's a slippery character. I'm sure he takes bribes." Aurelian's unfriendly look did not alter and she had a feeling of helplessness. She knew that her words must sound like fantasy. Since Aurelian's return, Eros had shown an exemplary demeanor; he was quiet, self-effacing, sedulous to please. Not a trace of that obstructiveness, that effrontery, which had been evident at first in his service to her. That, indeed, was a further reason for disquiet. There was something frightening about a man who could act such varied roles, adapt himself with such ease to the master of the moment.

"Look, Severina," said Aurelian, with the exasperating air of the man who makes an effort to be patient with an irrational woman, "Eros is a find. He's worth ten of the others. Of course, he's no pattern of virtue, but he knows better than to try any tricks with me!"

"Don't trust him!" she cried. "I tell you the man is dangerous!"

"You must leave me to choose my own servants," he said sharply. "By the Sun, Severina. I've had to learn to judge men. I've been picking them—and kicking them out—for years. Most of the time you've had only a tiny household of women to run."

She had gone pale at his brutal taunt. In a voice that despite its trembling showed that she was not to be intimidated, she answered,

"Eros was my assistant, too. I saw a lot of him. And I say he's capable of trying to deceive you—yes, even you, Aurelian!"

It was then that he made a concession, a grudging, empty one, but nevertheless a concession. "All right," he growled, "I'll keep a careful eye on him." At that she judged it best to leave the matter, though she saw that he had given way not because he took her warning seriously, but to put an end to her importuning.

Of the projects which increasingly absorbed Aurelian's energies, the most important was the campaign in preparation against Palmyra. He sought to keep his intentions secret at this early stage, but some of the measures being taken were difficult to conceal and before long Zenobia, who without doubt had her spies in the Capital and probably in the Palace itself, must have been aware of what was afoot. At any rate, an Embassy from this Empress of the East was already on the way to Aurelian's Court—ostensibly to bring her congratulations on his victories over the Goths and Alemanni.

The Army's strength was rapidly built up. Urgent orders went out to Imperial governors in regions whose inhabitants were hardy and of warlike temper, prescribing the number of recruits each area was to supply. Throughout the borderlands and deep into the Balkans there was a rush to enlist with Aurelian's proudly victorious Eagles. In Illyricum, the Emperor's homeland and nursery of the soldiers who had vanquished the Alemanni, ardent young volunteers besieged the depots.

Meanwhile, Diocletian was tirelessly at work reequipping the field army, whose weapons, armor, clothing, and stores of every kind were, after so many years of almost uninterrupted warfare, desperately in need of renewal.

These things hardly concerned Severina. But simultaneously there went forward a vast and costly public undertaking that caught at her imagination. As Empress-Regent she had sought to defend Rome by barricades in the suburbs. Now Aurelian directed that the city, excluding certain outlying districts, awkward to embrace within a defensive scheme, was to be surrounded by a mighty wall.

To Severina it seemed that the ghosts of the Alemanni were still marching on Rome. How hollow were these dazzling triumphs, when the victor hurriedly set about girdling his Capital with impregnable defenses! Rome, which had outgrown circuit after circuit of walls, had for centuries neglected her fortifications. Who could assail her, at the heart of an Empire whose frontiers were guarded by four hundred thousand invincible soldiers? Now it had come to this. The Mistress of the World trembled for her safety. Although, at the last moment, Aurelian had crushed the Alemanni, it was all too likely that sooner or later other barbarian hosts would break into Italy from the North and the day might come when only ramparts of massy stone would stand between the city and the fury of a conqueror.

Like other major projects of Aurelian, this one ramified endlessly. Military engineers with scrolls and wily-looking contractors were in evidence about the Palace. Parties of surveyors set up instruments in streets and gardens; valuation of properties to be requisitioned was pressed forward; quarries opened and prisons emptied to provide convict labor.

Soon the first demolition gangs were clearing the site of the future wall, disturbing neighborhoods with the crash of debris and parching clouds of dust.

While this and other enterprises were in train, a tremendous upheaval shook all classes in the city.

At a Council meeting attended by Severina, Eros read out a summary which he had prepared of reports on the situation at the Mint. It was a masterly exposition, thorough and lucid. Clearly drastic measures were demanded. Years of anarchy, during which the Emperors had been drawn away from Rome to fight invaders and rebels, had weakened control over the administration. With prices soaring and valuable stocks of metal at hand, the temptation to the superior personnel of the Mint had been irresistible. An elaborate routine of theft had developed in which not only the principals, but also overseers and higher-grade craftsmen participated. Substantial quantities of silver and bronze had been regularly withdrawn from the storerooms and illicitly disposed of, while the alloy from which coins were struck was adulterated by the inclusion of lead, tin, or zinc. In respect of weight and content of precious metal, and even of workmanship, the money issued at Rome was decidedly inferior to the product of other Imperial mints.

To the chief organizers of this extensive racket it yielded a huge fortune, much of which they were obliged to disburse in bribes and goodwill payments. The conspiracy had lasted long enough to acquire a sort of respectability and to give rise to a whole complex of vested interests. One particularly grave feature was the number of persons of standing directly or indirectly involved in this systematic defrauding of the Treasury; among them was a group of Senators.

Eros read on and on in an expressionless voice. As Severina listened, the thought came that he, too, might have some connection with these rascals. If so, she reflected bitterly, he would have used his cunning to cover up his tracks. In the next instant she admitted to herself that she knew nothing to warrant such suspicion; the fact was that since her difference with Aurelian on his account, her animus against Eros had grown until she was ready to impute to him any kind of knavery.

Aurelian did not interrupt Eros, but his look boded ill. As soon as the summary was finished, he spoke.

"The Senators—I want all the names."

Eros extracted a document from the batch before him and recited over a dozen names. Severina bit her lip. They included several well reputed Senators, one of whom she had personally entrusted with responsible tasks while Empress-Regent.

"Here!" Aurelian threw out a hand as he uttered the brusque command. Unnaturally loud in Severina's ears, the chair scraped as Eros rose to take the document over. There was a tense hush when he sat down again. The Council members watched Aurelian while he debated somberly with himself and one minute, then another, passed.

He put the document on the table; his hand rested on it; Severina saw his fist slowly clench.

"With effect tomorrow morning, the Mint will close—until further notice!"

The cold and pliable officials at that table were accustomed to

Aurelian's swift and radical decisions; they knew and feared his impatience when criticism of these was voiced. Nevertheless, at his words there was a perceptible stir which could only mean dissent. For a few moments they shifted in their places, looked at one another or, more hopefully, at Severina. She sat with eyes downcast. It had been her hope that Aurelian would find it possible to stamp out the frauds and reform the Mint without resort to mass dismissals. Still, though she was alarmed at the extreme course he was taking, she could not oppose her husband before his own ministers.

"Have I Your Majesty's permission to speak?"

A thin, dry voice had suddenly raised itself, none too confidently, for Aurelian, at the other end of the table, could hardly catch the words. He leaned forward, ill-humoredly, hand to ear.

It was Philip the Epirote, a skinny little figure, with bulbous bald head and wizen face, one of those arid, prematurely aged officials who seem to have had no youth. Though everyone respected his formidable mental powers, he had played a passive part in the Council's deliberations, never venturing a controversial view.

Aurelian's grunt was an affirmative. Philip sucked his scraggy lips and began carefully, "I would urge the Augustus to reconsider his decision. As Controller of the Corn Supply, I have had the opportunity of learning a little about different sections of the populace, including the Mint workers. I would respectfully ask that the following considerations be taken into account. First: that like all men of their class they have the greatest terror of unemployment. Second: their leaders have no respect for the law, since they have been breaking it for a considerable time. Third: they have a strong corporate sense, for they have their own Mint Workers' Association, and they are used to acting collectively. Fourth: their numbers make them formidable and they live concentrated in one district, on and around the Caelian Hill. It is reasonable to draw two conclusions, namely, that if they are thrown out of work, they are likely to riot; and that if they riot, they will not be easy to suppress."

Under Aurelian's glare Philip blinked and sucked again noisily; but he went on obstinately with his tabulation of points. "There are three other factors with a bearing on the situation. The City Police are under strength and inefficient—and, further, the report we have just heard makes it clear that some of them have been beneficiaries from the frauds. Again, if rioting breaks out, the Mint workers are likely to be joined by other elements of the population, particularly the unemployed."

A grating noise came from Aurelian.

But Philip still had one item left on his list of arguments. Pedantic habit carried him on, although his voice had developed a nervous squeak.

"Lastly, Your Majesty, during the recent military emergency, quantities of arms disappeared from the militia depots. We can assume that some, at least, of these would quickly find their way into the hands of the Mint workers."

Aurelian's abrupt gesture conveyed that he had listened long enough. He nodded curtly to Eros. "Message to the camp. The Thunderers are to be alerted. Leave stopped. Men ready to parade, short notice, full battle order!"

Severina saw Philip make a faint grimace. He looked at Aurelian and then at her and shook his head slightly. She could read his thought: You kept the city quiet all through a military crisis; this heavy-handed soldier is provoking a rising in time of peace!

Opposition was now silenced and the Council passed to other matters. Still, an atmosphere of foreboding persisted, to which Aurelian alone appeared insensitive.

When the officials had withdrawn, Severina quietly asked, "How strong are the Thunderers?"

Aurelian gave her a sharp glance. He reflected a moment. "Seventeen . . . eighteen hundred. They were nearly twenty-three hundred before the battle."

"They won't be enough," Severina said matter-of-factly.

His look showed irritation. "They're first-class troops. They broke the Alemanni!"

"That was an open battle," she replied. "This would be a confused struggle in a maze of streets and alleys. They wouldn't be able to keep formation."

He frowned. It was obvious she had made some impression.

"Then I'll bring up more troops," he said. "The whole Army if necessary!"

With heavy sarcasm, he added, "Would twenty thousand men be enough?"

Severina met his angry gaze without wavering. "Yes," she said. "Twenty thousand men would be enough."

Within three days the Palace had become a military base, with troops standing at arms in the courtyards, officers hurrying to and fro, mounted couriers leaving and arriving at the gallop, dejected prisoners being marched under escort to interrogation.

The tramp of soldiers echoed in many streets. While the main operations were directed against the Mint-workers' quarter, squads of Praetorians marched up to the mansions of the wealthy. Senator after Senator and other notables suspected of complicity in the frauds and the violent uprising that had followed the closing of the Mint were dragged away.

The Thunderers, indignant at being sent against a city rabble, slouched through the almost deserted streets and carelessly approached the Caelian Hill. They found the district converted into a bristling fortress. In a shapeless melee, which spread along narrow, twisting lanes and into gloomy alleyways, the conquerors of the Alemanni were beaten to pulp. Barely a third staggered back under a rain of stones, tiles, bricks, stools, flowerpots, and improvised darts, pursued with taunts and hysterical screaming by hordes of brawny artisans and their viragoes of womenfolk.

Severina was present when an officer with blood still trickling from a cut in his cheek brought word that one of Rome's most famous Legions had been shattered and its survivors put to flight by a mob of slum rioters. A look of bleak incredulity came over Aurelian. He sprang up, grasped the officer's shoulder and stared speechlessly into his face. Then he drew back, his expression ominous.

His voice, when he found it, clanged with fury. First of all, he issued orders for the entire field army to enter Rome. As soon as he had given one of his aides the message, Aurelian motioned another. "I want squads of fire fighters organized—at once! Soldiers as well as the city fire brigade. They're to follow close behind the fighting troops."

Severina, who had been standing silently at a distance, heard him rap this instruction. "Fire squads!" she exclaimed.

He turned his scowling gaze on her. "This is a revolt. I'm going to smash it. The troops will storm the tenements. Where they can't break in, they'll set fire to the place!"

She stared at him, appalled. "But the slums—all those buildings crowded together! Whole blocks will burn!"

"I'll only use fire as a last resort," he said. She could see that, in spite of his terrible anger, his habit of mind as a great commander had reasserted itself and he was coolly appraising all the factors. "But if I can't get those rebels out any other way, I'm going to burn them out!"

Severina could only wait passively while Aurelian was away directing the storming of the Caelian Hill. Much as this bitter and prolonged battle of the streets distressed her, she knew that it would be fought to a conclusion; nothing she could do would affect its course. What both aroused her horror and determined her to intervene were the sweeping arrests and the executions which continued in Aurelian's absence. When he returned, the strain of the struggle showed in his stiff gait and worn, somber face. But she would not delay until he had rested. As soon as he had cleansed himself, she approached.

"Soon be over," he said heavily. "The troops are mopping up."

She came straight to the point. "These arrests, Aurelian—there are far more than I expected."

He cast her a hostile look. "Only criminals—and their associates."

"Associates is a very broad term," she retorted warmly. "Everyone in Rome associates with criminals—innocently, without knowing it. I myself have had dealings with some of these men. Dozens of people are being rounded up on nothing worse than vague suspicion. And the guilty ones are so many! Must they all die? Aurelian, I implore you—show mercy! The worst of these men are not really dangerous. They're rascals and deserve punishment, but let it be within reason. If they're mixed up with the Mint frauds, make them

397

disgorge. But wholesale executions—it's unworthy of you. And unwise. You're still a new Emperor. The Senate's goodwill can be of use to you."

"The Senate's goodwill!" His laugh was unpleasant. "What's the matter, Severina? Can't you understand? They've no goodwill for me. They hate me. To them I'm a vulgar upstart, nothing more. But I'll show them! Mercy, did you say? They'd only despise me for it. And why should I spare them? I tell you half the Senate is compromised in this affair—half your fat, greedy, crooked patricians!"

He said this with such vindictiveness that once she would have been struck mute. But now she feared his anger without being quelled by it. His outburst only excited in her more strongly the impulse to oppose his cruel will.

"You were warned not to be too hasty over the Mint." Deliberately she chose words that would penetrate his masculine self-conceit. "You overrode that advice. Don't brush all advice aside as a matter of habit. I'm your wife, Aurelian. I've a right to speak. For your own sake, show clemency. Execute the ringleaders, if you must. Impose fines—crippling fines, if you like—on those who have plundered the Treasury. But don't pour out a river of blood!"

"That's easy woman's sentiment," he said. "Sloppy phrases—gush! Face the facts. These Senators deserve death, every one of them. They're guilty—and now they've been caught. Why all this fuss over a few slimy old bastards who've bloated themselves on their country's misery? I tell you, Severina, I've seen thousands of men— fine, brave soldiers—go down in a single day on the battlefield. To the world it's just an item in a bulletin. Do you get excited over that? Some wretch from the slums, who's never had a real chance, steals a few times. They throw him to the wild beasts. Where's the cry for mercy then? There's not a murmur from you—until your friends are in trouble!"

His vicious tone and, in particular, his final phrase, agitated her deeply. "What friends?" she demanded.

"Oh, never mind," he answered wearily. "The fact remains that it's only when this particular gang is concerned that you're all for mercy!"

398

She tried to speak with calm, but could not quite restrain her voice from trembling. "It's obvious enough. When your soldiers die in battle, they give their lives for the Empire. Nobody blames their deaths on you. When a criminal is torn to pieces in the Arena—and I must say it strikes me as senselessly cruel—it's done in the name of the Law. It would happen no matter who was Emperor. These Senators are being killed at your express command, in your name, Aurelian. I hate the thought that my husband's name is reeking with blood!"

"Blood! Blood!" he shouted. "What of the blood they're responsible for? Thousands of my best troops are casualties!"

His ugly vehemence broke her caution down. "Mithras doesn't seem to have remembered His Elect!" she said bitterly.

Having spoken, she gasped. But she could not recall the gibe. Rage distorted Aurelian's face. He took a step toward her and slowly raised his right hand. Sick with fear, she stood her ground. Dreadful moments passed . . . Aurelian's eyes glittered; he was breathing audibly. Then his hand dropped to his side. For a little longer they confronted each other in silence. "Aurelian," she murmured at last, appalled lest her sacrilegious words had opened a gulf between them.

Another interval went by before he answered. His face still bore the mark of strong emotion, and he spoke hoarsely.

"I am not worthy to be His Elect—and yet—and yet He did not forsake me. How else could I have crushed this conspiracy? He has been with me all the time. I wonder you do not feel His Presence— a sensitive woman like you."

She drew back, conscious of the violent aura of this man, the invisible pulsations of a force truly strange and strong enough to be daemonic. But her instinct prompted her to seize the moment and turn his change of mood to advantage in their tense and fateful debate. "No," she said staunchly, "I do not feel His Presence. I smell death in this room. Tiberius Piso—Valens of Tarentum—the elder Crispus, a man of seventy-five, Aurelian, and sick—and Lentulus Afer—more than a dozen gone already. And all those others under arrest, scores of them, men of every rank, threatened with execution."

"All right," he said abruptly. "I'll spare them."

She clenched her hands at her sides, so strong was the impulse to clap them. "Drusus, too? He should never have been rearrested. He was only complaining about the loss of his property."

"Dead already," answered Aurelian, showing no remorse. "But the others will stand trial. Those with means will have to make good the Treasury's losses. The guilty will go to prison. I'll remit any death sentences."

"Oh, Aurelian," she said softly, finding in her heart not only inexpressible relief but also compassion for him.

He looked at her earnestly. "Believe me, Severina. I don't want to be a butcher. But the rot's everywhere. I have to be severe with the enemies of the State. Still, I've given this gang a lesson they won't forget in a hurry. I should be free now to get on with my plans against Palmyra. That's a Roman Emperor's business—not storming slums and chasing slippery old blackguards!"

Severina did not answer. Her relief had given way to sadness. Her whole nature shrank from these bitter struggles with Aurelian, yet she knew that she would have to nerve herself to contend with him again and again. He would drive on, in his own ruthless way, to restore the greatness of Rome and many would suffer. She more than anyone, perhaps she alone, could sway him to mercy. Between her and this man so heavily tried, to whom she longed to be all tenderness, lay the shadow of inevitable conflict.

By the time the embassy from Palmyra arrived, Rome was again tranquil. The repression had been thorough; disaffection dared not raise its voice. Moreover the city had been regaled with a gladiatorial show on a spectacular scale, with no quarter given; and now it was glutted with bloodshed, exhausted with the prolonged orgiastic excitements of a mass death struggle outside its own doors, below its own windows.

The chief Palmyrene envoy, one of the desert capital's Romanized nobility, was called Caius Metaballus, a name which enshrined that of the great Syrian deity, Baal.

He was closeted with Aurelian for about an hour, ostensibly to felicitate him on his victories, but in reality—as everyone knew—to seek confirmation of Zenobia's authority as ruler of the Roman East.

Many at the Palace pictured the meeting as an unequal contest between a rugged Illyrian soldier and an Oriental aristocrat of seductive tongue, the master of subtle and ingenious argument. Severina knew better. She was not surprised to learn, later, how from the start Aurelian had dominated the brief negotiation.

Conscious that no splendor of trappings or ceremony would dazzle the Arab diplomat, accustomed to the florid magnificence of the Palmyrene and Persian Courts, Aurelian resolved to impress him with a Roman Emperor's warlike simplicity. Metaballus was received in a modest room, before whose door stood guard not a showy Praetorian but a plain Illyrian legionary of the field army, the butt of his javelin resting on the bare wooden floor. Aurelian, dressed in a clean but well worn military tunic, sat on a stool at a little table. He was flanked by Probus and Diocletian, both bareheaded and in unadorned body armor.

To the flowery compliments of Metaballus Aurelian returned terse, plain thanks; he heard with an impassive face the protestations of Zenobia's desire for friendship and cooperation. Then, briefly, avoiding any expressions of goodwill, he requested the withdrawal of all Palmyrene garrisons from Asia Minor, from Syria, from Egypt.

When Metaballus courteously pointed out that the issue was a complex one and sought to begin a discussion, Aurelian cut him short. "The issue," he said, "is a simple one. There are foreign garrisons on Roman territory. I want them withdrawn."

Several times, exerting all his diplomatic skill, Metaballus endeavored to present the situation from Zenobia's standpoint; each time Aurelian brushed his clever arguments aside. He was not to be diverted from his demands. The one concession he offered was to renew the traditional alliance between Rome and the City State of Palmyra, but only on condition that Zenobia without delay recall the forces she had stationed in the Imperial provinces.

"There are no differences between Rome and Palmyra," said Metaballus, "which cannot be resolved with goodwill—the same goodwill that has always existed between us. My Queen is convinced of it and is ready to seek a settlement in a spirit of reasonable compromise. Am I to report to her that Your Majesty's only response to all her efforts for peace is—an ultimatum?"

"Call it what you like," said Aurelian. "Only make my meaning plain!"

Metaballus politely expressed the hope that this would not be the Emperor's last word; then he begged permission to withdraw.

To Severina's surprise, a letter reached her the following day from Metaballus, soliciting an interview. At once she informed Aurelian, who said, "I know. He is being watched. No harm in seeing him."

Metaballus was ushered into the Imperial apartment and made an obeisance to Severina lower and more graceful than a Roman noble's, lifting his slim and shapely right hand in a fluent movement to his heart. He was a tall, fine-boned, and sinewy man, with brilliant black eyes and proud aquiline profile, and he wore the heavy ceremonial toga with elegance.

"Ah, Augusta!" he exclaimed, beaming as if the sight of her fulfilled some long-cherished ambition. "In my Queen's Court, we speak with equal admiration of the Emperor Aurelian's military genius and of the wisdom and courage of his beautiful Consort!" His Latin was mellifluous and extravagant phrases seemed natural to it.

With his polished yet predatory look she decided that he resembled a refined eagle. "You pay charming compliments, Metaballus," she answered with a smile, "but you came to Rome for more serious business than to make flattering speeches to women."

His face lit up in too facile pleasure at her quick rejoinder, but she was aware that those admiring eyes were carefully appraising her. He leaned forward, still with that ingratiating look. "Dear Augusta, Gracious Majesty, have I your permission to speak with candor?"

"I prefer it," said Severina. "Leave the flatteries out and you can be as candid as you like."

He gave her a flashing smile. "Do you know, Augusta, that in Palmyra—and, as I am told, elsewhere—they say there is an Opposition Party at the Court of Rome"—Severina looked at him sharply —"and that its leader is—you?"

402

"Explain yourself!"

"They name it the Clemency Party. May I venture to suggest that the Emperor Aurelian is known for—well, what some people would call his severity. So there is scope for such an Opposition here. Indeed, such a Party should exist in every Court!"

"My wits are too pedestrian for these subtleties, Metaballus," replied Severina with a little irritation. "Please come to the point."

"The point, dear Majesty? Only that, like my own Queen, you abhor bloodshed—unnecessary bloodshed. That is why I appeal to you to help avoid the calamity of a war between Rome and Palmyra!"

Severina did not answer at once. She looked at him soberly. "On that subject it is not for me to speak," she said. "I imagine the Emperor has already told you what is in his mind."

He made a deprecating gesture and said, "You have great influence, noble Lady—use it for peace. It is common knowledge how you feel for those in distress. No, Your Majesty, this is no flattery. Many Senators' wives and any beggar in the streets of Sirmium will confirm that I am speaking simple truth. Well, now two great peoples, multitudes of innocent folk in many lands, are in distress. . . ."

Though she could sense the cool and calculating mind which guided the persuasive voice, the argument was one which could not fail to move her.

"They look to you, Augusta. Speak on their behalf. Rome at war with Palmyra—what torrents of blood that means and how unnecessary! Only the Persian King stands to gain from it. Rome and Palmyra should be equal allies, one warden of the West, the other of the East. That is how it was. Why not now—and always?"

"Your plea is an eloquent one, Metaballus," said Severina quietly, "but it ignores certain vital facts. Palmyra can have peace, simply by making restitution. Return to Rome what is Rome's—what you took from us in the days of our weakness—and there need be no conflict. Zenobia is a brilliant woman. She does not need an Empire in order to shine."

For the first time Metaballus spoke with the force of passionate conviction. "My Sovereign Lady was born to rule a great Empire!"

Severina saw that it was no mere courtier's phrase. She answered without irony. "Personally I have no ambition beyond that of the average woman—to keep her husband safely at home. I admire Zenobia's dazzling accomplishments, believe me. But I would recommend her to look at the facts in the same sober light as I do. The Emperor only wants his own back; that he is determined to have. Why not give way in time? War would be averted and the whole world would applaud Zenobia as the woman who preserved peace."

"These are not conditions, Augusta," he said, still speaking with unfeigned directness; for a little he had set his diplomatic mask aside. "They are a summons to surrender, when surrender is impossible. One cannot just step down from a pinnacle!"

"One can fall from a pinnacle, Metaballus."

"Better to fall!" he answered vehemently. Then, recovering himself, he gave her one of his flashing smiles and went on with his former professional smoothness, "As you know, my Queen has a son who is already associated with her in the government. It is his heritage she protects. Some sensible frontier adjustments she would be perfectly willing to accept—I have her authority to make proposals. But she regards it as a sacred obligation to her son to ensure that Palmyra's dominions remain substantially intact."

"You asked me a while ago if you might speak candidly. Forgive me if, in my turn, I speak with bluntness. The heritage you mention is a stolen one. One way or another it will be restored to its rightful owners. If Zenobia tries to hold on to it, she will lose not only Asia Minor and Syria and Egypt—she will lose Palmyra itself."

"So, Augusta, you believe it must come to war?"

"I am still hoping that your Mistress—your Queen, as you call her—will be persuaded to accept our terms while there is time."

He drew himself up, his lean, dark face stern. "The Emperor, your husband, used a more insulting term—he called her my Chieftainess. But Chieftainess or Queen, we Palmyrenes will guard her against any injury. We are not naked and helpless to supplicate Rome. It is not through weakness that we offer concessions, but in order to renew the alliance of East and West which has been of such benefit to both. Still, dear Majesty, if the armies are to conclude this discussion, pray remind your husband that my Sovereign

404

Lady disposes of immense forces, far more powerful than those with which we broke the Persian invasions. Rome cannot show the like of our famous Syrian archers nor of our Cataphracts, the same mailed cavalry who chased the Great King over the frontier—after he had received the capitulation of a Roman Emperor!"

Severina could not but admire the arrogant desert warrior who had emerged from the polished and supple envoy; yet for her these ringing vaunts had a pathetic undertone. "The Emperor needs no reminder," she replied calmly. "There is something else which should not be forgotten. You have the Cataphracts—we have the Illyrians. They are the world's finest soldiers. I mean no scorn of the tens of thousands of brave men ready to die for Zenobia when I say that they are no match for the Illyrians. I tell you, Metaballus, the old genius of Rome for war has been reborn in them. Why must we prove under the walls of Palmyra what you already know in your heart?"

"There is in my heart only devotion to my Queen," he said. "I am a Captain in her Lifeguards and with my last strength I will defend her life and her greatness. Noble Lady, I wish that so good and wise an Empress could have been the friend of my Queen. Since it is not to be, I must bid you farewell with sorrow and, may I say, with profound respect."

He bowed low and with another graceful movement caught the hem of her robe and raised it to his lips. Then he stood upright. "Be happy, Augusta!" he said, with melancholy in his smile, "and continue to lead the Opposition!"

After this, preparations for the campaign went forward in the open. The legionary camp outside Rome gradually emptied as unit after unit set out along the roads northward on its way to the assembly area near the straits dividing Europe from Asia. There they absorbed big batches of recruits and trained assiduously, while awaiting the Emperor's arrival.

Rome was relieved to see the Illyrians go. The period of inaction had been too long for their truculent and insubordinate spirits. Once the plunder of the Alemanni had been squandered they began to grow restive. Rome had to be placed out of bounds and this acted as a further irritant to their already dangerous tempers. Savage fights, sometimes with a toll of dead, sprang up between group and group, even between comrades. Travelers were waylaid on the neighboring roads and robbed with violence. There were raids on nearby farms in which the actual thefts were less serious than the wanton damage caused. It took several executions and public scourgings before Aurelian could reimpose strict discipline.

Rome was glad also when Aurelian rode away with the last of the field army. He took with him the bulk of the Praetorians and his chief civilian officials. The curses of thousands of widows and orphans accompanied him; and even those who had not suffered personally in the grim suppression of the rising felt their spirits grow more easy at the thought that Aurelian no longer brooded over the city from the Palatine Hill.

Severina bade Aurelian farewell at the Palace. In his splendid armor, with his imposing height, straight veteran's back and powerful shoulders, he made a proudly martial figure. He was in good bodily health again, braced by the prospect of honorable action and supremely confident. For a long while he had not spoken of his sense of being Elect, nor, as far as she could judge, given any other sign that its influence was active; and she hoped that this profound disturbance in him had wholly subsided.

Still, their leave-taking was not like the last one, in the Balkans. Then their affection had been unclouded and the years had brought them into a harmony which Aurelian's frequent absences had not impaired. This time, although their bond remained indissolubly strong, the old accord was missing. Ever since his return from the Gothic and Alemannic wars, there had been occasions when she could detect a reserve on his part toward her that she found baffling.

Also memories of sharp contentions, with words spoken to hurt, now burdened their relationship.

Aurelian patted Julia's shoulder and kissed her, rather awkwardly, on the cheek. She did not show emotion at the parting, but merely said in a clear, firm voice, "Good-bye, Father!" He turned to Severina and said, with an attempt at jocularity, "She's getting so big, we'll have to find her a husband soon!" Severina he clasped in

406

his arms; it was she who, pressing herself against him, gave ardor to their farewell embrace.

"You've nothing to worry about," he said. "Rome will be quiet. I've given the fat, pampered whore a thrashing she won't forget!"

"It's not Rome I'm worried about," Severina answered in a low voice.

He weighed her remark for a few moments; then, with an understanding she had not expected, said, "When we reach Palmyra, come and visit me. Come alone," he added quietly, indicating Julia with a nod. "It's a bad climate out there."

Severina could only think the painful thoughts, speak the instinctive words of any woman when the husband she loves is leaving for war: "Look after yourself—and come back quickly!"

"As quickly as I can," he said with a grim smile. "After Palmyra, I've got to settle with Gaul!"

29

SO AURELIAN resumed his march of conquest. He came now with forty thousand legionaries at his back. Before him sped the legend of his prowess, his severity, his invincible fortune. It leaped the straits and raced along the great highways eastward, invisibly breaching walls, sounding a dread drumbeat in the ears of city councillors as they sat in anxious debate whether to resist or submit.

Nothing withstood Aurelian. The rich towns of Asia Minor, long docile under Palmyra's sway, flung their gates wide and nervous deputations hastened to his camp to affirm with what impatience their citizens had awaited the legitimate ruler of Rome.

Before long Aurelian's unchallenged Eagles were winding down from the defiles of the Taurus Mountains and across the hot Cilician lowlands. The motley armies of Zenobia streamed north to meet them—swarthy archers from the warlike Mesopotamian marches;

droves and droves of bewildered peasants and unenthusiastic urban militia, trudging with pike or sword and buckler; and, core of the huge array, the clanking squadrons of Cataphracts, ponderous lancers sheathed, man and mount, in steel.

In two fierce encounters they were shattered. After the first, Syria suddenly remembered that she was a Roman province; her dignitaries prostrated themselves with glib felicitations before the man who, with forty thousand irresistible swords at his command, was beyond doubt their rightful Emperor.

On to Palmyra. The embattled city stood in a scarred and waterless plain, devastated by its own defenders. Thirst and distance and the raids of elusive Bedouins on his communications could not check Aurelian. The siege was initiated and pressed with relentless vigor. With her dominions shrunk to the circuit of the walls and hunger already taking toll among the common people, the proud defiance of Zenobia gave way to despair. In the dead of night, with a few companions, all mounted on fleet dromedaries, she dashed through the Roman encirclement out into the open desert and headed for the Euphrates and the safety of the Persian frontier. In the alerted Roman camp Moorish horsemen swung onto their bareback ponies and set out in hot pursuit, guided by the freshly patterned tracks which stretched across the sand. They rode back the following day through throngs of wildly cheering soldiers, with a pale, dejected woman in their midst. Soon after Palmyra opened its gates. Installing a garrison of archers, Aurelian turned for home with the humbled Empress of the East and the stupendous spoils of her empire in his train.

To Palmyra again. The captive but untamed city had risen and slaughtered its Roman garrison. When a courier overtook Aurelian with the news he had already reached Europe. But before the rebels could consolidate themselves, he was upon them. The Legions were let loose on the panic-stricken population and the glory of Palmyra was expunged forever.

To Egypt. Here Aurelian overturned the throne of a new usurper called Firmus, who sought to recover for his country the independence from Rome which she had enjoyed under Zenobia. As the legionaries flowed in an awe-inspiring spectacle of martial power through Alexandria's gleaming marble streets of temples and palaces, the populace crowding the sidewalks looked on in heavy and hostile silence. Again Aurelian met the estranged spirit which had perplexed and angered him at that other extremity of the Empire, Dacia. In Egypt, too, native traditions had never died and local loyalties claimed the heart's allegiance. Rome was an alien, hated for the harshness of her yoke.

Bred in a rugged country, amid a taciturn folk, Aurelian felt a baffled revulsion against the neurotic insolence of these garrulous Alexandrians, their leering ribaldry, their hysteria. Worse even than the bastard Greeks of the shameless, beautiful city were the Egyptians of the old stock, sullen and superstitious serfs, fanatically attached to their senile and repulsive cults. Many times conquered and pitilessly exploited, they had never acquiesced in their subjection and yielded up only what brute force exacted.

Like other Roman commanders in this land of stale antiquity and shrill, violent mobs, Aurelian reestablished the Empire's authority with an iron hand. The penalty for revolt was savage and widespread devastation in the city. For the moment cowed, the Alexandrians went back to their private affairs—until the next nervous gust of their irreconcilable hatred should sweep them into new, murderous seditions against Rome.

To Gaul. The reigning usurper, Tetricus, had no desire for a trial of strength with the conqueror of the Alemanni and Palmyra. He sent secret messages offering capitulation. But the fiery Gallic Legions, recruited in the province, were ardently attached to its independence; they clamored to be led to battle. Their courage and élan could not prevail against the cold ferocity of the Illyrians. One day's tremendous carnage gave Aurelian mastery over Gaul.

So grimly ravaged by the barbarians was this greatest of the western provinces that it was now far gone in decline. The exposed countryside had suffered even worse than the towns. In many places, whole villages stood empty and rotting amid weed-grown fields. The peasants, doubly afflicted—by the raiders and their own rapacious absentee landlords—had simply abandoned homes and holdings and taken to the wilds, where under the name of Bagaudae they had set up a widespread and invisible republic of outlaws, permanently at war with settled society.

The astonished world beheld itself reunited. All that Aurelian had not recovered were the outlying positions between the Rhine and Danube, and the foundered province of Dacia. To the Romans his reign appeared an almost unbroken recital of victories. At last, after years of unspeakable agony, the Empire was at peace. Every pretender, every usurper, every rebel—save the hungry groups of Gallic runaways skulking in their woods and hills and marshes— had been overthrown. Every invading host, every marauding band of barbarians had been exterminated or bloodily repelled. After the slaughter of their bravest fighting men, the Goths needed years to recruit their strength and, at any rate while Aurelian lived, their primitive code of honor would also restrain them from taking up arms against Rome. The Alemanni were prostrate and the report of their paralyzing disaster froze the other German tribes and confederacies in their forests. Palmyra's ransacked wealth and the renewed stream of gold from the rich Asiatic provinces for the moment overflowed the Treasury. Egypt, though disaffected and obedient only to the naked sword, was as ever prodigally productive. The cargo ships, their hulls deep with her corn, wallowed in the sea lanes to Italy.

This glorious redemption of the Empire, so long overrun and fragmented, a prey to the hundred horrors of anarchy, was supremely the work of one man. When Tacitus rose in the Senate to propose that Aurelian be saluted as Restorer of the World, for once the cynics did not secretly smile, for once an Emperor's achievement was equal to the servile assembly's adulation.

Half Italy seemed to have crammed itself into Rome for Aurelian's Triumph. For hours the procession poured like a proud and colorful river between the dense-packed banks of spectators; for hours the acclamations sounded over the rooftops.

No one, not the oldest, could recall the like for magnificence and

410

variety. The plodding bulk of a score of elephants led the way; there followed a whole menagerie of rare animals and company after company of gladiators, with muscle-rippling bodies and brutalized or devil-may-care faces. Then the heaped trophies and the captives of many races and lands, chief among them the fallen Queen of Palmyra, slowly pacing with set face and downcast eyes, the gleaming royal gems which bedecked her mocked by fetters of gold. After the captives, the captor: Aurelian himself in a Gothic chariot drawn by four stags. With his stern face and tall, imposing figure, still unbowed by the burden of years and battles, he appeared a living image of the implacable god of war.

Behind came the grave ranks of the Senate, mostly elderly men with hoary beards and all dignified by the purple-striped official togas they wore, a plausible imitation of the august assembly which had guided Republican Rome to greatness. Picked units of the Army, horse and foot, brought up the rear of the immense procession.

So Rome, which he had made again the capital of a united Empire, beheld the plenitude of Aurelian's glory. He next arranged that she should see the magnitude of his power. After days of carnival, of lavish distribution of food and money, of gladiators in the Arena glutting with their wounds and dying spasms the bloodlust of the frenzied tiers of spectators, Aurelian held a grand review of the Army.

In a level extent of country not far from Rome, two parallel, breast-high barriers were erected, stretching for several miles and demarcating a broad channel along which the march-past was to take place. For Aurelian a saluting stand was set up, a simple wooden platform, draped in purple cloth and ascended by railed stairs.

His retinue of generals in ornate parade armor halted at the foot. He mounted alone and walked, a towering figure resplendent in gilded helmet and breastplate, to the platform's edge, from which he looked far over the restless and murmuring sea of heads, split by the wide and empty causeway.

Distant trumpets plucked at the ear. Slowly the hubbub stilled.

Myriads of faces turned toward a trampling sound that grew to rhythmic thunder.

Stately, behind their rigidly upheld ensigns, whose burnished metal ornaments flooded back the sun's brilliance, the Legions swung past; an endless onpouring of marching men in faultless order.

The Roman populace had cheered other great military reviews. But in the bearing of these soldiers was something that stamped them as different from all Rome's other armies in that generation. They carried themselves with the arrogant assurance of conquerors.

When the officer leading each formation had almost reached the saluting stand, a curt command rang from him. His sword flashed from the scabbard and came to rest upright before his face; the whole array of helmeted heads, in a single movement, jerked round and all eyes stared toward the Emperor.

Aurelian stood at the salute upon his platform, his face impassive, but his heart straining with exultation. No Roman army of the past could rival what these men, his men, had accomplished. Not Julius Caesar's, with the resources of the unvanquished Republic to nourish them and contending with enemies unversed in scientific war. Not Trajan's, so numerous, so well provided, so free to concentrate upon one foe at a time. This huge totality of martial power slowly, massively, surging past had expanded from his own hard-beset Illyrian handful making war against heavy odds in a ravaged frontier region of the dismembered Empire.

No wonder the multitudes blackening the fields around hailed him as Restorer of the World. He had found the world in collapse. With none on earth to help, he and his Illyrians had taken their stand, hurled back the floods on every side, freed the Empire of invaders and usurpers and reasserted its unchallenged authority from its Atlantic rim to its moat of Syrian sand.

In all this achievement the favoring Hand of God was plain. The Radiant Soldier of the Heavens had been with him from the day they brought word that Claudius Gothicus, dying of plague, had besought him to take up the burden of the broken Empire. Even long before that, on half-forgotten battlefields, there had been moments when he felt his body glow as the God entered and took possession. Now, more intensely than ever before, he felt the Presence and Power of Mithras burning within him.

The review ground opened up to embrace the unmeasured Earth. The noise of the multitude below increased and diversified into a clamor of unnumbered peoples bathed in the invisible streaming of force from the God enshrined in his heart. Benign yet stern, a Sun that kindled Rome to life and scorched her enemies, He rayed out over the world to its far girdle of stormy waters, the God manifest through his Chosen, triumphant after long travail.

Endlessly the Legions tramped below, endlessly the cheers and cries and murmurs of a million spectators swelled, subsided, reared again; the noise floated like incense clouds round the platform where the Emperor stood transfigured, godlike and a vessel of the God.

30

THE next day Aurelian woke with a racking headache. He moved about as if dazed, with an unwonted pallor, turned from food with a grimace and stayed morosely silent, except for an occasional grumpy few words.

A young maidservant came in with a timid air carrying a polished wooden casket of trinkets from which Severina wished to select a birthday gift for one of Julia's classmates. At the slight noise of her entry, Aurelian swung round, glowering. Unnerved, the girl stumbled and clutched at a little table, which overturned. With a squeal, she went sprawling; the casket shot from her hands and necklaces, bracelets, brooches, rings, and other glittering baubles swished and scraped across the floor toward Aurelian's feet. He kicked at them viciously. "You clumsy bitch!" he yelled. "Get out—I'll have you whipped!"

Almost fainting, she pulled herself onto her knees, one hand instinctively going to her barked shin, the other making an irresolute movement toward the nearest trinkets.

"All right, leave them there. Just go," Severina said quietly. The girl scrambled up, stood unsteadily a moment, gaping white-faced at Severina, and then hurried out.

"I'm going for a ride," declared Aurelian abruptly. "Call off the Council meeting." He strode from the room, which seemed still echoing with his fury. Before long brisk commands faintly reached Severina from the Great Courtyard—the picked Illyrian troopers of the Imperial bodyguard were mustering.

Though its violence had left her shaken, the explosion had not come altogether as a surprise. During the week she had watched with concern how the strain of the endless ceremonies had been telling on Aurelian—and, in particular, yesterday's grand military review, an ordeal of hours, from which he had returned spent and glassy-eyed, hardly able to talk coherently. In spite of her worry, she was glad that he had abandoned his duties for the present to go riding in the cool of the morning.

She picked the casket up and began to replace the scattered ornaments.

The freshness of morning passed; the sun grew hot; long hours succeeded one another; the sun waned—and still Aurelian had not made a reappearance. Very anxious now, Severina got the Palace Guard Commander to make discreet inquiries. All he could discover was that a troop of Guards cavalry, going at a purposeful canter, had left Rome quite early in the day by the Via Valeria, which led eastward. He made his report in person and added that Herennianus was in the Palace for an interview with the Emperor, now almost due. In the circumstances would the Augusta receive him instead?

It was a deeply bronzed, sober, and reserved Herennianus who, with no hint of the former easy terms between them, gave her a respectful salutation. He explained that he was about to leave on an extended recruiting tour—the Cavalry Corps was being brought up to strength after the severe losses of the Gallic campaign—and there were a number of points about his itinerary still to be settled with the Emperor.

414

"He should be back soon," Severina said, conscious of some embarrassment. "Do sit down and talk, Herennianus. We haven't had a word together since the siege."

It was the siege of Palmyra she meant. Once the Roman blockade had been firmly established round Zenobia's capital and refuge, Severina had visited the Army and, in accordance with tradition, had been proclaimed Mother of the Camps, although she felt herself the least warlike of Empresses.

The visit, on which she had set out eagerly, had disappointed her hopes. Operations were not going satisfactorily when she arrived. The Palmyrenes had made some daring and successful sallies, and there was concern over reports that a strong mobile force was fitting out a little distance inside the Persian frontier. Aurelian himself was absent for the greater part of each day. Although his aides made her cordially welcome, she was aware that her presence at Headquarters during this difficult period must add to their trials.

Herennianus she met only twice—and then briefly and in public. Either his duties took him elsewhere or he deliberately avoided her.

The heat round Zenobia's desert citadel was suffocating. Straight from the depths of the waterless Arabian wastes blew a wind like the breath of a furnace. The most torrid hours of the day Severina spent alone, restless and sticky with sweat, in Aurelian's Spartan living quarters. Flies were everywhere; in a minute they settled black on any scrap of uncovered food. In any case, she had no appetite for the only fare available—stodgy soldier's porridge or meat stew filmed with fat, washed down by tepid but potent Syrian wine.

Of Palmyra she had seen nothing but an arc of lofty wall at a distance, with tiny anonymous figures slowly moving on the ramparts. The Roman artillery was only just being installed. The few catapults in position were making no visible impression; the great stone barrier appeared to flick their puny missiles contemptuously away.

Not long after her arrival at the camp, a tour of inspection was arranged for her. She insisted, however, that no warning should be given and no special preparations made; her desire was to see the troops under everyday conditions. An imposing cavalry escort accompanied the litter, so that contrary to her wish the progress round the camp was a noisy one. Soldiers resting after their spell in the siege works poked sleepy, resentful faces out of tents and bivouacs as she passed. The lines of the regular troops were orderly and clean, but she choked at the stench from the encampment of the wild Bedouin auxiliaries. Swarms of their slatternly women and naked children came running out to raise a mournful cry, which the escort commander explained was for alms. The troopers beat back with their lance butts the most forward of the women, some of whom, with their lustrous black eyes, raven hair, and sinuous carriage, were beautiful in spite of their filthy rags. Severina had her purse emptied among them and the cavalcade moved off, leaving the crowd struggling and screeching on the ground.

Her circuit of the camp had revealed a most formidable concentration of ordered military power, but it was this painful closing spectacle that stayed longest in Severina's memory.

Such experiences would have weighed on her spirits less had she been able to reestablish her relations with Aurelian on their old footing. It was her failure to draw close to him again, as she longed, that made other trials hard to bear. Yet it was not indifference that he showed her. He had greeted her with obvious pleasure, was solicitous of her health in the enervating heat, spoke to her frankly of his problems and heard her views with respect. Only, within the strong attachment that continued to unite them, she was aware that in some indefinable way he had withdrawn himself. Even when they were alone together and he was most relaxed, she could sense this separation from her.

She told herself that the circumstances militated against intimacy. An armed camp is no substitute for home, and war has a prior claim on a soldier husband's attention.

However, as her litter headed over the sands toward the settled regions of Syria on the first stage of her long journey back to Rome, she felt relief from one anxiety. Despite the unceasing pressure on the commander of a great army in the field, Aurelian appeared in robust health—of mind as well as body. Severina had discovered that a Mithraeum, a subterranean chapel where Mithraic rites were practiced, was situated not far from the camp and that Aurelian sometimes attended. But she had not been able to detect in him a trace of that intense and somberly exalted state in which he had spoken of his Revelation.

His speech had been concerned with strictly practical matters; his manner had been as it always was in war—brisk, incisive, masterful.

Herennianus took the seat that Severina indicated. Once he began to speak, it was with his former vigor and fluency, though his look remained serious.

"It's a pity, Augusta, that you didn't pay your visit at the end, when we captured Zenobia. There were some extraordinary scenes, I can tell you. They were brave men, those Palmyrenes. You should have seen them when the Emperor condemned them to death for counselling Zenobia to make war on Rome. Not a flicker of emotion! They stood like swarthy statues, while our troops raised a bloodthirsty howl.

"I was senior officer at the executions—and I must say it was a nasty business. By the way, one of the Palmyrenes asked leave to speak to me. He said he had been an envoy here. Do you remember him, Augusta, a tall, wiry man, very dark, with a thin, finely curved nose—yes, and magnificent eyes? His name?—that's it, Metaballus. He said, very coolly, 'Will you be good enough to convey my profound respect to the Empress Severina? Please tell her that my last words were: Long live the Opposition!' There was plenty doing after that—I forgot all about him, until you mentioned the siege."

In a low voice she asked, "Did many die at that time—with Metaballus?"

"Many! The field looked a shambles when the headsman had done. Funny thing—Zenobia herself denounced them. A strange woman, that. . . ." He checked himself on the point of growing too familiar in tone and rose. "I have pressing duties, Augusta," he said formally. "Do you think His Majesty will be much longer?"

As in the old days, Severina had found the company of Herennianus congenial and the impulse to talk freely to him was still strong in her. She reflected, then said, "Please don't go yet." Omit-

417

ting any reference to the painful scene over the trinket box, she told Herennianus of Aurelian's departure so many hours ago from Rome.

"Via Valeria?" Herennianus murmured. He glanced away, evidently searching his mind. "Why, of course—Tibur!"

Even as the word escaped, he must have regretted his unguarded tongue. He shot a scared look at Severina; instantly it woke the suspicion that he had blurted out a name of secret significance.

"Why would the Emperor be going to Tibur?" she asked quickly.

"Tibur?" he repeated with an affectation of surprise that would not have deceived a child. He did not meet her eyes.

"Stop this nonsense, Herennianus!" Her tone brooked no further evasion. "Whom has the Emperor gone to see at Tibur?"

He swallowed, frowned at the floor, glanced at her pleadingly, then evidently made a decision. "His Gothic woman," he muttered.

Three brief words, barely heard, yet they made a breach with all the past. The stricken silence prolonged itself. Dully Severina wondered why the blow was not more shattering, why these words, which should have burst over her like a roaring wave, left her capable of thinking with a stunned calm.

"Tell me everything, Herennianus, please," she said quietly. "From the beginning. . . ."

She saw his face crease with his feeling for her and his lips reluctantly moving. He leaned toward her as he spoke, but his voice, low-pitched, hesitant, apologetic, came to her from far away.

What Herennianus was unwilling to impart in narrative zest, her own imagination feverishly supplied. The scenes unrolled themselves before her wounded gaze. The mutiny with its fearful stresses; the savage battle against the Goths; the breakdown of discipline as the victorious Romans sacked the camp; the parade of captive women; Aurelian's surrender to that impulse of—what was it?—cruel revenge—lust—participation with the men in mass animality? All this she saw with painful clarity. But strain as she would, she could not picture the blonde Northern woman who had supplanted her.

"Don't make too much of it, Augusta," Herennianus said unhappily. "The Emperor—well, he's not like he used to be. He's got too much to bear—he can't keep himself in so well. It's like this, if you see what I mean. A soldier needs a woman—you'll pardon me—in a simple way. A soldier's a fighting animal and he gets the urge to couple like an animal. Just like he wants to fill his belly—crude, satisfying stuff—nothing subtle—no nonsense about it—no questions asked." He spoke rather shamefacedly and she appreciated, with a little stir of gratitude, that he was laying bare his own debasement in order to excuse his Emperor.

"What is she like—this—do you know her name?"

"Hunilda."

Severina repeated the name, as if the barbarian syllables might yield up the woman's hidden personality.

"I suppose you'd call her beautiful," Herennianus went on. He could not guess how deep a stab the word inflicted. "That is, if you care for these big, voluptuous Northern women. I can't say I do—a primitive creature—healthy—placid. Her head's stuffed with heroic lays and dragons and enchanted maidens and evil dwarfs. She prattles away in her queer lingo. I don't think the Emperor bothers to listen."

Aurelian preoccupied and silent—that her imagination could vividly depict, but not the Gothic woman whose body he had used and who chattered, unheeded, in the room.

"He doesn't see much of her," added Herennianus coaxingly. "Only now and then, when he seems to get a bad spell. He still needs you—you're his wife, his equal, his link with the world. I think he'd have dropped her long ago, if it weren't for the boy."

"The boy!" Now the wave roared over her and she felt herself drowning.

"Augusta, are you ill? Severina, please . . ." Herennianus had risen and was bending over her bowed head.

Pale, she looked up. "Tell me about the boy—yes, I insist," she managed to say.

Herennianus watched her with distress. He spoke hesitantly. "He must be—let me see—three—four years old. A sturdy kid. Very active. His mother's got some outlandish name for him, but the Emperor calls him Claudius."

She fought the dreadful pang mutely, eyes downcast. It was she who should have given Aurelian a son to bear the name of the dead colleague and Emperor he must in his own dour way have loved.

As moments went by, the pain grew unbearable. A tremor passed through Severina and she moaned, a sound inexpressibly shocking to Herennianus, who knew her proud, uncomplaining nature.

"Please, Augusta, try to understand!" he urged agitatedly. "The Emperor's been under a superhuman strain. He'd be less than natural if he didn't give way now and then. I sometimes think he's drawn to this Hunilda just because she is a Goth. The Goths, you know, killed his father. To treat one of their women like this—a princess at that—it gives him a kind of perverted revenge, don't you see?"

An earlier phrase of his had embedded itself in her memory, resisting dissolution. "What did you mean—'his link with the world'?" she muttered inconsequentially.

He hesitated. "There are worse things for an Emperor than an occasional lapse of this kind," he answered. His tone gave these enigmatic words, which found an echo in her own mind, a solemn and sobering purport. "For his sake—for ours, don't take this thing too hard. He needs you—perhaps more than he knows. Only you can help him!"

She was aware of him stooping over her, of his silent but ardent compassion enfolding her. "I had better go now," he said, very gently. "Pardon me, dear Augusta, for hurting you so. Perhaps, when the Emperor returns, he will send me word when to wait on him."

Severina answered only with a little lift of the hand. Already her mind was busy along the trails which his revelation had opened. At last she could account for her persistent feeling of estrangement in Aurelian, of a hidden barrier between them. Her uncle's behavior, too, had become intelligible. With contacts in the highest military circles, he must long ago have been informed of what Herennianus had just disclosed. His affection for her was strong, with a jealous quality. He was a man of irascible temperament and no respecter of persons. It was possible now to understand the almost brutal rudeness he had shown Aurelian—and also Aurelian's untypical mildness in response.

420

She did not relish her uncle's championship. It only added to her distress that her humiliation was known to him.

Aurelian came back late the following afternoon. She resisted her first inclination to shun him on his return, to make of absence a reproach or punishment. Between her and Aurelian too much had happened; she simply could not now permit offended pride to govern her behavior.

Nevertheless, she had a struggle before she approached him. A sleepless night and, since then, other weary hours of confused thinking had left her quite uncertain what to say. She searched his face for guilt or self-satisfaction—and saw only that he was an aging man to whom the years had given little rest. He met her gaze rather absently, nodded, and said, "I'm sorry. I was detained." It was a casual phrase, she could see—not consciously misleading, without effrontery.

"How are you feeling now, Aurelian?" she asked, hovering between concern and irony. Standing before him, noting his faint, familiar changes of expression, she just could not think of him as fresh from some sensual escapade. He appeared to be making an effort to comprehend her simple question. "Oh, I'm all right," he said. "There's trouble, Severina. A dispatch has come in from Probus in Gaul. Another mutiny—a whole Legion this time." She knew now that he was contemplating distant, violent scenes and problems that had no relation to her. Mutiny made infidelity trivial; to tax him at this moment with his night at Tibur would be absurd.

"Ah, well," he said with a shrug, "Eros has a big batch of reports waiting. I'll look them over and join you later." He gave her a smile, friendly but still a little preoccupied, and walked away.

It was late in the evening when Aurelian came back to their apartment. Though he looked tired, he began at once to talk, freely. At first he touched on minor topics, but before long, by a natural transition, he was speaking of the mutiny in Gaul, which evidently was very much on his mind.

From Gaul, he ranged elsewhere in the Empire. Wider and wider themes opened up as his forceful monologue developed.

Listening, Severina perceived—and it was a painful admission to make—that Tibur had provided him with a salutary release, restored his equilibrium, enabled him to shed his edginess and his burden of thunderous anger.

At first she heard him rather inattentively, distracted as she was with her own reflections. Her position was one in which a wife finds it hard to be magnanimous. "Try to understand," Herennianus had urged. "He still needs you. . . ." She struggled to understand. Did Aurelian really need her? Obviously the man he had become, no doubt the man he had to be as ruler of the world, had needs which she was poorly equipped to satisfy.

Perhaps every so often some primitive purgation, a plunge into sensual oblivion, was necessary to him. It might be his only escape from the unending pressure of his responsibilities. She knew her own inadequacy. For a blind, raw, self-forgetful bodily release he would be obliged to turn elsewhere. She herself had never had the charms or the arts to evoke it.

But it was to her that he now was speaking with such intentness, such emphasis; she who was helping him search for light on the great issues that were paramount in his mind. It seemed as though two opposite tendencies were simultaneously at work in him. On the physical plane, where his long absences on campaign had contributed to his alienation from her, a stranger gave him solace. But it was to his wife that he came with his cares and his problems, his schemes and his dreams.

The thought occurred to Severina that the woman at Tibur, by setting him free of his intolerable stresses, had sent him back to her.

Time passed and his flow of comment continued, Severina making only those brief and pertinent interruptions at intervals that enabled his ideas to maintain their impetus. Gradually what he said compelled her closer interest and she ceased her private debate.

"Reserves—there's the trouble. We need masses of them," he was saying. "Take Cannae . . ."

"That battle against Hannibal centuries ago?" she asked in surprise.

"That's it. Rome lost her whole field army in one single day. Scores of thousands of trained men. What happened? She created another field army—just as good, better perhaps. The little Republic had reserves. Our huge Empire hasn't! If we had a Cannae, if we lost the entire field army in a day—and it could happen any time—we would probably just go under!

"As it is, fighting's getting more and more bloody. The barbarians have changed. They're learning from us—it was bound to happen. We're changing, too. When I was a recruit, every infantryman was issued two heavy javelins. Well, you can't chase Goths lugging those around. We're cutting down the load on the troops—even armor's being reduced. The barbarians are meeting us on more equal terms. Casualties are bound to be high."

Severina found a hopeful implication in his words. "So we must have a long period of peace to build up reserves," she suggested.

"It's not as simple as that," he answered, frowning. "We need the reserves, but we can't afford to wait too long. The soldiers are so used to bloodshed now that they soon grow bored and restless without it. The Illyrians worst of all. That's the real reason for this mutiny. If peace lasts, they'll get completely out of hand—I know them!"

It was sinister truth he spoke. The main threat to the stability of the Roman State was the insubordinate spirit of the Roman Army. Here and not in respect of courage and fighting skill (in which the Illyrians were equal to the finest soldiers of history) lay the fatal inferiority of Rome's latest Legions to those of her prime.

Aurelian had paused. He appeared to be weighing his next remark. Suddenly, as Severina watched him, she felt apprehension grow. An intuition told her that all he had said that evening had been tending to one point. Even before he spoke, she knew to what grim climax he was coming.

"We must find them a foreign war," he said, "or they'll find a civil war for themselves."

There was a somber relish in his tone. He did not find the prospect unwelcome, she saw. He, too, was an Illyrian soldier, inured to bloodshed, craving violent action.

She clung to the hope that he had spoken in general terms—and, in general terms, the force of what he said was undeniable. She stood up, meaning to bring this ominous conversation to a close before he committed himself to some specific intention.

423

With a slight, imperative gesture, he stopped her. Deliberately, he went on, "We shall have to have another war—and pretty soon. There can be only one enemy."

A sick excitement made her tremble. From those phrases death and destruction would advance far over the world.

She breathed a name.

"Persia!" he confirmed, giving the syllables an altogether more threatening sound. "We don't need a pretext. There's a long, long score to settle with them!"

Again his point was a weighty one, impossible to dispute. Rome had taken the measure of Parthia, which had been content to survive the offensive of Trajan and never again represented a major threat. Its successor, the Sassanid Empire, a resurgence of the old, bitter, militant Iranian stock, was a different proposition—the perpetual enemy. One could make a truce with it, but with the certainty that, sooner rather than later, its fierce drive to reach the Mediterranean would be resumed. The Goths had slain the Emperor Decius in battle. The Sassanids had inflicted even worse ignominy on Rome. They had taken the Emperor Valerian prisoner and on his death, so report said, had flayed the poor corpse and stuffed the skin with straw.

Severina roused herself from her quiescence. She could no longer passively listen—merely, as it were, feeding his soliloquy—while he pursued his argument to such terrifying conclusions. A war with Persia could tax the exhausted Empire to the uttermost and might bring upon it fresh, perhaps irretrievable, disasters.

"Surely," she exclaimed, "not a full-scale war—not an invasion! You mean a demonstration on the frontier?"

"We shall see," he answered. She suspected that his mind was already made up, yet the form of his remark left the issue nominally open. She determined to oppose, with all her resources, the notion of this unnecessary war. With the clarity of fear, she could see the implications. To begin with, Aurelian himself—he would be involved personally. Imagine him, a man of sixty, in active command of an army contending with a fierce enemy of inexhaustible numbers in a land of scorching plains and arid mountains, which stretched far away into the depths of Asia!

424

"Aurelian," she said, "Persia is a mighty Empire. Rome's worn out. We haven't had a proper chance to recover. Can't you find the soldiers an easier war? The Great King won't attack. He's too scared. But if the Persians had to fight—and on their own territory—who can foresee the outcome?"

Aurelian rose. "The outcome?" His voice vibrated through her. "Can you doubt it? I have Help, Severina! It has never failed me. Of course the Persian King is scared. He is lost, I tell you. He will be delivered into my hands!"

A cruel elation showed in his face. His look, harsh and triumphant, was painful to sustain. She felt a sinister power pulse from him. With chill in her heart, she recognized beyond doubt that his sense of Election was still working in him violently and that it was a primary factor in his designs against Persia.

She heard again the urgent tones of Herennianus: "You're his link with the world . . . for his sake, for ours . . . only you can help. . . ." Aurelian, the great general, had been talking military folly. Against an enemy such as Persia there could be no question of victory predestinate. As best she could, she must try to win him from these perilous dreams.

Severina understood now that she had an adversary infinitely more potent than the woman at Tibur. It was with the God that she must struggle—for Aurelian's mind.

31

WITH every day that passed Aurelian grew busier. Tax reform, the issue of new coinage, the construction of the great wall of Rome, which was lagging far behind the stringent timetable he had laid down, the reorganization and expansion of the Army, long-overdue repairs to the road system binding the Empire together—there were a thousand and one activities to be planned and supervised. A river of petitions and complaints flowed into the great building on the Palatine and a team of secretaries toiled late into every night to sift and annotate them and prepare the cases for the Emperor's personal attention. Everywhere he probed he brought to light incompetence and corruption. Toward inefficiency he was severe, visiting offenders with stern reprimands, dismissals and, in more flagrant instances, imprisonment. Toward corruption he was ruthless; his cleansing instrument was the executioner.

It was Justice, an unbending, pitiless Justice, that was enthroned. Not for many years had the Empire enjoyed such an honest administration and Aurelian's rule was popular, save with the guilty and their families and friends.

Of these, however, the number was very large and it was impossible for a reasonable person to refuse many a measure of sympathy. Justice, even in a hurry, should calculate its penalties to the circumstances. Aurelian seemed determined to make every sentence an exemplary one.

More than once Severina recalled the words of the unfortunate Metaballus. An Opposition—if a name so forthright could be given to the widespread but unorganized element in Palace, Administration, and Army of those who cautiously expressed their revulsion and misgivings—had come into existence. She could have no formal contacts with it, but she reflected its sentiment and might have been called its voice.

It was during the evenings, in the privacy of their own apartment, that her will contended, subtly and persistently, with Aurelian's. Often enough he was tired and irascible; sometimes he dozed. On other occasions she would encourage him to talk and, while skillfully avoiding a dispute, would try to induce him to moderate the harshness of some punishment. Though most of her efforts failed, she had her successes and almost each of these meant a life or number of lives no longer forfeit.

As regards the woman at Tibur, with the lapse of time Severina had become incapable of making an issue of the matter; inwardly she had accepted her rival. In any case, she could now less than ever contemplate an open conflict with Aurelian. Her distress would have been harder to bear in silence had his conduct been flagrant. But the facts proved as Herennianus had intimated. Aurelian did not visit Tibur for weeks at a stretch. Plainly, what drew him there was not ordinary sexual passion.

But occasionally there occurred the brief disappearance which Severina knew, without further inquiry, was accounted for by a stay at Tibur. As far as she could make out, it was when the overload had become unendurable, when the exasperations to a man of his exacting standards and impatient temperament of governing supine millions through a clumsy and obstructive bureaucracy had mounted to a peak, that the urge for release mastered him.

Then, without a word, he would ride away to the fleeting sensual oblivion in which he shed his tensions. This woman—Severina was certain—would have no reproaches for him, in word or look; she would not seek to thwart him with clever arguments. If she had heard about his cruelties, she would not regard them with horror. Instead she would submit to him, soft, responsive, solacing, setting him free of himself.

The picture Severina formed of her rival was at first shadowy. Little by little, with painful efforts of her imagination, she endowed the Gothic woman, if not with features then at least with something of personality. Though daughter of one tribal chief and wife to another, Hunilda must long ago have come to accept her humiliation, as Severina now accepted her own. After all, that was life as people knew it, Roman and barbarian alike. Men so often died violently and women learned to consider their subjection to the conqueror as part of Nature's order.

Of warrior stock, Hunilda was bound to admire Aurelian with his aura of virility and his martial renown. The ancient pride of barbarian women must stir in her that from her womb had come a sturdy, big-limbed boy, sired by a mighty war leader.

It was upon the boy that Severina's imagination most eagerly played. If only she herself had borne Aurelian a son! That would have gratified his deepest instincts and been a fulfillment of his manhood, as the Throne was of his valor and his victories. He would have founded a dynasty, a breed of conquerors.

Julia would one day marry and merge herself in her husband's family. She was no substitute for a son.

Whom did the boy resemble? Not his mother, probably. Learned doctors held that a woman was only the agent of birth. The infusion of life, the strongest imprint of personality, comes from the father. And when the father was Aurelian, how much more must this be true! His image must be stamped deeply on his son. More and more Severina came to think of the child as distinctively his father's—and so a natural object for her own sympathetic concern. The very name, Claudius, attached him to Aurelian and separated him from his foreign mother.

Severina felt no desire to see her rival; as time passed, the longing grew in her to set eyes on young Claudius.

One evening, Aurelian came into their apartment rather earlier than the hour at which official business normally ended. His step was brisk and his look showed eagerness. He approached her and held out his hand; on the palm lay a silver-bright coin. Severina saw it was an antoninianus, of the new, improved series Aurelian was issuing to replace the debased coinage of his predecessors.

"Look at it!" he urged, raising his hand.

Severina took the coin, which was reverse upward, and examined it. The design showed a woman presenting a wreath to the sceptered Emperor, a symbolism which accorded with the proud legend: RESTORER OF THE WORLD. She looked up into Aurelian's living face and, a little troubled by the expectancy there, turned the coin over.

Inscribed on the obverse in well executed letters was: AURELIAN BORN LORD AND GOD.

In itself the assertion of a living Emperor's Divinity was nothing novel; it was an act of state, without far-reaching spiritual implication, just as Emperor-worship was little more than a formal public expression of loyalty. But her intuition grasped at once the significance this coin held for Aurelian. It affirmed, in the strongest form, his conviction of being specially Chosen and Endowed.

Another illumination came to Severina. The inscription announced his claim to a power that made him invincible; it was a promise of victory. Then it linked directly with the theme which she knew was dominating his thoughts—the projected war against

Persia. Here was his answer to the opposition she had voiced—and to what, as her insight told her, now made her opposition formidable, his own awakened doubts.

For doubts he must have. All his previous wars were by nature rescue operations—to recover an Empire that largely had been lost. No patriotic Roman, least of all Aurelian himself, would have questioned their entire justification. But the kind of war he was contemplating, no matter what his pretext and the provocation, was essentially aggression. Above all, as she had reminded him, it was a perilous undertaking, which might easily miscarry, as other wars against Persia and, earlier, against Parthia had done.

This little silver shape resting on her fingers had betrayed Aurelian's inner conflict. On former occasions when he weighed the issue of war, he had not needed to buoy himself with such arrogant affirmations. A sobering interval had elapsed since, under the heady influence of his spectacular Triumph and the great military Review, he had boasted that the Persian King would be delivered into his hands. For the first time in his career, Aurelian stood uncertain. Her intervention now might be decisive. This was the opportunity she had sought.

His searching eyes were still on her as Severina returned the coin. "Well? Well?" he demanded.

"I've seen better workmanship," she answered coolly.

He looked taken aback. "Oh, it's not from Rome. It's from a provincial mint—Serdica, you know, in the Balkans."

"I should have thought it was not from Rome!" Her tone was sharper than she intended.

"Never mind that!" He spoke irritably. "You know what I mean . . . the inscription."

She shrugged. "Other Emperors have done the same thing. Domitian, I believe . . ."

His face showed such anger at this comparison with one of Rome's most infamous and hated rulers that she saw she had overreached herself.

"Domitian?" he growled. "Everyone knows he had delusions!"

It would have provoked him too far to retort, "You, also, have delusions!" Desperately she sought for arguments that would pierce deep without arousing his fury. His look, at once anxious and exasperated, forbade further delay. She replied indirectly:

"I suppose this makes me a goddess—of sorts!"

He peered at her. The implication, clearly, had not occurred to him.

"Well," she resumed, smiling faintly, but careful to keep overt mockery from her tone, "I don't feel in the least a goddess. Does a goddess get sick headaches? Does a goddess find her feet swell when she stands too long? Does a goddess get monthly pains—you know how bad mine are for a day or two? Besides, a goddess would have kept her figure better than I have! No, Aurelian, I'm afraid I'm a very ordinary woman."

He was frowning as he listened, but did not interrupt. She could see that he had taken her point—that by detailing her own deficiencies she meant to allude to his own.

Does a god grow old and gray? Does his mouth hold discolored stumps and does he sometimes wince with toothache? Is a god unable to control his fury, so that he clenches his fist and yells at some cringing offender? Do lost battles revisit a god in nightmare, making him start from sleep, heart hammering, throat dry, brow damp with sweat . . . ?

Her oblique reasoning had powerfully moved him, she could see. His face had become a battlefield where the forces of his divided nature openly contended. She watched him in silence, pitying him from her heart. At last he bent stricken eyes on her. "But—but" he began, "why don't you understand? Look what I've been enabled to do—a man like me—a Pannonian peasant—poor—with no schooling. How can you explain it?"

"Some men do godlike things," she said quietly. "You're one of them. Better to be a great man than an imitation god! Rome has plenty of gods, anyway—nobody is going to be impressed by another one. Listen, Aurelian. It means nothing to the people of Rome that you think yourself the Elect of Mithras. It means nothing to the Persian King—he thinks himself favored by his own god! The whole world knows that what you have done you owe only to yourself—your own courage, your own talent. You don't need these claims to be Chosen. You don't need these inscriptions. They don't add to your glory. They can't! Why, in ages to come people will salute your work who would smile at this coin and not even know what god you worshiped!"

He looked down at the coin; his fingers closed on it, slowly.

"I tell you," he said in a voice that was almost a groan, "I've seen the God—with these eyes—heard His Voice. I feel—somehow—changed!"

Obviously he was shaken. She was distressed for him, but she dared not show mercy. "This idea of yours is dangerous. It is taking you away from us. It is leading you to do rash things—to make war on Persia, for one. Just imagine if our Army met disaster. It could happen. Other Emperors, other rulers, believed like you that some God was on their side—and were defeated, all the same! Oh, yes—you'd beat the Persians in the field. No one doubts that. But what if your army wastes away with thirst and plague somewhere far beyond the Euphrates? This coin won't help you, then! This coin won't save us if the frontier's left wide open. And you know it! You're the Emperor of Rome, Aurelian. The sole responsibility is yours. Elect or not, ask yourself whether you have the right to take such risks—and in a war that isn't even necessary?"

He gazed at her a while in silence. "I'll send instructions to the Mint," he said at last in a subdued voice and, putting the coin away, he went heavily from the room.

For a number of days people at Court remarked among themselves that the Emperor had grown absent-minded. They noted, too, with some relief, that he showed himself less harsh and abrupt than usual, even a little uncertain. At the Council he would sit staring at the officials in turn, until they shifted in their seats uncomfortably.

The change in him at first elated Severina; her words must have penetrated deep—to the very basis of his convictions. It was time. He had become a dangerously lonely man, doubly isolated, pinnacled on the Throne of the World and self-withdrawn yet further by his sense of closeness to Deity.

After a while, however, her first facile jubilation gave way to renewed anxiety. It struck her that Aurelian was in a kind of waking trance, attending to affairs with a portion only of his mind, while with the remainder and all the intensity of his soul engaged on strange, unhappy, inconclusive speculations. More than once she saw him look at her with a mute sadness that she felt as a reproach; and when he spoke, it was as though he were, at the same time, trying to catch some elusive voice.

One evening Severina was waiting restlessly for Aurelian in their apartment. The day's last official business—an audience with some visiting Gallic notabilities—was over hours ago, yet he had not made an appearance. As his absence drew out, the fear grew in her that he had gone to pass the night at Tibur. When she could not bear to stay inactive any longer, she set out on a quick and unobtrusive tour of the Reception Hall and the neighboring chambers where he might conceivably have been delayed; he was nowhere to be found. She then sent for the Guard Commander who, with surprise, assured her that the Emperor could not have left the Palace.

Something at last prompted her to try the Council chamber—a most unlikely place, since no meeting had been held that day. She went there at once, though without any expectation of finding Aurelian. As soon as she opened the door, she saw him lolling in his great chair at the far end of the table. Stertorous breathing sounded across the dim, empty room.

She hurried over. Aurelian's eyelids were glued together, his mouth hung open. His head was jerking—slowly—down. A tremor passed through him and, abruptly, he raised his head; within a few moments it began to droop again. For an anguished minute she stood without moving, afraid to rouse him, afraid to let him sleep on. Finally, she placed a hand lightly on his shoulder and whispered, "Aurelian . . ."

The painful motion of his head stopped, instantly. His eyelids opened and staring eyeballs raised themselves to her. He gave a long, hoarse sigh. His breathing grew easier and his flickering gaze suggested that he was aware, in a puzzled way, of Severina bending over him.

"It's dark in here," he mumbled, screwing his eyes against the gloom, as normally one does against dazzle. He turned his head with an effort from side to side, identifying his surroundings. "I came here"—she leaned closer to catch the indistinct sounds—"it's

432

quiet—I was tired. . . ." His brow furrowed with the struggle to recapture from these preliminaries some lost experience whose effect was still strong on him. Suddenly he sat upright. An expression she could only think of as rapt made his face still and his eyes strange and luminous. He gripped her forearm with hooked, rigid fingers.

"Severina . . . are you listening . . . ?" he murmured. "I . . . I have had a vision!"

Severina did not disengage her arm. She was too agitated to feel the nails biting her flesh. Groping with her free hand for the table edge, she let her weight sink against it.

"A vision?" she echoed.

He nodded, gazing at some point beyond her, and continued slowly, "I was walking . . . a long time . . . hours, days . . . in wide courts paved with marble. There were tall pillars . . . they stretched on and on . . . clouds floated past, all round stars were blazing. They turned night into day . . . everything glittered!"

His grasp, which had for a few moments relaxed, tightened again on Severina's arm.

"A great company watched me. . . . They stood in groups, to either side as I walked . . . shining figures in flowing white robes. Some were beardless . . . smiling youths, with noble faces—just like statues come to life. . . . Others were old . . . old and stately. They had long beards. Their eyes gleamed at me. . . . All were full of majesty . . . radiant . . . like gods. They were gods, Severina!"

He paused, contemplating the visionary scene; then he went on, more quickly:

"I heard a great Voice. It came pealing like thunder . . . it froze me, but my heart was full of joy. 'Aurelian!' The sound of it rolled through the sky. Then all that company, all those shining figures, shouted in a mighty chorus, 'Aurelian, the Restorer of the World!'

"I looked at them—my heart was banging—but the courts began to reel . . . and break up . . . and sink. The stars swung all around . . . they exploded . . . darkness rushed in. . . . The figures . . . everything vanished . . . I felt a hand, your hand . . . your voice was saying, 'Aurelian. . . .'"

433

He stood up, shakily, releasing her aching arm, and looked down at her. There was a glare of such concentrated potency from his face that she shrank back and wished there was light in the room. She thought, "He is possessed—by what?"

"Can you doubt it any more, Severina? The gods themselves have acknowledged me!" He spoke quietly, but with triumphant certainty. Still unsteady, he turned and walked across the darkling room to the door.

The next day, orders went out for the Army to mobilize for an invasion of Persia.

Aurelian's vision, as Severina came to recognize, was the final relapse. The obscure, irrational forces within him had prevailed against her reasoning. He would do what his essential nature, the dark daemon in his soul, compelled.

She knew her battle was lost. He would go his own way, whether or not she gave him the support of her belief in his more than mortal destiny.

Strangely, there were no more visions. It was as if this convulsion of the soul were needed to throw off the last influence of her mind, with its alien logic and light. Once the daemon had asserted its mastery, it was no longer violent. It drove him with a steady, unresisted hand.

From the start Severina had been heartsick about the projected invasion of Persia. One could call it a war of revenge, even a preventive war—the fact remained that it was a foreign war, meant to be pressed far over the frontier against a warlike people in an inhospitable land, whose climate could be more deadly than its armies.

Now the mobilization had begun, she and the ministers who had counselled a long interval of peace and recuperation were powerless. She understood that an inexorable process had been set in motion. Legions, reinforced and reequipped, exhorted with speeches, spurred by the promise of plunder, were tramping along the roads; barbarian auxiliaries were crossing the Rhine and Danube; military magazines were being stocked; towns on the Emperor's route were busily arranging billets and the supply of provisions. A vast, interlocking mechanism was extracting soldiers and supplies all over the

Empire—and beyond—and assembling powerful formations in advanced state of war readiness at strategic points eastward.

When war was joined, the clash would be tremendous. The whole world tensely waited. Everyone knew that Aurelian took an enemy by the throat, neither giving nor asking quarter. He would fling the concentrated might of Rome into Mesopotamia and go storming onward.

Previous campaigns Aurelian had planned with a grim, purposeful calm. This one, to be the most spectacular in his career, perhaps in that of any Emperor, excited in him at times an ugly vehemence.

He could still discuss in a temperate manner the grand maneuvers by which he hoped to bring the Great King's armies to battle. But too often he would sit back in his chair in their apartment, talking slowly in a kind of gloating soliloquy, the intensity of his brutal purpose giving a sinister eloquence to his matter-of-fact words, making vivid his march across the map. His voice, harsh and complacent, brought before the eyes long columns of legionaries with the dust of Mesopotamia, of Media, on their armor and gear, a moving pattern on the parched brown earth edged by the swirling lines of his Moorish light cavalry.

His strategic aim was less conquest than destruction; his weapons the torch and spade and pickaxe, as much as the sword. Sometimes, smiling balefully, lingering over the spectacle he evoked, he would talk of the overthrow, the eclipse, the obliteration, of this restless and ambitious kingdom which had inflicted such dire and shameful loss on Rome. He would point a spear at Persia's heart and thrust it home with the united power of sixty thousand legionaries. He would march in; slaughter the armies; batter in the walls of the towns; let his troops loose to kill, with no mercy shown, to plunder, to burn. He would fire the villages; trample the harvests he did not carry off; chop down the orchards; choke the wells and the canals. Vast areas of Persia would be left an unpeopled wilderness. It would be a long time before a land so devastated could again mount a full-scale war.

The pressure on Rome's eastern frontier would cease. Rome would abut on a vacuum.

435

These lurid dreams were indulgences for the evening. From soon after dawn and through most of the day, Aurelian labored with unsparing energy, driving his personal staff until they were worn out. Already the witticism went the round of the Palace that the first casualties of the Persian war were the Emperor's secretaries.

Edict piled on edict. No matter what the effort cost, Aurelian was determined to leave the Empire's affairs in sound order when the time came for him to take command in the field.

During this frantic final period, Severina saw little of him each day until well after nightfall. About noon he would come in to snatch a meal—a light one, for even his iron stomach was growing rebellious under the strain. Then away to further sessions with his generals and ministers or to examine petitions together with the commentaries his staff had prepared on them. Though beset with preparations for a great war, he still preferred, where possible, to deal personally with appeals to the Throne, for among his civilian officials he had complete confidence only in Eros.

His coarse brown hair was turning white. The furrows of his brow deepened. His skin took on a sallow tinge. It was as though the life-energy were draining out of him to transfuse itself into the half-moribund Roman State. Most people at Court held him in fear. His look was irritable, his tongue harsh, his judgments, always tending to severity, grew more rigorous.

The momentum of events was such by now that Severina could only wait and watch with foreboding. The hours, which passed so swiftly for Aurelian, for her were leaden. She was pleased therefore when one afternoon a servant brought a message from Eutropius, who had just concluded an audience with the Emperor, requesting leave to call and to present his nephew. Eutropius, warmhearted and attached to her, was the only Senator for whom she felt a cordial friendship.

It happened that Julia was with her when the visitors were shown in. Behind the beaming Eutropius came diffidently a good-looking young man of sturdy build, with bright, intelligent dark eyes and a fine forehead.

With solemn pleasure, Eutropius explained their presence in the

Palace. His nephew (the relationship was on his wife's side) hailed from the Tuscan hill country. The district of which his family were the principal landholders had been involved since the days of Gallienus in a dispute with the Treasury over tax arrears; and the young man, Hortensius by name, had been one of a delegation chosen to lay their grievances before the Emperor. Eutropius himself had been their advocate.

They had approached the Emperor with apprehension. To their astonishment, he had shown himself readily accommodating and almost affable. With his usual dispatch, he had canceled most of the arrears and spread repayment of the balance over five years. The reason for his lenience, Severina knew, was one these rural dignitaries never would have suspected. Aurelian, unbending as a rule toward offenders and prone to insist on the full requirements of the law, tended to take a tolerant view of tax default. He sprang from a class which was accustomed to regard tax collectors as the worst of oppressors and tax evasion as legitimate self-defense.

Julia had made to leave as uncle and nephew entered. But Eutropius, exuberant from his success and the Emperor's unwonted graciousness, begged Severina's permission to present Hortensius to her daughter.

The Princess, who was emerging from the more awkward phase of adolescence and was already viewing men with a deliberate interest easily mistaken for poise, looked keenly at the handsome, sunburned youth. He was obviously a little dazzled by the splendors of the Palace but, though country-bred, he was of noble family and a becoming dignity already showed in his bearing. The well proportioned girl, with her clear and steady, gray eyes and healthy complexion, seemed to make a lively impression on him. He and Julia stared at each other for some self-forgetful moments.

Both Severina and Eutropius observed that look—and they, in turn, exchanged a glance. Well, thought Severina, startled but not displeased, she is over fourteen—and mature for her age!

After Eutropius had described the interview with the Emperor and received Severina's congratulations, he launched on a labored comparison between Sassanid Persia, with whom war was imminent, and its ancient predecessor, the Achaemenid Empire, which the Greeks had defeated at Salamis. He quoted the Messenger's speech from *The Persae* of Aeschylus, lost the thread, and turned with an expectant smile to Hortensius. The youth, bowing first to Severina to crave her indulgence, rounded off the passage—a fairly long one—without faltering. Severina noticed that Julia listened intently. She herself heard with pleasure his musical voice follow the splendid measures with confidence and true feeling.

With an innocent vanity, Eutropius commented, "He is a very good scholar, Your Majesty—he speaks classical Greek fluently!" Hortensius looked embarrassed.

"I wish I could say the same of my daughter," observed Severina smiling. "Still, she has done quite well at her other studies."

The boy and girl smiled shyly at each other, though neither ventured to speak.

Afterward, Severina thought deeply about this little episode. She had been attracted by young Hortensius. His look was manly; he was intelligent, well educated, and of what struck her as an amiable character. His manner was pleasantly diffident, without being awkward. He came of good family, all the more commendable in her eyes for living at a distance from Rome and for not being prominent enough to excite jealous attention. Even the tyrant Emperors of the last century had not molested them.

Well, why not?

Once Severina would have rounded fiercely on a proposal to marry off a young girl, as she herself had been married, by an arrangement between elders. Now the words she repeated to herself unconsciously echoed those of her own parents, years ago, and indeed those of parents from ages immemorial when a daughter approached ripe womanhood: "It is time she were betrothed!"

With this frightening Persian expedition looming nearer, she could see that to place Julia—a freely consenting Julia, naturally—in the shelter of a prosperous country family, of modest style of life, might well be the wisest provision for her future.

When an opportunity offered she raised the matter, very guardedly, with Aurelian. He heard her at first with an absent look; but soon his changed expression showed that the significance of what she said was penetrating. For a while he brooded in silence, once or twice shooting her a suspicious glance. Finally he said in an inconclusive way that raised her hopes, "She's a bit young . . . that's a fine-looking young man . . . good shoulders . . . sensible, too—make a good officer. Pity it's a Senatorial family. . . . The girl like him? . . . Well, we'll see. . . ."

In Severina's mind Hortensius was now established as a possible son-in-law. She sent Eutropius a note saying that she would be pleased to see his nephew at Court again. A little experiment encouraged her to persist with her tentative matchmaking. Once, when Julia was present, she mentioned Hortensius in an apparently casual way to Aurelian. Immediately the girl looked round; and though she then bent over a ring which seemed to be chafing her finger, her heightened color showed how much she was interested.

Rome was agog when the appointed day came for Aurelian to leave for the East with a powerful contingent of Praetorians. For the war there was little enthusiasm—the Empire had known too many wars, and it was weary. Yet everyone recognized that great issues hung on this campaign. The prospects were that Rome's most formidable rival would be struck down for at least a generation. People felt that victory was assured. Though the Empire had put more numerous armies into the field, it had never assembled one more efficient and battle-hardened, nor one dominated by a will more potent. The soldiers did not love Aurelian; they simply believed in him. At his bidding, they would cut the Great King's finest troops to pieces.

Rome knew it; the soldiers were convinced of it; the Persians themselves suspected it.

In the great Mesopotamian capital of Ctesiphon there was fear bordering on panic. While the Roman vanguard was still a thousand miles away, the city prepared feverishly for siege. The arsenals clanged twenty-four hours a day. Tanks were dug to store water for a huge garrison. Trains of provisions poured in. Throughout the realm the levy of soldiers was pressed forward. From rocky pastures in the old Persian heartland the shepherds, exchanging their crooks for bows and spears, took the dusty tracks to the little market towns appointed for the local musters. The powerful feudatories of Media each equipped an army of retainers. The barons on the Oxus called in their bands of redoubtable light cavalry. The semibrigand chiefs of Afghanistan rode west with retinues of wild hillmen.

Over the borders sped the call for fighting men. Indian Rajahs stowed bags of Persian gold in their treasuries and sold off companies of dusky swordsmen for warfare in the Unknown beyond the Hindu Kush. Bedouin Sheiks, avid for loot and battle, led horse and camelry to the service of the Persian King.

Two assault corps formed the main strength of the immense array laboring westward to the Roman frontier. The first consisted of scores of towering war-elephants; the second, of the heavy regiments of Cataphracts, lancers fully mailed on bulky chargers. In the van surged clouds of light horse; and, blackening the earth for miles around, trudged masses of infantry, ranging from the splendidly accoutered Royal Footguards to half-naked peasants.

It was as brave and well ordered a host as Persia had ever summoned to arms. But the Great King and his generals and even many of the soldiers had a foreboding that it would not be enough. Soon a grim conqueror, invincible as Alexander of Macedon, would be bearing down on Mesopotamia—and bitter would be the restitution he would exact for all the injuries and insults which Persia had inflicted on Rome.

32

IN THE concentration area near Byzantium tens of thousands of Roman soldiers of all arms were encamped, ready to cross the straits into Asia as soon as the last substantial contingents from the West had joined them. Meanwhile, strenuous training continued. From soon after dawn every day, drill instructors drove sweating squads on the parade grounds; and before morning was far advanced, units in full battle order already maneuvered and charged each other in the neighboring fields. Hour after hour, the barked commands, the continuous crash of big formations marching, bugle calls and ferocious yells of men engaged in mimic fighting drifted across the lines to the tent which was the office and sleeping quarters of Eros.

Early one afternoon he sat there alone, unaware of these noises. His shoulders were a little bowed. His face had a sickly color and a muscle twitched every now and then in his right cheek. The hands he rested on the table trembled. At times his look moved aimlessly about, but for the most part he stared at the tent flap with a dazed expression, as though an apparition had entered.

Twenty minutes before, Eros had still been the coolly self-confident Imperial Secretary who had not only taken advantage of his influential post to sell favors, but had even found a relish in the deadly risks. Though under his present terrible master he had at first acted with extreme wariness, as years passed and no shadow of suspicion fell on him, he had tended to neglect his earlier strict precautions. His long immunity had given him an almost superstitious faith in his own cleverness. The corrupt and crafty official who despised men of honor as slaves to empty fancies had himself succumbed to the most dangerous of illusions—that he could never be found out.

Now the impossible had happened—and with crushing suddenness.

The Emperor had sent for him about an hour after midday. It was not the time for a routine summons. Still, Eros was untroubled as he picked up his tablets and a batch of returns he had summarized for the Emperor and walked briskly round to the Praetorian Tent.

Even the Emperor's bleak and menacing look as he entered did not warn him. He had seen it often enough before. Indifferently he thought, Somebody's going to catch it! "Ready, Your Majesty," he said and approached the table.

Harsh and deliberate, the Emperor's first words stopped him short. "You have been accused of taking a bribe. Have you anything to say?"

441

A gush of terror went through Eros. The grave had opened at his feet.

It was some moments before he could begin to master his panic. "A bribe!" he stammered, through lips gone ashen. "Oh, no! Your Majesty. No!"

The Emperor regarded him stonily. "Do you know Leonidas of Byzantium—a cattle merchant?"

It was hard to think clearly, hard to seek out plausible words, under those eyes that had looked unmoved on so much death. Eros shivered. His brain, usually so nimble and resourceful, had turned traitor. He plunged . . .

"I have never heard of him!"

The Emperor stirred a little. "You can tell him that to his face. He is being brought to the camp tomorrow. Meanwhile, here's his statement." A document lay on the table. The Emperor pushed it forward.

Eros did not move. He stared at the document dumbly.

"You had better find your tongue," the Emperor went on. "The charge is a capital one! Last week over forty men of the Seventh Gallic Cavalry reported sick after eating some meat. Two died. I ordered an inquiry. The meat was traced to cattle supplied by this man, Leonidas. Something else was discovered. He was not on the list of dealers recommended by the authorities at Byzantium—he has been in prison for fraud. His name was added later—on your instructions, Eros. The order is signed by you!"

A faint sound came from Eros. The Emperor waited, but as Eros did not speak, he resumed after a little:

"I had him questioned. They soon made him talk! His statement names a go-between. Some shady character, called Pamphilus, who's disappeared. There was a pass to the camp in his lodging when they searched it . . .

"I trusted you, Eros!" the implacable voice continued. "I gave you a free hand. You signed that order—why? If you can't explain, then you did it for a bribe. It won't have been the first time, either. It will certainly be the last!"

A short interval followed these lethal words. "Still nothing to say? . . . Very well, you are under arrest. Get your files ready to hand over. On no account leave Headquarters lines. All pickets and sentries have been warned."

From far off Eros heard the curt dismissal, "That is all." He had a confused recollection of stumbling out, of soldiers staring. Somehow he had made his way, without collapsing, to his own tent.

He sat there almost overcome, unable to rally himself, until his glance, wandering without direction, fell upon the hourglass. He blinked, aware in a blurred way of a message from it beating against his brain. Suddenly, his eyes widened and he started back. Nearly an hour had passed since the Emperor's summons! Tomorrow, his confrontation with Leonidas, the short, hurried trial, the inevitable verdict and, before another day had passed, the sword flashing down on his neck—all were nearly one hour closer!

Almost sobbing, he seized a sheet, on which he wrote two shaky lines. He screamed a name.

One of the clerks, an elderly, meager-looking man with a deferential air, hurried in and found Eros scribbling the superscription on a sealed note. "Take this, at once. He's somewhere in the camp. Hurry, damn you! Hurry!" The clerk gaped at the shrill impatience of his normally cold and aloof superior and at his ghastly pallor.

Before the clerk had left the tent, Eros had snatched another sheet and was feverishly writing.

Twice Eros reversed the hourglass before the entrance flap was thrust aside and Mucapor ducked in. He scowled at Eros, for whom he had never hidden his dislike, and strode up to the table.

"Well, what the thunder is it?" he growled. "Don't you know I'm in the middle of inspections?" His truculent manner did not disguise a certain uneasiness.

Eros had had time to bring himself under firm control. He eyed Mucapor steadily. He had always felt contempt for these rough and ignorant soldiers, so slow-witted in everything that did not pertain to war. A simple tough promoted to command a Legion, that was Mucapor. He'd never rise higher—he hadn't the brain for anything more complicated.

But would he be stupid *enough*?

Well, the chance had to be taken. The only hope was to scare

Mucapor into acting. Scare him badly enough to shake his dumb loyalty to that butcher. For Mucapor had everything a crude parade-ground bully could dream of—liquor, women, fancy badges, the chance to throw his weight about—and all of it he owed to the Emperor.

"Come on, man!" rasped Mucapor. "I haven't got all day! Out with it!"

Eros opened a drawer in the table and slowly drew out a long sheet, which he held up toward Mucapor. "I found this in the Praetorian Tent—in one of the Emperor's personal files. Read those names. . . . No, hands off, General—I'll hold it."

Mucapor glowered but, stooping a little, began to read the list wavering in Eros' clutch; his lips slowly formed the syllables.

"Here, what's this?" he demanded. "Probus . . . and my name's there. Ventidius, too, near the top . . ."

"Probus has already left for Egypt, or I'd have sent for him," said Eros. "My own name's there—lower down," he added with a little, sickly smile. Mucapor frowned and began again to scan the list with painful concentration. "That's right," he agreed, after a while. "There's half the generals." Obviously he was not concerned about the few civilians at the foot of the list.

"What's it all mean?" His rough tone was troubled.

Eros swallowed. "Death!" he said with a twitch. "All of us—I've seen the instructions. Arrest tonight, after Lights Out. No trial. Execution, dawn tomorrow!"

Mucapor's face went purple. Bloodshot eyes bulged at Eros who watched him in a suspense that was almost unbearable. It was a little while before Mucapor could bring words out.

"But why—why?" he choked.

The shrug of Eros conveyed that there was no accounting for a madman's savage caprices. "You know the Emperor," he said. He emphasized the "you." The simple flattery convinced Mucapor as no evidence could have done.

He grabbed at the list, but Eros whipped it away just in time. "Give me that!" demanded Mucapor thickly. "I want to show it to Ventidius and Constans. They're on it. Give it to me, I tell you!"

444

His seamed forehead glistened. "Only for an hour—I'll bring it back."

"All right," said Eros, grudgingly. "Just an hour. If he finds out!" He contorted his face in a grimace expressive of stupefying wrath.

"He won't find out," Mucapor muttered, folding the list with fumbling fingers.

He shambled toward the entrance with head bowed, a man who had aged ten years in the last minutes. At the tent flap, he raised his head and turned, showing his teeth. "Don't you worry," he said hoarsely. "He won't find out!"

Alone in the Praetorian Tent, Aurelian was frowning over the day's returns of sick and absentees, when a quick, shuffling sound caught his ear. He looked up angrily as five men came pushing in together. At once his expression changed. Though their hands were empty, he read their errand in their taut, scared faces and averted eyes.

They stood in a ragged, silent line, confronting him. Mucapor stepped forward and grasped his sword hilt. A few moments later five naked blades pointed unsteadily at the Emperor.

Now all were moving toward him.

Aurelian sprang up. The table overturned, the papers went flying. "Guard!" he shouted. The faces before him gave no sign and he knew that the sentries had been ordered away; nobody was within earshot. He did not remember then that he was the Elect of Mithras, proclaimed on coins as AURELIAN BORN LORD AND GOD. The pang that assailed his heart was the fearful realization of a mortal man that his time was come. But he roused himself to die fighting. Round he swung and snatched up the chair. He glared at the conspirators, who closed in slowly as if enacting some ancient ritual of reluctant killing; then, he fastened his fierce and bitter gaze on Mucapor, who was still the foremost, and flung the chair at him.

Mucapor dodged. It skimmed past and thudded on the ground some distance behind.

Bare-handed now, Aurelian stood warily, head thrust out, fists clenched. Mucapor was drawing back his sword arm. His eyes,

445

which would not meet Aurelian's, flickered as though he were dazed.

Aurelian launched himself forward, flinging out a hand to seize Mucapor's wrist. His fingers closed on air. Fire split his chest. A long, hoarse gasp came from him. He drew himself up shuddering, his face twisted, unaware that after Mucapor the other conspirators were striking at him. For a few moments he towered among them; then he sagged a little and pitched over.

They jumped back to avoid the heavy body. The crash with which it hit the ground almost unnerved them.

Speechless, they gazed down at their handiwork. Mucapor was the first to stir. He looked from the red sun swelling round Aurelian's heart to his own dripping sword and back again. I killed him! he thought with a heartbroken and baffled guilt, I alone killed him! See . . . those cowards! They all swore they would share the killing, but they only struck at his shoulders and arms!

Now the others were staring at him, mutely imploring some word that would set them free from their awful spell.

"We had to do it!" Mucapor muttered. "It was him—or us!"

As soon as the courier from the Army reached the Senate, Eutropius was deputed to break the news to the Empress. In the Palace the lamps were already being kindled. He entered the Imperial apartment, his simple, kindly face clouded with sorrow, not for Aurelian, whom he had admired with trembling, but for the bitter grief he was bringing the Empress. At the sight of his pitiful expression, she stood up, hand to her breast.

He gulped, then said, dragging the words out, "Augusta . . . the Emperor . . ." He gestured despairingly. "He's dead." Unhappily he gazed at the white-faced Empress, who had not moved. "They assassinated him. . . ."

She did not ask who "they" were. What did it matter? Aurelian was gone. He would not return.

"The Senate is trying to ascertain the full facts. A delegation will wait on Your Majesty—tomorrow, early."

She began to sway a little and the tears welled out and trickled down her cheeks. Mistily, she saw Eutropius bend toward her and she motioned him to go away. Poor man, she thought, feeling even

446

in this moment of agony that she had been less than courteous to a good friend who had undertaken a distressing duty through affection for her. "Thank you, Eutropius," she muttered towards his dejected back.

Aurelian dead! How could it be true? Yet it was true! She would never see him again—speak to him—hear his voice that made "Severina" sound the name of a conquering Legion!

She felt the steel that had killed him embed itself in her own breast and bowed herself, writhing. Sob after sob made her shudder. She sank down and abandoned herself to the tears that were pouring now in an irresistible flood.

After a while her women, peeping in, saw her lying almost inert, save for an occasional long tremor. Frightened, they ran to fetch Julia. They found the girl surrounded by her mute, awestruck classmates. She did not move as the women approached, but sat staring straight ahead. It was less grief that dazed her than a shock of incredulity that death should take away her father, such a tall, strong, grim man, feared by everyone. Dimly she had a feeling that an act of earth-shaking impiety had taken place, that Nature had committed treason.

The women led her gently to her mother. Severina must have heard her step or sensed her presence, for she raised herself and turned her pallid face as soon as Julia came in. The girl stumbled into her arms and they wept together, comforted by each other's closeness.

Eventually Julia, worn out by so much violent emotion, fell asleep with her head in her mother's lap. Severina tried not to disturb this calm and healing sleep of youth. But as time went by Julia's weight became more and more oppressive and she called her women, who roused the girl with some difficulty and carried her off to bed.

Severina sat on alone. Confusedly she thought of her years with Aurelian, every fresh memory quickening her anguish, and tried to grasp that he was lying somewhere far away, collapsed and lifeless. He had vibrated with force; his energy had galvanized an Empire. Now there was not a breath, not a flicker in him.

His murder would be a heavy blow to Rome. Yet, apart from herself and Julia and his few companions in arms, would anyone

447

mourn Aurelian deeply? Severina wondered dully what his death would mean to the Gothic woman at Tibur. Always as background to her thoughts was an awareness of the huge Palace, wakeful with the news. Many in it, she had no doubt, were openly exulting. She and Julia were already strangers in what that morning had been their home. They were no more now than the widow and orphan of an Emperor; soon others would come pushing in to take his place and theirs.

Weighted with pain, the gray hours stretched slowly out and passed. Severina was startled to observe that light had begun to grow. She longed to call back the darkness that was ebbing from the world. Night should have lingered to hide her sorrow, day refused to dawn.

With a new desolating pang, she reflected that it was yesterday when she had learned of Aurelian's death. Yesterday! It consigned him to the past. In the next instant she had unconsciously accepted the fact that he had fallen out from her life for ever.

By full light she was calm again. Sorrow had exacted its first overpowering tribute and she had wept herself empty. Already she had begun to philosophize. Aurelian had escaped her before his assassination. The sane and sober soldier she had married had vanished in the possessed and daemon-driven Emperor.

She let the women bathe her face and hands and took a few sips of warm milk. Then she changed her robe and went to receive the deputation of which Eutropius had spoken; headed by Tacitus, it brought condolences from the Senate.

The old man's sympathy was genuine, she could see that. Yet it was possible to detect relief and even elation in some of the others. By the world Aurelian would be remembered as the restorer of Rome's greatness, but the image he had left in the minds of most Senators was rather that of a heavy-handed autocrat, of relentless driving power, who had shown contempt for their privileges and whose swift, rigorous justice had not spared members of their own order.

"The Empire is now without a formal head," said Tacitus. "However, it is the unanimous wish of the Senate in the present unhappy circumstances that Your Majesty be regarded as holding the supreme place in the Roman State for the time being."

"As it is your unanimous wish, very well."

"Of course," went on Tacitus, "in this period of mourning, dear Augusta, you cannot be expected to devote yourself to the exacting business of government."

She looked at him with ironical eyes until he appeared a little disconcerted.

"Naturally," she said.

"The Senate has already appointed a committee, of which I have the honor to be chairman, to administer the State until more permanent arrangements can be made."

He waited, rather uncomfortably, for Severina to comment. She merely gave a slight shrug.

"I regret that we must intrude further on Your Majesty's sorrow," he resumed. He held out a letter with its seal broken. "This message arrived yesterday by special courier from the Army near Byzantium."

In her unsteady hand the lines blurred. The Senators watched in silence as she read:

"The brave and fortunate Armies to the Senate and People of Rome. The crime of one man and the error of many have deprived us of the late Emperor Aurelian. May it please you, venerable Lords and Fathers, to place him in the number of the Gods and to appoint a successor whom your judgment shall declare worthy of the Imperial Purple. None of those whose guilt or misfortune has contributed to our loss shall ever reign over us."

She looked at Tacitus. "What does this mean?" No effort could keep her voice from faltering.

"The courier is outside, Augusta, if you wish to question him. But, briefly, this is what appears to have happened . . ."

Tensely she listened to the aged, tremulous voice. At its tale of cunning and folly, of scared men striking desperately, loathing what they did, her grief was darkened by horror. She had not dreamed that among his murderers were members of Aurelian's innermost circle!

The least surprising name was that of Eros. Curiously, she felt

449

no clamor of hatred at the thought of him. His fatal role had almost the appearance of having been foreordained. She should have dismissed him from the Palace before Aurelian set eyes on him, but she had been too weak. She had warned Aurelian about him, but he would not listen. Eros had proved too clever for her—to Aurelian's undoing and his own.

But Mucapor! His was the stupefying name!

Aurelian had been his idol. Though rough and insensitive, he had felt that potent quality of leadership in Aurelian and responded with an honest devotion. This attachment had been reinforced by a heavy debt of gratitude for benefits received over many years. Aurelian had picked him out, given him the opportunity to distinguish himself, opened his way to advancement and honors. But for the man he had murdered, the chances were that Mucapor would still be an obscure Centurion, without a hope of rising higher in the Service. She never could have imagined that anything would make him turn against the Emperor to whom he owed so much.

Nor could she ever have imagined such a panic reaction to the lies of Eros on the part of so tough and brutally courageous a soldier.

Ventidius, too, who had served her so well, whose promotion she had so vigorously recommended. Till now she would have thought of him not only as a brave and intelligent soldier, but also as an intensely loyal one, touchingly proud that his birthplace was near his Emperor's.

How can you guard against Fate if the ministers of its injuries are those you have yourself raised up, enriched, made close to your person?

She forced herself to heed what Tacitus was saying. ". . . Even in our grief, Your Majesty, we feel deep gratification that the Army has remained faithful to the constitution of the State." His tone was unctuous and behind him heads were nodding. Indeed, what had happened was very strange. The soldiers, in their dismay and bewilderment at Aurelian's murder, had resigned the privilege they had usurped for a hundred years and now were actually calling on the Senate to nominate an Emperor. How ironical that Aurelian, who had hated the Senate, should—by reimbuing the Army with its ancient discipline—have been responsible for the restoration of this traditional right!

No wonder there was undisguised exultation on the faces of some of the Senators. Visions of renewed grandeur for their Assembly and their class, so long deprived of real power, intoxicated them.

Their folly was of no importance to her. Her one concern at the moment was to hear the fullest account of how the soldiers had turned upon the murderers of their Emperor. What had led them to compose that extraordinary message to the Senate?

"Have the courier brought in, please," she requested Tacitus.

A wiry, brown-skinned man, with darting, observant eyes and an air of confidence, was shown in. He answered Severina promptly. "It was like this, Your Majesty . . ."

When the news flashed through the camp, the men were thunderstruck. It couldn't be true. Not Aurelian! Not old Hand-on-hilt! Only when a junior officer went the rounds, shamefacedly announcing that Mucapor was going to address a full parade, did they emerge from their stupefaction. Hardly anyone obeyed the summons. They milled round, waiting for a lead.

It came from the Centurions, who—reversing their customary role—incited the men to rise. In ugly mood a great crowd poured into the Headquarters lines. One of the clerks was seized and roughly questioned; from him they discovered that Mucapor and his confederates were in the Praetorian Tent. As the soldiers came surging in, they found the general with Eros, gazing at him in consternation. Mucapor looked wildly round; then pointed to Eros and groaned, "He put us up to it, the lying bastard!" Two men grabbed at Mucapor, but with the face of a madman he flung himself past them and dealt the cringing Eros a blow that split his lip and sent him staggering against the wall; his knees buckled and he slumped to the ground. Amid uproar the generals were arrested; two or three drew their swords and had to be overpowered, but Mucapor made no resistance. A couple of enraged legionaries stooped over Eros, from whose bloody mouth came moans for mercy; they yanked him up and dragged him away toward the Guard Tent. They were followed by a mob of shouting soldiers, who pummeled and kicked at him, until his body went limp.

451

The generals were marched to Mucapor's tent, round which a strong guard was posted.

Rough but reverent hands washed the Emperor's corpse. It was laid out on his own simple camp bed and covered with one of his purple cloaks. Four First Centurions mounted a Guard of Honor.

After that, thousands of soldiers flooded on to the main parade ground. A table and stool were carried there from the Headquarters lines. Watched by the immense, silent throng, one of the Emperor's secretaries, who had been found hiding among the clerks, was escorted up to the table, before which three senior Centurions had stationed themselves. As soon as he sat down, they began arguing loudly in an effort to decide the terms of a Declaration from the Army to the Senate; at intervals one or another would turn to shout at the secretary. Their wrangling went on until he raised his hand to ask their attention and assured them that he understood exactly what they meant. They fell quiet, while he transcribed in his own elegant writing and polished phrases the gist of their muddled dictation.

He stood up. The hush deepened. Straining his voice to reach as many as possible of his huge audience, he read slowly and distinctly from his tablets.

There came back a tremendous roar of approval.

Once the courier had finished his terse and lively narrative and had been dismissed, Tacitus put on a very solemn expression.

"Our next duty, Augusta, will be to arrange for the late Emperor's apotheosis," he announced. "He has been acknowledged as most worthy to rank among the Gods. Everything should be in order for the ceremonies to begin tomorrow."

Severina found it hard to restrain a bitter smile. Poor Aurelian! So at last he was to be indisputably a god—by virtue of some empty ceremonial performed by petty men who were secretly relieved at his murder!

"Now finally, Augusta," Tacitus said briskly, minute by minute more emancipated from the deference which, as the living Aurelian's Empress, she had inspired in him, "there is a strong sentiment among the Senators that you yourself should have a voice in the matter of your late husband's successor. It is felt that—ahem—a

452

choice approved by you would—er—recommend itself more readily to the Army."

They all stared at her eagerly, except Tacitus, who looked modestly down. It was easy to see on whose behalf they were soliciting her support; hard to see this prosy old man, amiable and well intentioned but without force of character, bearing the burden which had crushed younger, far stronger and abler men; hard to see that palsied hand wielding the sword of Aurelian.

"Choose Probus!" she said.

They looked sour. Tacitus wrinkled his face and pulled nervously at his beard. He exchanged a glance with his colleagues. "Your Majesty's proposal," he said without enthusiasm, "will be communicated to a full assembly of the Senate."

Severina heard him with indifference. What did it matter if that ancient wore Aurelian's crown? It would not hurt Aurelian nor bring him back to her.

She was not surprised when, after weeks of interregnum and anxious and irresolute debate, during which the Army and people waited obediently and she was accorded the honors of a reigning Empress, the choice of the Senate fell on Tacitus.

33

BEFORE many months, Tacitus having been murdered in his turn, the Legions threw off their unaccustomed docility and proclaimed Probus Emperor. He hurried to Rome to formalize his accession and to prepare for a campaign in Gaul, which was being inundated by barbarians from across the Rhine.

An embassy of Gothic nobles rode into the city not long after him. They brought congratulations from their High King to the new Augustus—and a request that, having regard to the fidelity with which the Goths had observed their treaty with Rome, their hostages and numerous captives in the Empire should be restored to them.

The move was shrewdly timed. With a fierce struggle of uncertain duration opening in Gaul, it was politic for Probus to retain the goodwill of the Goths even at the cost of a humiliating concession. He accepted the embassy's demand and at once began the necessary arrangements. Among the most important of those to be repatriated early was Hunilda, who following Aurelian's death had managed to get a message through to her father, the kinglet of one of the Gothic subtribes; he had long given her up as dead.

To Severina, who was living in already obscure retirement at the villa in the Alban Hills which had been her first home with Aurelian, came an invitation in pressing terms to the Palace. Probus had written in his own hand and the letter was brought early in the day by one of his personal aides. Accompanied by him, Severina set out immediately for Rome by litter.

Unfamiliar guards were at the Palace gate, under a strange officer. Neither they nor the few domestics she encountered in the corridors, while being conducted to the Imperial presence, recognized in this veiled, soberly dressed woman, with something of a country air, the Empress of less than a year ago.

Probus received her in the very apartment she and Aurelian had occupied. Here nothing had changed. Tacitus had enjoyed no respite to settle down in the Palace; Probus was merely camping there for a number of days while the field army completed its concentration. Yet, though everything was as she had left it, she felt the place alien to her. It had never been truly a home, the scene of a tranquil family life, of the mild, wholesomely monotonous domestic routine, made up of many small and intimate things, so deeply satisfying to a woman. Here, with the dregs of her energy, she had grappled in Aurelian's absence with continuing crisis. Here, on his return, Aurelian had worn away his strength with labor at an impossible task and lost himself in fantasies of destruction.

Once she had thought of this vast and complex ornate structure, reared by megalomaniac Emperors, as peopled with the malevolent or pathetic ghosts of Rome's Imperial past. Now her own ghosts thronged there, all pitiful—Aurelian himself—Mucapor, who had loved and murdered him—Eros, all his cunning no defense against the executioner—Ventidius, her right arm in an emergency of the utmost peril—Tacitus, climbing on shaky old legs to the fatal summit of the world—and how many others?

Everything in her rejected this place of evil associations where the wounds she had thought were healing became raw again.

Probus greeted her warmly, taking her hand in his strong clasp. He had altogether lost his boyish look; on his lean and sternly handsome face Severina's experienced eyes could read a conscientious Emperor's inheritance—a hundred problems simultaneously urgent and a dozen that were desperate.

With genuine concern, Probus inquired about her health, but she appreciated that this and his felicitations on Julia's approaching marriage were preliminaries to matters of greater moment to the Emperor of Rome.

Soon he was alluding to affairs of state. She listen attentively, waiting for a clue to the reason for her summons to the Palace.

"I shall be leaving for Gaul—day after tomorrow. It's going to be a stiff campaign. The Franks and the Lygians—they're howling savages—have poured in. Tens of thousands of them. The Burgundians, too, are on the move."

Severina nodded. Her imagination was accustomed to vivify the clipped, practical phrases of a soldier Emperor. With her own eyes she had witnessed the havoc of barbarian invasion. All too graphically, she could now conjure up the blackened villages, the suburbs blazing round the ill-defended walls of towns. The Franks were an old and dangerous adversary poised against Northern Gaul. The wild Burgundians had broken their way through to the Rhine from somewhere on the Baltic. As for the Lygians, they were a ferocious horde, untouched by civilization, from the dark heart of the primeval forest of Central Europe.

She gazed at Probus with pity. Short of conquering first all Europe, then perhaps much of Asia, there was no final solution to the problem of the Empire's security. For when the tribes pressing against the frontier had been defeated and weakened, they became unable to resist the drift or thrust of still more savage tribes from the interior, also on the move west and south toward the rich lands beyond the Rhine and Danube. Obscure convulsions, such as those which had ejected the Goths onto the Sarmatian plains above the Black Sea, were in progress in the vast wilderness of woods and swamps stretching between the Baltic and the Roman borders. Probus, it appeared likely, would have to do much of Aurelian's work all over again.

There was a little pause. Probus was looking at her with some constraint. Abruptly he said, "There's something else I want to talk to you about—I'm afraid you'll find it rather painful."

He explained about the embassy from the Goths and went on, a little awkwardly, "You know, don't you, that Aurelian had a son by a Gothic woman, some princess of theirs, called Hunilda?"

Severina did not look away. A few moments passed. "Yes," she said quietly.

"The point is, Severina, we can't let the boy go with his mother. Aurelian's son, a Roman Emperor's son, in the hands of the Goths—you see how dangerous it would be. Barbarians don't take much account of legitimacy, anyway. It could lead to untold trouble."

"I see," murmured Severina, beginning to catch his drift.

"That's not all," resumed Probus. "If the boy stays here, he might also fall into the wrong hands. Plotters might use him—it's a tricky problem. Of course, it would be easy to do away with him, but I'd like to avoid that. An innocent child—and Aurelian's son! Look here, Severina. You can help me. Everyone knows you could have had the woman killed or at least turned out of her home, once Aurelian wasn't there to protect her. You left her alone, her and the child. There's nothing petty in you. You can even forgive an injury like that. That's why I'm appealing to you now." He touched her arm in what was almost a supplicating gesture. "Couldn't you take him—this boy? Look after him, bring him up? You I could trust absolutely!"

He paused, uncertain of her reaction. "Think about it," he urged. "After all, your own daughter will be leaving you soon. Forgive my haste—I've sprung this on you—but I must settle the matter one way or another before I go."

In agitation she told herself, this boy should have been my own

456

son—now he is being offered to me! She had never set eyes on him, yet he was no stranger to her imagination. She felt herself soften at the thought that he had need of her. And she, for her part, had need of him, of his tender youth, his helplessness. For soon she would be alone, with little but memories to occupy her. In three weeks Julia would become the bride of Hortensius and once she was gone the villa, though modest in size, would seem enormous and empty. Severina had no desire to share a home permanently with the young people; to do so would impose a strain on all three of them. Nor could she contemplate joining Drusilla (who, in any case, was still engaged in her grotesque and pathetic love affair and would not wish to have a relative as witness). There was Crinitus, of course. He was always pressing her to come and stay at Baiae. But she shrank from his bitter tongue, which had not spared even Aurelian.

Claudius would be the answer to her loneliness. He would enable her to maintain a home of her own. To care for him would restore a purpose to her life.

Still, she hesitated. He was the child of the woman who had drawn Aurelian away from her; every glance at him would be a reminder. Even more than this, the thought of Hunilda's loss weighed with Severina. It was hateful to be the instrument of another woman's bereavement. She was being offered ample revenge— but she had never sought revenge. After all, Hunilda had not deliberately wronged her.

A phrase of Probus' bored into her mind that made these considerations suddenly irrelevant: "It would be easy to do away with him." Aurelian's son—butchered! She stared at the intent face of Probus. He was a better man than Aurelian, though not so great, so vehement of will, so dominating. Yet he would obey the stern command of duty. He would kill with reluctance, but kill he would if he judged that reasons of state made it imperative. And soon he would be on the march! The child's life hung on her "yes" or "no."

"Very well," she said with a sigh. "I'll take him."

"Good!" he said heartily. "I'm sure you won't regret it. I'll send straight away to collect the boy."

She could not help smiling. How like an Illyrian, getting necessary things done promptly, but in a peremptory, roughshod way!

"The problem's solved, so there's no reason to be in a hurry, Probus. Just let her—the mother—know that I am to have the boy. I'll go a little later on and see her myself. Perhaps I should have done that already."

He pressed her hand, wishing to bring the interview to an end for other urgent matters waited his attention, sorry to deprive himself of her company.

"You won't regret it," he repeated. "Good-bye, dear friend!"

"Good-bye—and good fortune in the war!" She regarded him in silence for a few moments, this handsome, capable and confident man who could find time amid a grave emergency to be merciful. Then she said, "Look after yourself, Probus. The Empire needs you." They were commonplace phrases, but she knew he understood what she meant them to convey.

"Don't let them kill you—as they killed Aurelian!"

The villa proved to be a short distance outside Tibur on a little-frequented road. It was an inconspicuous place, doubly screened by a stone wall of a man's height and, within this, by numerous well grown trees. An aged porter received Severina at the gate and led her along a winding gravel path to the modest one-storey house with its simple portico.

As the litter grounded in the courtyard, a sturdy blonde young woman emerged from behind one of the pillars. Severina knew her at once for Hunilda. Her figure was too substantial and her limbs too large for gracefulness, but she moved with an assurance that made Severina think of her as stately rather than buxom. Making no obeisance, she greeted Severina with composure in halting, guttural Latin. Severina returned a brief, formal answer. Hunilda conducted her to a pleasant, spacious room, where two chairs—one deep and high-backed, with carved armrests, the other low, plain, and comfortable—stood facing each other. "Please sit," said Hunilda, indicating the tall seat—it must have been Aurelian's—and herself sat down opposite.

There was a little, strained silence while the two women took stock of each other. Hunilda's gaze was cool and steady; she held

458

herself erect and betrayed no awe of her visitor's exalted rank. The phrases of Herennianus came back to Severina: "I suppose you'd call her beautiful . . . these big, voluptuous Northern women." Hunilda's thick, glinting flaxen braids were coiled round her head, accentuating its broadness. Her skin was a flawless white and pink. The deep-blue eyes coldly regarding Severina were set wide apart under brows too pale. In her red lips, plump and a little pouting, was a hint of sensual ardor.

A beautiful face, Severina conceded, though a trifle florid, a trifle heavy, without much animation. For her body, too, Herennianus had found the right word: voluptuous. Those big, firm breasts and generous flanks invited hearty caresses.

Not a subtle character, not a character to have troubled Aurelian with her thoughts and moods. But she must have ministered to his pleasure with the zest of her own ripe body. Union with her must have been mindless and drowning, coupling on the most primitive level.

Soon, however, Severina began to feel ashamed of this uncharitable scrutiny. To harbor malice against Hunilda was foolish and unfair. Aurelian was dead. What was there left to resent, to envy, but some memories? After all, Hunilda had not sought to take her place; she had had no choice but to submit. More and more she appeared a pathetic figure.

"You know why I am here," Severina began suddenly.

A shadow passed over Hunilda's face. She inclined her head.

In that moment pity finally vanquished hostility in Severina. Poor Hunilda! she thought—doubly wronged. Ravished and then robbed of her child!

"I am glad I met you before you went home." Severina spoke slowly, so that this foreign woman could follow. "I want you to believe that I had no part in forcing you to give up your son. But I will try to love him and keep the memory of his mother alive in him."

Abruptly, her self-possession forsook Hunilda. The look she gave Severina was harsh with pain. Her eyes glittered, but they remained dry.

"I do not blame you. I understand that Aurelian's son must not

459

be brought up among the Goths," she said, helped by the tardiness with which the Latin words suggested themselves to keep her voice under control. "It is hard to bear. But I know that you will be good to him." She spoke without warmth, almost grudgingly. "They tell me you have a heart full of kindness."

At this the tears welled into Severina's eyes. Hunilda could not resist the contagion. She stood up, her mouth twisted. A desolating moan escaped her. She stared wildly at Severina, who rose and put out a trembling, compassionate hand to her hot cheek. For a few moments, Aurelian's Empress and his concubine looked at each other without reserve or pretense. Then they drew apart, both ashamed of having acknowledged their kinship in suffering.

After an interval, Hunilda said in a manner less unfriendly than before, "No, do not keep my memory alive in Claudius. It is enough that I shall remember him when I am far from this land. It is enough that I shall long for my son and weep for him when I am alone at night." Hunilda's halting delivery and mispronunciations did not make her words less poignant in Severina's ear. Her heart ached for this afflicted mother.

"Perhaps you will marry again and have other children," she said gently. "Other sons—I myself," she added with a sigh, "never had a son."

"Of course I shall marry again and have other children," answered Hunilda, not hiding her scorn for this barren Roman woman. "The High King will find me a Gothic hero, a prince among warriors, and I shall bear him brave and handsome sons!"

Severina saw that Hunilda's was not a case for unmeasured pity. Her wound would bleed, but it would heal. A fertile barbarian wife, she would gradually forget her grief for her lost Claudius in the joys and cares of rearing an ample brood.

One last question, Severina decided, before she asked to see the boy. It was painful to put; perhaps painful to answer. Better come straight to the point. "Did you love Aurelian?" she asked quietly.

Hunilda's brow wrinkled in her search for Latin phrases.

"How could I love him—a Roman who had slain my husband of less than a year and made a slave of me, a princess of the Goths? At first I hated him. I tried to kill him with his own dagger, but he was too quick and strong. Still, he was very kind to me and made me many gifts, rich gifts—my sisters will be jealous when I show them," she added, with a little, complacent smile. "And he was a famous warrior, greater even than our own champions! I liked him very much, at least after Claudius was born."

She paused and her expression hardened. "But Rome I have always hated!" The words came with an arrogant ring. "One day we shall come again, we Goths. This Probus, he will die as Aurelian died. There will be no one to stop us. We shall take revenge then for all our dead and for all the Goths Rome has made slaves. And we shall stay and rule, for the strong must always rule the weak!"

Severina had flushed, but she choked back the impulse to retort with Roman pride to this crude and cruel vaunting. There was no point in bandying taunts with somebody who spoke as though the Goths had been the victims of aggression—and who, in the same breath, claimed for them a natural right to conquer and enslave! In any case, she could afford to be tolerant; this untamed savage was the mother of Claudius. Ignoring Hunilda's outburst, she said with calm authority, "Send for Claudius, please. I want to spend some time with him every day, so that when you go he will not feel he has been left among strangers."

A little later, Claudius stood shyly before the simply dressed, strange lady with her gentle, searching dark eyes, and reassuring smile. He did not draw back when she took his hand and he gazed up at her with interest when she spoke to him in a pleasant voice, free from the roughness he was accustomed to in his mother's.

Severina's first glance at him had dispelled her instinctive fear. Claudius strongly favored Aurelian; decidedly he was not a copy of his mother.

"Don't use such baby talk," Hunilda said brusquely. "He's getting on for five." Severina knew then that she had betrayed too much softness at sight of the boy—her eyes had already taken possession of him. No wonder his mother suffered, looking on. Indeed the boy, with his big frame and firmly defined masculine features, would have seemed older than five, but for his innocent blue eyes and white, almost girlish skin.

461

"You must not spoil him," went on Hunilda, her tone still sharp. "Claudius is going to be a soldier. That is what his father wished. He told me so," she added with spiteful emphasis, "many times!"

"We shall see," answered Severina mildly. "But don't worry about my spoiling him. I have made up my mind to leave Italy. Claudius will live with me on a little estate of my family in Spain. He will get a nobleman's education, but he will learn to farm and work with his hands like a Roman of the old school. When he grows up, he will be free to become a soldier, if he wishes. But I intend to bring him up as a Christian and it is not easy for Christians to serve in the Army."

"I did not know you were a Christian," said Hunilda. She spoke indifferently, for these Roman religions meant little to her.

"No, I'm not—I'm not anything. Belief is difficult for someone like me. I've got a skeptical—a questioning—kind of mind," explained Severina patiently, feeling that all this was going over Hunilda's head. "I might have become a Christian once, but Aurelian forbade it. I was young then; to believe was easier. Now I'm used to living without faith—I suppose I've come to prefer it. Still, it is hard for a child if you tell him the sky is empty. Claudius will be happier if he has something to hold on to. I cannot teach him to believe in Rome's old gods. They are dead. People are turning to new religions. I have chosen the best of them. I know quite a number of Christians. They are mostly good and upright persons. I should like Claudius to grow up like them."

Hunilda had listened without much interest, though what she had understood left her a little puzzled. It was prudent to observe the ancient ritual and not to stint the gods of their due sacrifices; then they would prosper the harvest and protect the herds and flocks and—though less certainly—help the tribe in battle. But she could not see what they had to do with being good and upright.

Smiling faintly, Severina continued, more to herself than to Hunilda, "Besides, I have an absurd feeling that before Claudius is an old man we shall have a Christian Emperor on the Throne!"

Some time after Hunilda had started on her homeward journey, a letter from Herennianus reached Severina. ". . . The campaign is going brilliantly. Probus is an inspired general. We've smashed the Lygians. . . . What is this I hear about you leaving Italy? Why not stay—and let me join you? Just say the word, Severina, and I'll quit the Army. You know that I am yours to command. I ask nothing in return but to be near you and be useful to you. I am no pattern of virtue, but there is one person for whom I feel a pure and disinterested devotion—and you know who she is."

Severina reflected for a long while over this letter, though the thoughts it prompted were concerned more with Claudius than with Herennianus. Stay in Italy? No. Spain, a less exposed province, would be better for the child. One day, the Goths or some other fierce invaders from the North would come storming deep into Italy. Rome with its accumulated riches would always draw the hungry tribes.

Again, Claudius would be a Christian in a household partly Christian. Perhaps the persecutions would begin once more. There could be few places safer from the attentions of a state inquisition than a small manor house in Southern Spain.

These, however, were not decisive considerations. The main reason why she must go into virtual exile from her family lay in the brutal fact that there never could be security for Aurelian's son in Italy. Even the humane and sympathetic Probus had been gravely disturbed by his existence; even he was troubled lest conspirators use Claudius. And what if Probus died—suddenly, as Roman Emperors were wont to die nowadays? Overnight the Throne might pass to some bloodthirsty soldier untouched by reverence for Aurelian's memory.

At once Claudius would be in peril. Not Julia—even a suspicious tyrant would hardly regard her as a potential rival. But a former Emperor's son might easily attract the interest of some group or faction seeking a candidate of their own for the Purple. Few in Rome would be surprised if the reigning Emperor preferred to take no chances with Claudius.

There was another danger—from Claudius himself. As he grew, he might feel the temptation of his glorious parentage. The prospect of the Purple could dazzle a young man. In Italy, with Rome the terminus of at most a few days' travel, the mirage might appear very real. In distant Spain, his horizons would be limited. Rome would represent little more than a glamorous legend, the Throne something far beyond the sweep of his imagination.

The conviction had by this time taken root in Severina that it was Aurelian himself who had entrusted Claudius to her safekeeping. Now as when he was alive, she would not fail him. She would accept the obligation he had laid upon her, with all its consequences —the foremost of which was that she must retire from Italy and settle down with Claudius in Spain.

In that distant, tranquil countryside his boyhood would not be overshadowed. No one would trouble about his paternity. No one would consider him a threat. No one would seek to kindle dangerous ambitions in him. He would be lost to sight of Rome, its Rulers and its politicians. In Spain both she and Claudius would be forgotten; only in that lay safety for him and the chance of happiness.

As for Herennianus, she had been fond of him, but he could not possibly take Aurelian's place. No man could. Aurelian had been a Titan in strength, will, and achievement; toward the end a tormented Titan, in bondage to grandiose and violent dreams. Even his faults were on the heroic scale. Once such a man has your heart he will never release it; even in the grave he holds it fast. She had no remnant left of love to give to any other man. The truth was that Aurelian, living or dead, would brook no rivals; the thought of him extinguished them. Set against his memory Herennianus, gallant and gifted cavalry captain though he was, shrank to nothing.

Her refusal would have to be uncompromising. That Herennianus had written with complete sincerity she had no doubt; he was convinced of his own disinterestedness. But he was an ardent man, in the full vigor of his years. She could not imagine him long content with the self-denying role which he had proposed for himself.

That same day she penned her answer. "You were born to be a soldier. It is the only possible career for you. Your offer has reminded me what a generous heart you have, but I cannot possibly permit you to sacrifice so much for my sake. I ask you to stay on in the Army. Probus is a noble Emperor—serve him as loyally as you served my husband. If, unhappily, we lose him, attach yourself to Diocletian. I feel his hour is coming.

"Guard yourself well, dear friend, and may you find some day the happy love you deserve. As for me, I shall always think of myself as Aurelian's widow."

Her farewells were quickly over. A year ago she had been an Empress, but of the throng who surrounded her then, few had any interest left in her; courtiers have short memories for those no longer great. The Illyrian commanders whose affection for herself she cherished were away in Gaul, fighting. She had no close ties with any of the Senatorial families, save that of Eutropius, to which Julia now belonged because of her marriage with his nephew, Hortensius.

The worthy Senator had aged considerably since that crowded lifetime ago (though no more than six years by the chronicles) when he had escorted her from Sirmium to Rome. He was deeply affected by her decision to leave Italy and repeatedly warned her about the danger of the long, burning Spanish summers to her health, which he pronounced already far from satisfactory. In his simple way he showed a sympathetic understanding of her motives and a shrewd practical sense that surprised her. "Don't cut yourself off altogether, dear lady!" he implored. "If not for our sakes, for the boy's. Something might happen"—he was afraid to put his forebodings about her into explicit words—"and he may have need of friends."

Severina pointed out that she was not cutting herself off altogether from Italy. She would be leaving behind dear relatives who were unfit to travel and it was her intention to return at intervals, very quietly, to see them. Even this did not allay his anxiety. However, he appeared a little more cheerful when she invited him to accompany Julia and Hortensius on their first visit to her in a few months' time.

Julia did not exhibit keen distress at the prospect of a long separation from her mother, both because she was not demonstrative and because for her the parting was not an excessively painful one. Their temperaments were dissimilar and a true intimacy had never grown between them. At this time, too, Julia was largely absorbed in her own new happiness. Married younger than Severina had

465

been, she enjoyed the advantage of a husband of amiable nature, well suited to her in years and tastes and who ardently returned her feeling.

However, Julia's wedded happiness had not prevented her from feeling considerable mortification over young Claudius. From the start she would have nothing to do with him. Severina was hardly surprised by her shame and resentment at the sudden intrusion of a bastard half-brother. She could only assure Julia that her own interests would not suffer on account of him. The Alban villa would pass to her as soon as her mother left for Spain. In due course she and her children would inherit the bulk of the family property of all kinds. Claudius would be only a minor beneficiary under Severina's will (though she was determined, while she lived, to give him love without stint).

While Julia remained adamant in her refusal to acknowledge Claudius, Hortensius soon made friends with him. Once, during a visit of the newlyweds to the Alban villa, Severina, who had gone to her bedroom to fetch a bracelet which she wished to give Julia, caught the voice of Hortensius, slow and very distinct, coming from the garden. She went to the window. He stood not far away with a hand on the shoulder of Claudius, who listened engrossed while he explained in simple terms some design he was tracing with a stick on the ground. When he had finished, Claudius turned his head and looked up at him; the two exchanged a grin of comradeship.

It was a disappointment to Severina that she herself had been unable to reach a closer understanding with her attractive and talented son-in-law. He always showed her great respect—too much for spontaneous affection. She sensed that he was never quite at ease in her presence. His first and probably abiding impression of her had been formed when she was a reigning Augusta and Consort of an Emperor held in fear by the whole Senatorial class. She could not deny that she was accustomed to giving orders and had the reputation of being exceptionally strong-minded, even a little eccentric. A spirited, independent young man, with a new, adoring wife, was bound to feel himself cramped in the society of such a mother-in-law.

It would not be without regret that he would say good-bye to her aboard her ship at Ostia, but her departure would be something of a release and he would think of her with more warmth in her absence.

Severina found Drusilla in the midst of griefs more shattering than the voluntary exile of a step-daughter. Marcellus the Steward, her favorite, had absconded, taking with him her little serving maid, Myrrhina. His desertion and the discovery that he had been deceiving her with a girl of her own household had so demoralized Drusilla that she was even neglecting the sacred rites of her toilet. She received Severina in an ill-fitting robe of bygone fashion. Gray streaks showed in her raggedly piled hair. Without their accustomed paint her cheeks were sallow and coarse-grained and their flabbiness was accentuated. Her eyes, puffy with weeping, filled once more as she poured out her incoherent story to Severina. The unhappy woman hardly listened to what Severina had to say, but came back again and again, inconsequentially, to her own distresses.

A new steward had been appointed. Severina sent for him, to get a clearer account of what had happened. He was an elderly man, stooping and goat-bearded, and his breath was odorous with garlic. In despair, he unfolded an incredible tale of the consequences of Drusilla's doting trust in Marcellus. Revenues had been embezzled wholesale. Estate property had been sold and the proceeds had simply vanished. These depredations, once cautious, had become unbridled during the past year; their scale of late was such that Marcellus must have found it increasingly difficult to hide them, even from the unsuspicious Drusilla.

An exact estimate of the losses would be impossible, added the steward. The accounts were in a hopeless muddle. Nor could the servants be relied on to give honest information; the entire household had been involved, one way or another, in the plundering. "I shall have to get rid of the lot!" the steward lamented, clutching his beard.

Severina grew more and more anxious as she listened. However, just before he finished, she had an inspiration. She would report the situation to the senior member of Drusilla's family, an aged but still active cousin, known for his shrewd, ruthless and immensely profitable manipulations of the Egyptian corn supply. Even his distant supervision of the estate would be some protection for his giddy and improvident relative.

When Severina announced her intention, the steward pulled a long face. She had the impression that he, too, would soon be robbing his foolish mistress, but probably in moderation, not exceeding what was customary and even respectable among stewards.

The last of Severina's visits of farewell was to Crinitus at his villa in Baiae. She found him propped up on a couch by a window overlooking the sea, his body almost helpless now, but the sharp-boned, irascible face under its heavy forehead still making an effect of formidable character. Benjamin, the Hebrew physician, took up his station just out of earshot. He had warned Severina not to overtax his patient and that he would signal the moment he judged the interview had lasted long enough.

The unchecked progress of her uncle's infirmities had in no way diminished the caustic fluency of his tongue. After listening to her, with obvious impatience, for a little while, he began in his thin, wavering invalid's voice, which suggested a petulant wrath, such a flow of tart commentary that she looked worriedly at Benjamin, whose answering gesture she interpreted as, "Don't argue with him!"

Against Spain Crinitus inveighed with brutal derision. The climate was atrocious, the people boors. It was the most backward of the provinces, worse even than Britain! The towns were dreary enough, but the countryside—it was mostly rocky wilderness inhabited by savages. The only sensible thing their family had ever done was to emigrate from Spain to Italy!

"As for you, Severina—you're a fool! Always running off somewhere. First, there's Sirmium. Then you bury yourself in the country, in your villa. Now this lunacy about Spain. Why don't you stay here? You could bring that wooden daughter of yours, if you like. Oh yes, of course, she's married to some yokel in Tuscany. Well, bring him, too.

"You've nothing to say? It's a funny thing, Severina. You're the

468

only person I've ever really cared for—apart from myself. But you've never cared for me, have you? Come, own up!"

"Oh, I have, Uncle!" Severina exclaimed, despite her anxiety not to contradict him. "I have always been very fond of you!"

"Not really, not deeply!" retorted Crinitus. "Aurelian, yes—you loved him. Julia, too—it's natural, I suppose—you're her mother. And now she's off your hands, there's this half-barbarian brat. Still, I don't think there will be another man. I can't see you marrying again!"

Severina thought of Herennianus. "No, Uncle. I will never marry again."

"That I can understand," he said, surveying her with a kind of sour sympathy. "It's better to be Aurelian's widow than the wife of some nonentity."

"That's not exactly how I look at it," Severina began. She broke off and rose. Benjamin was motioning. "Good-bye, Uncle dear. I'll write. . . ."

He screwed up his face in an angry and despairing grimace and struggled to raise himself from the pillow. "Come and see me— d'you hear?" He strained his scraggy throat in a vain effort to shout. "Don't go away for good—promise you'll come back. . . ." His voice shook more and more. "Next year—just for a few days. Promise, Severina!"

"Oh, of course, Uncle," she whispered, terrified. "I'll come and see you, I promise. There! There!" Benjamin hurried up, alarm in his expression.

"Don't forget!" Crinitus muttered; he sank back on the pillow and closed his eyes. Benjamin felt his pulse, arranged the coverlet and accompanied Severina to the door.

Outside, she said, "Will he—shall I find him here, if I come back —say, next year?"

The physician shrugged. "Who knows? He is an obstinate man— though I must admit that he obeys my instructions—and he is determined not to die. Anyone less stubborn would have been dead years ago. He is living on willpower alone. One day, naturally, his body will just refuse to carry on. And then. . . ." Benjamin spread his hands in an eloquent gesture. "Meanwhile," he added, a wry smile wrinkling his refined, aquiline dark face, "he boasts of having outlived his previous doctor. Perhaps he will also outlast me!"

Already the twilit room had a forlorn air, having been stripped of almost everything that was to accompany Claudius on their journey. Severina stood by his bed, hearing faintly the servants bustling about the house with their preparations for tomorrow's move. Claudius lay breathing gently, his upraised fists alongside his head in the attitude of infant slumber. One lock of his coarse brown hair, Aurelian's hair, had tumbled over his forehead.

Looking down on him, Severina thought how many factors met in the life of this dear and innocent child. Rome's tottering greatness, built by so much valor, endurance, statecraft; the surging energy of the fierce Goths from somewhere among the glaciers and tempests of the North; the shrewd and stubborn courage of hardy Illyricum; the enlightenment of brilliant ages, living on, though feebly, in the culture of her own patrician house; the deep spiritual stirrings and strivings that found their voice in the Christian faith. Surely something noble must grow from such a mixture. The elements mingling in this boy were not irreconcilable. There might one day emerge a type of man, an order of society, blending wisdom with vigor, discipline with freedom, tradition with daring enterprise, a rational and restless intellect with profound and passionate convictions. The Roman, the Goth, the Illyrian, the Christian, all had something wholesome and of high value to contribute, something that might be necessary to the complete man. Perhaps the future would fuse together what was good and great in them and eliminate what was evil.

But that future was a long way off. Before its radiance brightened the horizon, the Empire would undergo many—and ultimately fatal—disasters.

Rome would go down in the end, of that she was convinced. Aurelian's work and that of the other Illyrian Emperors, Claudius and Probus (and any that might follow), would prove in vain. The men with the Sun emblazoned on their ensigns would in the long run be vanquished by the men from the sunless North.

470

In some ways the catastrophe would actually be of benefit. The unrelenting pressure of the tax gatherer would cease; life would no longer be one continued squeeze. There would be no more Courts of Oriental remoteness and magnificence to maintain; no more of those fantastic, brutalizing, insanely costly butcheries in the Arena; no conscription; no spies in every quarter.

But all alike would be ignorant. There would be ever-present violence. The majestic Roman Law would be supplanted by crude tribal codes. The Baths would molder into ruin; people would grow brutish and filthy. The splendid city life of the classical past, the great beacon flame of Athens, the artists and the architects, the philosophers and the poets, the dramatists, the historians, the men of genius and their works—all would pass into oblivion.

Severina shook her head. The losses need not be everywhere so great, nor need they be irretrievable. For vital gains had been made. The Illyrian Emperors had staved off Rome's downfall. With their victories they had won time. Aurelian had told her once that the barbarians were learning Roman warcraft. They must surely be learning other things from Rome, more valuable than warcraft. Profound changes were at work among them. Though they would return to the attack again and again, their final triumph had been delayed so long that before they established themselves in the Empire's ruins they might well have thrown off the worst of their savagery and acquired the rudiments of civilization. The darkness, then, need not be total. The Illyrians might prove to have saved not Rome herself, but what was most precious in Rome.

That would be a supreme achievement, of immeasurable significance for the future.

The longer Severina's thoughts dwelt on it, the more her confidence grew. Whatever befell the Empire, much of the inestimable value would never now be lost. The work of Aurelian and his comrades in arms would preserve enough to make a fresh start possible one day and perhaps brilliant advances. No, the superhuman struggle of Rome's fighting Illyrian Emperors would not be in vain. The Unconquered Sun would help to illuminate new ages.

As she looked at Claudius, he turned abruptly round and pressed

471

his cheek into the pillow with such a vigorous motion that she feared he would awaken. But his eyes remained closed; he slept on, breathing quietly as before. "Bless you, my darling!" she whispered, as gently she arranged the covers again. The great themes that had filled her reverie faded from her mind. The Empress of Aurelian was lost in the woman bending over her sleeping child.